BOOKS 4-6

Crimes of the Fae

MELISSA A. CRAVEN
M. LYNN

Edited by Cindy Ray Hale
Proofread by Caitlin Haines
Cover by Covers by Combs

For those who tell us a realistic story has to have cursing.
Gosh. DARN it. We never listen.
:)

PRISON REALM

NORTHERN VATLAND

LOCH VILLANDI

FARGELSI KINGDOM

SOUTHERN VATLAN

DRAGUR FOREST

VINDUR CITY

ISKALT KINGDOM
EASTERN VATLANDS
ELDFAL
SANDUR
SOL LOCH
UR KINGDOM
TEOTANN OASIS
ELDUR DESERT
CH LANGT
RADUR CITY

FAE'S PRISONER

MELISSA A. CRAVEN
M. LYNN

Chapter I

Ten years of cruel darkness and starvation.

Ten years of scraping by in a prison realm, of bowing before a king who liked nothing more than seeing his people on their knees.

But Griffin O'Shea had no delusions. He deserved his fate, deserved the punishment that sent him across the powerful barrier surrounding the fae prison realm, to have everyone outside that barrier forget he ever existed.

He tried to forget too, tried to put his brother from his mind, to forget the woman he'd married—not that she'd wanted to marry him. He'd felt it all those years ago, the moment their marriage bond shattered the day he left his old life behind.

There were only two ways to get out of a fae marriage.

Death.

Or a fate worse than death. The prison realm.

Griffin's anger had long since subsided over the fate his brother and his wife allowed him to choose, the one they'd accepted without a fight. There was no time for hatred anymore, no time to do anything but survive.

Which was what Griffin tried to do.

The cheers from the gathering crowd reached him where he leaned against the cold stone wall of the tunnel beneath the castle. For ten years, he'd managed to avoid the notice of King Egan Byrne, but that wasn't possible anymore, not when the people he'd grown to care about were in danger.

But he'd failed them.

Failed to infiltrate the castle, failed to save the little girl who looked to him with so much trust.

He pushed off the wall and paced the length of the tunnel.

He didn't deserve Nessa's trust. When Nessa's sister, Shauna, found him on his first day here, he hadn't deserved her kindness or her friendship. She'd saved his life that day.

But he deserved this day, now.

The crowd, come to watch the newest battle, would assume Griffin had betrayed King Egan. He supposed he had, but that wasn't why Griffin wanted this, why a fight for his life was long overdue.

If they knew the true reason he was here in the prison realm, he'd lose their trust.

He'd been an ally of Queen Regan O'Rourke, the now dead sorceress of Fargelsi. If word got out, not even Nessa would look to him with trust.

Because the queen he'd spent most of his life in service to sent a good many of them here—to a realm the rest of the fae world forgot existed. The fourth kingdom of Myrkur. The realm of the Dark Fae, where it was always night and Griffin O'Shea held no magic.

If he died today, he would die still feeling like a traitor.

Light footsteps echoed through the tunnel behind him, and he lifted his head to find Gulliver, an orphaned kid Griffin found about a year after joining Shauna's village. They'd been together ever since.

But he shouldn't be here. "Gullie, what in the name of all the realms do you think you're doing here?"

Gulliver narrowed his cat-like eyes. His tail curled around his middle. He wasn't the first Dark Fae Griffin had met with such features. Before crossing the prison barrier, he hadn't thought fae like him existed.

But they did. Here in Myrkur some fae had tails or tusks, others had horns or wings. They were the Dark Fae, exiled to this realm generations ago.

"I came to see you." Gulliver crossed his arms, trying to project strength like he always did when he thought he was in trouble.

Griffin sighed. He didn't want his last words to his twelve-year-old charge to be a chastisement. "If the king or his men catch you here—"

"I know. I know. They'll take me as an indentured servant to work in the mines." He flashed Griffin a grin. "Good thing they never catch me."

"Yet," Griffin grumbled. "They haven't caught you *yet*." Gulliver was a thief. A good one. He had the ability to move around unseen, unheard. And his tail was lightning quick, shoving his stolen bounty away faster than a blink. It came in handy. "Were you trying to sneak up on me?"

"No. That would be useless. You always seem to know I'm there." Gulliver kicked at a rock on the ground before lifting his vulnerable eyes to Griffin "The crowd says you're going to fight the king's greatest warrior."

"Gullie, I'm going to be okay."

"Do you promise?"

Griffin sighed but didn't respond. They both knew it was a promise he wasn't sure he could keep. "You've never seen me fight." He'd had many chances to wield a sword over the years but mostly to protect their secret village from other Dark Fae. There was a difference between that kind of fight and single combat with a trained swordsman. "Have you seen my competitor yet?"

Gulliver shook his head. "Do you think it'll be a Dark Fae?" His eyes narrowed to slits. "Or Tuatha De Dannon?"

"Probably Dark Fae." The king only took Dark Fae into his employ. Light Fae, those like Griffin, were more likely to be indentured servants, and the Tuatha De Dannon were land fae, like Gulliver. An ancient race of fae born here in Myrkur but enslaved all the same.

"What if it's a mountain ogre? Or a Slyph with great bat wings?"

Griffin planted a hand on each of Gulliver's shoulders and dipped his head to look him in the eye. "I don't want you watching this fight."

"But—"

"When you leave here, find Shauna and get as far away from the castle as you can."

Gulliver's bottom lip quivered. "What about Nessa? The king still has her."

"Practice patience. I will do my best for Nessa but I don't want my fate to be yours. You're a good man, Gulliver, but I need to know you'll be safe."

He puffed up his chest even as he fought back tears. Griffin yanked him into a hug, not wanting to let go.

Since entering the prison realm, Griffin had found what he'd sought his whole life, what he'd once deluded himself into thinking he'd found with Regan—the queen who raised him.

A family.

He had to fight for them now, to honor them until his last breath.

Which could very well be today.

Releasing Gulliver, Griffin pushed him back the way he'd come. "Go before someone sees you."

Gulliver took a strengthening breath, giving Griffin one last look, before running down the tunnel, leaving Griffin alone once more.

He'd never been strong in his convictions. At least, not until coming here. He'd had a tendency to let people down, never being who they wanted or needed him to be. The day he'd found the three-year-old Gulliver sleeping on the street, he'd made a vow to himself. He would always be there for him, and he'd try to be better, to do better. For the kid.

But now, it was time to break that vow.

It was time to say goodbye to the best friend he'd ever had, Shauna. Time to leave Gulliver as he promised he never would.

Time to give up on saving the young Nessa, who'd only had eight years of freedom and would spend the rest of her life in captivity.

He'd failed them all. Because he wasn't going to win this fight.

The crowd outside grew louder, their stomps over the tunnel making dirt rain down on him. They came to see a battle, to see blood.

Footsteps echoed through the tunnel from the arena ahead, and Griffin turned to see the king himself approaching, the short tusks protruding through his beard made his smile seem even darker.

Griffin didn't bow, instead he straightened his shoulders and narrowed his eyes.

A loud clang echoed as King Egan threw a sword at Griffin's feet. He bent to pick it up, examining the rusted blade and cracked hilt.

"The great Griffin O'Shea." The king crossed his arms.

Griffin didn't make a habit of sharing his last name, but something told him he didn't want to find out how the king knew it. Yet... "You don't get to speak my full name."

"Your little Nessa has been a great wealth of information."

Griffin lunged for him, slamming the king against the stone wall. "What did you do to her?" Even as a kid, Nessa wouldn't have given information freely to this man, information only Shauna was supposed to know.

The king smiled. "The child is strong in her convictions. I quite like that. She wouldn't give me information to save herself. But to save you..."

Griffin cursed. Nessa must have thought telling the king Griffin was of royal blood would earn him a place of power. She was wrong about one thing. Griffin didn't want that power.

The king pushed Griffin away and righted himself. "It doesn't have to come to this. Join me now and this all goes away. I could use a soldier with the royal blood of Iskalt running through his veins."

Royal blood. The blood of Iskalt, one of the other three fae realms where his brother now held the throne. But Griffin had never honored his blood. He hadn't chosen Iskalt in the war that brought him here. He'd served the Fargelsi Queen all his life, fighting against both Iskalt and Eldur.

"I will never join you." Griffin spat.

King Egan's lips ticked up into a pleased smile behind his unkempt beard. "Let's make this interesting, shall we? I don't believe you will win, but if you do, the girl's contract is yours, and you're free to take her home."

"The girl... you'd give Nessa to me?"

His smile widened. "Of course. Though, she could have value as an indentured. She's beautiful. A bit young and weak, but perhaps she'll prove useful in many ways."

Griffin gripped the hilt of his sword tighter, wishing he could drive the rusted blade straight through Egan's belly. But it was no secret the paranoid king surrounded himself with loyal servants who wouldn't let Griffin take his next breath if he slayed the king where he stood.

Griffin stepped closer to Egan, dropping his voice. "One day, I'm going to kill you."

A booming laugh echoed against the stone. "Well, my boy, you must win this day first. I'll see you in the arena."

When he was gone, Griffin leaned his head back against the wall, finding a new strength in himself. If he won today, maybe he wouldn't fail Nessa after all.

This was for her and every other fae who'd made Griffin one of their own.

He ran a hand through his long auburn hair, adjusting the ribbon that held it away from his face.

Ogres were big and dangerous but also slow. He could use that to his advantage. A Slyph however, with their powerful wings, they were fast and difficult to catch.

A key rattled in the lock at the end of the tunnel that led into the arena. A bald man dressed in the king's colors stepped in. Black ragged wings protruded from his back. "It is time." The Slyph spoke with a gravelly voice that matched his countenance.

Griffin was ready. He would save Nessa or die trying.

He stepped away from the wall and followed the man through the opening. Rough stone turned to fine sand beneath his feet.

He couldn't make out the faces of the crowd in the inky darkness, but that wasn't unusual. The sun never rose in Myrkur. It was one of the harshest things about this broken and cruel realm. Griffin had almost forgotten what it felt like to have sunlight warm his skin.

Or magic sparking at his fingertips.

Upon entry into the prison realm, all magic vanished from those who could wield it. Griffin hadn't been able to call forth his own magic in more than a decade.

Torches lined the arena and the platform on which the king sat, creating a circle of light. Griffin wiped a sweaty palm on his linen pants before tearing his white shirt off over his head and tossing it to the ground.

The crowd chanted and cheered along with the rhythm of a heavy drumbeat coming from somewhere behind the king.

The king stood, and the crowd quieted, straining to hear his every word. "My fae friends, thank you for coming today." Egan turned to the crowd, raising his hands at their applause.

Griffin wondered if the crowd was full of only Dark Fae, the ones who were loyal to their king. Or had they forced others to attend these macabre fights?

The king continued. "This morning, the young man before you was given a choice. Serve me or face his own mortality."

The crowd booed and hissed at Griffin.

But he wouldn't let himself become an indentured servant to a corrupt king. He'd faithfully served Regan despite knowing it was wrong.

Never again.

"And he has chosen death!"

The crowd roared with anger at Griffin's audacity to deny their king.

Griffin refused to look at the fae calling for his demise.

The king held up a hand to quiet the cheers. "Now, I am not a heartless fool. On the chance Griffin manages to defeat my best warrior, he will win the contract of my newest servant, Nessa." His eyes drifted to Griffin. "The rules are simple. Fight to the death by any means necessary."

If Griffin managed to kill an ogre, he'd have no regrets. He'd take Nessa home, and they'd tell stories of tonight for years to come.

The thick metal grate blocking the entrance to another tunnel lifted. Griffin braced himself, ready for whatever fae beast came for him.

Out of the shadows came a warrior.

Not an ogre.

And not someone Griffin wanted to kill.

Chapter 2

Griffin had never laid eyes on Riona Nieland, but that didn't mean he couldn't recognize her.

Unlike the crowd chanting her name, Riona had no smile on her face, no indication she took pleasure in this fight.

She stood with her back to him, her face lifted in respect to regard the king on his dais far above the arena floor.

Griffin had none to give either of them.

"My king." Riona lowered herself to her knees as if this was a practiced performance. The crowd quieted, leaning forward to hear her words.

Riona was the king's most loyal soldier, despite her youthful appearance. She'd made a name for herself overseeing village raids when those villages refused to pay the king's high taxes that demanded too much of their meager yields.

Bright tattoos in an array of colors and ancient symbols wound up her arms, disappearing under the capped sleeves of the thin shirt she wore under her chain mail. The tattoos seemed to breathe, like they had a life of their own.

As the king's warrior, she had the advantage of proper armor and weapons.

Griffin only had himself and a rusted sword with a crack running the length of the hilt.

The balding winged man who'd led Griffin from the tunnel clamped a hand on the back of his neck. "Kneel to your king." He tried to force Griffin to his knees, but Griffin stood his ground.

"That man is not my king."

"Did you say something, prisoner?" King Egan perched on the edge of his half rotted throne, looking down his long nose into the arena, waiting in anticipation for Griffin's words.

Griffin strengthened his voice. "You are not my king. I have no king."

It was the truth. Griffin was a man without a home. With Queen Regan dead and her niece, Neeve O'Rourke, on the Fargelsian throne, that kingdom was no longer his. In Eldur, Queen Alona most likely cursed his name for everything he'd done to harm her people.

And his brother... Lochlan held the throne of Iskalt, but he'd be the last person to welcome Griffin.

So, it came down to the king of the prison realm, the man starving his people and forcing them to fight to the death when it amused him. Griffin would never call such a man his king.

Egan stroked his long wiry beard. "Well, it's no matter now. Even kingless men can die at the order of a king."

Riona shot Griffin a venomous look over her shoulder before focusing on Egan once more. "I will do you proud, Majesty. Please allow your humble servant your blessing this day." She pressed her forehead to the ground before Egan.

The king stood and lifted a hand. "Riona Nieland, you are blessed. This fight will end when one of you dies. Should Griffin prevail, he wins the contract for the indentured child, Nessa." He stared down at Riona with a lecherous gaze. "Should my favored warrior, Riona succeed, she will earn herself a promotion in rank."

"Thank you, sire." She lifted her face to him, gazing at him through the veil of her lashes, as if she welcomed his attention. "You honor me."

Griffin snorted, but he doubted anyone heard him. Even when he was loyal to Regan, he wouldn't have groveled like this woman. But Egan demanded such fawning from his loyal subjects.

She pushed to her feet, and Griffin faced her, the rusted sword firm in his grip.

Riona gave him a fearful look as she slid her sword free. Was she scared?

Griffin dropped his sword to the sand. "I won't fight you."

Riona cocked her head to the side. "That's a shame because I will fight you."

She lifted her sword in a wide, uncontrollable arc, missing Griffin entirely.

"Have you ever gone to battle?"

Riona narrowed her eyes. "There is no need for battle in Myrkur."

"Maybe not in the castle." Had she lived a comfortable life being told her sword skill could beat anyone's?

"Fight her, Griffin!" Gulliver's scream rose above the crowd.

Griffin couldn't find his charge in the dark, but he sighed, wishing the kid would heed his command to leave. For once.

"I won't fight you," he repeated.

She advanced on him, tossing her sword from hand to hand, her eyes narrowing. That was when he saw them.

The wings unfurling from her back.

Riona Nieland was a Dark Fae. A Slyph, and a rare one at that. He couldn't take his eyes from the fine white lace-like wings that spread in a wide arc around her. Delicate and beautiful, they looked out of place in the dirt arena. With a sweep of his rusted sword, he could sheer her wings right off her back and leave her lying helpless in the sand.

How was this woman Egan's prized warrior?

The crowd cried out for blood, for violence.

And all Griffin wanted to give them was surrender, peace.

This time, when Riona lifted the sword, Griffin had to duck her attack from above.

"You cannot win if you do not fight," she growled, landing behind him.

Nessa's face had been a permanent fixture in his mind since she was taken. Normally, thinking of her made him feel vulnerable. A reminder that he couldn't save her.

But now, those thoughts gave him strength. He still had a chance to walk away from this.

Griffin lunged back from Riona's air attack, sprinting to where he'd left his sword. Riona wasn't far behind. As soon as he gripped the hilt and whirled around, he blocked her sword, the blow far heavier than he'd expected from such a small fae.

In the orange glow of the torches, they danced together, her wings fluttering like a dragonfly's.

"I thought you weren't going to fight me?" she grit out as their swords clanged once more.

When Griffin didn't answer, she went on. "What changed your mind? Fear?"

"I'm not scared of you." He drove her back with another attack.

"You should be."

He met Riona's cold blue eyes. Ebony hair fell loose from her single braid.

He didn't want to fight her, even though she was loyal to Egan. He'd been in her shoes once before.

But still, this was for Nessa, for his makeshift family.

"Why aren't you scared of me?" She jumped back to avoid his blade.

"Because." He kicked her, sending her sprawling to the sand. "I have something to fight for."

They were the truest words he'd ever spoken. For the first time in his life, he wasn't torn between what was right and what was his duty.

And it was freeing.

"The girl?" She jumped to her feet, sword in hand. "She means something to you?"

He didn't answer as his chest heaved with his labored breath.

Riona didn't look as tired as he felt. She circled him, her breath even and her brow free of sweat.

The crowd jeered above them, but even that noise faded away, and it was just Griffin and Riona.

Sweat ran down Griffin's face as they circled each other, neither making a move.

"Fight!" the king yelled.

They both ignored him.

He might rule the prison realm, but down in this pit, there were only two people who got to decide what happened next.

With a growl, Riona sprinted toward him, her sword raised. He blocked her attack, the momentum pushing her back. She came again, this time sweeping her sword at his legs.

He jumped over the blade and ducked her sudden move into the air above him.

Something clattered to the sand, and they both looked up to see a jewel encrusted dagger the king threw for his champion.

Riona looked from the dagger to Griffin.

"Go." He clenched his jaw. "I never expected this to be a fair fight."

She shook her head. "There will be honor in your death. I will not cheat to bring it about." She wasted no time advancing on him once more.

Pain seared up his side as her blade glanced off his ribs. Crimson blood trickled along his bare skin.

Pushing the pain aside, he blocked her next attack, twisting to the right before jumping toward her with his sword raised. She slipped out of the way just in time.

Griffin's wound opened wider, letting blood pour down his side. But there was nothing he could do about it. Not now.

Now, all he could focus on was staying alive long enough to end this fight.

Commotion on the king's platform stole his attention for a moment. Nessa appeared carrying a tea tray for the king.

If Griffin failed, that would be her life if she were lucky. More likely she'd end up in the opal mines or worse.

Nessa's eyes drifted to him for a brief moment, and Griffin wished he could see her more clearly, that he could know if she was okay.

With renewed energy, he rushed for Riona, meeting her move for move. His body began to recall his former training, like muscle memory.

She had nimble feet and lightning fast wings, yet he suspected she had an even quicker mind. But everyone was beatable.

"I won't let her become you," he bit out. Riona groveled before the king, flattering him and taking whatever scraps he gave her. Today it was a jeweled dagger, but tomorrow it could be rags.

The words surprised Riona, and she paused long enough for her sword to drop just the slightest bit.

He knocked the sword from her hand, kicking it across the arena. She'd duped him in the beginning. "You weren't scared before. Do you feel it now?" He rested his sword against her throat and a hand at her back, gripping her wing joint. One twist, and she'd never fly again.

She swallowed, the truth evident in her eyes. She knew she'd lost.

She closed her eyes for a brief moment before settling them on Griffin. "At least grant me a warrior's death."

Griffin nodded and pushed her down to kneel before him, his sword still at her throat. He stared down at his rusted blade as the sounds of the crowd swept over him.

They wanted someone to die, and to them, it did not matter who.

The king rose from his seat, anger flashing across his face.

Griffin ignored him as he wiped sweat from his face. His entire body was hot, exhausted. Not only from the fight but the days leading up to it. Finding Nessa, trying to set her free, knowing he'd lost when the king's men found him.

It all brought him to this moment. He glanced from Riona to the crowd chanting for her death. Only moments ago, they'd cheered for her to prevail.

He circled her, lifting his sword. He rested the tip on her back, her tattoos disappearing and reappearing along her arms. This was what she wanted, what the people wanted.

He lifted his voice to the crowd. "You want her death? You call for her blood?" He sucked in a breath. "This isn't right. The people of Myrkur should not be fighting each other. We're all stuck here, we're all forgotten. And yet ... you wish for barbaric practices." He looked to the king. "I reject your demands."

He lowered his sword and threw it across the arena to join Riona's. "I reject death. I reject blood." He circled Riona again, and she lifted her eyes. They weren't icy as before, only confused. Anger coursed through Griffin as he watched her odd markings snake along her arms. This was what his life had become, a constant struggle for survival. And he had no one to blame but himself.

If he wanted to end the cycle of struggle, he first needed to change himself.

Dropping to his knees, he winced at the pain in his side. Blood oozed out with nothing to stop it. He focused on the girl in front of him. "I will not kill you today." His voice was meant to be soft, reassuring.

Riona's eyes narrowed, and a scowl formed on her face. "You are a fool, Griffin." Her voice was so low only he could hear. "There will be consequences."

"There always are." He lifted his voice once more so the crowd could hear him. "I will not kill Riona Nieland." Cheers and boos provided a mixed reaction, but they weren't Griffin's concern. The little girl standing next to the king was. "I won this fight and the prize."

He stood near the platform, his eyes never leaving Nessa's fearful brown ones.

"Griff!" Gulliver's yell of warning was enough to make Griffin turn as Riona ran for him, sword in hand.

Griffin scrambled for his own sword and managed to block a series of rapid attacks. His strength out dueled her waning speed.

Ice raced through his veins as he readied for another attack. But it didn't come. Riona stopped, her hand drifting up to cover her mouth. "Your eyes."

"My eyes?" It took him a moment to realize what she'd meant. He'd felt the surge of magic in his veins. The ice. But it wasn't possible. The prison barrier meant anyone who crossed it did so without their magic. It had been a cruel part of his imprisonment, and one he hadn't expected.

Only one thing could have stopped Riona's attack. Magic. The Dark Fae feared magic because they'd never had it.

His eyes flashed violet, a reaction to the Iskaltian magic he wasn't supposed to have. It was fleeting, only enough to surprise Riona into stopping her attack. Then, it was gone.

The king lifted a hand. "I declare this fight over. My greatest warrior lives. Though Griffin has bested her. For that he has earned his freedom."

Griffin stiffened. "No, not my freedom. I did this for the girl. I won her contract."

The king stroked his tangled beard. "And yet, Riona still lives. I don't think you're in a position to negotiate."

Riona stepped in front of Griffin, a thoughtful look on her face. Griffin braced himself for her to reveal what she'd seen. Instead, she met the king's gaze head on.

"Sire." She spoke loud enough for the king to hear but not the surrounding crowd. "It will benefit you to be seen as merciful and honest. It's just one girl."

Griffin looked from Riona to the king and back again. Moments ago, they'd tried to kill each other, and now ... now, she was his only hope of saving a girl he loved like his own kin.

The king's gaze softened as he considered Riona's words, studying her face with a fondness that surprised Griffin.

Egan's expression brightened, and he snapped his fingers. "Excellent idea, dear. Nessa, come here."

She took a tentative step forward but didn't say a word.

"Do you want to be released?"

She nodded.

"No one can say I'm not a merciful king." Griffin saw it happening in slow motion. King Egan shoved Nessa forward. She teetered on the edge of the platform before he pushed her again. Only air greeted her on the drop.

Griffin ran past Riona as Nessa's cry rang in his ears. He lifted his arms, but the momentum of catching her drove him onto his back with Nessa thudding into his injured side. Pain seared through him, but it didn't matter. He had her. He hadn't failed this time.

Nessa's little hands clung to him.

Griffin sat up, keeping a hold on her. He brushed a hand over her hair, down her shoulder, looking for any sign of injury. "Are you okay, Ness?"

She nodded as tears slipped down her cheek.

The world grew hazy, the sounds fading away into the dark. He tried to look around, assuming Riona had already left to join the king. A pool of dark red blood seeped into the sand at his side.

Blackness crept into his vision.

"I've got you," he whispered to Nessa.

But it may have been a lie because his arms slipped from her and weakness tingled throughout his body.

He put a hand to his wound, trying to stem the bleeding. Blood oozed between his fingers moments before he fell into a different kind of darkness.

It was an immense thing: Dying. A life could be summed up in one's final acts. At least, he hoped so. No one remembered the Griffin who'd chosen the wrong queen and done truly evil things. The prison magic wiped those memories from the realm.

The Griffin O'Shea the prison realm would remember, the one it would mourn, was a man who'd protect the people he loved no matter the cost.

And he figured that was a pretty darn good way to leave this life.

Nessa's sniffling receded into the distance as Griffin fell onto his back, letting his last sight be of the stars overhead.

A stabbing pain shot through Griffin's side, and he came up swinging, fearing he was still in the king's fighting pits.

"Calm down, you big baby, it was just the first stitch." Shauna pushed him back down on the table in her kitchen—a kitchen where he'd eaten most of his meals since his arrival in Myrkur. The day he'd stepped through the border magic that separated the three fae realms from the prison world, Shauna basically saved his life. She'd brought him to her home before the king's guards could take him to the castle. As a new arrival, he would have had a rough initiation into Myrkur society as an indentured servant.

She'd guided him through the mountain pass where it grew darker and darker until they arrived in a land where the sun never shone.

"Are you trying to flay me alive, Shauna?" Griffin grit his teeth as she bent over his injured side.

"No, the king's favorite did that for you. Hold still, you've got a gaping hole in your side." A frown marred her face as she went about her work. Even after ten years without magic, his first instinct was to call on his power to ease his pain.

"This is how the humans do it." He reached for the bottle of spirits she'd used to clean his wounds, taking a long drink before she wrestled it away from him.

"That's my last bottle." She set it back down and passed him a wineskin instead. "Tell me one of your humantales. It will distract you." Shauna had lived her whole life in Myrkur and stories of humans were as bizarre to her as fairytales were to humans.

"It's more likely to entertain you than distract me." Griffin glanced down at the long gash from arm pit to waist, hoping it would grow numb soon.

"Humor me." Shauna leaned closer to see in the candlelight. He hated to waste her candles. They were such a precious commodity in their small community.

"They have this place," Griffin began. "A sort of tavern called McDonald's."

"And this Mr. McDonald serves good ale?" Shauna asked, stabbing her needle through his skin again.

"No ale." He winced, taking another drink from the wineskin. "He serves a sort of sweet, bubbly drink called Coke. Ice cold and refreshing on the hottest days."

"Your humantales always revolve around food and drink." Shauna's stomach gurgled.

"But that's not the best thing Mr. McDonald serves." Griff sneaked one last sip of her spirits. "The food. Oh, Shauna, the food is divine at McDonald's. Cheeseburgers and fried potatoes with ketchup and salt."

"I know what cheese and salt is, but that's about it," Shauna murmured.

"Imagine thick slabs of meat between slices of soft bread and melted cheese with onions and pickles. And ketchup is this tangy tomato sauce that makes everything taste better. And for the kids." He turned and smiled at her, the spirits warming his face. "They have Happy Meals that come with a toy."

"Now you're just making things up." Shauna shook her head with a smile.

"I'm completely serious."

"This Mr. McDonald can just afford to give away toys with a meal?"

"The human world has so many wonderful things. I used to think I could never give up magic to live there, but I've since changed my mind." He winced as she pulled her thread tight. "Tell me she's okay, Shauna."

"Nessa? Of course she's as right as rain, tucked into her bed, dreaming of her hero, the great Griffin O'Shea." She smoothed his hair back from his face. "Thank you for bringing my sister home safely. Even..." She sucked in a breath. "Even though she eavesdropped on our conversations and relayed parts to the king."

"She's just a kid. I can't hold that against her. You know I'd do anything for you two, but I sure thought I was going to fail this time. How did I get out of there alive?"

"Gulliver, who else?" She went back to her stitching.

"Of course." Griffin sighed. The boy was going to find himself at the end of a hangman's noose one of these days.

"After you passed out, the guards dumped you and Nessa in the slums outside the castle gates. Gullie found you just as some scumbag was trying to take off with Nessa. He stole a cart, and they managed to get you in it and pushed you all the way back here before you could bleed to death. It took them most of the night."

"Guess I should probably go easy on the boy."

"Seeing as he saved your life, probably so."

"Where is he now?"

"I fed him some scraps for dinner and sent him to bed an hour ago."

Griffin scoffed. "I've never known that boy to do anything he's told. He's probably out skulking around for his breakfast, the little thief."

"You take good care of him, Griff. You take good care of all of us in Fela."

"That's not how it works, and you know it. In Fela, we take care of each other." Their village was unlike any other in all of Myrkur. Those in the castle lived well on the king's wealth. The indentured who served him ... did not. And the ones who refused to work for the king, or were cast out as useless, lived in slums and poor villages throughout the kingdom, each doing the best they could to survive.

Not everyone in the prison realm was a criminal. There were good fae here. Some were born in Myrkur—the descendants of those criminals sent here from generations past. And some were sent here for small crimes, while others were the Dark Fae of Myrkur, imprisoned here in their home realm long ago simply because they were different from other fae, the Light Fae Griffin had always known.

When he first arrived in Fela, it barely qualified as a town. But it always had one thing all the other places lacked. People who still cared about each other's well-being and weren't simply out for themselves. In the years since, Fela had grown into a community where everyone worked together for the good of all their citizens—right under the king's nose. Hidden among the rockiest mountains of Myrkur, the valley they called home was known only to those who lived there.

"You nearly done?" Griffin's words slurred a bit from the drink. He wasn't much of a drinker anymore. Once upon a time, when he lived among royalty, he drank nothing but the sweetest wine. It was much harder to come by here, and he'd lost his taste for it.

"Not yet, keep drinking. We're going to be here for a while longer," Shauna murmured, focused on her task.

"Where's Hector?"

"At his mother's. Hush now, I need to focus." She prodded his arm, pulling the mangled flesh back together as best she could.

"When's he going to make an honest woman of you?" Griffin took a long pull from the wineskin, grateful his side had grown numb.

"He has a family to take care of already, and I have Nessa. The little ones need him now that his father is gone."

"So, you're both going to sacrifice your youth to care for your families and not seek a little happiness for yourselves?"

"We are happy in our own way, Griff. And we don't need any more mouths to feed."

"I'm just saying you love him, Shauna. You deserve to be

together. He's a good man, and I only say that because I am drunk. On any other day, I'd say no man is good enough for you."

Shauna snorted, pulling her thread tight again.

"Are you done yet, or do you intend to knit a sweater out of my hide? I'd like to sleep in my own bed at some point tonight," Griffin said with a grimace.

"You'll sleep on the floor in front of the fire when I'm done with you. You can go home after I'm sure there's no infection. But you will hold still if you ever want to move properly again. There is muscle damage here."

"That damnable Slyph woman and her sharp sword." He growled as Shauna tied off the last of her stitches and splashed mineral spirits across the inflamed wound before she wrapped it with clean linens.

"You'll heal, you stubborn lout." She stood to stretch her tired limbs. "And just where do you think you're going?" She eyed him as he tried to stand.

"I need to check on Gullie."

"Gulliver is fine. You can check on him after you've had your tea." She moved to her small counter where she crushed herbs and made potions for everyday ailments for her family and their neighbors. She was both midwife and healer for their small community, and she'd worked hard to learn her craft from her mother before she passed.

"Fine." Griffin shoved off the rough-hewn table and staggered to the rocking chair across the room by the fireplace. The room started to spin as he collapsed into the chair.

"Drink this." Shauna shoved a warm cup of herbal tea into his hands.

"Mmm." He took a long sip and sighed, leaning his head back. "You shouldn't waste your honey on me."

"It tastes awful without the honey." She propped his feet up on a stool and checked his bandages.

"Stop fussing over me, I'm fine." He sipped the fragrant tea, letting its warmth ease his tensed body.

"Thank you for saving Nessa, Griff." She leaned down to kiss his forehead. "But don't you dare get yourself killed, you hear me?"

"Yes, ma'am." He slurred and frowned. "What'd you put in the tea, Shauna?"

"Just a little concentrated lavender and elderflower syrup to help you sleep, so you don't run off when I'm not looking and re-injure yourself."

"Shauna." He groaned, his eyes drooping.

"Hush and finish your tea so you can sleep and let your body heal."

Griffin leaned his head back against the headrest and did as she said.

"Night, Shauna," he murmured as she went to find her own bed.

Griffin gazed around the small room that was as familiar to him as his own home a stone's throw from Shauna's door. It was funny how it had taken a prison sentence to give him a life he could be proud of. They didn't have riches or power, or even magic, but they had what mattered. Friendship. Community and family. And that gave him a reason to get up in the mornings. Still, Myrkur wasn't the kind of land dreams were made of. Far from it. It was always night in the realm of the Dark Fae. And that meant precious little grew here, so they relied on the few crops they could cultivate, hunting and gathering. Whatever they didn't have, they either went without or improvised.

It wasn't always that way for the people of Myrkur. Only a few generations ago it was a land like all the other fae realms. A kingdom of its own, ruled by the Dark Fae kings who were good to their people. But the Dark Fae didn't always get along well with the Light Fae. Particularly those from Fargelsi, where Griffin grew up. For the Dark Fae, their magic came from their defining characteristics that allowed them the power to fly or the ability to see in the dark or a host of other physical traits that made them different.

Over the years, Griffin had pieced together the history of how Myrkur had become a prison realm. Queen Sorcha O'Rourke of Fargelsi—Queen Regan's grandmother—was often at war with the

Dark Fae kingdom who shared a border with her far to the north. She persecuted those Dark Fae within her borders.

Her persecution grew so heinous that the other fae realms, Iskalt and Eldur fought against her in a great war that no one outside Myrkur could remember. To protect the Dark Fae from annihilation, a treaty was signed among the four kingdoms, agreeing to isolate Myrkur behind a barrier spell to protect the Dark Fae from Queen Sorcha and those like her. To save the last of his people, the Dark Fae king agreed, and the boundary spell was erected around Myrkur, utilizing the magic of Fargelsi, Eldur, and Iskalt—only Queen Sorcha changed her part of the spell, causing everyone outside the boundary to forget those on the other side. In the generations since, Myrkur came to be known simply as the prison realm—a place fae criminals were sent as punishment for their crimes, knowing the world and all those who loved them would forget they ever existed.

In the years after the boundary went up, the Dark Fae began to thrive again in their own kingdom. But there were many who hated the king for agreeing to the boundary, and a rebellion ensued. Anarchy and chaos reigned for years until a new king seized the throne. King Egan's grandfather. Under the Byrne Kings, Myrkur had become exactly what Queen Sorcha wanted it to be, a prison.

Griffin's eyes drooped as he set his empty mug aside. His belly was warm, if not full, and his mind fuzzy from Shauna's herbs. He fell into a dreamless, peaceful slumber in front of the fire.

He hadn't slept long when the back door crashed open. Griffin was on his feet before he was fully awake.

"Get inside you little thief, before Chieftain Kvek's men come to drag you to the gallows." Hector marched Gulliver into the kitchen by the scruff of his neck.

"What's he done now?" Griffin yawned, ignoring the ache in his side.

"Stole a hoard of food from the Chieftain of Drykur." Hector crossed his arms over his chest, letting out a snort of disapproval. With his great bullhorns and the ring in his nose, Hector was an intimidating presence.

"Just a couple of eggs and a ham." Gulliver squirmed in Hector's grip, the flat of his tail thumping against his captor's chest. "That greedy old Kvek had at least forty hams in his smoke house, he ain't going to miss one, is he?" Gulliver broke free of Hector's hold.

"Just a ham and eggs?" Griffin stared down his long nose at his charge. "Empty your pockets."

"Come on, Griff, the old toad doesn't need all that food." Gulliver pulled a dozen eggs from his hat and a smoked ham he'd tucked inside his worn coat.

"It doesn't matter how much Chieftain Kvek has. The point is that food isn't yours, and it's not worth your life to risk taking what doesn't belong to you."

"But look at it, Griff. It smells so good." Gulliver stared at the ham, practically drooling. The flat, leaf-shaped end of his tail tapped against Griffin's face. "You can't tell me we're not going to eat it. Besides, you brought Nessa back home. I thought a nice breakfast feast would be a good way to thank you."

"Gullie." Griffin bent to Gulliver's level. "Next time you want to thank me, just do your chores."

"What's he done now?" Shauna shuffled into the kitchen, her hands on her hips.

"Stealing food, as usual." Griffin folded his arms across his chest, trying to keep a stern frown on his face.

"You listen to me, young man." Shauna cuffed him on the back of the head. "When you stay at my house and I send you to bed, you stay in that bed until you're called for. You don't sneak out. Griffin almost died trying to save Nessa, and that's the thanks you give him?" She tapped her foot on the stone floor as Gulliver hung his head in shame. His long wiry tail thrashed in agitation behind him.

"And don't flick that tail around my kitchen either." Shauna went to brew a pot of tea.

Gulliver grabbed his tail, and the end of it snaked around his arm, twitching with his pent up frustration. Gullie could never hide his feelings. His tail gave him away every time.

"Empty your pockets," Griffin repeated.

"I did." Gulliver's voice went up a few octaves.

"Your other pockets are bulging, Gullie." Griffin pressed his lips together.

Heaving a sigh, Gulliver pulled a loaf of bread from his coat pocket, followed by a wedge of cheese and a string of sausages from under his shirt.

"Bring your mother and sisters over, Hector." Shauna settled a skillet on the stovetop. "They can help us eat the evidence."

Chapter 4

Griff stretched his arm over his head as he ran a hand along the wound in his side. It ached when his skin stretched and pulled, but he'd had worse pain since coming to the prison realm.

Nearly a week ago, he'd almost died. Almost faced the fact he'd leave this world with few people to remember he'd ever been there at all. His brother, Lochlan, wouldn't mourn a brother he couldn't recall.

The woman he once called wife wouldn't cry for him.

He stood in the center of their rudimentary village, watching his people going about their daily tasks. He wasn't sure when it happened, but the people of Fela were his family now.

A group of men and women walked along the dirt path through the village carrying buckets of water in each hand, water that would be boiled and made safe for drinking. The nearest water source was a small mountain spring near the cliffs that bordered their land.

Life here in the night realm wasn't easy. He glanced down at his hands, a prince's hands, that had been made rough with work. He cleaned, cooked, harvested meager food supplies, and ventured out to nearby villages for trade. Here, nothing was beneath him. There was something freeing in that thought. No one expected him to change anything or make the hard decisions.

For the first time in his life, there was no pedestal under his feet. He was truly one of the people.

"You should still be resting." Shauna stepped up beside him.

"It's been almost a week. I've had enough rest. There's work to be done."

"There's always work," she scoffed. "But we also need to take care of ourselves. These people count on us."

That was their first mistake. Even a decade later, Griffin didn't think of himself as someone to be trusted or relied upon.

A sigh rattled through his chest. He'd done his penance, ten years of it, so why did he feel like it would take the rest of his life to earn the forgiveness he wanted?

His eyes found Nessa trying to help unload one of the trader's carts. Leaving Shauna behind, Griffin snuck up behind the kid. "Ness."

She screamed, and he laughed.

"Relax, Nessa. It's just me."

She turned around, a frown turning her lips down. "Don't sneak up on me."

He sent her a wink. There weren't many people who could drag smiles out of him. Nessa was one of them. Once upon a time, he'd been a happier sort.

But he was a young fool back then.

"Come on." Griffin lifted a crate of eggs into a small wagon. "You can carry the torch and help me make some deliveries."

Nessa's eyes lit up. For some reason, the kid idolized Griffin. He wanted to tell her he wasn't the kind of man who deserved adoration, but he held his tongue, not wanting to break her heart.

To her, he was the man who'd risked his life to protect her.

He didn't need to look to know she followed him. The first house they came to looked like a strong gust of wind might topple it. Griffin gestured for Nessa to knock, and she did, placing their torch in the old cracked urn in the yard.

An older woman with tiny horns on top of her head answered, a bright smile on her face.

"Lady Walsh." Griffin bowed.

The woman laughed. "I ain't no lady, Griff, but I could get used to your bowing."

He rose. "Not a chance, my dear. But who needs a bow when they have eggs?"

Mrs. Walsh opened the door wider. "You should have led with that. Come in, come in."

Griffin nudged Nessa forward into the house.

Mrs. Walsh pursed her lips. "And just how many of these eggs do I get?"

"As many as your heart desires." Griffin winked. The old women of the village saw right through his charm. "Seems our foragers were lucky on the morning hunt."

They hadn't had eggs in weeks other than the occasional ones Gulliver pulled from his pockets. One day, Griffin would have to deal with his thievery.

"I'll only take a few quail eggs." Mrs. Walsh reached into the bin Griffin brought in from the wagon. "Others need them much more than an old woman like me."

Griffin had never before lived in a place where each and every person thought of the other residents before themselves.

"Now scoot, children. I have some meditations to do." Once Griffin stopped at the door, she called to him. "Oh, Griff, you might want to check in on Sinead. She hasn't been feeling well, and those children of hers are quite useless."

Griffin nodded. "I will. Thanks."

Once outside, his eyes found the glow of the cook fires in one of the communal shelters at the center of town. Large pots hovered over the fires, filled with water for boiling.

"Ness, you think you can make some deliveries while I go check on Sinead?"

Nessa pushed a dark lock of hair behind her ear and nodded.

Taking the torch in one hand, she pulled the wagon behind her with the other.

Griffin put a hand on her head. "You know what to do."

Even the children in the village pitched in, just trying to survive. There was no such thing as a childhood spent playing games and running amok. Not here. This place forced them to grow up fast.

He watched Nessa make her way over to Mrs. Walsh's neighbor and turned to cross the street. Lifting a hand, he knocked on Sinead's door.

No one answered.

He knocked again before pushing it open. Griffin's eyes found Sinead. She lay in a small bed with a flattened straw mattress, and the remnants of a thin blanket covered her. Bright red hair clung to the sweat on her face.

"Sinead?" Griff rushed forward. She was even worse than Mrs. Walsh implied. Sinead Ryan wasn't much older than Griffin. He scanned the one-room home, looking for her three boys.

Sinead shook as a coughing fit overcame her.

"Where are your boys?" Griffin knelt beside the bed and put a hand to her forehead. She was burning up.

She coughed again. "They were assigned to the harvest today."

Their village had small fields near the cliffs. They didn't yield much, but what they did was vital for their winter stores.

Griffin closed his eyes. It wasn't the first time in the last ten years he wished they had access to healers from the other three realms. Sinead wasn't the first villager to fall ill over the last year. It had happened more and more frequently. A few recovered. Most did not. Yet, they hadn't found the cause.

In Myrkur, lives were brutal and short. It was everything to survive one day at a time. He'd buried too many friends, too many good fae.

And he knew just by seeing her, Sinead wouldn't cling to life much longer.

"I'm going to get Shauna." He pushed to his feet. "She can help you."

He practically ran from the room until he reached the fresh air. It was happening again, the loss. But he couldn't tell anyone how sick she was.

He sprinted across the village, finding Shauna surveying the pots of boiling water as they were poured into wineskins to be rationed out for the day.

Stepping up to Shauna, he dropped his voice. "I need you to come with me without causing a commotion."

She looked to him in question. "Has your wound reopened?"

"No. It's Sinead."

Shauna's eyes widened. "Show me."

Together, they made their way back to the sick woman. Shauna lowered herself next to the bed. "Hello, darling." She pushed hair out of Sinead's face, a tiny smile on her lips.

But there was something about the action… Shauna looked at Sinead the way Griffin had once looked at his wife.

A wife who'd never truly loved him, but that hadn't seemed to matter at the time.

It made so much sense now, why Shauna and Hector were only friends. She was in love with someone else. Someone she might lose. Tears streamed down her cheeks.

The door opened again, and Nessa slipped in.

Griffin blocked her path. "Ness, you shouldn't be in here." The fewer fae exposed to whatever ailed Sinead, the better.

Shauna looked over her shoulder at Nessa. "Run home and get my kit."

Nessa nodded and disappeared.

"You should go, Griffin." Shauna lifted a tear-stained face to him. "Did you touch her?"

Griffin shook his head.

"Okay, good. Now, go."

Griffin didn't make a habit of disobeying Shauna. The people looked to her as a leader. Shauna was their healer, and she protected them.

Griffin no longer wanted that kind of responsibility. He'd seen what true power did to him before. He couldn't handle it. In his experience, power corrupted those who wielded it.

He walked back through the village, completing the deliveries Nessa didn't get to. He greeted everyone by name, taking pleasure in the familiarity of the act. Small tasks suited him, they made him feel useful even as his thoughts turned to Sinead.

He returned to the cart loaded with the available goods and moved all the meat into the main cellar beside the cook shelter.

This haul would feed the village for at least a week. More if they were careful.

A young boy streaked through the village, colliding with Nessa who was racing back to Sinead's house with more supplies for Shauna. The boy picked himself up off the ground.

Griffin reached Nessa and helped her up so she could run along to help Shauna.

"Sir." The boy met Griffin's gaze.

"I'm not a sir." Not anymore. He searched for the name in his mind. "Patrick?"

The boy nodded. "That's my name, si—Mr. Griff. I was with Gulliver just now," he gasped. "We was just playing on the road through the mountain pass, and they came."

"They who?" He stepped closer to Patrick. "You were playing outside the gates?" Fear sliced through him.

"Yes, sir. Sorry, sir—Mr. Griff. The king's soldiers. They was with Chieftain Kvek." His voice dropped. "I hid among the trees, but Gullie..." His voice shook.

Griffin took a fortifying breath. "Are you saying the king's men have Gulliver?"

Patrick nodded. "They was saying he'd hang for his thievery."

Griffin's gaze hardened. The king had taken so much from them, he wouldn't have Gulliver. "Patrick, fetch me a horse."

"You can't be meaning to go up against the soldiers, Mr. Griff?" The boy trailed along behind him.

"That's exactly what I mean to do." For Gulliver. He'd save him and then never let the boy out of his sight again. They'd always known his thievery would catch up to him one day. Today was that day.

Patrick ran for the village stables which only consisted of three stalls and a small exercise pen. Cart-pulling mules took up two of the stalls. And the third... an aged horse that was better suited for the pasture.

Well, staying here suited Griffin too.

Hector jogged toward him before matching his stride. "I just heard. Griffin, I don't care how good you think you are in a fight, it's only been a few days since your injury. You are not at full strength."

"You sound like Shauna." He pushed into his own small home, one he shared with Gulliver.

Hector followed him in. "I'm coming with you."

Griffin raised one brow before bending to pull his sword free from its hidden place beneath his bed. "Going to walk now, are you? Kvek's stronghold is only a few hours away by horse, but longer on foot."

"I still won't let you go alone. I'll take one of the mules."

Griffin straightened to regard his friend. Over the years, he'd developed a relationship with Hector, similar to the kind he wished he'd had with his own brother. "Okay."

Griffin used to think magic made a fae who they were, but then he'd come to the prison world. He'd met fae like Hector who'd never had magic. Nor had he ever seen the sun. He was a Dark Fae who'd lived in this realm his entire life. And he was Griffin's friend, a brother. Magic didn't matter so much when no one had it.

Once outside, Hector ran for the stables.

Patrick led the ragged horse to Griffin. The village took good care of the horse they'd named King, but still, this was a kingdom that beat down even the noblest of its creatures.

A kingdom that let fae like Kvek carry out the king's justice anyway he liked. If he got his way, Gulliver would hang. And soon.

Griffin only hoped he wasn't too late.

Pain seared through his side as he pulled himself onto the horse.

Hector joined him a few moments later, pulling his large frame atop the mule.

By the time they left, word of Gulliver's fate had made it around the village, and fae stepped from their homes to wish them well.

The journey to Kvek's stronghold and the village surrounding it seemed to take forever, though it was only a few hours. Griff didn't know what time it was, but his eyes had become adept at seeing in the dark over the years.

They reached the far pass where stone walls rose high. Kvek was a loyalist, never forsaking his king, and he was well compensated for it. Hours from here, fae struggled just to survive.

And Kvek lived like a king. Beyond the stronghold, a village stretched into the distance, many times as large as Fela.

Hector whistled low and long. "And just how do we get into the stronghold?"

Griffin scanned their surroundings. He blew onto his hands to warm them as he thought back to the first time Gulliver came back with stolen goods from Kvek. Griffin told him it was too dangerous, that thievery never ended well.

He'd been right.

"We need to get around the stronghold to the village." There was a way in, he was sure of it. He pictured the dripping wet clothes Gulliver had come home in, despite the hours-long ride on the horse he'd stolen the year before.

The horse Griffin currently rode. Gulliver had been sneaking into the stronghold for years. "Did you know Gullie was the one who brought us King here?" He patted the side of King's neck. Gulliver named him, saying he looked like King Egan himself.

A fact Griffin did *not* share with Egan when he was his prisoner.

He shook his head with a laugh that didn't belong here. Shauna might have saved his life all those years ago when he first arrived in the prison realm, but Gulliver had saved his spirit. Before Gullie, Griffin hadn't wanted to survive. He hadn't known if he had the strength to make it in such a place. Everything he was had been stripped down to the core, leaving behind a version of himself he hadn't recognized.

Until he found the tiny, malnourished Gulliver. The kid gave him a purpose, he gave him strength.

"We need to take the high mountain road to get in." Griffin pointed to the hills in the distance.

Hector didn't argue. His mule would do much better than Griffin's horse on the high road with its narrow path and sheer drop.

Griffin clicked his tongue, and the horse climbed. And climbed. When it got too narrow, he slid from the saddle in favor of leading the horse.

Rocks shifted beneath his feet, falling down into the pass.

Griffin could hardly breathe as the path started its descent. The closer they got, the more he could make out smoke coming from chimneys, turning the dark sky into a hazy gray. He spared a glance for the stronghold with only two sentries manning the tower.

An ogre paced down below, looking for any wrongdoers. Griffin had only faced an ogre once before on a trading trip to a village near the shores of Loch Villandi. He'd led his party too close to the ogre encampment. That ogre was the first Dark Fae blood he'd ever spilled.

But it wasn't the last.

The path widened, and Griffin looked back at Hector to make sure he was still with him.

They both mounted up, preparing to ride into the village. The small cottages were in much better shape than any Griffin had seen in other villages, proving riches poured into this part of the realm.

Griffin spent ten years refusing to pledge an oath to the king. Maybe if he had, life wouldn't be so hard for his people.

But he was done compromising his morals.

He was done seeking riches and power.

Now, he only wanted to be left alone with his family and friends.

The ogre had his eyes trained on the horizon ahead, leaving his back turned to the mountains, allowing Griffin and Hector to slip into the village unseen. A river ran straight through the center of town and under the stronghold. That was their in.

He tried to remember everything Gulliver once told him.

There was a thick metal grate blocking the entrance from the river, but the spikes didn't reach the river bottom.

"Hector, I hope you know how to swim." He waited for Hector to catch up on his thinking before the two shared a smile.

They backed up into the trees obscuring the end of the path from view. They slid down and tied up their mounts. If everything went well, they'd be back in no time.

But one thing Griffin learned in the war of the fae queens... nothing went according to plan.

The two men walked through the village as if they belonged. Stone roads cut through town instead of the dirt paths he was used to. Long bridges spanned the river at intervals.

And looming over everything was the seemingly impenetrable fortress.

They reached the bridge closest to the stronghold. The current rushed beneath them but not in the direction Griffin needed to go.

He studied the water for a long moment before making his way down to the riverbank under the bridge, heaving a sigh before slipping into the cool dark water. Hector followed without a sound.

It took every bit of strength Griffin possessed to swim against the current. And that strength? It was much less than he'd once had outside this dark world.

"Griffin!" Hector yelled. "I can't..."

Griffin spared a glance behind him where Hector was losing his battle with the current. "It's okay," he yelled back. "I won't fail this time!"

Whether Hector was with him or not, Griffin had to do this.

For his own heart as well as Gulliver's. As he neared the grate, his eyes caught on the gallows, built right up against the walls. No one would ever forget who hanged the enemies of Myrkur.

And Gulliver could be next.

With renewed energy, his arms sliced through the water, the chill of the river numbed his wound until he reached the grate blocking the tunnel under the keep. Gripping the metal bars, he let himself rest a minute.

This was for Gulliver, he reminded himself before plunging below the dark water, using the metal bars as a guide. Water pushed at him, trying to make him loosen his hold.

He pulled himself deeper and deeper until he felt the spikes on the bottom of the grate.

Gulliver was right. They didn't reach all the way down. His lungs screamed for air, but he didn't turn back.

Instead, Griffin kicked against the current, pushing himself deeper, using the metal spikes to swing his legs under before pulling the rest of his body free.

He kicked as hard as he could, his head going fuzzy.

When he broke the surface, he gasped for breath, letting his lungs fill again and again, gripping the grate as the current rushed against him.

He wiped the water from his eyes, and that was when he noticed it. The torchlight.

He wasn't alone.

He searched the open landing beside the rushing river until his eyes fell on someone he never expected to see again.

Riona crouched near the edge of the river, swirling a hand in the water. She didn't look at Griffin as she spoke. "When one of my men alerted me to the man in the river, I didn't expect to see you." Her voice held no emotion, no indication of what she'd do.

"Did you call the guards?" he asked. "Or Chieftain Kvek?" Griffin hesitated to move closer to the landing.

Her nose scrunched in distaste. "Kvek is sleeping. If I wake him, I won't get to be the one who decides what to do with you."

Griffin knew almost nothing about Riona other than she was the king's favorite and a heck of a swordswoman. "I've come to make a deal." A deal he hadn't told anyone about. "Kvek holds one of my men, a boy really. Gulliver is young. He doesn't deserve to hang. Me, however... Kvek would do just about anything to get his hands on me."

He didn't know if that was true, but Griffin was willing to divulge his connection to Regan if it meant he could switch places with Gulliver.

Riona stood, torch still in hand. "Climb up here. You can wait."

She turned and left without an explanation, locking a heavy wooden door behind her.

Griffin pulled himself from the water, wringing out the bottom of his shirt. He wasn't afraid of his own death, not when he knew he was already living on borrowed time. Shauna once told him the past couldn't haunt him forever.

He'd proven her wrong.

Griffin watched the door, waiting for guards to arrive and arrest him. He wished he'd said goodbye to Shauna, to Nessa. They'd hate him for his decision to sacrifice himself. But there was no other option for Griffin.

His eyes drifted to the river, and thoughts of Hector worried him. He hoped the man had made it back to the horse by now.

The lock rattled before the door opened, and Gulliver stumbled in.

Griffin lurched to his feet, his healing wound twinging in pain as he wrapped the boy in a hug.

"Ew, you're wet." Gulliver laughed, but he didn't push Griffin away.

"We have to get you out of here. Take the river." He pulled away.

Gulliver smiled. "You have been listening to me, haven't you? I told you it was a good way in."

Griffin scanned Gulliver's face, taking in the bruises stretching over his boyish face. He didn't deserve to live in a world like this.

Riona entered the room, and they froze. Her tattoos shone in the orange glow of her torch.

Griffin gave Gulliver a sad smile. "You go home and tell everyone I love them, okay?"

Gulliver looked from Griffin to Riona, his eyes lighting with understanding. “No. Griff.” Tears gathered in his eyes. “This is my fate. You can’t take it upon yourself.”

Griffin put a hand on each of his shoulders. “I can, and I will. This is what we do for the people we love. Take care of our fae, Gullie. Be what they need. Always.”

Gulliver’s lips quivered as tears spilled down his bruised cheeks. “No... I...”

Griffin pulled him into one last quick hug before pushing him toward the water. Gulliver didn’t take his eyes from Griffin as he submerged himself. It wasn’t until he ducked under the water that their eye contact broke, shattering something in Griffin. He always knew he’d die at a king’s order. Winning in the pits was only a delay.

He turned to face Riona and held out his wrists. “I won’t fight you if you need to chain me.”

Her brow furrowed. “You... care for that boy? You’d sacrifice yourself for him?”

Griffin looked to the water once more. “I’d do anything for him.”

She stepped forward, her eyes studying him. “Go.” She jerked her head to the water.

“What?”

“I said go, Griffin O’Shea. You spared my life in the fight, now I repay my debt to you. Next time I see you, I *will* kill you.”

Griffin raised a brow. “You’ll try. What about Kvek?”

“He’ll wake to find his prisoner gone, and he will search for him. Hide that boy well.”

Griffin didn’t know what to make of this soldier, one who was loyal to King Egan, yet let Griffin live. Twice.

He slipped into the water. “Thank you.”

She didn’t respond as he pulled himself under the grate and let the current take him to the boy he’d give up everything for. The boy he’d raised as his own.

The boy who’d be in danger until Kvek grew tired of the search.

Hide him well.

He intended to.

Griffin ran up the trail through the mountains to catch up with Hector and Gulliver, his clothes dripping and sodden, making him shiver in the darkness. He didn't trust Riona at her word, that somehow by releasing him the score was settled between them. It was too easy. And nothing was ever easy in Myrkur.

"Griff loves you like you're his own son." Hector's voice reached him across the rocky terrain. He could just make out their forms ahead. Gulliver's tail dragged sadly behind him, and his shoulders drooped.

"Griff would never let them hang you, Gullie. He'd die first before he'd let anything happen to you." Hector draped a strong arm across Gulliver's slim shoulders as they led the horse and mule along the narrow path.

"But it's all my fault, Hector. He's going to die because I was careless."

"And you best remember that next time." Griffin jogged to catch up with them. "I'll not make the same sacrifice twice." Though Griffin knew he'd do it a hundred times over to save the boy he'd grown to love as his own.

Gulliver turned at the sound of his voice. "Griff!" His tail swished, slapping Hector's face side to side.

"Gulliver." Hector yanked on the boy's wayward tail.

"Sorry." He snatched his tail out of Hector's grasp and ran for Griffin. "You escaped!"

"Something like that." Griffin swept the boy up in his arms. "Don't ever scare me like that again, kid." He hugged him tight.

"I won't if you won't." Gulliver squeezed him back, his tail wrapping around Griffin's neck to thump against his head.

"Mind your tail, Gullie. You're choking me." Griffin made a strangled noise in his throat.

"Oh, sorry." Gulliver forced his tail to behave.

"I can't believe we both got away with it." Gulliver lunged ahead with a spring in his step. All worry gone from his mind.

"That's the lesson you take away from this?" Griffin dragged him back by his shirt collar. "We didn't get away with anything, kid. We've got to hide you. Chieftain Kvek will not be happy if he doesn't have someone to hang come morning. He'll send his men out to look for you."

"Aw, don't make me do it, Griff." Even Gulliver's pointed ears seemed to wilt along with his tail at the mention of hiding.

"Oh, you did it to yourself this time. You know where to go once we're home. There'll be plenty of supplies in the cellar. You stay put until I come get you, or so help me, I will hang you myself."

Gulliver heaved a dramatic sigh. "Can Nessa come visit me at least?"

Griffin paused on the trail just on the outskirts of the valley where Fela lay hidden from most of Myrkur. He bent down to Gulliver's level and placed a hand on each of his shoulders. "This is serious. You will stay in the cellar and not make a sound, you hear me?"

"Yes, sir." Gulliver's head fell forward.

"Your life depends on it this time. We got lucky tonight. We won't get a second chance to save your neck again, so for the sake of us all, try to sit still for once in your short life."

Gulliver made a face at that and ran ahead to open the gates that no one outside of Fela would even notice were there.

"You know it will be a miracle if that boy makes it to adulthood alive." Hector slapped Griffin on the back, shaking his head. "It's good to see you alive, Griff." He shuffled along behind Gulliver, leading the mule through the open gate.

"If he does make it, I'll surely have a head full of white hair, or none at all," Griffin murmured as he tugged on the horse's reins, pausing to close and lock the heavy gate behind them. The gates were an engineering marvel and brilliant camouflage that protected the existence of Fela from outsiders. Made of rocks and vines on the surface, it blended with the landscape, making it look just like the cliffs and crags surrounding the narrow entrance to the valley where they lived. Passersby would never know a valley lay behind the false cliff.

Underneath the camouflage, a strong metal structure held it in place with a lock only those of Fela knew how to open, and they guarded that secret with their lives.

"I'll see to King." Hector took the reins from Griffin. "You see Gullie settled in the cellar with something to keep him busy."

"And quiet," Griffin added. Villagers were already up and moving about their homes in the stillness of the morning. When Griff first arrived in the night realm, he struggled to adjust to the constant darkness. It had always felt like endless night to him, but over the years, he'd learned to see the subtle nuances of a Myrkur morning, and this was shaping up to be a beautiful one. In the absence of sunlight, mornings here were cool and calm. There was a serene stillness about the dawn in Myrkur just before the birds began to sing, and the morning dew covered their world in a clean blanket of sweet smelling freshness. It was Griff's favorite time of the day.

It was late morning before Griffin made his way to the small orchard where Gulliver was to hide until the danger had passed. Naturally, he was out climbing trees and not hiding below ground in the natural cellar they used to store their seasonal provisions. It occasionally served as a hideout as well.

"Gulliver, what will it take to get through to you this is no game?" Griffin stood beneath the oiche fruit trees. The dark tangy fruit was one of the few things that grew hearty and healthy in the land without sunlight. Griffin and several of the men from the village had worked hard to plant the seedlings and cultivate them into a viable orchard over the years. They'd only just reaped the benefits in the last few years as the trees grew strong enough to yield a harvest. This year's harvest would be the best yet. If the village boys didn't pick them clean before harvest time.

Gulliver dropped down from the branches, dark juice running down his chin. "I was hiding, Griff. I swear. Just up in the air instead of underground."

"I saw you from the road, and my night vision isn't like the Dark Fae's. If Kvek's men come for you, they'll find you with little effort."

"No one knows about Fela though. So, why can't I just hide at home?" Gulliver crossed his arms over his thin chest, his tail swishing behind him, swirling up a cloud of dust.

"It's called being extra cautious. Now, get below. I brought you something to keep you busy while you're here."

"Is it work?" Gulliver reluctantly followed him into the woods surrounding the orchard.

"Of a sort."

"You know how I feel about work." A clear spring trickled through the woods, disappearing into a crevice in the rocky ground at the base of a sheer cliff. It was the farthest corner of the valley, their most protected spot. Griffin stepped through the thick creeping vines that covered the cave opening.

At first glance the space seemed nothing more than a mountain crag worn away from erosion as the spring ebbed and flowed with the rains. And anyone looking for a hiding spot would seek somewhere with less mud and muck.

Just as the gates that guarded the pass into the valley shielded

Fela from the eyes of the king, the rear wall of the crevice protected their winter stores. Together, Griffin and Gulliver shifted the false wall to create an opening they could slip through.

Beyond the wall, a huge cavern opened up before them. Crates of provisions the villagers had managed to put up for the coming winter season stood along the far wall. The underground spring surged and gurgled at the back of the cave where a small mossy field of mushrooms, root vegetables, and onions grew in the dim light of the glow worms that illuminated the ceiling.

"When I was a kid, I would have jumped at the chance to play here." Griffin gave his ward a little shove into the room. "You can hunt for the biggest mushrooms, pick shadow berries by the stream. Collect a couple of glow worms, and you can catch some fish for your dinner. You can even go swimming and wash up in the spring. You could use a good wash."

"It's boring here." Gulliver kicked at a barrel of cider.

Griffin smiled at the sullen boy. He didn't do well without playmates to get in trouble with. "Let's sit, and I'll get a fire going for you in the oven."

The camp at the back of the cellar had everything Gulliver would need while in hiding, but he had to be very careful with the fire. Hector had engineered an underground oven that would keep the camp warm. It would funnel the smoke through a mud brick chimney that dispersed it through the mountain tunnels and crevices, but it could only handle a very small cook fire.

"Look in my bag," Griffin said as he fanned the small flame in the deep fire pit. "It was going to be your name day present in a couple of months, but I thought you could make good use of it now."

Gulliver rooted through the bag to find a rock carving kit Griff had traded for with the cooper in Drykur. He'd also collected an assortment of ivory and jade stones.

"This is mine?" He ran a hand over the smooth wood of the box. "Thanks, Griff!" Gulliver settled down on a log stump by the fire to examine the tools. "What should I make?" He held up a large jade stone from the box, his eyes round with delight. Gulliver was a talented craftsman. Give him a stick and a knife and he'd whittle the most beautiful figures faster than one could blink. If the boy ever lived to become an adult, he could make an honest living as a tradesman.

"I thought you could make us a chess set." Griff stoked the fire and slid a large flat rock over the pit to hide the flames and heat the stone for warmth later in the night.

"What's chess?"

"A human game. I've sketched the figures we'll need. They're in the box."

"Will you come teach me to play when I get it done?"

"Of course." Griffin sat on the log opposite him. "I'll stay the night with you tonight and come back soon to check on you, and we'll have a lesson then."

Gulliver was already busy shaping the largest rock with a flat-edged chisel.

"I'm sorry to have to ask you to stay here, Gullie."

"It's okay, Griff. I know I messed up." Gulliver swiped the flat end of his tail over the stone that was already taking shape under his skilled fingers.

"It's not just that, kid. You know who I am," Griffin said gently. "Who I really am."

"You know I'd never betray your secrets, not like Nessa—but she's young so you have to forgive her. So, you once loved and respected Queen Regan. She was your sort-of mother, and you didn't know she sent innocent people here. Of course you loved her. It's like how I love you. We don't have anyone else, you and I. But together we're a family."

"That's right." Griffin smiled. "And I know you'd never betray me. But I followed Regan even when I knew she was wrong."

"She took you in after your real parents died." Gulliver shrugged as if it were that simple. To him, it was.

"The point I'm trying to make is that I don't want to ever see you in a position where you'd have to tell my secrets."

"Well, you don't need to worry about that because I wouldn't tell."

"What have I told you a thousand times?" Griffin leaned forward.

Gulliver snorted, narrowing his cat-like eyes at him. "If I'm caught and anyone asks about you, I'm supposed to spill my guts."

"That's right. You tell them what they want to know about me, and I will handle it. You're not to put yourself at risk for me."

"Why is that? Didn't you put yourself at risk today to save me? What's the difference?"

Griffin smiled at that. "I'm the adult, that's why. It's my job as your—whatever I am—to look out for you. Not the other way around."

"You can say it, you know." The tip of Gulliver's tongue poked out between his lips as he concentrated. "You're my father."

Griffin headed back to his small cabin early the next morning, feeling confident Gulliver would stay hidden this time. For a moment, the light along the horizon reminded him of long-forgotten sunrises. And then he smelled the smoke. Thick, dark clouds billowed into the starlit sky, tinged with the light of flames.

Soldiers were in Fela. Griffin ran, ignoring the pain in his side from his still-healing wound, the wound that hadn't fared well in his river rescue. "Shauna!" he shouted as he ran to where her house had gone up in flames right next to his.

"Griffin." She stumbled to reach him. "They're here for Gulliver." She clutched his shirt in her fists, her eyes wild with fright. "They must have followed you here."

"Gullie is safe." Griffin grabbed her hand, trying to make sense of what he saw. The village was gone. Everything they'd worked so hard to build had gone up in flames. The king's men swarmed the center of Fela, rounding up its inhabitants. His gaze zeroed in on the woman in the midst of the chaos.

"Riona." He stalked toward her, rage consumed him just as the fire consumed everything he and his neighbors had. "We had a deal!" He slammed into her, knocking her to the ground.

She lifted a hand to halt her men as she picked herself up, flicking her delicate white wings behind her. "That was yesterday." She narrowed her dark eyes at him. "Before you led the king's men to a secret village that shouldn't exist. You're all guilty of theft."

"Theft?" Griffin crossed his arms over his chest. "Taxes you mean?"

Riona nodded. "Half of everything you own belongs to King Egan."

"We are just surviving here. There's nothing left for the king." Griffin refused to live in a world where one man took half of everything. That was why he and the others built Fela into the communal village it was. They couldn't survive without each other.

"The wealth you've accumulated here says otherwise. How have you managed it with such small numbers?"

"Wealth? We barely get by." Griffin's hands balled into helpless fists at his sides. This was why they went to such lengths to hide their community. There were countless villages all across Myrkur who slaved away to pay the king's taxes, leaving little for themselves and their families.

Riona glanced around at the villager's sooty faces. "Where are the rest of them?"

"The rest?" Griffin shook his head in confusion.

"Surely there are more of you. These few families can't account for the large crops and livestock—the mill and the smithy. Where is your chieftain?"

"We have no chieftain." Hector stepped forward. "We are a communal village."

"Communal?" She scoffed at the very idea that they would all work together for the good of the community.

"Everything you've burned belonged to Fela." Griffin moved to stand with his neighbors. "Nothing we have here belongs to any one fae, and certainly not to a chieftain—therefore, no taxes are owed, and no crime has been committed." They were careful to adhere to the letter of the king's law in that regard. It was a loophole they'd found that gave them the idea for the communal crops and farmland to begin with. If no one owned it outright, then no one was responsible for the taxes. "You're welcome to take half of what each family owns, but seeing as you've burned it all, there is nothing left."

"What about your grain stores?" Riona demanded.

"You burned the grain house," Hector said.

"Surely each family has their own stores for bread making."

"No, ma'am." Hector's mother, Kiaran stepped forward. "The grain is stored at the grain house. The women gather there once a week to bake bread for the village, and the children deliver the loaves to each of the families."

"You just give the food away?" one of the king's men asked, scratching his head in confusion.

"Yes," Kiaran said. "It is our way."

"It is your way no longer." Riona wiped a hand across her sweaty brow, her ebony hair falling over her shoulder. "You may rebuild, but you will pay the king's taxes, or we will return, and you will all wish you'd never been born. Now, where is the boy?"

"What boy?" Shauna lifted her chin, shoving a sobbing Nessa behind her.

"The thief with the twitchy tail. He escaped his punishment and led my men here. He will pay for his crimes in service to the king."

Griffin was grateful he'd left Gulliver where they would never find him and only hoped the boy would stay put.

"I've got the wee pest right here, lady." One of the soldiers entered the village center with a wriggling Gulliver hanging from his meaty palm by the scruff of his collar. "Caught him trying to shoot your men with a slingshot."

Griffin's heart stopped in his chest. This was what it was like when a parent knew their child was in danger and could do nothing to intervene. He turned pleading eyes to Riona. She'd let him go once.

She shook her head. "I tried. It's beyond my control now. I'll see to it he doesn't hang from Kvek's noose. The king will have use for his skills. That is the best I can do for him now.

"Move out." Riona shouted to her men, leaving Griffin and the inhabitants of Fela to the ashy remnants of the village they'd called home.

Chapter 6

Griffin couldn't take his eyes from the road. The dust kicked up by the horses settled back down to the ground, and still, he watched.

He could hear Gulliver's pleading until one of Riona's soldiers knocked him over the head to shut him up.

Riona, the soldier who'd let him escape Kvek but came back to do what? Get revenge? He refused to believe she was powerless to stop what happened. The soldiers listened to her as a favorite of the king's.

The same king who now had Gulliver.

"Griff." Shauna gripped his arm. "I know what you're thinking."

If anyone knew his mind, it was her. He hadn't hesitated to infiltrate the castle when Nessa had been taken. And he'd ended up in the fighting pits facing Riona. Now, it was Gulliver in the king's grasp. He'd do no less for the boy he'd raised as his own. But this time, he had no illusions that the king would allow him to win his freedom.

Shauna kept talking. "You can't go after him."

"I have to." He turned his gaze on Shauna.

"Look around, Griff. You're needed here."

He turned, taking in the still-burning structures that once served as homes for their people. Many gawked at the flames, frozen in shock at their meager possessions now turned to ash.

The village never had much, but now they had nothing.

"Sinead." Shauna ran toward the two men carrying the dark-skinned woman away from the burning flames of her home.

Griffin followed his friend and looked down into Sinead's golden eyes. "How is she?"

Shauna crouched down at Sinead's side. "Not good. Before the king's men came, I tried all my herbal remedies on her, but they didn't seem to make a difference. I don't know what's wrong with her."

Nessa sprinted across the broken village, barreling into Griffin's legs and wrapping her arms around him. "We didn't know if you'd come back."

Griffin bent to look into the angelic face. "I'll always come back to you. I'll always save you, protect you, and teach you to protect yourself."

Griffin had known many strong women who didn't need him at all. If he had any say in it, Nessa would grow to be just like them.

But she wasn't the only one he'd made promises to.

He straightened and turned to address the gathering crowd. Heat from the flames licked along his skin, and he knew they'd burn long into the night until there was nothing left. "Have we lost anyone?"

Hector came to stand at his side. "We'll get a count."

Griffin nodded. Since coming to this village, he'd always said he didn't want to be a leader, that he couldn't trust himself with an ounce of power. But his people needed someone to lead, especially with Shauna worried over Sinead.

Hector sucked in a fortifying breath. "Gather what you can. We'll move to the caverns at the orchards until we can rebuild."

"Rebuild?" Kiaran's voice was so quiet only Griffin could hear. "Now that they know we're here, there's no point in rebuilding. They'll come again."

"You know that, and so do I, Mother, but right now our people need hope." Hector squared his shoulders and gathered his family close to him.

"What do you need, brother?" Hector asked.

Gulliver. Griffin needed Gulliver. But he didn't say it, didn't reveal his secrets. Because the truth was, Griffin changed because of Gulliver, became a better person for a child who needed him. If something happened to him... it scared Griffin... what he might do. The lengths he would go to save Gulliver.

There was a darkness inside him, a darkness that lost him everything he could have had and sent him to this horrible place where not even an innocent child was safe.

"I have to go to him." Griffin looked from Hector to Shauna and the rest of their people. He'd break into the castle a thousand times to save his people. "Hector, I need you to hide our people, protect them. You're their leader." He always had been. The people looked to both Griffin and Hector, but most of the fae here were Dark Fae. Hector was one of them in a way Griffin never could be.

"I don't like the sound of that. Don't speak as if you aren't coming back."

Griffin sighed. "Would you rather I lied to you?"

First, he'd save Gulliver. If he survived that, he'd find Riona. This was her fault, and he'd make sure she faced consequences for betraying his people in favor of a king who cared nothing for them.

Goodbyes were never easy, especially when one didn't know if they'd ever see the people again. He left the caverns days ago on a morning marked by dewy grass and a cleansing breeze. He'd long stopped measuring his days by the rising and setting of the sun.

He'd spent the previous night trying to call on his magic. He'd felt it in the fighting pit, he was sure of it. And Riona had seen his flashing eyes.

How had it returned? And why was it so weak he couldn't use it?

Had the king seen it?

But now, the magic wouldn't come. It was as dormant as it was the moment he stepped through the barrier into the prison realm.

What would Brea think of him now? Would she be proud of her husband—if she knew he existed?

It had been a long time since he'd done something purely because he hoped to erase some of the deeds of his past. He'd learned it wasn't possible, that good did not outweigh bad.

Yet, that wasn't the reason he headed to the palace now.

This was for his family.

Hector stayed behind to take care of their people, and Shauna wouldn't leave Sinead's side as long as she was ill.

So, it was just Griffin. Alone.

How it was meant to be.

He reached the king's forest near the castle early in the evening, but he spent another day scouting the area. Tomorrow morning, he would make his move. Beyond getting inside and finding Gulliver, he had no plan. Before, when trying to save Nessa, he'd stolen the clothes of a king's guard. It got him in, but hadn't offered him any protection.

That wouldn't work this time. It barely had last time.

The closest village to the castle stood at the edge of the king's forest and showed all the signs of prosperity that came with loyalty to the king. But the slums that rose up just outside the castle gates were proof of what happened to those who fell out of favor.

Griffin set up his camp right outside the slums, blending in with the teeming crowds. He tied King beside his camp and lifted his saddle off. He didn't dare leave it out in plain sight for the thieves. Weary to his bones, Griffin didn't bother to start a fire or eat the meager food stores he'd brought before he bedded down for the night. Failure weighed on his mind, more prominent than he'd ever felt before.

When would it stop? When would the king let his people live in peace?

Griffin wanted to be done with fighting. If he never picked up his sword again, it would be too soon.

He rolled over on his hard bedroll, resting his head against King's saddle, thinking of all the people he'd let down in his life. It was hard to think of his former life as belonging to him because it was a different world. He closed his eyes and pictured the cottage in the idyllic Fargelsi countryside he'd once called his own. It was surrounded by rolling hills and green grass, like an image from a painting.

So different from the dark and mountainous Myrkur.

He'd started drifting off when footsteps had him jerking upright. He couldn't make out a face in the dark until the man grew closer. The first thing Griffin noticed was his uniform. One of the king's men.

"What do you want?" Griffin reached for his sword, pulling it free of the scabbard.

"I have a message from Riona Nieland. Are you Griffin O'Shea?"

"That's me."

"Riona will meet with you in the woods near the northern gates." The man turned away, and his footsteps grew quiet as he faded into the darkness.

"Wait," Griffin called. "When will she be there?"

The man didn't respond.

Griffin cursed as he rolled to his feet and made quick work of saddling King. He didn't bother packing his belongings. Things could be replaced, but he wouldn't miss his one chance to rescue Gulliver.

He pulled himself into the saddle and clicked his tongue, nudging King forward. Together, they raced across the night.

It was most likely a trap. He knew that just as much as he knew Riona couldn't be trusted. Her loyalty to Egan was bone deep.

He reached the trees, slipping under the canopy cover to avoid being seen by the guards in the northern tower. He slipped off King, letting him take a rest in the relative safety of the forest.

Riona wasn't there.

For what seemed like hours, Griffin paced back and forth, one hand on the hilt of his sword. It was hard to keep track of time in the prison realm, and he didn't know how long he'd waited before snapping twigs alerted him to another presence.

Griffin pulled his sword free, brandishing it in the direction of the noises.

Someone groaned and fell to the ground. Griffin would recognize that groan anywhere.

"Gullie?" He sprinted toward him, finding the kid sprawled on the forest floor, his eyes closed. Fear gripped Griffin as he dropped to his knees and patted the side of Gulliver's face. "Hey, buddy, wake up. You can do it. Open your eyes."

Another groan was the best thing Griffin had ever heard.

Gulliver's eyes slid open, and Griff couldn't take his gaze from the puffy bruises circling each eye.

"Stay with me," Griffin whispered, bowing his head.

"G-Griff." Gulliver's chest heaved like breathing was the most difficult thing he'd ever done.

A tear slipped down Griffin's cheek, and he wiped it away. The prison realm hardened people, and Griffin was no different. This boy was the only person who could bring tears to his eyes.

"What did they do to you?" Griffin checked Gulliver for further injuries, finding raised red stripes along his arms and back. "They whipped you?" He couldn't keep the horror from his voice. King Egan's punishments were legendary, but Griffin doubted he'd have gone to such lengths to punish a small crime against a chieftain.

No, this had another purpose.

Information.

A cry left Gulliver, and tears built in his eyes. "I betrayed you, Griff." He closed his eyes. "They wanted to know all about you."

"The king already knew I was an O'Shea."

"He didn't care about that. I told them everything, Griff. I tried not to, but it hurt so bad, I just wanted it to stop. They... they..." He moved slowly as if everything caused him pain as he rolled onto his side.

Griffin didn't understand at first. He looked for further injuries before his eyes landed on what was missing.

His eyes widened. "Gullie."

The king's men had cut off half of Gulliver's tail, the thing that made him who he was. The flat leaf shaped tip was gone.

Having never known Dark Fae existed most of his life, it took a while to get used to seeing wings and horns and tails.

But he knew what those features meant to the people who had them. It was their version of magic.

The remaining part of his tail didn't flick with Gulliver's emotions, it didn't wrap around him. Instead, it sat lifeless, dormant.

"I'm going to kill them for this." Griffin grit his teeth. "One day, Gulliver, we will rid our home of the noose the king places around us."

"Don't say that," Gulliver whispered. "I didn't come alone."

Griffin's eyes shot to the trees as soldiers materialized.

"Back away from the boy." One of the soldiers aimed an arrow his way.

"He's hurt. I can't."

The soldier stepped closer. "You will do as we say."

Griffin leaned down to speak to Gulliver, ignoring the soldiers. "I guess this is where I sacrifice myself."

"No, Griff. You can't. They'll kill you now that they know you were one of Queen Regan's loyalists."

The only thing Dark Fae, prisoners, and the king agreed on was their hatred of the Fargelsian royal line who developed the magic that trapped them here. That he'd served one of their queens made Griffin an enemy of all who resided in Myrkur. "I'll be okay. Do you think you can ride?"

Tears flowed down Gulliver's cheeks. "I…" He paused as a sob shook him. "I can ride."

"That's good." Griffin brushed hair back from Gulliver's forehead. "Our people are in the caverns. You'll be safe there."

"But you? How will you be safe?"

Griffin didn't answer. He didn't deserve safety, didn't deserve mercy. It took ten years for his deeds to catch up with him in the prison realm. And now that they had, he welcomed the end of his torment. If this was how he could atone for his mistakes, then he'd gladly go with the soldiers.

As he stood, he broke all the promises he'd made to the people he cared about. That he'd be okay. That he'd return to them.

They were impossible words.

Two soldiers gripped his arms, pulling him away from Gulliver. "You're going to be okay, Gullie."

Gulliver struggled to sit up, his eyes never leaving Griffin. "I'm sorry, Griff. I failed you. This is because of me."

Griffin shook his head. "Don't ever blame yourself. The king wants me because of the actions in *my* past, not yours."

Gulliver got to his feet. "No, Griff. Nothing you did matters. Not here."

"I wish that was true. Don't wait until you're too far down a dark path to become the person you want to be." Griffin didn't fight the men holding him. He deserved this fate. "Be good, Gulliver. Whatever your life becomes, be a good man. Because there are no regrets in goodness. And regrets can shatter the soul."

Gulliver leaned against a tree for support as the soldiers chained Griffin's wrists together.

Griffin spent the last ten years trying to make up for the person he'd been before coming to the prison world.

But in the end, redemption didn't matter.

Chapter 7

"I'll admit." King Egan poured Griffin another glass of bitter red wine. "I was a bit surprised when my guards told me they'd captured the man who'd fought for his freedom in the fighting pits." The king's toothy smile and thunderous laughter made Griffin cringe with disgust. The man was vile, but this reception was not quite what he'd had in mind when the king's soldiers dragged him into the castle. "For a moment, I regretted not letting you keep your freedom. But just for a moment."

Griffin grew up in the finest palace across the three realms, but the Myrkur castle was little more than a crumbling ruin. What was once a mighty fortress was now a hovel the king and his loyal servants called the Great Castle of Myrkur, the seat of the lord of the prison realm. The drafty halls and fortified battlements seemed as if one good storm would level the whole structure, but the king concealed those flaws under a layer of fancy furnishings crafted with gold and silver-plated designs.

Even now, the ancient oak table was covered in the finest linens, stained with wine and what looked like blood but fine, nonetheless. What infuriated Griffin was the veritable feast laid before the king. A prime cut of beef, roasted vegetables, fried fish, stuffed peppers, fresh crusty bread with melted butter, and three kinds of pie for dessert. It was enough to feed all the people of Fela for several days, and most of it would likely go to the pigs when the king was finished.

"Another steak, O'Shea?" Egan carved a thick slab of meat from the rare and bloody roast at the center of the table. "That one not to your liking?" Egan gestured with his dagger at Griffin's full plate. He refused to eat from the king's table.

"No, thank you." Griffin took a sip of dark red wine from the gaudy silver goblet at his elbow. He recognized the flavor of oiche berries. He watched as the king cut his meat, stabbing it with his ruby dagger before stuffing it into his mouth. The rich juices dripped down the short tusks protruding from his jaw and flowed into his beard.

When one thought of a fae king—even a Dark Fae king—Egan was not the image that came to mind. Rough around the edges, dirty and without the benefit of a single table manner, he disgusted Griffin.

Egan leaned back in his throne-like chair, propping his feet up on the table and resting his plate against his broad barrel chest where he continued to shovel food into his mouth. "The O'Sheas of Iskalt were a mighty clan long ago. You are the last of them. You and your king brother."

"We are." Griffin didn't feel the need to mention his uncle, Callum O'Shea, who was currently a prisoner in the deepest darkest cells of Iskalt.

"I could have use for a man like you." Egan nodded, managing to chew his food with his mouth closed for once. Taking a deep gulp of his wine, the king spilled more into his dark gray-streaked beard than he managed to get into his mouth. His hair wasn't much better than his beard. Long and stringy and threaded with braids and bits of leather and beads, he looked more like a battle-worn warrior than a king. Griffin supposed that was what it took to control a prison realm once ruled by true kings. "I could offer you and your lady friend a comfortable position at my court."

Griffin snorted at that, taking up his wine goblet to cover his sneer. This was no royal court, and Egan was no true king. And

Shauna would have a few choice words to the king about being any man's *lady friend.*

"I apologize, your Majesty." Griffin pasted on a smile. "What lady friend?"

"They call her Shauna, I believe. Her and her little girl. The one you fought for. Bring them to the castle, and they'll have everything they could ever want."

"And what role would you have me play among your... court?" Griffin leaned forward as if he was highly interested in what the king had to say.

"The O'Sheas have a singular magic, I am told." The king abandoned his meal in favor of more wine. "I can offer you much wealth for the use of your magic."

"I have no magic, your Majesty." Not anymore. Griffin folded his hands in front of him. He'd grown weary of this dance.

"Magic can be restored," the king said with a wave of his hand. "Did you like your taste in the fighting pits?"

That was him? Griffin met his dark gaze. "You..."

"Yes, though I am but a lowly Dark Fae, I managed to return a sliver of your power, just enough for you to feel it, for you to trust me. I can return it all."

"How?" Griffin would never trust this fae, but he needed answers. Griffin ran through everything he'd learned about the Dark Fae in his mind. If one of them had magic, it changed everything. Was that how the king kept his throne?

The king shrugged. "I have my ways. There is a spell that even a Dark Fae can perform, if you know the words that will direct the magic back to its owner."

Egan leaned forward, droplets of wine hanging in his beard. "You will serve me."

"At what price?"

"Serve me." The king leaned forward. "Give me your loyalty, and I will restore a portion of your magic to you. To use in my service, of course." His rough voice shifted like gravel in his throat. "You are a nobleman, O'Shea. I can give you your life back. Wealth. Status. I can restore you to power... of a sort. You and your woman will rise head and shoulders above the rest of my court. I can give you riches beyond your wildest dreams." He sat back as if he'd just offered Griffin the world on a silver platter.

"And what do you believe my magic can do for you, your Majesty?"

"You can create portals, yes?"

Griffin's brow furrowed. "What do you want with the human realm?" That was the only reason he'd want Griffin's portal magic.

"You will learn in time."

There was no way Griffin would bring this man into the human realm. None.

"And if I can't open a portal?" He didn't completely believe the king could return that much magic to him.

"Then, you are useless to me. It is well known what happens to those who prove useless to the king. Particularly those with a past loyalty to Queen Regan O'Rourke." Egan refilled his goblet, sloshing wine onto the tablecloth.

The king's outcasts either ended up dead or living in a slum unable to get work. Those rejected by the king were the untouchables of Myrkur society. To help an outcast was to become one. They didn't live long.

"And what of my ward?" Griffin drummed his fingertips on the table.

"Ward?" The king frowned.

"The boy your people tortured for this information you've discovered about my past. The one you nearly killed to get to me."

"The slum rat?" The king paused with his goblet halfway to his mouth.

"Your men cut off his tail." Griffin slammed his fist against the table, itching to get his hands on the king's dagger. To the Dark Fae, their unusual features were a matter of pride. What they'd done to Gulliver was blasphemous and cowardly.

"Aye, I can see how that might anger you. Didn't realize he was your ward." Egan ran a finger over the smooth ivory tusks that were his defining feature, in addition to his pointed fae ears and smooth flawless skin—under a layer of dirt. "We shall do what we can for him. He will live here at the castle with you and your woman."

"And if I refuse your kind offer?" Griffin folded his arms across his chest.

"Then, you are free to go." Egan shrugged. "You are welcome to try to outrun your secrets, but things have a way of catching up to a man in Myrkur when he has nowhere left to hide."

"I see." Griffin drained the wine from his goblet. He was screwed either way.

"Walk with me, Griff." The king rose from his chair and led him from the dining hall.

Griffin followed him down a long corridor, the floor strewn with crumbling rock and litter gathered in corners from years of neglect and a general disregard for cleanliness and good housekeeping. The air was stale and hot. Too little fresh air came in through the arrow loop openings in the walls.

"You're an honorable man, I can see that now," Egan said. "You aren't motivated by the riches and comfort you see here. I can respect that." The king clapped him on the back as they stepped through an open gate into the castle bailey—an inner courtyard behind the safety of the castle walls—what remained of them. The dark green grass spanned the width of the courtyard. The night air was thick with sweat and the musky scent of too many unwashed bodies.

"Stay the night and think on my offer. We can talk again over breakfast. Donal here will see you to your rooms." The king left him with a stooped young man with no remarkable features. An indentured servant.

"This way, my lord." The man bowed.

His formal address took Griffin by surprise. He hadn't been addressed as such in more than a decade. He'd once responded to such epitaphs as "your Highness," or "my lord" as was his right by birth. To hear it now though, it sounded foreign to his ears. That wasn't his life anymore.

Griffin followed the steward across the bailey to the soldiers' barracks. The move was strategic. Rather than wow him with the *elegant* comforts of a guest suite, the king chose to put Griffin in with the soldiers. Egan wanted him to see his army. And see it he did. Hundreds of men and women trained in the inner courtyard. Dark Fae creatures he'd never seen before stood in organized ranks. Great lumbering ogres with their long arms, saber teeth, and mottled moss-like skin. Tall men and women with ram's horns or tusks like the king's. A sea of winged Slyph trained in the skies above the castle. And beyond the castle walls, stretching toward the Black Sea, were thousands upon thousands of soldiers, Dark Fae and indentured, criminals and non.

Beyond the land, to the sea, were the Asrai. What Brea had once called mermaids. He'd scoffed at his wife's human notions of the fae back then. The Asrai were natural habitants of Loch Villandi, the pristine lake that separated Fargelsi and the Northern Vatlands. But when Queen Sorcha banished the Asrai to Myrkur, they made their home in the Black Sea. Griffin didn't know much about them or the Slyph of the sky, but something told him he should find out.

Not only did Egan have a vast army, but he had a navy and air-force too. The king had big plans, and those plans now included Griffin and his ability to portal to the human realm.

Chapter 8

When Griffin walked into the dining hall the following morning, the atmosphere had changed dramatically. Scores of tables stood where none had the evening before. Egan's court raised a ruckus as they broke their fast on glazed ham, eggs, bacon, and fresh baked bread—more food than Fela had seen in a month. As Griffin made his way to the king's table, his "court" cheered and raised their flagons of ale, calling out Griffin's name like he was already one of them.

"Lads, bring our guest to the table," the king roared above the din. "He's just in time for the morning's entertainment." Egan's jeering smile sent warning bells off in Griffin's mind.

Meaty hands grabbed him by the shoulders and dragged him to sit in the chair beside the king. They bound his hands with shackles and strapped him to the chair.

"I take it you've had a change of heart, your Highness?" Griffin arched a brow at the king.

"You had your chance to accept my offer last night, and you didn't take it." Egan shrugged, spearing a slab of ham on the end of his dagger. "I thought you could do with some proper motivation." He gestured toward the end of the hall with his greasy knife.

Griffin struggled against his restraints, gripping the arms of his chair until his knuckles turned white. At the apex of the hall, Shauna and Nessa were tied to blood-stained posts, their backs bared to the waist. Angry red welts stood out on Nessa's smooth dark skin, but Shauna had taken the brunt of the punishment. Blood streamed down her back, and her head hung limp between her shoulders. Gulliver was nowhere in sight. "Let them go." Griffin turned angry eyes on the king.

"Aye, she's your woman." Egan's thunderous laughter joined that of his court. "Is the wee one your get?"

"What are your terms?" Griffin growled. As he'd suspected the night before, he was screwed either way. He had no choice but to follow the king's lead.

"Your women will work for me as indentured. As long as you serve me loyally, they will clean and see to my chambers. They will eat well and rest easily under my protection. Should you defy me, I will send them to the brothel tents, where they will serve my soldiers, to breed along with the other women of little use."

"And what shall you have me do, my king?" Griffin's voice dripped acid. He would die before he let that happen to Shauna and Nessa, and Egan knew it.

"Walk with me, young Griffin." The king swilled the last of his ale and gestured for his soldiers to release Griffin from his shackles.

"My... women." Griffin glanced to the end of the hall. He couldn't meet Nessa's terrified gaze. Thankfully, Shauna had passed out.

"The healers will see to them immediately." Egan gave a careless wave in their direction, and Griffin let out a strangled breath when soldiers moved to release them from their restraints.

Griffin followed the king from the hall, surprised when he guided him into his private chambers. He'd expected a pig's sty but was surprised again to see the king's lounge was neat and orderly with simple furniture and not a speck of dust in sight.

"Sit." Egan lowered himself on a chair covered in supple leather, gesturing for Griffin to take the one opposite him. He reached for a sleek ebony box, retrieving an elegant pipe from its velvet-lined interior. He packed the bowl with pungent tobacco and bent to light a long splinter from the low burning fire in the brick fireplace.

He offered the pipe to Griffin, but he declined.

"Your queen's grandmother was responsible for turning Myrkur into a prison." He leaned back in his chair, puffing on his pipe. "Have they truly forgotten us?"

Griffin nodded. "To the outside world, Myrkur never existed, and Dark Fae are the stuff of human imagination. They believe Myrkur is a prison world, created as a punishment for those who break the laws of the fae. The torment of knowing you will be forgotten by all those who once loved you is widely considered the worst possible punishment."

"Sorcha was responsible for that. But her granddaughter is as bad as she was from what I hear."

"Was," Griffin said. "She is dead."

"I suspected." Egan nodded. "We noticed a substantial drop in new citizens a few years ago, and it has be a very long time since I've welcomed someone of your stature into my fold. It is good news to hear she is dead." He leaned forward. "Tell me, who rules each of the realms now? Your brother is King of Iskalt, but is Faolan still Queen of Eldur? I heard some nonsense from an indentured who came here only a few years ago that a human woman rules Eldur now."

"It is a long story, but Queen Alona is Faolan's human daughter. She's inherited the throne."

"And Gelsi?"

"King Brandon's daughter, Neeve O'Rourke is Queen of Fargelsi now." Griffin gave the facts as they were and offered nothing more.

"Aye, another O'Rourke woman." Egan spat into the fireplace. "We have been captive behind the walls of the border spell for far too long. I mean to bring it down."

"And how am I to help with such an endeavor?" Griffin asked. The thought of bringing down the barrier spell sent both fear and excitement through him. Then, he thought back to the army Egan was building. What happened if they got loose in the three realms?

"We cannot pass through the barrier, but I believe you can portal from Myrkur to the human realm."

"What do you hope to find in the human realm? There is no magic there."

"A backdoor," Egan said. "Open a portal to the human realm and from there—"

"You want me to open a portal into any of the fae realms," Griffin finished for him.

"It can be done?"

"There's only one way to find out," Griffin said. "But magic has rules. When I travel to the human realm, I can go anywhere I've been before. But when I portal back to the fae realm, I can only return to my original location, which means if I leave from Myrkur to enter the human realm, I have to return here. But with the magical barrier in place, my O'Shea magic might not allow me to pass through the barrier spell."

"That sounds awfully convenient," Egan replied.

"Rather inconvenient for Shauna and Nessa, if you ask me," Griffin said. "I need some assurances, your Majesty. If I am unable to do what you ask, what will become of them?"

"Best you succeed so we don't have to find out. It would be a shame for such a fine young girl to end up in the tents at such a tender age."

"And if I manage to create this backdoor, where would you have me go?"

"Fargelsi. There, you will search for anyone who knows what went into creating the barrier spell. Then, you can find a way to bring it down."

"You want me to search all of Gelsi for a person who might remember what happened three generations ago?" The task was impossible.

"I suggest you start with Brandon O'Rourke."

"And if I may ask, what do you plan to do once the barrier falls?"

"Take my revenge on the Light Fae." King Egan took a deep pull of his pipe, the tendrils of smoke drifting up to the ceiling.

"These young kings and queens will have no chance against my army."

Griffin nodded as if in agreement. But he knew one thing Egan didn't. The new generation of Fae rulers might be young, but they were united in a way the realms had never been before. Egan wouldn't see that coming.

The king stood, dashing out the contents of his pipe into the fireplace. Standing behind Griffin, he placed his huge hands around the base of Griffin's skull and recited words Griffin couldn't understand. Long-forgotten but familiar magic surged within him, filling a hole that had stood empty inside him for more than a decade. The icy tendrils of O'Shea magic stretched inside him, lighting the violet fire in his eyes.

Iskalt magic was night magic, and in the night realm, Griffin O'Shea should have been more powerful than he had ever been, but something was missing. He stared down at his hands, trying to create a ball of light or anything so simple. Nothing happened.

"I have returned your portal magic. Nothing more."

Griffin looked to him, wanting to destroy him for everything he'd done, but he couldn't think past the O'Shea magic surging through him.

"You will leave in two days' time for the human realm," Egan said, stepping away from Griffin. He was weakened after returning Griffin's magic to him. "One of my trusted soldiers will accompany you on your journey. You will carry out my wishes, or I will hear about any disloyalty, and your woman and her child will suffer."

"I will serve you well, your Majesty. I will find a way to do as you ask, but I have a few requests. Something to give me some assurance while I am away."

"You may ask, but you try my patience, young Griffin."

"I just need to know that while I am away, Shauna and Nessa will come to no harm."

"I give you my word as king that they shall remain untouched while serving in my household as long as they behave."

His word meant next to nothing, but Griffin pushed on. "And my people? Your men destroyed our village."

"Ah, yes, Fela, I heard about that. Sorry business, taxes. If they pay, I see no reason to deprive them of the crown's assistance in rebuilding. Is that all?"

"One more thing, your Majesty." Griffin paused. Making another request was tricky, but it wasn't about him this time. "I would like to take one of my men with me on this journey. Between the human realm, Fargelsi, Eldur, and Iskalt, we have much ground to cover. I would be grateful to you if I may take a man I trust to help me along the way." Was that enough groveling?

Egan nodded. "Very well. My steward will see to your provisions for the journey."

"We will need money while in the human realm."

Egan snorted his annoyance. "You will be there but a moment."

"Your Majesty is aware that Iskalt magic only works at night?"

Egan nodded. "So, leave at night."

"Time is skewed between the fae and human realms. It will be daylight when we arrive in the human world. We will have to wait for nightfall. There are things we will need for this journey that we can only get there."

"Fine. I'm sending one of my people with you. They will have the means to purchase whatever you may need while in the human realm." Egan urged him toward the door.

With that, Donal appeared from the king's inner chambers and whisked Griffin back to his rooms in the castle. Once alone, Griffin paced the confined space, running his hands through his hair in frustration.

"How did I get into this mess?" He tried the door but wasn't surprised to find it locked. He had little more than a day to figure out how he was going to accomplish an impossible task. He didn't want to think about the possibility of failure. At least not while the king had Shauna and Nessa in his clutches.

But even more, he didn't want to think of returning to a land where his own brother wouldn't know him.

Griff couldn't stop moving. He sat. He stood. He paced in the moonlight streaming in through his window.

The prison realm was supposed to be a one-way ticket. The magical barrier kept it that way. As soon as a prisoner set foot across it, their magic disappeared as did the world's memory of them. No one could explain the ancient magic that had doomed them all.

But now... Griffin stared down at his hands, willing himself to do something, anything. The magic sparked along his fingertips, a familiar and unsettling feeling.

He'd resigned himself to his fate, to living out his days among prisoners and the Dark Fae, all united in one thing.

No one else knew they existed.

Griffin tried the door again. He tried to summon his magic to force his way out. But the power didn't come. The king returned his O'Shea magic, the kind that opened portals to the human world, but it wasn't enough. Griffin had the tiniest taste of the magic that left him many years ago. And he wanted more.

Uncurling his fingers, he flattened his palm against the scratchy fabric of his pants.

Images flashed through his mind. Shauna and Nessa and their

terrified eyes. The wounds they'd suffered because of him. It was his fault, their captivity.

And he'd do anything to set them free.

The images changed to people he'd done his best not to think about for years. Regan. The woman who'd been like a mother, the evil queen he'd abandoned too late and wouldn't be waiting for him in Fargelsi.

He'd known Queen Neeve as a servant girl, the one offering kindness in a palace devoid of such things. They hadn't known then she was the daughter of King Brandon, or that Brandon was even alive. Not even Griffin imagined Regan locking her brother away in a cell for almost twenty years.

That would be the smart place to go in search of a way to bring down the magic surrounding the prison world. The histories of Fargelsi were no doubt lost when the palace crumbled in the final battle of the Queen's War.

But there was one person there who might be able to help.

The question was would he? What lie would Griffin have to tell? The prison realm had been created for a reason. None of the three kingdoms would want to mess with that magic.

The image changed yet again, and this time, he saw the people of Fela. A mixture of Dark Fae and those unfortunate enough to be sent to Myrkur. Didn't they deserve for the Light Fae to know they existed? To know that the three kingdoms didn't only belong to those with traditional magic.

For them, he'd do this. For them, he'd seek a way to bring the barrier down just enough to create an escape route for the good people of Myrkur. And if it didn't work? If Griffin helped to set all those in Myrkur free to ravage the kingdoms he'd once called home? What would he do then?

The kingdoms would have to prepare for war.

Most inhabitants of the prison realm wouldn't want a fight, but tell that to the king's horde of an army eager for war.

The horrors he might unleash on the three kingdoms would be unimaginable.

And yet… he covered his face with his hands. His O'Shea portal magic turned his blood to ice, chilling his skin in a way he hadn't felt in too long.

Still, the portal magic reminded Griffin of his past and where such powerful feelings led. He jumped to his feet and paced the room again. Turning on his heel, he let all the anger, the desperation rise up as a scream trapped in his throat. Without the rest of his magic, he couldn't fight Egan, fight the plan he had for Griff. He picked up a cracked vase and threw it at the door. It shattered, raining shards of glass onto the floor.

"That's one way to greet someone." Riona's eyes widened as she examined the vase. "You must get your anger under control before we leave."

"We?" He snapped his eyes to her.

Riona shrugged, running a hand over the narrow braids creating an intricate design on the top of her head. The tattoos peeking out the sleeves of her shirt seemed even more pronounced on her dark skin, like they had a mind of their own. "The king has graciously allowed me to go on an adventure with you."

Griffin snorted. Graciously. The king's people were more loyal than Griffin thought because Riona voiced the words with a straight face.

"You mean he's sending you to watch me." He crossed his arms, glaring at her and wishing Egan had sent anyone but *her*.

The woman who'd tried to kill him in the pits.

The soldier who'd let him escape Kvek's stronghold.

The loyalist who oversaw the burning of Fela and the eventual trap for Griffin.

To say their relationship was complicated would be an understatement.

"If you're done gawking at me, we have to prepare. We leave tonight." She turned and walked out of the room, her steps measured like that of a soldier always marching to the beat of their master's drum.

Griffin chased after her, her white wings fluttering in his face.

"We can't leave for the human realm tonight. The king made me a deal."

Riona's posture stiffened, and she didn't stop walking. "One thing you must learn, Griffin O'Shea, is that the king does not owe you anything, and he does not make deals."

But he had. He'd promised... Griffin shook his head at his own stupidity. Egan only told him what he wanted to hear. There was never an intention of letting Griffin bring one of his own men along. He didn't need a deal when he had Shauna and Nessa in his clutches, knowing Griffin would do whatever it took to see them safe.

"Come." Riona ducked through a doorway into a long corridor with no decoration, only an endless monotony of crumbling gray stone.

"Quaint," Griffin muttered, kicking a pebble out of his way.

Riona shot him a glare over her shoulder. "Myrkur Castle is the greatest castle in all the fae realms." She spoke with a monotone voice as if the words had been programed into her.

But she'd never seen the high waterfalls of Fargelsi or the magnificent sandstone structures of Eldur.

And Iskalt... he had an image in his mind of what the ice palace looked like, but he hadn't been back there since he was a small child. He shut down that train of thought. Missing people who wouldn't know him was useless.

The king was sending him to Fargelsi, a place that held so much pain, so much regret.

Riona led him out into another courtyard before stopping and turning to him. Torches hung along the wall, casting them in an orange glow. For a moment, Griffin pictured what Riona would look like with sunlight reflecting off her dark skin and through her translucent wings.

She crossed her arms and dropped her voice. "What deal did the king make with you?" Concern flickered across her face.

"Why are you asking if it won't be allowed?"

"Because I've known many like you, men who thought they could challenge the king. And you know what happens to them?"

He could guess.

"They die. And their families die. And their associates die. The king will not hesitate to hurt the girls he is holding captive. That's the first lesson I will teach you. He is ruthless, and he is powerful. Do not cross him. If you do what he asks, he will keep his word. They will be safe in his household."

Griffin curled his fingers in. "And he has just returned my power to me. At least a portion of it."

Riona frowned. "Don't be fooled. I know what he returned to you, the single aspect of your magic. It will do you little good once we are where we need to be."

Griffin leaned against the wall. He wanted to ask where it was Riona thought they needed to be, but he pushed the question away. She'd only lie. "And what is the next lesson you need to teach me?"

"Not all who do the king's bidding are without honor." She started walking again.

Griffin didn't know where they were going until they reached the stables right inside the rusted castle gates. A few soldiers lingered nearby, and the stable boys rushed to and from stalls where dozens of ragged old beasts with dull coats looked out at them. They were the finest horses he'd seen in all of Myrkur, but nothing flourished in a land where it was always night.

Griffin once owned beautiful, strong horses, but since coming to the prison realm, he'd only seen malnourished nags and old mules.

But just like the king's people, these horses were taken care of in ways the villagers could only dream about. And still, it was nothing like the bounty that awaited them when they returned to Fargelsi.

A boy walked toward them, leading two horses by the reins.

"Why do we need horses?" Griffin reached out, running a hand along the coarse black hair of the horse's scraggly mane. "I can portal from the castle."

"Like I said." Riona mounted a gray horse and patted its neck. "Some of us have honor. We make sure deals are kept." Giving a click of her tongue, Riona nudged her horse through the gates.

Griffin scrambled to mount his horse and catch up to her. *Some of us have honor?* Was the loyal Riona questioning her king?

Something like that could be useful in the future.

Home. It was a feeling Griffin had only felt in one place before. The cottage he'd left behind in Fargelsi. If he'd been smart, he'd have kept to the rolling hills rather than becoming someone he never wanted to be at the palace.

But now, as they neared Fela after hours of hard riding, his heart ached with the knowledge that his new home was destroyed. A few structures stood tall, black marks snaking up the wood. But that was it.

The community he'd helped build for the last ten years was gone, turned to ash.

He couldn't look at Riona, refused to see if there was an ounce of regret in her eyes. "You stay here." He couldn't reveal the caverns to her, not for anything.

To his surprise, she didn't argue. He squeezed his thighs and urged his horse toward the orchards, thankful when the trees hid him from Riona's sight. Sliding down off his horse, he felt along the cliff face at the far side of the orchard, leading his horse through the vines covering the opening. Griffin left his horse in the cave entrance and stepped to the false wall concealing the caverns from potential foes. Hefting his weight against the stone, the wall moved and silence echoed from within.

"It's just me." Griffin called as he stepped into the chamber, pushing the wall back in place in case Riona came looking for him.

A cacophony of sounds and voices echoed off the ceiling as the inhabitants came out of their hiding spots.

His eyes scanned the gathering, trying to get a read on how many people took to hiding here. It was less than half of Fela's numbers.

Hector saw him first, his eyes lighting up in surprise. In three long strides, he reached Griffin and pulled him in to a hug, squeezing the air from his lungs. "We thought you were dead." Griffin pulled away as all chatter ceased and eyes fell on him.

"Where is everyone else?"

Hector's gaze turned sad. "They left."

No, his people wouldn't do that. They wouldn't abandon their community instead of rebuilding. "Not possible." Griffin wanted to search the entire cave system, he wanted to make himself believe the family that had become his life wasn't broken.

That Shauna and Nessa weren't being held by the crown.

That their village was not full of ghosts and ashes.

But this place, this prison realm, was meant to beat fae down, to strip them of everything they loved until there was nothing left. And it was all Egan's design. Not for the first time he wondered what Myrkur could become under a benevolent ruler. But he suppressed thoughts like that. It only led to wonderings of how he would do things if he were that benevolent ruler. A slippery slope for one like Griffin O'Shea.

Griffin tried to call on his magic again, finding only a single strand with a single purpose. The portal. Yet, power was no substitute for family. It couldn't erase pain that came from the very soul.

Guilt washed over him. This was all his fault. He looked to the people huddling around the smoldering fire in the hearth meant to warm only a few. They looked to him like a leader come to tell them how to get their homes back. He'd failed them, and they knew it, yet still they trusted him. He didn't deserve such loyalty.

And now the woman responsible for so much waited for him back among the ghosts of Fela.

Looking to Hector, he sighed. "I've brought two horses with me. Sell them to pay the village taxes and then rebuild. We can be what we once were, working together to keep our community whole and cared for. But we will have to pay the king's taxes each quarter now that he knows about us."

The villagers murmured in worried tones. It would be a difficult, if not impossible task, and they all knew it. But what choice did they have?

"Hector, these are your people now. You must lead them."

Hector narrowed his eyes. "That sounds ominously similar to goodbye."

Griffin couldn't explain his mission to people who had little knowledge of the outside world. His eyes caught on two sleeping figures near the back of the cave. One, a woman whose pale skin was slick with sweat. Sinead. He walked toward them, giving nods to the others lingering about.

"She's why they left." Gulliver didn't open his eyes as he spoke.

"What do you mean?"

His eyes slid open—well, as much as they could with the bruises. "Some people worry it's a plague. Every ache and pain they blame on Sinead. Only Hector will touch her and help her now that Shauna is gone."

Griffin slid down the wall to sit next to Gulliver. "She's going to be all right."

Gulliver snorted. "That's a lie."

"Yes, it probably is." He leaned his head back against the cool stone.

"The king's men came. They didn't find most of us, but Shauna and Nessa were collecting herbs to help Sinead. They took them, Griff. They let me go to get to you, but they truly do have you now, so what's the point of keeping them alive?" His gaze settled on the ground. Gulliver was a smart kid, he knew when there was no hope. "They offered you your magic back, didn't they?"

"How—"

"Your eyes. They flashed violet when you came in, but then the color disappeared. You're the one who taught me all about the magic of the three kingdoms, yet, I think the color is supposed to last longer. The king did not give you everything."

Griffin didn't know how the kid was so perceptive. "I'm not the king's man, Gullie. I made a deal to keep Shauna and Nessa safe."

"A deal with the king is never a good thing, even when protecting the people you care about. He will always twist it. Want to know who taught me that?"

He nodded.

"Shauna."

Shauna and Nessa were born in the prison realm. Their grandfather was a criminal sent to Myrkur ages ago. That was their only crime—the crime of their birth to a daughter of a criminal. A daughter who'd died giving birth to Nessa. There was no before for them, not like so many others. Like Griffin. They didn't know anything but struggle.

Shauna wouldn't want him to help the king.

But he refused to lose another friend.

Griffin leaned in real close and dropped his voice. "I'm going to the human realm."

Gulliver's eyes widened. "But... how?"

"The magic you told the king my family possessed."

Gulliver looked away and swallowed. "I didn't want to give you up. You told me before that no one could learn you're descended from a royal line, let alone the royal line of Iskalt. I'm sorry." Tears welled in his eyes.

"Gullie." Griffin bumped his shoulder. "One day, the king or maybe Kvek will come for you again, and I won't be here to protect you."

"I can protect myself."

One corner of Griffin's mouth curled up. "I know you can. But this realm has become too dangerous for you. You're coming with me."

Chapter 10

Gulliver stared at Griffin like he didn't believe the words. "You want..." He shook his head, wincing at the movement that caused him pain. "But I'm... I don't belong." He took a deep breath, and it shook on the way out. His eyes glassed over, but Griffin didn't know if it was from the pain of his missing tail or the shock.

"Gulliver, if you stay here... I'm afraid what will happen to you when I'm gone. I can't protect you when I'm not in this realm."

"But..." He wiped away a tear, probably hoping no one saw it. When he spoke again, his voice was nothing more than a whisper. "I'm not someone who gets chosen. You can't risk whatever it is you have to do by taking the orphan kid with half a tail and nothing else to call his own."

Griffin understood his hesitation then. Gulliver wasn't scared of venturing outside the kingdom he'd known his entire life. He didn't think he deserved to go.

This kid... he had a way of breaking Griffin's heart.

Griffin turned to face him fully and completely, not letting Gulliver look away. "You haven't been an orphan for almost ten years, not since I found you. You and me, Gulliver, we're a family. And I'm not leaving you behind." He had no choice but to leave Shauna and Nessa. But this, right here, was his choice, the one the king tried to take from him by going back on his word.

He groaned, thinking of Riona. He was going to have to thank her, wasn't he?

A commotion at the mouth of the cave drew his attention as Riona herself walked in, her steps echoing off stone walls. She stood at the opening that should have thwarted her, a permanent scowl on her face.

The reeling people of Fela jumped to their feet, but they didn't yell or confront Riona. They would never forget the king's warrior who destroyed their home.

And now, her eyes took in the cavern, probably noting the meager stores, the malnourished fae backing away from her. Her gaze settled on Griffin. "We must leave."

She was right. They'd been here too long. Griffin stood and held a hand down to Gulliver. He took it and let Griffin pull him up.

Hector stood behind Riona, one hand on the hilt of his rusted sword. Griffin didn't have the heart to tell him Riona could kill him before he even drew his weapon.

What if this entire mission was wrong? He was supposed to lead a dangerous person into the three realms who'd won their peace ten years ago when they defeated Regan and the people who served her —people like Griffin.

But he'd heard no news since then. Had the peace lasted?

Was he searching for something that would divide them once again?

Griffin approached Riona, towering over her. It wasn't fear racing through him necessarily, but more of a wariness. He had to keep his guard up around her. "We leave the horses here. Hector will see to them."

"But—"

Griffin cut her off with a snarl. "We are not taking horses into the human realm. We'll have no need of them there." He reached a hand back, snatching a handful of Gulliver's threadbare shirt that was once blue but had faded to a dull gray. "And this is my man you so honorably said I could bring."

"Man?" Riona didn't bother stopping Hector from leaving to gather the horses outside the cavern. "This thief-child?" Her cold eyes slid over Gulliver's bruised face, her distaste evident. "He can barely hold himself up. No, Griffin O'Shea, we will be better off just the two of us."

A few of the villagers neared, their anger plain. "Griff." Hector's mother, Kiaran clenched her jaw. "You've led one of the king's soldiers to the only place we are safe right now?"

He put a hand on her shoulder. "We are leaving." It was time to give all his fae an explanation. He pulled back his hand and sighed. "The king has tasked me with a mission."

"Since when do you do missions for the crown?" Daniel, a Dark Fae not much older than Griffin, spat.

These people knew so little about him. There was a time when everything he did was for a crown. If his community, his family learned of his past deeds, they'd never forgive him.

"King Egan thinks it's time the world was reminded we are here." He wished he believed his own words. "He is sending us through a portal to the human realm, and eventually into Fargelsi where I will search for a way to end the magic keeping us trapped in this land of perpetual night."

And what would they learn of the other kingdoms? War? Egan was anxious for it. And his armies were ready.

The villagers talked over one another, trying to make sense of this news. If they ever did, he hoped they'd tell him because he didn't know anything. Most of all, he didn't know what would happen if he actually managed to bring down the magic—which he very much doubted he could do without the full use of his own magic.

Riona tapped her foot. "We must leave." She turned on her heel. "The thief can come, but if he passes out or slows us down, you're carrying him."

Gulliver gripped Griffin's arm. "I won't let you down. Not ever again."

Griffin didn't blame Gulliver for revealing his family's magic to Egan. He put a hand on his shoulder and urged him to the opening. "I know you won't."

Hector stopped them. "This mission is dangerous, right?"

"What? Going into a realm where no one knows who I am and asking around about the prison magic?" He shrugged. "Easy."

It was a lie, and they both knew it.

Griffin never imagined he'd set foot in Fargelsi again, but now that the opportunity was there, he longed to lie in the grass and look at the puffy white clouds. He longed to feel the heat of the sun beating down on him.

But mostly, he couldn't shake the hope that he'd see the people he'd wronged again, that he'd find some sort of redemption.

But that was a dream from another lifetime.

Riona waited for them where the road wound along the outer edge of the orchard. The silver light of the moon guarded their steps. Griffin stopped beside her. "Not here." Not where any of those in the cavern could sneak out to watch. He didn't need them to see he was the one with the magic to open portals.

He made sure Gulliver was following before returning to the ruins of their village. Here, there was much better shelter, much more privacy.

"You're going to use magic, aren't you?" Gulliver's amber eyes lit with excitement, which made an odd contrast against his bruises.

It was hard for Griffin to remember sometimes that the Dark Fae living here had never seen magic. When prisoners arrived, the first thing they experienced upon entering the darkness of Myrkur was the absence of their magic.

Magic was the stuff of bedtime tales to fae like Gulliver.

Griffin nodded. "I need to create a portal." He needed a familiar place in his mind. He'd been to the human realm many times, and he loved every bit of it. His favorite place was somewhere called Ireland, a land of rocky crags and welcoming people. There were many places that looked out over the ocean. He could sit there for hours. Sometimes, he had. When he wasn't sent there on missions for Regan, he enjoyed exploring the human realm on his own.

"Get ready to step through the portal, I'm not sure how long I can keep it open."

Gulliver wasted no time in stepping up beside him, but Riona's scowl never left her face.

"I'm not diseased." His mind went back to Sinead, but the prison realm couldn't be his worry when he left. He had to focus on one problem at a time, and right now, that meant keeping himself and Gulliver alive.

Riona stepped to his other side. He shot her the kind of smile the old Griffin would have worn. Sometimes, he was able to catch glimpses of the man he was, the one that hadn't yet been hardened by this place.

Was there an old version of Riona?

His magic made the hairs on his arm stand on end as it gathered and pooled in his belly. He kept a firm image of Ireland in his mind. Gulliver would love it, but they couldn't stick around long enough for anyone to see his tail.

He counted backward in his head before the magic exploded from him in a flash of violet.

The blast sent Gulliver and Riona tumbling to the ground.

"Did it work?" Gulliver asked, looking around, excitement in his eyes. "Or does the human world look identical to ours?"

Riona pushed to her feet. "No, it doesn't. Griffin failed." Her accusatory glare cut through him, but he wouldn't back down.

"I've been without magic for ten years, so excuse me if it takes a while to get used to it again." Maybe this was a mistake.

Maybe the king put faith in the wrong man.

Or maybe, Griffin's magic knew something he didn't.

"Let's try again."

This time Gulliver hesitated, standing farther back from Griffin's side. Riona didn't move. Griffin let the magic free, but it didn't blast out of him like before. This was more of a slow trickle. One that, again, produced no portal.

"Maybe you're thinking of the wrong place." Gulliver shrugged.

"Gullie." Griffin's grin stretched wide. "You're a genius." If he was going to create a portal for the first time in ten years, one strong enough to breach the magic of the prison realm, he needed to choose a place that had more meaning to it. A place he'd visited more times than he could count.

Gripping Gulliver and Riona's hands, Griffin closed his eyes, picturing green pastures just outside a small town. And a broken-down barn where the girl he would forever love used to play. A smile curved his lips, and when the magic rose up in answer, it felt right.

A gust of wind blew the hair from his forehead. He stepped forward without opening his eyes. Dry and cracked dirt turned to fresh grass beneath his feet. The cool night breeze stilled, and Griffin's magic stuttered and faded as the bright sun greeted them.

When he opened his eyes, pain surged through his head at the brightness of the sun. Shielding his eyes, the first thing he saw was the small white house that needed more than a few repairs, and the unused barn.

The lawn hadn't been cut recently, and it curled around his feet. He'd let go of his companions and turned to watch the two Dark Fae revel in the first sunlight they'd ever felt.

Both stood, clutching their hands to their eyes.

Ten years of hard living in a realm without light was difficult for him, but they'd never seen the sun before, and it was too much.

Still, even Riona smiled as she squinted into the sun. Mimicking Griffin and lifting a hand to shield her eyes, her entire posture relaxed.

"You did it." Gulliver beamed a proud smile. "We're... free."

Griffin pulled him into a side hug, not wanting to ruin this moment with thoughts of all those they'd left behind. This wasn't a trip of joy.

They had a purpose, people to save.

A peace to destroy by opening the borders of the prison realm.

Likely, Griffin had just taken his first steps to bringing war to his world.

And once again, he was on the wrong side, because someone who didn't deserve his loyalty pulled the strings he had to dance to.

He chanced a glance at Riona, knowing she was here to keep him in line.

First, he had to survive. Do what he could to free Nessa and Shauna and all the others.

Then, maybe he could change his fate.

He could be a good man, choosing for himself where his loyalties would lie.

There was nothing to be done about that from the human realm. "Come on." He took off toward the barn, already knowing there'd be no animals inside. "We need to stay hidden until the sun goes down and I can portal us into Fargelsi."

Gulliver matched his stride despite the obvious pain it caused him. Griffin would make sure he saw a healer in Fargelsi.

"So." Gulliver grinned, his tail showing no signs of life. "Why does a human farm mean so much to you?"

Griffin opened the door and ushered them through. Riona collapsed onto a hay bale. "I miss the dark."

Of course she did.

"The sun is intense. Am I supposed to see black spots in my eyes?" Gulliver asked.

Griffin grunted. "What you're supposed to do is not look directly into it. Trust me, you'll feel a lot better once you've adjusted."

Gulliver climbed onto a stack of hay bales and grinned down at Griffin. With his bruising, it looked sort of menacing instead of happy. "You didn't answer my first question."

Griffin sat and rubbed a hand along the back of his neck. "The woman I once loved used to live here."

"You fell in love with a human?"

He shook his head. "Brea Robinson doesn't have a human bone in her body. She was a changeling."

Riona scoffed. "Changelings are myths. Don't listen to him, boy. He'll have you believing nonsense."

Griffin shrugged. They'd learn for themselves, eventually. The story of Brea Robinson and the human she'd been exchanged with at birth—Alona Cahill—was told far and wide in the fae realm.

Because the girls in question sat on thrones in two of the three kingdoms—and Brea's half-sister sat on a third.

But that history was for another time.

Griffin leaned his head back and closed his eyes.

This time, the image that filled his mind was one he'd tried to erase from his subconscious.

He'd lost that battle, because all he saw was Brea walking toward him and accepting Griffin as her husband.

She hadn't known how fae marriages intertwine magic and love.

Fae marriage bonds lasted forever. And the only way to break them was through death or a trip to the prison realm.

It had been ten years since he felt their marriage bond snap. But time did not erase all feelings.

Gulliver looked down on him and lowered his voice. "Don't worry, Griff. I believe you. That's what matters."

In that moment, as he pushed memories of Brea away, it was.

No matter who he spoke to or came across, they wouldn't remember him, and it had to stay that way for him to survive it.

Chapter 11

Griffin leaned back, letting the sunlight warm his face. He couldn't get enough of it. Yet, Gulliver sat in the shadows of the barn, shielding his face from the sun's rays streaming in through the window. His cat-like eyes ran with tears from the brightness of the late afternoon light, but he couldn't stop himself from looking at everything he could see.

"When will this misery end?" Riona's voice sounded muffled under her wings she'd shielded herself with.

"A few more hours, but it's fading. You'll be fine once the sun begins to set, and then we'll go into town for provisions."

"Do it again, Griff." Gulliver begged. "Open a portal."

"I can't right now, I must rest for a while and wait until night." He glanced at Riona, wondering if she understood the limitations of his power.

"Stop your endless chatter," Riona grumbled, burrowing deeper into the last moldy bits of hay they could find in the abandoned barn. Sometime over the last decade, Brea's parents had moved away. A foreclosure sign faded with age sat in the front yard where Brea used to play as a little girl.

"We should let Riona rest. Let's go for a walk in the shade."

Griffin tilted his head toward the door. "Keep the hood pulled down low over your face, and you'll be fine."

"Don't go far," Riona warned.

"Where would we even go, Riona? We'll be just across the yard." Griffin led Gulliver toward the house, guiding him with a steady hand until they entered the shade of the house.

"Will we get to see any humans, do you think?" Gulliver asked, searching the yard as if a human might appear at any moment. He held a hand up to shield his eyes and stumbled over his own feet—which was unlike the steady thief.

"We will when we go into town this afternoon." Griffin chuckled at his eagerness. He reminded him of Brea and her certainty that dragons had to be a thing in Eldur—the land of fire. "But I need you to be very careful while we are there. Humans don't have things like tails and wings or cat eyes. You must promise to listen to me and do exactly as I say."

"Promise."

Griffin moved to sit on the back porch steps, gently pulling Gulliver down to sit beside him. His tail was bandaged, and the poor kid couldn't get comfortable anywhere.

"Tell me more about magic," Gulliver pleaded. Where the boy was delighted with what little magic he had seen so far, Riona seemed terrified of it. A fact Griffin tucked away for the future.

"There are three fae realms," Griffin began.

"I know that already," Gulliver interrupted. "In Fargelsi, it is always spring. The lands of Eldur are dangerous with hot deserts and beautiful oasis. And Iskalt is cold and dark, but not as dark as Myrkur. I want to know about the magic."

"Well, fae magic is as different as the people who wield it," Griffin said. "In Fargelsi, the people draw their magic from nature. They must speak the spells to bring forth their power. They can grow buildings right out of the ground and light fires with a single word. And in Eldur, where the fire fae live, they draw their magic from the sun. During the day they are far more powerful than Fargelsians who have use of their magic at all times. But at night, when the sun fades, so does Eldurian magic, leaving its people powerless until the sun rises again. And in Iskalt, where I was born, we draw our magic from the moon, which is why we're stuck here until night falls."

"Wow, I bet Eldur and Iskalt hate each other," Gulliver said.

"We did for a long time. But my brother is king of Iskalt now, and he grew up in the Eldur queen's court. The new Eldur queen was like a sister to him. And my wife, Brea… I guess she's my ex-wife now—such a human thing—is a princess of Eldur *and* Fargelsi, and she's probably the Iskalt queen too. Brea's half-sister is the queen of Fargelsi now, so they are all friends. These are things I need you to know so you're prepared for whatever we might face, but let's keep that knowledge between us. The less our traveling companion knows, the better."

"I don't think she likes magic." Gulliver nodded toward the barn where Riona stood in the doorway with her jacket draped over her head and her wings tucked under her long shirt in case any humans happened by. "She definitely doesn't like the sun."

"Is it this bright every day?" Riona walked toward them, shielding her eyes.

"You'll get used to it."

She looked up at the run down two-story house with a frown. "Do all humans live in such nice houses?"

"This is actually an old abandoned house." Griffin wasn't sure how to explain the things she would see on this trip. To someone who'd grown up in Myrkur, Brea's old home looked like a mansion.

"Abandoned?" She scowled. "Two families could live here and never see each other. Ugh, how do the humans not burn up here?" She moved back into the shade, tying a strip of fabric around her long braids to lift them off her neck. "It's so hot here." She fanned her face. "It is like this in Fargelsi?"

"I'm afraid the sun is brighter and hotter in Gelsi." Griffin elbowed Gulliver, letting a small smile cross his face. It was bad parenting to so obviously enjoy her discomfort, but it wasn't like she hadn't earned it.

Her shoulders fell. "I can't do this." She shook her head. "My eyes won't stop running, and it's like a sword stabbing into my head every time I open them."

"That's why we're going into town soon. We need some supplies before we leave for Gelsi."

"And how do you intend to pay for these supplies?" Riona frowned.

"The king said he would give you enough money for the journey." But Griffin sighed. Of course that promise was just another lie. He wondered how Egan expected loyalty when he gave none.

"I brought some small gemstones with me, but I don't know if they will be worth much to humans."

"Surely we have something of value to trade. Something that wouldn't be suspicious to a human." Griffin began to feel the futility of this mission. They would never get anywhere without the means to purchase what they needed.

"I stole this from the man who took my tail." Gulliver held up a gold ring with a stone the size of a fire nut.

A triumphant smile lit Griffin's face. "That's my boy." He took the ring, thinking he wasn't so great at this parenting thing. "Stealing is wrong, but in this case, I will allow it. We will fetch a fine price for this at the pawn shop in town. It won't bring back your tail, but it's the least you deserve for what that man did to you. Today, you're going to learn what a cheeseburger is."

Griffin held his breath as the human peered through a thick lens at the stone in Gulliver's ring. Griffin kept a hand on Gulliver's shoulder to keep him from wandering around. In his current state, he was like a nervous horse in a house, knocking things over and tripping on his own feet.

"Beautiful opal, and the gold is twenty-four karat. I can offer you two hundred store credit and two hundred cash." The man set the ring down.

"Deal." Griffin nodded and went to look around, grateful to see a large selection of sunglasses.

The man behind the counter gave them odd looks as Gulliver pulled the hat down to further conceal himself. It only sort of did the trick but if the man noticed anything different about them, he didn't say.

Riona hadn't taken her eyes off the human yet. "Stop staring," Griffin whispered. She looked uncomfortable with her wings stuffed inside her jacket. All her clothes were made to accommodate her wings with slits in the back. She would need a better disguise.

Griffin searched through the sunglasses for styles that wouldn't stand out. Something that looked like it came from an apothecary or a smithy. And the lenses couldn't be too dark. Just enough to conceal Gulliver's eyes and give them both some comfort from the sun's bright light. He even grabbed a pair for himself.

Riona and Gulliver watched as Griffin searched for clothes that wouldn't be too conspicuous in the fae world. He gathered an outfit for each of them and let them choose a backpack to carry them in. He spent about half of their credit. The other half he used to buy some extra supplies. It was the best he could do given that their "king" hadn't provided them with the means to do the job he'd sent them to do.

"Thank you, sir." Griffin ignored the way the man eyed them suspiciously and accepted the money that would buy them one of the best meals they would ever eat. "I must warn you of something before we get to the tavern. McDonald's has what I can only describe as a torture park. I went to examine it many years ago, climbing into this structure where children hit me on their way by. There was an entire area with little balls they threw at me. And then a group of human females started screaming at me that I wasn't supposed to be there. It was my first experience with human torture. I will protect you from it."

Gulliver gave him a relieved smile. "Thank you."

"Here, put these on." Griffin passed the sunglasses to each of them as they left the store in their new clothes. He tucked his into his shirt pocket.

"What is this contraption?" Riona stared at the glasses. "I don't need spectacles."

"Put them on." Griffin insisted.

"Ohh." Riona sighed in relief as she slid the glasses in place. "That's so much better."

"Hey, I can see!" Gulliver's eyes stopped watering almost immediately.

"These should make it easier for you until you adjust to the sun." He passed them each a backpack with their old clothes and a few tools that might come in handy later.

As they walked along the sidewalk, Griffin kept a close eye on Riona. He still didn't trust her, but she was clearly unnerved by the human world.

"I always heard they didn't have magic." She eyed the cars coming and going along the street, and he imagined none of it made any sense to her.

"I guess in a way they do have magic, but they call it science and technology."

"They just ride around in their metal beasts like it's nothing." She shook her head in wonder.

"I think you're going to need to learn to just go with it, Riona," Gulliver said as they crossed the street to McDonald's, his eyes wide and unblinking trying to take it in all at once.

"The kid is right. The human world is overwhelming in its own way," Griffin said. "But when you're faced with magic, real magic, you're not going to have time to react with fear and distrust."

"I'm starting to see that," she murmured, following Griffin into the too bright fluorescents of McDonald's. "I just don't like it."

Griffin glared at the bright blue torture structure across the restaurant. Once he ordered their food, he made them sit as far as possible away from it, casting suspicious glances whenever he saw someone enter the area with the torture balls.

In the end, Gulliver ate four cheeseburgers and two apple pies before he was finally full and sleepy.

They managed to avoid the human torture balls and made their way back to the farm just as darkness fell, and Griffin's magic came alive inside him once again.

"Do it again, Griff." Gulliver giggled, actually giggled. It was the most child-like sound Griffin had ever heard from the boy.

Griffin couldn't help his answering smile as he began to open a portal between his hands, squeezing it down to a pinprick of light and letting it swell into a sphere the size of his head.

"Stop your horsing around." Riona stepped away from Griffin, the violet light of his magic reflecting in her dark lenses.

"You can take those off now, you know. It's dark."

"Not dark enough with all your flashing lights," Riona muttered as she tucked her glasses into her bag.

"I'm practicing." Griff pulled on his magic, feeding more into the beginnings of a portal in his hands. "It's been a decade since I last held my magic, and portaling into Fargelsi is going to be difficult. My magic requires that we return to the place where we last were in Myrkur. I'm counting on the border magic not allowing that. Otherwise, this mission is doomed before it truly begins."

"Might as well give it a shot here," Gulliver said, looking around the Robinson's overgrown drive.

Griffin guided them to the open field where the moonlight shone brightest. Chills ran down his spine when he realized it was the exact spot he'd portaled to when he first came looking for Brea Robinson all those years ago. It felt like another lifetime. A time when he was just a young kid with a head full of all the wrong ideas.

"Wait!" Riona took another step away from Griffin. "I need a second." Her voice shook with anxiety.

"It's okay." Gulliver took her hand in his. "It's just like stepping through a doorway."

"Right." She lifted her chin but stayed where she was. Probably not a bad idea for them to keep their distance since he had little confidence this would even work.

He lifted his face to the moonlight, letting it revive the magic within. It felt good. Like he'd found a missing piece of his soul. With a deep breath, Griffin called on his O'Shea magic, the violet light sparking at his fingertips as he pulled his hands apart, opening a dark black portal... to Fela. His hands trembled as the magic rebelled against him, and the portal collapsed.

Riona gave a startled gasp, and Gulliver groaned, kicking a clump of grass in frustration.

"No, that was good." Griffin wiped a clammy hand across his brow, feeling faint from the effort. "The magic around Myrkur won't let me in. That's what we want."

"So, what now?" Riona asked.

"Now, I need to focus." Griffin rubbed his hands together, clearing his mind of thoughts of Myrkur. For years, he never let himself think about Fargelsi. About the home he'd left behind. Not the palace where his adopted mother reigned, but the small cottage on the shores of Loch Villandi. How might his life have played out there if he could have contented himself with the simple life of a farmer?

He couldn't dwell on what ifs now. He let his mind recall the days he'd spent with Brea when she first came to Fargelsi. Their time at the cottage were among the happiest memories of his life.

Violet light crackled under his skin, sparking at his fingertips as he once again pulled his hands apart, creating an opening in the atmosphere, like a tear in the fabric of the human world. Late afternoon sunlight spilled through the opening, and the scent of home filled his senses.

Riona groaned, scrambling for her sunglasses.

"You first, Gullie." Griffin nodded for him to step through the portal. Riona followed.

With a last look at Brea's childhood home, Griffin returned to his.

Chapter 12

No air smelled as sweet to Griffin O'Shea as that of the Fargelsi countryside. As the portal closed behind him and his magic faded once again, Griffin took a deep breath. He was home. He could see the hillside cottage Queen Regan had given him when he was still only a young man. She'd recognized his need for his own space away from the chaos of palace life. In those moments, she had been good to him. A true mother who cared for the young Iskaltian prince she'd taken as her charge when he was just two years old. Those moments made it difficult to think poorly of her even now.

Griffin turned away from the cottage to find Gulliver running in circles in the thick green grass of the open pasture, a huge smile on his face, and the first flicker of movement in the remnant of his tail.

"Slow down, Gullie, you're going to—" Griffin shook his head when Gulliver tripped over his own feet. Losing his balance, he stumbled head over heels down the hillside.

Griffin jogged to catch up with the boy when Gulliver fell over again trying to stand.

"You all right?" Griffin leaned down to help him up.

"I'm fine." Gulliver dusted himself off. "Everything's just off kilter without my tail. I don't feel like me. You think I'll always be this clumsy oaf now?" His slim shoulders drooped. "I feel so useless."

"You are going to be fine, Gullie." Griffin bent down to his level. "It'll take some time to heal, but you'll be okay, I promise. Now, come help me make camp in the woods. It's been a long day for us already, but sunset's not far off. We'll rest up tonight, and then, in the morning, we'll see if we can buy some horses from one of the farms in the area." He turned to see Riona standing with her arms crossed over her chest and her sunglasses perched on her nose.

"You all right?"

She nodded. "Just tired. I don't know how I'll manage in this cursed daylight." She followed Griffin and Gulliver along the trail and into the forest.

"Loch Villandi is just ahead. We'll camp there where it's cooler, but do not touch the water. You hear me, Gullie?" Griffin raised his voice. "No matter what, you don't go near the water. I don't want you falling in. Loch Villandi's waters are deceptively beautiful, but dangerous. Stay away."

"Yes, sir." Gulliver said over a huge yawn as he rubbed his belly. "We have any leftover cheeseburgers?"

"Why can't we just portal to the palace?" Riona stomped through the underbrush early the next morning as they made their way up to the cottage. Griffin had scouted ahead to find a young family lived there now.

"Griff has O'Shea magic," Gulliver explained. "He can open portals to the human world but not from place to place inside the fae realms, right, Griff?"

"That's right, buddy. Besides, it's only a few hours to the palace. If we leave soon, we can start making inquiries in the Dragur Village this afternoon." He had no idea how he was supposed to get an audience with the former king when no one knew Griffin used to be a royal himself, but he'd have to think of something soon.

"Very well." Riona rooted around in her bag. "Use these." She handed him three small dark gemstones. They glittered in the morning light. At first, they appeared black and then a deep garnet and purple.

"Myr opals. They're worth enough to purchase horses and whatever else we might need for travel. That is, if you can even find anything worth purchasing out here in the middle of nowhere."

They reminded Griffin of fire rubies from Eldur. They would fetch a good price well beyond the cost of horses and provisions.

"You two stay here while I go talk to the farmer and his wife."

"Not going to happen." Riona shook her head. "I don't trust you."

"If you think I'm going to leave Gullie behind just to ditch you, then you haven't been paying attention." Griffin set off along the path to the cottage.

The farmer met him along the way.

"Saw your campfire this morning." The young fae man tilted his hat in greeting. "Where you headed?"

"Vindur City. We have need of horses and provisions if you or any of your neighbors have any to sell." Griffin fished the gemstones from his pocket, letting them catch the light so they sparkled like fire in his hand. The farmer's eyes widened at the sight. He could trade the stones for enough coin to plant his crops for the coming season and line his pockets with the rest.

"Aye, I have a couple of horses I can spare. Come with me to the barn, and I'll see you properly outfitted for your journey." The man was kind and chatted easily with Griffin about the way to Vindur. The ease with which the man trusted caught Griffin by surprise. The Fargelsi of his past was not a land where neighbor trusted neighbor, much less a veritable stranger.

After a drink of fresh cider at the farmer's wife's insistence, Griffin made his way back to camp with two saddled horses and plenty of food and cider to fill even Gulliver's belly.

Griffin smiled at the parcel of silver figs the farmer's wife brought him. He'd planted the fig trees himself when he lived here. They were his favorite fruit. He liked them fresh from the tree, warmed by the Gelsi sun.

"Griff!" Gulliver called when he returned to their camp. "Look what I found!" He ran up to Griffin, his cap full of ripe Gelsi berries.

"You didn't eat any of these, did you?" Griffin asked in alarm. The magic-blocking berries were Regan's favorite weapon. She'd used them to subdue her people and stifle their magic.

"No, Riona said we should ask you about them first, but there are hundreds of them, Griff. I've never seen so much fruit. There's not a dead bush among them."

"Riona was right. You can't eat these." Griffin dumped the contents of Gulliver's hat onto the ground. He wasn't sure what they might do to Dark Fae. Gulliver and Riona didn't have magic, but they were magical beings. "New rule. Don't eat anything in Fargelsi without checking with me first. Actually, scratch that. Don't *eat* anything or *touch* anything in Fargelsi without asking if it's safe. The prettier a thing is, the more likely it's dangerous."

"I was hoping we could feast on berries for breakfast."

"How about sun warmed figs and fresh cheese instead?" Griffin handed him the package from the farmer's wife.

"You got food *and* horses?" Gulliver's tail gave an awkward flick behind him causing him to leap back like something goosed him on the rear.

"Settle down there, kid. That tail of yours seems to be waking up. How's it feel? You need fresh bandages?" Griffin checked over his various bruises and cuts, glad to see they were healing.

"It's kind of numb." He sighed. "Like it's not quite there, so it surprises me when the feeling comes back."

"We'll find a healer we can trust and see what they can do for you." Griffin popped a silver fig into his mouth. He'd have to do some creative lying to explain the presence of the kid's tail to a fae who'd never seen such a thing before.

"Is everyone in this land so rich they can afford to sell their best horses and provisions on a whim?" Riona examined the fine pair of geldings and their sleek leather saddles.

Griffin offered her some fresh fruit and cheese and went to retrieve his bag from their camp. "I think, Riona, you will soon learn a hard lesson. It's not wealth you see here, but you have seen so much extreme poverty you don't know the kind of lives average fae can live here."

She scowled at him. "You forget I live in the king's fortress and want for nothing."

"The king's castle is a hovel. Just wait. I'll show you a true palace." Griffin left her to mount her horse. "Gullie, tuck your tail in and keep your glasses on. If we meet anyone along the way, remember, the fae here have never seen the likes of you."

"Am I that strange looking?" Gulliver asked over a mouthful of cheese.

Griffin pulled himself up into the saddle and reached to haul Gulliver up behind him. "You're a handsome lad, but in this land, people look like me. Boring and plain with only pointed ears and shining eyes to set us apart from the humans. You are far more interesting."

He turned to Riona. "That goes for you too. Keep your wings hidden, and if we run into anyone on the road, let me do the talking."

"Very well, but don't forget for a moment, I am in charge of this mission."

"I sincerely doubt you will ever let me forget it." Griffin nudged his horse along the trail toward the road to Vindur City.

"The heat is insufferable here." Riona dabbed at the sweat running down her face as the cool Gelsi breeze stirred the tall grasses along the rolling green hills around them.

"It feels quite cool to me," Gulliver said, munching on a snack of hard tack and nuts. The boy hadn't stopped eating since they left Myrkur. "You sure you're not just complaining to have something to talk about?"

Griffin chuckled at his honest assessment of her constant grumbling. "I think maybe she's having a harder time because she's a Slyph and you are Tuatha De Danann." The Tuatha De Danann were Dark Fae of the land, and Griffin long suspected they were among the oldest fae creatures in all the realms.

"My mother was a Slyph, but I am not," Riona said, matter of fact.

"I thought all fae who fly were Slyph," Gulliver said.

"How many Slyph have you seen with white wings and dark skin?" Riona raised a brow at Gulliver.

"None." Gulliver shrugged and fished around Griffin's bag for more figs.

"Will you stop eating? Save some for the rest of us." Griffin swatted his hand away.

"So, what kind of fae was your father?" Gulliver asked in that way kids could get away with but adults never could.

"Gullie, that's rude."

"What? She's pretty, I just want to know how she got white wings."

"My father was Asrai," Riona said. "My mother was of the sky, and my father, the sea. There used to be many with such origins all living together." Her smile turned sad.

Griffin found himself studying her face for any sign of Asrai features, but he didn't know what to look for. He suspected her Asrai blood was the cause of her discomfort in the sunny climate of Gelsi. Asrai blood ran cold, and they preferred the depths of the seas and lakes they inhabited.

"We will reach the Dragur Forest soon. You'll be more comfortable in the shade." Griffin picked up their pace.

"Remind me of our new rule, Gullie?" He cast a glance over his shoulder at the boy.

"Don't touch anything or eat anything. I got it, Griff. I am twelve, you know."

"Well, that rule is extra important in the Dragur. It's an ancient place filled with dangerous creatures and poisonous plants. Once we reach the village on the other side, we'll find a room for the night and inquire at the palace to see if the queen takes audience with her subjects the way the Eldur queens do. That's our best hope of getting in to see Brandon. And if that goes well, we'll see about finding a healer to look at your tail."

"It's throbbing something fierce after sitting in this saddle all day." Gulliver fidgeted behind him.

As the afternoon wore on, Gulliver dozed against Griffin's back, and Riona fell silent, leaving Griffin to enjoy his homecoming. As much as he'd missed the sun, he welcomed the cool shade of the Dragur Forest.

"I don't think I like this place." Riona rubbed her hands over her arms. "It feels... wrong."

"They say the forest was once haunted," Griffin said, giving her a sympathetic look. "It's always rubbed me the wrong way too. But if we keep to the road and reach the other side before nightfall, we will be fine. You don't want to let the sun go down on you in the Dragur."

"I don't think I like Fargelsi. It is beautiful and so green and lovely. I just can't quite decide what it is that I don't like—besides the sun. The glasses help, but it's just so infernally bright. I'll never get used to it."

"I used to say that about Myr," Griffin said. "In those first few years, the darkness haunted me. I found it deeply depressing until I began to see the beauty in it. It's never felt quite right to me, but I adjusted. I still missed the sun and the vivid colors though."

"Well, I don't plan to be here long enough to adjust." Riona shifted in her saddle. "But I can see how much you've missed this place." She scowled down at a row of bushes along the side of the road. The blood-red flowers bobbed in the breeze. "I think it's the colors that bother me. Everything looks so unnatural it hurts my eyes."

"Open your mind, Riona." Griffin laughed, stretching his arms out wide. "Take a moment to experience the land and culture that is not your own. Yes, it's different and very foreign to you, but maybe you can find a way to enjoy this adventure. You can still think the colors are weird and the smells strange. That doesn't make them wrong."

"Perhaps you have a point." Riona lips twisted into something resembling a smile.

Familiar landmarks sent Griffin's heart racing as they approached the outskirts of Dragur Village. It had grown in the years of his absence. The trees were taller, thicker. There was an abundance here that wasn't here before. The inhabitants of the village lived in the trees, using their magic to grow their houses from the trees themselves.

Griffin watched the wonder cross Gulliver's face as he saw the villagers come and go from their tree houses, using the winding stairs made of bark and vines to reach the heights of the village in the canopy overhead. That was where most of them lived, while the businesses flourished beneath them on the forest floor. Rock buildings rising from the ground now stood between massive tree trunks with open doors, welcoming weary travelers into taverns and inns that had grown prosperous in the intervening years.

As they approached the palace, Griffin experienced a moment of extreme confusion. Everything was so different. But of course it would be. The Gelsi Palace he knew as a child was destroyed in the battle between Regan and Brea. His wife had turned the palace to rubble. Of course the new queen would have built a new one in its place.

"Woah." Gulliver gazed up at the twin waterfalls. That detail hadn't changed. Nor had the vine bridge that stretched from the forest across the Villandi River, though it wasn't quite the same either. These vines were white with the palest blue flowers.

Riona reined her horse to a stop as she stared in awe at the towering ivory structure. The new palace held hints of the old, but it was lighter... somehow happier than the palace of his memory.

"It looks as if it grew from the ground," Gulliver said in wonder.

"It did." Griffin smiled at his open-mouthed stare. "That is how the magic of Gelsi works. The people of this land speak an ancient language of power that can call forth anything they want from the land itself. They have only to learn how to ask."

"I never knew such riches existed," Riona murmured. "You were right, my king's fortress is a hovel in comparison to this sheer beauty."

Griffin couldn't take his eyes from the place that was so like the one he'd once called home. Pale ivory towers seemed to reach for the clouds, taller and stronger than the ones that stood there before. Bright blue tiles gleamed from the domed roof of the central structure. Hundreds of crystal clear windows glinted in the sunlight, letting the fresh Gelsi sunshine sweep the halls inside. White vines with bright green leaves crept up the sides of the towers to wrap around the spires. The twin waterfalls fell at each side of the palace, crashing to the river below.

"Time to go see if we can bluff our way inside." Griffin nudged his horse forward.

"You grew up here?" Gulliver whispered.

"This palace is new. The one that was here when I was young was similar and every bit as grand as this one."

"You think they'll let us inside?"

"Somehow I doubt that." Anxiety gripped his chest as they made their way across the bridge. Part of Griffin expected Regan to show up any moment, screaming at him for his absence all these years. But somewhere behind those walls, beyond the palace to the gardens, lay the grave of the woman who'd raised him. Against his better judgment, love for that woman still stirred in his heart.

"State your business at the palace." The guards at the open gates halted their approach, staring wide eyed at Riona and her unusual tattoos that never seemed to still along the surface of her dark skin. He should have known hiding her wings wasn't enough.

"We are here to speak with your queen and her father, Brandon O'Rourke. You will let us pass." Riona spoke with authority as she reached for her sword and unfurled her wings.

Blast that woman for not listening to him.

Her white wings spanned the width of the bridge, blocking the guards on the palace side from those on the village side of the river.

Delicate like lace, the filmy membranes of her wings seemed as if the slightest pressure would tear right through them. But a Slyph's wings were like armor, and Riona was prepared to wrap them around Griffin and Gulliver and force her way past the guards.

"Riona, no!" Griffin stepped in front of her. "This is not the way. These people are not our enemies."

"What is she?" the queen's guards murmured, drawing their weapons. Uncertainty and fear spurned their actions, and Griffin knew they were about to find themselves in a dark cell far beneath the palace. Maybe then, Riona would stop complaining about the sunlight long enough to realize she'd ruined everything.

"Griffin O'Shea." A familiar voice cut through the tension as the guards parted for the last person Griffin ever expected to see again.

"Myles?" Griffin shook his head in confusion. Ten years, and the boy he'd once abducted from the human realm still wore that stupid smirk on his face.

"It's been a while, Griff." Myles shrugged, waving the guards away. "I see you've made some interesting new friends." He eyed Riona with curiosity before turning to Griffin with a smile. "Do you have any idea how weird it is to be the only person in the whole fracking fae world who remembers you?"

Chapter 13

Griffin had no words, no actions as he stood frozen on the vine bridge that was once destroyed in an epic battle between his wife and his surrogate mother.

Their family was... complicated.

Especially because he assumed said wife was now married to his brother.

Complicated indeed.

But... no one was supposed to know who he was. He'd come to terms with the three realms not knowing he ever existed, to being a stranger in their midst.

And yet, the smirking human gave him hope.

Griffin stayed quiet as Myles ordered the guards to take Griffin and Riona's horses to the palace stables and turned to walk back into the palace.

Myles threw a look over his shoulder. "Well, come on then. The day Griffin O'Shea shows up is a special one." He looked to Gulliver. "Do you know why?"

Gulliver shook his head, not taking his eyes from the human.

A smiled widened Myles' lips. "Because, dear boy, it means I get to prove to my wife I was right. That there really was a red-headed dude who abducted me and then married by best friend, trying to trap her with wonky fae vows that don't allow for divorce. I mean, seriously Griff, it's the twenty-first century." He skipped, literally skipped, down the gleaming marble hallway.

Next to Griffin, Riona kept a hand on the hilt of her sword. She'd pulled her wings in, but they were still visible, causing every servant they passed to stop and stare.

Myles pushed open a heavy oak door, held in place by a series of flowering vines. Griffin had never forgotten how beautiful Fargelsi was, how full of life.

But he had forgotten how it made him feel. Here in this kingdom, he could breathe.

Riona hesitated on the threshold. "I don't like it here. Why is he smiling so much?" She paused. "And singing? Something isn't right with this man."

Griffin peeked into the sitting room where Myles hummed a song as he poured goblets of wine at a table in the back. "There are many, many things wrong with Myles." He shook his head with a hint of a smile. "But right now he is our best hope." He was their way in, their way to an audience with Brandon.

Gullie pushed past Griffin and flopped onto the couch. "Oh." He sighed. "This is comfortable."

Sometimes Griffin forgot people like Gulliver that had never been outside the prison realm didn't know there was anything better than the squalor they'd always known.

And Griffin wasn't sure if that ignorance was a gift or a curse.

"What are you singing?" Gulliver sat up.

Myles looked to him and grinned. Riona was right. He smiled too much. But then, Griffin had once been a man liberal with his smiles.

"Just a little Beatles."

Gulliver removed his sunglasses, oblivious to the gawking that came from Myles. "Beatles? Like a bug? You're singing about bugs?"

A laugh burst free of Myles. "I like you, cat man."

"Cat man?"

Myles joined him on the couch. "Like a superhero. Someone who saves the day. They're always different from anyone else, but that's what makes them special."

"But I'm not different. In Myrkur, all the Dark Fae have distinguishing features. Horns, tales, wings..."

"Myrkur?"

"We don't have time to tell each other everything we don't know." Griffin snagged a cup of wine. "Because with Myles, that's a lot."

Myles opened his mouth to protest but shut it and shrugged. "Here's my order of knowledge importance. One, will knowing something make my wife mad? Two, will not knowing something make my wife mad? Three, will—never mind, let's just say I want to keep her happy."

"So, that's how you came to be here? You married a fae woman?" Griffin still couldn't fathom how the human came to be here in Gelsi.

Myles jumped from the couch. "Oh yeah." He walked toward a bookshelf. "I was in here earlier and forgot it."

A golden circlet made to look like a ring of vines rested on the shelf. Myles picked it up and set it on his head. "I'm sort of King of Fargelsi. Sometimes, I forget."

Riona scowled. "How does one forget they're king?"

But Griffin knew how. He was Myles.

Myles shrugged. "I mean, the queen is ruler of Gelsi. She handles the diplomacy stuff. The last time I tried to help, I accidentally gave the farming rights of the same plot of land to three people. Before that, I organized the solstice party and ordered the wrong kind of wine. The queen usually waters it down for that night to keep it somewhat classy. Well, I didn't do that, and let's just say pandemonium ensued."

"We sure this guy is a king?" Riona gave him an incredulous stare.

Myles lifted one shoulder in a shrug. "King Consort. I have duties of state, and I assist my wife in making decisions. Though, I prefer to sit on the throne and look pretty while she rules the kingdom."

"That doesn't seem fair." Gulliver gave him a thoughtful look.

"That's my specialty." Myles smiled. "I'm really good at doing nothing and looking pretty. Though, I do dabble in mediation between tenants and landowners from time to time."

Griffin had a feeling Myles was very good at that. Hearing him speak made Griffin long for better times. When he wasn't beholden to a cruel king who held Shauna and Nessa captive. He couldn't take a moment of relief being back in Gelsi because he knew the conditions his people were living in back in Myrkur.

Griffin drained the rest of his wine and advanced on Myles. Myles scrambled away from him.

"Hey, remember when you kidnapped me?" Myles' voice shook. "That was fun, right? We don't want to spoil it with a repeat."

Gulliver's brow creased. "Griffin wouldn't do that."

Griffin could feel Riona's eyes burning into him, seeing him in a new light. "Gulliver," she started. "I think you'd be surprised what people do when they have no other choice."

Was that about Griffin or her? It was the first crack in Riona's armor, and he couldn't help wondering what King Egan held over her.

Turning his attention back to Myles, Griffin ran a hand through his hair and sighed. "You aren't supposed to remember me, Myles. That's what I signed up for. The prison realm erases people from the three kingdoms as though they'd never existed."

But one person remembering him meant others had been told of Griffin the traitor, the abductor. The man who'd loved a girl so completely, he'd paid the price of her freedom, entering the prison world of his own accord to break their marriage bond and let her go.

Myles' eyes darted from Griffin to Riona and back to Gulliver. "Why have you returned? More importantly *how* have you returned?"

Griffin scowled. "King or not, you will answer me when I ask a question."

"I didn't hear a question."

He pushed out another sigh. Myles had always been difficult. "How do you know who I am?"

Myles put a hand on the back of the couch as if to steady himself.

"We don't know for sure. For the longest time, everyone thought I made you up as a joke. Once I managed to convince a few people I was actually serious, Brandon went through his books. It took months, but he found a bit of buried information. We knew it wasn't because I'm human. If that was the case, Queen Alona would remember you too. And she doesn't. I've asked."

Griffin didn't interrupt him, instead nodding for him to continue.

"There was one difference between me and Alona. When you went into the prison realm and crossed the magical barrier, I was already back in the human realm."

Griffin took a step back, not meeting anyone's eyes as the thought rolled through his mind.

The prison magic, as powerful as it was, didn't reach into the human realm. A smile slid across his lips. "Myles, I think I love you."

Myles smirked. "Well, whatever floats your boat. But I do have to warn you I'm married to a queen, so it's going to take a lot of presents to win my heart."

Riona looked accusingly as Griffin. "This human is an idiot. You couldn't have found *anyone else* to help us on our quest?"

"Don't you get it?" Griffin asked. "This is the first piece of the puzzle, the first chink in the magic. No magic is infinite and all powerful. And if the barrier magic around Myrkur, the same magic that steals memories and magic alike, can't penetrate the human realm, it means it has a weakness, two weaknesses since we were able to portal into the human realm through the barrier magic. And when there are two, there are more."

Riona pursed her lips. "You're talking to two fae and one human who have no magic. At least, I hope the human doesn't have magic because he'd probably light the entire world on fire. Explain what you mean."

Griffin couldn't contain his excitement. He smiled as he spoke. "Think of chain mail. You're used to that, yes?"

She nodded.

"Good. Each link is connected to another, to many more. And it's strong." He demonstrated with his hands. "So, think about the links and what would happen if a handful of them failed, if they didn't stay linked. What would you get?"

Understanding lit in her eyes. "A vulnerability."

"Exactly." He paced the length of the room and back again. "Exactly." His feet stopped moving. "We need to find the next vulnerability."

Myles' eyes widened as he looked at them. "You did break out, didn't you?"

Riona straightened her spine. "I am one of King Egan's trusted soldiers. We have no need to break out."

Griffin thought for a moment. "We didn't escape from Egan, but we did break out through the magic."

"King... you mean the prison realm has a king?" Myles turned to Griffin in surprise

"Of course." She scowled. "How else would we survive?"

Griffin held his tongue, trying to keep his ideas of surviving from ending this quest before it really began. Riona lived in Myrkur, truly lived. She had everything she needed while the people of Fela and other villages barely had enough to eat. It was something she'd never understand. He knew that because the old Griffin wouldn't have known. He was blind to the hardships of the people Regan trapped in Fargelsi with a border magic that...

Gulliver's eyes narrowed. Riona stopped moving.

And Myles, well, he watched them with a new distrust in his eyes. "You're trying to bring the prison magic down, looking for its weak points like Brea did with the Fargelsi magic. Only this time... you want to release all the criminals."

It was a statement more than a question. Griffin saw it in his eyes. Myles knew the truth. Well, not the entire truth. He thought Myrkur was a land of criminals, not the Dark Fae.

"You don't understand." Griffin pointed to Gulliver and then to Riona. "Have you ever heard of Dark Fae?"

"Of course."

Griffin leveled him with a glare. "Outside of the children's stories."

"Fine. No. But they're not real."

"Aren't they? Try telling Gulliver his tail is a fake. Don't let Riona know you think those wings are a trick of the light. The Dark Fae are fae just like me and that wife of yours. And they too have been forgotten by the world. Yet, unlike me, they never deserved their fate." He had so much more he wanted to say, but Myles wasn't the right person to tell of the king who was dying to start a war once the magic was gone. And he certainly wouldn't say it in front of Riona.

"All of them?" Myles rubbed the back of his neck. "They're all real?"

Before Griffin could answer, the door burst open, and four children ran in, the last of which stumbled with each step.

"Papa." One of them lunged for Myles.

The tension vanished from his posture as he picked up two squealing girls and threw them on the couch. "Now, girls, Papa has to talk to these nice people."

Griffin couldn't wrap his head around Myles being a father, something Griff wouldn't get to do if he couldn't bring the magic down. There was no way he'd ever bring a kid into the prison realm.

But this... the excited chatter, constant babbling, and endless smiles... it fit the joyous human.

"Papa." A tiny girl with thick ebony hair tugged on his sleeve. "We heard there was someone with wings in the palace." She stared at Riona in awe.

One of the other girls walked to Riona and reached up to touch her tattoos. "These are pretty."

Even Riona softened at that and gave the kid a smile.

"All right, girls, how about you go find the triplets? I do believe they might have a snack ready for you."

Wings forgotten, their high-pitched voices talked of cookies and cakes as they ran from the room.

Myles closed the door after them, his casual smile fading from his lips. He took a deep breath. "I don't only remember you, Griff. I remember everything you did. They're not actions I will ever forget. I was locked in a dungeon because of you. My best friend almost traded her life for mine because of you. I'm glad Brea and Lochlan don't remember. It would only bring them pain."

Griffin couldn't respond because every word he said was the truth.

That was the problem with truths.

They cut deeper than any sword.

Gone was the Myles of a few moments ago. In his place stood a man version of the boy he'd once known.

"None of us are the people we were ten years ago."

Myles shook his head. "Our appearances might be different, we might have new goals, but our souls, Griff, who we are inside doesn't change."

Griffin hoped he was wrong, that a yearning for power could be washed away.

But who was he kidding? Here he was in Fargelsi trying to bring down magic at the behest of a king just as bad as Regan. Possibly even worse.

It seemed history was repeating itself.

But this time, Griffin wouldn't let his mistakes define him.

He stepped closer to Myles and looked down on him. "You're wrong." His voice came out gravelly, raspy.

"For the sake of the three kingdoms, I sure hope I am, Griff. The next time you betray someone I love, I'm going to kill you."

He'd try, at least. But if Griffin did lose his way again, he might sharpen Myles' blade himself.

Chapter 14

Griffin followed Myles to his wife's throne room. What a strange thought that was. Myles Merrick. A human of little importance was now the king of Fargelsi—a title Griffin once aspired to. One he thought was owed to him as the son of a king. Nephew of a king. Brother of a king. It was in his blood.

But ten years in a prison realm had chased away all ambition. In Griffin O'Shea's world, the most he aspired to was his next meal. A safe place to sleep at night. And a better future for the boy who was as much a son to him as any born of his flesh. He was not that man anymore. At least he hoped not.

"Wait here." Myles nodded as he approached the queen, busy in a meeting with her nobles. They sat around a table together, the queen's throne across the room on a raised dais—seemingly there for tradition's sake as a symbol of her power.

"What is it, Myles?" Queen Neeve asked as Myles bent to deliver the news. "What? Lochlan doesn't have a brother." Neeve frowned as her gaze wandered into the shadows where Griffin stood between Riona and Gulliver—tails and wings secreted away under their clothes.

"She has what? Myles have you fallen asleep while reading one of your fantasy books again?"

"Not lately, darling," Myles said, his good humor as rock solid as ever. He murmured some additional information for her ears alone.

"Oh, I see," the queen said as she stood at the head of her table. The other nobles rose to their feet out of respect. "Everyone, I must ask for your patience." She smoothed an ink stained hand down the length of her simple ivory gown. "It seems an important matter needs my immediate attention. Might we adjourn until tomorrow?"

"Of course, your Majesty," one of her nobles replied as they each gathered their documents and maps and matters of diplomacy for discussion. The governing of Fargelsi had changed dramatically since Regan was in charge.

"Father, please stay. I think—I hope you'll bring some sense to this conversation," she muttered, her gaze drifting to Riona.

"Of course." Brandon crossed to the door to see the others out.

Griffin hardly recognized the man who looked so much like his sister. Brandon had aged over the last ten years, but he was no longer the malnourished, beaten down version of himself he had become during the years of his imprisonment. This man had a fire in his eyes —a fire Griffin found startlingly familiar. There was much of Regan's countenance in her older brother.

The queen waited until the room was cleared before she spoke again. "Myles." She paced the room. "Seriously... what?" She placed her hands on her hips. "I'm going to need more information than 'we have visitors from the prison realm.'"

"Griffin O'Shea has returned, and he has need of an audience with you and your father." Myles nodded in respect toward his father-in-law.

"And I'm supposed to know who this Griffin O'Shea is?" She tapped her foot in irritation.

"No, you've forgotten him, darling." Myles flashed a brilliant smile at his wife. Clearly, he was enjoying himself. "But I've told you about him before. You just choose not to listen to my 'humantales' as you call them."

"Myles."

"Oh, fine. Ruin my fun." Myles dropped to an empty seat at the table. "Griff is Loch's brother. Everyone has forgotten him but me because I was in the human world failing to learn to live without you when he was sentenced to the prison realm for his crimes. Griffin was Queen Regan's foster son in the way that Lochlan was Queen Faolan's."

"Skip to the important part, Myles." Griffin stepped forward.

"Right." Myles scratched his jaw, taking an insufferable moment to think before he continued. "Let's just focus on the fact that we have three visitors from the prison realm, and one of them has a spectacular set of wings, and the other, I hear, has a tail in need of some medical attention." Myles winked at Gulliver, and the boy blushed to the roots of his hair. He seemed unable to take his eyes off Neeve. She was beautiful, and Griffin realized Gulliver had probably never seen a woman quite like her before.

"She has wings, really?" Neeve quirked a smile at her husband. "Or are you just fooling me?"

"She has wings." Riona stepped forward. Slipping her long coat from her shoulders, she unfurled her delicate white wings, letting them shimmer in the candlelight from the chandelier overhead.

"Oh my." Neeve stumbled back, falling into the chair she'd just vacated. "You're Dark Fae?"

"Yes, your Majesty," Riona said, surprised. "I had not expected to find those who knew of us outside of Myrkur."

"I-I've read of such fae from histories and mythologies, but I never anticipated seeing one with my own eyes. You said you are from Myrkur? Where is that... I apologize, where are my manners? What is your name, dear? And, oh my, your wings are just so beautiful." She leaned forward, a glint of mischief in her eyes. "Can you really fly?"

Riona cast a wary glance at Griffin, unsure what to make of the queen's ramblings.

"I am Riona... Majesty," Riona stuttered. "Myrkur is the night realm of the Dark Fae, you know it only as the prison realm. And yes, all Slyph fly... ma'am."

"Slyph? Fascinating." Neeve's eyes sparkled with interest.

"And you are?" Neeve's attention turned to Gulliver, and Griffin nudged him forward.

"Take off your glasses," Griffin whispered.

Gulliver took a clumsy step forward and whipped his sunglasses off so she could see his cat-like eyes. "Gu-Gullie, your Majesty." Gulliver tried to dip into a courtly bow, but he over-corrected and face planted on the rug in front of her.

"Oh my, are you okay?" Neeve shot out of her seat to help him up. "Myles you said this child was injured?"

"It's nothing, my lady." Gulliver leaped back to his feet. "Just my tail is all."

"Your tail?"

"Yes, ma'am. I am Tuatha De Dannan. Dark Fae of the land." He lifted his chin with pride.

Griffin stepped forward, placing a hand on Gulliver's shoulder. "He was captured by some men from the prison realm, and they tortured him for information, your Majesty. They cut off part of his tail."

"What? When was this?" Queen Neeve put a motherly hand to Gulliver's face, checking over his faded bruises.

"A week ago, but it still pains me something terrible," Gulliver said, his bottom lip trembling for effect.

"Of course it does, you poor dear." Neeve folded him into her arms. "Myles will take you to see my personal healers right away. Are you hungry, darling?" Neeve steered Gulliver to the table of refreshments set for the nobles and made him a plate herself.

"It *has* been a while since we last ate," Gulliver said. Griffin chuffed the little liar on the back of the head.

"Myles why don't you take Gullie to the healers and help Riona get settled in her rooms for the night."

"That is not necessary, Majesty," Riona tried to protest. "We planned to find a room in an inn."

"Nonsense. You must be exhausted. I will speak with Griffin this evening, but we will see you both at breakfast in the morning."

"I am afraid I am here as my king's envoy." Riona stood unmoving, her arms braced behind her back. "I must insist I stay."

"And I am afraid I do not know your king, Riona. This is Fargelsi, I am queen here. We will speak further tomorrow."

Riona seemed ready for a fight, but Griffin shook his head, trying to reassure her without words that this was how it needed to be. This was the chance he'd hoped for, and he wasn't going to let her screw it up. He needed to speak with Neeve and Brandon alone.

"This way, Riona." Myles guided her toward the door, not giving her a chance to defy the queen any further. "Gullie, bring your snacks, and let's go see a man about a tail."

With a sigh of frustration, Riona did the only thing she could, she followed Myles from the room.

"You really are Griffin? O'Shea?" Neeve studied his face. "I don't see much of a family resemblance with Lochlan. All these years, Myles has talked of you, and we've all thought it was just one of his elaborate pranks."

"I never expected to return to find anyone had remembered me." Griffin finally found his voice. "I expect it will make all of this more difficult. But I have much to explain—preferably while we are alone." He glanced over his shoulder to make sure Riona was gone.

"Please, have a seat." Neeve offered him a chair at her table. "Why have you come? Actually." She frowned as Brandon moved to join them at the table. "*How* have you come here from the prison realm?"

"It is a very long story." Griffin sighed. "But I desperately need your help." He launched into an explanation of the events that had led him here, taking a grateful sip of wine when the queen served him herself.

"This King Egan seeks to bring down the barrier around Myrkur?" Brandon frowned. "And he's sent you to find out how it was created?"

"I know how this must seem," Griffin began. "I'm a stranger to you, come to tell you an outlandish story, and I can't assume you will help me accomplish this impossible task I've been sent to do. But the lives of two people who are everything to me are at stake. Egan will make Shauna and Nessa wish for death if I fail. I don't intend to give Egan what he wants." He glanced at the door again, expecting to see Riona's shadow on the other side.

"You are safe here, Griffin," the queen said. "Myles will not let her out of his sight. Ask me what you must, and I will do what I can to help you."

"Help me free the innocent people of Myrkur who do not deserve the prison sentence they have been dealt simply because an O'Rourke ancestor decided the Dark Fae must be removed from your world. Help me find a way to save my family from a terrible fate. Once they are safe, I will not rest until Egan and those like him are brought to justice. I do not want to bring the barrier down—that is not my goal, though my traveling companion must think otherwise—I only want to free those who deserve a better life." He didn't tell them of Egan's vast army. Right now, all that mattered was Shauna and Nessa and the people of Fela.

"And you believe I can help you?" Brandon asked. "That is why you came to Gelsi, is it not?"

"I hoped you would be able to point me in the right direction." Griffin felt the futility of this request. Brandon spent twenty years as a prisoner. What could he know about any of this?

"I don't know much of my grandmother's history. She died long before I was born and her deeds were... frowned upon by those who came after her. I can only imagine the barrier around Myrkur is similar to the one that once stood around Fargelsi. Regan learned the barrier spell from somewhere, and I imagine that had something to do with Queen Sorcha. They were close when she was a child."

"Regan kept her spellwork private," Griffin said. "She didn't share it with me except to teach me simple things."

"She truly was like a mother to you, wasn't she?" Brandon shook his head, baffled by the magic that had removed Griffin from their minds.

"She was the only mother I ever knew. My mother, the Queen of Iskalt, and my father were killed when I was only two years old. The arms that held me when I was scared... the hands that dried my tears and nursed me when I was sick... they were Regan's."

"And Lochlan sentenced his own brother to the prison realm for remaining loyal to the woman who raised him?" Neeve frowned, a look of sympathy on her face. "It just doesn't sound like something he would do."

It was strange how they saw things differently now. No one had sympathy for Griffin when Regan's crimes were still fresh and raw in their minds.

"I chose to go to the prison realm as my punishment for working against Iskalt and Eldur. I had my reasons for making such a choice." But none of that was important now. "Regan's grimoire may have had answers, but it would have been destroyed when Brea brought down the palace—I'm sorry, I've forgotten myself—Queen Brea."

"Don't call her that to her face." Neeve grimaced. "My sister has never wanted to be queen of anything."

"That sounds like Brea." Griffin smiled.

"I do not know if she was in possession of any of Sorcha's spells or where she'd have gotten them," Brandon said. "And you are right, everything was destroyed after my sister died. Whatever she learned of barrier magic likely came from somewhere dark. It took Brea's magic to destroy the barrier around Fargelsi. Someone with both Eldurian and Fargelsian power. But she still needed the help of many magic wielders." Brandon paused to refill their wine glasses.

"We have precious few records about the origin of the prison realm," he continued. "Perhaps that is because those who were present at its creation forgot everything they knew about it when it was completed?"

"From what I understand, that was not something that was supposed to happen," Griffin said, taking a long sip of wine. "Egan believes it took the magic of all three realms to create the barrier, but the magic that made everyone forget, that was Sorcha's doing."

"So, it stands to reason that it would take the magic of all three realms to see it destroyed," Brandon added, sharing a wary look with his daughter.

"You don't think it's as easy as that?" Neeve glanced at her father.

"I wouldn't call what we did to end Regan's rule easy," Brandon said.

"Of course not, but it can't be as simple as doing the same thing all over again?"

"No." Brandon frowned. "We are dealing with older, much more complex magic this time. A spell like that grows stronger with time, and three generations is a very long time for this barrier to take on a life of its own. It's evolved. It will not be easy to breach this magic—if that is even possible."

Neeve shared a nod of agreement with her father before she turned to face Griffin. "This King Egan likely hasn't put all his trust in you," Neeve said. "That is why he's sent his envoy with you. We cannot allow an unknown king to flood our borders with the criminals we have so ignorantly sent to Myrkur. And Griffin is right, we owe it to the innocents to help them in any way we can."

"Thank you." Griffin let out a strangled breath, and his body relaxed for the first time since he'd left Myrkur. He hadn't realized how much he'd anticipated their refusal to help.

"You have Fargelsi in your corner," Neeve continued. "But you will need Iskalt too. This will take the combined effort of all our strongest magic wielders across the three kingdoms. You must go to Iskalt and tell the king and queen everything you've told us," Neeve said. "In this matter of magic, Lochlan will stand for Iskalt and Brea will stand for her sister, Alona, Queen of Eldur."

"Thank you, your Majesty." Griffin dipped his head, surprised at how quickly she trusted him, and knowing if her memories were intact, she'd have him thrown from the palace.

"We will all work together to find a solution, Griffin. That is what we do now." She placed a cool hand over his, but Griffin couldn't hear anything she said over the beating of his heart. She was sending him to Brea. To the woman who was once his wife—now married to his brother.

Returning home was hard enough, but he wasn't sure he had the strength to face Brea, knowing she would never recall the memories of the life they'd once shared.

Chapter 15

Griffin had never spent much time with Brandon O'Rourke, the king who'd been locked away in the palace dungeons the entire time Griffin had grown up.

Regan hadn't let anyone in on that secret, the fact she'd captured her own brother, the rightful Fargelsian king, the only person who could have defeated her until Brea Robinson came along, prepared to burn everything to the ground to end her aunt's rule.

Brandon led Griffin from the throne room and down a long hall. It was strange to be in a completely different palace where Regan's had once stood. Griffin's gaze slid to the tapestries hanging along the walls, the wood underneath his feet. This palace suited Neeve, the woman who'd grown up as a servant in the very kingdom she now ruled.

"It's strange, isn't it?" Brandon didn't look at Griff, keeping his eyes trained on the hall ahead.

Griffin released a long sigh. "I used to run through Regan's palace, dodging servants and guards." He'd only seen a few such servants since stepping inside this palace.

Brandon was quiet for a long moment. "My daughter doesn't like others to serve her. She pours her own wine, keeps her rooms tidy, and even makes Myles carry water from the well to their rooms."

Griffin pictured the Neeve he'd known. She would have been intimidating with her height if she hadn't kept her eyes trained on the ground. She'd barely spoken except to Brea. But this queen version of her met every one of his looks with one of confidence. "She's a good queen, isn't she?" Somehow, he knew she couldn't be anything less.

Brandon stopped walking and turned to Griffin, the smile fading from his face. "She is. I don't know you, Griffin, but I trust Myles, and I probably know more about the prison realm than anyone in this world. Even if I didn't believe you, that woman with wings and the kid with a tail are proof enough. So, I'll say this, my trust lasts up to the point you betray either of my daughters. If that happens, I will make sure there's no prison realm for you, only death. Do you understand me?"

Griffin stared at him, wondering just how much Myles had told them of his past transgressions. It was enough for Brandon to feel the need to protect Neeve and Brea—both daughters he hadn't known until they rescued him more than ten years ago. "I don't intend to betray them." He'd never intended for any of his betrayals to happen, but that hadn't stopped them before. He kept that part to himself. "I also don't expect you to remember my relationship with your sister, but you have to know one thing. I betrayed Regan when I helped Brea, Neeve, and you escape Fargelsi through the swamps of the Southern Vatlands. I let you through the queen's barrier."

"Even if that is true, Griffin, one heroic act does not forgive a hundred cowardly ones." He started walking again, leading Griffin up a spiral staircase. He didn't knock as he pushed open a door. "We will talk more in the morning." And then, he was gone, leaving Griffin on the threshold of a sitting room. This was no ordinary sitting room though. It looked... human? An overstuffed leather couch sat next to a reclining chair.

Gulliver was on the couch, and Riona had taken the chair. Myles stood in front of them like he was telling them a story. Griffin inched closer, trying to hear what he was saying.

"Then, there was a battle, and none of us knew what side he was on. He sort of fought for us, but then, he tried to save Queen Regan when my bestie was tearing her palace apart stone by stone with her magic."

Riona pursed her lips. "What is a bestie?"

"A friend." Myles laughed. "A best friend. She once thought she'd killed me because Griffin told her I was dead."

"Myles," Griffin growled, stepping farther into the room. "What have you told them?"

Myles turned slowly as if wishing Griffin weren't standing right behind him. "Oh, erm, nothing much. Just how glorious we all thought your red hair was. It really matches your... er... pale skin tone."

Neither Gulliver nor Riona laughed at that. By the way Gulliver stared down at his hands, not talking, Griffin knew what tales Myles was spinning. Tales of a man who'd betrayed everyone who ever loved him. Lochlan. Brea. Even Regan in the end.

Myles kept talking as if he hadn't just shattered the fragile bonds between the three of them. "So, these are Brea and Lochlan's rooms when they come."

Griffin's eyes widened. No wonder everything looked so human. Brea would never fully leave her upbringing behind.

"We would have put you in guest quarters, but with the minimal staff we keep here, Neeve wanted you in rooms that were already made up. I'll play tour guide."

Griffin followed the human to the hall where the bedrooms branched off from the sitting room.

"Make yourselves at home. Just don't... break anything, yeah?" He turned away from Griffin and walked toward the door into the hall. "We will talk again in the morning, Griff."

Once he was gone and the door shut behind him, Gulliver stood and walked toward one of the bedrooms without saying a word.

"Gullie," Griffin called after him.

"Give him some space." Riona walked to the hearth, the wood had grown up from the floor, complete with flowering vines. Inside, a fire struggled to gain momentum. She crouched down to stoke the embers back to life.

"This castle is cold." Her wings fluttered as she stood and backed away from the fire.

To Griffin's surprise, she didn't go in search of her bed. Instead, she took a seat on the couch. Griffin joined her and stared into the dancing flames. He closed his eyes and leaned back against the cushion. It was odd finding comfort here. Yet another thing he had to thank Neeve and Myles for.

"I've heard stories of Queen Regan."

At Riona's words, he opened his eyes. "Most in Myrkur have. She sent a lot of people to the prison realm." He sighed. "When we cross that magical border, we know the world will forget us, but do you ever wonder if it would be better if we too forgot?"

Riona was quiet for a long moment. "No." She paused. "If we forget the evil we do, how are we ever supposed to atone for it?"

"Do you really think there's atonement for people like me?"

"I have to."

"Why?" He turned his head to look at her.

"Because you and I are the same, Griffin. And I refuse to believe I can never make things right."

"Why do you serve Egan?"

She met his gaze. "Why did you serve Regan?"

In all the years of his imprisonment, he'd tried to answer that very question. Why had he served someone he knew was evil? Why did he hold captive the very people who wanted to save the realm?

Only one answer had ever made sense to him. "Because she was all I had."

"Do you ever wonder if what makes a person good or bad is just circumstance?"

"All the time."

This was the first honest conversation he'd had with Riona, and there was small comfort in the fact he wasn't alone this time. Riona was trapped in the same cycle he'd been in most of his life.

"Tell me about your wife."

His wife. Brea. Another sigh rattled from his chest. "Brea is Regan's niece. I captured her from the human realm where she'd lived her entire life for protection. But she saw me as her savior, not her captor. At least at first." He smiled, thinking about spending time with Brea at his cabin and riding horses.

"You loved her?"

Griffin nodded. "As much as I was able. I was raised by a woman who had expectations and conditions that came along with her love. I thought I could love Brea even when I was hurting her. She escaped once—thanks to Queen Neeve, actually. So, I was sent to retrieve the one person who could get her back to Fargelsi. Myles Merrick, the person she cared about more than anyone."

He hadn't told this story in the years he'd lived in the prison realm. No one was supposed to know about his connection to Regan. It would have put a target on his back.

"Keep going." Riona leaned forward, resting her elbows on her knees.

Griffin sucked in a deep breath. "It worked. She exchanged herself for Myles. When Regan told me I was to marry Brea, I never thought Brea would have been kept in the dark."

"About what?"

"Fae marriage."

Curiosity lit in Riona's eyes.

Griffin shoved a hand through his hair. "A fae marriage is a magical bond. It tied Brea to me whether she loved me or not. It created that love in her."

"What happened?" Riona stared at him, hanging on his every word.

"Our entire world imploded. War came to Fargelsi, a war led by Brea herself. She was the most powerful fae I've ever seen. And she was in love with my brother. Lochlan never would have sent me to the prison realm. He hated me, but I think he loved me too."

"If he didn't send you..."

"It was my idea. My uncle sits in a cell in Iskalt so the people will never forget what he did to them. I didn't want that, but mostly, I did it for Brea. As soon as I passed through the magical barrier, our marriage bond severed. I felt it the moment it broke."

Riona sat still for a long moment, too long. Griffin was not a fae to trust, not like she'd ever have trusted him anyway.

"What does it feel like?" Riona's voice was so low he wasn't sure he heard right at first.

"What?"

"Love. What does it feel like? It seems in your previous life, you had much of it. Regan, as bad as she sounds, obviously loved you. You said yourself your brother wouldn't have sent you to the prison realm. And this wife of yours, I'll bet she cried for you. I just..." She took in a deep breath. "I'm curious. I want to know what that feels like."

"It's painful. Love has led to the most painful experiences of my life. I didn't just love Regan, I followed her down a dark path—always hoping she would make better choices, and I made excuses for her when she didn't. Loving her destroyed me. I think my brother would deny loving me. And Brea... there was a point I think she truly did feel... something for me, but I betrayed her worse than anyone. So, I guess I'm saying love is the great destroyer. But it's also the most amazing feeling in all the worlds."

Tears gathered in his eyes, but he blinked them away. He'd known coming back would be hard, that being surrounded by people who didn't remember him would crush what was left of his soul.

Riona reached over and took his hand. He turned his head to look at her. "And your king... he's going to kill my family." What was left of it. No matter what happened outside the prison realm, he couldn't lose sight of what was at stake. He was no longer Griffin O'Shea of Iskalt. This wasn't his world anymore.

"I'm sorry."

Griffin sighed. "I don't understand you, Riona."

"You're not the only one who has done evil. Egan..." She didn't finish.

Griffin turned, still not letting go of her hand. "What does he have on you?" He skimmed his gaze along the tattoos covering her arms. They told a story he couldn't decipher. "Who are you?"

She pulled her hand from his. "We all have secrets to protect, Griff. And mine would only put you in greater danger."

"Danger? Riona—"

"I'm tired, Griff. I think it's best if we all get some sleep." She didn't look at him as she walked away.

Griffin heaved himself to his feet and headed toward the third bedroom. Stopping at the door, he realized Gulliver's door was still open. He pushed it wider to find Gulliver sitting against the wall next to it, tears streaming down his face.

"Gullie? Are you hurt?" He looked to the tail that was wrapped with fresh bandages courtesy of Neeve's healers.

Gulliver shook his head. "I don't think I know you at all, Griff."

"Were you listening to our conversation?"

"I'm sorry. I just..." He released a breath.

Griffin slid to the floor next to him. "I never wanted to put you in danger."

Before Gulliver could respond, the door opened again.

"Gullie? I heard crying." Riona's gaze found Griffin's. "Oh, I'll go and let you take care of it."

"*You* came to help Gulliver?"

She shrugged.

"Please stay." Gulliver stared up at her, his eyes shining.

Riona hesitated for a moment before lowering herself to the floor in front of them. Griffin could barely see them in the dark, but they were all creatures of the darkness now.

"We shouldn't be here, Griff." Gulliver wiped a hand across his eyes. "These people... you did bad things to them, and I... I... I don't even know you."

Griffin heard Neeve promise to help, they even told him where to go next, but he wondered when it came down to releasing Myrkur from the prison magic... would they help then? Once they learned of the existence of ogres and all manner of Dark Fae, would they choose to remain in their peaceful world?

He hadn't missed the distrust in their eyes. Probably thanks to

Myles' stories. Griffin put an arm around Gulliver's shoulders. But their current situation wasn't the one that had Gulliver crying.

"Hey." Griffin nudged him. "You know this version of me better than anyone."

Gulliver shook his head but didn't utter a word in response.

"I need you to trust me, Gullie. I don't want to do this without you. We have to go to Iskalt where my brother and my ex-wife will show no recognition. It's going to hurt. A lot. But our mission isn't about me. This is for Shauna and Nessa, remember?"

Gulliver nodded and wiped the tears from his eyes.

Riona studied both of them. "Iskalt? Why?"

He wasn't sure if Brea and Lochlan would help him. It seemed too simple, too familiar. Ten years ago, Brea brought down the barrier around Fargelsi. There was little chance that was all they needed to do this time. Yet, it was a start.

But he knew of one other person who also studied boundary magic with Regan. He would prove unwilling to help, but he also happened to be in Iskalt. "We must speak with my uncle."

Gulliver looked up at him. "But Myles said your uncle was a bad man."

"He is."

"He said you used to be a bad man too."

Griffin sighed. Myles needed to learn to keep his mouth shut. "Listen to me, Gullie, I will never hurt you, and I will *never* betray you. No one in the three fae kingdoms knows what we have been through in Myrkur, they do not understand what it is to live in darkness, to fight for everything we have. But we do, and that knowledge binds us."

Riona scooted forward and took their hands in hers. "The three of us against the fae realm."

Griffin didn't show his surprise as Riona dropped the wall that had existed between them. Now that they understood each other, she seemed more real.

"These people don't remember me," Griff said. "And maybe

that's a good thing. But they will feel no loyalty to me, no love. We can't trust any of them."

"Only each other." Gulliver nodded.

Griffin squeezed him tighter. "We will one day have to go back to Myrkur and resume our roles fighting one another, but out here, we fight for the same thing."

Riona didn't release their hands. "Here, we fight for each other."

Chapter 16

"Griff!" Riona's scream tore through their suite of rooms, sending a spike of fear right into Griffin.

He raced from his room, across the sitting room, and slammed open Riona's door to find her standing before a looking glass in a mess of ocean blue that left her arms bare. The tattoos normally painting her dark arms were gone.

As in, vanished, leaving behind beautiful unmarked brown skin.

"How?" Griffin couldn't take his eyes from her arms. "You yelled for me? I thought you were dying."

Riona sent a scowl over one shoulder. "Someone is going to die if they don't get me out of this ridiculous dress."

Griffin's expression softened. He'd known another girl ten years ago who'd hated the Fargelsian styles when it meant she couldn't live in her riding pants.

"You look..." He couldn't finish the sentence as his eyes traced the body-hugging bodice that flared slightly at the waist before raining down in multicolored panels.

"Ridiculous?" She groaned. "I look completely and utterly ridiculous."

The door opened again, and Gulliver let out a low whistle. “Riona, you look beautiful.”

Yes, that. Those were the exact words Griffin had tried to get out and failed.

She softened a little at Gulliver’s praise. “How am I to wear a sword with this dress? I don’t even see anywhere to hide a knife.”

Griffin crossed his arms and leaned against the wall. “And who are we knifing tonight?” He couldn’t look away from her tattoo-less arms.

“I don’t know, Griff. You seem to have made every fae in the three kingdoms your enemy.”

“Doesn’t count if they don’t remember they’re my enemies.” He woke in a much better mood today surrounded by the finery he was once accustomed to. Then, the guilt came. Nothing here should make him content. He’d wanted to leave for Iskalt right away, but Neeve asked for one day. Griffin wasn’t sure why she needed the time.

Riona reached behind her, trying to tighten the laces of her backless dress, but her wings created an obstacle the dress wasn’t made for.

Griffin pushed off the wall and batted her hands away. “Let me do it.” His fingers brushed her skin as he began at the bottom, tightening her bodice. When he reached the top of the dress just under her wing joint, his finger brushed over a raised scar, and he froze.

He could only imagine what kind of punishment created such a scar on a Slyph. It seemed someone tried to take her wings. Anger rushed through him at the thought of such a gruesome injury that could have robbed her of the ability to fly.

Riona’s wings fluttered, slapping him in the face until he backed away. “Riona... I—”

“Leave it alone, Griff.”

“But—”

“It was a long time ago.” She turned back to the mirror.

Gulliver, oblivious to everything, smiled. “At least they left us clothes that accommodated us.” His tail had been coming back to life. The healers believed it would soon grow to the length it was before.

Griffin didn't step back from Riona. He had so many questions. "You smell like rosewater." Those words were not supposed to leave his lips.

Riona's face flushed. "I had a bath this morning while you were out exploring the palace."

"Did a servant bring you water?"

"No, but the queen did."

Griffin's eyes widened. "Riona... you can't have a queen bringing you water."

"Why not?"

"She's a queen! There are rules."

Riona shrugged. "She didn't think there were rules when she showed up at my door with buckets of water." She ran a hand over the top of her tight braids. "At least they let me refuse to have my hair done for this dinner. Seriously, who dresses like this for a meal?"

Griffin had to agree. He looked down at the light blue trousers and silk shirt they'd foisted on him. When Regan ruled here, this kind of dress was required to be in her presence.

But Neeve seemed different.

At least, he'd thought so.

There was a knock at the door to the sitting room, and Gulliver ran to answer it.

Griffin couldn't take his eyes from Riona. Lifting a hand, he ran his fingers down one arm. "Where are your tattoos?"

She turned toward him. "They appear when I choose."

"You can control them?" He gripped her wrist and pulled her arm closer. She didn't free herself, instead, letting him examine every inch of skin between her fingers and her shoulder.

"The tattoos are a part of me." Her voice was low. "All my people had them."

"If they're a part of you, why would you hide them?"

She turned back to the mirror. "You should go see who is at the door."

He stepped closer to her, the woman he'd once fought with in the king's arena. They both owed each other so much. The night before, he'd told her more than he'd told anyone in the prison realm, and he knew why. They were the same.

Putting a hand on one shoulder, he leaned in. "Don't hide any part of yourself, Riona."

"Isn't that what you do with your secrets?"

It had been. "Yes. Be better than me. Do better. There's still time."

Her entire body shivered, and he turned toward the bed for her cloak, settling it over her shoulders. She closed her eyes, releasing a sigh, and the tattoos returned.

"What do they say?" He traced a pattern of lines on the back of her neck.

Her eyes opened, and she stared at him in the mirror. "I'm dangerous, Griff. I don't know what they say, but I get this feeling. Whatever it is, it's not good. These tattoos that tell my path, it's my future actions they foretell. Not my past. And I can't help thinking whatever it is I'm meant to read in them will change everything for me." She bit off the last word and sucked in a long breath, sparing one more glance for Griffin before brushing past him to walk into the sitting room.

She was dangerous. Griffin ran a hand through his hair as he followed her and found Gulliver, Riona, and Myles waiting.

"So, here's the thing." Myles clapped his hands together. "My wife doesn't trust you. I don't trust you. But for some reason my father-in-law wants to talk to you tonight. Hence the dinner. Neeve promised she would help you, but I've got to admit, Griff, I've spent the last ten years filling her ear with stories about you. When you're the only person in the world who remembers something like that, you go out of your way to make sure you never forget."

"Now, who wants a nice dinner? It's taken me a while to get used to royal food, but who is up for something that sounds just as gross as it tastes?"

Myles didn't know that Griffin and Gulliver weren't used to having many food options at all, so they'd eat whatever was put before them.

Riona shrugged, tucking in the bit of vulnerability she'd shown Griffin and instead became the stoic woman who'd fought him so expertly in the pits.

Griffin smiled to himself. He liked the fierce version of Riona. He liked the contemplative version. And the version that was curious about him, about Brea.

And then, there was the one who'd sat on the floor of Gulliver's room the night before, accepting the truth that the three of them had to work together, had to protect each other. That Riona... he liked her the most.

"Her tattoos are back," Gulliver whispered. "I like them."

Griffin slid his arm around the young man's shoulders. "Me too, Gullie. Me too."

The dining hall wasn't what he'd expected. Instead of the long table that could seat too many people, Brandon sat behind a shorter mahogany table near a blazing hearth. Two candelabras provided light for the table. Griffin's gaze slid up to a chandelier casting flickering light across the room.

Just like everything else in this palace, the room held an easy comfort Regan's palace never had. She never wanted her guests to get too used to her palace.

All night Griffin had stayed awake in bed wondering if Regan was going to walk through his door. In those moments, he wished he'd taken Gulliver and run from Egan. They could have escaped into the human realm and lived there, far away from the people he didn't want to face.

Footsteps ran toward them like a bunch of tiny drumbeats followed by squeals from the children who weren't dressed as nice as Griffin and Riona.

Brandon stood to greet them, a reserved smile on his face. "Take your seats. The queen will be here shortly."

Myles snorted. "Eventually, she might make an appearance. It's month's end, and you know how she can't resist, Brandon."

Brandon sighed, but his smile belied his annoyance. Both men obviously adored Neeve.

Griffin took a seat and gestured for his companions to do the same. "What's month's end?"

"It's the lantern festival." One of the children—a tiny blond girl hopped onto a chair and snagged a roll.

Brandon sent her a scowl for her table manners, but it was with obvious affection.

Myles sat next to his daughter and proceeded to imitate her in taking a roll, slathering butter on it, and stuffing it into his mouth. "The lantern festival is an ancient Fargelsian custom that was abandoned in the time of Queen Sorcha." He swallowed. "You don't know how it was in Fargelsi after we defeated Regan. The people were free of the boundary spell, but they couldn't be free of everything she put them through. Many had been forced to work for her, others lived for years in the dungeons, their families never knowing where they were. So, we restarted a few old customs to bring joy into their lives again and to highlight the peace we'd fought hard for. The lantern festival was one."

Griffin tried not to let Myles' words strike him as hard as they did. He'd had a hand in keeping the Fargelsian people in line.

The kids around the table chattered about going to watch the lanterns rise after supper.

Gulliver asked the question Griffin wanted an answer to. "What happens at this festival?"

A festival was something Gulliver would never have seen before, Riona either. But Griffin remembered the many parties Regan had thrown. Those were the good times, the times he couldn't make himself regret.

Myles smiled. "For three nights straight, the people of Fargelsi use their magic to launch glowing lanterns into the night sky."

"Why would they do such a thing?" Riona couldn't keep the scorn from her lips.

Red crept up Myles' neck. "Well, they're supposed to carry our worries to the skies above. Once a lantern stops glowing, it means the worry has faded from the fae who launched it."

"But that's ridiculous." Riona lifted a brow. "You can't get rid of what ails you by sending it to the sky."

Myles opened his mouth to respond, but the doors slamming open stopped the words. A messenger crossed the room to reach Myles.

Myles pushed his chair back and stood. "What has happened?"

The messenger leaned down to whisper something in Myles' ear and pressed a message into his hand. Myles nodded. "Please find the queen and bring her to our chambers. Brandon, can you get the kids fed and back to their nanny? Then, we will need you to join us as well."

"Of course." Brandon stood. "What's going on?"

"I'll explain later. Griff, you're with me. Now."

Griffin followed him out into the hall with Riona and Gulliver on his heels. "I didn't have to wear this ridiculous dress," Riona whispered. "Did I?"

"Probably not." It was most likely a test. Neeve wanted to know how pliable Riona was, how far she was willing to go to please the queen.

Griffin sped up to walk at Myles' side. "Where are we going?"

"My rooms. We need to talk." Myles' jaw clenched, and he uncurled his fists. "You have not told us everything it seems."

Griffin didn't know what to say to that, but Myles was right. There was plenty they kept from the people of Fargelsi.

Myles slammed open the door and ushered them inside. He waved toward the white settee in the sitting room. "Have a seat." He turned his back on them and unfolded the parchment.

No one broke the long silence until the door opened once more and Neeve entered. She peeled gloves down her arms, releasing her hands as she set the gloves on the mantle. Myles handed her the message, and her expression didn't change as she read it. She lifted her eyes to her husband, and he gave her a short nod.

Neeve untied the front of her cloak. "We are at peace now in the three kingdoms." She draped her cloak over the end of a chair and lifted the hem of her gown so she could sit. "We've had this peace for the last ten years. My husband tells me this coincides with you, Griffin, entering the prison realm." She tapped a finger against her chin before lifting her other hand that held the message. "We received a note tonight telling us of a breach in the prison magic."

"A breach? How would anyone know?" Surely there weren't powerful enough fae to be able to spy on the people the world had forgotten.

Myles slumped into a wing-backed chair, crossing one leg over the other. "Darling queen wife, I think we need to tell them."

Worry flashed across the queen's face. "We do not know them."

"Yet, you've already given your support to Griff. Maybe it's time he had our secrets too." Myles turned tired eyes on Griff. "Regan is gone. You are a man without a master. Some probably call that freedom, but you... maybe not."

Griffin didn't take his eyes from Myles. "Whatever happened in the past is done. I am not that man anymore."

"No. I don't suppose any of us are the same." He rubbed his eyes. "It started when she was six."

"What started? Who was six?"

Myles sighed. "My niece, Tia."

His... "Brea and Lochlan's daughter?"

"Yes. She's powerful, Griff. Maybe even as powerful as her mom. She's ten now, but for the last four years, she's been plagued by dreams. They change, but the themes are always the same. Darkness. Fae with all sorts of features. Wings. Tails. Horns. She even dreamed of a giant green beast."

"An ogre," Gulliver piped in. "That's what they're called."

Gulliver was right. These images could mean only one thing. Tia saw the prison realm in her sleep. "But how? No one who enters the realm returns."

Neeve's shoulders dropped. "None of us know. At first, we

thought they were simple nightmares, but then there was one constant."

"You." Myles met his gaze. "Tia described seeing you over and over. But I'm the only one who remembers you, the only one who could prove that Tia's dreams weren't just dreams."

Griffin rubbed his face. "This isn't possible."

"You haven't met this little girl. With her, everything is possible."

Griffin looked to Neeve. "And the message? Why did we have to leave dinner so suddenly?"

"It's from Iskalt, from Brea." She held it out.

Griffin's hands trembled as he unfolded Brea's words.

The dreams are growing worse. Tia spent all week in bed, mumbling about a man who has to come. One who has to save her. I don't know from what, but she's scaring me with tales of a breach in the prison magic, allowing this man she sees to escape.

Why does my girl need to be saved? And by this stranger? I can't help feeling something is coming for us, sister. Something more evil than we've faced before. Tia has taken to sitting in the north tower watching for this mystery fae to come. She claims she'll feel him moving toward her, and that will allow her to return to us, to her twin brother.

Please be on the lookout for this new evil, Neeve. Protect Myles because we all know he's the most likely one to do something stupid.

I love you both.

Brea

Griffin read the note three times. This child, his... niece... she saw him in her dreams?

He passed the note to Riona who read it to Gulliver. Griffin wasn't a hero, he wasn't the man to save a child, yet this child believed in him. She knew he'd come, and he'd save her from some unknown evil.

Neeve rubbed her eyes. "Griff, I know there's a lot to think about, and you need to be smart about this."

Emotions warred within Griffin. A desire to follow the path that led to taking down the wall with the most powerful magic wielders in the realm. And an invisible pull toward this little girl.

"We were going to Iskalt, anyway." He stood. "We leave in an hour."

"You can't possibly consider going through the marshes in the dark." Neeve chimed in. "The Vatlands—"

Griffin cut her off. "—are not our way to Iskalt."

"Griffin." Myles crossed his arms. "You cannot be thinking what I know you are."

"We must cross Loch Villandi. I won't waste any more time. If we leave tonight, we can reach the shores by morning and hopefully get a fisherman to take us to Iskalt."

"No fisherman will risk their ship in the dangers of the Iskalt sea."

Griffin met Myles' gaze. "Everyone has a price."

CHAPTER 17

"Do you know who Queen Sorcha was?" Neeve leaned against the doorframe, watching Griffin prepare to leave. She'd brought him provisions and then stayed. Griffin had known Neeve before when they both resided in the Fargelsian palace. He didn't know if he'd ever get used to her being a queen, but somehow, it fit.

"I've known a little of her. She was Regan's grandmother, but Regan didn't speak much about her family."

Neeve met his eyes. "Sorcha was the most powerful Fargelsian to have ever lived. She could do spells none of us can even dream of. You obviously know how Fargelsian magic works. We have to speak the words of a spell to let it free. Well, Sorcha is said to have performed dangerous magic, the kind that would kill the average Fargelsian. But her spells were hidden away inside a book. Though, most Fargelsians think the book is a legend."

Griffin stopped packing the food and turned to her. "But you don't?"

Her brow furrowed. "I... I don't know. My father seems to think it is real, but I have a hard time believing the story."

Griffin crossed his arms. "What does the legend say?"

"Sorcha had a twin sister who knew she had to do something to stop the path Sorcha had set them on, spreading darkness across the kingdoms. So, she stole the book and hid it in the human realm with a network of guardians." She studied him for a long moment. "Rumor has it Regan searched for the book for decades."

He tried to remember a time when Regan revealed this to him, but she'd kept him in the dark. Griffin hated how much that hurt. "But she didn't find it?"

Neeve shrugged her shoulders. "We don't really know. The spells she used for the border wall were certainly more powerful than most. We assume they came from the book, but I don't know how she got them. Her arrogance may have prevented her from thinking the book was with mere humans."

"She wasn't—" He bit back the words, wishing he didn't still feel this urge to defend her.

"There's more." Neeve stepped into the room. "Sorcha created the prison realm."

He already knew that, but he started putting the pieces together. "She—" He stumbled back. "Are you telling me this book could bring down the prison magic?" It was exactly the kind of lead he'd been looking for.

She pursed her lips, thinking before speaking. "I believe it's the most logical conclusion."

"I need to find that book." He shoved the last item in his pack and slipped it over one shoulder. "Thank you, Neeve, for your hospitality."

"Griffin?"

He stopped in the doorway and looked back. "Myles' stories about the great Griffin O'Shea... I wouldn't trust that man with this information."

"Then, why do you trust me?"

She gave him a soft smile. "Because I know what it's like to spend years in captivity. Our prisons were different. But I fought against mine, and I managed to do good even with the oppression I endured. I very much hope you're planning to fight against yours."

Riona and Gulliver walked down the hall to join him as he gave the servant queen one final look. "For any wrongs I may have done you, your Majesty, I am more sorry than you could ever know."

She didn't remember his status in the palace or the fact he played a hand in keeping the Fargelsian people trapped in their kingdom, but the words weren't for her. He'd needed to say them.

"Wait for me!" Myles sprinted down the hall with a too large pack dangling from one hand. He panted as he joined them.

Neeve smiled at her husband. "Myles will be accompanying you to Iskalt."

Griffin's brows drew together. "That's—"

"A great idea." Myles grinned. "Yes, Griffy-Griff, I agree. No need to thank me for leaving my wife and kids to help you. They understand we have a special bond."

Griffin grunted. "We do not."

Myles slid an arm around his shoulders. "Now, is that any way to talk to the only person in the three kingdoms who even knows who you are?"

Neeve gave her husband an indulgent laugh before pulling him away from Griffin. He wrapped his arms around her, and Griffin shifted between his feet, uncomfortable with the moment between them.

"I'll be back as soon as I can," Myles whispered, resting his forehead against Neeve's.

"I don't like this, but it feels important. I can't shake that feeling. Whatever they find, it's going to change everything."

"Not everything." He kissed her long and slow.

Griffin cleared his throat. Myles pulled back with a sheepish grin.

Neeve stayed where she was as the four of them walked down the hall. Myles walked backward, not taking his eyes from his wife. "I love you, Neever Beaver!"

Griffin choked on a laugh. "That's your nickname for her?"

Myles gave one last wave and turned to join the group. "I mean... it's better than douchy Loch. And there aren't even any beavers here in the fae realm, so she just thinks I'm rhyming her name."

"What's a beaver?" Gulliver asked.

Myles ruffled his hair. "We're going to have a lot of time to talk on this adventure, little man. I'll tell you all about the humans."

"Oh joy, time to talk to Myles." Griffin shared an exasperated look with Riona. They walked across the bridge and took the horses Neeve promised them. Once they headed for the Dragur Forest, the tension winding through Griffin eased. The palace wasn't the same as Regan's, but he couldn't help seeing her around every corner.

Ahead, Myles and Gulliver chatted, but Griffin hung back, thoughts of the spell book Neeve told him about rolling through his mind. Maybe it wasn't people he needed to gather to help bring down the prison magic.

Maybe it was words.

They rode across open ground, away from the swampy Vatlands Myles suggested they travel. Griffin knew that way was safer, but it was also much slower across Eastern Eldur to the Sea of Iskalt before they would reach the Ice Palace. It would take weeks. And weeks were something they didn't have.

There was only one other way into Iskalt. And none of them would like it. They stopped occasionally and rested only when they had to.

As soon as Griffin laid out his plans, he'd seen Myles' face grow steadily paler. Griffin didn't blame him. Their journey would be risky. It was not an undertaking many supported.

Riona and Gulliver didn't quite understand Myles' fear. Riona was born for the water. And Gulliver... he tried putting a brave face on for everything.

They reached the ramshackle dock at the southwestern edge of Lake Villandi which spanned the distance between Fargelsi and Iskalt. Crossing here would allow them to bypass Eldur—except for the mountain pass through the tip of the northern Vatlands that stood between Iskalt and the shores of Villandi.

Griffin slid down from his horse and peered into the crystal clear water. He couldn't see any of the mysterious creatures that lived in the depths, but he knew they were there.

A dark-skinned woman with pink magic flashing in her eyes walked toward them, her hands on her hips. "And who might you be?" Her expression wasn't unfriendly, just... wary.

Griffin walked toward her. "Griffin O'Shea." He stuck out a hand.

She clasped it, one eyebrow raised. "I didn't know there was another O'Shea in the world other than that blasted ice king."

"So, you're not a friend of Iskalt's?"

She smiled. "Oh, I'm a friend of Iskalt's, just not the royal couple."

Griffin could make that work, but before he spoke, Gulliver jumped down. "Well, my friend here is about to blow up their world, so he could use your help."

Now, she looked interested. "And how can I be of service?" She scanned each of their faces. Myles tried to obscure his with the hood as he dismounted.

"We need passage to Iskalt."

That surprised her. "What's a pretty boy like you going to do in Iskalt? Do you realize how cold it is there?"

Griffin had nothing to say to that. He was Iskaltian, he was born there, but he hadn't set foot in his kingdom since he was barely old enough to remember. Could he even claim to be a Prince of Iskalt anymore?

The woman laughed, a full laugh. "That question wasn't supposed to initiate a deep period of thought. Of course, I can give passage to anyone who pays."

"Get us to Iskalt without being captured by a royal vessel, and you can keep our horses. They're good stock and will fetch a good price."

She rubbed her chin, letting the sun glint off a ruby ring. "So we're clear, my cargo is illegal. If you are caught on this ship, you may be sent to the prison realm."

Griffin and Riona shared a look.

Only Myles took issue with that. "How illegal?"

The captain ignored his question. "Welcome aboard. We leave tomorrow at first light. I'll take those horses now. My men can sell them when we're gone. With beasts like that, they may even fetch a price at the palace."

The captain's people led the horses away while Griffin made camp near the edge of the lake. He wished they had another means of getting into Iskalt, but even most fishing vessels avoided Lake Villandi, leaving them with few options but to trust a smuggler—the only fools brave enough to face the difficult crossing.

"What do you think she's bringing into Iskalt?" Gulliver asked.

"It's probably better if we do not know." He turned to Gulliver. "How's the tail?"

"The queen's healer sent me with some salve. It's helping."

"Good. Let me know if anything goes wrong, all right?"

Gulliver nodded, and Griffin clapped him on the shoulder.

The night in the palace of Fargelsi came back to him, the moment Riona decided she was in this with them. Griff didn't yet know what was at stake for her, but they all had things to lose if they didn't find what Egan wanted.

That night, as he looked to the stars above, he thought of Shauna and the strong will Egan would try to break. Of Nessa, the little girl who'd never deserved any of this. It was for people like them that propelled him on this journey. He'd give them a real life, even if it meant unleashing Egan to do it.

His last battles were about kingdoms and who sat on the three thrones of the fae realm.

This time, he fought for people, for freedom.

For ideals that were larger than himself.

He shifted to watch Riona in her sleep. Was there a part of her that wanted to fight for the same things?

Maybe they were always meant to be on the same side.

Chapter 18

Griffin watched Myles lean over the side of the ship, heaving as the contents of his stomach streamed into the lake below.

"I hate you, Griffin O'Shea," he grumbled in between bouts of nausea as the ship rocked. "I hate you so freaking much."

Riona chuckled from her spot sitting beside Griffin on the deck. "I don't think the king likes you very much."

"King Consort." Griffin didn't know why he corrected her. Maybe it was because Myles had risen to the position Regan once meant for him. He wasn't sure how he felt about that. "Where's Culliver?"

Riona shrugged. "It's not my job to watch the boy."

The rocking intensified as water sloshed over the ship's side. Griffin lunged forward, tackling Myles' to the deck as water crashed over where he'd just been standing. Griffin had seen what happened when the average fae touched the Lake Villandi water. He'd once lived near the Villandi shores, and he'd seen many fishermen who thought they could master the lake throw themselves in to the waters after only touching a few drops.

Myles kicked him off. "I don't need you saving me, O'Shea."

The words stung, but Griffin only grunted and sat back on his heels. "You're welcome, human." He settled back next to Riona. Sanity said they should head below deck, but that only made Myles' sickness worse.

"Are all humans so rude?" Riona crossed her arms.

"No. And yes. Myles is just seasick. I don't pretend to know all humans, but the ones I've known can be pretty rude. My wife..." He let the words trail off, better left forgotten when they were only a day from setting foot in Iskalt.

"I thought the passing was supposed to be easy."

Griffin sighed. He hadn't properly prepared any of his companions. Only Myles had known what was in store for them. On the Fargelsian side of the expansive lake, the water appeared calm, beautiful—deceptively so. The closer one sailed to Iskalt, the more the waters churned, trying to keep ships from their shores. Some thought it was a kind of magic, but Griffin wondered if it was an omen for what lay ahead.

Iskalt held no hope, no warmth. At least, it hadn't before. If Lochlan was king now, why did the waters still churn?

The cracked wooden door slammed open, and the Captain screamed at them. "Below deck. Everyone. I won't have idiots accidentally touching the water and not-so-accidentally throwing themselves overboard."

"Not arguing with that." Myles, looking pale and tired, followed her.

Griffin tried to steady himself and get to his feet. He reached a hand down to Riona. She shook her head, her braids clinging to her face. The colorful tattoos danced along her skin. Riona followed his gaze and pulled her sopping cloak to cover her arms.

"I'm not going inside," Riona yelled above the wind. "I belong out here." She closed her eyes as another blast of lake water smacked her in the face. Griffin tried to get to her, to push her out of the path of the water, but he wasn't fast enough. Yet, nothing happened. She didn't jump to the depths or hang over the side of the ship.

Griffin studied her for a moment longer, stumbling as the boat reared up. He lowered himself beside her, his hands searching for something, anything to hold on to. "You told us you were Asrai but it was hard to believe with our feet on solid ground." A fae of both Slyph and Asrai descent seemed like the stuff of legends.

She didn't hear him over the howling of the wind. She seemed to be mesmerized by the water, but not controlled by it.

"Griff!" Gulliver's worried face appeared as he opened the door. "It's too dangerous out there."

"He's right." Riona shoved Griffin's shoulder. "Go, be safe. I'll be fine out here."

Griffin met Gulliver's gaze. "I'm not leaving her." He'd left people behind before. If she meant what she'd said—that they needed to fight for each other in a world that had forgotten them—then this was him fighting for her.

The storm raged around them, turning the sky black as a torrent of rain pounded down. Another wave sloshed over the side of the boat. "Riona, please!" Griffin reached for her as she stood at the side of the deck, looking down into the water.

A bolt of lightning seemed to crack the sky in two, and it snapped Riona from her trance. Her eyes widened as they landed on Griffin. "Yes, you're right. We need to get below deck."

He wouldn't tell her he'd been saying that all along.

Riona pushed him toward the door as the wood beneath their feet creaked. They both stumbled down the narrow staircase to where the crew sat leaning against the cargo.

Griffin shook his head, brushing the rain soaked locks from his face. Riona did the same with her wings.

Gulliver sat with a number of the sailors, his face not nearly as green as Myles'. He jumped up when he saw Griffin. "Hey, Griff. You want some ale?"

"No. And neither do you." He took the mug from Gulliver's hand and passed it off to Riona. "Is there tea?"

Gulliver's shoulders dropped. "Yes, there's tea."

A crash sounded above, making every fae present jump. Smugglers took their chances on the massive lake, but they knew the risk. If this ship went down, it wasn't the water that would kill them.

Only the creatures in it.

"Do you hear that?" Riona asked.

Griffin tried to listen above the boisterous sailors. "What is it?"

"A melody." She turned to the stairs. "I need to get back up there."

"No." Griffin grabbed her wrist. "Stay here."

She ripped her arm out of his grasp. "Where is the music?"

Griffin and Gulliver shared a look. "Riona." He tried to listen. "Is it something in the water calling to you?"

She shook her head and yanked open the door, running back up into the rain.

"What is she doing?" the captain yelled. "I don't care if she does have wings, she's going to get herself killed."

Griffin couldn't let that happen. He sprinted up the steps, yelling back down. "Don't let the boy follow me." Because he would. That was Gulliver. Griffin ignored the rain pounding into him as he searched the deck for Riona. A wave crashed over the side, and he jumped up onto a crate, never stopping his search.

He shielded his eyes against the rain, and that was when he saw it. A movement in the sky. Riona battled the storm, her wings working furiously to keep her in the air. It was the most incredible sight he'd ever seen.

And it terrified him.

"Riona!" He didn't move from atop his crate as lake water flooded the deck. What was she doing? His eyes followed the path it looked like she was trying to take. The rain let up just enough for him to see the crags of Talam.

That wasn't right.

Their path wasn't meant to take them anywhere near the island. Movement atop the cliffs overlooking the beach had Griffin trying to get a better look. A man stood on the uninhabited island.

The water receded from the deck, and Griffin jumped down, yanked the door open, and thundered into the safety below deck.

"Captain," he called. "There's an island out there."

"Not possible," the captain yelled. "We aren't anywhere near

Talam." Her eyes pinned on Griffin. "Unless... the storm sent us off course. We need to get out there, but I refuse to risk my men. Where is your little winged friend?"

"By now, my guess is she's *on* the island."

The sound of splitting wood surrounded them, and horror flashed across the captain's face. "I have to go above deck. I need to save my ship." She climbed the stairs before disappearing out on the deck.

Wood cracked. Griffin didn't know much about boats, but he knew that wasn't a good thing.

She was going to need help. Griffin ascended the stairs to help the captain, but what he found...

"A wave crashing over the rail hit me." Fear shone in the captain's eyes as she climbed up onto the wooden rail.

Griffin ran toward her, trying to catch her by the legs, but he was too slow. Lifting one foot, the captain let it dangle over the dark waters.

Griffin's scream died in his throat as the captain stepped off the rail. As soon as she hit the water, something dragged her under.

Horror sliced through Griffin as he backed away. He looked to the island just in time to see the ship crash onto Talam's black sandy beach.

Chapter 19

Riona

As soon as the ship crashed, the storm faded away, letting the waters return to the glassy calm depths as they'd seen in Fargelsi.

The music went the way of the storm, no longer calling Riona. She flew down to the shipwreck, knowing how lucky they all were to have more likely beached the ship instead of crashing into the rocky shores at the north of the island.

The storm had caused damage, but Riona had other priorities. She lifted higher in the clearing skies, wondering if what she'd seen was an apparition or a product of magic.

Yet, as she neared where the man watched the ship down below, she knew it was real. She gave one flap of her wings, hovering over the ground before touching down.

The man didn't move.

Riona took his silence as a chance to marvel at how closely he resembled her. No, he didn't have dark skin. The opposite actually. But his pale, almost chalk-white skin was covered in tattoos just like hers. And the wings may have been black, but they could only belong to someone of their species.

"I thought I was the only one." Riona studied him from blond hair to odd clothing. "The song... was it you?"

He nodded, pulling out an odd instrument she'd never seen before.

"You caused the storm." She didn't know why she was so sure of it.

He didn't respond to her except to dip his head. "Your friends." His voice was lower than she'd expected. "They have all survived. Except the captain, unfortunately."

She had many questions for this man who was so like her. Where had he been all these years she thought she was the only one of their kind? But she had a more pressing matter. Giving him one last look, she kicked off the ground and flew toward the shipwreck.

"Griffin?" She landed on the deck. "Gulliver?"

Someone stumbled from the stairwell. The human. "That was quite the ride." Myles held the side of his head where blood seeped through his hair.

"Where are the others?"

"Coming." Myles fumbled his way off the boat and collapsed onto the black sand. Gulliver emerged next. "Where's Griffin?"

"Wasn't he with you?" Riona looked behind him.

Gulliver shook his head. "He went after you."

No. He wouldn't have been that stupid. A cough alerted her to someone else's presence. Running the length of the deck, she found Griffin leaning against a crate with blood trickling down his cheek.

"Riona!" Gulliver yelled. "Griff! There's someone coming."

The fae with the music. Riona extended a hand down to Griffin, pulling him up. He gave her a grateful smile, but she'd already looked past him to the waiting fae.

"Griffin O'Shea." The man rushed toward him, one hand out in greeting.

Griffin took it, confusion flashing across his face.

"Welcome to Talam. I was hoping to have visitors while I was here, but some of you were not expected." He sent Riona a look she couldn't decipher. "Come, come. I have a camp in the forest."

Griffin's jaw clenched. "We aren't leaving our ship."

"What if I promise to repair it if you come with me now?"

"Dark Fae don't have magic."

The man smiled. "True. But then, I never said the magic was in me." He tapped the instrument against his leg. "I'm Nihal, by the way."

"Well, Nihal," Myles started. "What is a Dark Fae doing in human clothes?"

"Ah, very good question. You're intelligent for a human. The truth is, I live in the human realm. No, I won't tell you why or how I traveled here. We will meet again one day and those answers will come."

Riona looked to the sailors who seemed lost without their captain.

"Stay with the boat," Griffin ordered, giving Riona a shrug. "Someone had to take charge." He lifted his voice again. "There should be some wares that are okay to eat in the galley. Just... be careful of the water."

Nihal had a skip in his step as he led them through the garden of boulders to the trees where he'd set up one meager tent.

Riona raised a brow. "This is where you live?"

Nihal smiled. "Only for one night. Then, I'll be back in my village in the human realm."

Emotions rolled through Riona, warring for supremacy. There were differences, but none so profound as their similarities.

"Why don't your tattoos move?"

"Ah." He grinned. "That is an answer for another time. We don't have long."

"Why?" Riona crossed her arms.

"Because there are things happening in Iskalt."

Griffin huffed out a breath. "We were on our way there. You delayed us."

He shook his head. "Your ship was headed for the smuggler's coast, and those men you're with would not have just let you go."

"What do you mean?" Myles asked.

Nihal gestured to the ground around a fledgling fire. "I received word of your departure from an ally in the Fargelsian court. As I started asking around the docks if anyone had seen your party, a common name surfaced. Captain Murphy."

Griffin averted his eyes at the name. Had he seen her perish?

"A king consort of Fargelsi." Nihal pointed to Myles then Griffin. "A forgotten prince of Iskalt. A woman who is one of the last of her kind. In joining together, you made yourself easy pickings."

Riona scowled. "Says the man who wrecked our ship."

Nihal sighed and pulled his instrument onto his lap. "Trust that I wouldn't have done so if there were another choice."

"Ever thought of not playing?" Riona wouldn't let this go.

"I have thought of it many times, yes. But I do not play for my pleasure. The piccolo allows me to perform magic I could not otherwise do. I do not use it lightly."

Riona rubbed her eyes. Between the rough seas, the flight through the storm, and now a cryptic fae who looked like her, she was ready to go to sleep and forget it all.

Nihal's eyes rolled back into his head, and his body slumped forward. Griffin scooted near him. "He's breathing."

Nihal's arm bent up with the piccolo in his grasp. He put it to his lips, and a sweet melody replaced the awkward air around them. A gust of wind blew through the trees. Riona ran to the edge of the cliffs, but the sea below still held its calmness.

Shouts came from the beach, but she couldn't make out the words. Jumping into the air, she flew toward the noise and touched down. "What happened?"

One of the sailors stared at her in disgust. "Ship's healing itself. Not even my magic could do that."

The piccolo's song reached the beach, and Riona could get lost in it. She flew back to where she'd left the others.

"The ship is repairing itself. We'll be able to leave at dawn."

Griffin opened his mouth to speak, but Nihal set his instrument down and spoke as if nothing had just happened. "Dawn it is. Good luck on your journey."

That was it? That was all he had to say for himself. A Dark Fae who could make magic with his piccolo?

"I suggest you stay up here for the night rather than with those men." Those were Nihal's final words to them.

Riona looked to Griffin and nodded. Something inside begged her to trust Nihal.

And they were all too tired to do otherwise.

Chapter 20

Griffin

Griffin woke the next morning to find Nihal standing atop the cliffs, looking into the rising sun. His dark wings stretched wide, making him a sight to behold.

Wiping the sleep from his eyes, Griffin joined him, his gaze going down to the beach and widening. "The smugglers. They're gone."

A pit opened inside him. Was this where they lost, where they failed? Was it because of a winged fae with magical music?

A smaller boat anchored not too far from the beach. "Is that a... fisherman?"

Nihal nodded. "That's Liam. He comes around here every few weeks to see if I have need of him to run messages for me."

"Messages for who?" When he didn't respond, Griffin nodded. "Right, another answer we'll get in time."

Nihal shrugged. "Did your clothes dry adequately over night? I don't exactly have a tune for that."

"They did, thank you." Griffin and the others had been soaked to the bone when they'd arrived, but Nihal had dry clothing waiting for them. "I don't suppose you'll ever tell us why you forced us into coming to Talam?"

Nihal shook his head with a hint of a smile on his lips. "Come. We must speak with Liam."

At the beach, a tiny wooden boat had been hauled from the water, and a man with gills running up his arms and neck smiled wide. "Nihal." He pulled him into a back-thumping hug.

"It's good to see you, Liam. Have you met my new friends? Griffin, Riona, Gulliver, and Myles." He cupped his hands around his mouth to whisper, "He's human."

"The human has ears." Myles didn't look offended.

Liam released a booming laugh.

Griffin couldn't take his eyes off the strange features. He'd thought all Dark Fae were in the prison realm, and here were two free ones standing right in front of him. How many more were there?

Nihal and Liam waded into the water, an act that seemed unnatural to Griffin who'd spent his life avoiding it. They spoke in hushed tones before returning. Nihal grinned wide. "Liam will take you to the shores of Iskalt. No need to land on the smuggler's coast because his boat carries the royal seal of Iskalt."

Liam nodded. "The king tasks me with many things."

"And I'm sure the king will thank you for this. You are bringing his brother home, after all."

Just hearing the words struck something in Griffin's gut. His brother. Home.

But Iskalt had never been his home.

"Nihal." Griffin stuck out a hand. "I don't think I'll ever understand you."

Nihal shook his hand. "Griffin O'Shea, you and I will cross paths again to find the secrets you seek." His eyes found Riona. "If things were different, my dear, you and I would be able to spend time comparing our upbringings as the last of our kind." He bowed. "Be safe. You think the storm yesterday was rough... well, the waters of Iskalt have drowned many men. Good luck." He lifted into the air with a giant flap of his wings and flew to the top of the cliffs, watching them for a moment longer before disappearing through a portal he shouldn't be able to make.

"That man..." Riona shook her head. "He caused the storm that almost killed us, yet... I want to trust him."

Griffin knew the feeling. But like Nihal said, he fully expected to see him again.

Griffin wondered if Nihal's final words had been a lie. Since leaving Talam, they'd had nothing but smooth sailing. Liam operated his boat alone, always running to different areas to keep them on track.

Griffin leaned against the rail, letting the sun warm his skin.

"You were with Captain Murphy before?" Liam asked.

Griffin nodded. "Well, until she died."

"How'd she die?"

"Jumped from her own ship."

Liam let out a low whistle. "The woman has a reputation even outside the smuggler's coast. She abducts those with well-connected families, the nobility, sometimes even humans. If no one will pay for them, she pushes them from the boat to die in the dangerous waters."

Griffin could hardly process the information. "She..." Was that what she had planned for their group? Myles was the only one anyone would pay for. A chill raced down his spine.

"Nihal..." Was that the reason he created the storm? "He saved us."

A grin slid across Liam's face. "He tends to do that. Calls himself a conduit, not like I know what that is. He was the first fae like me I've met. You know, dark." His eyes slid to where Riona and Gulliver soaked in the sun. It seemed even the hard Dark Fae enjoyed the warmth after the gray skies the day before.

"You'd be surprised what kind of fae exist."

Liam grunted. "Not sure anything can surprise me anymore."

Griffin pushed off the rail. "Can I ask you something?"

He nodded.

"Nihal said the second half of our journey would be more difficult. But this... the breeze and the glassy waters."

Liam grimaced. "We are still in Fargelsian waters. Wait until we reach Iskalt. That's where many ships sink."

Griffin began thinking they should have taken the weeks to cross the Vatlands and Eldur on horseback.

The first iceberg marking the entrance to Iskalt waters stood in their path. Liam tried his best to steer around it, enlisting the help of Myles who claimed he'd taken two sailing lessons as a kid, but they were too late. The wooden boat scraped along the iceberg, sending shards of ice raining down on the deck followed by freezing cold water. Griffin tried to steer clear of the water, but it got him anyway. He waited for the compulsion to jump but it never came.

"Iskalt spells their waters to keep the Fargelsian dangers out." Liam ran from one side of the ship to the other.

"They should spell their icebergs," Gulliver yelled.

"We're going to lose the ship!" Myles yelled.

Riona's eyes widened as the ship rocked sideways, trying to break free of the ice. She jumped to her feet, walking with deliberate steps to the side of the ship.

What was she doing? Griffin tried to rise, but the ship dug farther into the ice, knocking him back on his butt. The cry was stuck in his throat as Riona climbed onto the railing and dove into the icy waters with a mesmerizing grace.

He scrambled to his feet and stumbled to the railing to peer down into the dark, frothing water battering the iceberg on all sides.

"What was that?" Liam yelled.

Griffin searched for Riona, his heart beating rapidly. A loud crack filled the air as boards broke apart.

Liam took in a deep breath. "We can't take much more damage before we sink. Bring me the oars." Griffin didn't know what he planned to do with them, but he wasn't focused on him, not with Riona down in the freezing water.

Only months ago he'd faced Riona in a fight to the death. Now, he needed her to be okay. "I can't do this on my own, Riona." She was loyal to King Egan in a way only Griffin understood. He'd been there. She just needed to see she was worth so much more than what he deigned to give her.

But first, she needed to live.

Time stopped—or at least it felt like it.

Gulliver joined him at the rail despite Griffin's insistence he stay away. But if the ship was doing down, at least they'd be together.

Gulliver put a hand on Griffin's arm as time ticked on. Liam passed Griffin a long oar to use as leverage to try to break the ship free of the ice.

It wasn't working.

Until it was.

The ship groaned and cracked as it was freed of the ice.

And still, she didn't resurface.

No one other than Egan would miss Riona. Her kind had been forgotten by the realm, and the only one like her lived in the human realm.

"She's going to be okay," Gulliver said. "She's Riona."

Griffin couldn't take his eyes from the dark waters, he couldn't stop looking for the woman who'd saved them.

"Griffin," Liam shouted. "Is that... there's a body in the water."

Griffin ran the length of the ship, stopping next to the captain. "Get her out."

"Nets!" The captain ran toward where the net hung at the bow of the ship and got them into the water.

Griffin and Myles pulled the nets up and Riona with it. Her entire body shook, proof she still lived. "Get me something dry to wrap her in," Griffin pleaded as he gathered Riona in his arms and headed for the stairs. He laid her on the table, not knowing what to do next. "Liam?"

The captain appeared in the doorway. "What is it?"

"I think we need to undress her, get her warm. Will you fetch

Myles for me?" The human knew more about how to take care of someone when you didn't have magic.

Griffin blew out a breath. Myles groaned when he walked in. "I kind of hate you, Griff. I mean, who takes a ship across this cursed lake? You got us shipwrecked, almost killed by smugglers, and stuck on an iceberg." He sighed. "But what do you need from me?"

Griffin looked down at Riona and the tattoos fading from her skin as if draining her very life. "You packed clothes for the journey, right?" Griffin only had what was on his back.

Myles rummaged through his bag and handed Griffin a pair of linen pants and a cotton shirt.

Together, they managed to remove Riona's clothing—keeping their eyes averted out of respect.

"She really saved us?" Myles tugged the shirt over her head.

Griffin focused on drying the icy water from her hair and wings. He wished Egan had returned all of his magic. Then he'd have her dry in no time. "Riona is half Asrai and half Slyph."

"I have no idea what that means."

"Humans," Griffin grumbled. "They may resemble what you humans call mermaids."

"No way." Excitement laced his tone. "Riona is a mermaid?"

"Half-mermaid. She doesn't have a tail like the creatures of your stories, but she is drawn to the water."

"How did I not know such a fae existed?"

"They've been forgotten, just like many other kinds of fae trapped behind the prison barriers. Prisoners aren't the only fae being forgotten. It's why we're on this mission. We're going to change the world."

Griffin didn't sleep that night. The rocking of the boat subsided the closer they got to Iskalt as the waters calmed.

And still, he couldn't let himself rest. Riona woke up twice, but each time she could barely open her eyes. There were no fires on this vessel for obvious reasons, but Griffin wrapped her in whatever he could find.

He'd watched her most of the night as the blue faded from her lips, and her beautiful dark skin regained some of its undertones.

Gulliver tried to stay up, but he ended up passing out on a wooden bench next to Griffin. Liam was up on deck watching for any other dangers.

The air chilled as they neared the Iskalt shores, the biting cold burrowing deep into Griffin's bones.

For now, everything was calm. The fear that had lived with him about facing Brea and Lochlan was replaced with a new fear. He hadn't wanted to lose Riona. They were in this together. Did that make them... friends?

Her eyes fluttered open as if she could read his thoughts.

"Hi." Griffin smiled down at her. "Can I get you some water?"

She shook her head.

"You saved us." He knew without a doubt she'd pushed the ship away from the iceberg. "I didn't know you were that strong."

She coughed, and when she spoke, her voice held a weakness that was so unlike her. "Only when I give in to my Asrai nature."

"In the palace, many were afraid of me. And then there's you," she whispered. "You've never been afraid of me. Not even as we fought in the pits. Why?"

He had so many answers for her. Because he thought he deserved every punishment. Because he was fighting for Nessa, for all his people.

But neither of those answers seemed sufficient, honest.

He looked into the flickering light of a single candle. "Because I know what it is like to be feared." He dropped his voice. "Fear is worse than hatred."

"It is." Her eyes fluttered shut again.

He looked from a sleeping Gulliver to a dozing Myles. Here, for once, neither of them had to be feared.

"Is Riona going to be okay?" Maybe Gulliver wasn't asleep.

Griffin softened his voice. "I think so."

They sat in silence for a long moment. "Griff?"

"Speak, Gullie."

"Do you ever regret the things you've done?"

Griffin's brow scrunched. "Is this what's keeping you up?"

"I think I know you. You raised me. But I've started wondering if I only know one side. Maybe there's a part of you—the part that followed the evil queen—you hide from us."

Griffin turned to face him, the flickering of the candle highlighting the shadows on his face. "I will regret the things I did for the rest of my life." He sighed. He owed Gulliver the truth. "I like to tell people I'm not the same man I was, but I've never tested myself to see if what drove me all those years ago could get ahold of me now." He would soon once he saw Callum. Would the real Griffin finally show up? "I think... I think the two sides of me have merged. The one who cares about our people in Myrkur, who doesn't go a day without fearing for Shauna and Nessa... he's real. You've always had the real me."

He sucked in a breath. "But... I think Regan had the real me too."

Two halves, both wanting different things. Gulliver's expression fell like he didn't appreciate the complexities of that answer. Griffin had to constantly fight the side of him that sought power and adoration.

But he did, he fought it. And most of the time, he won.

"I need some air." Gulliver slid off the bench and headed up the stairs. Now that they were past the rough waters, the lake surface was calm.

Griffin relaxed back in his chair. "He's never going to think of me the same way."

He hadn't thought Riona was awake, so her voice surprised him. "You cannot change your nature, Griff. But you can fight it. He'll figure that out one day. You and I have darkness in us. We make little sense to someone with such obvious light."

The difference between him and Riona was that Griffin had people to yank him out of Regan's orbit, to make him question her when she still lived.

Who did Riona have to pull her from the darkness?

To make her see King Egan as he was.

Someone who could show her she deserved more than the bloodshed he foisted upon her.

She'd fallen asleep again, and he looked down into her face. "Me, Riona. You have me."

The biting cold wasn't something Griffin would ever forget. He was a child when he last set foot in his home kingdom of Iskalt, before his uncle took his father's throne. Before Lochlan reclaimed it with an Eldurian army fortified by the Iskaltians still loyal to the royal line.

And Griffin hadn't been there. He should have stood at his brother's side, should have fought for their family.

Instead, he chose to forsake the only other person who mourned his parents the way he did. He barely remembered them, but he knew they'd have wanted their boys to fight for each other, not against each other.

They'd have been ashamed of him.

Riona stood at his side, wearing an outfit of Myles' that fit her awkwardly. Her wings were hidden underneath her shirt, folded in on themselves. Griffin never wanted her to hide such an integral part of herself, but it was her decision.

Just like it was her decision to let the tattoos fade into her skin.

Riona would do anything to secure the secrets of the prison realm, and Griff would do anything to bring those secrets down.

It seemed they were meant to be at odds, but just like everything else, their animosity faded into the sea. For now, they had similar goals.

"Griff." Gulliver's teeth chattered. "Is it always this cold in Iskalt?"

He looked sideways at Gulliver. "Most of the time, it's worse."

"And here I thought the icebergs were just friendly greetings from the ice king."

A laugh burst out of Myles. "More like a warning to keep smugglers from nearing the Iskalt shores. That's why they sail to the smuggler's coast north of here and then travel over the mountains to the villages from there. But I'm definitely telling Lochlan fae are calling him the ice king. It fits."

Their ship had made it through the rough waters to the calmer inlet and run aground on a sandy beach. It wouldn't be setting sail again anytime soon.

Their group trudged up the narrow path from the cove and stared across the expansive field of snow that spanned the distance between the palace and the nearest village.

Liam had grown quiet behind them, maybe mourning his boat.

"What will you do?" Griffin asked him.

He shrugged. "It was just a boat. We all survived, and that's what matters. Nihal will make sure I'm compensated."

Griffin nodded, amazed at the faith he had in the Dark Fae they'd met back on the island.

"What is this stuff?" Gulliver's eyes widened as he leaned down, his hand hovering over the snow. "It's not going to kill me, is it?"

Griffin laughed. In Fargelsi, many things were deadly. Here in Iskalt, life was difficult, but the fae weren't surrounded by potential dangers. "It's snow, Gullie. Go ahead. Touch it."

A look of glee flashed across Gulliver's face. It reminded Griffin how young this boy still was, how ill prepared he was for what lay beyond the prison world he'd known all his life.

He stuck one finger in the snow. "It's cold!" He laughed as he scooped up a handful and then another. He took off running through the field, his steps leaving grooves on the smooth surface.

A snowflake hit Griffin's face, and he looked up to see the tiny flurries blanketing the sky.

Gulliver tilted his head back and caught snowflakes on his tongue, laughing each time.

Griffin could have watched him for hours. There was no snow in Myrkur, just like there'd been none in Eldur or Fargelsi. It was one of the wonders of Iskalt. Griffin shook the snowflakes from his hair, leaning down to scoop up a handful of snow. With a grin he took careful aim and landed the snowball against Gulliver's back.

Gulliver whirled around, trying to look at his back. "What did you *just* do?"

Griffin laughed when another snowball hit Gulliver's front, and he turned to see Riona's eyes dancing with humor.

"No way, you're both dead." Gulliver scooped up a snowball, and chaos ensued as all three adults ganged up on the kid.

Liam only watched them with a look of amusement.

Gulliver's shrieks of laughter did wonders to lift Griffin's mood. If nothing else, at least the kid got to experience his very first snowball fight.

Myles stepped up beside Griffin, his face flushed red from the cold. "We should keep moving and get to the palace. We aren't exactly dressed for this weather."

Griffin shook his head as he caught sight of Riona hopping through the snow drifts with tentative steps, a look of awe on her face. "Just give them a little longer Myles. In the prison realm, in Myrkur, these kinds of moments don't exist."

"What kind?"

"Wonder." In Myrkur, there was only survival. Here, in the safety of Iskalt, there was room for them to breathe.

A few travelers on the road winding through the field gave them odd looks, but Griffin didn't have the heart to interrupt Gulliver or Riona.

Liam clapped him on the shoulder. "This is where I take my leave of you."

"Will you be okay?"

The fisherman nodded. "A friend has an inn in the nearest village. I'll go there and try to find an Iskaltian ship heading back to Fargelsi."

"Go to the Fargelsian queen." Myles stepped in. "Tell her Myles sent you. She will see you are compensated for your ship."

"I don't know who you folks are, but from the moment Nihal introduced us, I knew you were working for good. Or else, he wouldn't have orchestrated your survival."

Griffin shook his hand, and Liam turned down the road, trudging through the snow.

Griffin let his gaze wander across the fields to the imposing palace at the other end. No one would ever call the Iskalt palace comfortable. It wasn't soothing and airy like Fargelsi. It didn't hold the beauty of the exotic Eldurian palace. Instead, it stood like a fortress meant to intimidate, to threaten.

At least, it had while his uncle Callum claimed it.

Now, it held a new kind of intimidation for Griffin. Behind those walls, Brea and Lochlan lived their life in ignorance, never knowing he'd once stood between them.

Griffin gestured for Myles to follow him, and they joined Gulliver and Riona. Gulliver's cheeks and nose were bright red, but he seemed impervious to the cold.

Riona's breath curled in front of her face, and she couldn't stop staring at it. "I've never seen magic other than your portals, Griffin." No one in Fargelsi had used it around them. "Is it always like this?"

Myles snorted. "That's not magic, it's science."

She turned to him, confusion tugging the corners of her lips down. "Science? I do not know this term."

"The cold air meets the warm moisture in your breath."

"Moisture? I did not spit."

"No..." Myles shook his head. "You know what, screw it. Yes, it's magic. Isn't it wonderful?"

Griffin held in a laugh. "We should head toward the palace."

"Do you think they'll give us an audience with the king?" Riona's fierce gaze met his. "Or do we have to fight our way in?"

"Whoa." Myles held up both hands. "No one is fighting their way into my best friend's castle. Dude, if you told me I'd be saying a line like that ten years ago..." He laughed. "We'll get in to see the king *and* the queen."

"How do you know that?" Riona crossed her arms.

"It's called bestie privilege."

Riona opened her mouth to speak again, but Griffin cut her off. "Don't try to understand human speak, Riona. It usually makes little sense."

Myles only shrugged and walked toward the snowy path that would take them to the palace. "We're not going through the front entrance."

"Probably a good idea." Griffin brushed snow from his hair. "We don't need our presence here discussed throughout the villages. Gulliver, keep your sunglasses on once we're inside. Don't take them off until I tell you it's okay."

Gulliver nodded, checking to make sure his tail was still tucked away.

The closer they walked to the palace, the more Griffin wanted to turn around and brave the rough waters of Lake Villandi again. But he couldn't. Not this time.

"It's so big." Gulliver stared up at high stone towers and the fortified walls that wrapped around the palace. It was a fortress, but it was also beautiful in its own way.

The guards at the front gates watched them pass, but didn't speak as Myles led the group around to the south side of the palace grounds. They rounded the corner to find a frozen pond. Memories rushed in to swirl in Griffin's mind. He'd been so young when he left Iskalt as a child, the memories were normally only fragments. But he could see his brother so clearly running across the frozen pond with his friends.

Now, there were two children playing a game Griffin didn't recognize. They had blades strapped to their feet and sticks in their hands.

A smile stretched across Myles' face. "That would be the prince and princess."

Suddenly, Griffin couldn't breathe. He'd known Brea and Lochlan probably had kids, but it still felt like a lance shot through him at the sight of them. His eyes followed the princess across the ice. She used an odd stick as she chased a black toy. "What are they doing?"

"Playing hockey." Myles laughed. "I made Lochlan take me to the human realm to get skates and sticks. If the kids had to live in a freezing kingdom, they'd at least get the benefits of it." He cupped his hands around his mouth. "Nice shot, Tia!"

Two guards obviously sent to watch the kids looked their way but didn't move. They kept a distance, probably at Brea's insistence. She wouldn't want her kids feeling smothered by security.

Tia jerked her head up. She was older than Griffin thought at first. Maybe eight or nine?

"Uncle Myles!" She dropped her stick and wobbled as she tried to run with the blades on her feet. Griffin saw it then, the complete adoration. The kid loved Myles... her uncle.

A relationship Griffin would never have with his brother's children.

Tia reached them and flung herself into Myles' arms. "What are you doing here? Mom said you were busy with your own brood—her word, not mine."

"It's a long story, but your cousins had to stay back in Fargelsi."

Her expression dropped. "Oh."

Myles put her down and wrapped an arm around her shoulders. "I'd like you to meet some friends of mine. This is Griffin."

She lifted her chin, regarding each of them with keen eyes. "Hello. I'm Tierney."

Griffin's gut clenched at the name. Queen Tierney. She'd been married to Brea's mother in Eldur. Until... Griffin met Myles' gaze in understanding. They both knew what Tierney's death in battle had done to Brea. It gave her the anger, the hatred she'd needed to defeat Regan.

Griffin bent down to meet the little girl's gaze. "Hi Tierney." She stared at him, recognition on her face.

"I wondered what your name was," she whispered. "I knew you'd come today. It's why I came down from the tower. Griffin." Power swirled in her intense gaze.

Griffin couldn't look away as the message Brea sent Neeve came back to him. Tierney saw the prison realm in her dreams, saw him.

One side of her mouth curved up. "You're going to save me. Not here. Not now. When the time is right. But I wish you'd save my brother instead."

The intensity left her eyes in an instant and she became just a little girl again with snow clinging to her strawberry blond hair and melting on her rosy cheeks. She gave them a full smile and turned to Gulliver. "Who are you?"

Griffin couldn't take his eyes off her as she chatted with the others. What did she mean he'd save her but not her brother?

Snapping out of his daze, Griffin dropped a hand on Gullie's shoulder. "This is Gulliver."

She scanned Gulliver from head to toe. "Gulliver is an odd name."

He raised a brow. "So is Tierney."

Tierney pursed her lips. "Okay. You can play hockey with us."

Before Gulliver could accept the invitation, a cry reached them followed by a splash.

Griffin didn't stop to consider what had happened. He ran as shouts filled the air. The ice cracked, dragging the prince below the surface.

"I'm coming, Toby!" Tierney's little voice rang out behind Griffin. She muttered a string of words he couldn't make out.

The ice undulated, sending fissures through every part of it. Magic. It had to be. But the only people who could have magic here were the guards. Unless... He cast one more glance toward the frantic kid whose lips hadn't stopped moving. The hair on Griffin's arms stood on end as another wave of erratic magic filled the air.

The prince pulled his head above the ice before a wave of magic sent him back under.

Griffin reached the edge of the pond and tested the ice with his foot. Cracks spidered out from his weight. He'd never wished for his magic to return more than in this moment.

Tierney skidded to a halt beside him, her hair sticking to her face.

Griffin could feel it. Her magic. The power she possessed. He turned to her. "Pull your magic back in."

"I need to save him."

"Kid, you're going to get him killed." *Think, Griffin.* He couldn't remember how to reverse Fargelsian magic. "Just don't utter another word."

The guards reached them, and Griffin gestured to Tierney. "Get the princess away from here."

Fat tears slid down her cheeks, but the guards pulled her away, taking orders from a man they didn't know.

A man who had to save Brea's son.

What had Tierney called him? Toby.

"I'm coming, Toby." He couldn't stand in any one place too long, or the ice wouldn't hold him. Sucking in a breath, he stepped out onto the ice, now broken by a little girl's uncontrollable magic.

With light feet, he hopped across the surface. The prince hadn't come up in too long. Adrenaline spiked through Griffin as he reached the hole in the ice Toby had fallen through. There was no sign of the prince, no sign of life at all.

Griffin stuck a hand down into the icy water, trying to find him. Myles, Riona, and Gulliver waited at the edge of the pond, yelling for Toby.

"Stay off the ice!" Griffin ordered. He unclasped his cloak around his neck and threw it onto the ice behind him.

He was Iskaltian. The cold shouldn't bother him.

And yet, he hesitated.

Sucking in a deep breath, he plunged into the water, letting it sting his eyes as he kept them open. The pond wasn't deep, but it was dark, only letting light through where the ice cracked above.

Griffin's entire body went numb from the cold. He kicked his legs as he searched everywhere for the young prince. Even after ten years, he couldn't let anything break Brea's heart the way the death of her son would.

His lungs squeezed, desperate for more air as his heart beat uncontrollably.

And then he saw him. The young prince with his dark hair, so unlike his sister's. Griffin reached for the boy, relief flooding him. He wrapped an arm around Toby's waist and dragged him back to the opening in the ice.

A hand reached down to help lift the prince. Griffin took the help without thinking where it could come from with the ice so splintered.

Whoever it was dragged Toby from the water. Griffin gripped the jagged edges of the ice and hauled himself out of the icy pond. His entire body shook as he tried to crawl toward the shore. The cracks surrounding him widened, and that was when he saw her.

Riona, wings unfurled behind her set Toby on solid ground before returning for Griffin. From the air. She was flying, showing her otherness to Iskalt with no thought to what could happen.

Griffin had only seen her fly to get to Nihal. The Slyph rarely used their wings to fly. Only when faced with battle would they take to the skies.

Yet here, to save his life, to save a prince she didn't know... she was Griffin's guardian, come to his rescue. As his eyes slid shut, her hands lifted him from the ice. The last thing he remembered was soaring through the sky.

Chapter 22

Warmth enveloped Griffin, and a smile curved his lips. Warmth could only mean one thing. He was safe in Fargelsi with Queen Regan, the only woman who'd ever taken care of him.

And Brea. His wife.

A sigh rattled through his chest as he pulled Brea against him. She fit him like nothing ever had before. The marriage magic was only a few days old, but they'd have a lifetime to explore what it meant, to come to terms with the binding force that could never be torn away.

And Griffin didn't plan to do either anytime soon. In the coming years, Brea would grow into her role as a Fargelsi royal. And their children... he smiled at the thought. They'd be remarkable children, holding the magic of all three realms within them. Brea was of Eldur and Fargelsi. Griffin could command Iskalt power. As long as they remained together, no one would defeat them.

"Brea," he whispered on a sigh. His Brea.

Regan had forced her into the marriage, taking advantage of her naiveté, but the magic made her feel things for Griffin. He knew it did.

"Griffin." Her voice sounded far off, like she wasn't lying right beside him.

"I love you, Brea."

Pressure pulsed in his chest as if someone slammed their fist into it. Warmth hit his lips, and he sighed into the kiss.

"Griffin, if you don't wake up right this freaking second..." That was Myles. Wait, he shouldn't be there. Brea had traded herself, her freedom to make sure Myles and Neeve were released from Fargelsi.

His eyes slid open slowly, painfully. He sucked in a breath, but his lungs were raw, and pain rippled through him. And there she was, Brea Robinson. The girl he'd abducted from the human realm, the one who was now his wife.

He reached up, sliding his hand to the back of her neck. Brea froze. "Sir, I—"

Griffin cut her off by pulling her closer and rising up to meet her kiss. She didn't stop him at first, giving in to the irrational pull between them.

And then she punched him and shot to her feet, one finger on her lips. "Saving my son does not give you the right to kiss your queen."

The fog in Griffin's mind cleared. He wasn't in Fargelsi with Regan and Brea. Regan had been dead for ten years, and Brea was no longer his wife.

No one spoke for a long moment as Griffin realized what he'd just done.

"Myles," Brea growled. "I will not banish your friends from the palace." Her suspicious gaze slid over Riona who'd left her wings bared. "They saved my son. But they are your responsibility."

Myles smirked. "I am a king too. You can't just order me around."

She stepped toward him. "Care to bet on that?"

They stood in a silent stand off for a long moment before Myles pulled Brea into a hug. "I missed you."

She rested her chin on his shoulder. "I missed you so much I don't even care that you brought a pack of bizarre strangers with you."

Strangers. That was what they were to her.

The door to the sitting room burst open, revealing the king—Griffin's brother. Lochlan's gaze darted between the fae huddled near the fire. "Where's my son? Tobias... he... I heard. Is he okay?"

Brea nodded. "He's in his rooms sleeping. One of the healers is keeping a watch by his bed, as is *your* daughter."

Lochlan's brow shot up. "What did she do? You only call her mine when she's causing trouble."

Griffin wanted to laugh at that because it should have been the other way around. Brea was the troublemaker. But right then, he felt like an intruder on their family moment.

Brea sighed. "Someone has to teach Tia to control her magic—better yet, not to use it—or we're in for many years of this sporadic destruction before she takes any of her Fargelsian classes seriously. And heaven help us when she gains both her Eldurian and Iskalt powers. That child... She could have killed her brother today."

Lochlan rubbed tired eyes. "That girl is going to be the death of me."

Brea's expression softened as she stepped toward her husband and wrapped her arms around his waist. "We will get through it. We always do."

Myles groaned. "We should probably go before you guys start with all the kissing and the self-sacrificing vows." He put a hand to his chest. "I would die for you, my douchey Loch." He deepened his voice. "Brea, you are the stars in the sky. Yada, yada, puke."

Lochlan leaned into Brea. "Why do we let him visit again?"

She only smiled and shook her head, exhaustion weighing her down. "It's not like he and Neeve aren't the same way."

Myles laughed at that. "No, our relationship goes something like this. Myles, I need you to do a thing. It's a hard thing, but you're the manliest man I know, so it has to be you." He shrugged. "Then, I do the thing."

Ten years, and these people hadn't changed a bit. Griffin watched them interact, knowing he could have been part of their lives if he'd made different choices. This could have been his family.

"These people are strange," Riona whispered.

"That's always been the best thing about them." A shiver raced down his spine, and a thought struck him. "How did I end up in dry clothes?" He looked to Myles.

Myles pointed to Riona who gave him an unapologetic look. "It was either strip you or let you die. You did the same to me. Now we're even."

The ensuing silence told him Brea and Lochlan no longer chatted with Myles. Instead, both sets of eyes settled on Griffin. "Do I want to know?" he asked his wife.

"I'm not sure yet." She pursed her lips. "Go to Tobias. He and Tia need you. I'll figure out what's happening here, and then I must go nurse Ciara."

Lochlan swept his eyes through the room once more before turning and shutting the door behind him.

Brea took a seat in a high backed wooden chair that looked almost like a throne. It suited her.

Griffin scooted closer to the fire.

"If I told my husband you kissed me, you'd have more than just the one black eye." She crossed her arms. "And yet, I do not wish you harm. Who are you, sir, and why did it feel wrong to hit you?"

When no one answered, her eyes settled on Myles. "What don't I know?"

Myles sighed. "Well, this is the second time I've been abducted by Griffin O'Shea."

"We did not abduct you," Griffin protested. "I'd have been happy to leave you at home."

Brea's eyes widened as they bounced from Myles to Griffin and back again, ignoring Griffin's words to focus on Myles'. "You mean the man from your stories?"

"No, the man from our histories. Brea, I've been telling you about Griffin since he crossed into the prison realm."

"My husband told me there is no way out of the prison realm. So, I ask again, who are you?"

Griffin pushed himself up despite the ache in his bones. He held back the bit about being the man her daughter saw in her dreams.

Brea probably didn't even know they were more than dreams. "Many years ago, I was your husband."

Why was Griffin such an idiot? He had to lead with the husband bit. But looking into her eyes, he couldn't hold it back. Brea Robinson was every bit as beautiful as he remembered. Dark hair framed her pale skin. Her eyes... he sucked in a breath. They would forever haunt him.

And her kiss... he couldn't bring himself to regret that. The marriage magic might be broken, but he still felt the small tug of it, pulling him to her.

He had to remind himself he wasn't here to catch up with old friends—or enemies. They needed information and quickly if he was to save Shauna and Nessa. They were his family now.

Brea left them hours ago, not letting him finish explaining who he was. She hadn't wanted to hear much beyond, *I was once your husband.*

Myles led them to the suite of rooms he and his family normally used when visiting. Servants bustled around—many more than in Fargelsi. They opened drapes, pounding the dust from them, and started a fire.

Griffin barely had the energy to stand, so he lowered himself to the woven carpet before the hearth, letting the flames thaw the ice inside him. He'd thought a lot about what it would be like seeing Brea and Lochlan again.

He'd never counted on it hurting this much.

Riona busied herself cleaning up in the washroom while Gulliver lounged on the bed, his eyes sliding shut. Myles left them to their own devices so he could check on the kids.

Griffin stared into the flames, letting them clear his mind. He was like Myles once, all charm and hilarity. He'd been an easy person, one who liked jokes and smiled every chance he got. The prison realm tore that out of him, leaving behind a man who worried too much, cared too much, lost too much.

Riona stepped from the washroom, her face impassive—a mask she seemed to have perfected. She sank onto the carpet beside him and stretched her wings to the flames to dry them.

"Did you grow up in this palace?" she asked.

He shook his head. "I was young when I left. My mother and father were killed."

She flicked water from a wing tip. "My mother and father died when I was young too." She stretched her arms out, sighing as the tattoos darkened, the vibrant colors returning to the surface.

"Does it pain you to hide them?"

"Yes. But I do it because out here, outside Myrkur, they don't understand what it is to be different. Eldur, Fargelsi, Iskalt… sure, there's a difference in how they use their power, but if one fae from each kingdom walked toward you, would you be able to tell the difference?"

"Probably not." Eldurians often had darker skin, but then, so did some Fargelsian fae. Even in Iskalt, skin color varied, but at the end of the day, it didn't separate them from the fae of other kingdoms. Not like Riona's tattoos and wings.

"That is why this Queen Sorcha didn't only wish to send prisoners away. Anyone who is different has been forgotten by your world."

"Is that why you accepted this quest for Egan? To bring all fae together into the light?"

She took a long moment before responding. "No. I came because I had no other choice."

A knock on the door interrupted them. Griffin pushed to his feet and crossed the room. He pulled open the door, surprised to find Lochlan on the other side. His brother had changed more than Brea had over the years. Fine lines creased his brow.

And a kid dangled from one of his arms, squirming to get free. "Papa, down."

Lochlan looked to Griffin like he was just another father who knew the way of children. "As soon as I put her down, she's going to run."

"Do you... want to come in?" He didn't know what answer he hoped for.

"I have to get back to my son's side, but you and I need to talk. Please, come with me." He hoisted the little girl into his arms. "This is Kayleigh, the kitchen's worst pastry thief. Which is why she's with us." He chuckled to himself. "She stole an entire pie yesterday and shared it with the stray cats in the stables."

Seeing the serious Lochlan smile and wrestle with his daughter wasn't something Griffin ever thought he'd witness.

Lochlan gave him a brief smile, another thing Griffin rarely earned in their lives before.

Griffin followed him down the long hall where colorful portraits adorned the walls. This castle was once his home, yet he knew little of it. They reached a series of doors and stopped at the one in the middle before Lochlan pushed it open.

Tobias slept in an ornate four-poster bed. His sister had fallen asleep in a chair beside it.

"Can you hold Kayleigh for a moment?" Lochlan passed the kid over before Griffin could tell him how not a kid fae he was. The only one he'd ever been drawn to was Gulliver. Kayleigh got an impish look on her face before trying to break free. Griffin tightened his grip.

Lochlan bent to lift Tierney and put her in bed beside her brother. He placed a kiss on her head and straightened.

Brea appeared in the doorway and froze. She was in the middle of nursing a baby. "Sorry, I didn't mean to interrupt you two." She looked to Griffin. "You can put Kay down."

Griffin did as he was told, but Kayleigh didn't try to run off again. Instead, she took her mother's hand. When they were gone, Lochlan shut the door with a laugh. "Those kids obey my wife much more than me." He gestured to the two chairs next to the bed. "Sit. Please."

Where was the commanding Lochlan Griffin had known, the *douchey* Loch—as Myles called him.

"So." Lochlan rested his elbows on his knees and leaned forward.

"Myles told me about your perilous journey to reach our shores. Not many ships brave the Iskalt bays anymore." He paused, rubbing his chin. "In fact, we found a smuggler vessel capsized about a mile out to sea from what they call the smuggler's coast."

Griffin's face paled. The other ship... He thought back to Nihal and the music with a mind of its own. Was that the true reason the music wanted them on a different vessel?

"You look pensive."

Griffin snapped himself out of the dark thoughts. "I am, sorry. It's been a long journey to reach Iskalt."

Lochlan offered him a tentative smile. "Myles has been entertaining us with stories of Griffin O'Shea for the last ten years. He claims I had a brother who was sent to the prison realm. I didn't believe him."

"And now?"

"Now, I am sitting face to face with someone who strongly resembles my father and escaped the prison realm—which is supposed to be impossible. We don't know much about the magical barrier, but crossing it is supposed to be a one way trip. It doesn't let anyone leave. You portaled out, didn't you?"

Lochlan had always been the smartest among them. "We did."

"I knew it. Only an O'Shea can open a portal to the human realm." He paused. "Myles says I should thank you for saving my son's life."

Griffin shrugged. "I did not do it for your thanks."

"You did it because he's your nephew."

"No. He was a kid in danger. I had no thought to his blood relations."

Lochlan rubbed the back of his neck. "Are you sure you're the Griffin from Myles' stories? Because that man wouldn't have jumped into a freezing pond to save a random stranger."

"I'm not sure who I am anymore." The truth slipped out. Maybe it was the kind of thing he wanted to be able to say to his brother and have him understand. He wanted to tell him of his life over the last ten years. "But I do understand loss. I wouldn't wish it on anyone."

"Are you a father? I'm sorry, I don't know what's possible in the prison realm."

"I have not sired children if that's what you're asking. But one thing I've learned is that it doesn't matter who gave birth to the child or sired them, only who loves them with their entire heart. I have people who are counting on me."

Lochlan nodded, but his eyes glazed over like he was deep in thought. "Were we good brothers? I know the stories about Regan and your loyalty, but was there any point where we were truly a family?"

The question surprised Griffin. He wasn't ready for it. "Those moments were fleeting. I wish I had a different answer for you."

"Over the last ten years, I've tried to remember you. I even traveled to a few of the places Myles said we were together. I don't understand how every memory could have just vanished without a trace left behind."

Griffin stared at the serene faces of the sleeping children. They didn't yet know how dangerous this world was. "I think, no, I know that it's probably a good thing you don't remember. If you did, you'd never trust me, and this conversation wouldn't happen."

Lochlan's brow creased like he was thinking too hard. "The only blood relation I have—other than my children—is sitting in my dungeons."

Griffin studied his brother, trying to see if the years of separation had been good for him. They weren't the kind of family who was there for each other or the kind to offer encouraging words. But Lochlan didn't know that. He didn't know that when Griffin put a hand on his arm, it was the first time he could ever remember wanting to take his brother's worries.

Pain lanced through him, but it wasn't a physical type of pain. The world continued to churn. As Griffin was erased from the collective memory of the three kingdoms, life went on without him—as if he'd never been there at all.

"Brea won't let Myles discuss you in front of her." Lochlan sighed. "But I've seen it every day. There is something missing from her. And she chooses to ignore it. To some people, she's a queen. To me, she's a wife. To my kids, she's a mother. But to herself... I think that's where she gets lost. This pain, it's the only thing she holds back. Our marriage sealed her in a new magical bond, but Myles tells me she once married you. Sometimes, I fear pieces of the bond between you never went away."

"Why are you telling me this?" Griffin met his gaze. "You don't know me."

"But I do." A breath rushed out of him. "Myles comes to me when he needs to visit his parents in the human realm. For ten years, we've been making trades, each one the same. I take him to visit his parents, and he tells me more of this man he says is my brother. I know about your perverse loyalties and that you switched sides, fighting against Regan's soldiers with me. You saved Brea, Alona, and Brandon. And you loved my wife."

"With everything I had." Memories rushed in at him. He'd done what Lochlan said, breaking Brea and her father, Brandon, out of the palace along with Alona, who now sat on the Eldurian throne. These kingdoms owed him for their peace, but he'd never deserved thanks.

Lochlan's haunted eyes met his. "I'm thankful. If you did not love her, I wouldn't have Brea at my side. Is that odd? That I'm glad you loved my wife?"

He said loved in the past tense, but just seeing Brea had brought all his old feelings rushing to the surface.

Lochlan reached forward, pushing a lock of strawberry blond hair from his daughter's face. "Sometimes, I wonder..." He shook his head. "I used to wish for family. I had two moms growing up, despite our lack of a blood relationship. I had a girl who was like a sister and a best friend. I found Brea... but sometimes, I think of the brother Myles claims I can't remember. I never thought I'd meet you."

A long silence stretched between them before Griffin leaned forward. "I wonder too." He wondered what his life would be like if he hadn't chosen Regan, if he'd grown up in Eldur like Lochlan instead of Fargelsi.

Would he be free?

Would he be happy?

"You may not think you deserve thanks for saving my son, but you have it. Any request, anything you need from me during your stay here, you only have to ask. I may not know you well, Griffin." Lochlan stood and clapped a hand on Griffin's shoulder. "But I do believe you're my brother. Whatever that means for us... we'll figure it out. I'm not leaving Tia and Toby, but you should return to your people and get some rest."

Thoroughly dismissed, Griffin left Lochlan behind. A presence loomed near the doorway in the darkened hall. He expected to see Brea, the woman who didn't like to see people hurting.

Instead, when the figure turned, his eyes clashed with Riona's.

Griffin sucked in a deep breath, trying to calm his rapidly beating heart after the single best conversation he'd ever had with his brother. He stopped moving, his feet refusing to go forward as the emotions he'd held at bay for the last ten years toppled the carefully constructed walls around his heart.

He hadn't let himself miss them. Brea and Lochlan. Because if he missed them, he'd have to admit to himself he loved them, that he'd made so many mistakes that had hurt the two people he cared about most.

Tears gathered in his eyes, but he didn't let them fall.

Riona said nothing as she approached, and Griffin was thankful for her silence. He didn't know what she'd heard, but it didn't matter.

He was used to loss. He'd come to terms with leaving his family behind, but he was never supposed to get them back.

Chapter 23

Griffin straightened his tunic—borrowed from his brother, the king. The ice blue cloth was fine with simple navy embroidery along the shoulders that were a little loose on his narrow frame. A decade in the prison realm had robbed him of the strong physique he'd once had. The trousers were comfortable and simple. Not the clothes of a king.

Making his way down the wide, stark hallway from his rooms, Griffin studied the tapestries along the way to the dining hall. Depicting the history of Iskalt, he wished he'd had memories of walking this hallway, of living in this palace, but he was so young when he'd been forced to leave.

Sounds of laughter drifted from the dining hall.

Griffin had dined in the halls of many palaces where kings and queens were attended by their court. Iskalt was different, and he suspected that was Brea's doing. He peered into the dining hall, watching Brea and Loch with their young family at the lone table at the opposite end of the room. Toby and Tia sat on either side of their father, vying for his attention—which, like a good father, Lochlan divided equally among them.

Kayleigh sat beside her mother, who balanced baby Ciara on one arm and poured a tumbler of juice for Kayleigh with the other. They were a beautiful family, happy to entertain their strange guests.

"You have a tail," Tierney said, eyeing Gulliver's bandaged tail flicking nervously behind him. Griffin didn't realize he'd stopped hiding it.

"I do," Gulliver said. "I'm Tuatha De Dannan, land fae from Myrkur."

"You just said a lot of things that don't make sense," Tia said, picking at her dinner. "And you have cat eyes."

"Is that okay?" Gulliver asked, frowning as if not quite sure what to make of the assertive princess.

"It's cool." Tia popped a green bean into her mouth. "You just don't see that every day."

"What happened to your tail?" Toby asked, leaning around his father to stare at Gulliver's bandages.

"Tobias, that is a rude question," Lochlan said.

"It's okay, your Majesty. It got cut off." Gulliver examined the strange contents of his plate. It looked suspiciously like human food. "Some bad people did it, but Griff saved me."

"Will it grow back?" Tia asked.

"I sure hope so." Gulliver's truncated tail thumped against the back of his chair. "It used to have a mighty fine tip, flat and shaped like a leaf. That's where all the feeling was. I feel a bit clumsy without it."

"That's so cool," Toby said. "I wish I had a tail."

Griffin smiled as Gulliver puffed out his chest. It was nice to see the royal twins had accepted Gulliver so easily.

"Oh, no, no, your Majesty. I couldn't." Riona's terrified voice caught Griffin's attention.

"Just hold her for a minute." Brea shoved Ciara into Riona's arms. "She won't break."

"Are you sure about that? She's so tiny." Riona held the princess like she was made of glass. "And such a sweet face." Riona scowled down at the little girl in her arms. "Just don't cry, okay?"

"Don't let that sweet innocent face fool you," Brea said. "That one is a little monster. And spoiled rotten. We can thank her father for that." Brea bent over Kayleigh's plate to cut her meat into small bites she could manage on her own.

"Don't linger in the doorway, Griff." Myles clapped him on the back. "I'm starving." Myles moved past him and stopped at the head of the table. "Really, Brea? Fish sticks and green beans? Did you send your husband grocery shopping at Target again?"

Ciara started to cry, and Riona groaned. "No, baby princess. We had a deal. No crying." Myles took pity on her and rescued the squirming child from her unfamiliar arms.

"I grew up on this stuff. I want my kids to like simple food and not the fancy stuff the kitchens insist on preparing for them." Brea shrugged.

"So, all those preservatives and fillers are okay? You know there's like hardly any real fish in those things."

"They taste like the scum at the bottom of a fishing vessel," Lochlan said. "But thanks to Brea, fish sticks are one of maybe three things they'll eat without a tantrum."

"Hers or theirs?" Myles asked with a smirk.

"Both." Lochlan refilled the twin's glasses with more juice, topping off Gulliver's too without a second thought. It was strange to see Lochlan being a father.

"You going to linger over there and watch this poor excuse of a dinner, or are you going to join us?" Lochlan cast a glance over his shoulder at Griffin.

"Not quite what I had in mind when the king of Iskalt invited me to dinner." Griffin took the empty seat beside Riona.

"We will eat after the children are done." Brea pushed Kayleigh's plate back in front of her child with a frown that said 'finish your vegetables.'

"Can we take Gullie sledding tomorrow?" Toby asked. "Can you believe he's never been?"

"It doesn't snow where Gulliver comes from," Lochlan said. "You'll have to show him all our favorite winter games. But not tomorrow, you and your sister are coming with me to visit the northern villages to investigate the border at Loch Villandi. You love seeing the icebergs."

"Aw, Papa, can't we stay and play with Gullie?" Tia begged. "Your king trips are boring."

"They aren't boring, they're educational."

"That means boring, Dad," Toby said.

Griffin snorted into his wineglass, trying to cover up his laughter.

"My children amuse you?" Lochlan turned to him with a smirk.

"You know what they say about kids speaking the truth." Griffin shrugged, enjoying the rare opportunity to give his brother a hard time. He had to remind himself over and over that this was not his family. Not anymore. They were kind and receptive, but they didn't know him. He was a stranger they were compelled to reach out to, but if they knew the sins of his past... Griffin would be left out in the cold before he could blink.

"Okay, kids, go with Nicola," Brea announced as a servant entered the room. "She's going to take you to the kitchens for dessert." Brea stood and lifted the sleeping Ciara from Myles' arms to hand her to Nicola.

"Come with me, children." Nicola held out her hand for Kayleigh. "Let's let your mother and father have a nice dinner with their guests."

"You're a lifesaver." Brea regarded her servant with a sense of gratitude few in her position would have for those in their employ.

A small hand tapped Griffin's shoulder. He turned to find a pair of violet eyes staring at him.

"Thank you for saving me, Uncle Griff." Tobias threw his arms around Griffin's shoulders and patted him on the back.

Startled, Griffin returned the hug.

"Goodnight, Uncle Griff!" Tia hugged his other side. "Can Gullie come with us for dessert?"

"Yes, he can, if he wants." Griffin eyed Gulliver, not willing to make him go if he didn't want to. But Gulliver followed the twins without a second glance at Griffin. When food was involved, that kid would go anywhere.

After the kids retired for the evening, Griffin actually enjoyed the meal with Brea and Lochlan. It was surreal, telling them stories of his childhood in Fargelsi and hearing similar ones of Lochlan's in Eldur. Riona seemed to enjoy the stories, but she had little to add to the conversation. Her childhood experiences were a million miles away from theirs.

"These two princes had it easy," Brea said, laughing at Lochlan's story about growing up with the Eldurian princess, Alona, and having to share a tutor. "We had to go to school with all the commoners, right Myles?"

"Who are you kidding? We were the commoners." Myles snorted, sipping on his wine after dinner. "Though, I was the popular one. Most everyone else just thought Brea was weird."

"I was fae in the human realm who spent too much time in mental hospitals because I saw fae everywhere I went, of course I was weird!" Brea threw a half-eaten roll at him.

"Oh, you grew up in the human realm?" Riona asked. "That explains a lot."

"I didn't know I was fae until I came here when I was almost eighteen." Brea's eyes went glassy as her memory glossed over the details of her arrival in the fae realm. Griffin had been the one to bring her here, but her memories wouldn't reflect that detail.

"And you are now Queen of Iskalt?"

"I am not a queen." Brea stood to refill their wineglasses. "My husband is the king. I just live here."

Griffin couldn't take his eyes away from her. She was still so... Brea. Still the same woman he fell in love with and married all those years ago. He found himself hanging on her every word, eager to hear more about her life.

Myles was the first to retire and then Riona. Soon, it was just Brea and Griffin after Lochlan left to go check on the kids.

Brea moved to clear the table herself rather than call a servant to do it at this late hour.

Griffin chuckled as he watched her.

"What's so funny?" She quirked a smile at him as she wiped the crumbs off the table.

"That was always one of the things I loved most about you, Brea. You never gave up your human roots just because you found out you were fae. I'm glad to see marrying a fae king hasn't changed that about you." Griffin took a sip of his wine, unable to keep the smile from his face.

Brea frowned at him for a moment before she gasped. "You're G. From the letter."

"What letter?" Griffin asked, unnerved by her startled expression.

"*Number seven. I love that none of this scares you. I miss you. -G.*" Her voice was barely a whisper.

"Ahh, number seven. The one you never received." Griffin nodded. "I once told you one of my top ten reasons for loving you, and you made me tell you the other nine, but I gave them to you slowly over time. I left that one for Lochlan to give you, but he never did."

Brea leaned back in her chair. "I like this time of night. The palace goes quiet, and I can just be."

Griffin chuckled. "You never wanted to be a royal, yet three kingdoms tried to make you theirs."

She looked to him with a smile. "First, it was Regan wanting to use me as a puppet. Then, Eldur. My mothers tried very hard, but that was never meant to be my throne. Iskalt though... It's..."

"Cold? Ugly?" Griffin laughed.

"Yes." She laughed. "But it feels right."

One corner of Griffin's mouth tipped up. "I missed your laugh. More than anything about you. Ten years without Brea Robinson's laugh is a tragedy."

Her smiled turned sad. "I get the feeling you and I have been through a lot together."

"More than you could imagine."

She reached over and put her hand over his.

He wanted to tell her their entire story, that they'd once shared a life together, but he couldn't get the words out. Something told him it wasn't the right time.

"I'm happy you're here. I'm happy to see you and Lochlan getting along. It feels like our family is complete with you here, but I can't recall why."

"Without the memories to go with those feelings, I can imagine it must be disturbing." Griffin withdrew his hand from under hers.

"I don't like it," Brea said. "So, maybe you can tell me our story, help me relearn the memories I've lost."

A pang of horror shot through Griffin at the suggestion. "No, you don't want me to do that, Brea." He scooted his chair back, preparing to stand. "You should keep your memories happy. You don't want to remember me as I was." His hand cupped her cheek and the familiar sensation of her skin against his came crashing back to him.

"You are my husband's brother. My children's uncle." Brea stood. "And to me... I don't know what you are. I mean, I know what you've told me, but I'm missing so much. That's the problem, Griff. It's me. Was I in love with you?"

The words sat on the tip of his tongue, but he swallowed them and stood, breaking eye contact with her. "I'm sorry I don't have the answers you seek." The words were like acid on his tongue.

Her shoulders fell, and she nodded. "I suppose you are just as confused as the rest of us. I must leave you now if I'm going to kiss my kids goodnight." Her strained expression didn't match her words.

With that, she turned and fled the dining hall.

Griffin stayed behind to finish his wine—and the pitcher, trying to forget the pull toward his brother's wife. By the time he shuffled back to his room, he was unsteady on his feet and convinced he was going to ruin his second chance.

"What are you doing?" Riona stuck her head into the hall. "You're making a racket out there."

"I am?" Griffin turned bleary eyes on her. She was a vision with her white wings fluttering behind her and her swirling tattoos pulsing across her dark skin. But she wasn't Brea. He swayed on his feet. "Did you come out here to annoy me, or have you decided you like me? I think you like me." A hiccup escaped his lips.

Riona pressed her lips into a thin line. "You're hardly likable, particularly in this state." She moved to catch him before he stumbled.

"I'm in love with Brea, did you notice?"

"You're drunk. I noticed *that*." She draped his arm over her shoulder.

"Yes, very drunk." He grinned down at her. "That's the only thing you can do when you realize you're still in love with your ex-wife who is now married to your estranged brother. Wine. Copious amounts of wine."

Without a word, Riona stepped into his arms, and rose up on her toes, giving him no warning before she kissed him. Her lips were warm and inviting, and she fit perfectly against him. Griffin's heart pounded beneath his ribs as he reached for her, letting a hand trail down the length of her delicate wings. A shiver ran through her body at his touch, and he very much wanted to make her do that again, but she stepped away.

"Did you feel something when I kissed you?" She peered into his gaze.

"I did." He closed the distance between them, but she pressed a hand against his chest.

"Then, you aren't in love with Brea. Maybe you never were."

"How can you know that?" Griffin wanted it to be true. Needed it to be true.

"You were young and fancied yourself in love with the girl she was, but maybe you were just infatuated. Maybe you're recalling how you once felt about her, and you just want to feel like that again—but not necessarily with her."

Griffin frowned at that. For ten years, he'd struggled day to day just to survive. Being here with Brea brought back memories of being in love—memories of a short time when he was happy before everything fell apart. Who wouldn't want to recapture those feelings if given a chance?

"I hope you are right, Riona." He stumbled into his room with her assistance where he collapsed on the bed. "I don't want my brother to have to kill me for falling in love with his wife. Again."

Chapter 24

"Do you have many memories of Iskalt? Or were you too young?" Lochlan asked as they rode along the palace trails through the woods. Griffin was helping Lochlan "survey the land," but it was really just an excuse to spend some time together so Lochlan could figure out how he felt about Griffin's return. His brother had always been nothing if not predictable.

"Nothing concrete, but I do remember flashes of mother and father and you." Griffin rode quietly beside Lochlan along the winding trail that wrapped around the lake where the kids were ice-skating when Griffin first arrived only a few days ago.

"You remember me?" Lochlan glanced at him. "You couldn't have been more than two years old when they died."

"I have a vague memory of the day of their funeral. Callum wanted you by his side, but no one could find you. So, I wandered away, looking for you. I found you down here by the lake."

"You walked all the way down here on your own, and no one stopped you?"

"That's usually the way it goes with spare princes. No one notices the second born too much."

"I remember coming down here alone," Lochlan said. "I was only four." He shook his head. "If any of my children wandered off like that, I'd kill them."

"Callum probably didn't send anyone after me, hoping I'd disappear." Griffin suspected that was what Callum would have preferred of both boys that day.

"And then, he sent you to live in Fargelsi and me in Eldur. Were we ever friends after that?"

"Not really. We were so young, and I think we both had to think of ourselves at the time. New kingdoms. New families."

"And Regan was truly your family?" Lochlan gave him a skeptical look.

"I was a child, Loch. Hardly more than a baby when I lost my family. She's all I ever had, and she was good to me. She was my mother as much, if not more than Faolan was to you. I didn't learn of Regan's true motives until I was a grown man."

"And by then, it was too late, you already loved her."

"I did," Griffin managed in a whisper. Could it be possible that without the biases of their memories, the people he wanted to love might actually understand his past actions? "I owed her my life and my loyalty."

"As much as I owed the same to Faolan and Tierney. They raised me as one of their own. I would die for them."

"Had they proved to be evil as Regan, can you imagine how torn you might be between doing the right thing and fighting for the women who raised you?"

"An impossible choice, brother." Lochlan led them down the trail to the north side of the lake.

"I need to speak with Callum." Griffin urged his horse to follow. He'd come to realize over the last few days that if Regan had been searching for Sorcha's book as Neeve claimed, if she'd found it—there might only be one man alive who knew where it was.

"I will go with you. We will find the information you need. We cannot release the whole of Myrkur, but we can and should free those who do not deserve to be there. I shudder to think of all the awful fae we've sent there over the generations thinking there was nothing but a prison waiting for them on the other side." Lochlan stopped at the center of the path, gazing across the lake. "What is that blasted child doing now?" He dug his heels into his horse's flanks and charged down the trail around to the east side of the lake where the kids were playing.

Only, two of them were on the ice, again.

"Gullie!" Griffin galloped behind his brother, his heart racing in his chest at the sight of Gulliver on skates with the petite Tia trying to teach him.

"Tierney Enis O'Shea, get off that ice this instant!" Lochlan flung himself off his horse and marched out onto the ice. It cracked under his weight, and he jumped back.

"I tried to talk her out of it, Papa," Toby said. "You know how she is."

"It's okay, Papa. I fixed it." Tia skated in circles around Gulliver, showing him how to balance his weight on the blades. "He's never skated before, we had to teach him so he can play hockey with us next time."

"Gulliver, come back here, now." Griffin tried to keep the panic out of his voice. He had images of Gulliver falling through the ice and never seeing him again.

"I'm not so good at the moving part, Griff." Gulliver tried to turn toward the adults.

"Don't fall!" Lochlan and Griffin yelled at the same time.

"Papa, it won't break this time," Tia insisted, a wave of magic hit Griffin in his chest, and for a moment, he couldn't breathe.

"Tia, rein in your magic, sweetheart," Lochlan's voice was calm and commanding. "Just like we've been practicing. Now, help Gullie skate toward me." He crouched down on the ground.

Tia rolled her eyes and took Gulliver's hand, guiding him toward the shore.

A loud crack echoed across the lake, making the frozen surface tremble beneath the children's feet. A huge shelf of ice broke just behind them, floating away to crumble and sink into the frigid waters below.

"Papa?" Tia's voice shook as she clutched Gulliver's hand.

"It's okay, Tia. Keep coming toward me." Lochlan's hands shook as badly as Griffin's. He wanted to run out on the ice and snatch Gulliver up in his arms and bring him to safety.

"Tia, wait!" Gulliver cried as he lost his balance and crashed to the ice. Cracks spidered out around him.

"Tia, run to me, baby," Lochlan said. "We'll take care of Gullie, but you have to get off the ice."

"I'm sorry, Gullie." A big tear ran down Tia's face as she ran to her father.

"Gullie, can you crawl toward us?" Lochlan asked. "Keep your weight distributed across the surface, and it won't crack anymore."

He wasn't far, but Griffin knew he was frozen in fear.

"You can do it, Gulliver. Just inch your way toward me." Griffin belly crawled out onto the ice. He was so close, but they were running out of time. "Just do what I do." He inched forward, prepared to take another dive into the lake if that was what it took.

Slowly, Gulliver crept toward him, bright tears shone in his eyes. "That's it, son. I've got you." Griffin swept him up in his arms and ran for the shore just as the ice shattered around them.

Gulliver clung to him like he did when he was just a little boy, and Griffin held on tight. "You're okay, you're okay," he murmured, refusing to let him go after they reached the safety of the shore.

"Tierney, what do you have to say for yourself?" Lochlan towered over her with his arms crossed over his chest.

"I'm sorry." She lowered her head, sniffing back tears. "I thought I could keep it from breaking again."

"The problem is you don't think." Lochlan knelt before her. "You have magic no one else has. We can't teach you how to control it if you don't listen to us."

"I'm sorry, Papa." She wiped her tears away. "I won't let that happen again."

"See that you don't." Lochlan stood and scooped her up in his arms, taking Toby by the hand. "You are not allowed to even look at the lake without adult supervision. Is that clear?"

"Yes, Papa," the twins said in unison.

"I'm sorry, Gullie." Tia sniffed again. "Sorry, Uncle Griff."

"Is he okay?" Lochlan asked as they made their way up to the palace, leading their horses behind them.

"Just shook him up a little. He's fine." Griffin carried Gulliver up to the palace kitchen for hot chocolate to warm him up. He was too old to carry, but he'd scared Griffin half to death.

"After your hot chocolate, you go find your mother and tell her what happened," Lochlan instructed.

"Do we have to?" Tia's bottom lip trembled. "She'll be so mad."

"Yes, you have to. And I better not find out you've given her an embellished version of the tale either."

"You okay, or do you want me to stay and have hot chocolate with you?" Griffin set Gulliver down and crouched to his level.

"I'm okay, Griff."

"Maybe try not letting Princess Tia talk you into anything dangerous again."

"She's kind of bossy," Gulliver whispered.

"She gets that from her mother." Lochlan gave him a wink.

"Truer words have never been spoken." Griffin stood to follow Lochlan from the kitchen.

"I had thought Gulliver was a kind of servant, but he's a son to you, isn't he?" Lochlan asked as they made their way down into the depths of the castle.

"I found him when he was just three years old living in a slum just outside the Myrkur Castle. We've been together ever since." Griffin wasn't sure when it had happened, but somewhere through the years, Gulliver had become his child. "Blood doesn't always matter when it comes to family." He thought of Shauna and Nessa back in Myr, and it renewed his urgency to speak with Callum.

"It's the people that matter," Lochlan agreed. "He's a good boy."

"Just mind your valuables when he's around. He likes to collect things that aren't his." Griffin slapped Lochlan on the back and handed him a jeweled knife. "Pretty sure that belongs to you. I found it in his room last night. I try to remember to shake him down every couple of days to make sure he hasn't stolen anything truly valuable. He's been on his best behavior since we arrived."

"Well, since mine tried to kill yours, I think we can call it even." Lochlan tucked the knife into his belt. They walked along the dank corridors lit with torchlight.

"Callum's been down here for the last decade?" Griffin shivered in the cold. He couldn't imagine living out a sentence like that. "Why not send him to the prison world with all the other prisoners?"

Lochlan frowned at the question. "I didn't want us to forget what he'd done. How much harm he and Regan brought to our people."

Griffin nodded. "It is wise not to allow yourselves to forget the past."

"But what I don't understand is why I sent my own brother to the prison realm."

"That's what you think?" Griffin turned to him in the dim light.

"Someone sent you." Lochlan shrugged as if the weight of the three realms rested on his shoulders. "You are a Prince of Iskalt, your punishment would have fallen to me."

"It was my choice, Loch. I knew I had to pay for my crimes, but I chose the path that would be better for everyone." Really, the path that would end the marriage magic between him and Brea. But he didn't say that.

"You sacrificed yourself for our happiness?" Lochlan stopped and turned toward his brother.

"I did so much bad. I didn't belong in your lives after that. It was better for you to forget the pain I caused."

Lochlan grew silent as they traveled deeper into the dungeons with only the torchlight to guide their way. Myrkur might not be the best place to live, but at least Griffin hadn't been confined to the freezing dungeons of Iskalt for the last decade. Sure, Myrkur was always dark, and that in itself could be stifling to a man used to the sun, but at least there was a sky. Fresh air and companionship.

"You've brought me a guest, nephew? How unlike you." Dirty hands with cracked nails gripped the cell bars, humming with the magic keeping Griffin's uncle from portaling to his freedom in the human world.

"Your nephew has come to speak with you," Lochlan said.

"Another one?" Callum peered out at Griffin in confusion.

"I've come from the prison world, so you do not remember me," Griffin explained, taking a step forward in the torchlight. "But I am an O'Shea."

"Why don't you portal me out of this hell hole, and maybe I'll be inclined to believe you?"

"Nice try, old man." Lochlan moved to stand beside Griffin. "My brother has some questions for you. Should you answer them honestly, I'll see to some improvements to your accommodations."

"I want a fireplace, two new blankets, and some whiskey. Lots of it," Callum said.

Lochlan nodded for Griffin to continue.

"You once attempted to create a magical boundary around a village in Iskalt. Where did you learn such magic? I need you to tell me everything you know about boundary spells."

Callum's hands dropped from the cell bars, and he stepped back into the shadows. Lowering his gaunt frame onto a wooden stool, he leaned back against the wall with a sigh. "Boundary magic? That will cost you a lot more than a blanket and some whiskey." His seldom-used voice grated in his throat.

"If your information helps my brother, I will increase your comforts as I see fit. Now, talk."

"Regan knew of such magic. She created the spell around Fargelsi. Complicated magic, that was. She tried to teach me, but I failed to construct the spell properly."

"And you killed an entire village of Iskaltians in your experiment," Lochlan muttered.

"Where did she learn how to create the barrier around Gelsi?" Griffin pressed. "Did she have a page from the book of Sorcha?"

Callum's eyes widened. "You're looking for the book. Now, tell me why an O'Shea strives for such power?" When Griffin didn't answer, Callum leaned closer to the bars. "Are you looking to destroy a boundary spell, boy? Now, what is the most powerful boundary in the realm?"

He tapped his chin, a smile curving his lips. "The prison realm."

Griffin crossed his arms. "I do not know why my king wants the book."

"Your king?" His grin widened. "I smell lies, nephew. Why are you lying to me?" He muttered to himself as he drifted away from the bars. "A king. The prison realm has a king. What might he offer to bring down the magic?"

"Get to the point, old man." Lochlan growled. "Can you help Griffin or not?"

"Help him steal the most powerful book in existence?" He crossed his arms. "No. You don't want to play with that book, boys."

Griffin crouched down to meet his uncle's gaze in the dim light of his cell. "That book has led to the suffering of thousands. We need to find it so we can end that suffering."

Callum barked out a rough laugh.

"If you ever wanted to make amends for the wrongs you've done, this is your one chance," Lochlan added.

"Aye." Callum nodded. "I know where the book is kept, but you won't find it. Sorcha's twin hid it in the human realm. Her ancestors safeguard it now." His hands balled into fists as if aching to get his hands on the book once more. "Regan managed to find it long before she ever did anything with the spells. I took her to study it, to find what would give her the power she sought to overtake her brother. But the keepers of the book wouldn't let her copy any of the spells. It wasn't until years later when an odd fellow appeared in Fargelsi with scrolls containing powerful spells that Regan gained access to the power she sought. Those spells were going to make the strongest alliance in history. No one would have been able to defeat us."

Griffin met the cold eyes of his uncle. "But you were defeated, Uncle. And now, you'll be able to watch the book you wanted for your own personal gain create peace instead."

"So you know where it is kept?" Lochlan folded his arms across his chest.

"I do not. The location changes. I only know who is protecting it. But I'll let you boys find that out for yourselves."

"Papa!" Tierney's screech echoed along the dungeon walls.

"Papa?" Toby and Tia stumbled into the room, their breath billowing into a cloud of white around their pale faces.

"Twins?" Callum stood, grabbing the bars of his cell. "O'Rourke Twins?"

Griffin wanted to contradict him to tell him the twins were only of Iskalt, but that wouldn't be true. Not when their grandfather was an O'Rourke.

"What is it, Tia?" Lochlan crouched in front of her.

"It's Gullie!" she wailed, throwing her arms around her father's neck.

"What happened now?" Lochlan directed his question to his son.

"She tried to fix his tail." Toby stared at his feet, not meeting his father's eye.

"Who is that?" Tia sniffed her tears back, staring at Callum.

"I'm your great uncle Callum, sweet girl." He tried to smile, but between his grating voice and the layer of grime covering his face and hands, he was a gruesome sight.

Tia clung to her father even tighter, burying her face against his neck.

"Don't speak to my daughter, old man," Lochlan growled.

"Go to Ireland," Callum said suddenly. "An old fishing village called Bealadannan. Look for a Gelsi woman by the name of Ashlin Carrik. She will guide you."

Toby stared at Callum, eyes wide with horror, like he'd seen some awful omen in his great uncle's eyes.

"What's wrong with Gullie?" Griffin asked, breaking Toby away from Callum's ferocious gaze. It seemed Princess Tierney O'Shea was determined to 'help' Gulliver into an early grave.

"She grew his tail back," Toby said proudly. "But now, he won't wake up."

Griffin scooped Toby up in his arms and ran for the stairs, Lochlan and Tia right behind him.

"We aren't done with this conversation, boys!" Callum bellowed behind them. "You'll both be needing that book now." His maniacal laughter rang out behind them.

"Gulliver?" Not sure what to expect, Griffin raced into the royal nursery where the kids played most afternoons.

"Griff, look at it! Isn't it beautiful?" Gulliver swished his new tail around.

"Are you okay?" Griffin went down on his knees to inspect Gulliver for any injuries. Magic gone wrong could lead to any number of issues. Some that might not be visible at first.

"Griffin, I am so sorry!" Brea wrung her hands. "That child of mine has a mind of her own."

"Kind of like her mother," Griffin said wryly, trying not to let his worry for Gulliver lead to anger with the strong-willed princess.

"Tia is so stubborn, and I just don't understand it." Brea paced the nursery with baby Ciara cradled in a human looking contraption she wore like a sling over her shoulder. The baby princess slept through her mother's anxiety. "It's like we don't speak the same language. Her Gelsi magic is so volatile. Even Neeve has never seen anything like it. She soaks up her lessons like a sponge, and she's constantly trying things she can't possibly handle at her age. I shudder to think what she'll be like when she comes of age and inherits the magic of Iskalt and Eldur as well. By then, she'll likely be easier to reason with. It's hard to reason with a ten year old who thinks she knows everything."

"I'm fine, Griff," Gulliver whispered. "Better than ever." His tail snaked up over his shoulder, and the freshly grown tip—shaped like a leaf—patted Griffin on the face. "I'm not so sure the queen is though." He watched Brea's furious pacing.

"Why don't you go find Riona and show her your new tail? And maybe stay away from Tia for a few days," he added under his breath.

Gulliver nodded. "She didn't mean to hurt me, Griff. Something weird happened when she used her magic. It was like it... bounced off me at first."

"Loch," Brea sighed when her husband joined them. Tia still clinging to his neck. "What are we going to do with her?"

Lochlan marched into the room, setting Tia on her feet before her mother. "Apologize to Uncle Griff." He stood, sighing with regret.

"I'm really sorry, Uncle Griff." Tia sniffed, her big dragon-sized tears tore at his heart.

Griffin crouched down to her level. "I'm not going to say it's all right, Tia. You have to listen to your parents about using your Gelsi magic. You know, I grew up in Fargelsi, and children there learn the words of power as they grow up. But you are very strong. You learn fast, but that doesn't mean you're ready to use your magic whenever you feel like it." Griffin glanced up at Brea and Loch, hoping he hadn't overstepped.

"Maybe it will help to hear it from someone new." Brea shrugged, urging him to continue.

"I'm afraid I can't let Gullie play with you anymore, Tia. Not without adult supervision." Griffin stood to his full height to tower over her.

"I would never hurt Gullie, Uncle Griff. Not on purpose." Tia's bottom lip trembled.

"Then, you should think about that, sweetheart." Brea took her hand. "You can't experiment on your friends. It's not safe."

"I wasn't experimenting." Tia jerked her hand out of her mother's grasp and ran from the room.

"I'm sorry," Griffin said. "I was too hard on her."

"No, she needed to hear it from you, brother. Gulliver is your child, you have to protect him. Even from pint-size princesses with too much magic and not enough sense."

"What about Toby?" Griffin asked. "He doesn't seem to give you any trouble with his magic."

Brea's eyes filled with tears, and he wondered if he'd said the wrong thing.

"Toby doesn't have magic," Lochlan said. "Not of his own. His only power seems to be in amplifying Tia's. Now that he's old enough to understand, he seldom helps her outside of their lessons."

"We won't be gone long, Brea," Lochlan insisted. "Just a couple of hours to glamour a few humans and ask some questions. We'll be back before you know it."

"You're always too cavalier about glamouring humans," Brea huffed. "I was one of those humans you glamoured for half my life."

"You. Have. Never. Been. Human," Lochlan growled, and Griffin stifled his laughter behind a pastry he stuffed in his mouth. Those two deserved each other.

"You know what I mean." Brea glowered back at him. "For almost eighteen years, I thought I was human."

"Don't blame me for doing your mothers' bidding. You know they just wanted to keep you safe."

"I know. I just like giving you a hard time for it. Bring me back something Irish—and Myles, don't let him forget the usual."

"I know, I know. Starbucks frapachinos and Godiva chocolate." Myles pulled on a human jacket over his stylish human clothes.

"You three are an odd sort of royal." Griffin shook his head.

"So not a royal," Brea called over her shoulder as she left them.

"We better hurry, Gullie wants cheeseburgers." Griffin stood to grab his coat he'd bought at the pawnshop.

"I thought we needed to make this a quick trip so your lady friend doesn't find out we were gone."

"She's not my *lady friend.*" Griffin scowled at his brother.

"Seriously, Loch, who says lady friend?" Myles grinned and nudged Griffin playfully.

"Only old, out of touch, uptight kings, I guess." Griffin nudged Myles back. He enjoyed needling his older brother. For the first time, it felt like they truly were brothers. He planned to enjoy it for however long it lasted.

"Well, whoever she is, we better get going before she shows up." Lochlan shoved them both toward the inner courtyard where night was falling.

"And *we* are going where again?" Riona marched in with a guilty looking Gulliver behind her. Both were wearing their human clothes and had their bags tossed over their shoulders. Ever since Griffin had the nerve to speak with Callum without Riona, she had taken to following him everywhere and listening in on his conversations.

"We are just following a lead we got from Callum," Griffin admitted with a sigh. He still wasn't sure he could trust her. As far as Riona knew, they were seeking a way to bring the border around Myrkur down so they could take that information back to Egan. But Griffin had seen that done before. The moment Brea and her army broke through the Gelsi border magic, the entire barrier failed and thousands of Fargelsians, previously trapped, flooded into Eldur and Iskalt. He would not let that happen with Myrkur. Not until they found a way to separate the criminals from the innocent. If they were going to do this, they were going to do it right.

"You will tell me about this lead when we get to this Ireland place." Riona's wings bristled with annoyance.

Griffin quirked a smile at her. She was so easily annoyed, and her wings always gave her away. Just like Gulliver's tail. He found it oddly... alluring.

"Yeah, it'll be a miracle if we get any actual work done on this trip," Lochlan muttered as he followed them into the moonlit inner courtyard.

Chapter 26

They portaled into the human world atop a grassy green hill on the rocky shores of Ireland. They were greeted with blue skies and bright sunshine. And Finn Donovan, the king consort of Eldur.

"Finn? What are you doing here?" Griffin looked between Lochlan's friend to the Kings of Iskalt and Fargelsi in confusion.

"Finn has been doing some... research for us in the human realm," Lochlan said. "I asked him to meet us here."

"Who's this the guy?" Finn lifted his chin at Griffin.

"My brother, Griffin. This is my... other brother, Finn," Lochlan said awkwardly.

"Can we dispense with the whole I don't know you because I forgot you explanations and just go with, it's nice to meet you, I know you're my brother's best friend?" Griffin gave Finn a nod. "We don't have much time here, and we need to make the most of it."

"I don't like this," Riona said.

"Of course she doesn't." Lochlan rolled his eyes.

"There are too many people involved." Riona glared back at him.

"Which is why I tried to tell everyone it should just be me and

Griff on this trip, but no one listens to me," Lochlan grumbled, crossing his arms over his chest.

"Riona, Gulliver, don't move until Finn glamours you."

Finn stepped in front of them and lifted a hand. "What?" His eyes bounced from Riona to Gulliver before landing on Griffin. "You said they have no magic."

"They don't."

"My glamour won't work. Something is blocking it."

Myles shrugged. "Could be because they're already glamoured.

All eyes turned to him. "Speak, human," Lochlan bit out.

Griffin stepped closer, seeing Riona as the fae she always appeared to be. He rounded her to examine her wings.

"You wouldn't have noticed last time you portaled because you didn't have a human with you. Look at me, I'm a human glamour detector." Myles smiled proudly.

Lochlan met his gaze. "It's not a glamour. Finn's magic didn't work."

"Then it's something they're doing on their own. Maybe Dark Fae have like a... natural glamour? How cool is that?"

Griffin looked to Riona. "You... do Dark Fae glamour themselves without magic?"

She shrugged. "As long as no one can see, we're good. You all should do something about those ears though." She pushed past him.

She was right. They didn't have much time. Finn glamoured himself along with Griffin and Lochlan.

Lochlan met his friend's gaze. "Any luck, Finn?"

"I found her, but she's not exactly cooperative... or competent."

"Who?" Riona demanded.

Lochlan turned to Griffin with hands fisted at his sides. "Catch her up to speed, will you? Her infernal questions are getting us nowhere."

"Callum gave us the name of a woman who might lead us to the source of the boundary magic," Griffin whispered a hasty explanation she would like. "If all goes well, we might actually find something that will please Egan when we return."

He didn't miss the look of disappointment on her face.

"She's not going to like a troop of Fae descending on her all at once," Finn said. "She's really old and kind of cranky."

"Griff and I will go with Riona," Lochlan said. "Gulliver, you stay here with Myles and Finn."

"We'll be right back," Griffin said. "No stealing anything while I'm gone."

"Yes, sir." Gulliver rubbed a tail Griffin really hoped no one else could see.

Griffin and Lochlan walked down the hill toward the village, Riona following quickly behind.

"I will do the talking," all three of them said at the same time.

Lochlan sighed. "Let's agree to let Griffin speak."

"Was it necessary to bring him?" Riona asked. "You can portal here just as well as he can."

"Enough, you two." Griffin picked up the pace. The sooner they finished this, the sooner he could put some distance between Lochlan and Riona. They didn't trust each other and had taken an immediate disliking of one another.

The village of Bealadannan was old and crumbling, like some historical site come alive after a long dormant sleep to join the modern world. Cars and cellphones looked out of place in a village like this.

"Finn says she lives on the cliffside near the edge of town."

The town was little more than a few cobblestone streets and a marina where fishermen came and went with their day's catch.

Ashlin Carrik turned out to be an old crone of a fae woman. She stood waiting on her dilapidated front stoop, her cane tapping against the cracked concrete.

"If you're after Sorcha's book, you'll have to do better than a couple of O'Shea princes." She turned back into her house, leaving the door open for them to follow. "Or has one of you managed to become king of Iskalt?"

"I am Iskalt's king, madam." Lochlan gave the old woman a curt nod.

"Sit, sit." She gestured at the table in the corner of her one-room home. "I'll tell you what I know, and you can be gone with tonight's moon." She busied herself making tea and stoking the fire in the already too warm room.

"You're the one who married the O'Rourke girl, then?" She lowered herself into a seat beside Lochlan.

"My wife is the daughter of Faolan and Tierney Cahill."

"And Brandon O'Rourke is her father. She's the Eldur-Fargelsi weapon, and she's had a few children, hasn't she? That's why you're here seeking the O'Rourke book of spells. You want to understand twin magic, yes?"

"Twin magic?" Lochlan frowned, stunned into silence.

"How do you know so much about us?" Griffin asked, casting a wary glance at Riona, wondering again if he could trust her.

Ashlin just smiled—an act that took years from her weathered face—and shrugged.

"We are here to ask about ways to destroy—" Riona said, but Lochlan held up his hand to stop her.

"What do you mean by twin magic?"

"The O'Rourke line is riddled with twins, or didn't you know?" She poured them each a steaming cup of tea, the aromas of lavender, citrus, and lemongrass hung heavy in the air. "I suppose it has been a while. Regan never had children, so the last twins were Sorcha and her sister, Grainne, until your twins were born that is." She passed around a tin of biscuits, but no one was interested.

"What have my children to do with this book?" Lochlan managed to ask in a choked whisper.

"The O'Rourke book of spells holds many secrets to dangerous magic. High on that list is twin magic. When did you notice your girl had great power?"

"How do you know this?" Lochlan's voice shook with fear.

"I am old, dear. And I may choose to live in the human realm, but I am not useless. Not yet, anyway." She stirred honey into her tea and took a careful sip. "Your girl? She is strong, yes?"

"Very," Lochlan said.

"And your boy has no magic to speak of. Only enough to boost his sister's, yes?"

"Yes."

"In the right hands, the O'Rourke book of power can teach the best ways to raise such twins. To teach them how to control their magic *together*. That is key."

"And in the wrong hands?" Griffin asked.

"It can teach an O'Rourke woman how to break free of the twin who holds her back."

Riona kicked Griffin under the table.

"Where might we find this book?" Griffin asked, shooting Riona a glare. They didn't need to ask this woman about the barrier magic. They just needed the book.

"Grainne brought the book here to the human realm to keep it from any future O'Rourke twins. Her descendants still watch over the book."

"Where is it?" Riona asked. "It would help his majesty and his wife a great deal if they could learn how to help their twins now, before they are grown and it is too late."

"To my knowledge, it was buried with Grainne in the village cemetery. Hers is the largest headstone at the center of the churchyard."

"Thank you." Lochlan reached for the woman's hands. "If there is anything I can do for you..."

"Leave me be." She gave him a sad smile. "The happenings of kings and queens no longer concerns me. Just... watch your back, your Majesty. And take care of those twins."

After an hour of digging in the fading afternoon sun beside Finn, Griffin's arms ached. Grainne's grave was old, and the ground was hardened with time and erosion.

"It's clear." Griffin called up to his pacing brother. "Myles, help us lift the lid, it's heavy."

The three men lifted and groaned as they slid the stone sarcophagus lid aside.

"Is it there? What do you see?" Lochlan leaned over the grave.

"Nothing." Myles climbed out.

"No book?" Lochlan's shoulder's drooped.

"No body." Griffin climbed out and offered a hand to Finn.

"We should go back and ask the old crone to explain this," Riona said.

"She's right, Loch. This is the lead we've been looking for. We need that book."

"You've been looking for something to help the twins, haven't you?" Griffin put it together. "That's what Finn has been researching in the human realm."

"We couldn't find answers in any of the three kingdoms." Lochlan rubbed a tired hand over his face. "We've known for a long time that Tia needs more help than we can give her. We can't keep a magic tutor for longer than a few months."

"It was my idea, to research human folklore," Myles said. "Finn and I have taken turns researching for the last five years, but this is as close as we've ever come to an actual answer."

"Then, we need to go back and ask more questions." Griffin tossed his shovel down.

"We'll stay and fix this. You three go," Finn said. "We'll meet you there when we're done."

Riona and Griffin followed Lochlan back across the village to the old woman's home, but when they arrived, she wasn't there.

"We'll wait until she comes back." Lochlan sat down on the front step.

Griffin walked around the old cottage. Something wasn't right. The back door stood ajar, and he peeked into the empty room, his heart hammering in his chest.

A teakettle hung over the fire with steam pouring from its mouth.

"Loch!" Griffin raced around to the front of the house. "Time to go."

"What? No, I'm not leaving until I have answers."

"We're not going to get them here." He rested a hand against Lochlan's shoulder. "She's hiding from us. Something isn't right."

"She's just an old woman. She can't have gone far."

"No, Loch, she doesn't want us here. I think this was some kind of set up. It could be a trap. We need to get back home."

"Brea!" Lochlan called the moment he stepped through the portal into the palace courtyard they'd left from only hours before. Moonlight was fading from the early morning sky.

"Loch!" Brea sobbed, stumbling across the grassy courtyard to reach him.

"What happened?" He gripped Brea by the shoulders, peering into her bloodshot eyes.

"Callum," her voice shook. "He's escaped."

"How?" Griffin wanted to go to her, to comfort her, but that wasn't his place anymore. Never had been. "His cell was magically sealed."

"I didn't know it, Loch. I should have been paying more attention. What kind of mother am I? I didn't know they were going down to visit him. They never knew he was in the dungeons before the other day. Tia was curious. You know how she is." Brea's shoulders shook with the effort to speak.

"What happened, Brea? You're scaring me." Lochlan pulled her into his arms.

"He took them, Loch. Our babies. He... He must have talked Tia into letting him out. She would have taken it as a challenge to break through the magical barriers."

"He has Tia and Toby?" Lochlan's hands shook.

"Yes. What does he want with them, Loch? They're just children! You have to find him." Brea shoved her husband back into the fading moonlight. "Give him whatever he wants, just bring them home."

"He wants the book, Brea. He's going to use our little girl as a weapon."

Epilogue

Tierney

Three months later

Tia focused on the warm pressure in her hand to remind herself she wasn't alone as she stared at the rocky crags of a place Callum called Ireland. She'd clung to each of his words, hoping he'd reveal a plan to bring Tia and Toby back to their parents, back to where it was safe.

But she'd started wondering if there was a safe place for her in either of the worlds.

Magic was her constant companion, thrumming through her body, looking for weaknesses to break through. It took all her willpower to keep from uttering spells that would set it free.

Energy traveled up her arm from Tobias' hand, and she tore hers away so violently she fell back onto her butt. The grassy shore softened her fall, but nothing could soften the confusion in her twin's eyes.

Tia gasped for breath as if a hand squeezed her lungs.

At ten years old, her magic should lay mostly dormant inside her, but it never had. Her earliest memories were of her accidentally using it on servants and friends. It was why she no longer invited friends to the palace. Once, she'd even tried distancing herself from her brother, but he didn't let her.

Below the cliffs, water twisted and frothed. She peered over the edge, wondering if there was a way to end the desperation of the last three months. Behind her, Tobias never took his eyes off her. She could feel his measured gaze. He was the calm twin, her safety. Yet, his touch made her magic grow and coil inside her.

Turning, her eyes met his. They had always been together in all things, but this time was different. "I can't..." She steeled her gaze. "You can't touch me, Toby. Because every time you do, it feels like I'm going to explode."

He pursed his lips. It had taken a long time for him to believe he amplified her magic because he couldn't feel it. When she spoke Fargelsian words of power, he didn't feel the flashes of invincibility that roared through her.

Toby was just Toby, a boy who might never fit into the world of magic, but one she'd protect with everything she had.

Tierney didn't know why Callum took them, why they'd hidden in the human realm for months.

She only knew it couldn't be good, that he had a use for her.

And whatever that use was, it would most likely hurt the people she loved.

Turning away from her brother, a brother she'd almost killed many times with her errant magic, she peered down at the waves. An icy breeze lifted the hair from her neck, sending a shiver down her spine.

Straightening her posture, she didn't let the cold get to her. She was an Iskalt princess. Brave. Loyal. Fierce. Everything her mother taught her. Her father tried to instill discipline and work ethic, but she would always be more like her mother. A rebel.

"I'm sorry, Toby," she whispered, wondering if the words would haunt him the rest of his life. "This is all my fault." She leaned in, careful not to touch him. "We need to run." She glanced back at the stone cottage where Callum poured over maps and old legends. "When the time comes, we need to get away. Will you be ready?"

He nodded, his face growing ashy. Tia hated the life Toby had to live because of her. She wanted more for him. Running away wouldn't get them back to the fae realm, but at least they'd have a chance. They only had to wait for their moment.

As if hearing their conversation, Callum walked outside and stood looking over the cliffs. "Want to see what happens when you run from me, young fae?"

Tia swallowed, inching closer. Fear kicked her heartbeat up a notch as she pushed Toby behind her, muttering under her breath. Her Fargelsian magic, the only kind she could draw on, pooled in her fingertips. But she didn't know the words to set it free. Callum reached out and yanked her toward the cliff. Her scream died in her throat as he held her leaning over the edge. His words were soft enough for her ears alone.

"If you defy me, it won't be the brave magical princess paying the price. I will take your brother, and you will never see him again."

Toby's scream sent relief flooding through her. He yelled her name, and she met Callum's dark gaze. For now, her brother was here with her and she could protect him.

"Do you understand now?" Callum loosened his grip, and she tried not to stare at the rocks below. She nodded and he pulled her back, releasing her.

She dropped to her knees, her entire body collapsing in on itself. "Yes. I understand. Please, just don't hurt Toby."

Callum lifted his eyes to the dusk. Tia didn't have access to her Iskalt night magic yet, but she saw the moment her uncle's came alive in his eyes.

He turned, swiping his hand through the air and shoving Toby through a portal before closing it, swallowing Toby's scream.

"Please," Tia yelled. "Bring him back. I'll do whatever you want."

A smile curled his lips, and a portal opened nearby. Toby fell through, his entire body shaking. Tia crawled toward him. "Tell me you're okay." She wanted to take his hand, to drag him in to a bone-crushing hug. But she couldn't control her magic while touching him.

Toby rolled onto his side as his body heaved, and vomit splashed the grass.

Tia pulled her knees up to her chest, tears stinging her eyes. "Toby, I'm sorry."

No more dangerous escape plans. Tia would never again risk her brother's life.

Callum's boots bent the grass as he walked toward them. A look of disgust twisted on his face.

Tia met his gaze, not daring to look away.

"If you try to run from me, I won't be so generous in your punishments." Callum's scowl never left his face. It had been three months since he pulled them into the human realm, three months of him refusing to tell them why.

Tierney backed away from Tobias, letting the power settle inside her.

Toby rolled onto his back. "What do you want from us?"

Callum rubbed the back of his neck and glanced over his shoulder to the tiny cottage they'd been staying in. "Supper is ready. Eat or don't. I don't care. In the morning, I'm leaving for a few days."

Callum left them periodically to chase down leads on whatever he was searching for. Those were the worst times because he spelled the cottage to not let them outside.

Tierney pushed herself to her feet and followed Callum inside. Her magic begged for release, for her to choose a target and let go. But there was something forcing her to hold it back.

Portal magic, a gift she hadn't yet received.

If something happened to Callum, the twins would be stuck in the human realm forever.

Which was why they sat quietly at the table eating, their eyes never leaving their plates.

Today's plan failed, but Tierney would find a way to get them out of this. All her reasons for running still mattered. But as Tobias grabbed her hand under the table—ignoring her request to stop touching her—she realized there was another way.

She squeezed Tobias' hand, letting magic flow through their

connection. Tierney would spend every moment Callum was gone teaching herself to control her power.

Until the day came when she could let it out.

She would save Tobias. She would save her parents and everyone else. Tierney had always wanted to be just like her mother.

Now, she too had been abducted for reasons she didn't yet know.

They say history is doomed to repeat itself. Her uncle Griffin came to mind. The three kingdoms trapped prisoners in the prison realm, forever forgetting what it was they did. Tierney heard stories of Queen Regan of Fargelsi. She'd heard stories about her mother's heroics.

But they didn't have the full tale.

If you forget the very fae who caused so much turmoil, how are the kingdoms supposed to learn from it? How are they supposed to be better?

As Tierney chewed on the remnants of her stale bread, she let her magic boil and turn to anger.

Whatever it was Callum sought, she'd make sure he didn't get it.

Because if he did, something told her it would be the end of the peace the three kingdoms had fought so hard for.

She shared a weak smile with Tobias. The world saw them only as kids, but she knew they were different, more.

She could feel it in her bones.

The story continues in
Fae's Power: Queens of the Fae Book Five.
Turn the page to dive in.

QUEENS OF THE FAE
BOOK FIVE

FAE'S POWER

MELISSA A. CRAVEN
M. LYNN

CHAPTER I

RIONA

I'm losing my patience.

Riona read the words as they appeared in front of her, wishing she could wipe them from her mind as easily as she could from the spelled journal.

I'm losing my patience.

She knew what would happen to her and Griffin if they didn't return to Myrkur soon.

King Egan. He was the only king she'd ever known until stepping foot outside what the Light Fae called the prison realm. Egan raised her from a small child. He'd given her a purpose, a calling. And at one time, she'd loved him for it.

Maybe not in the way a normal fae loves. She'd watched how Queen Brea looked at her children, the heartbreaking agony she'd felt when Callum O'Shea tore them from her. Riona had never felt that way about anyone. With Egan, she'd appreciated all he'd done for her and let herself be blinded, unable to see the cruelty.

His words sent a shiver down her spine.

Glancing toward the door of the bedroom she shared with Gulliver, she watched for any activity in the hall. She couldn't afford an interruption now. Riona pulled out the inkless quill and began to write. Living her life without magic had left her vulnerable to awe. Like the first time Egan showed her the set of books that could communicate with each other.

Despite the lack of ink, black words appeared as she wrote.

This is not an easy task, sire. But we will not let you down.

She'd written to Egan every chance she got, telling him stories of the world beyond their borders where beauty was more than the stars in the perpetually dark sky.

She stared out her window overlooking the Iskalt fields. Children chased each other through the snowy courtyard, reminding Riona why she was still here. She cared—which was a new sensation for her.

Two months ago, the twins of Iskalt were stolen away. In the aftermath, it was like Iskalt lost its soul. The entire kingdom mourned two royal children they most likely had never met.

It was a far cry from Myrkur where citizens stole from each other, only caring about themselves.

Riona wiped a hand over her words, and they disappeared. A knock sounded on her door, and she shoved the book under her pillow and stood, smoothing out the dress the queen had given her. The woman had even been nice enough to have it altered for Riona's wings.

Where did such kindness come from?

Stepping into the hall, she found a grim looking Griffin waiting for her. He'd changed since the kids were taken. Even if no one here remembered him, he was still their uncle.

"Have you been in there all morning?" He tried to peek around her, but she moved to shut the door behind her.

"I needed a rest."

He ran a hand through his unkempt auburn hair and pushed out a sigh. "I know what you mean. I'm exhausted."

"Then why don't you take a rest as well?" She studied him closer, examining the signs of his weariness that grew each day. Dark circles under his eyes. Pale, ashy cheeks.

He leaned against the wall as if he needed it to hold him up. "I can't. Not until we find Tia and Toby."

"You'll be no good to them half-dead."

He closed his eyes and leaned his head back against the wall. "That's what Brea keeps saying. She's become the voice of reason for the O'Shea men. Never would have seen her as the reasonable one."

Riona wasn't sure what to make of the Iskaltian queen. She was kind and thoughtful, but there was a layer of distrust beneath everything else. Life had made her wary, like it did for most fae, and losing two of her children exacerbated the feeling.

"Griff." Riona nudged his arm. "Was there a reason you came to get me?"

"Yes." His eyes slid open. "I wanted to make sure you were okay."

Over the last two months, they'd made the jump to the human realm ten times, following leads that never panned out. It was hard on all of them, but they couldn't stop. "I'm fine, but you look like you're about to keel over."

"That's because I am." He stumbled, and she caught him around the waist.

"Come, you need sleep." She tried to lead him back into her room, but he pulled away.

"No, they need us in council chambers."

Riona sighed. Another meeting discussing leads and trying not to give in to the hopelessness of their task. The twins could be anywhere, and it wasn't like the human realm was small.

Taking Griffin's arm to steady him, Riona led him down the long hall. And then another. And another. The palace of Iskalt was a labyrinth of never-ending stone walls, colorful tapestries, and elaborate carved doors and statues. Torches burned in brackets, lighting the way, and braziers smoldered in corners, warming the hallways. There were no windows this deep in the palace aside from the bed chamber that abutted the outer wall, and Riona had started longing to see the sun everywhere she went. As soon as their mission was complete, they'd return to the darkness of Myrkur, and the sun would be just another memory of her time here.

When they reached council chambers, the magnificent carved doors stood open, and voices poured out into the hall.

Lochlan, sounding just as tired as Griffin, argued with a man Riona hadn't seen in months as he'd chased his own leads. Finn, King Consort of Eldur, had refused to return to Iskalt until he had something to tell his friends. Brea stood across the table, staring down at a set of maps.

"Lochlan," she snapped. "You aren't making any sense. You'll be no good to the twins if you die trying to find them. Go."

"Did she just give a king orders?" Riona whispered.

Griffin nodded, the first hint of a grin appearing on his face. It dropped when Lochlan stalked toward them. He sent an icy glare Riona's way, and she felt it all the way down to her toes. The distrust. The King of Iskalt did not like her much.

If only he knew how right that instinct was.

Magic flooded Riona as she watched Lochlan walk away. Not her magic—that would require her to have some. No, this was by Egan's design. A powerful spell. She'd seen him recite it once from a scrap of ancient looking paper he kept under lock and key. It allowed him to steal magic from the barrier, but as Dark Fae, she never understood how he wielded it.

She held back the cry trying to push past her lips as the magic pulled at her, sending a searing pain into her chest. She dropped Griffin's arm and backed away until her butt hit the wall.

What would Griffin say if he knew?

She betrayed him with every breath she took.

Because Riona would always belong to the king of Myrkur, and the magic he'd placed around her like a noose reminded her of that at every turn.

Brea spoke about something, but Riona couldn't concentrate with Egan's magic squeezing the life out of her. He wasn't happy with her response in the journal. She closed her eyes, counting backward from ten. The magic loosened and faded. Egan never went too far to remind her she was his, at least not yet.

Riona searched the room to make sure no one noticed her distress. Griffin gave her a worried frown, and she averted her eyes.

"Finn." Brea sighed. "You saw him. He can't keep going on like this."

Finn scratched his chin. "Do you think he'll actually rest?"

"He needs to." She shot Griffin a pointed look. "As do you."

"Not a chance. I'm ready to go back into the human realm when we have a new lead."

Brea rolled her eyes to the ceiling and grunted a word that sounded way too much like "Men!"

Riona moved closer to the table where maps were strewn over the surface. "This is the human realm?"

"Part of it." Brea ran a finger over a land mass. "The problem is they could be anywhere. Callum is an O'Shea, he can open portals anywhere in the human world so long as he's been there before. We don't know where in Iskalt he left from. If we did, we could wait for him to return."

"Do we know how he escaped yet?" The investigation had been going on since he left.

Brea nodded, her hand curling around the edge of the table. "My girl..." She sucked in a breath. "We think Tia released him. It may not have been on purpose, but there are traces of her magic in the cells. It's the only logical answer."

Tia released her own kidnapper?

Riona never wanted to feel for these people. She didn't want to worry about Griffin or find herself thankful Gulliver hadn't been taken along with the twins.

Yet, here she was.

"Do we have another lead?"

Finn stepped forward. "Of a sort." He scratched the top of his head where Riona knew a crown sat when he was in his home kingdom of Eldur. He'd married Queen Alona, but apparently these Light Fae royals just dropped everything to help each other. Who did that?

"Finn." Brea sighed.

"Right, Lochlan dropped me in the human realm a few days ago after you all came back—in Ireland again. My time there was more enlightening this time. Humans chronicle every bit of history, including strange happenings. If Sorcha's book has been in the human realm for a while, there would be evidence in the form of things humans couldn't explain, a power they didn't understand."

Griffin dropped into a chair near the table. He gave Finn a wary look. Was he another fae who'd forgotten Griffin? "What did you find?"

At first, they'd tried to search for the kids in the human realm, but they'd eventually realized it was a futile search. There was only one thing Callum would truly want—Sorcha's book. If they found that, they'd find the kids.

"I'm not really sure." Finn rubbed his eyes before reaching into his pocket and pulling out a folded piece of odd-looking parchment.

Riona stepped closer. "What's that?"

Finn unfolded it. "It's what the humans call paper." He slapped it down on the table, making Griffin jump.

A series of numbers stretched across the lined page. "I don't understand."

"There's a story most humans don't believe to be true, yet they still documented it in the Irish archives. There is a local legend that tells about a small village that disappeared three hundred years ago."

"What do you mean disappeared?"

Finn fixed his eyes on her. "It's just gone. Archeologists from all across the human realm have studied the location intensely, trying to figure out what happened. They never did. But stuck in between pages of an old book recounting the story of this village, I found these numbers. I don't know what they mean, or really if they have any meaning at all, but right now, they're the only clue we have. I think it could be a coded message."

Brea wrapped an arm around Finn's waist and leaned into him. "Thank you for coming when we needed you."

Riona studied them, wondering how this queen could be so open with her affections. It didn't make a lot of sense. Emotions were something to be contained and controlled. Egan had taught her that. Show someone your emotions, and you showed them your weakness.

"You should go home to Eldur and my sister, Finn. You've done enough here, and she needs you."

No one argued with Brea, it seemed. She took careful care of many grown men—kings even—as well as small children. There was something so ... human about that, at least what Riona had heard of humans. She didn't possess an ounce of fae cruelty or wicked tendencies. She wasn't cold like her husband.

Riona looked down at Griffin, whose eyes hadn't left Brea and Finn. He stared at them with a longing that tugged at her—this time without magic.

Griffin wanted them to remember him, but she'd seen a reluctance in that as well. He'd told her enough for her to know he'd supported the wrong queen on the wrong side of a war. If the people he loved remembered him, they'd also remember everything he'd done.

"I don't think there's anything more we can do today." Riona gave Brea a pointed look before flicking her eyes to Griffin.

Brea nodded. "We'll come back at this with fresh minds tomorrow. Griffin, you have to rest." She rounded the table and put a hand on Griffin's shoulder without saying anything.

Riona helped him from the chair, and together they went back the way they'd come.

Riona pushed open the door to their sitting room to find Gulliver asleep on the settee.

Griffin sort-of smiled when he looked at the boy, his tail curled around his legs. "He has the right idea."

Riona led Griffin to his room before dumping him on the bed. His hand shot out to snatch her wrist.

"Griff..."

"Please, Riona. Don't leave."

She'd never heard such desperation in Griffin's voice before.

"I have so many images running through my mind every time I

close my eyes." He turned glassy eyes on her. "I can't sleep in the human realm. I can't sleep here. There's so much at stake, and all I can see are Shauna and Nessa. We've been gone too long. What do you think he's doing to them?"

Riona couldn't leave him, not with a question like that hanging over him. Bending down, she unlaced her boots and kicked them off before climbing on to the oversized bed. Her wings curled in against her back, letting her settle on her side.

"You're afraid," she whispered.

He nodded. "I'm supposed to be finding Sorcha's book, and we keep coming to dead ends. What if Egan decides enough is enough? What if he assumes we aren't coming back, that we've escaped?"

The truth was on the tip of her tongue. She could never truly escape Egan, not with his magic in her veins.

But she couldn't tell him.

"Shauna and Nessa are survivors, Griff."

He nodded. "That won't stop Egan. And now Callum has my niece and nephew. You don't know the man. He is everything that is wrong with this world. I'm scared for them, Riona." He didn't mention the dream they'd all come to a silent agreement not to speak about. What brought Griffin to Iskalt so quickly months ago was news that Brea's daughter was dreaming of him, of the prison realm.

Of the fact he was supposed to save her. Griffin didn't say it, but Riona knew it drove him.

She reached forward and put her hand over his heart. "Fear is the biggest motivator. We'll find the children, and then we'll bring Egan the book and save your family."

His eyes slid shut. "But what if bringing Egan the book ends up killing us all?"

A chill raced through her from the tips of her wings to her toes. She knew so little about magic, about this book, but what if Egan used it to start a war?

The man sleeping beside her had done a lot of evil, and he was paying for it now.

But for the first time, she wondered if they weren't playing on the same side.

Griffin would complete Egan's mission, he'd find the book. She was sure of it.

But would he hand it over to Egan? Or would he get them all killed?

CHAPTER 2

GRIFFIN

A crack reverberated around the room as Griffin slammed his fist into the table. "I can't break it."

It was the middle of the night, and they'd had the sequence of numbers since Finn returned days ago. Most of the palace slept—including Gulliver and Riona.

Lochlan looked up from where he was dripping wax onto the numbers for some unknown reason. "Maybe if you helped me, this would go quicker."

Griffin eyed the tomes surrounding him. He had every book on magic in Iskalt surrounding him, and Lochlan thought the solution was playing with wax?

Standing to stretch his stiff limbs, Griffin joined Lochlan at the table. "I don't really understand what you're doing."

Lochlan didn't look up. "A couple years ago, we found how Callum and Regan were passing messages. There were two ways. They had a set of books she'd spelled. Write in one, and it would show up in the other. For anything official that would need a paper trail, Regan sent messages on parchment spelled to react to hot wax."

Griffin stared at his brother, wondering how many discoveries they'd made in the last ten years. Regan didn't tell Griffin about her secret communications, and for reasons he couldn't understand, the thought burned.

He'd always clung to the fact that one fae had trusted him completely, one fae had loved him.

He leaned forward to peer at the paper. "Is it working?"

Lochlan sighed. "No." He put the candle back on the table. "But something has to. It's just code. We've broken plenty such codes before."

"Yes, but if this is a human code, magic won't decipher it."

Lochlan leaned back in his chair. "How do humans live such frustrating lives?"

"They aren't frustrating to them because they never knew any different."

"Stop trying to make me feel bad about being mad at the humans for this." Lochlan darted a glare at him, but his lip turned up into a wry smile.

Griffin chuckled and rubbed his eyes. "We need to get creative."

"My wax idea was creative."

"Maybe we need more eyes. I can wake Riona. There's only a seventy-five percent chance she'll punch me for it."

"No." Lochlan shook his head and leaned forward. "Griffin, I may not remember you, but you *feel* like my brother—if that makes sense. And brothers always have each other's backs, so I know I can trust you."

Griffin squirmed, stepping away. In his world, brothers stood on opposite sides of a war. But he couldn't tell Lochlan. This was the first time his brother had ever trusted him, and Griffin didn't want to give that up. "So ... you don't trust Riona?"

"You told us yourself she's an agent of the king we're supposed to hate in Myrkur."

He thought back on the journey he'd shared with Riona, where he could almost forget who she was beholden to. She'd kissed him, making him realize he wasn't truly in love with Brea. It was the biggest revelation of his life. And yet, here was Lochlan voicing the exact concerns he'd once had about Riona himself.

"I don't know if I can trust her. Did I ever tell you how we met?"

Lochlan shook his head.

"It was in the fighting pits."

"Fighting pits?" Lochlan swallowed.

"I was fighting to free Nessa—the first time she was captured. Such things are a common occurrence in Myrkur. I won, but it was close. The rules dictated one of us had to die, but I refused to kill her. In return, she later let me go when I broke into a stronghold to save Gulliver. But then she led men to destroy my entire village."

Lochlan rubbed a tired hand over his face. "The prison realm ... it's a very different kind of place, isn't it?"

"Well, first, there's no sun, only constant night. The king's men roam the countryside capturing people to become indentured servants to work in the king's mines." One corner of his mouth turned up. "But there's a place—or used to be—where the villagers worked together to keep everyone alive. We were a family. And now Egan has two members of that family and the rest are homeless and likely starving. So we will try everything, Loch. We will break this code, so that one day I can return to free my family and rebuild my home."

"I wish I remembered you, Griffin. I wish I knew our history, because something tells me you're someone I cared about deeply."

Griffin didn't tell him the truth, he couldn't. Lochlan had never cared for him as brothers should.

And that had been Griffin's fault.

Griffin crawled into bed as the sun rose on the horizon. He didn't bother to change his clothing before his eyes slid shut.

Almost immediately, he could see them. Shauna and Nessa. His family. As much as he loved being around Lochlan and Brea, even when they barely knew him, they weren't the people he worried for most.

He was killing himself trying to find the twins because that book was his way back to the people he loved most.

As he drifted off to sleep, he could hear Egan's voice calling to Shauna, his best friend, the girl who'd saved him in the prison realm. She hadn't asked what he'd done or if he was dangerous. The day she found him, she'd only asked if he was hungry before bringing him to the village that had served as his sanctuary for nearly a decade.

Not everything was bad in the prison realm. It was the first time he truly understood what it was to fight for other people, to care for them.

If he was going to be fatalistic, he could almost say the prison realm saved him. It allowed him to become a better version of himself. One Lochlan could respect.

Egan's words drowned out every other thought in his sleepy mind.

"Stay away from her," Griffin groaned.

A warm hand slipped into his. "Griff?"

His eyes popped open. "Egan, he's going to kill them."

"Why? He has no reason to." Riona climbed over him to get to the other side of the bed. Her silky soft wings brushed his arm.

"We have to find this book, Riona. And these kids."

She sat still for a long moment, her breath the only sound in the room. Pulling back the covers, she slipped underneath. "You won't find anything if you're half-dead from sleep deprivation."

Griffin's entire body relaxed. She was right. Her presence should remind him of what they had to do, of who she worked for, but instead, it calmed him. "I'm going to save them."

Riona's tattoos moved and swirled as if they wanted to tell him everything Riona held back. "Sleep, Griff."

He closed his eyes once again, and this time, he didn't see Shauna and Nessa in their cells at Egan's palace. He saw the villagers he loved like family, the ones left behind to rebuild what was taken from them.

Griffin didn't know what time it was when he woke. Riona and Gulliver were nowhere to be found, so he took his time shaving with the blade Lochlan had given him. He bathed and changed into a pair of thick black woolen pants and a vest over a long-sleeved white linen shirt.

His stomach growled as he yanked his boots on. When had he last eaten? It wasn't yesterday afternoon. Maybe the morning? He was starting to lose track of the days in Iskalt and in the human realm. Every action bled together to create a nonstop quest.

When he reached the dining room, only Brea sat at the high table. The sight of her made his breath hitch. Even if he knew he wasn't in love with her anymore, he never wanted to stop feeling confident in her presence. She'd always given him strength, and he needed it now more than ever.

"Good morning, Griffin." She smiled, but he'd always been able to spot her false expressions.

"Good?" He lowered himself into a chair next to her. "Maybe we should stick with morning."

"Well, it's almost lunch, but the kitchens know to keep breakfast running late for me each morning."

"Because you're lazy?" He forgot for a moment that he couldn't joke with Brea like that anymore.

Brea lifted one brow. "Because I'm a mother who spends most of the morning with my children."

"That too." Griffin nodded to the man who set a water goblet in front of him. He took a long drink before setting it down. Neither of them mentioned she had two fewer kids to prepare for the day.

Brea called a servant over and whispered something in his ear. The servant nodded and walked away.

"There was a time, your Majesty—"

"Don't call me that."

"—where you'd have laughed at the idea of servants catering to your every whim."

"There was also a time I thought I was human."

Griffin searched the hall, his eyes landing on all the servants waiting to be given an order. "You told me it was a flaw to like you."

"That sounds ... yes, I can see that." She chewed on a lip. "I wish I remembered, Griff."

"Sometimes I wish I'd forgotten it all."

A servant placed a plate in front of each of them. Griffin surveyed their fare. Salted fish, berry pastries, poached eggs.

Brea chewed on a bite of egg before looking toward him once more. "I don't think you really want that. It hurts, Griff, to know someone was so intwined in our lives, and yet we don't even recognize them. You brought me from the human realm. You changed my life, and I've wracked my brain trying to see your face in any of my memories."

"If you remembered me, you wouldn't have invited me to your table."

"No. You can't believe that. Everything inside me is screaming to trust you. I don't understand it, but it's like I know you're the only fae who can repair my family. We aren't whole without Tia and Toby. And now, I'm wondering if a part of us has been missing this entire time. Maybe we aren't whole without you either."

"Please don't say that." He scooted his chair back and stood, his appetite suddenly gone.

Brea ran after him. "Griffin? What did I say? Is it so wrong to want to love you? To want you in our family?"

He turned on his heel so quickly she almost slammed into his chest. "Yes."

"Why? Why can't I trust you?"

"I'm not a good man, Brea." Or at least he didn't use to be. "Regan was like a mother to me, and I chose her over you again and again. I tricked you into a fae marriage you didn't want. I didn't just bring you from the human realm, I abducted you on Regan's orders." He leaned down, staring into her wide eyes. "I abducted Myles after making you believe he was dead." That was the deal breaker for the Brea he knew. She could take everything else, but the lies about Myles hurt her the most.

Brea's eyes hardened, and Griffin waited for her to throw him against the wall with her magic, or at the very least, yell at him. Instead, she stepped forward, sliding her arms around his waist.

He stiffened, figuring she was going to crush him with her power. There were so many things she could do to him.

After a long moment, he realized it was the worst kind of punishment of all.

A hug.

There was no pain to satisfy him, nothing that could serve as his penance.

After a while, his arms threaded around her as a tear leaked from the corner of his eye.

"I don't know who you were, Griff," she whispered, gazing up at him. "But I'm beginning to see who you *are.* We are all capable of so much bad. Bad is easy. It's the good that's hard, change is even harder."

Her voice tapered off, but she didn't end the hug. Silence stretched between them as the image of Brea shifted in his mind. Could he really be part of two families? Was it possible to get Lochlan and Brea back?

No.

Not while they were still without their memories.

Brea released him and stepped away. "You're going to save them. I know it. And those kids will get to love you too. I refuse to believe I'll never see them again. Promise me you won't give up, Griff. Promise you'll find them? They need to know their uncle Griff."

It would be a false promise, they both knew that. But he needed to say it just as much as she needed to hear it.

"I will bring your children back to you."

Her face brightened the slightest bit. "Good, now come and eat."

He shook his head. "There's someone I need to see."

She gave him an understanding nod before he sprinted down the hall, backtracking to his room. When he slammed open the door, he found Gulliver and Riona sitting on the floor playing some game with marbles.

Riona was mesmerizing with her moving tattoos and dark eyes. Her white wings made her a contradiction, and it fit her. The light and the dark. The good and the bad.

This time, he was hoping for a little of the bad. Only Riona would have the information he needed.

Gulliver smiled up at him. "Griff! You want to play? All you have to do is pick up marbles in a sequence, creating your own pattern. I can show you."

Griff knew the game. It was how they taught kids to break codes in Fargelsi.

"I'm sorry, Gullie. Maybe later. I need to speak with Riona."

Gulliver shrugged and went back to playing.

Riona gave him a quizzical look as she pushed herself off the floor. Griffin led her into his bedroom and shut the door before turning on her. "How much do you know about Sorcha's book?"

Riona's stern look fell away into surprise. "Just as much as you—"

"Don't lie to me. You were Egan's champion. Before we met, I remember every time I saw you sitting atop your steed next to the king, bowing to his every whim."

"You don't understand." She sidestepped him and sat on the bed.

"Then make me." He took a seat beside her. This wasn't supposed to be an argument. The accusations fell past his lips before he could stop them. But he knew Riona, he understood her like few others could.

Because she was just like him.

Riona rested her elbows on her knees and hunched forward. "I don't know anything about the book, but he has a spell that allows him to wield magic from the barrier."

Griffin knew there was a reason Egan was able to return his portal magic to him. This wasn't news, and there was no proof the spell was from the book.

"What about you?" Riona's eyes pinned him with her glare. "Regan never told you about the book while you were subjugating the Fargelsian people?"

She hadn't. But she also hadn't had him turning the human realm upside down for it. Which meant Brandon might be right. Regan knew where it was. She'd studied it, had spells from it. He tried to recall the memories he'd pushed to the back of his mind, realizing how much she had kept from him.

He hadn't been her son or her champion. Not her partner—that was Callum. So, what was he?

Gullible.

He sighed. "She didn't mention it or where it could be."

Riona lifted her face to his. "A book with so much power wouldn't be in the human realm without protections. We don't even know what this book can do, how much power it can wield."

"Riona," he whispered.

Her eyes locked onto his, her voice softening as she nodded. "If it's truly as powerful as we've been told, what if it can not only bring the magical barrier around the prison realm down, but this book ... have you ever wondered if it can make the world remember?"

His heart thundered in his chest whether from Riona's nearness or the questions that rolled through his mind. What if he could restore memories and cease being the forgotten prince, the one everyone felt like they knew but never would without their memories?

He flopped back on the bed. "Why is it that every choice feels like another set of chains?" Lies wrapped around him like steel tightening until he gasped for breath.

If they found this book, the truth would be right at his fingertips.

Riona lay beside him, her thigh brushing his. "I don't have all the answers, Griff. But we'll find this book. We'll save the twins and return to free Shauna and Nessa." She sat up, letting her eyes meet his before she stood. "We won't fail, because you won't let us."

He stared after her as she left him behind. She was right, they'd find it. But Griffin knew they couldn't give it to Egan.

He only wished Riona agreed.

He needed to talk to someone—someone who preferably couldn't talk back. Ruffling Gulliver's hair on his way past, Griffin stepped into the hall and turned the opposite way of the main hall. He'd rarely spent much time in this palace, but it still felt familiar. It called to his roots.

The library wasn't far. Griffin ducked into the stone archway to see solid oak bookshelves lining the walls. He skimmed the dusty leather spines on his way to the back corner where a forgotten portrait hung.

There were many paintings of his parents around the palace grounds, but none were like this, so lifelike it stirred memories he couldn't possibly have. Neither he nor Lochlan hung on these walls. A royal child in Iskalt got their first portrait done on their sixth birthday. They'd both been gone by then, living in separate kingdoms.

He sat on the arm of a nearby couch and studied them. His father had auburn hair just like Griff's, but Lochlan favored their mother.

"What would you two think of me now?" he asked. It would have broken their hearts to see him choose Regan's side against his brother. But if they were here, they'd have forgotten him too.

"I want my family back. But the moment I have them, they're going to abandon me. I'm sorry. For everything. I'm just ... sorry." He buried his face in his hands.

Words failed him as his back shook. His parents were the only ones who got to see him cry. He had to be strong. For Riona and Gulliver, for his brother and his children. For Shauna and Nessa. Brea.

For everyone who'd end up hurt or dead if Egan got his hands on the book.

"I'm going to save them all." And then he'd disappear into the prison realm again to let his first family live their lives without him. Even if he could return their memories with Sorcha's book, these people ... they'd never forgive him.

CHAPTER 3

GRIFFIN

Griffin stared at the rumpled and stained page with a series of numbers he couldn't make sense of. They'd tried every magical solution known to them. They'd applied all of their combined knowledge—which was considerable—to crack the code, but were still missing something vital. He could feel it, right on the tip of his fingers if he could just grasp it.

The numbers started to blend together, and Griffin wiped a weary hand across his bleary eyes, hoping for a moment of clarity that never came.

5416201721015 4768

In all likelihood, the numbers were just numbers, and they were chasing a dead end, but it was the only solid lead they had. It had to yield something. Some clue to the whereabouts of the book or the twins, or both. Something to make the last weeks of research fruitful.

When Finn returned from the human realm with the code, they were all excited, convinced they had the information they were looking for. But that excitement quickly yielded to frustration.

They'd sent copies of the code with trusted messengers to the Fargelsian and Eldurian queens who were also hard at work trying to interpret the numbers themselves. Alona and Finn stumbled upon a source in the Eldurian palace library that confirmed a possible name for the vanished village in Ireland. *Aghadoon.* It could hold the secrets to Sorcha's spell book, or it could be another false lead. If Aghadoon once existed somewhere in Ireland, and if Callum knew of the village and its connection to the book, then it was likely he'd be somewhere in Ireland as well.

"It's useless." Lochlan balled up the sheet of parchment he'd spent the last hours poring over and tossed it into the fireplace. "It's time we search elsewhere. We've lost too much time as it is." He tugged a hand through his tangled blond hair, looking exactly like a desperate father. "Brea is inconsolable today, and I'm worried for her health. We've had to call in a wet-nurse for Ciara. Brea's under so much stress she is struggling to feed her enough."

"Maybe you're right. We should send two parties and continue our search of the human realm." Griffin leaned back in his chair, his limbs stiff from too much time bent over parchment. It was like looking for a needle in a haystack the size of the palace. Impossible. But he'd made a promise to Brea he intended to keep. He would bring her children home.

"We can each lead a search party. I'll take Finn, and you can take Myles. We'll cover more ground that way." Lochlan flipped through pages of research and files containing copies of everything they'd discovered. His end of the dining table was covered in the intel they'd collected.

"Loch, you know you have to stay here. You have a kingdom to—"

Lochlan's fist slammed against the table. "I don't care about the kingdom. My children are missing. I have advisors who can handle the day to day business of Iskalt."

"A king must keep his people first and foremost in his mind. I know that's not what you want to hear, but Iskalt needs you."

"My children need me too."

"You will serve them better here while those you trust do everything in their power to find Tia and Toby and bring them home. With Callum on the loose, you cannot be seen as a weak king or he will take your throne when you're not looking, and then where will Iskalt be?"

"Spoken like a true prince of the realm." Lochlan sighed. "You are right, brother. My resources are at your disposal. You will lead the next excursion into the human realm. But you will keep a close eye on Riona. Her interest does not lie with ours."

Something tugged at Griffin's cold heart at the strength of Lochlan's trust in him. With everything he had, Griffin did not want to betray that trust.

"Myles, stop dragging me." Brea's voice echoed in the hall. "At least let me take Ciara back to the nursery."

Lochlan was already out of his seat when the human came barging into the dining hall turned study, Brea, clutching a sleeping Ciara, trailing along behind him.

"Bring her with you, she'll want to hear this too." Myles rushed across the room, looking half crazed and as sleep deprived as the rest of them.

"You realize she's just eight months old, right?" Brea followed him, catching his sense of urgency.

"You reek of horses, human." Lochlan took in Myles' travel-stained clothes.

"I figured it out." Myles beamed at them.

"Figured what out?" Brea tried to shove him into a seat. He looked near collapse from what was likely a mad dash across two kingdoms to bring whatever news he had for them.

Lochlan poured him a glass of wine, but Myles waved it away.

"It's in Ireland like we thought." He slammed a human map onto the table, a grid of red lines drawn with a careful hand across the Irish island. "It's coordinates."

"What?" Lochlan and Griffin asked as Brea gasped in surprise.

"Location coordinates." Myles reached for the parchment Griffin had been staring at for hours. "It's not a code or a random series of numbers." Myles sat down in Griffin's chair, scribbling the numbers into a formula.

"5 4 1 6 2 0 1 7 2 1 0 1 5 4 7 6 8 is actually 54° 16' 20.172" North by 10° 1' 54.768" West." Myles sat back with a triumphant grin.

"Of course." Brea snatched the map to study the area circled in red ink. "What's there?"

"The question is what's not there," Myles said.

"Aghadoon?" Brea gasped.

"There's a castle ruin at these coordinates."

"And you think we can find it? The real Aghadoon?"

"It has to be there. We'll find it, Brea. I promise."

"If you two are done speaking in code, do you think you could share it with the rest of us?" Lochlan's fists rested at his sides, but his body was tensed like a mountain cat ready to pounce.

"Map coordinates, Loch." Myles stood, placing his hands on the king's shoulders. "The numbers lead to an exact latitude and longitude location in Ireland. It's a lead. A good one."

"You leave now." Lochlan took the map to study the location. "You said there was an old castle?"

"It's a ruin." Myles nodded. "But it should be a good place to look for our next lead. It can't be a coincidence that we're looking for the vanishing village of Aghadoon, and these coordinates lead where they do. Someone wanted it found. There's no other reason the coordinates would have been left in that old book."

"Myles needs to rest," Brea interjected. "He's dead on his feet, and it's noon, anyway. No one is going anywhere until the moon rises. Go find a bed, Myles—and a bath, you reek. We'll be ready for you when you wake."

"Thank you, Brea." He seemed to wilt before their eyes now that his message was delivered.

"Thank *you.*" Brea passed Ciara off to Lochlan and pulled her best friend into her arms. "I don't know what I'd do without you."

"Good thing you'll never have to figure it out." He wrapped his arms around her.

After he'd gone, Lochlan glared at his wife. "We?"

"Yes *we*." Brea took in a deep breath, a sign she was preparing to win an argument. Griffin knew that look all too well. They were in for a fight.

"I'm going with Myles and Griffin this time."

"No, you aren't." Lochlan passed Ciara back to her. "Our youngest children still need you."

"We have a wet nurse now, you'll manage without me." She passed the baby back to him. "Ciara will adjust to the wet-nurse."

"And Kayleigh? Will she understand when her mother leaves? She's not handling the absence of Tierney and Tobias at all."

The little Iskalt princess was beside herself with the missing twins. She stuck to Lochlan and Brea like glue and wouldn't leave her remaining sister's side. The nanny had her hands full with keeping Kayleigh in the nursery when her parents weren't there.

"I know." Brea's shoulders fell in defeat, taking her daughter back from Lochlan's arms. "They're my babies, Loch. I feel so useless staying here and doing nothing."

"Join the freaking club." Lochlan growled, the human phrase sounding odd on his lips. "We have to trust our friends to do this, Brea. I know you're capable of storming the human world and taking on Callum all by yourself, but we don't have that luxury this time."

"I know." Brea's brow furrowed in disappointment and anger.

"Will you watch over Gulliver while I'm away?" Griffin asked her. "He's awfully fond of you," he teased. It was no secret the lad had a bit of a crush on the Iskalt queen. Not that Griffin could blame him. But Gulliver had several crushes these days.

"No way, Griff. I'm coming with you." Gulliver marched into the room with a pastry in each hand and berry filling smeared on his face. Gulliver spent a lot of his free time in the kitchens, and from what Griffin had heard, the cooks loved the boy with the tail.

"You're staying here." Griffin folded his arms across his chest, quite sick of this argument he'd had three times in the span of an hour. "You don't belong in the human world."

"Haven't we already figured out I'm an automatic glamourer—is that a word? Being Dark Fae does have some benefits, you know. Like humans being too blind to see the tail attached to my butt." Gulliver crammed half a pastry in his mouth.

Griffin bent down to pluck the second pastry from his hands. "I was referring to your penchant for saying things humans don't understand. We can't glamour your mouth shut, though that is an intriguing idea."

"I'm going." Gulliver mimicked Griffin's pose. "We're in this together, Griff, and the twins are my friends. I want to help you and Riona."

"Go pack." Griffin sighed.

"Perhaps you can leave before she realizes..." Lochlan suggested.

"She'll be more suspicious if I leave her behind." Griffin turned back to Brea. "Am I a bad parent for wanting to keep him with me so I can know he's safe even if we end up in a dangerous situation?"

"In my book that makes you a good parent." Brea kissed him on the cheek and turned to go.

Griffin made his way back to his rooms, eager for a nap before they traveled after moonrise. It felt good to have a plan again. To be doing something that would take him another step closer to freeing Shauna and Nessa from Eagan's grasp.

"Packed already?" Griffin peeked into Riona's room. She was resting on her bed, writing in her journal. She did that a lot.

"Ready to go." She ran a hand across her page and closed the cover. "Gullie caught me up to speed."

"I wish I could make him stay here where it's safe." He lingered in the doorway, feeling anxious for her company. "But I'm also relieved he'll be with me."

"Come inside, Griff." She laughed at his transparency. "I have a question for you." She patted the bed beside her.

He left the door cracked but welcomed a moment alone with

Riona. He enjoyed moments like this when she was in a good mood. It happened so rarely.

Griffin dropped down onto the bed beside her, toeing off his boots and letting them slide to the floor. "What's your question?"

Riona glanced at the hallway. "You didn't see our little eavesdropper out there did you?"

"No, I made him go take a nap, but he's probably out waiting in the moon garden so he can be sure we don't leave without him. Or he's out hunting for things to steal before we leave." Griffin massaged his temples. "What's on your mind, Riona?"

"Are we still working on the same side?" she blurted.

"What? Of course, we are." Griffin moved to grab her hand, but they weren't hand-holding, reassuring kinds of friends. At least not yet. "I'm with you, Riona. My mind is always on Nessa and Shauna. They are my family."

"It's just a little confusing seeing you bond with your brother and his wife. They're your family too, and I can imagine it's difficult to choose between them."

"I'm not choosing Shauna and Nessa over my brother's family." Griffin sighed. "I want to help bring the twins back, but I'm not losing sight of our mission."

"Even if it means betraying your brother and Brea?" Her voice took on a hard edge.

Griffin heaved a weary sigh. "I'd like to think there's a way to do what we came here to do and help my brother at the same time." He was walking a dangerous line with Riona. He could never forget she was Egan's envoy in this venture. He wanted to trust her, but at the same time, he couldn't divulge all his intentions to her.

"It's just ... if you screw this up, he will blame me, and I can't ... won't allow that."

"I won't let that happen. No matter what."

Griffin would do whatever it took to save Nessa and Shauna and every innocent inside the magical walls of Myrkur. But he would not allow Egan to bring his army into this realm or open the floodgates for every criminal sent to the prison realm to come back for their revenge.

He just had to figure out how to do all of that, save the twins, free Shauna and Nessa from Egan's clutches before he could figure out what Griffin was up to, and keep the book out of the wrong hands. And hopefully not lose Riona in the process.

Chapter 4

Griffin

Myles was the last person to stumble through the portal before Griff closed it. He groaned as he pitched forward, landing on his knees. "Griff, why is it so much smoother when Lochlan opens portals?"

Griffin smirked down at him. "Your human body can't take it?"

Myles pushed himself up from the grass and crossed his arms, but the guy couldn't be menacing if he tried.

Griffin shielded his eyes with his hand and stared into the bright sky, not taking his eyes from the faint outline of the moon. Before being sent to the prison realm, his Iskalt magic rejoiced in the light of the moon. That was when it could play. His fingers curled into his palm as the buzz from opening the portal wore off, leaving Griffin weak. Like a human. No strength pulsed through his veins, but he could still remember how it had felt.

Like he could do anything.

Griffin turned to make sure Riona and Gulliver were okay and watched them pick themselves up off the crunchy grass. If he'd had his way, they'd go directly to the coordinates Finn found. But when did he ever get his way?

Lochlan didn't want his brother walking into a trap, even with his kids at stake.

And this woman they'd come to see, this Ashlin, she was the only fae any of them had met who knew anything about Sorcha's book. She had to know of the secret village. He thought back to the last time they visited her, the way she'd lied to them and then disappeared. Griffin wouldn't let that happen again.

"Surprised you listened to Loch and brought us here." Myles brushed grass from his butt. "We've been trying to catch Ashlin at home for months."

Exhaustion wound through Griffin, and he had no comeback for Myles. The portals used to be easy. Griffin could open them with a flick of his wrist. But that was before his magic had been taken from him.

"Is this how humans feel?" He directed the question to Myles. "Tired and weak all the time."

Myles shrugged. "Pretty much. Maybe the vampire king took too much from you?"

Griffin wasn't sure what a vampire was, but he could guess who Myles meant. Egan. The Dark Fae King hadn't really taken Griffin's magic, but the prison realm had robbed it of him nonetheless, leaving their group unprotected in the human realm.

Myles circled Gulliver.

"It's gone again, right?" Gulliver's eyes followed him.

Riona knocked into Myles' shoulder on her way by. "Just like my wings have been every time we've come."

Griffin had trouble trusting something he didn't understand, and it seemed he wasn't the only one because Myles shot him a suspicious look. The Dark Fae features were invisible to humans in the human realm.

How was that possible when Griffin had to rely on Lochlan's glamour to hide his ears?

Myles' face softened when he met Gulliver's gaze. "Yes, you look normal. Like me."

Griffin snorted. "Human is not normal."

"Well." Myles started forward. "Let's go forward on our vampire king/ice king mission. Hey, they should meet. That would be epic."

"What's a vampire?" Gulliver whispered to Myles as they walked toward the village.

"They're this wicked cool creature who drinks blood and can only come out at night."

"Drinks blood?" Riona shook her head in disbelief. "And humans find this entertaining?"

"Oh, totally." Myles grinned but there was fear behind it.

"We need to move faster." The ruins of Bealadannan looked as desolate as Griffin remembered it from the first time they'd come in search of the twins, when they'd learned about the lineage of O'Rourke twins—Sorcha's lineage.

Griffin kept his hands clenched, his jaw firm, as they walked through the dirt streets of the village. Crumbling buildings stood on either side, and the people who lived in them didn't peek out their windows like they had before.

At the other end of the village sat a single house on the cliff's edge.

They reached the stone cottage. Smoke curled up toward the sky, billowing out of a chimney. Someone was home. But when they got closer, they realized the door stood open.

A foreboding feeling wound through Griffin, and he picked up his pace, running the rest of the way. When he reached the cottage, he peered inside. Ashlin's belongings were scattered around the cottage, spilling out through the door. A fire raged in the hearth, the tea kettle hanging over it, this time not piercing the air with its song.

It held a similarity to how they'd found the place two months ago when they'd returned. Since then, each time they came looking for Ashlin, everything had been tidied, but she was never home.

Riona, Gulliver, and Myles joined him.

"Do you think..." Myles didn't finish the sentence as he covered his mouth with his hand.

Griffin examined every part of the cottage, looking for clues. "Did someone ... take her? Everyone, get inside."

They hadn't expected much from the old woman after she'd sent them on a fool's errand to an empty grave, but Griffin had hoped she'd give them more information when he presented the numbers to her. He couldn't storm a disappearing village if he knew nothing about it.

Griffin surveyed the cottage, wondering who could want to abduct an old woman. A folded parchment sat atop the bed. He bent to pick it up and unfolded it. One line of text stretched across the page. "Follow the numbers." He whispered the words again. "We're on the right path."

"Griff." Riona's tattoos spiraled fiercely, not sitting still on her skin. "I can't help feeling we needed her."

She was right. They'd just lost someone who could have been an ally.

He turned on his heel and walked to the door, hat in hand. "We need to leave." *Follow the numbers.*

They were trying.

Stepping outside, he gulped in fresh air, needing to remind himself they had real clues this time. He wasn't sure if he could take another dead end.

"Myles," he barked. "Bring the map."

Myles reached into his bag and retrieved the rolled-up map of Ireland. Griffin took it and spread it out on the ground, kneeling beside it.

"We're here." Myles pointed to a star that marked Ashlin's cottage.

"And where do we need to be?" Riona joined them.

"Here." Myles tapped the area that was circled. "Eastern Ireland, but lucky for us, I'm guessing it's only a three or four hour cab ride."

"Cab?" Riona gave him a confused look.

"Yes. We can't portal back to the fae realm and then the human realm again to get there faster because Griff has never been there. Plus, you all see him. He's barely standing."

"Not true." Griffin wobbled as he took a step forward.

Myles crossed his arms. "We don't have a choice. We have to take a cab that'll cost an absolute fortune." Myles shrugged. "And I listen to Loch. Well, sometimes. He told me to look out for you."

Griffin couldn't seem to process those words. Lochlan wanted to make sure he was safe? "I've seen cabs before." Griffin looked to Riona and Gulliver, needing anything to distract him from his self-pitying thoughts. "You are going to see a lot of things that scare you, but I promise they're safe. Myles, you brought human money, right?"

"Sure did. I had a feeling you were going to be an expensive date, Griff."

Griffin rubbed his chin. "We don't have time to figure out what happened to Ashlin, but we can assume it has something to do with us, with this book, so we must move along. We need to get as close to these coordinates as we can and find an inn. I don't feel comfortable checking out the village during the day. Even without my magic, the moon fortifies me."

Myles rolled up the map and pulled out another contraption Griffin had seen before.

"What's that?" Gulliver leaned closer.

"A cell phone." Myles hit a series of numbers and brought it to his ear. "Hello, I'm in need of a cab outside Bealadannan. Yes. Okay. Thank you."

He slipped the phone back into his bag before realizing they were all staring at him.

"Was he talking to himself just now?" Riona asked, turning her gaze to Griffin, like she worried for the human's sanity.

"What? I called the cab company to send a car." Myles shrugged.

"This is magic?"

"My phone?" He laughed. "No. But sometimes Lochlan takes me into the human realm so I can call my parents when we don't have time to visit. That's a kind of magic you could say."

Griffin wished he saw the world the way Myles did. He considered being able to talk to his family as good as magic. It had a purity to it, a purity that meant he was a good man.

Griffin didn't know what he was, but he'd never considered himself good.

They walked through the crumbling village to reach the other side where a paved road greeted them. He tried to remember his first time in the human realm. It seemed like a place where anything could happen. They didn't have fae magic, so they created magical objects instead.

Like the yellow cab pulling up in front of them.

A string of curses flew from Riona's mouth.

Gulliver stared on in awe.

Griffin only shrugged and opened the door as he greeted the Irishman in front. "Good afternoon." He always resorted to formal speak, the words of a prince, when talking to humans he didn't know.

The man smiled. "Dinna just stand there, lad. Tell me where I can take ye."

Griffin ushered the rest of the group in and gestured to Myles. Myles leaned forward between the seats. "We're headed for Dublin."

"Ah, Americans. Knew ye looked funny. Kidding. Kidding. Dublin ye say? That's quite the drive."

Myles pulled out a wad of human bills. "Got anything better to do today?"

The man's eyebrows shot up. "No, sir. Guess I'm headin' to Dublin with a load of Yanks."

Myles patted his shoulder and relaxed back into his seat, squished between Riona and Griffin. Gulliver sat up front, a giant grin on his face as his eyes darted to each of the human surroundings they passed.

When the cab started moving, Gulliver squealed and clapped his hands together.

Riona remained quiet, a green pallor to her cheeks.

Griffin had an acute awareness of his companions. Their mission rested on them being able to blend into the human world.

Myles stretched his arms along the back of Griffin and Riona's seats, oblivious to the venomous looks sent his way. "Griff," he whispered. "When you first abducted me in the human world, did you ever think I'd be so integral to your future?"

Griffin grunted. "You are not integral."

"Sure I am. Tell him, Riona."

Riona's jaw clenched. "Get your arm off the back of my seat, or I'll fly you into the sky and drop you."

The driver looked at them in the rear-view mirror.

"Riona." Griffin raised a brow.

She crossed her arms but didn't respond.

Myles smiled as he started humming a song Griffin hadn't heard before. It was all a grand adventure to him. The king consort of Fargelsi hadn't changed a bit in ten years. He was still the boy with too much laughter in his eyes, too much joy that didn't belong in a fae world that could cause such pain.

Griffin settled back in his seat, preparing for the long drive to Dublin—wherever that was.

Riona and Gulliver stared at the cab as it drove away like it was the last lifeline they had.

Griffin had spent a lot of time in the human world, but he'd never seen one of their big cities. They'd driven through dusk, reaching their destination as the moon claimed the sky. Even in the dark, this place put fae cities to shame.

Maybe if the book truly could restore memories, he could live in the human realm, at least until Lochlan stopped trying to kill him.

Though, the Lochlan he knew now, the king of Iskalt and father of four was so very different from the cold, hard brother who'd only had scorn for Griffin.

"What do we do now?" To Riona's credit, she didn't seem scared of the cars driving down narrow streets. Tall buildings lined the sidewalks, giving the city a closed in feel.

Yet … it was beautiful in a way so completely different from the fae kingdoms.

"We get ourselves a room. Myles, what time is it?"

Myles pulled out his phone. "Eight PM."

"Okay, let's rest tonight and do more tomorrow. We should find a room at one of the inns." The driver had dropped them off in front of a building called the Holiday Inn. "This one may be appropriate." It had inn right in the name, but the huge building looked nothing like any inn Griffin had ever seen.

No one argued, so Griffin went inside. They walked across white tile to where a human sat behind a desk.

"I'll handle this." Myles and the woman at the desk struck up a conversation Griffin couldn't understand. Bed sizes? Smoking?

The human world was always overwhelming, and Griffin wasn't sure how much more he could handle tonight.

To his surprise, Gulliver clutched Riona's hand.

Myles returned to them and held out a small piece of plastic to Griff.

"Do I look like a dust bin?" Griffin eyed the plastic card.

"It's your room key. I got us two, because I am *not* sharing a bed with you. Come on. We're on the eighth floor."

Myles led them to a set of silver doors. He pressed a button on the wall and then waited. When the doors slid open, Gulliver jumped back.

Even Griffin stayed where he was.

Myles stood on the threshold. "Come on. It's just an elevator. It's safe. I promise." He urged them inside the closet-like room.

Griffin looked back at the woman who was watching them. They had to do this. "Myles is the human. We need to trust him." Words he'd never imagined himself saying.

Once the four of them were inside, the doors slid shut, and Myles pressed a button on the wall.

Gulliver screamed as the elevator moved. Riona pressed herself back against the wall, barely breathing until the doors slid open again. The rooms outside the magic closet were different this time. Griffin and Riona peered into the hallway.

Myles walked out first. "I choose Gulliver as my sleeping buddy. He's more tolerable than you two." He stopped at a door. "This is us. You guys are next door."

Griffin watched the way Myles slid the plastic into the slot to open the door, so he followed suit. It took him a few times to get the door open. Riona reluctantly followed him inside.

"I don't like this place." Riona set her small sack on one of the beds as her eyes scanned the foreign place. "I don't like it at all. There's too much magic everywhere." She fanned her hands out, gesturing at all the human gadgets around the room.

"I keep telling you it's not magic. Humans would call it science or engineering."

"I don't care what they call it. I don't like it."

Griffin sighed, having no energy for all the human things in this room. "Let's just get some rest. Tomorrow, maybe it won't look so daunting."

She didn't look like she believed him.

Riona's scream jolted Griffin from his restless sleep. At first, he'd thought it was Shauna screaming in his dreams. It took him a moment to wake up. A sound came from the bathroom, the reason for the scream.

Griffin kicked the blankets off his legs and heaved himself from the bed. He rubbed his eyes as he approached the closed washroom door. He knocked, not sure she could hear him over the noise inside.

The door opened, revealing Riona sitting on the closed toilet—he knew that one from previous visits—in a fluffy white robe with a contraption blowing hot air.

Griffin leaned against the door frame, and she turned off the air blaster, putting it on a hook on the wall. "You okay?"

She nodded. "I couldn't sleep so I decided to examine the human magic. Did you know they can make water fall from the sky just by turning a handle?"

He did know that. "It's called a shower."

"Their chamber pot cleans itself."

"A toilet."

"But the most miraculous item is this contraption that blows hot air. Do they use it to dry their bodies, do you think?"

Griffin chuckled. "I haven't seen one of those before." He sighed. "I've been to the human realm countless times, but..." It had lost the awe for him. How did he admit that to someone who still only saw magic?

Riona bound her long braids on top of her head and smiled. It was such a rare sight, Griffin wanted to savor it. How could Lochlan not trust this woman? All she needed was someone to give her the chance to be good, the chance to fight on the right side.

Griffin had watched her change over the last few months. She talked more now and had become protective of Gulliver.

"What's that smile for?" she asked.

He shrugged, guilt gnawing at him for spending a single moment not thinking of Shauna and Nessa and how Riona had played a part in destroying his village.

Leaving the bathroom behind, he crawled back into his bed, wanting the conflicting emotions to disappear. If he closed his eyes, he saw them, the two girls in the prison realm he had to save. But ... it wasn't only about them anymore.

Riona emerged and climbed into her bed, her eyes closed.

"Riona?" he whispered.

"Yes?" She turned onto her side, the back of the robe bulging with her wings.

"What do you see when you close your eyes?" He needed to know, to believe in her, to know she believed in him.

Riona didn't answer for a long time. "Long ago, before you came to Myrkur, there were rumors. I was a child at the time, but I remember everything so clearly. My people lived near the water as we were children of the sea and sky, feared for our ancient ways but also revered. You ask what I see at night? I see fire and blood. I see my people on their knees as the wings were ripped from their backs. Griff, I see the moment I should have died."

"But you didn't."

"No. Instead, I got to live with the memories as an indentured servant to Egan. Some say it was a fate worse than death. To be the last of my kind—or at least to think I was the last." None of them had forgotten Nihal.

"Yet, you're loyal to him."

She closed her eyes, but he knew she wasn't sleeping.

"Do you want to know what I see?"

She didn't respond to his question.

"I see destruction and ruin. I see a scared people huddling together, unable to even find enough food to eat. I see you sitting atop your horse."

Her eyes blinked open.

"But then I see you saving Gulliver, saving me. And I see Shauna and Nessa, my family brought to the king's palace. I have so many conflicting images in my dreams. I understand you, Riona, because I have been there. But I have changed. I won't serve another tyrant with my eyes shut. Can you say the same?"

She rolled over, her back to him. "I do not know."

It would have to be enough for now.

An incessant knocking sounded on their door way too early in the morning. Griffin grumbled to himself as he pulled it open.

Gulliver darted past him with a plate piled with food. "Griff, did you know this inn has *free* food in the morning? That means you don't have to pay for it."

"I know what free means." Griffin rubbed the sleep from his eyes.

"They let you have as much as you want."

Myles walked in after him. "I knew the kid would like that."

Gulliver climbed onto Riona's bed, offering her a plate of eggs and toast. She shook her head.

Their conversation from hours before stuck in Griffin's mind, but he needed to trust her.

"Riona." Gulliver beamed. "I like your dress. It looks soft. I had one like that in my room, but there were no trousers with it."

Myles held back a laugh. "Gullie, that's not a dress."

"It's not?" Riona looked to him.

Myles bit his fist until he had his laughter under control. "It's called a bathrobe. No one goes into public in those."

She frowned as if she didn't believe him.

Griffin flopped back onto his bed, and Gulliver threw him a pastry.

"Humans have the best food." Gulliver crammed long thin pastries into his mouth.

"Those are called French toast sticks." Myles perched on the end of Griffin's bed. "What's the plan for today?"

Not for the first time, Griffin wished he had use of his magic. "We have to stay in our rooms until nightfall when I can hide my fae features more easily."

"What about me?" Myles asked. "I'm the normal looking one—"

"Yes." Sarcasm dripped from Riona's words. "Humans are the normal ones."

"No, Myles is right." An idea formed in Griffin's mind. "The coordinates are outside Dublin, probably an hour's cab ride. You could go see what's there. We know the village has disappeared but look for clues. Ask around about the local legends. Anything."

"Can I go?" Gulliver's eyes lit up. "No one can see I'm not human." Griffin frowned, and Gulliver answered his own question for Griffin. "No, Gullie. It's too dangerous for little old you."

"I'm sorry, kiddo." Myles offered Griffin a salute. "Human at your service." He stole a pastry from Gulliver and practically skipped from the room.

Riona groaned as she lay her head back. "Your human is odd."

"Very."

"And you trust him with this task? I could fly to Aghadoon and make sure no one saw me." She sat up, the tops of her wings poking from the collar of the loose robe.

"Have your wings always been dark?" Gulliver asked through a mouth of food.

"Dark? They're white." She frowned at him.

"Not the tips."

Griffin's eyes widened as he noticed what Gulliver had pointed out. Black shadows speckled the top of her otherwise pure white wings.

Riona shot to her feet and ran into the bathroom. A scream echoed from her. When she returned, she had a shirt on that fit around her wings in the back. "Griff, what do you think it is?" She sounded scared.

Griffin stood and walked toward her. He ran a finger over the black tips, and she shivered.

"Griff," she whispered. "This isn't supposed to happen. The darkness ... I don't know what's caused it."

Griffin pulled her into a hug. "We'll figure this out. I promise."

He'd have to add it to the growing list of promises he'd already made. But what if, at the end of the day, he couldn't keep a single one of them?

CHAPTER 5

GRIFFIN

"There's nothing there? What do you mean there's nothing there?" Griffin stared at Myles wanting to throttle him for wasting the whole day.

"Just what I said. There is *nothing* with a capital "N" at these coordinates." He tossed a worn piece of paper onto the table. The numbers carefully written in his human codes of latitude and longitude.

"No village or town?" Griffin frowned.

"Not even a house."

"Are you sure you looked everywhere?" Riona asked.

"Trust me. There is nothing there but a lot of grass, a hill, and some old ruins that used to be a castle."

"What about around the area? Did you check in the nearby towns?" Griffin asked.

"Listen, guys." Myles gave a patient sigh. "We can go back tonight, but I'm telling you, there is nothing anywhere near these coordinates. It's miles and miles of just ... Ireland. Craggy hills, stumpy grass, some rocks and the occasional goat. That's it. So unless some of the human tales were right and the Fair Folk actually do live under the hills, then we're at a dead end."

"What is he rambling about?" Riona turned to Griffin for a translation.

"What's a Fair Folk?" Gulliver looked up from playing with the bedside lamp. He was fascinated with the on/off switch.

"You're a Fair Folk," Myles answered absently, sinking down to the bed beside Gulliver and kicking off his shoes.

"She said to follow the numbers." Griffin paced the hotel room. After a full day inside, he was climbing the walls, eager to do something. Anything other than waste more time.

"It's almost sunset." Riona bent to look out the window for the millionth time. "We'll go to this place and see if we find something the human overlooked."

"I'm right here, you know." Myles glared at her.

"I see you." She stared blankly back at him.

"You do know I am the king of Fargelsi, right?"

"Yes, but you are not my king." Riona returned to her bed to rummage through Gulliver's bag. He'd taken everything from his room that wasn't nailed down.

"Really, Gullie, do you need to take the clicky box?" Riona tossed a long black rectangular device back onto the bed.

"I like the buttons."

"That's a remote control." Myles ran a hand through his hair and rolled his eyes to the ceiling.

"Which is why I want it." Gulliver snatched it up. "It controls things."

"It doesn't control *things*." Myles wrestled the remote out of Gulliver's hands. "It controls a television. That television in our room specifically. Without the TV, it's useless."

"It's not magic?" Gulliver frowned.

"Nothing here is magic. Truly." Myles seemed like he wanted to beat that knowledge into their heads.

"I don't care what you call it, it seems like magic to me," Riona said stubbornly. "And I've decided I don't much care for it."

"Just because you don't understand something, doesn't mean it's magic," Myles said. "You two would do well to remember that."

"Then how will we know when something really is magic?" Gulliver asked.

"I will tell you. And if I'm not around, then Griffin will tell you."

"Like right away?" Gulliver gave him a pleading look.

"The moment I see real magic, you'll be the first to know."

"Let's go." Griffin finally said. "By the time we get there, it will be dark."

Myles gave him a long look. "You look less exhausted than this morning at least."

Griffin only shrugged in answer. He didn't want to admit how the moon strengthened him, how he'd never fully recovered from opening the portal the day before, and the day seemed to drain the life right out of him.

"Is that wise, to risk you being seen without a glamour?" Myles asked. "We should wait for dark before we leave this room."

"I have a hat." Griffin yanked a hat over his head. The wide brim provided cover for his ears.

"And that looks ridiculous. People are going to stare at you for the dorky hat and catch sight of the ears." Myles pushed him back down onto the bed. "We wait."

"Fine." He'd liked Myles better when he wasn't a king. He'd gotten bossy in his old age.

For the next hour, Griffin watched Myles teach Gulliver and Riona about the science and technology behind the things they perceived as human magic. He was only half listening, trying to call on his strength in the fading twilight.

"I get what you're saying, Myles, but it still seems like a form of magic, this technology," Riona said. "I understand the bat-ery makes the clicky box work and the sensor-ma-gig in the box tells the tele-thing what to do. But that's just like the way Griffin's magic is powered by the moon, and he tells it to open a portal."

"No." Myles shook his head, clearly aggravated. "That's not the same thing at all."

"I'm pretty sure it is." Riona relaxed against the headboard on her bed. "Humans have magic, it's just a little different. But fae magic is all different too. Iskalt magic is not the same as Eldur, and Fargelsi magic is even more different. So is human magic. Myrkur is the real land without magic." She shrugged like it was all that simple.

"No, no." Myles stood. "That's so not it, Riona."

"As entertaining as this debate is," Griffin interrupted before Myles was moved to tears. "The moon has risen." He could feel his strength returning with the fading of the light. In a matter of moments, the weariness left him.

Myles dug an article of clothing out of his bag and threw it to Griffin. "Wear my sweatshirt. It has a hood."

Griffin slipped it on. "How do I look?"

"Handsomely human." Myles grinned. "And a stylish one at that."

Griffin turned to Riona and Gulliver. "Are their features still hidden?"

Myles nodded. "We're good to go."

"This human is useful." Riona pursed her lips. "But I still don't like him."

"He'll grow on you." Griffin nodded. "Let's go."

It was still an event getting everyone down the elevator and into a cab without causing a stir among the humans passing by. Their elevator companions thought Riona was quite strange when she exclaimed, "It goes down too?" Not that Griffin liked the ride any more than she did.

"It might have been cheaper to buy a car than take cabs everywhere," Myles muttered as he paid the driver.

"You lot want me to wait for you?" the cabbie asked, staring down the empty road. "There's not much ter see 'ere at night. Not much ter see period," he muttered.

"Um, yes. Please. We just fancied a walk by the ruins tonight and don't want to get stuck." Myles closed the door.

"Bit odd of a place for a walk."

"Err, a friend said it was lovely. Just ... wait here. But don't come closer. Please. We'll come right back to this spot."

"All right." The cabbie shook his head grumbling something about Americans as they walked away.

"See, there's nothing here." Myles turned to the roadside. "Just some goat paths that go up the hill through those crumbling pillars." He pointed to the tallest hill where the remains of a castle sat looking ready to collapse. "And more of the same on the other side of the road."

Riona turned around in a wide circle, her wings fluttering in the breeze. "How far did you go in each direction?"

"Several miles. I walked all day."

She nodded. "I will take to the skies and see what I can find. You may not have looked far enough."

Griffin settled a hand on her arm to keep her from flying away.

"What is it, Griff?" Riona frowned at him. He stood, staring at the hillside Myles had spent the day exploring.

"What's wrong, man, you look like someone stepped on your grave."

"You don't see it?" Griffin turned toward them, hardly able to take his eyes away from the sight.

"See what?" Riona scowled. "It's as the human said before, there is nothing here."

"The human has a name. You may call me Myles, or your Highness, either works for me." Myles' tone took on a razor-sharp edge.

"As I've said before, you are not my king."

"Stop bickering, you two." Griffin's hand tightened on Riona's arm. "You really don't see it?"

"See what?" Gulliver asked.

"The village. It's right there." Griffin pointed to the hilltop. "Just beyond those old pillars."

"You can see it?" Myles turned around, peering into the darkness as if he could will himself to see what Griffin saw.

"The vanishing village." Griffin grinned. "It's not vanished at all. You just have to be Iskaltian to see it in the moonlight." Griffin stepped off the road to make his way up the hill.

"Gulliver, that's magic right there," Myles said.

"No, it's not, I can't see anything."

"That's why it's magic, because Griff sure sees something we don't."

"Wait, you're not going into an invisible village alone." Riona raced after him.

"It's not invisible to me." Griffin kept moving.

"You've lost your mind." Riona ran ahead, squinting for all she was worth. "Nothing is there, Griffin."

"There is a quaint little village at the top of that hill. I can see it clear as day."

"I don't like this."

"She doesn't like much, does she?" Myles muttered.

"Just wait here and let me investigate. Ashlin said to follow the numbers, and those coordinates led us right here. I have to look."

"Be careful, Griff," Myles said. "We'll wait here for you."

"I won't be long."

"Take me with you, Griff," Gulliver begged. "I want to see the magic village."

"I need to go in alone this time, buddy." Griffin bent to meet his gaze. "Stay here with Riona and keep an eye on her and Myles for me. Make sure they don't kill each other. I'll take you next time if it proves to be safe."

"I never get to do the fun stuff." Gulliver kicked at the ground.

"And don't steal anything while I'm gone," Griffin called over his shoulder.

"What am I going to steal, Griff? Rocks?" Gulliver's voice rang out in the quiet night.

"Are we sure he hasn't gone mad?" Riona whispered, watching him make his way up the hill.

But Griffin was as sane as he'd ever been.

The village was old to be sure, and he couldn't see anyone out and about, but the place was well cared for. Lights flickered in windows all around the town center. It had a distinct Fargelsi aura about the town. As if a Gelsi village had been lifted up and transplanted in the human realm. But for what reason?

The goat path turned to cobblestone streets with tufts of grass growing between the stones here and there.

"Hello?" Griffin called, startled to see a young man driving a mule-drawn cart right toward him. "Good evening, sir. Might I have a word?" Griffin asked. The driver seemed to look right through him as he passed. "I was wondering if you could tell me about this place?" Griff raised his voice.

The man gave him a horrified look and flicked the reins, driving his mule into a trot.

"Please, just a moment of your time?" Griffin tried to follow him, but the man turned down another street, driving his cart as fast as he dared.

"Get to yer chores, lads, or there'll be no pie for you come supper." A woman's voice sounded behind him, and Griffin turned to find a fae woman sweeping the front steps of her cottage. Her three young boys scampered to the rear of the house where a barn leaned precariously to the left.

"Madam, might I have a word?" Griffin took a step toward her, and she screamed, running into the house and slamming the door behind her.

The reception was the same wherever he went. Few were out and about, most likely preferring to be inside with their families. He was beginning to think no one would speak to him and worried the village would fade with the sunrise, and he would have to come back tomorrow evening.

"You have caused quite a stir, young man." An elderly fae gentleman walked along the cobblestone street toward Griffin. He walked with a cane and a slight limp as he approached warily. "My people are frightened."

"I can't say I blame them," Griffin said. "I'm a little frightened myself."

"Where do you hail from?"

"Iskalt." Griffin didn't see a reason to hide that fact.

"You should return." The man turned to leave.

"Wait, please. I've come a long way to this place."

"What you seek can't be found, young man. You should leave at once, you and your friends on the hillside."

"Tell me what this place is, please?" He needed to get this man talking. "Ashlin sent me here."

"Ashlin?" The wiry fae peered into his eyes, searching for something Griffin couldn't fathom.

"She told me I would find what I'm looking for here." Well, she'd told him to follow the numbers. That was close enough to the truth.

"She should know better than to send strangers into our midst. There hasn't been an unknown descendant in generations. Not in this world or any other."

"Descendants? Descendants of whom?" Griffin asked. "I am of Iskalt, I can see your village in the moonlight."

"Only the descendants can see through the magic that shields this village—day or night. You must go, young sir. We do not trust outsiders here. And Ashlin is no friend of ours. Not any longer."

"What descendants? Tell me that, and I will leave," Griffin begged.

"The direct descendants of the O'Rourke."

"Which O'Rourke? Sorcha?" Griffin took a step closer.

"Do not speak that blasphemous name here, lad. The O'Rourke was her twin. The lady Herself was our ancestress. If you can see this place, you must carry at least a drop of her blood. But it is of no matter. You must leave and forget you ever saw or heard the name of Aghadoon." The man tapped his cane against the cobblestones, and he and the village faded into the rising mist.

Chapter 6

RIONA

"What the heck is he doing?" Riona sat in the field, letting the high grasses obscure her from view. Griffin was a small figure at the top of the hill. He used his hands like he was talking to someone, but there was no one there with him.

"I always knew something wasn't right with Griff." Myles threw himself down beside her. "Maybe he's finally lost it, seeing villages and people no one else can see."

"Don't say that." Gulliver picked at the grass. "I'm sure there's an explanation for his behavior."

Riona snorted. "You, boy, are too young and too naïve.."

"Griff doesn't think so." His eyes narrowed. "He trusts me more than he trusts you. At least I never followed King Egan."

"The vampire king?" Myles looked to Riona, excitement in his eyes.

"Why do you keep calling him that?" She was sure she'd regret the question just like she regretted every question that spurred Myles' incessant talking.

"There's no sun in the prison realm, right?"

Riona's jaw clenched. "In *Myrkur* we live in perpetual darkness, but we have mornings and evenings just like you do. You just have to look close enough to see the subtle changes as our day fades to night."

"Well, Vampires can only come out at night. Hence the vampire king. When I lived in Ohio, Brea and I spent a lot of time watching shows on Netflix. Her absolute favorite was called *Buffy the Vampire Slayer*." He smiled and laid back to stare up at the stars. "She used to hide from her parents at my house." He rolled onto his side and propped his head up with one hand. "And now we're both fae royalty." A laugh burst out of him. "You should have seen my parents' faces when I told them I was basically living out my own fairytale."

Riona had never given much thought to humans or the secret fae world they knew little about. Yet, curiosity now warred with her distaste for the human. "How did they react?"

"Well, at first they didn't believe me. They're Ohio stock, you know."

No, she didn't know.

"What's an Ohio?" Gulliver asked, still not taking his eyes from Griffin up on the hill.

Myles waited a moment before answering. "It's home. Where Brea and I grew up. My parents still live there. Lochlan brings me home occasionally—if I catch him in a good mood. He has a soft spot for me."

Riona doubted that. The icy king had nothing soft about him. "So, they believe you now?"

He nodded. "It's been ten years, and I still look like I'm an eighteen-year-old senior in high school with the slower aging in the fae world. I still don't totally understand it, but my wife tells me I'll live much longer than I would have in the human world, so it's cool. Over the years, my parents were sort of forced to imagine the fae world did exist. But they refuse to come visit."

"I never knew my parents." Gulliver pulled his knees in to his chest.

"Let me ask you something, Gullie." Myles sat up. "Who makes you feel safe? Who helps you when you're hurt or makes sure you have food to eat? Who loves you?"

Gulliver glanced back at Myles before fixating on the top of that hill once more. "Griff."

Myles patted his back. "Then I'd say you know your father at least."

Riona's brow creased. "We can't just choose who our parents are." If all of what Myles claimed was true, didn't that make Egan a sort of parent to her? He'd taken her to the palace after her people were destroyed. He'd made sure she was safe and cared for. In his way.

Myles shrugged. "Sure, we can."

"It's that simple for you, isn't it?"

"Everything is simple if we try to make it so."

Riona shook her head but didn't respond. Her life was anything but simple.

Gulliver rested his chin on his knees. "I want it to be that simple."

In those words, Riona heard herself. She didn't want to be the indentured servant who couldn't escape the king. She didn't want the prison magic to fall, thrusting the Dark Fae into the realm of the Light only for them to be persecuted for their physical differences.

"Griff will change the world so everything can be simple."

Riona met Myles' gaze. She'd rarely heard the human say anything without a joking tone. Until now. "How do you have so much faith in him? Unlike the rest of your people, you know who he is, what he's done."

"I don't have faith in *him*. I have faith in *people*. Anyone can change if they try hard enough."

Riona tore her eyes away from him. "I don't believe that."

"Then I'm sorry for you." He drew in a deep breath. "I don't like what Griff did to me. I don't like how he hurt people I love, but that was ten years ago. And from what I hear, that was ten years of Griffin protecting the people he cared about, fighting for the ones who couldn't fight for themselves. I want him to deserve my faith, but for that, I need to give him a chance."

In the distance, Griffin started down the hill. Riona watched his every movement. "Your human ideals could be the thing that breaks you."

Myles shook his head. "No. My human ideals keep me grounded in a world so unlike my own. If I break, it will be because of fae duplicity. If you don't believe the best in people—or fae—it'll be a very lonely existence."

Gulliver jumped to his feet and ran toward Griffin. "Are you okay? Did you find it? What happens next?"

Griffin's face told Riona all she needed to know. He hadn't learned anything new. "The village wasn't really there, was it?" She crossed her arms.

Griffin put one hand on Gulliver's shoulder and rubbed his eyes with the other. "No, it was."

Riona climbed to her feet, wiping the grass from her trousers. "So, you were right? Your Iskalt magic allowed you to see it?"

Griffin sighed. "I don't know. They kept speaking of descendants of *the O'Rourke* being able to see it, but that's the thing. I don't have any Fargelsian blood in me, let alone Fargelsian royal blood."

"But you served a Fargelsian queen." Myles pushed himself off the ground to join the others. "Could that have something to do with it?"

He shook his head. "Regan raised me, but I had no real relation to her." He turned his gaze on Riona. "Before we leave, could you do a sweep of the area. Just to make sure we haven't missed anything."

"Yes." Her wings stretched to their full size, the night contrasting against the white brilliance of the wings, except for the dark shadows that crept along the edges. She thought there might be more darkness there now than there was earlier in the day, but she tried not to think about it. With a powerful flap, she jumped into the air, her entire body relaxing into the movement. Flying was a rare pleasure for her since she'd left Myrkur, and she'd missed it.

The damp air grew thinner the higher she went. She breathed it in as she changed direction and spiraled down toward the hill seeing nothing of the village Griffin claimed was there.

A light from something on the ground caught her eye, and she hovered over the hill, lowering slowly until her feet touched the grassy knoll. The light faded as if it was a dying magic, but Riona inched closer. Below where the light had been there was an odd-looking envelope. Wasting no time, she picked up the envelope and jumped into the air, letting her wings do most of the work.

Griffin looked up at her as she hovered above them. Myles grinned. "I don't think I could ever get used to watching someone fly."

Griffin issued a quiet "me either" but she was probably imagining the awe in his voice. Her face flushed as she set one foot on the ground and then the other. Her wings folded in naturally at her back.

"Did anyone see you?" Griffin asked.

"There would have to be people here to see me." She held out the envelope. "I found this."

Griffin took it and turned it over, having what seemed like the same thoughts as Riona. "It's clean."

Riona nodded. "Which means it was just recently left. There was a bit of light magic making sure I saw it."

"Open it." Gulliver bounced eagerly on his toes.

Riona couldn't blame him. They'd reached so many dead ends over the months that they were due for something helpful.

Griffin opened the envelope and pulled out a single square of colorful paper. "It's sticky on the back."

"That's because it's a Post-It." Myles smiled in excitement over a piece of paper. "On one of my trips to the human realm, Lochlan and I went shopping so Brea could have her human comforts. I bought a ton of Post-Its, and now my wife is obsessed with them."

"A queen is obsessed with a tiny piece of paper?"

Griffin's eyes focused on the odd little paper. "What does this mean?"

Riona took it from his hands and read it aloud. "Ashlin sends her regards. Come find us again to get the answers you seek."

"The old woman?" Myles rubbed the back of his neck. "The one who was abducted?"

"What if she wasn't?" Riona thought back to the cottage on the cliffs. "What if she only left in a hurry when she saw us coming?" Riona turned the paper over and froze. "More numbers."

"How many?" Griff asked. "Like the ones before? Myles, do you have your maps?"

Myles crossed his arms. "Yes, Griff. I brought them out into this field where we weren't supposed to have use for them."

"What about your phone? You said it could find things, information from someone named Google."

Myles tipped his head back, like he was searching the sky for patience. "Google is not a person, but we're in the middle of nowhere, an hour away from the city. I don't have service." He checked the time on the phone. "Let's go before the cab waiting for us leaves, and we really do get stuck."

Riona scowled, but there was no malice behind it, only a bone-deep weariness from chasing the smallest leads and still finding no trace of the book or the Iskalt kids.

They crossed the fields to get back to the road, and relief wound through Riona as she saw the yellow ... cab ... waiting for them. "If we had horses, they'd wait for us too." Sure, the cab was faster, but she couldn't shake the eerie feeling of sitting in something that didn't need a horse or water to move.

"Riona." Griffin released a weary sigh. "The human realm is different from ours, and we'll be here a while. I refuse to go back again without the twins or a way to save Shauna and Nessa. So, just get used to the idea that you won't understand most things here, and you need to trust me to know what I'm doing."

She climbed into the cab, not giving Griffin an answer. She wanted to trust him, everything inside her was begging her to tell him the truth. The problem was, once she did, he'd never trust her again. Once he learned of the book she used to communicate with Egan. When he knew of the magic tying her to the king.

He thought they were the same because they both served evil rulers, but it wasn't the same at all. By Griffin's own admission, Regan trusted him. Sort of. She let him go into the human world regularly or even to the other fae kingdoms.

But Egan ... Riona never got to be separated from him, she didn't get his trust, only his control.

Griffin would open his eyes to it one day and realize Riona didn't belong here with these people who would do anything to find the Iskalt twins. She didn't belong among the queens who'd defeated Regan. They were good, truly good. To their people, their friends, even those they didn't trust, like her.

Riona never got the chance to be good.

"You're quiet." Griffin nudged her as the cab bumped down the road. Her hand shot out to grab the door handle.

"These cabs give me stomach pains."

Myles leaned over. "If you puke, make sure it's on Griff, not me."

Griffin shot him a scowl. "Are you okay, Riona? Do we need to stop?"

In truth, it wasn't the cab making her sick to her stomach. She'd come to the realization that nothing in her life was a choice. Everything had been set for her.

And she would have no chance at doing good. As much as she wanted to be on Griffin's side, she knew she would obey Egan in the end.

They reached the inn while the moon still hung high over the city. The ride was only an hour long, yet Riona could have kissed the ground as they spilled out of the cab.

Myles paid the driver and waved to him before he took off. It was so ingrained in the human to be polite, to follow the rules of society.

"Are all humans like you, Myles?"

Myles cocked his head. "Like me?"

"You didn't trick the man to take less money. You smile at every stranger you see. You're ... nice to your fellow humans."

Myles laughed. "No, not all humans are like that. You should see where I grew up. People are a lot less trusting there."

Griffin ushered them all through the double glass doors. Riona took Griff's advice and tried not to be amazed at everything she saw. She clamped her lips shut when they rode the elevator, though she would have preferred to scream. That thing was *not* fun.

The four of them filed into Myles' and Gulliver's room. Myles immediately went to his bed where he'd left the map of Ireland. He unrolled it on one of the beds. "This is where we are." He pointed to a star. "Here's the last coordinates." He tapped a circled location. "I'm guessing the village is still in Ireland. I mean, I've seen some powerful magic, but none that could move a village across an ocean."

"Ocean?" Gulliver leaned closer.

"Giant body of water. They separate the continents. Ireland is an island in itself, which means to leave, one would need to fly across the ocean."

"Fly?" Gulliver's eyes lit up. "I knew humans had magic."

Myles groaned. "Not this again. Humans can fly in things called airplanes. It's technology."

Gulliver sank down onto the bed, his shoulders slumped.

"Griff, hand me the coordinates." Myles pulled his phone free. "I'll plug them into Google."

Riona still wasn't convinced Google wasn't a person. Maybe the one providing magic to all their technology.

"That can't be right." Myles stared down at the screen, his brow creased.

"What is it?" Griffin tried to see what Myles saw, but Myles nudged him out of the way. "What's wrong?"

"Nothing ... necessarily." Myles pushed a hand through his hair, worry dancing across his features. "Maybe ... I'll try again." His fingers flew over the screen while the three fae around him watched in awe. Humans had every bit of information at their fingertips. The thought of such a thing had Riona feeling very small. That box could do more than her. Her only magic was in the wings on her back.

Myles eyebrows drew together. "Same place. Let me pull up a bigger map."

"You're going to pull a map out of that ... phone?" Gulliver couldn't contain his interest.

"No, but it will let me see a map on the screen." He said nothing more for a long moment before lifting his face to Griff. "Ohio."

"Let me see that." Griffin took the phone, his jaw tightening. "Is this Grafton?"

Myles sat on the edge of his bed. "Griff, those coordinates can't be right. How does an entire Irish village just move to Grafton, Ohio?"

"What's in Grafton?" Riona's eyes went from one to the other.

"My parents, for one." Myles shook his head in disbelief. "And also the farm Brea grew up on. Lochlan purchased it years ago."

Griffin's eyes widened. "They've been there." He turned to Riona. "The first place we came to in the human realm."

"Where the sun nearly blinded us?" she asked.

He nodded. "Myles, when I was in the village, they kept mentioning me being a descendant of Sorcha's or her sister's. But ... I don't have Fargelsian blood."

"That you know of," Myles interjected.

"Yes, that I know of. But do you know who does have royal Fargelsian blood?"

"Brea." The name was a whisper on Myles' lips. "There has to be a reason their next coordinates were Grafton." His eyes widened. "And the twins. If Callum is after the book, he won't be able to see the village, but Tia and Tobey..."

"We have to get to Grafton. Traveling like humans will take too long."

Riona caught on to what they were saying. "Griff, if we want to portal there, we have to portal to the fae realm and then to Grafton hours later. Are you strong enough?"

Griffin rubbed his face. "I don't have a choice. Collect your belongings. We leave in half an hour."

Chapter 7

GRIFFIN

Griffin was able to open a portal to the moon garden at the center of the Iskalt Palace, the last location he'd portaled from. They arrived back at the palace at mid-afternoon, and Griffin was grateful he had the excuse of daylight to avoid making another portal right away. There was something very wrong with his O'Shea magic. Without the full use of his Iskalt magic to fuel his O'Shea magic, it was somehow running out of steam. It was getting harder and harder to travel between the worlds, and the time skew grew more extreme each time.

They spent the afternoon in Lochlan's council chambers catching the king and queen up to speed on their findings, and after a hasty afternoon nap, it was time to leave for the human realm once more.

Griffin was beginning to think traveling the human way would have been much easier.

In the end, he couldn't open a portal large enough to pass through, so his brother had to step in and create one for them.

"Your magic is weak, brother," Lochlan said before Griffin stepped through the portal. "It is not your fault. This Dark Fae king will pay for what he's done to you and your people. We will get your magic back, and you will be strong again." Lochlan clapped him on the back, and with a wordless nod, Griffin stepped through the opening into the human realm to a fresh wave of sunlight, high in the sky. He wanted to weep at the sight. He was so tired, he couldn't count how many hours he'd been on his feet.

Gulliver stood on the back porch of Brea's childhood home, the door open, but neither he nor Riona seemed inclined to step inside.

"Did you break in?" Griffin asked, eager to make a bed in the barn and forget this day wasn't over yet. He had another invisible village to find. "And where is Myles?" He glanced around for their human chaperone.

"He ran off to see his family," Riona said absently. "Said he'd be back by sunset."

"Get to the part where you broke into Brea's old house, Gulliver."

"Key." Gulliver held up a silver keychain with a set of house keys as explanation.

"Did you steal them, or did Brea give them to you?"

"Brea gave them to us, said she has someone in the human realm to keep the house clean and stocked. Brea came here earlier to get us takeout—whatever that means—and said we should make ourselves at home."

"Then why are we out here and not in there?" Griffin asked.

"I'm not going in there." Riona backed away. "I think I'd rather sleep in the barn."

"What's wrong?"

Gulliver pointed into the dark entryway, and Griffin peeked inside, startled to see two human machines whirling and banging in the small mud room.

He had more experience with human machinery than these two, but household contraptions weren't his specialty. Particularly ones that made noise. Still, he knew enough not to fear them. "It's just a machine." He stepped inside, hoping he could figure out how to turn them off.

He touched the white front of the spinning machine to find it was quite hot. Something was inside, tumbling around and around. The machine made a loud beep, and Griffin jumped back. He turned to see Gulliver and Riona were halfway across the yard.

"It's okay, it stopped," Griffin called. He opened the hot door and stepped back, expecting steam or hot air to sweep out of the machine. Nothing happened, so he bent to look inside.

"Oh!" He stood up, checking the other machine filled with water. "I know what this is!" He waved Riona and Gulliver inside. "It's okay, come in."

"What is it?" Gulliver asked, clutching Riona's hand. Griffin wasn't sure if it was for his own comfort or for hers.

"This one washes clothes, and the other one dries them. Look." He reached into the dryer and pulled out three sets of clean sheets for the beds.

Riona touched the fabric and pulled it close when she felt the warmth. "The smell is like a field of wildflowers." She buried her face in the sheet. "What's it for?"

"The beds." Griffin peered into the machine that was still washing something.

"What's the wet one for?" Gulliver asked.

"Probably for the blankets, but we should leave that for Myles. I don't want to blow Brea's machine up."

Riona stepped back again, still clutching the sheet. "Do they make a habit of exploding?"

"Not if we don't mess with it." Griffin steered them both into the kitchen where Brea had left them a note to make themselves at home and help themselves to the takeout in the fridge and that only Myles was allowed to run the microwave or other appliances.

"What's takeout?" Gulliver asked.

"What's a fridge?" Riona scowled at all the human contraptions around the kitchen.

"I know two of these things." Griffin opened the refrigerator to find takeout boxes of Chinese food for their dinner later. "Gulliver, you're going to love this ... once Myles gets back."

"Aw that smells good. Why do we have to wait?"

"It's better hot. I know that's what the microwave is for."

Griffin looked around the kitchen. "But I don't know which one that is, so we better not attempt it." Griffin put the food back in the fridge.

"I think we should try to sleep," Riona said. "My body thinks it's night." She swayed on her feet, holding her sheets like she wasn't about to give them up.

"Agreed." Griffin led them through the kitchen to the living room, feeling odd and a little uncomfortable in Brea's childhood home. "The bedrooms are probably upstairs." Griffin crept through the house like he shouldn't be there.

"Only one family lived here?" Riona shook her head in disbelief. "Brea's family must have been wealthy."

Griffin didn't have it in him to explain to her once again that what she saw was this world's version of borderline poverty.

"I get a bed to myself?" Gulliver's eyes widened at the queen size bed that used to belong to Brea's parents.

"You've been sleeping in a bed by yourself since we arrived in Iskalt," Griffin said.

"But that's in a palace," Riona said. "This is just a normal house, according to you."

"Make your beds and get some sleep." Griffin took a set of clean sheets from Riona and headed for the guest room, leaving Brea's old bedroom to Riona. He couldn't sleep there or in the room her parents once shared—a room she likely shared with Lochlan whenever they came here together. There were too many ghosts in this house already.

"What is this?" Riona stepped into his room holding a pink fluffy thing with a strap.

"Oh, Brea's note said she left you an eye mask on your pillow to help you sleep. Put it over your eyes, and it will block the sunlight."

Riona looked carefully at the sleep mask, nodding to herself. "I'm stealing this when we leave." She retreated across the hall to her room.

Griffin struggled with the sheets for much longer than necessary before he figured out how it worked. He hoped the others did better than he did. Collapsing in a heap under the cool, sweet smelling sheet, he fell asleep in moments.

Griffin woke to the sound of Myles' voice and the scent of something he didn't recognize.

His stomach growled at the memory of the Chinese food in the kitchen, and he rolled over, rubbing the sleep from his eyes. It was still light outside, but the sun was setting. He'd have his portal magic back soon, and he anticipated spending all night looking for the village somewhere around the rural areas near Brea's house. Possibly somewhere on the farm.

"Griff, you gotta try this 'umplin thing. It's so good." Gulliver's eyes lit with excitement when he joined them in the dining room.

"I think that's a dumpling, Gullie." Griffin took the seat beside him and grabbed the waxed carton with the spicy dumplings he liked.

"That's what I said." Gulliver slurped from a bowl of soup.

"Did you get to see your family?" Griffin asked Myles.

"Briefly." Myles yawned and patted his full stomach. "I fell asleep on Mom's couch, but it was good to see them."

Griffin helped himself to a little of everything, mixing the savory rice with the sweet red sauce he loved. Riona hadn't said much. She seemed to be focused on the food too.

Finally, she sat back and sighed, a contented smile on her face. "Gullie was right. Humans have the best food." She belched loudly and slapped a hand over her mouth, her cheeks flushing red before she burst out laughing.

Griffin laughed with her, happy to see her let her guard down. It happened so rarely, but he enjoyed the moments when he got to see glimpses of the real Riona.

His laughter froze as he looked past her through the window. He stood, shoving his empty plate aside as he paced to the window overlooking what was once a large pasture.

"What is it?" Riona leapt from her chair to join him. "What do you see?"

"It's here," Griffin whispered.

"What?" Gullie and Myles came to look at the yard bathed in moonlight.

"The village. It's right there in the pasture." Griffin pointed. "It looks just as it did in Ireland." The same crumbling pillars stood flanking a path through the tall grass, and he could just make out the cobblestone streets in the distance.

"Let's go then." Riona stepped toward the door.

"No need." Griffin's shoulders tensed. "Someone is coming here." A man made his way along the path through the pasture, looking over his shoulder as if he didn't want to be followed. "Stay inside." Griffin stepped through the kitchen and the mud room to the back porch. He wasn't too surprised when Riona ignored him and followed him into the yard. She stayed behind to watch as Griffin went to meet their mysterious visitor.

"You move across worlds quickly." It was the old man he'd met before. He came to a stop beneath the large oak tree at the edge of the pasture. A tire swing hung from the massive branches, and Griffin could imagine Brea playing there as a child.

"Someone was kind enough to leave directions." Griffin stood with his hands in his pockets, not sure how to proceed. He hadn't expected to find the village so quickly or to be confronted by the man who took it away before. His eyes flitted to the cane, preparing for the man to tap it and make the structures disappear, taking Griffin's hope with it.

"I told you to leave. You shouldna be here." The man's soft Irish burr took on a hard edge.

"Please, I don't know why I can see the village and my friends can't, but I'm supposed to be here."

"Yer a descendant. That much is plain." The man stepped forward, leaning heavily on his cane. "There was a time all descendants were friends." He held his hand out. "Seamas," he said simply.

"Griffin." Griffin shook his hand. "So, you're Fargelsian descendants?"

"I suppose we are at that." Seamas shrugged. "We're direct descendants of Grainne O'Rourke, Queen Sorcha's twin sister. And if you can see our village, then you are too."

"I can't imagine how. My blood is of Iskalt. I don't have Gelsi magic."

"Ye don't have to have the Gelsi power, but somewhere in your lineage yer linked with someone who does. Or did."

"What does it mean?"

"Ye know of the book?" Seamas asked.

Griffin nodded. "Though I'm starting to think I don't know nearly enough about it."

"Aye, that is true enough. The O'Rourke book of spells is powerful. Dangerous in the wrong hands. It is why I left ye in Ireland."

"Sorcha's book contains magic I desperately need." Griffin hoped this man would help him.

"It's na her book. She was keeper of it for a time, that is all. Its history reaches back further than just her or Grainne, though her descendants are the keepers now."

"You know where the book is?" Griffin glanced behind Seamas to the magical village he called home.

"Aye, it's there, and it's safe. That is all that matters. Ye canna have it. It's too dangerous and not mine to give."

"Can you show it to me?" Griffin asked. "I'd just like to see if it contains information to break a certain kind of spell. If it doesn't, I will move on and look elsewhere for a solution."

He didn't respond for a long moment, and Griffin was sure he'd tell him to leave and never return. But he didn't. "Come wi' me." Seamas turned toward the pasture. "Leave yer lady to watch over ye from afar."

Griffin followed the strange old man, waving to Riona not to follow.

"Ye canna see the book, Griffin. It's hidden within the village. I don't even know where it is, so don't ye ask. But tell me about this spell, and I'll do my best to help ye if I can."

Griff shivered as they passed through the stone pillars into the village. The magic of this place seemed to affect him more this time than it had on his last visit.

Seamas led him to a large building at the center of the village. Griffin was startled to find the place was a library. Dimly lit by candlelight, the large room was filled with shelf after shelf of aged books. Some leather bound and cracked. Some were mere scrolls of parchment and some were modern notebooks.

"What is this place?" Griffin looked around in awe. He could hear a faint whisper among the aisles of books. A sound like pages rustling as someone flipped through an open book.

"We are the keepers of magic," Seamas explained, putting his cane across the doorway, drawing Griffin's attention away from the books. "Ye canna enter here. We don't know ye, young sir. Descendants who want to join us must first undergo a wee bit of testing of yer loyalties. After ye were seen in the village before, our elders gave me a talking to. I was not ter turn ye away without telling ye who we were."

Seamas sighed. "Apparently, you aren't the first to inquire of late."

"So, you're the keepers of the book's magic?"

"No, boy. We're the keepers of *all* magic."

Griffin felt uneasy as he put a hand on the wall to brace himself. The whispering sounds grew louder as Seamas spoke. It was as if the sound were intent on overpowering Seamas' voice.

"The ancient powers have been largely forgotten through the centuries as knowledge passed down through families. What most fae use today pales in comparison to what they once knew in the distant past. The O'Rourke ancestors have always kept a complete record of their Gelsi magic."

"The book?" Griffin asked, trying to focus on Seamas' words.

Seamas shook his head. "The Book holds many spells, aye, but it doesna hold all the secrets to the ancient powers. This room is that record, and the book is the key to accessing these records. I can try to help you, Griffin, but then ye need to go and na come back. The elders will try an convince ye to stay, but ye need to go. This is not the place for you."

Griffin had no intention of staying once he found what he needed to know. He crossed his arms over his chest as he explained the boundary magic Sorcha placed around Myrkur.

"Aye, we know of the prison realm. It isna wise to bring it down. That kind of magic changes over time. Becomes something else. It's best left alone."

"Unfortunately, that is not an option." Griffin's ears buzzed with the whispering sound growing louder, like an alarm trying to warn him of danger.

"Yer na the first to come asking about dangerous magic. Another woman came looking for the book not too long ago. She was a descendant and knew of our village. We had to turn her away. Another man came looking. He wasna a descendent and couldna see our village. But the wee ones he had with him could."

"Children?" Griffin stood up straighter.

"Aye. Young ones. A boy and a girl."

"How long ago was this?" Griffin asked.

"A month or so ago." Seamas shrugged.

"Do you know where he went?"

"It doesna matter, the wee ones didn't tell him what they saw."

"It matters to me. To their parents!" Griffin slammed his fist against the rough wood of the door frame. "Did you speak to them like you spoke to me?"

"No, we let them pass from the village. There was no need to interfere since they posed no danger to the village." His eyes shifted away, and something about the tone of his voice made Griffin uneasy.

Griffin wasn't sure he believed him. "That man poses a threat to our whole world."

Seamas leaned forward his eyes narrowed to slits. "Yer contemplating magic that ought to be left alone. Can I not sway you to go home and not think of it again?"

"The lives of people I love are at risk if I do not find this book." The hair raised on the back of Griffin's neck, and he stood, backing away from Seamas toward the door. The whispering grew louder. He could almost make out a voice. A word.

Leave.

Griffin didn't need to be told twice. He turned and threw the door open.

"I'm afraid we canna allow you to leave now." Seamas followed him at a walk. Seemingly unconcerned with Griffin's quick departure from the library.

"I'm afraid you can't stop me." Griffin stumbled over the cobblestones.

"We are leaving this place. You will come with us." Seamas stood at the center of the street as an unnatural fog rolled in. "We must protect our knowledge, Griffin. The two worlds are at stake, and you're trying to play with dangerous magic."

Griffin panicked and did the only thing he could. He opened a portal to the moon garden at his brother's palace in Iskalt.

A hand gripped his shoulder at the last second and Griffin's heart thundered in his chest as he made the leap. Whoever grabbed him was coming to Iskalt with him.

Chapter 8

GRIFFIN

Griffin O'Shea had traveled by portal since he was a child. Traveling to and from the human realm was not supposed to be a difficult task for an O'Shea. But never before had he become stuck inside one.

The unfamiliar grip on his shoulder tightened as a long tunnel stretched out before him. Whispers echoed around him, beckoning him to follow. He moved slowly, as though engulfed in swamp water, the mud and muck making his movements sluggish.

Violet light flashed and flickered along the tunnel, like strikes of lightening from an angry sky just before a storm. A familiar, comforting sound filled his ears. Singing.

The whispering voices didn't like the song.

But this voice was sweet and melodic, drowning out the frightening whispers. He knew this voice as well as his own, but he couldn't recall how.

He could just make out her form in the distance, her blue dress billowing out behind her like watered silk. Her voice was angelic and powerful, as though it was the source of her fae magic. No creature of the human realm or of Myr could create such a sound. Such a sense of peace.

A lullaby.

One Griffin knew from his childhood.

Regan? He moved to follow her, but the hand on his shoulder held him back.

The woman turned to smile at him. She clutched a book in her arms, a tear coursed down her cheek like a fine drop of crystal.

Something pulled at Griffin's soul. The whispers chanted for him to follow her. To take back what was lost to him.

Dark clouds rolled in, and thunder shook the ground beneath him. She was gone, but her song lingered. Still the whispering called to him, begging him to find her among the swirling shapes and foreign sounds.

Tall buildings emerged from the clouds, their windows reflecting the brilliant light of the sun. Earthly sounds reached him now. Blaring horns, the odd human music he never seemed to understand no matter how often Brea had tried to explain it to him. Black city streets flashed by, the orange painted traffic lines as useless to him as ever. Flashing lights, too many people. Crosswalks. Odd human smells. Sirens. So much noise, Griffin would never make sense of it all.

Then he saw green grass. Trees. Birds. Familiar things, but it was only a flash of these things before the city returned. Loud and obnoxious, but somehow more pleasant. The aromas here were appealing, and the buildings less intimidating. The city streets flew past him in a grid pattern. Easy to remember, if only he could make sense of it.

The fae woman's song cut off abruptly, and the sounds of the city bombarded him. A scream chilled his blood, and the tunnel turned red.

The cloying scent of blood filled his senses just as Griffin stepped into Iskalt and his knees buckled beneath him. Unfamiliar arms lifted him from the ground and carried him inside the palace.

"Griffin?" Brea's voice called to him from the portal, urging him to come back.

Griffin's eyes fluttered open, and he sat up straight, making the room spin. "What happened?" He rubbed his eyes, trying to find his equilibrium.

"You made an unscheduled trip back to Iskalt," Lochlan said, peering over the edge of the settee with a frown at his younger brother. "You don't look so good."

Griffin took Brea's offered hand and moved to sit up. "I just arrived?" He shook his head, but the whispering still called to him.

"You arrived hours ago." Brea clutched his hand.

"And you didn't arrive alone," Lochlan added, his arms crossed over his chest.

Griffin grabbed his shoulder, remembering the moment before he leaped into his hastily made portal.

"Who is this ... creature you've brought back with you?"

"I am Dark Fae," the man said in a familiar voice. "The conduit."

"Nihal?" Griffin moved to stand up from the settee in Lochlan's study.

"It was time I left Aghadoon." Nihal shrugged.

"So it was you helping us? This whole time?" Griffin took a step toward the man, clutching Brea for support. "You gave us the coordinates?"

The big man nodded, his dark wings flexing. He reminded Griffin of Riona and the others he'd left behind.

"And you are?" Brea asked.

"I am Nihal, your Majesty." He gave a curt bow. "I am sorry I did not introduce myself before Griffin woke, but it was he I needed to speak with."

"And you have been helping my brother?" Lochlan asked.

"Several times," Griffin said with a shake of his head to clear the cobwebs from his mind. "We wouldn't have made it to Iskalt alive without Nihal's help." Griffin broke away from Brea and stumbled toward the Dark Fae to shake his hand. "Thank you. I think—no, I know—we would never have gotten this far without your aid." The whispering was fading from his mind, but the echo of the song was still with him.

"That was your music? In the portal? Did you do something?"

"That was all you, Griffin O'Shea. Something is very wrong with your magic. You are not well."

"We should let him rest," Brea said.

"No, Brea. He has them." Griffin shot her a look. "Callum was seen with Tia and Toby in the human world weeks ago. We cannot afford to slow down now."

"Are they okay? Who saw them? How are they?" Brea tugged on his shirtsleeve, demanding answers he didn't have.

"I don't know, Brea, but I think I know where we need to go next." He needed to find the woman he saw in the portal. Myles would help him find the right city. Griffin headed toward the garden, thankful the sun had set when he was unconscious.

"And where do you think you're going?" Lochlan followed him.

"I have to go back." Griffin stumbled across the uneven stones into the moon garden, Brea and Lochlan following close on his heels.

"You're too sick to travel." Lochlan tried to pull him back inside.

"I can't leave them there alone." Griffin shivered in the cold, his ragged hot breath puffed out around him.

"Please, Griffin," Brea begged, her cheeks stained with tears for her children. "Just stay the night with us, and then Lochlan will open a portal for you tomorrow at moonrise. You're not well."

"Listen to your family, Griffin," Nihal said. "Tomorrow will be soon enough."

"No, I have to leave now." Griffin wiped the sweat from his forehead, not pausing long enough to think about how he shouldn't be sweating in the cold Iskalt night.

"I had to come here to escape the village. Now that I've given you an update on Tia and Toby's whereabouts, I have to get back to work." He wasn't sure where Callum would take them, only that they were with him in the human realm, and the woman he saw in the portal was the key to finding them and ending this for good.

"If you won't open a portal for us, then I will." Griffin turned to his brother, knowing full well if he tried to open a portal right now, it wouldn't happen.

"Will you rest when you get back?" Lochlan asked. "Or do I have to go with you and make you?"

"I'll rest for a little while if I must." Griffin couldn't get the song out of his head. Even now, his mind throbbed with the melody.

"I'll see he arrives safely." Nihal stepped to Griffin's side to take his arm.

"Be careful, brother." Lochlan took a deep breath and spread his arms wide to open a portal to their home in the human world.

Griffin nodded, clasping his brother's hand one last time. He leaned on Nihal's arm, and together they stepped into the early morning light under the large oak tree in the yard where he'd left Riona. She sat there now, awaiting his return.

"What are you doing here?" Riona gaped at Nihal.

Griffin's mind swirled with whispers and songs from his childhood, but he looked to the pasture to see the village was gone. With a deep breath, he shook his head. "How long was I gone?"

"A long time," Riona said. "I saw you run across the pasture, and then you disappeared into your portal."

"When was that?"

"Yesterday."

Griffin swayed on his feet, his head spinning as he sank to the ground in a boneless heap.

CHAPTER 9

RIONA

Riona couldn't remember worrying about anyone. She'd never experienced the fear that came with illness or the waiting because she'd never cared about anyone enough to fear their death. That was the worst part. She didn't want to care. "Griffin." She knocked on the door again. "Are you okay?" She heard the water running before the door to the washroom opened, revealing a sweating Griffin who could barely keep his head up.

"I'm fine." He tried to brush past her, but his steps faltered, and he slammed his shoulder into the wall.

"You are not fine." She took his arm and guided him down the hallway to the bed he'd claimed.

Something happened when he went into that village she couldn't see, but he never had the chance to tell them. As soon as he portaled back to the house—with Nihal—he'd collapsed into a heap on the grass. It took all of Riona and Nihal's strength to get him up the steps and into the house.

Kicking open the door, Riona helped Griffin to the bed. He collapsed onto it with a groan. Indecision warred within Riona. A part of her wanted to let Gulliver take care of Griffin. Or Myles because it seemed like a very human thing to get sick. Or at least, she assumed so. She'd kept her distance from those who fell ill at the palace of Myrkur. She'd heard of the things that could happen to the sick.

She sat on the corner of the bed, watching Griffin as if she'd never seen him before. The fae she'd met in Myrkur was strong, resilient—though she'd never admit those things to him. Riona had admired him from the moment he refused to kill her in the pits.

Myles appeared in the doorway, his eyes going wide. "He's still not well?"

Riona shook her head. They'd expected him to recover quickly once the portal magic settled down.

Myles set a cup of water on the table beside the bed. "Right now, we need to get him hydrated. Eventually, we'll have to get some food in him since he's puked acid the last two times he's thrown up."

"Acid? How does one puke acid?"

Myles pinned her with a look. "You fae could really benefit from some science lessons. Maybe I'll start a college when I get back to Fargelsi for Muggle Studies." He snorted out a laugh. "Your stomach has acid in it that helps break down the food you eat. So, once he was done throwing up everything else in his stomach, only acid was left."

Myles rubbed his eyes. "I've seen so few fae get sick."

"I've seen many." Gulliver stood in the doorway, his eyes on Griffin's sleeping form.

Riona stood. "That's not possible. If there was some sort of sickness, we'd have heard of it at the palace." *We*. Gulliver's scowl told her exactly how he felt about that *we*. Riona and Egan. Egan and Riona.

Myles looked from Gulliver to Riona. "From what I've gathered, the real pandemic in Myrkur is extreme poverty. I'm not surprised you two had different experiences with fae illnesses." He looked down at Griffin. "Let's let him rest. I brought some food back from my parents' place." He stalked from the room, expecting the two fae to follow him.

They reached the kitchen where Myles opened a bag of bread—Riona couldn't believe it came in bags—and slathered a brown substance on it. "Peanut butter and jelly. I figured it was time you two try the most human food there is." He finished the sandwiches with a red gelatinous substance that did not look appealing and put them on the table.

Gulliver picked one up and took a giant bite, his smile growing as he ate. Riona tried hers in nibbles, but she wasn't hungry, not with worry filling every part of her. Though, it was delicious, she had to admit.

"Gulliver." Myles leaned forward in his chair and rested his folded hands on the table. "I have lived in the fae realm for a long time, but at times like these, I feel more like my human self in my ignorance. You say many have fallen ill in the prison realm?"

Gulliver set his sandwich down and swallowed. "Before we left, there was a woman in our village, Sinead. She couldn't get out of bed without help. Most people wouldn't go near her, worried it was some Light Fae plague."

"So, she was a prisoner?" Riona asked.

Myles shot her a scowl. "Isn't everyone behind that magic a prisoner?"

Riona sighed and looked away. "No. Most of the Dark Fae living in Myrkur are there because it was once their kingdom. Generations of them were trapped once the magic was put in place. But Light Fae ... yes, they're there for a reason, some crime they committed—or they are descended from prisoners sent there."

"And their magic is taken?"

"Yes." Riona focused her gaze on the table. "That's the way the border magic works. No Light Fae who enters Myrkur keeps their magic. It is how we keep the peace within our borders."

Gulliver slammed his fist on the table, startling both Myles and Riona. "That's not true, and you know it. The way to keep the peace is to let us live in peace. But you and your king can't do that, can you? In Myrkur, you destroy everything you touch. We Dark Fae are just as much prisoners as the rest. And now Griff is sick just like Sinead. I blame you. I blame Egan. You took their magic. Light Fae are supposed to have power running through their veins."

Riona had nothing to say about his outburst. Gulliver wasn't wrong. There was no peace in Myrkur because Egan wanted to keep them weak so he remained strong. Maybe they didn't deserve peace. But the Dark Fae? The ones whose only magic lay in the features that made them different ... she'd helped him keep them in line too. Rising from her chair, Riona met Gulliver's angry, cat-like gaze. "I'm going to make sure Griff drinks that water."

When she reached the quiet of Griffin's room, she leaned against the door, letting her heart return to its natural rhythm. Lifting one arm, she watched the tattoos slither and change with no reason she'd ever been able to find. There was one fae she could ask, but she couldn't bring herself to go in search of Nihal quite yet. Gulliver was right about many things. Riona was a Dark Fae, one whose secrets were hidden, even from herself. She didn't know why she was the last of her kind. Well, she and Nihal were the last. Yet, she didn't even know the meaning of the messages etched into her very skin.

Riona reached the bed in two strides. She stared down at Griffin's calm expression. In sleep, he didn't have a haunted look about him. She couldn't imagine how it felt to walk around in a home where no one recognized him.

Her fingers brushed auburn hair away from his face. His lips moved as if he had something to say. The water had only been an excuse. She wouldn't wake Griffin when what he needed most was rest. "Please be okay," she whispered. "I can't do this without you." And what was *this*? Find the book? Get it to Egan?

Or discover a way to free themselves completely from Egan's hold?

"Riona," Myles whispered. She hadn't noticed him opening the door. "We need to talk."

"Where's Gulliver?"

"He went out with Nihal for a walk. The kid needed to blow off steam."

She wasn't sure what the odd phrase meant, but she understood the sincerity behind it. Myles was one of the few people from Griffin's life who had stopped looking at her with distrust in his eyes. Did that make him more perceptive or less?

She followed Myles to the backdoor. He slid it open, and they stepped onto the wooden deck. From there, they could see much of the surrounding lands. Fields that went unplanted, equipment that sat rusting in the sun. "This place is sad."

Myles rested his arms on the rail. "The Robinsons were pretty awful people. The day Griffin abducted Brea and took her to the fae realm, it changed her life for the better—ultimately, I mean. Finding out the Robinson's weren't Brea's parents made a lot of sense. She was always meant for better things than living with people who never treated her like a daughter."

"It is odd to me that a fae queen lived in the human world."

Myles shrugged, his expression turning serious. "I have a theory about Griff."

Riona leaned her back on the rail beside him. "Is it a theory that'll get us killed?"

"I honestly don't know. This entire mission reeks of death to me."

"Okay, I just wanted to know in advance. Go on."

"Fargelsi has the most extensive library in the fae realm—my wife's doing. She didn't grow up a royal. Instead, she was a servant who didn't know her father was the rightful king. The servants to Queen Regan weren't allowed to learn. Now, my wife makes sure everyone has the chance at schooling."

"An honorable endeavor."

"Yes. There are a number of books for children in particular. They use them to teach children to read. One such book is called *A Power to Understand*. It tells the story of a woman who loses her magic. She spends the entire book trying to do good works, hoping it will be returned to her. As she goes along, she becomes ill. It worsens and worsens, but she can't stop her altruistic way of living."

"Does the illness go away?"

He nodded. "At the end of the book, she does one last deed before dying. Saving the life of the king. He sees to it that her magic is restored. Within minutes, the illness is gone. She still dies, but it's her age that kills her."

"But it's just a story." Riona's brow furrowed. "Right?"

Myles looked over his shoulder at the house. "I thought so. But Gulliver told me more about Sinead in Myrkur. I think Griffin might have the same thing, and it's made worse every time he opens a portal."

Riona turned to look out over the fields that should be teeming with life. The same could be said for Griffin. "So, what do we need to do?"

"Not me." Myles met her gaze. "I cannot help. But the story says the illness is triggered in some people by losing and then regaining only a portion of their magic. You see, the bodies of Light Fae aren't meant to remain stable without the full use of their magic. The power strengthens every part of them. Without it, they start to crumble. I'm guessing it is Egan's doing."

"How am I supposed to help?"

Myles shrugged. "You'll find a way."

Riona watched him re-enter the house, her chest tight. She sucked in a deep breath. Did Myles know she communicated with Egan? Did Griffin?

Closing her eyes against the sun, she exhaled, letting it empty her out.

Back inside, Riona went directly to her room, which she'd been told was Brea's as a kid. She rummaged through her bag until her fingers found the familiar cracked leather. Would the journal work between worlds? She'd only ever contacted Egan in the fae realm when his magic tugged at her.

Her eyes widened as she realized she hadn't felt his power since leaving Iskalt. The noose around her was gone. As long as she stayed in the human realm.

She opened the notebook and reached for the quill that would write her words without ink.

My King. Can you read this?

She waited with bated breath. Egan was the only fae who could save Griffin—if the children's story was true.

A few minutes passed before Egan's words appeared below hers.

You're late.

She was supposed to have contacted him yesterday.

I didn't know if the journal would work. And we've been busy following the village from Ireland to Ohio.

His response took so long she feared she'd angered him.

Have you located the book?

She stared at the words, not sure how he'd react if he learned they were still no closer to finding the book.

No. But we are close.

She could see his signature scowl in her mind.

Don't let me down.

This was her opening, she knew it.

There is something else, sire. Griffin has fallen ill. We think it's of a magical nature, and we know how to cure him. Without Griffin, we will not be able to bring the book to the fae realm.

Riona waited. And waited. Finally, a response came.

He needs his magic back.

How did he know? Were more fae in Myrkur ill?

Please, sire. We need him to accomplish our mission.

Egan didn't respond. After a few minutes staring at the journal for his words to appear, she slid a hand over their entire conversation, making it disappear with her touch the book recognized.

A throat clearing in the doorway had her shoving the book under a pillow. Gulliver stepped in, his arms crossed over his chest. "Riona."

She tried to erase the perpetual frown from her face, but Gulliver's words still wound through her mind. "Are you finished being a child?" He was young but youth did not excuse poor behavior. It was a policy they'd adapted in the prison realm.

He leaned against the doorframe. "Are you done betraying us?"

"Betraying you?" Riona sputtered. Her eyes flicked to where she'd hidden the book.

"We should be doing everything we can to help Griff, and you're in here writing in your journal. I don't know why Griff keeps insisting there's good in you. I see you in my dreams, Riona. Did you know that? I see the moment you almost killed Griff in the fighting pits. You didn't hesitate. Yet, he spared your life. I see you riding atop a dark horse—though, with wings, I have no clue why you'd need a horse—but you're destroying my village. You're what nightmares are made of."

His words shocked her, even though she knew the truth in them. She was not a fae to be trusted—she barely trusted herself—but she'd started thinking there was a bond building between her and Gulliver. The venom in his eyes was something she hadn't seen before. "Why do you say these things now?"

"Because Griff is going to die." Tears welled in his eyes. "He's going to die and leave me here with you until Lochlan finds us. You deserve to know that I will never hesitate in a fight. I won't let my opponent live. And those who betray me, betray Griff, will pay for it." With one final searing look, he pivoted on his heel and walked away, leaving Riona gaping behind him.

She was used to being hated by those in Myrkur. As the king's warrior, she knew what the other fae thought of her. She'd betrayed her race, the people slaughtered by Egan's men.

And yet, the hatred in Gulliver's eyes burned more painfully than any before.

She didn't want him to lose Griffin.

And her betrayal, her contact with Egan, just might be the thing that saved him in the end.

Chapter 10

GRIFFIN

Griffin found himself back in the fighting pits, waiting for the killing blow that would free him from the constant cycle of guilt and regret. Riona came at him, her wings stretching to the sky like she was an ethereal being, not mere fae. The tattoos along her arms spoke to him in a language he couldn't understand. He needed to find their true meaning.

But he wouldn't get the chance. He cowered as she raised a sword above her head. Before she brought it down, blackness crept along the edges of her wings, eventually spreading like spilled ink across blank parchment.

"Kill him," Egan commanded.

Nearby, a woman sang a familiar song, but Griffin couldn't quite make out the words. His surroundings changed, and he was back in Fela watching his people lose everything.

The lullaby strengthened, getting louder and louder until it was all he heard as the horrors of the prison realm flashed across his mind.

Shauna and Nessa with the red roadmap of a whip across their backs.

Gulliver and his truncated tail.

"You're going to be too late." Griffin didn't know who whispered the words, but they had his eyes shooting open. His chest heaved with labored breaths, and sweat dripped down his face.

"Too late," he yelped.

"Griff?" Gulliver sat in a low chair beside the bed.

"Gullie." It was a dream, but it wasn't. Everything he saw had come to pass, and now he knew he'd be too late to prevent the worst of it. He lifted a weak hand to brush damp hair out of his face. "What are you sitting on?"

Gulliver grinned. "Myles says it's called a bean bag chair. It's quite comfortable. Though, I don't understand why anyone would waste perfectly good beans on a chair. Maybe it's a way of storing them to eat later on." He shrugged. "Humans are very strange, aren't they?"

Griffin rolled onto his side to stare down at Gulliver. "How long have I been out?"

"Two days." He shot him a pointed look. "Riona wanted to wake you yesterday, but Myles and I didn't let her. There's also another man here. Nihal, do you remember him? The guy who accidentally shipwrecked us on that island and then refused to tell us anything. Yeah, him and Riona are getting along great." There was too much sarcasm in that last sentence for it to be true. Riona didn't get along with anyone.

But Nihal wasn't just anyone. He and Riona were the last of their kind.

"Oh." Gulliver stood. "Also, the village is gone."

Griffin nodded, grabbing his head as pain stabbed through his skull. "That's why I portaled back to Iskalt at the last second, they tried to move the village while I was still in it. They didn't take anyone, did they? Gullie, help me up."

"No, we're all still here." Gulliver crossed his arms. "Myles thinks you should say please when asking me to do things. Human manners. I quite like the idea."

Griffin groaned. Gulliver had spent way too much time with Myles. "Fine. Gulliver, will you *please* help up the man who raised you? The one who kept you safe all these years without human manners getting in the way."

"Jesus H. Roosevelt Christ, don't get your panties in a bunch."

That was it. "Myles! Get your human self in here right this minute."

Footsteps sounded outside the door before Myles opened it. "You're awake. Good." He looked too Gulliver. "Did he say please?"

"Myles, what have you been watching with Gulliver?" It was the only explanation for his new human phrases.

"Oh." Myles laughed. "Well, Brea left her copy of the *Outlander* series. She always told me Jaime was the only human as beautiful as the fae, but I've got to say, I'm not seeing it. I mean, he's okay looking."

"It's the hair." Gulliver pursed his lips as if deep in thought. "It usually looks like it's in need of a wash."

"You know ... you're right."

Griffin sighed. "Will you two stop debating Jamie's attractiveness and help me get up?"

Myles lifted a brow. "What do you say, Griff?"

Griffin growled. "Please."

A smile tilted Myles' lips. "Just be glad I'm not making you call me Majesty. Because I am a king, you know."

Gulliver nodded. "He is." He held out a hand to help Griffin from the bed.

Griffin slid his legs over the side of the bed until his feet hit the carpet. "If we're ever going to find the twins and the book, I have to talk to Nihal." Griffin didn't understand why Nihal was still here if the village left.

"Okay." Myles took his other arm. "Do you want to hear my theory of you being sick?"

"Are you going to tell me, or just let this awkward silence continue?"

"Someone is grumpy." Myles led him out into the hall. "So, I think this is a magic illness. Light Fae bodies are made to hold magic.

Without it, they can survive for a time—years even—before the illness is triggered."

"And how is it triggered?" Griffin focused on his feet so he didn't fall.

"By having only a part of your magic returned. Since that magic has nothing to latch on to, it sort of just floats in your body, causing harm every time you have to use it. Or even if you don't use it. It breaks down the magic wielder's cells."

Griffin didn't know what cells were or how Myles came to such a conclusion, but it made sense. Which also meant ... "The only way to cure me is getting my full power."

Myles nodded. "I think so."

But Griffin wasn't the only fae to fall ill. Sinead and who knew how many others had as well. "I need to talk to Riona."

Myles paused. "I thought you needed to talk to Nihal. He's outside. He won't come into the human house until you speak with him."

"I need them both." He looked to Gulliver. "Will you fetch Riona? Please."

Gulliver shared a smile with Myles. "I told you he could learn to be nice." He bounced away to find Riona.

Myles led him outside to where Nihal rested in the shade, his back leaning up against the trunk of a tree. He played his piccolo with his eyes closed.

As Griffin neared, the song grew louder, a familiar song. Griffin stopped moving.

"What's wrong?" Myles looked from Griffin to Nihal who'd stopped playing as he noticed them.

"Nothing." Griffin wasn't ready to share what had happened in his portal or the song and the whispers he'd heard.

Nihal stood, a smile gracing his young face. "Your Highness." He bowed.

Griffin had told him before not to address him as a prince. He didn't deserve that title. "Nihal." Griffin nodded.

"Sit, sit. We have many things to discuss now that you've

returned to us."

Myles helped him sit and then backed away. "I'll leave you two to talk about the dangerous stuff. Plus, we found a ball. I'm going to teach Gulliver how to play football."

He walked away with only a single glance back. Griffin studied Nihal, looking for similarities to Riona. He didn't look as if he carried the weight of their ancestors on his shoulders. His blond hair fell into his bright green eyes. Where Riona's skin was dark, his was pale, almost white. Dark wings stretched out behind him. But it was the tattoos that provided the largest difference.

Riona's featured many colors that looked like they moved along her skin. Nihal's black tattoos sat stationary on his skin.

Griffin snapped out of his thoughts as his eyes drifted to the field the village had occupied only days before. "You left the village."

Nihal shrugged. "It was time. As the only resident who wasn't a descendant of Grainne, I wasn't exactly wanted there."

"Then why were you allowed to enter? How did you even see it?"

"Those are good questions, but they aren't the right ones."

Griffin leaned forward, absently picking blades of grass. "What do you want me to ask?"

"It isn't about me. There are questions that will help you in your search, and others that will only hinder."

"How do I tell the difference?"

"Just ask what's in your heart, Griffin O'Shea."

Griffin waited a long moment. "The village ... if we find it again, will the outcome be any different?"

Nihal thought over his answer. "No. You will get no further information from the village."

"It's not only information I seek, but the book they protect."

Nihal scooted away from the tree and unfurled his wings. They weren't quite as large as Riona's, but their beauty was in their strength. "Is that really what is in your heart, or your head?"

Griffin had asked questions he thought were relevant, but were they really in his heart?

He drew in a deep breath. "Play it again."

Nihal stared at him. "Play what?"

"The song I heard, the lullaby. I need to hear it again. Please." He needed to feel like he wasn't losing his mind hearing a song inside his portals and again in his dreams. A song he knew in his heart but had no memory of. Nothing made sense in this trek across the human realm.

The village was important, and then it wasn't.

His portals worked, and then they tried to trap him inside.

And now, he'd returned to the one place that held so much memory and none at all. He'd never spent much time at the Robinson farm, but it was the place that raised the girl who saved the fae realms from her own aunt, and from Griffin.

Nihal lifted the piccolo to his lips and started playing. As he did, Griffin's weakness fell away, carried by the rushing current of the song filling him in the way magic should, healing him—at least for the moment. "How is this possible?"

Nihal finished playing and lowered his piccolo. "Because the song is from the book of power. It grants temporary strength, but every page of that book comes at a cost. Many such pages have made their way into the fae realm by people like me—people granted portal magic by the book."

"Then you can open the next portal." Griffin sighed in relief, knowing the safety of his people didn't rest entirely on him.

Nihal shook his head.

"Don't do that," Griff pleaded. "Don't tell me I'm wrong. We need so desperately for something to work in our favor."

"My portal magic allows me to travel from Aghadoon to Talam only. That is why I had to tag along with you to Iskalt. It was from the island I dispersed various spells across the kingdoms with captains I trusted."

It sank into Griffin, the hopelessness. Without the village, Nihal couldn't help, and the village was now lost to them, right along with the book. "Why have I heard that song before?"

"These questions, your Highness, are important, and I will give you answers. But first, ask me the thing your heart most desires to know."

"Riona," he whispered. "Why do her tattoos shift and dance while yours remain dormant?"

Nihal's lips twisted into a half smile. "Now, this is a question of the heart. Creatures like Riona, like me—fae of the sea and sky—who've long had their kin destroyed, we live for a purpose. There was a reason Riona did not die when her village was destroyed. There was a reason the book chose me as its conduit to the fae realm, able to carry spells through portals."

Riona crossed the yard toward them, picking up on the conversation. "A reason?" She stared down at the two of them. "Egan saved me."

Nihal's smile turned sad. "No, Riona, I'm sorry but that isn't accurate. Your magic saved you."

"I have no magic."

"Ah, you've been taught the great lie of the Dark Fae. You may not have magic pulsing at your fingertips like the Light Fae, but what do you call the figures dancing on your skin? What do you call the wings on your back? Or the fact that you appear human in this realm to human eyes in a way Light Fae cannot? So, yes, Riona Nieland, your magic is quite powerful."

He stroked the edges of his wings like he would a beloved pet. "To answer the prince's question, my tattoos no longer hold any magic."

"How is that possible?" Riona lowered herself to the grass.

Nihal surveyed them both. "Because their purpose has been fulfilled. The book of power holds the knowledge needed to interpret our markings, it can show us the purpose that has been chosen for us."

Griffin released a stream of curses. "And we just let the village disappear with the book. This time, we don't have an ally on the inside."

Nihal waited for all sound to cease, for Griffin to get ahold of his anger, for Riona to look at him with something other than disgust.

She lifted her face. "What did your tattoos reveal about you?"

"They marked me as a conduit, able to use certain spells in the book despite having no magic inside me. But that is not my only purpose." He looked to Griffin. "Don't worry, Highness. The village may be gone, but what they don't yet know is the book has already been stolen. I know this, because I helped steal it."

It made sense now—why Nihal let the village leave without him. He was a thief, one who'd stolen the most dangerous book in all the worlds.

"If you stole the book, where is it?" Griffin demanded.

Nihal shrugged. "I said I helped steal it, not that it was ever in my possession." He lifted his piccolo once more and played a new song, one that had the beat of Griffin's heart calming.

Griffin shook off the effect. "We need to go after the book."

"Yes." Nihal sighed, pulling the instrument away. "I suppose we do. You are not the only one looking."

"Callum," he breathed, meeting Riona's dark gaze. "Nihal, you must have seen the twins. How long has it been?"

"Three weeks, maybe four. I remember two children clinging to each other as they asked questions that obviously weren't for their benefit."

Griffin frowned. "Seamas told me they ignored the twins because they didn't pose a threat to the book. Callum eventually left because no one would respond to the twins' questions."

Nihal shook his head. "Seamas did not give you the full truth. He knew how dangerous the O'Rourke twins are to the book. The elders did refuse to acknowledge them, but they also cast them out of the village."

He wanted to ask why, but the book took precedence. If the book truly was no longer in the village, Griffin had to get to it before Callum could. He could save Shauna and Nessa.

Griffin stood, surprised by the strength the song gave him. He brushed off his pants. "We leave at nightfall. Nihal, you will lead us to the book." He was their only chance.

"Yes, your Highness. Ashlin took the book to protect it, but she can't continue to do it alone."

Ashlin? Griffin tried to recall where he'd heard the name. His eyes widened. "The old lady? She has the book?"

Nihal leaned his head back and closed his eyes. "When it comes to this book, this magic, not everything is as it seems. You'd be wise to remember that." He lifted his piccolo and Griffin walked back to the house, the music bolstering him.

Riona followed him down the long hall before a thought came to Griffin, the reason he'd wanted to see her earlier. He turned on his heel, and she almost slammed into him.

She didn't get mad or annoyed. Instead, she looked like she was trapped in her own thoughts.

"Riona." Griffin shook her shoulder. "Riona."

She snapped out of whatever daze she'd been in. "What?"

Griffin stepped away and rubbed the back of his neck. "Does Egan return parts of a fae's magic often?"

She shook her head. "You were the first. At least the first I knew of." But she wouldn't meet his eye.

That didn't make sense. Egan needed Griffin. He wouldn't risk doing something so volatile on him unless he knew it would work.

The truth sparked within him. Sinead. "He tested it." His jaw clenched. "How many?"

Riona looked like she was biting back a lie. "I really don't know, Griff. That's the truth. I know there were reports of sudden illness in seven villages, but I don't know if it has anything to do with … tampering with magic."

It had everything to do with Egan tampering with magic he knew nothing about. Griffin had never been so sure of anything. Egan must have experimented with returning small portions of power to Light Fae from different villages, seeing how far he could push them. He must have been counting on Griffin holding on until the book was back in Myrkur and he no longer needed Griffin.

"Myles," he called.

Myles appeared from the living room. "I'm sort of in the middle of the wedding scene right now."

"The what?" Griffin didn't take his eyes from Riona as he spoke to Myles.

"*Outlander*. Claire had to get really drunk to marry Jamie which is so totally not accurate. I mean, who wouldn't marry him? Well, I wouldn't. But plenty of others would want a piece of that? I'm definitely coming around on the hot knees thing."

"Myles." Griffin and Riona said it at the same time. "Shut up."

Myles shrugged. "Well, what did you want when you yelled my name?"

Griffin stepped away from Riona. "We leave at nightfall."

Myles' face sobered as he nodded. "We have another lead?"

Riona walked past them both. "You better be right to trust Nihal, Griff. I'm tired of dead ends."

Griffin sighed once she was no longer in sight. He couldn't quite figure Riona out. Sometimes she went out of her way to take care of him and others she wanted nothing to do with him. There was more pain inside her than he'd imagined.

Myles didn't move to go back to his show. "She's right, Griff. We can't keep chasing leads unless we find something soon. I'm a dad now as well as a king, and no matter how vital it is we get to this book, nothing is more important than my kids. They need me to come home."

Griffin stared at him as he walked back into the living room. He was right. They all had fae relying on them. Shauna and Nessa were never far from his mind.

But neither was the promise to Brea. He couldn't end this mission until Tia and Toby were safe at home where they belonged.

Chapter 11

RIONA

My Lord, we have a new path. Though Griffin has grown ill and struggles to use his portal magic. I fear his illness could become a hindrance to your Majesty's goals.

Riona was familiar with the stabbing pains of guilt that plagued her whenever she communicated with Egan now. She was torn. Torn between doing what was right and what her king demanded. If she defied him ... she was as good as dead.

She rested her head against Brea's old headboard. Her few belongings were packed, and it was time to move on. She likely wouldn't have privacy again for some time. Perhaps not until this was all over, and she was back in Myr where she belonged.

Riona didn't want to know what awaited her should she go against her king. Egan's reach was far, and his hold on her never failed to remind her whose creature she was. Even now, she absently rubbed her chest, just over her heart where Egan's grip tightened like a noose. His reply was a long time in coming. She stared at the page in front of her, her pulse pounding in her ears as she waited for his biting words.

So, the boy is ill. Let that be his motivation to end this once and for all.

The old Riona would have jumped to do his bidding, knowing that was the key to her survival. Egan had saved her and raised her in what she'd once thought was great wealth. In some twisted way, she'd felt a sense of loyalty to him for that. She'd learned a long time ago to harden her heart to the suffering of others, but she still saw it. Many times, she caused it. That was all she'd ever known in Myr. She'd never had anyone to care about other than herself.

As you command, my Lord. The magic you seek shall soon be within my grasp.

Finish the deed and return to me. I grow weary of waiting, and my patience runs thin at the news of yet another lead. See that this is the last one. Your place is at my side, Riona. I would have you near me once again.

Riona knew Egan fancied himself as her father. She'd used that to her advantage over the years. But she was just a possession to him. Something exotic and ferocious he could brandish like a weapon.

She knew better now. Her eyes were open to the possibilities that lay outside of Myr. Yet, she would never fit into the world of the Light Fae. And the human world frightened her. In a weird way, she was homesick. But Riona no longer knew where home was for her.

This creature of the night is tired of the sun. I look forward to giving you an update in person soon.

Ever your servant,

Riona

She slammed the book shut, disgusted with herself. It was easy to follow Griffin and let herself forget she was the bad guy.

The sound of Nihal's song drifted up the stairs to her room. Even she could feel the boost in strength the sweet melody gave her. It chased away her sense of guilt, reminding her that the words she'd written were just words meant to pacify the king. She didn't really believe in them. Yet, she couldn't seem to decide how she would proceed in the end. Would she have the courage to stand with Griffin and let Egan's hold on her destroy her from the inside out? Or would she think only of herself and run back to the master who held her chains? Hoping he didn't kill Griffin or the others she'd grown to care about.

"Riona?" Gulliver peeked into the room. "Are you ready?"

"All set." Riona slipped her journal into her pack and scooted off the bed, turning to smooth the wrinkles from the quilt. She would leave the room as clean and orderly as she'd found it. In all her life, Riona had never had such a room like this. Not even growing up in Egan's castle. She'd lived with the other children who were wards of the king. And later, she'd moved into her stark cold room in the barracks. No matter what Griffin said, privacy and comfort like this was a luxury for the wealthy.

"I'm worried about Griff." Gulliver leaned against the door, waiting for her to finish tidying up. "He's too weak to open another portal."

"Nihal is helping him with that, giving him strength." Riona laid a comforting hand on his shoulder. "He will be fine, Gullie. We'll make sure of it."

"Can you get the king to give him his magic back?" Gulliver crossed his arms over his thin chest, looking between her and the book she'd just returned to her bag.

"If I could, I would." She sighed. "Our best bet is to help Griffin find this book and get him back to Lochlan and Brea." She shooed him out of the room, hoping the boy's endless questions had dried up for now.

"He's all I have, Riona." Gulliver's tail drooped lifelessly behind him.

Riona leaned down, gripping both of his shoulders. "I will not let anything happen to Griffin, you hear me?" She didn't know if it was a promise she could keep, but something inside her hoped it was.

Gulliver nodded, and they made their way down the stairs to the sound of Nihal's lullaby.

Riona gasped when she stepped into the living room to find Griffin sitting on the edge of the couch with rosy cheeks and a smile on his face. The glow of good health was a shock. It was such a contrast to his state from a few hours ago, she only now realized just how sick he'd really been.

"Griff!" Gulliver ran to his side, letting Griffin wrap his arms around him in a hug.

"I'm okay, buddy," Griffin murmured into his hair.

"How long will it last?" Riona turned to Nihal.

"Long enough," Nihal said. "We'd better leave now. We will have a chance to rest once we return to Iskalt for the day."

Traveling between worlds was an exhausting business, but Myles said the alternative was flying to their destination in a human metal contraption. No one here seemed to think that a viable option other than the human, and he was out voted.

Griffin was in a cheery mood as he led them across the yard into the moonlight, his arm draped across Gulliver's shoulders. Riona didn't miss the way Gulliver's tail wrapped around Griffin's wrist as they walked. The kid was really worried about Griffin.

"Everyone ready?" Griffin called to gather them close.

Riona watched him for signs that they were asking too much of his limited magic. It never failed to astound her the way his violet magic appeared in his hands, growing as he spread his arms to open a portal into Iskalt—where it seemed to be another cold, but sunny day.

Riona muttered as she shoved her sunglasses on and followed Gulliver through the portal. It really was as easy as stepping from one room to another. It just felt so wrong, foreign to her Dark Fae experience. She wondered if she'd ever get used to that kind of magic.

Myles and Nihal followed her through, filling the small moon garden with too many bodies. Lochlan and Brea came to greet them even before the portal closed behind Griffin, and he fell forward in a boneless heap.

"Griff!" Lochlan scrambled to his side. "What's wrong with my brother?" He looked up to Myles for answers.

"He's sick." Myles went to Brea's side as Lochlan scooped Griffin up in his arms. "The best we've been able to determine is that having use of only his portal magic is destroying him from the inside out."

"Then why did you let him make another portal?" Lochlan growled, marching into his study just off the garden.

"We were in dire need, your Majesty," Nihal said.

"And who do you think you are to make such choices?" Lochlan glared at the man with wings and tattoos so much like Riona's.

"Enough of that douchey-Loch. Nihal is our friend. So we'll dispense with the pleasantries that aren't really pleasant with you." Myles followed him from the study, leading them all toward the royal residence wing. "Let's just get Griffin somewhere quiet to rest, and I'll catch you up to speed."

Riona and the others followed the king to a room opposite the king's suite.

"The twins?" Brea turned pleading eyes on Myles for news of her children, even as she turned the blankets down for Griffin.

"Nihal has seen them recently."

"They are well enough, your Majesty." Nihal bowed. "I believe they are frightened, but well physically."

"Where are they now?" Riona heard Brea demand as she retreated into the hall with Gulliver.

"I want to sit with him," Gulliver insisted.

"Let's take care of you first." Riona steered him toward the kitchens, counting on his empty belly to distract him for a little while.

CHAPTER 12

GRIFFIN

The lullaby haunted Griffin. It called to him in the darkness of his dreams, giving him strength. But there was something else too. The song fortified him, yes, but he wondered what such magic cost, and in the end, would it be worth it?

Screams echoed around him, and the music stopped.

"Keep playing. It soothes him." A voice he couldn't identify reached him through the fog. "I think it reminds him of our childhood."

It did remind Griffin of when he was a small boy running through the gardens of the Gelsi palace with Regan chasing him, laughing and offering him hugs and sweets. Showering him with kisses and the love of a mother he so desperately needed. Those memories chased away the distressing sounds that called for his attention now.

Something about those sounds—and the voice that made them—tugged at his memory, but Griffin was so tired. Tired of running from his fears. Tired of the screams that haunted him. Tired of the blood that covered everything around him. He just wanted to sleep.

"He is not well, your Majesty. There is only so much the spelled music can do to help him."

"Keep playing. Rest now, brother." A comforting hand pressed against his shoulder and Griffin succumbed to the music, letting it send him into a peaceful slumber for a time.

The screams were louder now, and blood streamed down on Griffin like a torrent of icy rain.

She was in trouble. The woman he'd seen in the portal. The screams—the blood—belonged to her. Something was wrong. They needed to find her before it was too late.

Griffin sat up straight, his eyes open, but his surroundings made little sense.

"Where am I?" The light of the bedside lantern sent a blinding stab of pain through his eyes.

"Iskalt." Lochlan said from his seat beside the bed.

Griffin looked at his brother in his wrinkled clothes and a scattering of discarded books around him.

"How long was I out?" He leaned his head back against the pillows trying to make sense of his dreams.

"Since your arrival this morning. The night grows late."

Griffin flung the blankets aside and attempted to sit up. They had to leave. Now.

"I know you're anxious to be away with the moon, but you're in no condition to portal anywhere."

"We have to go, Loch." Griffin moved to the edge of the bed, letting his feet brush the floor.

"Just give yourself a moment to finish waking up." Lochlan handed him a goblet of watered wine.

"How long have you been here?" Griffin sipped from the cup, blinking bleary eyes at his brother. As Brea would say, he felt like something the dog threw up.

"Since I carried you in here this morning."

"You've sat with me all day and night?"

Lochlan must have seen something in his face. The king of Iskalt scooted to the edge of his seat and laid a hand on Griffin's knee.

"You are my brother, Griffin O'Shea. You're my blood. And you remind me of our father." He hung his head. "The absence of my memories plagues me, Griff." He rubbed a tired hand over his face. "How could I have left you alone like that?"

"Like what?" Griffin stared at him, not sure what he meant.

"You were just a babe when our parents died. And I just left you? Let you grow up with that awful woman?"

The haunted look in Lochlan's eyes tugged at him. "You were just a child yourself, Loch. Only four years old. What could you have done? By the time either of us were old enough to make sense of anything, too much time had passed. I was of Fargelsi, and you were of Eldur."

"I should have done better by you. I'm your older brother. It was my responsibility to care for you when our parents were gone."

"It's ancient history, Loch." Griffin stood up, feeling better than he had after Nihal played his song the first time. He vaguely wondered if that meant it wouldn't last as long this time.

"I haven't thanked you." Lochlan stood with him. "Not properly anyway."

"For what?" Griffin lifted his pack over his shoulder.

"For working so hard to bring my children home." Lochlan swallowed, casting his eyes down to his feet. "I have had a small rebellion to put down in a southern village, and my council tells me it could cost many lives if I left Iskalt now. I don't know what we'd do without you."

"I'll keep good on my promise, Loch. I'll bring them home."

Lochlan nodded. "Home." He smiled. "I hope you know this is your home too now. We're your family. All of us. You have a place here. A purpose."

Griffin nodded, not trusting himself to speak. How long had he wanted to hear such words from his brother? And how long would it last if Lochlan ever got his memories back?

"The others are waiting for you." Lochlan crossed to the door.

"I'll open the portal to wherever you're going, and we'll set up a time and place to meet when you're ready to come home. I don't want you risking your health anymore. Not until we find out how to get your magic back."

Griffin nodded again, taking a moment after Lochlan had gone to collect himself. Was this what it was like to have a big brother looking out for him? Whatever it was, he didn't want to get used to it.

The woman's cries of agony still echoed in his mind. They had to move quickly. Griffin didn't know when it would happen or if it already had, but that woman was in trouble, and he was pretty sure Callum had something to do with it.

"Nihal." Griffin walked into the garden where everyone waited for him. "You know who she is? The woman in the portal?"

Nihal nodded. "We have met."

"Do you know how to find her? She's in trouble, and we need to hurry. I know she's in a big city with tall buildings and thousands of cars and busses."

"You literally just described every major city across the human world," Myles muttered. "Can you narrow it down some?"

"She is in a place called New York City." Nihal dipped his head in Myles' direction. "I can take you to her."

"I've never visited New York," Griffin said, frowning, trying to think of the closest place he had portaled to before.

"I have." Lochlan stepped forward. "Brea likes to shop in the city from time to time."

"I like the Christmas shopping," Brea said, flushing pink. "For the kids."

"Right. For the kids." Lochlan shook his head. "There's a place in Central Park where I can take you," Lochlan said. "It's private enough no one should see you arrive."

"That should be near enough to our destination," Nihal said. "She lives in a place called the Upper West Side."

"Can you handle this, Myles?" Brea turned to her best friend with a bit of a grimace on her face.

"Who me?" He rubbed a tired hand over his eyes. "Guide one

sick fae, two more stubborn ones, and a little boy with a penchant for trouble through one of the biggest cities in the human realm? Piece of cake. But I'm going to need a nice long vacation when this is over."

"Just try not to make a spectacle of yourselves, and you'll be fine," Brea said. "The Dark Fae will blend in with their natural glamours, but Griffin will need some help."

"Right." Lochlan approached Griffin, placing his hands on either side of his head to create a glamour that would last long enough for Griff to do what he needed to do in New York.

"We really need to get moving." Griffin couldn't explain it, but the woman needed help, and he didn't know how much time they had left.

Lochlan moved to the center of the garden and opened a portal into a land so green, Griffin could have sworn it was Fargelsi.

"This is a city?" Riona peered through the portal before she stepped through with Gulliver and Nihal right behind her. Myles and Griffin followed.

"Do not risk portalling back in your condition, Griff." Lochlan stepped through with them for a moment. "I will check back here every evening in case you have need of me," Lochlan said. "Leave a note pinned to the largest tree there with a time, and I will be here to bring you back."

"Thank you, brother." Griffin gripped his hand one last time before he backed away from the portal and into the quiet woods.

It was eerie, the way the forest cushioned the sounds of the city in the distance.

"Where to, Nihal?" Myles asked. "The Upper West Side is a big place."

"It is near something called West Fortieth and Fifth Avenue, between Grand Central Station and the New York Public Library."

"Okay. That was way more specific than I was expecting. Let's go. Chop, chop." Myles set off along a path through the woods. "We'll just hail a cab and be there in a few minutes."

"Minutes?" Riona glanced around them at the thick overgrown forest. They seemed miles away from anything resembling a city.

Griffin was as confused as the others, following Myles up a worn set of moss-covered steps to a wider trail. They encountered a few humans along the way. Such an odd thing to see them jogging along the trails with their dogs and their phones, going about their business in the middle of nowhere. As the trees began to thin and he could see the clear blue sky, anxiety gripped his chest. The woman had grown quiet. Whatever had happened to her, it was in the past now, and she needed help.

"We need to hurry, Myles." Griffin urged him to pick up the pace.

"Almost there." Myles glanced at his phone, following the directions the Google person gave him.

"Hey, Myles?" Griffin called.

"I know, keep walking." Myles ignored him.

"Are you sure Loch brought us to the right place?"

"Yep."

"But there's a castle. There, just up the hill. Like a fae castle."

"Do some humans live in castles?" Riona asked.

"Yep, we have castles here too sometimes, just ignore it." Myles led them up to a pair of iron gates at the head of the trail. Beyond lay a stone castle complete with a moat and a turret tower. A large plaque named the place as Belvedere Castle, but Myles had them turning off the trail before Griffin could see what the castle was all about.

For a moment, Griffin thought he'd stepped through another portal. Cars zoomed past them, blaring their horns, and pedestrians hurried around them.

"What just happened?" Riona took a step back, grabbing Gulliver's hand.

"Welcome to Manhattan." Myles raised his hand. "Some call it the best city in the world." A yellow car slowed to a stop in front of Myles.

"But we were just in the forest." Gulliver turned around in a circle. "Where'd this place come from?"

"We were in Central Park, smack dab in the middle of the city.

Now get in and just go with it. We'll be there in a few minutes." Myles slid into the front seat with the driver, leaving Griffin and the others to pile into the back seat with Gulliver sitting on Riona's lap. "Bryant Park near the New York Public Library. And step on it. I've always wanted to say that." Myles slapped the dash, and the driver whipped into traffic, speeding along a wide road lined with trees.

Griffin's mind whirled with images as the streets past by in a blur.

"Anyone else sensing the irony here? We're looking for a lady with a book and we're going to a library?" Myles glanced back at them, but if the others were feeling anything like Griffin, they were a bit shell shocked by the sudden appearance of the largest city he'd ever seen. It seemed to go on in an endless grid of streets and people —so many people. With buildings rising higher than any he'd ever seen before.

"Not a chatty bunch today, are we?" Myles chuckled.

"Here we are," the driver said a moment later. Myles tossed some cash onto the seat as he stepped onto the curb, ushering the others out of the back seat. The little yellow car pulled away to join the thousands of others just like it.

"Nihal, are we close?" Griffin asked. "Where does she live?"

"Do you have the address? I can just ask Google," Myles said.

"She is close." Nihal started down the street, past the stone steps of the library with its enormous columns and arches that wouldn't look all that out-of-place in Fargelsi.

"Here. This building is where she lives." Nihal pointed to an unremarkable stone building that reached toward the sky.

Myles whistled, shaking his head. "Right on the corner of Fifth Avenue? This lady lives in style." Myles marched across the street. "I don't suppose you know this mysterious woman's name?"

"No idea." Griffin shook his head.

"Course not." Myles gave Nihal a questioning look.

"The lady goes by many names," Nihal said.

"Well, you're just a big help aren't you Nihally." Myles took the steps two at a time up to the front of the building. "Wouldn't want this to be too easy."

A man dressed in livery with an odd hat perched on his head stopped them at the door.

"Hello, there sir," Myles said, pausing to shake the man's hand. "We're here to visit my aunt on the fifth floor. We won't be long. The old dear needs some help moving some furniture."

The man nodded with a huge smile and tugged on the golden door handle to let them inside.

Myles stepped into the grand marbled lobby like he owned the place.

"Did you give that man something?" Gulliver followed Myles to the elevators—not one of Griffin's favorite human inventions.

"I bribed him with a fifty-dollar bill." Myles pressed the call button. "But we're going to need to find this lady's apartment. We can't just go knocking on doors along Fifth Avenue."

"Does the number seven hundred four mean anything to you?" Nihal asked, pinching the bridge of his nose. "B. Number 704-B. I think."

"Going on instinct, are we?" Myles sighed, muttering something that sounded like 'fracking fae' under his breath before he stepped into the elevator and slapped the button for the seventh floor.

Riona braced herself for the elevator, grabbing Griffin's hand and squeezing tight as the small closet moved up in an unsteady climb.

Griffin's anxiety for this unknown woman sent his pulse pounding the closer they came to finding her. *We might be too late.* He hoped he was wrong about that. This woman had to have the book. He could just feel it. They were so close.

Griffin was the first one off the elevator. He looked down the long marble corridor, but he didn't have a clue what they were looking for.

"Over here." Myles called to them, standing in front of a black door with a golden plaque carved with the numbers 704-B. The door stood open.

"Looks like we're not the first ones here today." Myles' voice sounded unsteady and a little less sure of himself.

Screams shot through Griffin's head, and he saw blood. So much blood. "She's hurt." Griffin shoved the door aside, stepping into a small room with a high ceiling. The zigzag wooden floors gleamed in the light coming from the windows in the next room. Views of Bryant Park stretched in a picturesque panorama from the large windows in the living room. White marbled columns flanked the wide-open doorways leading from one room to the next. The house was quiet. The only movement came from the open balcony doors where curtains fluttered in the breeze.

Griffin stepped onto the long, narrow balcony, and he was momentarily stunned by the sheer size of the city sprawling out before him. He almost missed it. The drop of blood on the slate tiled floor. There was another one and then another.

"Here!" Griffin called to the others as he raced to the end of the balcony, shoving chairs and tables aside. Lying on the ground in a puddle of her own blood under the drooping waxy leaves of a potted plant was the woman he'd seen in the portal. She was so pale, and there was blood everywhere, but her chest moved, rising and falling with her labored breath. The dainty string of pearls around her neck were smeared with blood and bruises marred her lovely face.

"Let's get her inside." Nihal moved to grab her shoulders. "Careful with her head. She's had a nasty blow."

Myles met them in the living room with towels and helped them get her settled on the sofa. He dabbed at her head wound with a white towel that came away soaked in blood. "Guys, she doesn't look so good. We might need to call an ambulance to take her to the hospital."

"We don't know what happened, Myles. We can't take her to a human doctor." Griffin checked her over for signs of further injury.

"Wha-what happened?" the lady murmured, her brow furrowed in pain and confusion as she began to stir.

"Shhh," Griffin whispered, smoothing the blond hair from her face. "We're here to help you."

Her eyes flew opened, and she let out a shriek.

Chapter 13

Riona

Humans were strange creatures. Riona had never been in a human house before setting foot in Queen Brea's.

But that was not this.

This was a house in the sky overlooking a noisy city. In Myrkur, she'd always loved her quiet. When Egan let her have her space, she'd sit in the palace gardens under the oiche fruit trees. Before stepping into Fargelsi that first time, she hadn't known flowers could be any color other than black.

But she'd loved the black roses, loved the way their fragrant scent wafted through the gardens, and the softness of the petals in her hands.

But here, nothing was quiet. Riona examined the flowers on the balcony that grew from a pot instead of the ground. Was this more human magic?

If she were honest, she was tired of magic, tired of quests and information that didn't lead anywhere.

The music from Nihal's instrument drifted out through the open doors, wrapping her in a layer of warmth, of comfort that she didn't want. She didn't want to grow content among odd luxuries or happy with people she barely knew.

And yet the music had her stepping back inside, needing to hear more.

Nihal sat on the floor in front of the odd settee, playing a new song. It wasn't the song that gave Griffin strength, this one seemed ... more. The melody floated out of him. Griffin perched on the arm of the couch, a contented smile on his face. Part of her knew that wasn't right, that Griffin shouldn't be lost in the music when the woman who'd brought them here was dying.

"I love using human washrooms." Gulliver walked into the room and stopped. "What are we ... oh, that song is nice." He lowered himself to the floor beside Nihal.

Myles walked in from the kitchen carrying a glass of water. "I found some aspirin, but it won't really help with this kind of pain." He stopped. "What's wrong with you guys?"

None of them answered him, so he went on. "Riona, you're smiling. Stop. It's weird. Griffin, quit dancing or swaying or whatever you call that awkwardness. And Gullie..." His eyes zeroed in on Nihal, who appeared to be in a trance. "Hey." Myles put a hand on his shoulder. "Are you okay?"

As if Myles' words snapped Riona out of her stupor, she looked to Nihal, seeing for the first time the color draining from his already pale skin. His hair turned from blond to ashy gray. "What's happening?"

Griffin and Gulliver remained in their oblivious states, mesmerized by the song that no longer felt calming to Riona. "Nihal, what's happening?" She lowered herself at his side. "Stop playing. Please. This isn't right." Wrinkles appeared on his face and the darkness of his wings faded away, turning them to brittle white. "Nihal?" No, this couldn't be happening. "This magic is killing you."

And yet, he didn't stop.

Riona had been so wary of him after living her entire life thinking she was the only one of her kind remaining. "Please, don't do this." The fae was dying right before her eyes, and she wasn't ready. There were so many things she'd wanted to ask him, but hadn't. "No. I don't want to be the only one anymore." She blinked away tears.

Myles walked to the swaying Griffin and slapped him across the face. Griffin reeled back, the trance gone. "What was that for?"

"I've just always wanted to do it." Myles pointed to Nihal. "But you've been dancing to the song killing our new friend here."

Alarm flashed across Griffin's face, and he put himself between Nihal and the woman, crouching down to look into his eyes. "Nihal, stop."

They needed him. Yet, his body aged right before their eyes. Riona had to do something drastic to get him to stop. She reached around him for the tender spot she knew from experience was right below the joints of his wings. She reached up to hold his wing while finding the spot, but the wing tip broke off in her hand, crumbling to dust.

She backed away from him, her eyes glassing over. "He's ... killing himself."

As the music continued, Nihal slumped forward. Myles tried to pry the instrument from his lips, but the grip he had on it was too strong, like it was aided by the magic he performed.

His eyelids drooped and slid closed. And still, Nihal played.

The notes grew quieter as they watched the man they barely knew slide into unconsciousness. He fell, his back slamming against the marble floor seconds before his head hit and the piccolo skittered across the tile, still playing its song despite having no player.

"He can't be dead." Riona knelt beside the prone Nihal.

Myles dropped to his other side. "We have to save him." Even the human knew how important this man was. He pressed his hands against Nihal's chest over and over.

But the fae didn't open his eyes.

Myles sat back on his heels, listening to the sound still coming from the instrument. "He's dead."

The music slowed before stopping altogether, sending them into silence.

Gulliver finally snapped out of the trance and scooted away from Nihal. "What was that?"

No one answered him because none of them were quite sure.

Nihal's body shrank in on itself before turning to ash and disappearing before their eyes.

Riona clutched the edges of her wings, needing the comfort only they could give her. She scrambled from the ground to find space to collect herself, to keep anyone from seeing the tears in her eyes.

A cough froze her in her tracks.

And then another.

She turned on one heel, her eyes going to the woman who'd been all but dead. Her chest rose and fell, breath entering her lungs. Blood still caked into her clothing and her hair, but...

"The wounds." Griffin examined the woman. "They're gone."

Riona focused on the spot on the floor where Nihal's ashes had even disappeared.

The woman coughed again, but this time, her eyes slid open.

"Gulliver." Griffin commanded. "Can you find the light switch? I need more than this lamp."

Gulliver's brow furrowed. "What's a light switch?"

"I've got it." Myles turned on the rest of the lights in the room, but his face looked exactly how Riona felt. Confused. Sad. A little scared.

"Are you okay, ma'am?" Griffin hovered over the woman.

She nodded. "Water. I need water."

"Gotcha covered." Myles handed Griffin the glass he'd had before. Griffin helped her take slow sips.

"Where am I?" Confusion had her body tensing.

In the light, Riona got a much better look at the woman. Long blond hair and sparkling blue eyes. Even now in her weakened state, her gaze held an intensity Riona had felt few times in her life.

They explained what happened to the woman, but Riona didn't want to stick around for that. She slipped through one of the doors at the far end of this sky house, entering a bedroom that looked more like what Riona was used to. Yes, the bed was probably more comfortable than any in Myrkur, but unlike the other human places they'd gone to, this woman seemed to live more like a fae with few possessions.

Riona ran a hand over the soft blanket on the bed. Humans lived in so much comfort, she wondered how they left their homes every day to work. In the prison realm, getting away from the busy palace to visit the villages was her favorite part of the day.

At least in Myrkur, their villages didn't have buildings reaching into the sky. It was unnatural for those who couldn't fly to live so high up. She walked to the large window looking out on the thriving city. Was there ever quiet here? Peace? Or did one have to find stillness in the middle of so much activity?

She couldn't stop thinking of Nihal and the song he played to his death. Had he known he was to die?

She replayed his words while he sat underneath that tree at the Robinson farm. He was a conduit, able to use certain spells without having magic of his own. But he'd also said it wasn't his only purpose. Riona glanced over her shoulder to the closed door.

With a deep sigh, she turned to the table near the bed. Whoever this woman was, the only thing it seemed she cared about were the paintings in frames along the room.

There was a man with auburn hair, violet eyes and a crooked smile. He looked like he was causing mischief.

He featured in a lot of the paintings, always wearing a hat, but he wasn't the only one. Two little boys ran along a beach by the sea. In the next painting, they sat on their parents' laps. On the table, two frames were connected, one boy in each. Riona lifted it, peering closer so she could see the tips of their ears poking through their hair.

Riona's eyes widened as she stared at the images.

Fae children.

She wiped the remnant of a tear from her face and burst through the bedroom door, letting it slam behind her.

"She's fae!" Riona sucked in a breath. "Everyone, back up." Riona didn't know if she was Light or Dark Fae. But if it was the former, she'd have magic, and could use it on them. "Move. She could be dangerous."

Myles pulled Gulliver away from the woman, but Griffin didn't move. He knew more than anyone how they needed to be sure of who to trust, yet he inched closer, never taking his eyes from the woman. Reaching out, he tucked her hair behind her ear—her very fae-like ear—and nodded like he'd expected it.

Griffin removed his hand. "You didn't think Nihal would lead us to a mere human, did you?"

The mention of Riona's distant kin sent pain searing through her. She didn't need the reminder she was once again alone in both words.

The woman sat up, ignoring the blood now staining her settee. "Nihal?" A tear trailed over the curve of her cheek. "Your final purpose is complete." She bowed her head in respect.

"Is anyone else not worried about this unknown fae woman who just killed Nihal?" Riona couldn't believe the rest of them were standing so close.

"Riona." Griffin's gaze filled with a weary softness. "She didn't kill Nihal. She ... well, I'm not sure what she did."

"It was the song. Nihal transferred his life force to me, healing me. He completed his purpose." The woman looked more sad than pleased about that.

"And why was his purpose protecting you?" Riona held the paintings close to her chest.

"Because I am descended from the line of Grainne O'Rourke, yet I do not believe in keeping the book of power hidden. I assume that's why he led you here?"

No one answered as they waited for her to say she had the book.

The woman sighed. "Would this make you more comfortable?" She mumbled something under her breath, and her features changed to that of a familiar old lady.

"Ashlin." Griffin scowled, taking a step back. "You led us to a dead end."

"I did. But much has changed since then. I only wanted to give myself time to get to the book. That has been my purpose here for twenty-six years. Those spells, they are meant to be used, to allow the fae to flourish and to learn from their past mistakes."

"What are you holding, Riona?" Myles looked over her shoulder.

"There are many paintings in that bedroom, but these ones ... I think they have meaning."

"Those aren't paintings." Myles smiled. "They're photographs."

Riona couldn't fight the feeling that she needed to hide the paintings away, that letting everyone see them would change everything. Her heart hammered in her chest as she fought against the urge to destroy them. Sparing one look at the woman who'd returned to her normal features, Riona knew where the unfamiliar urge came from.

This woman was using magic to keep someone in this room from seeing the paintings she held.

Which made Riona fight harder. When Griffin's fingers took hold of the frame, the magic snapped, sending Riona flying backward.

Griffin landed on his butt with a grunt. His hands shook as he stared at the images. "It's me," he whispered. "Me and Lochlan." He lifted his eyes to the woman on the settee. "You're supposed to be dead, Mother."

CHAPTER 14

GRIFFIN

Griffin's life had never been easy. From forming a motherly bond with an evil queen, to having the entire fae realm forget him after his prison sentence, it all stemmed from a single circumstance.

His parents died.

There was never a question of either of them surviving, only who got them killed. Some said it was Regan, others claimed Callum had them murdered.

It was odd for the king and queen of Iskalt to leave the kingdom at the same time, but they'd traveled to the human world for a noble purpose, saving the daughter of their best friend, Faolan, the queen of Eldur, just like Finn now tried to do the same for Lochlan's children. That daughter? She was the weeks' old Brea Robinson. His parents exchanged her for a human baby, Alona—the same Alona who now ruled Eldur.

It was a profoundly important task because there were those who wanted Brea dead for having both Eldurian blood and Fargelsian—meaning, the potential for both magics.

And boy, were they right. Brea was the most powerful magic

wielder he'd ever seen. She pulled an entire palace down on top of Regan.

Griffin's parents never returned from that fateful trip to the human realm, and his life spiraled from there.

He couldn't stare at the woman he didn't know any longer, so he stood and crossed the room, yanking open the balcony doors. For once, he needed the noise, the activity of humans who were ignorant of the fae troubles unfurling right under their noses.

He stayed out there long after his supposed mother took a shower and retired for the night. Gulliver and Myles made themselves comfortable in a guest room.

Griffin closed his eyes, imagining how different his life might have been had he grown up in Iskalt with his mother and his brother after the death of their father. Would they have been happy? A family?

"Do you think she's the woman?" Riona joined him at the steel railing.

Griffin's grip on the rail tightened. He knew exactly the woman Riona meant. "She has to be." When he'd been trapped in his own portal, he'd seen a woman calling to him. It was his mother the entire time.

"She was exhausted. I'm sure she'll have more information for us tomorrow."

"I know." He did. He'd seen the injuries. Even if they'd healed completely, it would take a while for her to feel whole again.

Riona's wings curled into her back as she leaned over the rail. "I don't understand how they live so high in the air."

"You can fly. How are you afraid of heights?"

Riona stilled for a moment. "I'm not. But humans do not have wings. If they fell into the sky, they would crash down to the earth. Why don't they live near the ground where there's no risk of a building falling over?"

Griffin shook his head. "Most of the time, buildings don't just fall over. And there are too many people in this city for them all to live near the ground."

"That tells me they need to stop breeding."

A smile stretched Griffin's lips. He wasn't sure how Riona brought it out in him when he was still reeling on the inside.

"Are you angry with your mother?" Riona looked to him.

That was the question, wasn't it? All this time, his mother was alive, but without his father, she wouldn't have been able to open a portal home. But did that mean in all this time, she'd never found a way to get a message to them? Did she even try?

"I think I should be." He looked back over his shoulder at the dark room. "But I'm so tired of being angry." His met her gaze. "Aren't you?"

Riona hugged her arms across her chest. "I'm not angry."

"It's okay to admit it. To think of what your life could have been like if the people of your village hadn't been slaughtered. If Nihal..." His eyes turned sad as he paused. "If he was still here to answer your questions."

"Nihal's death doesn't make me mad, Griff. Only alone."

He got it then, the feeling he'd never understand. Riona grew up thinking she was the last of her kind. Nihal proved that to be a false assumption, but now, he too was gone. "Maybe we'll meet others like you."

She stared at him for a long moment, and he wondered what it was she searched for in his face. "No, Griff. I very much doubt we will. It's best not to craft hope out of nothing, because when it's gone, it takes a part of ourselves with it."

"Riona." Griffin edged closer to her and bumped their shoulders together. "You are *not* alone." It was the truth. They might have different end goals, different kings they wanted to be loyal to, but he couldn't imagine not at least trying to keep her on the right side of the fight.

The sides had become clear the longer they searched for the book. So many people wanted to keep it out of the wrong hands, and Griffin knew he had to be one of them. Once he freed Shauna and Nessa, he would defeat Egan.

He wasn't sure if this woman would be beside him or facing him across a battlefield, but right now, in the steady noise of a night in the human realm, maybe that didn't matter.

"Do you think she has the book?" Riona asked.

It was a question Griffin asked himself many times. "No. I don't." If she had it, he'd know, he'd feel it calling to him. He pictured the injuries on his mother. "Someone took it from her. Tonight."

Riona was silent for what felt like ages. "Egan won't wait forever."

"We can't return without the book." It was as simple as that. He couldn't give up until the book and the twins were in their possession.

Riona shivered. "I'm heading in for the night. I'll sleep on the floor of the room Myles and Gulliver took."

"You will not. Take the couch."

"The one with bloodstains on it?"

"Follow me. I'll show you a human trick." He re-entered the sitting room and went straight to the couch. "Humans need extra padding on their furniture because they don't like it when their bums hurt."

Riona gave him an incredulous look.

Griffin shrugged. "They haven't been bred riding horses or mules. All they know are their cars and sometimes these train things that go through tunnels. So, give them a break, okay? Humans aren't quite as ridiculous as you think."

"Says the fae pulling the bum pads off the settee."

"They call this a couch, actually." He held up one of said bum pads. "And this is a cushion." He flipped it and put it back on. "Now, the blood isn't a problem."

She marveled at the suddenly clean couch. "How did you learn that?"

"Myles. He got food on a cushion while we were at Brea's house. He flipped it over instead of cleaning it."

He walked to a door he'd seen his mother open for a towel. Searching through the linen closet, he found what he was looking for and returned to Riona. "A blanket."

She took it with a grateful smile. As Griffin turned away from her, she grabbed his wrist, forcing him to turn back to her. Her eyes studied him as if looking for something. "You're still not well."

"I'm okay." He swayed on his feet as if to prove her point.

"How will we help you without Nihal?"

He squeezed her hand but didn't let go.

Riona stepped closer to him. "Outside, you told me I wasn't alone." He waited for her signature snark or biting words, but they never came. "You aren't alone either, Griff. You don't have to figure everything out on your own. I believe in you, I believe in *us*. You, me, Gulliver, and even Myles. No one would think we could accomplish so much together, but we have. We've found your mother alive and come so close to the book. It's because of you. There's something I need to tell—"

Griffin didn't let her finish before pulling her toward him into a bruising kiss.

Riona tensed, her wings shooting out behind her in alarm. One hand came up, her fingers curling in Griffin's shirt. Instead of holding on like she'd meant to, she pushed him away so she could breathe. "Griff..."

His fingers traced over her dark skin. The tattoos swirled faster at his touch. "You can't say those things to me and not expect me to kiss you."

One of her fingers traced her lips. "We ... this isn't right, Griff."

"Why?" He leaned his forehead against hers. "You proved to me I didn't love Brea. You've trusted me during our journey even though I know you'd say there's no trust here. Do you know how much faith it takes to walk through someone else's portal?"

Her eyes met his, but she didn't speak.

"You earned my respect the day we fought in the pits. And again when you let both Gulliver and I go from Kvek's stronghold. Then you came to Fela and destroyed it, making me question everything about you."

A tear rolled down her cheek. "I didn't have a choice. I will never stop seeing the faces of your people in my mind. Destroying your village was a choice, my choice. But it's one that now haunts me. You should hate me, Griff."

He shook his head. "I know the worst of you. You know the worst of me. And yet, we're standing here together." His palm slid up one arm and over her shoulder to the hollow of her throat before pulling it back entirely. "There will be sides in the coming war if Egan destroys the prison magic, and I am pretty sure I know which side will have your loyalty. I've made that choice before. But until then, whatever this journey throws at us, we're in it together."

His fingers linked with hers before releasing her and stepping back. "Goodnight, Riona. Sleep well because I have a feeling tomorrow will change everything we know." He left her staring after him as he peered into his mother's room. She'd barely been able to speak after practically coming back from the dead. Shutting her door, he entered the room next to hers to find a pillow on the ground for him and Gulliver and Myles in the bed. Lowering himself to the soft rug, he closed his eyes, wishing he was the kind of man who deserved to give in to the feelings inside him.

Sleep never came for Griffin, and he was up long before the rest. His legs wobbled beneath him, but he gripped the kitchen counter to steady himself as he made his way to the fridge. He had to make sure Gulliver had something to eat when he woke. No one wanted to be around a hungry Gulliver.

Something tugged at Griffin and whispers echoed in his mind, not unlike what he'd experienced in his portal. He breathed deeply, trying to clear his thoughts.

Footsteps sounded behind him, and he turned, coming face to face with his mother. He stared at her, wondering how he hadn't seen the resemblance the moment they found her. She was the image of Lochlan.

Dark circles ringed her eyes, but she was otherwise unharmed.

"Griffin." She spoke the name she'd given him, slowly, like she wasn't sure she was allowed to use it.

"Most people call me Griff." He cast his eyes toward the floor, unable to meet her penetrating gaze.

She nodded, a smile coming to her face. She took a tentative step forward, and Griffin backed up. "I just ... can I get to the coffee maker?"

Griffin slid out of the way. "Brea is obsessed with coffee." He guessed his mother's fondness for it came from living around humans for so long. "Brea is—"

"I know who she is. The fae communities in the human world are not ignorant of all that has happened in the kingdoms."

"Oh. Right." He drummed his fingers on the countertop. "So, the book."

His mother heaved a sigh as she filled the coffee maker and hit a button. "I barely had it long enough to make a dent."

"A dent?"

She waved the question away as she reached for a mug. "It is out of our reach now. That is why I didn't tell you about it last night. I did not want you chasing after it."

"I can feel it." He rubbed a spot over his chest. "It's getting farther away."

His mother nodded. "That's because it is probably back in the fae realm."

"You..."

"There are a great many things you need to know." She waited for her coffee to finish dripping into a pot before pouring a mug and leading him from the kitchen.

In the sitting room, Riona had already tidied the couch and stood in the middle of the room stretching out her wings.

"Nihal used to do that." His mother smiled at the memory. "A Slyph's wings are like an extended muscle that must be treated well."

Riona caught sight of them and brought her wings in.

"Good morning." Griffin's emotions tipped from happy to see

Riona to confused at being in the presence of his supposedly dead mother. He couldn't wrap his head around it.

"Both of you, sit." Griffin's mother lowered herself to the ground.

The wearier Griffin sat next to Riona on the settee.

The woman sipped her coffee before setting it on the table between them. "I guess I should just start at the beginning. My husband and I volunteered to bring Brea Robinson to the human realm. An Eldurian noble then took Alona, the human child back to Eldur through my husband's portal where we were to follow."

"But you never made it." Griffin rested his elbows on his knees and leaned forward.

"No. We never made it. My husband—your father—was killed by the one fae he trusted most on his council."

Griffin knew what she was going to say.

"Callum. His own brother. I'd always seen through Callum, but my husband had a soft spot for his little brother."

Griffin thought of Lochlan. Brothers betraying brothers. Would the cycle ever end in Iskalt?

"Callum didn't kill me. Instead, he trapped me in the human world. I met Nihal four years ago. I'd been living in Aghadoon to be close to the book."

"I thought that village only allowed descendants of Grainne to even see it?"

She gave them a grim smile. "I am Fargelsian on my mother's side. I don't know if anyone ever told you that, Griffin. I wasn't known to be royalty—we kept the small amount of royal blood a secret—but your father and I fell in love. My father was a lesser Iskalt nobleman, though, in those days it was still quite the scandal for a prince to marry so far beneath him. And then when Brandon disappeared and Regan came to power, I made the choice to hide my Fargelsian heritage—until I needed it to get into the village."

She took a long drink, and it seemed to fortify her. "The book ... I don't know how Callum tracked it to me, but this time he didn't plan to leave me alive."

Griffin jumped to his feet. “Callum was here? He did this to you?”

She nodded.

“Did he have children with him?”

“I’m sorry. He didn’t.” She looked to Riona. “Are these the twins we spoke of when I was Ashlin? The O’Rourke twins?”

Griffin pushed a hand through his hair and paced the length of the room. “Yes.”

“My purpose in Ireland wasn’t only to delay you and give me time, I wanted you to know that no royal Fargelsian twins could be normal kids. Their power...

“What?” Griffin stopped walking.

“Brea is a direct descendent of the O’Rourke Queens. Any children of hers would be as well. In the O’Rourke line, twins hold a significance, but there haven’t been any since Sorcha and Grainne.”

“You told us this before.” Griffin was losing his patience. “What kind of significance?”

“There is much of the book only they will be able to read. And that kind of power is everything.”

Chapter 15

GRIFFIN

"Loch will meet us in the park in a few hours." Myles slammed the apartment door closed behind him. "We'll just take a cab straight there and be out of here in no time."

"And why is it Griffin can't create a portal?" Enis asked. "He was born with the O'Shea magic." She settled her clear blue eyes on him, and Griffin shrank beneath their steady gaze.

His mother's name was Enis O'Shea, and she wasn't dead. Griffin couldn't seem to wrap his mind around that truth. Nor could he stop staring at her.

"He's sick," Gulliver explained. "He gets sicker when he opens portals, so Loch won't let him do it anymore."

"You and your brother have remained close?" Enis looked at him with a bright smile and a healthy color in her cheeks. "I feared you would become strangers when you were torn apart."

"We've only recently become ... friends."

"Of course, you've been in the prison realm for a long time." She patted his knee. "Without the full use of your magic, it's no wonder you're ill."

It was a little creepy how much she actually knew about them. Part of him wanted to rage at her for not working harder to come back for them. How different all their lives would have been if she'd returned to Iskalt to raise her sons together and hold the throne until Lochlan came of age. How many lives might not have been ruined? But another part of him wanted to hold on to her and not let her out of his sight.

"Did you ... prepare him?" Griffin asked, giving Myles an imploring look. He didn't want to shock his brother with the news of their mother's ... not dead situation.

"Warn him his mother has come back from the dead?" Myles shook his head. "That's not something you tell a guy in a note pinned to a tree. I told him to meet us just after moonrise, and we had someone who would be returning to Iskalt with us."

"What's our next move?" Myles sat on the chair opposite the couch Griffin shared with his mother and Riona.

"We have to catch Callum before he tries to enter the prison realm with the twins." Griffin didn't want to think about what would happen if Callum were to get away with the book and the children he needed to read it.

"How does this twin magic work?" Riona asked, leaning forward to hear Enis' answer.

"O'Rourke twins are powerful," Enis began. "And if my assumptions are correct about Brea and Lochlan's children, then they will be even more powerful for having the magic of all three kingdoms. Yet we will not know that for certain until they come of age.

"The twins usually have a unique skill set. One twin wields powerful magic while the other twin has only the ability to enhance or stifle the other's. In the past, these twins have rarely worked together for a common goal. The twin without magic doesn't often survive long if he or she opposes the one with the power. That is why Grainne escaped to the human realm with the book of power. She went where her sister could not follow."

"My niece and nephew are just children," Griffin said. "They are young, and they love each other. We have to get them back before Callum has a chance to destroy their bond.

"Tia already has use of her Fargelsian magic." Griffin smiled, thinking of his niece's penchant for getting into trouble with her magic.

Enis nodded. "She will likely come into her Iskaltian and Eldurian magic when she is eighteen. The book will be the key to increasing her Fargelsian power. It will show her brother how best to work with her to help her. In the wrong hands, the book is dangerous. Even more so with O'Rourke twins added into the mix."

"If it's so dangerous, why not destroy it?" Griffin asked.

"Because the book holds as much good as bad. It holds the key to all of our magic. Much of what we no longer understand. It cannot be destroyed."

"But what does Callum want with it?" Myles asked.

"I think he wants to destroy the tentative peace our kingdoms have created in the last years," Griffin said. "Right now the three kingdoms are all friends because our rulers have become like family to each other. But what happens in the future when that friendship is no longer what holds them together? When others are in charge? Maybe Callum doesn't want to wait for that kind of division to happen naturally over time. I believe he wants to bring the barrier down between Myrkur and the other kingdoms."

"But why?" Myles frowned. "What will that accomplish?"

"Chaos. Conflict and division." Griffin rubbed a weary hand over his face. "He thinks if he can flood the realms with convicted criminals it will throw the kingdoms into anarchy—likely war, which is when he will try to seize power and create even more division among us."

"And he needs the twins and the book to destroy the boundary," Riona whispered, sharing a look with Griffin. That was why they were here. What would happen if Callum did the thing Egan sent them here to do? And what would Riona do now that she knew exactly what her king needed?

"I think I'd like to not return to the human realm for a while," Gulliver said the moment he stepped through the portal into a fresh sunny day in Iskalt. "I mean, I like pizza and donuts, and Coke, but I'm quite sick of the time shift between worlds. It's like we're losing time." He crossed the moon garden to Brea's side, giving the Queen of Iskalt a fist bump.

"I feel the same way about the human world." Lochlan followed him through the portal, letting it close on the inky black night in Central Park. "It's the worst part about traveling frequently." He rested a hand on Gulliver's shoulder, his laughter a rumble in his throat. But Lochlan's laughter quickly turned into a strangled sound when Enis lowered her hood, her face pale in the sunlight.

"Mother?" Lochlan's voice trembled in uncertainty. He shook his head and blinked as if to clear his mind of whatever vision he was seeing.

"Lochlan." She nodded, folding her trembling hands in front of her.

"She's not dead," Myles announced, slapping Lochlan on the back.

"I can see that." Lochlan took an unsteady step forward.

"After your father died, I was stuck in the human realm and another mission took precedence." She fumbled with her cloak.

"She was protecting the book," Griffin said. "Turns out she's been the one helping us all along. She's worked with Nihal for years."

"Where is Nihal?" Brea asked.

"He died saving Enis after Callum attacked her and stole the book," Myles explained. "We have a lot to catch you up on." He steered them all inside out of the cold.

Brea busied herself with getting them settled around the table in the dining hall as an early dinner was served for their traveling guests. She beamed proudly when Enis complimented her on the changes she'd made from the formal dining with the full Iskalt court.

"It always seemed a bit much in my day to have all the nobles in attendance every single night. It's exhausting."

"Right?" Brea laughed, bouncing baby Ciara on her hip while

princess Kayleigh had taken up residence on her long lost grandmother's lap.

"Now that we know Callum has the book, we can follow him." Griffin began the long process of catching them up to speed with everything that had happened. "We should leave as soon as we've rested for a little while."

"I'm sure it can wait until morning," Brea said. "You've not been well, Griffin."

"We don't have much time to catch up with Callum. I don't have time to be unwell. Tia and Toby will be beyond our reach soon."

"Who?" Brea cocked her head in confusion.

"The twins." Griffin's blood ran cold at the blank look on her face.

"What twins?" Lochlan asked.

"Not this again," Myles groaned. "We're too late."

"Too late for what?" Brea frowned. "What's going on, guys? Why do you all look so devastated? Who are Tia and Toby?"

"They're your children, Brea," Griffin said, rising to take Ciara from her arms just as they went limp with shock.

"What?" Lochlan frowned. "That's absurd, we don't have twins."

"Yes you do. Callum has them and he's taken them into the prison realm. It must have been before we left the human realm. The boundary magic has made you forget they were ever born."

Chapter 16

RIONA

"How could we let this happen?"

Riona watched Griffin pace back and forth across the palace library. "Seven."

He stopped and turned to her. "What?"

"That was the seventh time you said that. The answer won't change, Griff. We failed to get the book."

Red crept past the collar of his shirt and into his face. "You think I care about the book right now?"

"You should. We know now Callum took the twins to Myrkur, to Egan. Everything is different now. Egan doesn't need us. He doesn't need to keep your people alive."

Griffin collapsed into a chair. "Shauna and Nessa. How could I have forgotten about them? Since the moment I realized Brea and Loch forgot the twins, it's like I have this all-consuming guilt. And fear."

Pain seared through Riona, and she clutched her head with a quiet cry. The agony pulsed through her. She dropped to her knees. Egan. He must know she'd failed. "Callum," she panted. "He's reached Egan." That was the only explanation for the sheer anguish of his wrath.

Griffin scrambled from his chair and dropped to his knees in front of her. "Riona?"

The pain didn't go away like it had each time before. "It's him. The magic that ties me to him." Her wings shook as they folded around her.

And then another set of hands were on her, a comforting touch. Griffin pulled her to him, holding her as Egan's magic sought to remind her she didn't belong to herself or to Griffin.

Her body quaked in his arms as she burrowed closer, hiding her face in his chest. Her wings stretched to their full size and wrapped around them both like a cocoon. Riona hated relying on anyone else, she hated that Griffin had to hold her together.

But she didn't hate *him*. Maybe she never had. From the moment they met, Griffin had an honor about him.

"We've made a habit of saving each other, haven't we?" He rested his chin on top of her head. "How is the pain?"

Being in Griffin's arms, she'd barely noticed the pain ebbing away. "It's almost gone."

They stayed there beneath the shield of her wings as her heartbeat returned to normal and Egan's magic left her. For now.

Griffin's warmth soothed her, and she wasn't ready for the moment to end.

"We have to go back to Myrkur." Griffin's voice was no more than a whisper.

She leaned her head back to meet his gaze, wanting to contradict him, but he was right. "You need access to your full magic, or..."

"Or I'm going to die." He heaved a weary sigh.

It was a realization Riona had come to over the last week or so. Every time Griffin fell ill, it was a deeper sickness, more serious, and it lasted longer each time. Eventually, he wouldn't wake up.

He gripped her chin, his thumb moving over her lips. "There was a time you'd have welcomed my death."

She nodded because it was true. And since then, she'd followed a fae who was brave and selfless. One who didn't look at her tattoos and wings in disgust. "Egan once told me there was a reason the Dark Fae were trapped in the prison realm along with the criminals." Her wings retreated from around them and Riona sat back on her heels. "The three kingdoms weren't prepared for the likes of us. He claimed there'd never have been any kind of peace if Sorcha hadn't erected the magic generations ago. He claimed the Light Fae ... aren't supposed to mix with Dark Fae."

Griffin rubbed his chin. "That might be so. The Light Fae are not ready to find out there are ogres in this world and fae with wings or tails or horns. They may not understand how your magic comes from a different place than theirs. But..." He dipped his head. "Riona, look at me."

She lifted her chin to meet his gaze.

"Just because a fae is not ready for something doesn't mean it shouldn't happen. Egan wants the magic down so he can march his army through Iskalt and beyond, an army of Dark Fae who think the outside world has forsaken them. He thinks the only way to exist together is for one kind of fae to dominate the other."

"Isn't that the only way?" Riona frowned, unable to fathom a world where there was true peace among all fae.

"No. You do not know the lands of the Light Fae as I do. They do not yearn for conflict. Eldur's ruler is a human and Fargelsi's is a former servant. I think, given time, we could continue to be a world at peace, one who accepts all kinds of fae no matter how different they are."

Riona closed her eyes and released a long breath. "How do you do it, Griff?"

"Do what?"

"You lived in Myrkur for ten years, and yet, you have this faith, this hope."

"You wouldn't want to know the man I was before. I never questioned Regan even when she did things I knew weren't right. Not until a girl made me rethink everything I knew. I did my worst to her, even trapping her in a marriage bond. And yet ... she had faith in me. She was my anchor, the first fae who ever believed I could be more, good."

"You were lucky to have Queen Brea."

"I was. I can be that fae for you. Riona, you are not Egan's puppet. You don't have to continue to dance to his tune. Let me believe in you. Let my faith help you believe in yourself. I think you need me."

Tears welled in Riona's eyes, and for once, she didn't wipe them away. No one had ever told her she could be good, that she had more to offer than the pawn she was. She rose up on her knees and closed the distance between her and Griffin. One corner of her mouth curved up. "You're right about one thing, Griff." She steadied her breathing. If she was going to admit to this feeling, she had to be calm, confident. "I do need you." She leaned in, her last words only a whisper on his lips. "I don't know if I deserve your faith, but I want to."

Griffin pressed his lips to hers. Her body relaxed under his touch. This kiss, this connection was what they needed. Riona wrapped her arms around his neck, drawing him down on the library floor.

Both of them knew the dangers coming for them, that they had to return to the prison realm and there was a chance they wouldn't make it out again. Once they crossed the border, they would be forgotten once more, and this time, there would be no portals out unless Griffin got his magic back.

They didn't hear the door open, but Gulliver's snicker was undeniable. Riona pulled back to find Gulliver with Enis, looking down on them.

"So, is this what people do in the library once they know how to read?" Gulliver's smile spread across his lips. "I figured there had to be a good reason why anyone would sit in a dusty old library reading instead of exploring outside."

"Gullie." Griffin shook his head. "I'm going to make sure you learn how to read."

"Why would you do that to me?" Gulliver pouted. "Come on, we can make a deal. I distract your mother so you can, uh, continue, and you don't try to cram useless information into my head."

Griffin pushed to his feet. "Reading isn't useless."

Riona stood and met Enis' strange gaze. "Listen to the kid, Griffin. He's smarter than you."

Gulliver reached his fist out, and Riona bumped hers against it in the odd way Myles taught them.

"I'll let you guys talk." She tried to step around Enis.

"I actually wanted to talk to you, Riona." Enis smiled. Riona found she did that a lot, but something didn't feel right about it.

"Oh." Griffin's face fell. Riona knew how much Griffin wanted to spend time with his mother before leaving for the prison realm, but she'd been busy studying the few pages from the book of power found in the Iskaltian archives, presumably put there by Nihal years ago.

Enis led Riona out into the hall. "Would you like some tea? I'll have it brought to my rooms."

"How do you fall back into life as a royal so quickly?" Riona looked to her. "I'll never be comfortable in a palace."

Enis smiled. "Because I'm home. This palace hasn't changed. It still feels like my husband will walk around the corner or there'll be two little boys running through the halls."

Riona hadn't talked to Enis since they arrived from the human realm a few days ago. Enis assured them all it would take a while for Egan and Callum to understand the magic they wanted to use ... to understand the twins. Which gave Griffin time to rest.

Enis pushed into her rooms—rooms Riona had learned were hers all those years ago. A fire burned in the hearth. Enis stopped the servant on the way out. "Might we have a tea cart brought in?"

He nodded. "Yes, my lady. I'll fetch it myself."

Enis gestured to the white velvet settee, and Riona took a seat. She didn't know what the woman could possibly want to talk to her about. Without Griffin as a buffer, Riona had little to say.

Enis sat in a chair near the fireplace. "I don't know if I'll ever get used to the cold of Iskalt again. Especially after living in the human realm with a heating system where I only had to turn up the temperature on a little box to make it warmer."

Riona had stopped being amazed by human things. She'd

accepted their lives were just different. "Couldn't you heat this room with your magic?"

"Ah, my magic. I do not have Iskaltian magic like my boys. A long time ago, I was able to use Fargelsian power. But I'm out of practice and wouldn't be able to recall the right words without some time to study."

"You didn't memorize spells from the book?"

She shook her head. "It was in my possession for only a short time. I only intended to keep the book safe."

"Why? Wasn't Aghadoon protecting it?"

"That depends on what you mean by protecting. They had it hidden away unused, not accessing the enormous amount of information and spells it can reveal. Over the years, some of the pages have become part of the archives in the three kingdoms, like those found here, but we know so little of its true contents. We cannot have such a powerful book out there if we do not understand it."

"That ... actually makes sense."

Enis smiled. "Dear, I have spent so many years away from the fae realm, letting other kingdoms raise my children. Four years ago, I met Nihal, a Dark Fae who'd become a conduit of the book. He offered to bring me home, to let me give up on my mission. But I couldn't do that."

In a way, Riona understood her. Riona had spent most of her life on some mission or another for Egan. There'd been a time she thought the raids and the fights in the pit were part of loyalty to the king, and there was a nobility in that.

Enis stood and walked into the adjacent bedroom, returning a moment later with a small stack of parchment.

A knock sounded on the door, and Enis hid the parchment behind her back as she answered it and let the servant in. He pushed a silver teacart in front of him. Two sterling pots sat on top with china cups. A plate of pastries accompanied them.

"Thank you." Enis smiled. "We can pour our own tea." The servant bowed and left them in peace.

Forgetting the teacart, Enis sat beside Riona. "I learned a lot about your kind from Nihal, but he never told me where he'd come from. I now know it must have been Myrkur, but what I don't know is how he escaped the prison magic." She paused. "That is not why I asked you here." Enis stood and poured two cups of tea, not asking Riona how many sugar cubes she preferred. "There is a line almost hidden on this page." She handed a worn parchment to Riona. "Look at the bottom."

Riona leaned closer, trying to make out some of the smaller text. "A being from the land and the sea, born in darkness will bring out the music in the magic." She lifted her head to look at Enis. "What does it mean, 'music in the magic'?"

Enis set her teacup on the tray and walked to where her human sack she called a backpack sat. She pulled out a familiar looking instrument. "This music was not the purpose spelled out in Nihal's tattoos, but he was the only being I ever found who could bring about a sound from this specific instrument." She handed the piccolo to Riona.

Riona wrapped her fingers around the instrument. "And you think I can do the same?"

"To be honest, I don't know. I tried playing it myself, but no sound came. There was a page of the book that I believe now is displayed in Fargelsi. It isn't a spell, only an explanation. It says 'with music all spells are possible'."

"With music, all spells are possible," Riona repeated as she looked down at it. "But I don't know how to play."

"Try. Please just try."

Riona recalled watching Nihal play the instrument. She mimicked the image in her mind. But when she blew across the opening, nothing happened. No sounds, not even a squeak. "I can try again."

Enis slumped. "No, it will be no use. Nihal could play it instinctively. Like it was impossible for him to hit the wrong notes. It was the magic of the book."

Riona held out the instrument for her to take, but Enis shook her head. "You may yet find someone to play it in the prison realm.

Guard it with your life, Riona." She looked to the door as if making sure it was still closed. "I have one more request of you."

"What is it?"

"Those books you have that allow you to communicate with the Dark Fae king..."

Riona sucked in a breath. How did she know? "What do you want with them?"

"I want to speak with Egan."

CHAPTER 17

GRIFFIN

Failure came in many forms, but Griffin often wondered if he'd ever know what success felt like.

He sat on the snow-covered bank of the pond where he'd first seen Tia and Toby skating. Nessa would have loved that. She'd have loved the sun beating down on her, and the other children to run and play with. Even now when two of them were missing, the Iskalt palace teemed with the children of servants Brea allowed to play where they liked.

"You're going to catch a chill, brother." Lochlan lowered himself to the ground beside him. "In your condition, you need rest. Why don't we push off your journey a few days?"

Griffin snorted. "You wouldn't be saying that if you remembered your kids."

Lochlan's brow scrunched. "I've tried. Every night, I try to conjure images of them in my dreams. During the day is the worst though. Brea is mourning them, despite not remembering the kids we've lost. It's ... torture, Griff." Lochlan hunched forward, a tear rolling down his cheek.

Griffin couldn't remember ever seeing his brother cry.

"I'm sorry I failed you." Griffin stared into the distant snowfields across the pond. "You can't imagine how sorry I am." He'd made a promise to Brea to bring them home, a promise only he remembered now.

Lochlan shook his head. "I may not remember them, but I feel like I know you now. You would have tried your hardest."

For the first time in Griffin's life, that was the truth. There'd been no ulterior motives in his mission. He hadn't chosen to back the wrong king over his family.

And still, it made no difference.

"What is it like, Griff? The prison realm."

Griffin rested his arms on his knees. "I don't think you want to know."

"I do. I have to."

A sigh hissed past Griffin's lips. "It's always dark, but you get used to that part. Its inhabitants are stripped of magic. I think that was the worst part for me. We live in villages with the Dark Fae." He smiled as he thought of his people. "I lived in a place called Fela. We took care of each other, sharing what little we had, working for the good of the community. For more than ten years, we evaded the king's notice."

His shoulders slumped. "Before I left on the king's mission, we were attacked, our village destroyed."

Neither of them said anything for a long moment. Lochlan put his hand on Griffin's shoulder. "I'm sorry for the people you've lost."

That should have been the other way around, Lochlan needing consolation for his loss.

"My best friend was Shauna, our village healer." Griffin smiled at the memory, but it dropped quickly. "The king is holding Shauna and her young sister, Nessa, at the palace to make sure I return."

"I should have been there." Lochlan dug his hands into the snow. "If you were trying to rescue my children in the human realm, why wasn't I there with you?"

"You're a king, Loch. You couldn't just leave."

"But they were my kids. I don't remember them, but I feel their loss right here." He put a hand over his heart.

"You had a purpose here too."

"It shouldn't have mattered."

"But it did." Griffin turned toward him. "We have gathered important pages from the book because you and Finn traveled each kingdom, searching through the libraries and archives while I was busy in the human realm. We have much of our knowledge of the book because of you two."

Griffin never could have imagined the prison boundary to be as complex as they'd learned it was. This wasn't like Regan's boundary spell around Fargelsi. The greatest magic wielders from all three kingdoms came together to pick apart that boundary piece by piece. The prison boundary wasn't so simple.

"But is it enough to be any help?"

The scroll Lochlan and Finn found in the palace in Eldur contained their biggest clue yet. The wall itself was responsible for holding all the memories and magic. The page from the book of power claimed the exterior wall absorbed the memories, becoming stronger as more people crossed the boundary, while the interior wall absorbed the magic from those who entered.

"Griff!" Gulliver called.

Griffin turned to see him stumbling across the fresh layer of snow, his boots getting stuck in its depths. He waved a leather book over his head. "Griff." He panted as he reached them. "Riona, she..." He bent over, unable to breathe and handed Griffin the book.

Griffin gave him an odd look before flipping the cover open. "It's empty. Gulliver, what's going on?"

"Last. Page." Gulliver finally caught his breath. "Flip to the end. She didn't have time to erase it."

Griffin did as he asked, his eyes widening as he reached the page that had a line of black text scrawled across it. "My king, we have the knowledge you need. We're coming home."

Griffin growled. "Whose is this?"

"Riona's."

Something shattered inside him as the betrayal sank in.

"Griff." Gulliver's eyes flicked between Griff and Lochlan. "She's gone. And..."

"And what, boy?" Lochlan's icy gaze latched onto him.

"Enis went with her."

The brothers shared a look. Their mother?

"Follow me." Lochlan stood and together they trudged back to the palace. Griffin interrogated Gulliver as they stomped through the snow.

"Why did she leave this behind?" Griffin gripped the book in his fist, the evidence of her betrayal.

"Because I'd already found it." He huffed out a breath. "I hid it in my room this morning, and I watched her search every inch of her own room before Enis arrived and said they had to go."

"How long ago was this?"

Gulliver shrugged. "Enis did some Fargelsian spell to lock me in the room, but it wore off after a few hours."

"I thought Enis said she didn't have magic anymore." Lochlan's jaw clenched.

"Does it really surprise you she lied?" Gulliver's tail flicked with annoyance.

A guard opened the door for Lochlan, Gulliver, and Griffin. They made their way through the palace halls before stopping at the royal bedchamber.

Lochlan led them inside to find Brea rolling on the ground with her remaining children. A sad smile graced her lips, but it dropped when she saw her husband's stormy expression. She sat up. "What's wrong?"

Lochlan looked to Griffin. "Give her the book. If it's spelled to erase messages, it can be spelled to remember them."

"What's going on?" Brea stood and scooped the baby into her arms.

"We need your Eldurian magic. It's still daylight, and this has to be done now."

"Of course." She took the book. "What is this?"

"Riona's communications with the king of Myrkur."

Brea's face darkened. "The man Callum took my kids to?"

Griffin wondered if it was harder to deal with the kidnapping if they remembered the kids or not. It was a special kind of pain for a parent to know they didn't hold the one thing that connected them with their kids. Memories. The kind of memories that deepens love.

With Ciara in her arms and Kayleigh pulling at her leg, Brea concentrated on the book. A yellow ring of magic trapped it in Brea's power. The cover flipped open, and the blank pages flew past of their own accord until Brea reached the last page with the visible message. With a satisfied smile, she closed the book and handed it back to Griffin. The leather was warm in his hands.

It used to be moments like this when he fell more and more in love with Brea Robinson, but he knew now it had never been right. Without the marriage magic creating deeper feelings, he was left with respect. Respect and loyalty. He looked from Brea to Lochlan to Gulliver.

Riona betrayed him, and that crushed something inside him. But these people ... no matter what side Riona chose, he would never again go against his brother, his ex-wife, or the boy he'd raised as his own.

Griffin perched on the wooden arm of the settee and opened the book to find Riona's handwriting.

Brea leaned back. "I wasn't able to recreate the responses, but every message she sent is there."

Lochlan stepped closer, and together with Griffin, they read through Riona's growing betrayal. She'd kept Egan abreast of their movement, every progress they'd made. She'd told Egan about Griffin's illness, about the twins. Anger brewed in his gut. It was only days ago he'd told Riona he was so tired of being angry, yet he couldn't keep it from rising to the surface now.

Was everything fake? Designed to help her get close to him and learn all his secrets? The book fell from his fingers and tumbled to the ground, spine up.

Riona Nieland was now an enemy of the three fae kingdoms. She chose her side repeatedly, every time she wrote to Egan.

But Griffin ... was she an enemy of his as well?

The sun was still in the sky when Griffin returned to his room to prepare for the journey to the prison realm. He didn't have much to pack, so his mind was left to think about Riona, about their time in the library.

When he'd kissed her, he felt her respond. And her words ... Throughout his life, Griffin learned how to decipher lies from truths, but in those moments, he'd truly believed her, believed in her.

Just like she'd wanted him to. He slammed his fist against the wall, ignoring the pain in his knuckles in favor of the pain in his heart.

Was this how Brea felt when Griffin had chosen Regan over her again and again?

What about his mom? He barely had the capacity to think of her as being alive, let alone alive and a traitor.

Yet, she'd gone with Riona. Back to the man who wanted to bring the magic down to move his army across the fae lands. Griffin wondered if the Light Fae would ever be ready for the Dark Fae.

Griffin grabbed his bag as he stepped into the sitting room he'd shared with Gulliver and Riona to find Gulliver sitting on the settee, his back hunched.

Griffin dropped his bag on the floor and approached the boy. "Gullie."

Gulliver turned hurt eyes on his surrogate father. "You're leaving tonight." It was an accusation more than a question.

Griffin nodded, letting his anger at Riona fade away. Gulliver didn't deserve to stand in the path of his rage. But once it was gone, his energy slipped away as if it had been fired only by the strong emotions. "I am."

"And you're not taking me with you."

Griffin slumped onto the settee next to him. "I don't ever want you to enter that realm again. It's my job to protect you."

"But my friends are there. Shauna and Nessa are still trapped."

Neither of them said their real fears. The girls were trapped—if they were still alive.

"What about the twins?" Gulliver pleaded. "I want to help."

Griffin slid an arm around him. "I need to know you're safe. Going back there ... it scares me, Gullie. I might end up trapped forever if the magic remains in place. I might..." He sighed.

"Die," Gulliver finished for him. "You can say it, Griff. You might die." A tear leaked from his cat-like eyes. "Why do you get to risk your life and I don't? I can help you. I *need* to help you. I'm the last ally you have who remembers everyone. Riona has gone back to the king's side. Myles returned to Fargelsi to prepare his kingdom should the magic come down." He turned to meet his gaze. "It's always been you and me, Griff. That doesn't change just because it's dangerous. We're all we have left."

Griffin pulled the boy into a hug, not wanting to let go. "When did you get to be smarter than me?"

"I've always been smarter than you."

They both laughed as they released each other. If felt good to laugh.

Griffin studied him, the boy who'd had to grow up too fast. "Okay." He hoped he wouldn't regret it, but Gulliver was right. He needed to make his own choices. "We don't have much time. Pack your things. We're traveling the old fashioned way, no portals."

"Not a boat again?" Gulliver shrank back.

"No. There's only one place we can enter the prison realm. Be prepared for some long days in the saddle, Gullie."

Gulliver groaned. "I'm guessing I'll soon understand why humans need bum pads on their settees."

Griffin chuckled and bumped Gulliver's shoulder before pushing to his feet. "I need to see the king and queen before we go. I'll meet you at the stables at dusk."

"I won't let you down, Griff."

"You never have, Gullie."

He left Gulliver to prepare for the journey and found Lochlan and Brea in the moon garden.

Griffin approached cautiously.

Lochlan took one look at his eyes. "You're leaving, aren't you?"

"I must. We have to get to Myrkur before they figure out how to use the twin magic. I've promised this before, but this time, I won't fail. I *will* bring your kids home to you." Part of Griffin wanted to tell Lochlan to go to the human realm and stay there until Griffin passed the prison magic. It was the only way to remember him. But he didn't know how long it would take him to reach the border, and he'd never ask his brother to leave his family and his kingdom for that long, not for a brother he barely knew.

Brea gave him a sad smile. "Are we going to forget you again?"

Griffin nodded. It was the hardest part about leaving. "As soon as I cross the threshold, you won't know I was ever here."

He wondered how close Riona and Enis were to the magic barrier. They hadn't crossed yet if he still remembered them. But they were a future problem.

"Loch, if the magic comes down, the king will bring his force to travel across the realms unimpeded. I've seen his army, it's the stuff of nightmares. You must send word to Queen Neeve and Queen Alona. Your combined armies must be there at the border, ready to face whatever comes."

Lochlan nodded. "We'll be prepared."

This was the hard part. "I wrote this for you last night." Griffin handed him an envelope with the words 'You have twins and a brother in the prison realm you've forgotten. Read this now!' written in a hasty scrawl on the front. Inside, Griffin had left instructions for Loch and Brea. "You probably won't trust my instructions so as soon as I leave, write a letter to yourself about what must be done and who I am. Put it someplace you will find it."

Lochlan's brow furrowed as if he didn't like it, but he nodded.

Griffin gripped his arm. "Promise you'll do this. We will fail without your armies."

"You have my word."

Griffin stepped back. "I'm glad I got to see you both again. I don't think we'll meet in the future." Sadness exacerbated the weakness inside him.

Brea pulled him into a hug. "We may not remember you, Griff, but you will always be in our hearts. We will not fail you."

Griffin stepped back, his eyes glassing over. "We will not fail each other."

He tried to smile as he looked from his brother to the girl he once loved. "It was always meant to be you two. I'm sorry I ever tried to take that away." They didn't remember his actions of the past, but he'd never forget them.

"Right here." Brea placed a hand over her heart. "Always."

He ripped his eyes away, knowing if he stared at them too long, he wouldn't want to leave.

Going to the prison realm the first time had been for penance, maybe even redemption.

But now ... he was going for love. Shauna. Nessa. Tia. Toby. Even for Brea and Lochlan.

And that gave him a strength he'd never had before.

Chapter 18

RIONA

"The king's soldiers will be waiting for us on the other side." Riona stood, staring at the crumbling boulders flanking the path before her. Only a few more steps and she would be home, and everyone she'd met on this side of the border would forget she ever existed. Including Griffin O'Shea. "You can wait here and enter after they've taken me to Egan."

"No." Enis shook her head. "I go wherever the book goes."

"You realize he won't give it to you no matter what you do?" She glanced at the former Queen of Iskalt, still wondering why she'd come with her and not with Griffin.

"You let me worry about that." Enis took her final steps into the prison realm.

With a deep breath and a reluctant heart, Riona followed. Passing through the barrier magic was like walking through a cold shower. It left her shivering. She'd grown soft in the human realm with all its comforts.

Riona blinked in the dim light of the sun on this side of the barrier. Anytime she'd visited the border in the past, she'd thought the sunlight here was blinding. But in reality, it was like the softest of sunsets in this no-man's-land that wasn't Myrkur or the Northern Vatlands they'd just left.

"I thought it was always dark here." Enis glanced around the barren landscape.

"It will be when we get there." Riona waited at the center of the path. Egan's men would be along any moment on their patrol of the border. "The light fades the closer you get to Myr until it's completely dark, and only the light of the moon and stars will guide you. The palace is an hour's ride from here on horseback."

"Riona, ye returned." A garbled voice grated at her. "We didn't expect ta see yer lovely mug here ever again."

"Oh, my." Enis moved behind Riona, putting her between herself and the ogres heading their way. "What on earth is that?"

"Lady Enis, meet your first ogre, Uthar." Riona turned toward the loyal soldier. He was actually kind of a nice guy—as far as ogres went. "Uthar, can you take us to the palace? I have news for the king."

"Right 'way miss. Th' cart's just o're the hill." Uthar ran ahead to prepare for their ride to the palace.

"Good Heavens!" Enis gaped at the cloud of dust Uthar left in his tracks.

"Right." Riona turned toward Enis. "Ogres are faster than they look." Uthar and his brother looked like a pair of identical eight-foot-tall boulders come to life with their cracked gray skin and mossy green hair that grew down their broad bare backs.

"Told yer." Uthar grumbled at his brother Gunthar. "Her brought a lady queen wi' her."

"Hey Gunthar, how's it hanging?" Riona climbed up into the ramshackle cart the ogres used for transporting newly arrived indentured. Egan liked to scare the bejesus out of the Light Fae prisoners by having the ogres greet them.

"Er, wha'?" Gunthar stared down at her, scratching his armpit with long, knobby fingers.

"A human expression I picked up." Riona shoved him playfully. She liked the ogres. Most of them were fun, though some were just downright mean.

"You been 'round humans?" Uthar helped a shocked Enis into the cart, lifting her by the collar of her fancy riding dress. "Whas it like out there?"

"Big and scary," Riona said.

"Truly?" Gunthar snorted like a horse as he took up the harness to the cart.

"Bigger and scarier than Kaltrick on his grumpiest day." The Ogres' father was widely known as the meanest ogre in all of Myrkur.

"The little Slyph's having' a go at us, 'rother." Uthar's laughter sounded like rocks tumbling together.

"Hold tight." Gunthar called over his shoulder.

"He means it." Riona shoved a rope in Enis' hands. "Don't let go unless you want to fall out." The ogres took off, running up the winding road to the mountains that led into Myrkur.

Enis let out a loud yelp and clutched the rope, cowering down into the cart as the bland landscape passed them by in a blur. Riona stood at the helm of the cart, holding onto the reins behind their ogre mounts. "We'll be there in half the time this way," Riona called to her fae companion. Which didn't give her much time to decide her next steps, because Riona still wasn't sure which side she was on.

The ogre brothers dropped them off at the outer palace gates, which left them to make their way through the slums just inside the walls.

Riona had always turned a blind eye to those who lived among the tents, most of whom were the untouchables, cast offs from the palace. To her, they'd always been lazy fools who never worked hard enough to prove their usefulness to their king. But something had changed since she was here last. The filth and grime were worse. The smell of unwashed bodies permeated the air along with the night fires that kept them warm in the darkness of Myrkur. They'd truly fallen on hard times in her absence.

Enis walked beside her with a cloth over her nose, and a tear in her eye at the sight of young women and children starving and begging for the scraps the palace threw out. "I don't know what I expected, but this is heartbreaking."

"They bring it on themselves." The words were out of Riona's mouth before she could even contemplate them. It was something she'd said a million times before, but now she wondered how true that was. Was she just repeating what she'd heard others say about the slum rats?

"The palace is much better." Riona marched toward the inner gates, refusing to look anywhere but at her destination. How many times had she walked the main road and not seen what was happening right under her nose?

No one blocked her way as they passed through the palace gates. It wasn't as grand as the palaces she'd visited on her journey, but Riona had everything she needed and more in the barracks as one of the king's favored.

"Come with me." Riona led Enis up the grand staircase to the guest rooms. She scowled at the clutter in the halls. The staff had fallen down on their cleaning duties of late. "Let's get you settled. The king will meet with you in the dining hall this evening." That was protocol for guests—who were normally Myrkur chieftains.

"No, no, you're not leaving me in this hellhole." Enis hissed at her when she opened the door to their finest suite. Well, it was their finest, though it was rather bare in terms of what Enis was used to.

"I have something I need to do before the king knows I'm back. Just ... don't leave this room. You'll be fine."

"Riona, don't you dare leave me here." Riona shut the door behind her, twisting the key in the lock and pocketing it before she thought better of it.

Servants and guards had seen her return, so she didn't have much time to make her decision. If she knew Egan at all, Shauna and Nessa had started off serving him in his quarters, but for as long as Griffin and Riona had been gone, and as many excuses as she'd given him, they were likely working in the kitchens or the laundry by now. Both were terrible jobs, but still better than what awaited them should Egan decide Griffin and Riona had failed—and he would decide they'd failed when he discovered they had allowed Callum to beat them to the book and to the twins he needed to read it.

She also knew Egan well enough to know he'd forgotten the girls the moment they were out of his sight. Riona made her way to the kitchens at the rear of the castle, crossing the courtyard where punishments were carried out. She flinched at the familiar crack of the whip as two young boys were beaten for some slight against the king.

How had she let herself become blind to such things? Beatings were an everyday occurrence here. Riona used to sneak into the kitchens whenever she was hungry, and it had never bothered her before.

That was before she'd known another way. Another life where people didn't go hungry at the whim of a cruel king. Where children weren't orphaned and then beaten for stealing a loaf of bread when they had no other means of feeding themselves. Where indentured servitude wasn't even a thing. No one in Fargelsi or Iskalt had to spend their lives working in the king's opal mines until they were too old to be useful or died from lack of nutrition.

She found Shauna and Nessa in the washroom behind the kitchen, scrubbing filthy pots and pans, their hands cracked and dry from the harsh lye soap. Both wore the backless dresses of the female indentured. It was easier to punish them with the whips if they weren't protected with layers of clothing.

Shauna's back was covered in stripes from the whip master's attentions. Some had scabbed over, and some bled. Little Nessa wasn't much more than skin and bones, her back blistered from a recent beating.

There was no decision to make. It was already made the instant she laid eyes on the two most important people in Griffin's life. "Shauna?" Riona whispered, creeping into the washroom. Shauna looked up from the pot she was scrubbing. Sweat poured down her face from the heat of the water and the kitchen fires from the next room. Shauna backed away from her work, grabbing Nessa from the enormous cauldron she was busy cleaning. She shoved Nessa behind her.

"Don't you want to get out of here?" Riona bent so they could hear her whisper. "Griffin is coming back, and you need to be far away from the king before Griff gets here and does something stupid and heroic." She believed Griffin would do the right thing, and she wanted to give him that chance. And that meant getting his family to safety.

Shauna scrambled to her feet, taking Nessa's hand in hers. "You mean like trade himself for us?"

"Exactly."

"We have to get Hector too," Nessa said, her sweet face still managed to hold on to the innocence of youth. Something rarely seen in Myr.

"Hector? Who's Hector?" Riona growled.

"He's working out in the slums," Shauna said. "We can't leave without him."

"He's not in the castle?" Riona urged them to follow her into the darkness behind the kitchens.

"He's helping people escape the slums." Shauna limped behind her. "But he's also one of the king's indentured, patrolling the streets."

"Then he can help himself." Riona tugged Nessa's hand.

"He's here because of us," Shauna hissed. "We have to tell him we're leaving with you. That Griffin is returning."

"Fine." Riona rolled her eyes. "Where do we find him?"

"Follow me." Shauna led them around the outbuildings where the castle provisions were stored to a narrow dirt path that lead behind the castle to the rear gates.

"Get behind me." Riona moved to put herself in front of the indentured girls. "Put your heads down and act like you're scared."

"Won't need to act much," Shauna muttered, gripping her sister's hand.

"Where you heading with these?" An ogre soldier stopped them at the gates.

"These two are being put out for stealing food from the king's table." Riona gave Shauna a shove.

Shauna let out a pitiful wail, stumbling past the guards with a loud moan.

"Get her out of here." The soldier shoved her with a boot to her back. "And keep her quiet, I don't want to hear her wailing anymore tonight."

"She'll get what's coming to her." Riona sneered at Shauna's back, hauling her up by the tatters of her dress and marching her through the gates. Nessa rushed along right behind her.

Once through the rear gates, Shauna guided them into the slums far away from the night fires. From the back side of the slums, Riona noticed a huge difference from her prior visits.

"The tents here are empty. Why have the people moved so close to the main road?" Back here it was vacant and almost ... clean. Fresh grass now grew where mud trails once cut deep ruts into the ground.

"Hector has been moving people out of the slums, but we don't want the king to know yet. Every few days we move the remaining people closer to the road so it looks like it always does to those who pass by, giving little attention to the conditions here. A few disappear each day, but there are always more to replace them."

"And where are you taking them?" Riona glanced around. Curious how they'd managed to move so many people out without the king's notice. Not that many paid much attention to the cast offs.

"The villages where they'll be safe." Shauna cast a wary glance at Riona. She couldn't blame her for not trusting her.

"Kiaren, where is Hector?" Shauna stopped to ask an older woman Riona vaguely remembered seeing in Fela before it burned.

"Shauna, what are you doing out here?" The old woman grabbed her hand. "The king will have your head if he catches you gone from your duties."

"We're leaving, Kiaren."

"Finally come to your senses then?" The woman led her along the back row of tents. "He's just about to leave."

"Kiaren." Shauna pulled the woman to a stop. "Griffin is returning."

"Then you need to be anywhere else but here when he arrives. What is *she* doing here?" Kiaren glared at Riona.

"She is helping us."

"Why?"

"Well, she's been with Griffin all this time, so my best guess is his annoying goodness has rubbed off on her."

Riona snorted at that. Griffin would never have considered himself good, but these people obviously did. Before she could say anything, the women pulled her into a tent.

"Shauna?" A man with a ring through his nose pulled her into a hug. He was Dark Fae, with horns like a bull. He turned menacing eyes on Riona, an irritable snort escaped his nose.

"Time to get us out of here, Hector," Shauna said.

"That must mean Griffin is back?"

"He won't be too far behind me," Riona said. "As long as he believes Shauna and Nessa are under Egan's thumb, he won't think clearly. And as far as Egan is concerned, we've failed in our mission."

"And when Griffin shows up, Egan can't have anything to use against him." Hector nodded in understanding. "I'll get them out of here tonight."

"See that you do." Riona turned to leave.

"Wait, what will you do, Riona?" Shauna grabbed her arm. "You should come with us."

"I can't." Riona pulled away. "It's time I return to my king." She hung her head as she left them to their escape. Egan would kill her if he found out, but she owed this much to Griffin.

Back in the palace, Riona wrinkled her nose at the layer of ash and filth covering everything. Her accommodations within the barracks might have been more comfortable than those residing in the slums, but she was just as trapped as they were. Even more so, having the undivided attention of the king.

The king who would soon know she had returned. If he didn't already. Riona climbed the back stairs up to the guest quarters. Fishing the key from her pocket, she let herself into Enis' room.

"It's about time." Enis stood up from her seat on the bed. "What do you mean locking me in here?"

"I had something I needed to do first." Riona paced to the aged wooden chest in the corner and splashed her face with water from the basin. Checking her reflection in the cracked mirror, she thought she looked like the Riona Egan would remember. Though there was little of herself she recognized anymore. The black shadows creeping across her wings now covered half of the white membrane. Riona didn't know what would happen if they turned full dark.

"Don't think you can swoop in and steal the book out from under me. I've sacrificed too many years to let that happen."

"I don't want your book, Enis." Riona dabbed her face dry with what she'd once thought was the finest cloth. That was before she'd slept under the silken sheets in her room at the palace in Iskalt. "I just needed a moment to see to Griffin's family here before Egan knows I have returned." She crossed the room to face Enis.

To Riona's surprise, Enis didn't ask about this family of her son's. It was becoming harder to believe she would come to care for her children at all.

Riona pushed the thoughts away. They were for another time. "We're about to walk into the dining hall to meet with Egan and likely Callum too. They need to think I've come straight to them with you as my guest."

"Very well. You will introduce me to your king, and I will take it from there. It is important we find out where he is keeping the book."

"Don't forget your grandchildren are here too." Riona frowned at the former queen. She was as cold as ice.

"Of course. Their safety is obviously of great importance as well."

"Of course."

Chapter 19

GRIFFIN

"You ready for this?" Gulliver wrapped his arm around Griffin's waist, hoisting the bulk of his weight on his young shoulders. If it weren't for him, Griffin wouldn't have made it this far.

"Ready as I'll ever be." A coughing fit wracked his lungs.

"Hold on a little longer, Griff. We'll find Shauna, and she'll make you all better."

"Thanks buddy," Griffin wheezed. "Time to go home." Together they hobbled forward, through the barrier that would make all those he loved forget about him all over again.

He could feel the magic wash over him. Cold, icy tendrils trickled through his veins, searching for magic he didn't have, drawing out the last of his energy.

They were already waiting for him. Three muscular, bearded soldiers paced the barren land at the entrance of the prison realm, their ivory tusks jutting from their angular jaws.

Black spots danced in front of Griffin's eyes as they approached. "Gullie, don't let them catch you. Go find Hector." Griffin took a step toward the soldiers and collapsed face first onto the dry dusty ground.

Someone splashed water on Griffin's face.

His lids slid open, and he blinked the water from his eyes. Torchlight greeted him, along with the sounds of raucous laughter. Shaking his head, he realized that was the only part of his body he could move. His arms and legs were bound to a whipping post.

It all came back to him then. He was home. Back in Myrkur where he couldn't help but think he belonged.

Gulliver? He looked around, not seeing the boy anywhere. He could only hope the soldiers hadn't caught him after Griffin passed out. With any luck, he was a long way away from here where Hector and their friends from Fela were taking good care of him. Not that he'd ever known Gulliver to follow instructions.

"Ah, he's awake." A familiar voice sent a wave of revulsion through him. "Welcome home, young Griffin."

"Egan." Griffin managed to answer with a firm voice, though he felt as if the only thing keeping him upright were the ropes binding him to the whipping post.

"You forget your manners, Griff." The king's bushy brows arched at him. "I'll let it slide this time. I hear you've been through quite an ordeal."

That was when Griffin saw her. Riona stood behind the king seated at the high table. She wore an icy expression. Nothing of the woman he'd come to know was reflected in her countenance. She stood like a rock, not meeting his gaze.

He wasn't surprised to find his Uncle Callum seated at the king's table, eating his finest food and drinking the sour wine Egan boasted was the best in the land. It probably was, but that wasn't saying much.

Griffin was shocked to see his mother seated opposite Callum. He gave her a wary look but didn't speak. He couldn't fathom what she was up to, but her presence here felt like a betrayal.

"You've failed, Griffin." Egan sliced into a ham, serving himself and his guests from the same knife he used to eat his own food. The man was even more vile than he remembered. "I sent you through the barrier to collect what information I needed to destroy the magic keeping Myrkur in the dark, and you did not deliver."

"I never wavered, my king." The words were like ash in his mouth. "I nearly had it."

"Nearly." Egan stuffed a slice of ham into his mouth. "Nearly is not good enough, my boy. Your uncle has brought me all that I need, so what use do you serve me now?"

"Callum will never give you what you want. You would be wise not to trust him."

"Now is that any way to talk to your uncle?" Callum shared a scathing look with the king.

"You've betrayed everyone who ever had the misfortune to call you family." Griffin erupted into a coughing fit. Sweat trickled down his brow. He was dying and Egan knew it. "What do you want, Egan?" He was so tired, he just wanted an end to this torture.

"My healers tell me you have the sickness," Egan said. "Your magic is unbalanced. Supposedly, all you need is the full use of your magic, and all will be well again. Yet, I cannot return your magic to you until I know I can trust you. You see what a conundrum that is, don't you?"

"Uncle Griff!" A child's voice commanded his attention away from the high table. "Don't listen to him. He's a bad man!"

"Tia, Toby. Are you okay?" Griffin tried to get a good look at them, but they were just out of his line of sight. He could tell they were in some kind of cage on display for the whole court watching the proceedings with glee.

"We're okay, Uncle Griff," Toby called in a weary voice.

"Take good care of each other, kids. No matter what happens, that's your greatest strength." He hoped they were wise enough to understand what he was saying. No matter what, they needed to work together and not let the uniqueness of their magic tear them apart like it had for the twins who'd come before them.

"Uncle Griff." Egan chuckled and Callum joined him in a good laugh at Griffin's expense. "How adorable." Egan returned to his wine, draining his cup of the dark red, bitter wine he thought was the sweetest vintage.

"More wine, Callum?" Egan offered.

"Please." Callum barely concealed his grimace. He was clearly disgusted by the Dark Fae king with his scraggly beard, beady black eyes and ivory tusks. Not to mention his poor hygiene and even worse table manners. He was a king unlike any his uncle might have seen. Even Enis sat with a rough linen napkin over her nose to block out the malodorous scents wafting through the dining hall.

Griffin managed a wry smile. Egan thought he was an impressive king, trotting out his best food and wine to two Light Fae who'd spent their lives with luxuries Egan couldn't even imagine. They were appalled, and he had no idea.

"Where are Shauna and Nessa?" Griffin asked, fearing the worst. If Egan considered him a failure, they likely would pay the price.

"It seems they are unwell. Suffering from the plague sweeping through the villages. I can't imagine they will survive it, as weak as they are from the work they've been doing."

Griffin fought against his restraints. If he'd failed them so miserably, the only thing he wanted now was to take Egan with him when he died.

"Your Majesty, we've found the boy," a voice as familiar as his own stirred hope in Griffin's chest.

"Excellent work, Hector. Griffin, I believe you know my loyal servant of Fela." Egan's smile spread wide across his face.

Hector was once Griffin's closest friend other than Shauna. He was as close as a brother. But Hector was an indentured now, and he held a squirming Gulliver in his arms.

Many of the fae who'd ever meant anything to him were caught up in Egan's clutches now. Griffin had thought he could save them all. What an arrogant fool he'd been. He'd allowed himself to reach for power, only to fall flat on his face ... again.

No, this time it wasn't a throne he'd reached for. It was worse. This time he'd tried to become the savior of all those innocent souls trapped in Myrkur. And he'd failed every single one of them. Doomed himself and everyone he loved to a terrible fate.

Chapter 20

Riona

Griffin hated her.

That much was apparent every time Riona looked into his eyes, trying to say words she couldn't voice with Egan watching her every move.

"Sire, perhaps we should remove Griffin from the post."

Egan's hard eyes landed on her. They'd finished their meal, and Callum left to take the twins to their room while Hector carried Gulliver off to the cells. She'd never forget that image. Hector was supposed to be Griffin's friend. But then again, wasn't she supposed to be his friend too?

Egan, Riona, and Enis now stared at the auburn-haired Iskaltian prince who could only lift his head to skewer Riona with the betrayal in his eyes.

"Perhaps you've gotten too close to this man on your mission." His eyes narrowed. "A mission you didn't complete. Tell me, Riona, why shouldn't I tie you up next to our prince here?"

"No, Majesty." She dipped her head in response. "I am sorry. I only meant that he is weak, and you don't wish to kill him."

Enis stepped forward. "She is right. It isn't time to kill him yet."

The *yet* was the problem.

Egan stared at Griffin, and Riona could only imagine what he wanted to do to him. "Okay. I'll play by your rules for now, ladies. Enis, you may untie your son and take him down to the cells. But he will pay for his failures. Publicly. And soon." He turned toward the door. "When you are finished, Enis, come to my chambers. Riona, come with me."

She cast one final look at Griffin. As his mother untied him, he collapsed to the floor.

"Riona!" Egan stomped a foot against the ground.

She had no choice but to follow him through the palace Riona grew up in, the one she'd called home in the years after her village was massacred.

Egan sighed once they were alone in the safety of his private sitting room. He collapsed onto the black settee in front of the fireplace and rubbed his eyes.

Riona used to love times like these when it was just the two of them, when he brought her in to his confidence. She took her usual place by the fire that was never allowed to go out. Without even considering her actions, she reached for the wooden box on the mantel and began to pack his pipe.

"Griffin is really sick, isn't he?" Egan's king act faded away, leaving only the man who'd been like a father in so many ways.

Riona nodded, stretching her feet toward the hearth. "He's been ill for a while now. I wrote to you about it. Have the others with the sickness recovered?"

"One has."

Only one? Those weren't good odds.

He rubbed his chin. "A young man from Griffin's village. We had word he'd come down with the sickness after a portion of his magic was returned, but last week, he was part of a force that tried to burn their way in to Kvek's stronghold.

"Kvek?" There was only one way into the fortress. The river. Burning their way in wouldn't have worked.

Egan nodded. "We don't think they meant to take it. There have been raids all over Myrkur while you've been gone. I've had to send my soldiers to protect the chieftains."

That was a mistake. If Riona had been here, she'd have told him sending the king's forces would only sow more unrest in the villages. The people weren't happy as they starved and suffered under constant taxes and raids.

She pictured Fela and the destruction there. "Egan." She dropped the formalities as she'd always done when speaking with him alone. "Tell me, how close are you to bringing down the magic?" She handed him his pipe.

He let out a harsh laugh before he took a puff of his pipe. "The book is useless. Callum and I have tried to read parts of it. I thought it would help as much as the pages I had—"

"You had pages from the book?" He'd never shown her, but it was confirmation of what she'd suspected.

"I am Dark Fae, Riona. Just like you, I have no magic. But the pages I have ... they taught me how to direct magic from the wall back to the fae it belonged to originally."

So, that was how he'd returned Griffin's portal magic to him. They were right.

Egan stood and rounded the settee to reach a secret compartment in the wall. Riona was the only fae who knew it was there. He yanked it open and pulled out a thick leather tome. Walking back toward Riona, he dropped it to the floor at her feet. "Useless. May as well throw it in the flames."

Only useless as long as he couldn't read it. "Callum brought no answers?"

He shook his head. "He's been here for weeks, but all he brought was this book and two brats who say they know nothing of it."

A knock sounded at the door, and Egan answered it, letting Enis and Callum in.

Riona reached forward and lifted the heavy book into her lap. How could a book hold so much power? Did Egan even know what it contained?

Enis walked toward her as if drawn to the book. "May I?"

Riona shrugged and let Enis take it from her. This book had

changed everything in Riona's life. She now knew how wonderful life could be outside Myrkur, how the sun felt warming her skin. The taste of really good food. A full belly. Sweet wine and silk sheets. Her eyes were opened to the endless possibilities that lay beyond the borders of the only home she'd ever known. Could she give that up and go back to her former life? Leave it all behind?

Leave Griffin behind?

Gulliver?

If she had a choice, she'd free Gulliver from the cells and take him and Griffin far from this place, all the way to the sea where her ancestors once ruled. They didn't need magic if it only caused conflict.

Enis sat on the floor, running a hand across the broken leather. "I barely had the chance to examine it before Callum arrived." She shot Callum a scathing look before returning to the book.

Egan grunted. "Don't waste your time. It's written in some language that probably doesn't exist anymore. The magic in that book is useless."

Enis shook her head. "No, not useless. Just incredibly ... specific."

"What do you mean?" Riona barely knew this woman. On their ride from Iskalt, she hadn't revealed her motivations for betraying her children. But then, Riona hadn't either.

"The pages will open only to those they are meant for. Otherwise the language will appear as unreadable symbols."

A growl sounded in Egan's throat. "Speak plainly, woman."

Enis opened the book and flipped through the pages, landing on one with a hand drawn image of the instrument Riona had all but forgotten was in her bag.

Below that were a series of symbols. Riona leaned forward to stare down at the book as the symbols changed and morphed into lines of musical notes.

"What do you see here, your Majesty?" Enis lifted the book to show him.

Egan's brow furrowed. "Nonsense. How are we to know what those scribbles mean?"

"*We* aren't. Only Riona is. Because this page relates to her. Riona, what do you see?"

"Musical notes." She could practically hear the song in her mind.

Enis smiled, her eyes alight with ambition. "You see? You must find the parts that pertain to you. The information you seek is in this book, your Highness. You just need to find the people who can decipher it. The twins will be vital to the interpretation of much of this book since they have the magic of all three realms. Though it may be some time before they will be able to learn all this book has to teach them." She thumbed through the pages, her eyes scanning for those that might pertain to her.

Callum remained quiet, but his dark eyes never left the book. "Lord Egan, we need to see what the twins can read of this book."

Enis crossed her arms. "You mean to say you've had my grandchildren and the book all this time, but you haven't yet asked them to interpret it?"

He grimaced, his expression darkening.

Oh. Riona got it now. "They couldn't? You already tried."

"We went through every page." Callum sighed. "Nothing."

"Everyone out." Egan's words were so quiet they almost didn't hear him.

"What?" Enis shared a confused look with Callum, but Riona knew Egan's tempers more than most. She recognized a king ready to explode.

Red crept up Egan's neck. "You are all useless to me. I asked for a way to bring down the barrier magic, and you bring me a book I can't even read? Get. Out. Before I have you all whipped for wasting my time."

The three of them scrambled toward the door.

"Riona?" Egan called her back. "Take the damn book. But do not let it out of your sight."

Riona lifted the heavy book, feeling like she carried all the hopes of magic wielders everywhere.

Callum was gone by the time she stepped into the hall, but Enis leaned against the wall. She kicked away when she saw Riona with the book.

Enis held her arms out for it, but Riona shook her head. It was like the book called to her, not wanting her to let go now that she had it.

There were so many things Riona needed to do. Help Griffin. Find Hector and figure out why he'd brought Gulliver to the king. Free Gulliver and the twins.

Instead, she listened to the book, hearing its whispers grow louder and louder until it was all she could hear.

Not wanting to take the book into the barracks, she headed for Enis' room. She couldn't trust the woman when it came to Griffin, or the kids, but the book ... she'd never harm the book. Riona could see it in her eyes. These spells were the only thing that mattered to the woman.

Riona pushed open the door to Enis' room. It was much smaller than Egan's, with the sitting area and bedroom all one open space. Enis shut the door as Riona threw the book on the bed and backed away.

"How could you do it?" Riona hugged her arms across her chest. "Betray your family for a book."

Enis sighed. "If I remember correctly, you also betrayed them."

"No. I returned to Myrkur to save them. To make sure Griffin's people didn't suffer upon his return."

"And yet, you stood at Egan's side today. I know you wish for loyalties to remain clear, but life is more complicated than that."

"Why can I read the music?"

"Oh, I suspect there's a great deal you can read." She pointed to the book. "Every answer you've ever wanted is in this book. The purpose of your tattoos. The reason your wings grow darker each day. The truth to the prison magic. All you have to do is look."

Riona backed away until she hit the settee. "I ... no." It was all in front of her, this path she'd never asked for.

Enis' eyes changed from blue to black the longer she stared at the book she'd spent so long trying to steal.

The whispers entered Riona's mind again, and she clutched the sides of her head. "I can't ... make it stop." Her tattoos heated, sending bolts of electricity through her as they moved along her skin. Pain speared through her head. She couldn't do it, couldn't open the book.

Enis' eyes cleared as she looked to Riona. "I can save Griffin."

"What?" Her heart thundered against her ribs.

Enis moved to sit beside her and flipped through the pages before finding the one that spoke to her. "Many of the spells in this book are Sorcha's. But a few are from my ancestor, Grainne O'Rourke, her twin. I can see her spells. They call to me like the book calls to you. And this one ... has the power to restore magic."

"Egan has a page that has taught him to do that," Riona said.

"He is simply funneling pieces of magic from the barrier to the one who owns it. The spell he is using is very limited. The only real useful aspect of it is that it allows him to control those he's forged a magical connection with—even if they didn't have magic before. That is why people are getting sick. Abilities like Griffin's portal magic need something to hold on to—his root magic—Iskalt magic. Without it, he will die. And very soon. Others—like you—I suspect, he can't give magic to you, but he can form a magical connection that causes pain. He uses that to control those under him."

Riona thought to the times she'd felt Egan tugging on her, the pain in her head. Had he been using these spells?

Enis scanned the page in front of her. "The amazing thing about much of this book is one doesn't need Fargelsian magic to wield its power, only the words. This spell here is different. This is restorative magic. But ... I need Tia to do it. I don't know why the twins lied to Callum, but they have to be able to read most of this book. The barrier takes magic from Light Fae, but if I'm right, we can use this spell to fully restore it."

"You're forgetting one thing, Enis." Riona moved to sit beside her on the bed. "No one has magic here in Myrkur. Not even Tia, and I doubt Egan will return her magic in full. I don't even know if he can if his spell is as limited as you say it is. But if you can help Griffin..."

Seeing Griffin tied up, barely able to move of his own accord was an image Riona would never forget. "We have to convince the twins to help." Not only that, but they had to do it without Egan or Callum's knowledge.

Enis smiled. "Leave the details to me. I have a plan, but first, I must speak with Callum. Don't leave this room. There are people who would kill you for this book." With those words, she rushed into the hall.

Once the door shut behind her, Riona climbed up onto the bed. "Okay, whispering book. You have me here. What is it you want to show me?" A page flipped of its own accord and then another. Riona watched with wide eyes as the book came to life, stopping at a page at the back. "What's this?"

She leaned closer. The O'Rourke family tree. Riona read the text under the title explaining how the pages updated every time a new descendent was born—only the most direct descendants were recorded here. "That's kind of creepy." Yet, she couldn't take her eyes from the tree. Enis and her family were descended from Sorcha's twin, Grainne, but they weren't of the royal lineage, so they weren't recorded. Riona traced her fingers down ancestors dating back a thousand years before reaching Brea O'Rourke-Cahill-O'Shea, daughter of Brandon O'Rourke and Faolan Cahill, queen of Eldur. Each of Brea's children were represented with vines connecting them to Lochlan.

Riona's breath caught in her lungs as they begged for more air. Her finger shook as she traced the vine from Tierney and Tobias O'Shea. "This isn't possible."

But she couldn't doubt the accuracy of the book.

The twins controlling the fate of everyone in Myrkur were the children of Griffin' O'Shea.

Chapter 21

Griffin

The magical noose tugged at Griffin's neck as he followed Egan through the ranks of his soldiers preparing for battle. Experiencing the king's powerful hold for himself, he could almost understand Riona's betrayal. Almost.

Ogres and horned, hoofed Dark Fae fell in line as the king passed, while scaled Asrai fae took on their land forms to collaborate with the king's generals. A battalion of bat-winged Slyph flew overhead like a swarm of locusts.

"Even if the three kingdoms gather their armies once we've brought the borders down, they'll never match the might of the Dark Fae. Their magic tricks will be nothing against our brawn." Egan's barrel chest puffed up. "They won't know what hit them."

"It is true, the sight of such an army will shake them to their core, your Majesty." Griffin stood, defeated. He was too weak to act. Too weak to think. Egan gave him just enough magic to keep him alive, so he would get a front-row seat to the destruction of the Light Fae. Only, Egan truly had no idea what he was up against. He thought he understood magic when he'd never really seen it at work. He expected three separate armies. The weaker Fargelsians who had use of their magic at all times. The stronger Eldurians who had use of their magic during the day, and the Iskaltians with their night magic.

Egan's army was a fierce horde of brute strength, and they wouldn't go down without a fight. But the Light Fae were united in a way they never had been before, and at the helm of their collective massive army, were the strongest rulers the lands had ever known. They would defeat Egan with their magic. But at what cost?

And it was all Griffin's fault. He'd failed to find a way to free the innocents of Myrkur and remove the tools Egan now had in his possession—Griffin's own niece and nephew.

Egan tugged his leash, spurring Griffin to follow him as he regaled him with the feats of his army and his own prowess as a mighty ruler.

"What of their magic?" Griffin said in a disinterested voice.

"What magic?" Egan stared proudly at the thousands of Asrai soldiers—creatures of the sea come to do battle on land—with their vicious claws and teeth and scales that gleamed like armor in the torchlight.

"Make no mistake, the three kingdoms will come at you with the full force of their magic."

"What is magic against might?" Egan clapped him on the shoulder with a laugh. "We will come at them with the stuff of their worst nightmares. They will run at the very sight of the Asrai, and then my Slyph will pick them off like carrion."

"And what about the sun?" Griffin asked. The sunlight would blind them, just as it had with Riona.

"My soldiers are used to patrolling the border. They know of sunlight."

Griffin nodded. He had no doubt Egan would fail in his arrogance and willful ignorance. "Clearly, you have thought of everything, my Lord," Griffin murmured with disdain Egan was too distracted to notice. "So what need do you have of me?"

Egan shrugged. "Leverage. You and those kids." His laughter sent him into a coughing fit.

"Which you wouldn't have without Callum. Who wouldn't be

here if I hadn't gone into Iskalt and led him to the information he needed to gather the book and the twins." Creative truths.

"So you're saying you didn't fail me?" Egan's voice took on a harder edge.

"My mission might not have been a success, but it wasn't a failure either." Griffin turned toward the king of Myrkur. "The fact that my uncle walked into the prison realm with everything you needed doesn't mean I failed. It means you shouldn't trust him."

"And I should trust you instead?" Egan frowned. "Callum is in my pocket. We're two of a kind. He wants power. I shall give him Iskalt once I defeat your brother."

Griffin couldn't hold back his own laughter, which turned into a bout of coughing. Spitting blood on the brown grass at his feet, Griffin took a deep breath. "Callum won't be satisfied with that."

"You let me handle your uncle. I've plied him with my finest rooms and my best wine. He's dined on the riches of Myrkur. He's even developed a liking for Dark Fae women." Egan laughed. "He is my creature now. One I won't turn my back on."

"You truly have thought of everything, your Highness." Griffin shook his head, eager to see Egan hang himself with a noose of his own making.

"Indeed, I have." Egan turned his attention back to his soldiers. "Once Enis and those kids finish reading the book, we'll bring that barrier down. And then we march."

"With your bravest, most loyal servant at your side." The words burned like acid in his mouth.

"Riona's faith isn't what it once was." Egan sighed with something that sounded like deep regret. "I've gifted her to Callum. She will come back to me in time, but she needs to be reminded who and what she is. When Callum proves no longer useful, she will kill him."

"You did what?" Griffin choked on the tightening of the noose that seemed to grip his heart and lungs like a vise.

Egan laughed at the look of horror on Griffin's face. "She is my servant, to do with as I choose. She always has been and always will be. Now leave me, O'Shea. I have things to do."

The knot around Griffin's throat loosened, and he retreated into the castle. The king's men knew not to let him stray outside Egan's walls, but otherwise left him alone.

Griffin made his way to Riona's rooms, but she wasn't there. He hadn't spoken to her since he arrived back in Myrkur. Not since the sting of her betrayal hit him so hard. That she'd left him in Iskalt still hurt. But she didn't deserve to be traded like she meant nothing.

Griffin was almost running by the time he reached Callum's rooms. Though they may have been the finest Egan had to offer, they paled in comparison to what the former king would call luxurious.

The door stood ajar, but it was silent inside the room.

"Riona?" He pushed the door open, just waiting for Egan's magical tug that would send him back to his own pitiful rooms near the dungeons where Gulliver remained a prisoner beyond his reach.

A muffled sound of outrage greeted him in the dim light of the large, sparse room.

The furnishings were quite fine—for Myrkur. Clean and simple, but well made. The heavy four-poster bedframe lay in shambles on the floor, and the white linen bed curtains meant to billow in the breeze from the open windows, were wrapped around Callum O'Shea, binding him to the bed. A vibrant bruise marred his eye, and he was bleeding from various injuries, though a ball of fabric acting as a gag kept him quiet.

Riona sat in the lone chair by the window. Fury shone in her eyes.

"I saved him for you if you'd like to do the honors." She finally acknowledged Griffin. "I figured the least he deserved was a few more hours to fear his death."

"Did he touch you?" Griffin's voice came out rough.

"He thought to try, but he didn't get very far."

"Good for you." Griffin's mouth lifted in a hesitant smile.

"Griffin, I..." Riona trailed off like she was uncertain how to begin.

Griffin shook his head. A thousand thoughts passed through his mind, but the right words failed him.

Riona held a jeweled dagger clutched in her hands. Nothing so fine had ever belonged to Egan. She must have taken it from his uncle. He pried the knife from her blood-stained hands, letting his palm trace the furious lines of her face for a moment. He may have imagined it, but for a second she seemed to relax at his touch.

Turning to his uncle, Griffin gripped the knife and took a step toward the remains of the bed. From the bruises across his body, Riona must have thrown him against the heavy wooden bedposts as thick as young tree trunks.

Callum fought against his restraints, crying out in alarm as Griffin approached. He managed to shift the rag in his mouth, spitting it out as he took a deep breath.

"You're going to kill me, just like that, Nephew? Have your woman do the fighting and gut me like a coward?"

"She doesn't belong to me, or anyone else." Griffin scowled at the man he hardly knew. The man who was responsible for the path his life had taken when he was just a child.

"Get on with it, then." Callum sighed. "I can't take another moment in this hellhole with that absurd man who dares to call himself a king."

Griffin gripped the dagger and bent toward his uncle, sawing through the linens that bound him. "Leave." Griffin pointed toward the door. "I don't care where you go, but I never want to see your face again." Griffin's shoulders fell.

Callum scrambled from the shambles of the bed, adjusting his clothes until he found his dignity once again.

"You are as much as fool as your father," Callum spat.

Griffin smiled. "That is the highest compliment anyone's ever paid me."

"I take that back. There is much of me in you, Griffin." Callum's eyes darkened with menace. "Both second sons who would have made better kings than our brothers. Both with the thirst for power. Perhaps I should have kept you and raised you as my own."

"We are nothing alike," Griffin spat. "I love my brother and his family. I would never take what belongs to him."

Callum laughed in his face. "You really don't know, do you?"

"Callum, don't." Riona rushed forward.

Callum's laughter erupted, his eyes shining with tears of mirth. "The mighty Queen Brea's magical twins." Callum laid a hand on Griffin's shoulder. "They're O'Shea brats for certain, but they're not your brother's gets." His triumphant grin split his face. "They're yours." Callum's eyes widened, startled as he looked down to see the dagger protruding from his belly.

Griffin pulled back before plunging the dagger into his uncle a second time. "The first one was for me. That one is for my brother and father, and all of Iskalt, you worthless swine." He shoved Callum back on the bed.

Dropping the knife, Griffin left Riona staring at his retreat.

CHAPTER 22

GRIFFIN

"Where is Gulliver?" Griffin sat stiffly beside Egan at his table in the dining hall. He had little appetite with his waning health. If he had a choice, he would still be in his bed, but Egan's magic pulled him from the relative warmth and comfort he found there and forced him to join the king's court.

"The boy has taken up residence in my dungeons. Considering Shauna and the girl conveniently disappeared from the kitchens upon your return, your boy will take their place."

"I thought you said they were working in the mines." Griffin stared at the king.

"Mines, kitchens, what does it matter? They are gone."

"What do you intend to do with Gulliver?"

"If you please me in the coming battles, I may send him to work in the mines instead of the brothels. I'm told he has a talent for finding valuable things. Perhaps he will earn his keep."

"I haven't the strength to stand." Griffin sighed. "What makes you think I will be of any use to you?"

"You found the strength to kill your uncle." Egan raised a bushy brow at him. "My men discovered his stinking corpse this morning."

"It was I, my Lord." Riona's voice rang out across the din of the feasting soldiers seated below the king's dais. Riona captured Egan's gaze, making her way slowly, almost seductively, through the throng of staring men and women. "I found him rather useless, your Majesty." She took the steps up to the dais to his side.

Egan looked to her with pride in his eyes.

Dressed in fresh leathers, and her colorful tattoos drifting lazily across her skin, she looked every inch the warrior Griffin knew she was. With her increasingly shadowed wings fanned out behind her—the remaining white shining like a beacon, she was glorious.

"Your wings?" Egan reached out to touch the dark shadows along the edges of her diaphanous wings.

Griffin thought he saw her wince at his touch, but she recovered quickly, smiling for the king she seemed to adore. He couldn't stomach the look in her eyes.

"It is nothing, your Majesty." Riona folded her wings in, coming to stand beside Egan, completely ignoring Griffin. "I know I must accept my punishment for killing your man." She cast her eyes down.

Egan took her hand, chuckling. "You did me a favor, my dear. Callum O'Shea was baggage I no longer need. We have the twins, the book, and Enis is hard at work interpreting it. What need have we of a fool like Callum who couldn't seem to handle the prize I gave him." Egan's smile turned Griffin's stomach. "Besides, we have our own O'Shea here to open portals when we've need of them." Egan slapped Griffin's shoulder.

"I'm afraid he won't be opening any portals any time soon." Riona gave a hearty laugh. "Not without the use of his magic in full. He too, is useless. Though, as you say, I suppose we'll need him, eventually. As I told you, there are marvelous things to be had in the human world. Things you will no doubt want access to when the time comes." Riona bumped her hip against Egan's throne-like chair.

"One thing at a time, dear one." Egan joined her laughter. "One thing at a time."

"The humans have the best wine." Riona flashed her dark eyes toward Griffin, a perfect sneer on her face. "Rich and sweet. Perhaps you can keep this O'Shea strong enough to travel when you've need of him."

Without asking for the king's leave, Griffin stumbled to his feet and fled the dining hall to the raucous laughter of those Egan favored.

Griffin's mind reeled with thoughts of Riona. Of his uncle's warm blood on his hands, and the last word's he'd spoken.

Lies. It had to be lies. A final cruel joke. The twins couldn't be his. It wasn't possible.

But it was. They were ten years old. Not eight like he'd originally thought. Griffin had been gone for a bit over ten years. The math worked. Brea woke up one day and forgot she'd had another husband once. One she'd loved because the marriage bond made it so. He'd fooled himself into thinking that was enough, that one day she'd love him truly. But then she discovered she was pregnant. Naturally she would believe Lochlan to be the father. She would have no reason to think otherwise.

His gut churned in horror. It was bad enough that he'd let their sham of a marriage happen in the first place. Even worse, that he'd pretended for a short while that they were happy. But that there were now children involved? The possibility that he could be Tia and Toby's father ... it was heartbreaking to even consider it. That he'd missed their whole lives.

And the thought of telling Brea ... Lochlan. Griffin shook his head. They could never know. He wouldn't be responsible for hurting their family like that.

"Stop." Two of the king's guards blocked his path.

"I need to see them." Griffin gathered all the strength he had, desperate to see the twins. To search their faces for a trace of his own.

"They are resting. They spent the morning working with Lady Enis."

Griffin snorted in disgust. He could only imagine how hard his mother had driven the children—her own grandchildren—to find the magic she sought to learn from the book. That was all she cared about. Power. He supposed that was where he got his own thirst for power from.

Griffin searched his pockets, pulling a coin purse from his pocket. "Will this buy me a moment with them?" He handed the gold to the men who likely hadn't seen such riches in all their lives.

Together, they nodded, stepping aside and pocketing the gold without further thought.

Griffin charged into the room Tia and Toby shared. He heard sniffles coming from the bed where they lay hugging each other for comfort.

"Uncle Griff?" Tia sat up, wiping her eyes. "Is that you?"

Griffin crossed the room to sit between them, pulling them into his arms. "Yes, it's me." He ruffled the soft silky hair on their heads, one strawberry blond and the other a dark brown like Brea's.

"We're going to get you home." He tried to give them all the comfort he could. "I promised your mother and father I'd bring you back to them."

"I miss Papa." Tia sniffed. "And Mama."

"Of course, you do." Griffin held them tight, surprised by the severity of how much he wanted it to be true. That something so beautiful and good could have come from the travesty of his marriage to Brea.

He would never and could never take the place of Lochlan in their hearts. To the twins, he would always be Uncle Griff.

But he had to know. Somehow, he had to make it through all of this and make good on his promises to deliver Tia and Toby safely into the arms of their parents. And then he would find a way to discover if his uncle's parting words were more than just a cruel joke.

"I knew you'd come," Tia whispered, looking up at him with such trust. "Just like my dreams. You came for me."

He cupped her delicate cheek. "You knew I'd choose the right side in this before even I did." The words were mostly to himself, but Tia offered him a soft smile.

"Griffin, you can't be here." Riona's familiar voice brought him out of his blissful, too short moment with his brother's children. No matter what happened or what he discovered, he had to think of them that way.

Tia and Toby had been almost asleep when he found them, exhausted from their efforts to read the book that held the key to their escape from the prison realm.

Without a word to Riona, he tucked them into the large bed and kissed their foreheads. "I'll be back soon." He just had to lay eyes on them, just once, to know they were okay. Reluctantly, he turned to follow Riona from the room.

Once they were outside, crossing the empty courtyard, Riona slowed her pace to match his. "We have to talk."

She was more herself without the eyes and ears of the castle on her. This was the Riona he knew. The one he wanted to pull into his arms and erase the wide gulf standing between them. But she'd betrayed him right when he'd needed her the most.

Griffin's steps faltered as a realization struck him. He knew how Brea must have felt when he was the one who'd done the betraying. How much it must have hurt her to have someone she cared for turn against her when she'd had no one else to depend on.

For once, he was truly grateful Brea couldn't remember him.

CHAPTER 23

RIONA

Riona glanced back over her shoulder to the guards standing along the outer walls of the palace. They kept their eyes on those entering the palace, not leaving it, but she knew the Slyph patrolled the skies.

She'd never noticed how many guards Egan employed. Even a few Light Fae walked the grounds from the palace to the slums beyond.

"Are they indentured?" Griffin asked.

Riona had expected another question first, but she understood if he wasn't ready. "No, Griff. The guards come here of their own volition, choosing to work for the king. Indentured fae become servants, or take up roles as the king sees fit, others are sent to the mines, or worst, cast out as useless."

"We didn't know." He rubbed the back of his neck. "In Fela, we stayed out of the king's way, assuming the troops Egan sent to terrorize the villages and collect taxes were the worst of it. We knew about the mines ... but we just lived our lives, trying to keep each other going in our small corner of Myrkur." His shoulders stiffened as if he just remembered who he was talking to.

Riona sighed. She was so tired of playing this game, of trying to please a king who was never satisfied, one who'd unleash his army to destroy all the beauty Riona witnessed in the three kingdoms.

Which was why she was still here, why she'd betrayed Griffin. Egan needed to be stopped, and she wanted to be the one to do it.

Griffin's steps slowed as they reached the barracks. "Riona, whatever you need to say to me better be good because I can barely stand."

"We're almost there." She opened the door to the barracks and led Griffin to a room at the back. Dark Fae watched in curiosity. They'd probably tell Egan of this rendezvous, but Egan wouldn't care as long as he still believed she was loyal to him.

What were his words when he'd found out she killed Callum? Oh right, "Now you have to seduce the other O'Shea." He wanted information on the three kingdoms and their armies. Information he believed only Griffin could give.

Riona shut the door to her small room, so different from the suites she'd stayed in on her trip through the human and fae realms. A single bed sat along one wall with a short set of drawers for her few belongings.

"This is where you live?" Griffin eyed the cramped space.

"I don't need much." She pushed past him. "For now, we can speak in private here."

The door opened again, and Hector slipped into the room before closing it behind him.

Griffin looked from Riona to Hector. "What's going on?"

Riona took his arm and led him to the bed. "You look like death. Sit down."

Griffin took care lowering himself. "Hector..."

Hector grinned. "Bet you didn't expect to see me here?"

Griffin's eyes hardened. "You ... both of you betrayed me? Why am I here?"

They shared a look before Hector gave a short nod. "It was Gulliver's idea."

Griffin's hands clenched. "What was his idea?"

"For me to bring him here as a prisoner. While you've been gone, I became one of the king's men. The king wanted Gulliver, but I didn't want to let anyone else find him. I tried to hide him, to send him with Shauna and Nessa, but he wouldn't go. Not without you. Seems to think you need him to stay close. I have loyal soldiers watching over Gullie. He is safe."

"You mentioned Shauna and Nessa." He sucked in a breath. "They're safe?"

"They are." Hector put a hand on Griffin's shoulder. "You have your friend here to thank for that."

Griffin lifted his gaze to Riona's, a tear escaping the corner of his eye. All these months Griffin worried about the two girls, and now they were free. But Gulliver was in more danger than ever.

"You helped them?" Griffin's voice was small.

Riona hugged her arms across her chest. "I only got them out of the palace. Hector did the rest."

Hector sat on the bed next to him. "You've been gone a while, Griff, and to be honest, none of us knew if you were coming back. So, all this time, I've been thinking about what you would do to save our people. We have a network now." Excitement shone in his eyes. "We're focused on freeing indentured and Dark Fae who wanted to escape the army. It's the first time the villages and the king's own have worked together."

Exhaustion weighed on Griffin, but it wasn't natural, he knew that. The bits of magic keeping him alive weren't enough.

"Why am I here?" Griffin hung his head. "So you two can tell me you were only playing at betrayal?"

Hector gave him a long look as if comparing the Griffin who left with the one who'd returned.

Riona saw both. She saw a defeated man who couldn't save anyone with the lack of his magic draining him.

"How is Sinead?" Griffin asked.

Riona recognized that name, but it took her a moment to recall why. Sinead was one of Egan's test subjects. He'd returned bits of her magic and watched as she weakened.

Hector sighed. "She's dead, Griff."

Riona snapped her eyes to Griffin's. If Sinead died of the illness, they needed to find a way to recover Griffin's full magic as soon as possible. She couldn't trust that Egan truly understood the magic he was using to keep Griffin alive.

Hector looked to the door. "I have to go. I'm on patrol tonight."

Griffin grunted a goodbye, and Hector stood. "Take care of him."

Riona only nodded as he walked out the door, leaving her alone with Griffin. She paced the small room in front of him, not knowing exactly how to start. Every hate-filled look he sent her cut deep into her core.

"You really saved them?" He lifted his head to look at her, vulnerability in his voice.

"I..." She stopped moving. "Yes. It was the first thing I did when I came back."

He nodded as if he was unable to muster a smile. "I'm so tired of this, Riona. Tired of feeling the life drain from me every moment. Tired of not knowing who to trust or who has betrayed me."

She sat on the bed beside him, her shoulder brushing his. "Me. You can trust me."

"Can I?" He rubbed his eyes. "You left me, Riona."

"I needed Egan to think I was on his side. You, Griff, are important to him. I no longer am. If I wanted to survive this homecoming, I had to make it look like I betrayed you. That is what he expected me to do."

"And that makes sense logically. But Riona, I don't know what's happening in this palace. Shauna and Nessa escaped, but now Gulliver is trapped. The king doesn't trust me, yet he showed me the might of his army. Hector is somehow involved in everything. And you ... I don't know what your goal is."

"My goal?"

"Why are you doing this? We'll probably fail. A lot. I don't know if we can bring the magic back."

"We don't need to." She slid to the floor, reaching under the bed. "I found out how Egan, a Dark Fae with no magic, is giving magic to Light Fae trapped here." She pulled a thick book from under the bed.

"Is that...?"

Riona nodded. "The book of power. It's the key. It will show you anything within its pages that pertain to you and your needs." She dropped the book on the bed.

Griffin ran a hand along the worn leather cover. They'd spent so long searching for it, and now here it was, hidden beneath a bed in the prison realm. "How did you get this?"

"Egan gave it to me to guard. In his ignorance, he sees the book as useless because he can't read it, but he doesn't trust Enis with it."

"Yeah," Griffin sighed. "Neither do I." His mother was not the same fae who'd left her kids behind. She spent too long chasing this book. Now, it was all she cared about. He pictured Tia pouring over the book as Enis watched with a steely gaze. "Is Tia okay?"

"She's scared. So is her brother. They know they're special, but right now, they think it's because they can read most of the book."

He didn't think he'd ever understand the Fargelsian twin magic, but the thought of Tia and Toby in the prison realm was a nightmare.

Riona could see a question in his eyes. He wanted to ask her about what Callum said of the kids' parentage, but something held him back.

"Griffin." Riona turned to him. "I need you to make a decision right now. I know I betrayed your trust and broke the friendship we had, but that's in the past. And our future is bleak. It consists of keeping people alive long enough to thwart the king. So, right now in the present, you need to decide if you trust me, if you can work with me." Her eyes pleaded with him. "I can't do this alone."

Griffin stared at her for a long moment as if trying to see past the issues separating them. A sigh rattled from his lips. "I do. I trust you. At least I want to. Just don't make me regret it again."

Riona suppressed a smile and nodded as he pulled the heavy book into her lap. "Enis thinks there is a page missing."

"Lots of the pages must be missing. Spells from this book are spread across the three kingdoms."

"Yes, but this page is important. It infuses magic into someone who has none. Enis says Nihal believed the book could give out magic. But then she saw Egan, and she believed it too. The twins have scoured the book looking for this particular spell, but it isn't there. We think he's using it to siphon magic from the barrier. It's how he returned your portal magic and how he's giving you bits of it now to keep you alive."

"If he's funneling magic from the barrier, does that mean he can bring it down on his own?"

"I don't think so. I believe whatever spell he's learned is extremely limited in its use."

Griffin ran a hand through his hair and looked away. "What Callum said to me before ... is that in the book?"

It had been a few nights since Riona discovered the family tree, but she'd looked at it again and again. It never changed.

She flipped open the book, going straight to the last pages where the O'Rourke Queen's lineage was depicted.

"I don't understand. This is Sorcha's family?"

"The Iskalt queen was descended from Sorcha, so are her children..."

Griffin traced the lines before finding Brea's name. Below her were each of her children. Two of them had lines leading to Lochlan. The other two ... "The twins really are mine." He couldn't take his eyes off the names. "How is this possible?"

"I think you'll find a great many things are possible with this magic. The only thing stronger than the wall around Myrkur is this book." She closed the book and slid it toward Griffin. "We've discovered that each fae can only read the parts that relate to them. I wonder what the book will show you?" She lifted a brow in challenge.

Griffin stared at the worn cover.

"Go on. Open it."

Long fingers slid under the cover, flipping it open. And nothing happened. "Are you sure it's supposed to show me something?"

"Do you hear it? The whispers?"

His brow creased. "Whispers?" He closed the cover. "When I was trapped in my own portal, I heard them. And in Aghadoon outside the library. What did it show you before?"

Riona had been prepared for the question. Over the last few days, she'd gone through every bit of the book it let her read, but there was one part the book hadn't revealed to her, and she'd been too scared to ask the twins. She lifted a hand, watching the swirling marks dance across her skin. Nihal claimed the tattoos told of her destiny and that the book would help her discover what that was.

"Many things," she whispered, answering his question. "But not enough."

Chapter 24

GRIFFIN

Egan wanted Riona to seduce Griffin, to learn the secrets he had lurking inside him. Secrets about the queens and kings of the three realms, about their readiness and willingness to fight.

What he didn't understand was the kingdoms were used to battles, ten years of peace didn't erase their history of war with Queen Regan. Only now, all three kingdoms would have a common enemy. In all the histories of the fae realms, Griffin couldn't recall a time when Fargelsi, Eldur, and Iskalt bonded together as a unified army. If Lochlan heeded the letter Griffin left for him, they'd be ready.

Griffin just had to make sure those he loved on this side of the barrier were ready as well. He rolled onto his side, his body aching from spending the night on Riona's floor. When he left in the morning, the entire palace would assume he'd slept in Riona's bed, that she'd obeyed Egan's command.

Noise sounded in the dark, and Griffin sat up, trying to make out the figure.

Riona.

She stood with her bare back to him, her wings folded in. Griffin averted his eyes as she finished getting dressed.

"You can look now." Her words weren't hard, only resigned. "Today is going to be awful." She slipped a tiny dagger into her boot before letting her trousers cover it. Another knife hung at her waist next to her fire opal encrusted broad sword.

"That sword was a gift from the king." It wasn't a question, only a statement. The opals gave it away. Opals the indentured were forced to mine.

Riona swept her dark hair up out of her face, tying it with a black ribbon that matched the tight vest she wore over a dark shirt.

Griffin's eyes went to the single window. It was always dark in Myrkur, but the position of the moon told him it was still very early. "Where are you headed?"

"I must join the king. We have some duties to attend too."

"Is part of me trusting you not asking questions?" He looked up at her from his bed on the floor.

A pained expression flashed across her face. "Not today, Griff. You don't want to ask what I'm doing today." She wouldn't look at him.

Griffin considered what evils she might do in the name of her king. "It's a village, isn't it? You're being sent to get the fae in the villages to fall back in line."

"No, Griff. Today's mission is about one fae, no other."

One fae. He pushed himself off the floor with all the strength he could muster. "What are you going to do to him?"

Gulliver.

Riona stopped with her hand on the door. "I'm going to try to save him, Griff. But Egan wants to control you, and he knows the way to do that is through that boy."

And the twins. Had Callum told Egan they were Griffin's children? Gulliver was capable of taking care of himself.

"Help him. Please." He had to choose. Gulliver or the twins. But it was never a real choice. He didn't have a way to help Gulliver. Griffin's heart cracked in two as he pictured Gulliver tied to the whipping post.

Riona nodded once, scooped the book into her arms and left.

Griffin's legs cried out with weakness, and he fell onto Riona's bed. How was he good to anyone in this state? He'd fail them all. Riona. Gulliver. Brea. The twins.

But he wouldn't stop trying, not while he lived. He pushed himself up again and yanked open the door. Rows of soldiers slept on cots in the main hall of the barracks.

He crept through the sleeping soldiers, reaching for the main door right as it opened. Griffin reeled back as Toby's frantic gaze found his. His ... son? Griffin couldn't unpack those emotions right now, not when they were all in so much danger.

"What are you doing here?"

Toby cast a nervous glance behind Griffin at the sleeping soldiers. "I ... well, you see..." He couldn't get the words out as his voice trembled.

Griffin grabbed him by the shirt and pulled him into the barracks. He held a finger to his lips as he led Toby back to Riona's quarters.

Once they closed the door, Toby released a long breath.

"You shouldn't be here, Toby."

The kid kept his eyes trained on his shoes. "Tia told me I had to come."

What was that girl thinking? "Weren't guards watching you?"

Toby shrugged. "During the day they sit outside our rooms laughing and rolling dice. But our night guards usually fall asleep, and it's so early I managed to get out before they woke."

Griffin lowered himself to the bed. "Toby—"

"You can barely walk," he blurted, crossing his arms.

"I won't begin to guess how you found me here, but—"

"Oh, the entire palace knows you stayed in Riona's room last night. Why do they care where you sleep?"

"It's not about sleeping," Griffin muttered. "I'll ask again, why have you come?"

"We waited for you to find us. In the human world. Tia kept promising me you'd come. That you were one of the good fae who'd rescue us."

"I tried, Toby." Griffin scrubbed a hand over his face. "We

couldn't reach you. It wasn't until you crossed into the prison realm that I knew where you were."

"Is it true? That Mama and Papa have forgotten us?" His bottom lip quivered at the mention of his parents.

Griffin wanted to say no, to tell this kid his parents could never possibly forget him, but the lie stuck in his throat. Tears slid down Toby's reddened cheeks.

Griffin couldn't handle it anymore, he stood and pulled Toby into a hug, the kind of hug a parent gave. Toby trembled in his arms. "Are we ever going to see Iskalt again?"

Griffin pulled back and looked down at him. "I will do everything in my power to get you home."

Toby nodded, clinging to Griffin once more. Heat seared from his touch, but Griffin couldn't pull away as if the magic held him in place as it flowed from Toby, the twin born without magic.

"Toby, what's happening?" Strength wound through him, wiping away months of weakness, of feeling ill. Griffin had almost forgotten what strength felt like.

Toby pulled away. "We found a way. In the spell book, we found an entire chapter on Sorcha's prison boundary and copied it before they took the book from us. We don't understand most of it yet, but Tia used those pages to figure out how to isolate one fae's magic from the barrier that took it. She hadn't tried yet to direct it in to a real fae. Enis called it restorative magic."

Griffin stepped back, magic tingling along his skin, a familiar power. His own. "You could have killed me."

"The sickness would have killed you."

"But how? You don't have magic."

Toby stepped back, dropping his gaze.

"Kid." Griffin leaned down toward him. "Answer my question."

A small smile appeared on his lips. "You sound just like Papa when he's irritated."

Griffin didn't know if the twins would ever learn the truth, but now wasn't the time for family reconciliations. "Toby..."

"No one knows we can do it. Not even Mama."

"Do what, exactly?"

Toby rubbed his hands up and down his arms. A nervous tic. "Mama taught us a long time ago how I could boost Tia's magic, but that we needed to be careful. She said we should always agree on how to use our magic together as a team. She said my magic is just as important as Tia's even though I can't do much with it on my own and most people would think I don't have magic at all. But that's not all we can do. Tia ... she can funnel her magic *through* me when I'm not at her side. The spell that returned your magic ... Tia performed it just now, but I was her conduit."

All the implications of this rolled through Griffin's mind. The two of them could do great things together or they could be used for great evil.

"Toby." Griffin put a hand on each shoulder and looked into his son's eyes. "You can't tell anyone what you've done here today, that I have my magic inside the prison realm."

Toby nodded. "We know how to keep secrets."

"Good, then let's get to the palace before the morning guards take their shifts."

Ten years without magic, and Griffin hadn't lost a beat. He reveled in the feeling of the Iskalt power swirling within him. But he couldn't let it free. Not yet. Even during the day in Myrkur, the moon provided him with the power. If this realm wasn't so terrible, it could be an Iskaltian's dream.

He hunched his shoulders, trying to seem like he was as close to death as they all assumed.

Toby stopped in front of a door and knocked. A crashing sound came from inside before Toby knocked again, looking sideways down the hall. "Tia, it's me."

A grating sound echoed in the hall as Tia unlocked the door and ushered them in. Griffin tried to find something of him in there, but both kids were so like Brea.

A teacart lay on its side with a rusted metal kettle leaking tea out on to the woven carpet that surrounded the bed. Griffin righted the cart.

The book sat atop the bed, open.

"Uncle Griff." Tia wrapped long arms around him.

He rested his chin on the top of her head. "Thank you."

She smiled as she looked up at him. "It was Toby's idea that we test what we found on you."

Even now while performing no magic, the power swirled in Tia's eyes, stronger than he'd ever seen before.

"Egan returned my magic to me a few days ago so I could translate the passages he wants from the book." She shrugged. "He underestimates me. I learned his spell the moment he murmured the words, and that told me what to look for in the book so I could help you."

Griffin released her. The girl was young, but she had a good head on her shoulders.

A grunt came from under the bed. "Blasted wood." Gulliver slid out, clutching the top of his head. "Griff." He grinned up at him.

Griffin crossed his arms. "What are you doing under there?"

"We thought it was the morning guards knocking on the door."

Reaching a hand down, Griffin pulled Gulliver up and yanked him into a crushing hug.

"You're kind of cutting off my air, Griff." Gulliver's tail poked at Griffin.

"Sorry." He backed away. "How did you escape?"

Another grin slid across his lips. "Well, that was the easy part. Hector threw me in a cell just like we'd planned, but after I'd already stolen the keys from one of the guards. I stayed there for a couple days so I didn't cast any suspicion on Hector, but last night I saw my chance. My guard was part of the network Hector has created. He pretended he didn't see me escaping the dungeon. Tia has been hiding me all night."

"Good. We can get word to Hector to extract you."

Gulliver's cat eyes narrowed. "If you think I'm leaving my friends to fight this battle, you don't know me at all. I won't go, and you can't make me."

Tia intertwined her finger's with Gulliver's. "It's okay, Gullie. You don't have to go." She glared at Griffin as if challenging him.

"Fine." Griffin pointed at Gulliver. "But—and this goes for all three of you—you are not to try anything dangerous. If you need help, you will come to me, no one else. Not Riona, not Enis, not Egan."

Tia's scowl deepened. "But Riona has been helping us. Want to see?"

He let her lead him to the book on the bed. "Riona already told me how the book shows you what you need, but I've tried. I'm not important in this story." The book showed him the family tree he couldn't stop thinking of, but nothing else.

"No, you don't get it. The book doesn't show *you* what you need to see. It shows your magic what it needs. So, when you had such a small amount of magic..."

"But Riona doesn't have magic."

Tia shook her head. "You're wrong. The book says all fae have magic. Every single one, even those like Toby. Most people say he doesn't have a lick of magic, but he does. It's just different. The Dark Fae can't perform spells or open portals, but their magic is in their nature. Their wings and horns and even tusks. You could say they're more magical than even the Light Fae."

Gulliver looked to Griffin. "Try it. Now that your magic has been returned."

Fear ripped through Griffin, but he inched closer to the four-poster bed. He ran a finger along the spine before opening the cover. The pages started flipping of their own accord, and he jumped back in surprise. When they stilled, he forced himself to look.

On the page were familiar symbols. They flickered and shifted across the page before text appeared beneath them. He'd seen these before. "Why am I seeing this?" It was a symbol translation, the kind that could tell Riona the destiny her tattoos spelled out.

Toby climbed up beside Tia, stopping short of taking her hand.

"You're important." Tia shrugged. "Not in the same way as us, but no less. This book ... the people here, everything and everyone is preparing. You talked to Callum back in Iskalt, leading to our kidnapping and finding the book. Then you saved your mother, and she ended up here. Gulliver says Riona used to be an enemy, but now she too is ready to choose the right side. The book speaks of a single fae who sets it all in motion and is key to getting everything into place. A fae who knows everything that needs to happen, even if he doesn't know he knows."

Griffin shook his head. "I've done nothing. I didn't retrieve the book or save you."

Tia shrugged. "That's because you weren't supposed to save us yet, but it doesn't mean you haven't done exactly what you were meant to. And now the book is showing you the key to Riona's markings. There is meaning in that."

Griffin looked down at his niece—or his daughter. That term scared him more than the other. "Be careful, Tia. I think this book is more dangerous than we know. Be cautious trusting in something so powerful." He looked down at the book that was still open to the page of symbols. "Can I take this page?" He didn't want it to fall into Egan's hands or anyone else.

Tia nodded, carefully ripping it from the book.

Griffin turned to Gulliver. He didn't like that he was here, but if there was one fae who could move around unseen, it was him. "Do you think you can get a message to someone close to the king?"

"Of course." He nodded eagerly.

Griffin didn't want to do this. He'd rather Gulliver hid under the bed all day. And yet, here he was.

"I need you to find Riona. Tell her to come to my rooms tonight."

Gulliver's brow creased. "So, I'm a booty call messenger?"

One day, Griffin would get back at Myles for teaching Gulliver about human TV shows. "Just do it, Gullie." He turned toward the door. "And pick up this mess." He didn't want Egan to send an indentured to their rooms. "You're royals, not pigs raised in a barn."

"I'm not." Gulliver grinned. "I'm a dirty rotten thief."

"Well, Mr. Dirty Rotten Thief, help the prince and princess clean up the tea I'm sure you spilled."

Griffin left them to their mess. His magic buzzed along his skin, making him feel alive for the first time in so long. He clutched the page about Riona's tattoos in his fist as he pushed into his rooms.

It didn't escape his notice how he stayed in the palace—crumbling or not—and Riona lived in the army barracks.

With his new strength he wanted to run, to sit atop a horse, or simply walk down to the slums to find out more about Hector's network.

But he couldn't. Instead, he studied the page from the book of power and waited for Riona.

CHAPTER 25

GRIFFIN

Griffin couldn't sit still as he paced the length of his room. At least here there was no noise except the magic getting used to him once more. It filled his every sense, every part of him.

It was home.

He wasn't meant to live without magic, but it was a consequence of his prison sentence that he'd learned to accept. .

He walked to the window and clutched the frame, looking out onto the sleeping palace grounds. It didn't take long to grow used to the changing of night to day and day to night. When the sky remained dark, you had to use other markers.

Like the moon, perpetually full, hanging overhead. The stars scattered across the sky.

A knock sounded on his door. He steeled himself, letting his shoulders hunch and his steps falter before pulling the heavy door open.

Riona stood on the other side wearing the same clothes as before, but it wasn't her clothing that drew attention. Red lines stretched down her cheek and shoulders with blood crusting the edges. "Come in." He didn't take his eyes off her as he shut the door.

Riona held her chin up, not cowered by anything Egan did to her.

"He thinks I have come here to extract information, to lure you into your bed. So, we'll have most of the night."

"Riona," he whispered, reaching a hand to grip her chin and turn her head for a better look. "What did he do to you?"

She didn't push his hand away like he'd expect her to do. Instead, she stilled her quivering lip. "I'm okay, Griff." She sighed. "You'll be happy to know Gulliver has escaped. He's probably far from the city by now."

Griffin's brow creased. "He didn't get a message to you to come here?"

She shook her head. "I..." She released a breath. "He struck me ... Egan ... " She clutched her cheek. "When we didn't find Gulliver in his cell. He turned his whip on me, not stopping until Hector stepped in and calmed him down. But then ... what if Egan no longer favors me? That is when the real damage will happen."

His hands skimmed her shoulders and cheeks, up into her hair. "I won't let anything happen to you." He removed his hands and stepped back. "You asked me this morning to trust you. And I do, Riona. I trust you." He turned to the table where he'd set the page from the book. "Right now, I'm asking for the same. You and I will get out of here, we will save our families, our friends. That is our destiny. It doesn't matter what this page tells us. We choose our own paths."

Riona's wings gave an agitated shake, but her expression hardened. "Griff, what did you find?"

"If what Tia says is true, I found nothing. The page found my magic."

"Your magic," she breathed. "It makes perfect sense. The book didn't react to you because..." She stumbled back. "You have your magic now. All of it?"

He nodded, lifting a hand to show the power sparking across his fingertips. Riona approached him cautiously, rising on her toes to look into his eyes. "They're violet. Griffin, your magic ... it's beautiful."

He shook his head and held up the page. "Wait until I show you this."

Riona took it from him, her eyes scanning the symbols. "I don't know what it means."

"You can't read the symbols?"

She shook her head. The images on her skin moved with more speed than they had before. "My tattoos ... how?"

He stepped toward her. "I don't know why the book showed this to me. Tia has her theories. But it feels right. I think I'm supposed to have found it. I'm supposed to shape your destiny with the writing on that page."

Gathering every ounce of courage she possessed, she handed the page back to him. "Okay." She nodded. "I think I'm ready."

Griffin knew she'd been waiting for this her entire life. To finally understand what her tattoos meant.

Riona pulled every knife she had free, setting them on the table. She unbuckled her sword belt and let it fall to the ground with a clang.

The page said the symbols must be read in a specific order to spell out what Riona needed to know.

Griffin's magic directed him to leave the page on the table. He'd only read the symbols once, but the power inside him remembered. It wouldn't all make sense until he matched the symbols he'd read about with the ones sketched across her body.

"Give me your hands."

She held them out. On the left was a horseshoe. He rubbed his thumb over it before reading the second, a symbol that looked like praying hands. A human symbol.

"Faith will mean more to you than luck." The words poured out of him. "Faith in yourself and in the people around you." The two symbols kept swirling, unable to be still. Griffin leaned forward, pressing his lips against each. "I have faith in you."

Riona shivered. "Please, just keep going."

He ran his hands up her bare arms, finding the next marking and its equally vague meaning about loyalty. He bent forward to repeat the kiss on the tattoo on her arm. "You have my loyalty." Egan raised her, but she'd betrayed him so many times for Griffin. She chose to be good, and Griffin wouldn't forget that.

He moved up to her neck. "This row of white flowers means there is a purity about your task." She remained still as he pressed a kiss to the blossoms pulsing around her throat.

"Griff," she whispered, lifting her chin for him to move the kisses up. He pressed his lips to the mark of a whip across her face, and she closed her eyes, bringing her fingers to the laces of her vest. "Don't forget what we're doing."

He grinned against her skin. "Detours are allowed."

Her fingers shook on the laces, and Griffin put a hand over them. "Let me."

She nodded and dropped her hands. Griffin fought with the laces, and she helped him slid the vest and shirt over her head. He didn't stare at her nakedness, instead keeping his eyes on hers. His fingers skimmed her sides before settling on the next tattoo—a pattern of colorful lines weaving together. "You're going to change the course of fae history forever."

Riona held an arm across her breasts as Griffin's heated gaze left her eyes, trailing down to the single mark on her stomach. It reminded him of a compass rose with lines and arrows pointing in every direction. His fingers flitted over it, and his eyes flashed violet. "This one, right here, says a handsome fae will come into your life and make you question everything you thought you knew."

She smiled. "Well, it'll be nice when that happens."

Griffin laughed and pressed a kiss to the symbol. "It points to more than one path."

"That's impossible. You can't have more than one destiny."

Griffin rounded her to find the symbols on her back and stopped. His fingers skimmed across the raised welts, and she gasped at the pain.

"He did this to you?"

She nodded. "Egan loves his whip."

He stood, rounding her once more. "I will kill him one day. That I promise you. He will never touch you again."

She swallowed, her eyes glassing over. In true Riona fashion, she didn't let a tear escape.

Griffin moved back around her, letting his lips skim over the bruises between her shoulder blades. Rage raced through him, but the magic was stronger and it wanted him to continue.

He closed his eyes, touching the intricate knots swirling and curving over her sides. "You will be integral to much magic you were not born with. The instrument—"

Riona gasped. "Nihal's piccolo."

That part scared him. They'd seen first-hand how unpredictable and dangerous the music from the book was.

Griffin continued to read the clusters of symbols across her hips and back that held bits of information that wouldn't make sense until their true meanings were fulfilled. When he reached the last moving tattoo at the center of her back, he placed a palm over the colorful circle full of swirling blue and orange fae symbols, seeing flashes in his mind. "There's a crown." It came to him so suddenly he wasn't prepared for the onslaught of images racing through his mind. He fell back onto his butt. "Riona..." His eyes widened. "This tattoo speaks of your destiny." He stood, turning her to face him. "You are the keeper of Myrkur. That was once the role of your people in ancient times. Each generation a keeper rises. It is her responsibility to name the true heir of Myrkur and to guide them in their rule. When the time is right, you will know our rightful king or queen ... and you will place them on the throne. The keeper is ... a kingmaker." The tattoo revealed endless possibilities, but one thing was clear. They would defeat Egan.

Riona's face turned ashen as she trembled and dropped to her knees. She gasped, searching for her breath. "I feel ... empty somehow. This purpose, it no longer belongs only to me." She looked up at him, her eyes glassy and dazed. "You've set it in motion."

Griffin rose up on his knees, his hands shaking as he reached for her. "Naming a king or queen ... it's like having the power to end a war."

"Or start one."

He reached forward and tucked a braid behind her ear. "We don't know what the future holds, Riona. But now we know your role in it. And—"

"And what?"

"There have been so many misunderstandings between us, so many betrayals. And we're still here, still standing."

Griffin watched the war going on in her eyes. Without warning, she grabbed Griffin's shirt, pulling him into a bruising kiss. He kissed her back with everything he had, every bit of magic and power went into the kiss, sparking between the Dark and Light Fae.

Griffin ran his hands down her spine just beneath her wings, and she shivered under his touch. "Riona," he whispered against her lips.

"Hmm?" Her eyes found his.

"I think—"

"No." She cut him off. "We won't do the declaration thing. Because a war is coming for us, and we don't know what will happen."

Griffin pushed to his feet and extended a hand down. She took it and got to her feet. Griffin slid his shirt off over his head before pulling Riona to him once more. They collapsed onto the bed in a tangle of limbs and wings.

"Sometimes, Griff, moments are just that. Moments. A space in time that can never exist again."

Griffin pressed a kiss to her lips. "And sometimes moments are part of a lifetime, bigger than themselves."

He gave himself to her in every way, because she was right about one thing. They didn't know how much time they had.

That night, after Riona had curled against him under a fur blanket, the truth of her tattoos ran through his mind. She was a kingmaker, the only fae alive with the ability to recognize the true heir of Myr. If anyone else found out, they'd kill her.

He tightened his arms around her, wondering how a man who was sent to the prison realm after a lifetime of betrayals now had so many fae to protect.

CHAPTER 26

GRIFFIN

Griffin forced his hand to tremble as he lifted a spoon of porridge to his lips, nearly letting it fall back into his bowl before he managed to get the food in his mouth. Pretending to be a weakling when he had the full use of his magic was nearly as exhausting as actually being that weak.

They were finally learning the way the magic of the book worked, and how it revealed certain spells to certain people based on their need of the magic and their destiny. And the limitations of such magic in this realm. Egan had used the pages he and his forefathers had gathered to gain control of Myrkur. For the longest time, he was the only fae with any magic at all—with the ability to give and take magic, seemingly at will. It made him seem all-powerful to those without magic of any kind. But that wasn't the case. Now that Griffin understood Egan's limitations—it weakened the Dark Fae king in his eyes. He wasn't all-powerful, and now that Griffin had his magic back, he wouldn't rest until Egan was defeated.

He still maintained his hold on Griffin, but the king had no idea how strong Griffin was now—and Griffin meant to keep it that way.

"The troops are ready to move at a moment's notice, my king." Riona stood beside Egan's table in the dining hall. She never dined with them, but she was always there beside her king, ever the loyal servant. Except she was no longer loyal. Griffin could see that now. All her flirtations and menacing attitudes were a facade. Probably always had been. He doubted if Riona had ever shown Egan her true self.

"Very good, my dear. If we can ever decipher that cursed book, we'll be ready to march."

"I am told the child is nearly ready, my lord." Riona tilted her head toward her king, catching Griffin's eye, she gave a sly wink.

He ducked his head to hide a smile.

"I need you to understand something before we march for the border," Griffin said in a weary voice.

"For a man at death's door, you are quick to voice your *needs*, considering I am the one keeping you alive." Egan sneered as he stuffed his face with runny eggs, the yolks dripping into his beard.

"Tia is a child," Griffin reminded him. "The Light Fae are born with magic, but most will not have use of it until they are of age. Which Tia will not be for eight more years."

"I know all of this." Egan waved away his concerns. "The child is special—"

"Special though she may be, she is still a child," Griffin interrupted. "She, like all Fargelsian children, has use of her Gelsi magic she inherited from her mother and grandfather."

"Her magic will be more than enough to destroy the barrier once we have translated the instructions." Egan went back to his eggs, ignoring Griffin's concerns.

Griffin slammed his fist down on the table, making the king's plate rattle at the opposite end. Egan glared at Griffin, a hint of worry crossing his face, and Griffin could have kicked himself for displaying such strength.

"No," Griffin whispered, letting his shoulders slump forward and his voice grate in his throat. "It will likely not be enough. Fargelsi children Tia's age grow up learning the language of power, using it for simple tasks like lighting a fire or making flowers grow. It takes them a lifetime of study before they can master their power. What you are asking of Tia far exceeds reasonable expectations of a child her age. She is special, and she will try, and it might prove to be enough, but I need you to understand that magic is not a simple matter of wishing for results and willing them into existence. This could kill her if she is pushed too far. And if you care nothing else about her, remember this—she is a valuable tool now, think of what she will become if given the opportunity to live long enough to master the magic of the three kingdoms running through her veins. Do not waste her power, your Majesty. Think of how she may serve you in the future."

It was all he could do for his daughter right now. If he could sweep her and his sons far away from Myrkur and beyond Egan's grasp, he would without a moment's hesitation. They were trapped, and Tia would have to do this. But he would not see it kill her if he could help it.

"Very well." Egan sipped from his goblet, sloshing watered wine down his chin. "You make a valid point. But I will not be easily swayed—"

They all turned as Enis barged into the dining hall and marched up to the king's table, shoving her way past guards and soldiers. "It is done." She slammed the book onto the table. "We have deciphered the last of the spell work needed to bring the barrier down."

"And can the child actually do it?" Egan glared at Griffin.

"Of course, she can." Enis stood proudly. "My granddaughter translated most of the spells herself. She is more than capable."

"Then we march." Egan wiped his hands on a stained linen napkin and stood. "We leave for the border in an hour." He strode from the dining hall, yanking on the magical chain that held Griffin prisoner. He had no choice but to follow the king.

Torchlight flanked the king's entourage as they made their way along the main road to the border. Egan sat tall in his saddle. His feeble mount struggled under his weight, but the poor animal was the finest horse in the king's stables. Griffin rode on a mule behind him with Riona at his side. Enis rode in the king's carriage with the twins.

The horde of the Dark Fae army followed in their wake.

A sick sense of déjà vu swept through him as they neared the invisible barrier holding them captive. He'd been here before. Though last time a barrier like this was broken, he'd been on the wrong side of the battle. This time, he meant to be on the right side. He could only hope Lochlan had followed his instructions. If Tia managed to get the wall down, he prayed all the realms where there with their armies, waiting to flatten Egan's army with their magic. Magic Egan and his loyal soldiers couldn't fathom.

The king's party came to a halt at the entrance to the prison realm, marked by two large boulders on either side of the narrow path.

The dim sunlight shone here at the border, the no-man's-land between Myrkur and the Northern Vatlands. The king's army shielded their eyes, squinting into the light they weren't used to. If they only knew what awaited them on the other side, how many would turn back now?

Griffin watched as Enis led Tia and Toby from the carriage, clutching the book under her arm.

Riona and Griffin moved to dismount, but Egan stopped them. "We will wait at the ready."

Griffin took a deep breath, trying to find the patience to deal with the king's idiocy. "Your Majesty, we need to make camp."

"We will make camp on the other side. I will not spend another night in captivity now that I have the means to see it end."

"Your Majesty, this will take days, not minutes or even hours. This is the most complex magic most of us will ever see. It took the best magic wielders of all three realms to create this boundary magic hundreds of years ago. It has only strengthened over time. And we are counting on a child to break through it. It is not a simple matter of blowing up a wall made of brick and mortar."

"Griffin is right," Riona interjected. "I have seen the Light Fae use their magic. It is impressive, but it does take effort, your Majesty.

Perhaps you should send your army home and summon them when this is done?"

"No." Egan slid from his horse. "We will make camp here. I want my soldiers at the ready the moment that wall of magic crumbles. We don't know what awaits us on the other side."

"Very well, sir. I will see to the soldiers." Riona made it seem like making camp now was all the king's idea to begin with. She handled him well.

Enis approached the barrier with Tia and Toby at her side. She set up a podium to hold the book, lowering it to Tia's height. He could tell even from this distance that Tia was scared to death. She looked over her shoulder back at him, her eyes glinting in the fading light. "Uncle Griff?" She clutched her grandmother's hand.

"Your Majesty, may I?" Griffin gestured at the twins.

"You get two minutes, so make it count." Egan waved him toward the children as he sauntered off into the swarm of his army.

Griffin rushed to their side, pulling Tia and Toby close.

Tia threw her arms around him and buried her face in his shoulder. "I don't want to do this," she whispered. "It's wrong."

"It'll be okay, Tia." Toby patted her back.

"Toby's right." Griffin pulled back so he could see her face. "It's not ... wrong." He searched for the right words. "There are thousands of people stuck here that don't deserve it."

"Really?" She sniffed.

"So many." Griffin smoothed the reddish blond hair from her face. In the golden light here, her hair was redder. Like his. "Do the best you can, Tia. Trust your gut, and if you can't do it, we will find another way. I won't let anything happen to you."

"Don't fill the child's head with lies." Enis shook her head.

Griffin stood, holding the twin's hands. "You should try to remember that they're your grandchildren, and you're supposed to love them. Not sacrifice them to get your hands on the book you gave up your own children for." Griffin looked down at the twins. "I will be right behind you."

He backed away, a little piece of himself broke, leaving them to take on such an enormous task. Tia looked so tiny as she approached the podium, flipping through the book to find where she'd decided she should start.

While the others made camp, Griffin sat at the center of the dusty path that had led him here nearly ten years ago. A wave of dizziness washed over him, but he assumed it was exhaustion. He had slept little since returning to Myrkur.

"You know, you should go find your tent and get some rest." Riona came to sit beside him. "You said yourself this would take some time."

"I can't just leave them." Griffin shivered as Tia reached out with her magic, testing the boundary.

"I've ordered several tents to be set up right here, so you don't have to leave them, and you can make sure they're getting the rest they need."

"Thank you." Griffin reached for her hand but stopped. He wanted to wrap his arms around her, to let her give him comfort, but Egan had eyes everywhere, and he couldn't know about what truly happened between them. He thought he'd sent Riona to seduce him, that it would mean nothing. Griffin wasn't exactly sure what it meant, but he knew it wasn't nothing.

For hours, that first night, Griffin and Riona sat on the dusty road, watching Tia, grasping Toby's hand as she worked her way through the complicated magic. Griffin and Enis were the only ones who could see she was making progress, albeit slow progress. Every time she touched the barrier with her magic, it lit up the night sky for a moment, displaying the intricate and complex weave of spells that held them trapped inside Myrkur.

"This is utter nonsense." Egan paced furiously. "Nothing is happening, we should be well on our way to Iskalt by now. This child will not make a fool of me!" He kicked a pebble in the road, snorting and pacing like a big cat irritated by the confines of its cage.

"Will you be quiet, you fool of a king?" Enis turned, staring at him with her hands on her hips. "I've had quite enough bluster out of you for one night. This is highly stressful, complicated work you clearly don't understand, so why don't you go drink some more wine with your soldiers and leave the magic to us?"

Egan blustered some more, taking a menacing step toward the former Queen of Iskalt.

"My King," Riona interjected, putting herself between Egan and Enis. "Perhaps the children would feel less ... intimidated if you left them to it?"

Egan started to argue but thought better of it. "You are right, my dear." He patted her hand. He sought his tent after that, giving Enis one final glare that could cut glass.

Griffin wondered if his mother would make it out of Myrkur alive after that outburst.

Eventually, Griffin insisted they stop for the night, carrying Tia to her bed inside the tent she shared with her grandmother. Riona carried Toby, equally weary from his long day of amplifying his sister's magic—something Egan still didn't realize the boy could do. To him, Toby was useless, and Griffin wanted to keep it that way.

"Eat something." Riona shoved a plate of eggs and bacon into Griffin's hands. The sun was hardly up yet, and Tia was already hard at work again. The barrier flickered and darkened with every murmured part of the spell she spoke, sending wave after wave of magic against the wall.

"I'm glad Brea's not here to see this. It would kill her." Griffin ate mechanically, the food tasting like sawdust in his mouth.

"What do you mean, Tierney O'Shea?" Enis raised her voice, her face screwed up in anger.

Griffin set his plate aside, rushing to find out what was amiss.

Tia shrank under her grandmother's furious glare.

"What do you mean Tobias is your *conduit*?" Enis had gone red with rage.

"Take a step back." Griffin took his mother by the shoulders, moving her away from the twins. "You're tired and frustrated." He turned to find Tia crying. Her head braced on Toby's shoulder.

Griffin bent toward Toby, placing a gentle hand on his small shoulder. "Why don't you tell me what's going on?"

"Tia's scared." Toby lifted his head. "She's better when I'm with her."

"Of course, she is. You're the most important fae she has."

Tia nodded, sniffing back her tears.

"But if she doesn't physically *need* the boy here to funnel magic through him, then we could use him elsewhere," Enis insisted.

"I think we *need* to do whatever makes the twins comfortable. And we *need* to remember they are young children." Griffin glared at his mother, wondering how she'd become so cold.

"It's true, I am Tia's conduit," Toby said, squaring his shoulders. "She can do magic through me or take my energy to strengthen her magic."

"Right, we know that." Griffin nodded. "What seems to be the problem about that?" He played ignorant, hoping Enis wouldn't figure out he already knew how Toby's magic worked.

"The child said she doesn't need to *touch* him to conduct magic *through* him," Enis said, her shrill voice catching more attention from the bored soldiers than Griffin thought was necessary.

"Go take a walk, Mother. Get something to drink."

"I'm fine." She folded her arms across her chest.

"It wasn't a suggestion." Griffin's voice took on a razor-sharp edge.

Enis walked away, leaving Griffin alone with the twins.

"Why does this make Grandma so angry?" Griffin asked, kneeling down beside Toby.

Toby took a deep breath. "It means, she can send me to another part of the barrier, and Tia can whisper the spells through me. We can work to weaken the barrier in two places at once."

"I was told the boy doesn't have magic." Egan's gravelly voice nearly made Griffin jump out of his skin. "You know how I feel about lies, O'Shea." The noose tightened, squeezing around Griffin's heart as a reminder of who was in charge.

Griffin stood in front of the twins. "He doesn't have magic of his own," Griffin explained. "He is simply a conduit for his sister's magic."

"We will send him to another axis point of the barrier." Enis came up behind the king. "This is a good thing, your Majesty. It means we will get through this wall faster."

Tia started to cry when the king ordered a contingent of his soldiers to take Toby away. "Toby! No. The magic scares him when I'm not with him."

"It's okay, Tia. I will go with him." Griffin moved to follow his son, but the tears of his daughter cut right through him. How did Brea and Lochlan do this?

"Uncle Griff, stay with Tia. I'll be okay." Toby lifted his chin.

"I'll keep an eye on Toby," Riona whispered. "I'll fly to wherever he is and make sure he's okay. For now, I'll send someone I trust with him."

Griffin nodded and watched her walk away with his brave little boy, so like the loyal father who'd raised him.

He was proud of Toby. Proud of Tia. And wherever Gulliver was, he was proud of him too.

Chapter 27

GRIFFIN

Griffin felt so helpless, watching Tia work tirelessly, following the complex spell work from the book. She spoke the words of power until her voice was hardly more than a rasp in her throat. But Enis plied her with special teas and honey to give her the strength to keep going.

And now, somewhere at another part of Myrkur, Toby did the same while Biona watched over him.

"What is happening with the lights?" Egan came to sit beside him. "I can see it now, she's burrowing right through it, taking it apart piece by piece."

Griffin looked up at the night sky. It was late, far past the time when a ten-year-old should be awake still. Colorful lights flew through the sky. Reds and yellows, purples and oranges. Every color of magic he'd ever seen danced like the snúa aftur lights that danced along the over Eldur border. And in the distance, over the rocky mountains separating them, Griffin could just make out the lights glimmering over Myrkur where Toby worked.

"It's just as you said," Griffin lied. "As she burrows through the weaves of magic, she's discarding the substance the wall is made of. It will dissipate to nothing without the other pieces holding it together."

"It's quite beautiful," Egan murmured. With nothing else to do but watch and drink, the king was more than a little drunk.

"It's the most beautiful thing I've ever seen." Griffin smiled into his own goblet of wine. And it really was. Each of those fragments of light belonged to a fae inside Myrkur. Some living. Some long dead. But as the light made its way to its owner, it carried their magic back to them. All across Myr, Light Fae who were either sent here or born here were getting their magic back, right under the king's nose.

Griffin had watched for hours before he realized the barrier was made up of the magic it took from those who entered the realm, using it to strengthen the spell work Sorcha and her contemporaries had set in motion three generations ago.

And now, Tia was giving it back.

The king left him after midnight, searching for his own bed.

Just as Griffin carried Tia into her tent, he heard the unmistakable flutter of Riona's wings. She was back from checking on Toby.

"He's safely asleep for the night, and I've arranged to have a local woman watch over him." She smiled, clearly proud of herself.

"And who is this local woman?" Griffin asked.

"Shauna." Riona nudged him with her elbow. "She and Nessa are caring for him, so you can relax."

Griffin heaved a grateful sigh of relief, but he wouldn't relax until this was over and the twins were safely home with their parents where they belonged.

"I just don't understand it." Enis snapped the book closed with an irritable sigh. "Something isn't working."

Griffin and Riona joined her around the fire, taking a seat on the dry dusty ground. "It seems to be working just fine," Griffin said. "If not a little slow."

"It shouldn't be this slow. At this rate we'll be here for months." Enis wiped a weary hand over her eyes. "I've gone through every part of this book I can access and so has Tia and Toby. There is something important I'm missing. Something the book hasn't shown to those involved."

"Maybe there's another role?" Riona suggested. "Some aspect of the magic you haven't covered yet?"

Enis nodded. "It seems that way, but the twins should cover all the aspects of magic. They have Fargelsian, Iskaltian, and Eldurian magic. And if the book seeks more mature magic, I have Gelsi magic, and Griffin has Iskalt magic."

"What about the magic of the Dark Fae?" Griffin asked.

"They don't have magic, Griffin." Enis leaned back against the log behind her and stifled a wide yawn.

"Not of the traditional sort, but they are magical beings. Nihal certainly had his own kind of magic." He glanced at Riona.

"We've tried that. Riona couldn't read the pages."

"Well, Griffin read the pages concerning my tattoos," Riona admitted softly. "I understand what they mean now. Most of them."

It was as if Enis didn't hear her. "Nihal. That's it." Enis grabbed the book, flipping through the pages. "Can you read this?" She handed the book to Riona.

Riona's brow creased as she studied the page. "It's a song. There are bars of music here I recognize."

"Do you still have Nihal's piccolo?" Enis asked eagerly.

"Yes, I've kept it with me." Riona rummaged through her bag, retrieving the instrument.

Griffin looked over her shoulder, scanning the odd symbols on the page. "You can read this?" He frowned. It looked like gibberish to him.

"Try to play the song," Enis urged, ignoring Griffin.

"We've tried that. The piccolo wouldn't play for me."

"That was before you translated your tattoos. I take it you have discovered your purpose among your markings?" Enis asked.

"I have." Riona ducked her head.

"Your people draw great strength from the discovery of their life's purpose. It changes you. Griffin is right, *that* is your magic, Riona. I think the piccolo will respond to you now."

Riona held the instrument in unsteady hands. "How will I know what this song will do? How will I know if it will ... drain my life the way it did for Nihal?"

"Read the song before you play it. I believe its purpose will come to you."

Griffin watched as Riona studied the strange symbols on the page. As she lifted the instrument to her lips, Griffin stopped her.

"Are you sure?" he asked. "Don't do it if you're uncertain." He would not sit here and watch her fade to ash in front of his eyes.

"It is a song of ... destruction." She frowned at the words. "More like a song of undoing. It won't hurt me."

Griffin nodded, afraid to let go of her hand.

She gave him a reassuring smile, and she began to play.

Griffin clapped his hands over his ears. The sound was horrendous. Like a hundred cats fighting.

"I'm sorry." Riona pulled away. "That was awful."

"No, keep trying." Enis beamed at her. "It's working!"

"Oh." Riona stared at the flute again. "It didn't make a single sound last time."

"Try it again. Take your time."

It took her several nauseating tries—literally nauseating—but she finally made it through the song without making anyone sick.

"Play it again." Enis instructed as Riona finished her second nearly perfect play through.

Enis stood, gesturing for Griffin to join her. "Look." She pointed toward the barrier.

As Riona played the now sweet melodic notes, the barrier lit up in a soft white glow the color of Riona's wings. The intricate weaves of magic binding the wall began to loosen the more she played.

"Yes, yes, keep going." Enis fairly vibrated with renewed energy. "Let's get Tia." She turned toward the tent.

"No. Let's not." Griffin stepped in front of her. "It's late and everyone is exhausted and if you disturb my ten-year-old niece while she rests, we will have a serious problem, Mother."

"Oh, Griffin." She reached to touch his cheek, sadness filling her eyes for a moment. "You are right. I'm a terrible grandmother. Of course, she needs to rest. We all do."

"We will start again at dawn." Riona slipped the piccolo back into her bag.

Things moved faster with Riona's song. Much faster.

Griffin was relieved to find that Riona's playing not only helped Tia pick apart the magic holding the wall together, but it also calmed Tia, giving her a strength he hoped trickled down through the twin bond to her brother.

Griffin stood beside Tia, feeling useless as she murmured the spells, flipping back and forth through the pages of the book. Somehow, she knew exactly which pages she needed and when. To him, none of the words on the page made sense, but her eyes flew across the lines of spells that should be far beyond her years. This kind of magic was far beyond most adult magic wielders, and she charged through it like it was nothing. His girl was an impressive sight to behold.

Tia's voice suddenly rose into a crescendo, shouting out words of power he'd never heard in all his time living in Fargelsi. Wind swept through the camp and a rolling thunder boomed across the sky. Griffin stumbled as the ground began to shake, but Tia's voice remained as strong as Riona's music.

The soft white light that reminded him of Riona's silky wings, burst into a brilliant blaze to rival the sun.

Griffin covered his eyes until the wind died down and the ground settled beneath his feet. When he opened them, the white light of the barrier was gone. She'd brought the inner wall down. The layer made up of the magic of those held within its borders.

The outer wall shifted and swayed. The iridescent glow of the magical weaves seemed to flicker and gutter like a candle flame about to burn out.

"Toby," Tia whispered, her voice raw from shouting. At the

sound of her voice, the remaining weaves of magic seemed to turn toward Griffin's daughter, like a sentient creature recognizing its master. The bright light gathered into a serpentine streak, winding and twisting like a snake.

The last threads of the barrier erupted like a blast of white-hot fire and shot toward Tia, striking her through the chest.

"Tia!" Griffin's hands fell at his sides as he stared helplessly at the still form of his daughter lying in a heap at his feet.

CHAPTER 28

GRIFFIN

"Tia." Griffin dropped to his knees, turning Tia's body so he could see her face. He pushed the fine strawberry blond hair away with a finger, almost burning himself as he did.

His hand drew back in surprise. Her skin blazed with the heat of whatever swirled inside her. White ropes of power moved under her almost translucent skin as if something lived inside her.

"Griffin!" Riona yelled.

He jerked his head up to see what she'd seen. The white wall that had remained after the magic barrier was gone, and this was his only chance to save Tia. He had to get her out.

"Get to Toby!" He didn't know who he yelled that to, either Riona or his mother, but he could only save one of the kids. It was up to his allies to save the other. This was the moment Tia knew would come.

She'd never lost faith he'd save her.

Sliding his hands underneath her small frame, he lifted her and cradled her against his chest. Magic tugged at him, Egan's leash. Griffin could have broken the magic when he first recovered his power, but Egan would have known.

Now, with nothing left to lose, he sliced through Egan's hold on him. Griffin O'Shea was finally his own man again.

A man who had to save a little girl.

"It's okay, Tia. I've got you." He avoided touching her heated skin as her head fell against his shoulder.

He looked back at the army who could now sweep through the three kingdoms of Light Fae.

Not on his watch.

"Where are you going?" His mother cried.

Griffin didn't know. He had to get Tia out of Myrkur.

Tia murmured words that made no sense to Griffin as he took off, running toward the place where the barrier stood only moments before. He ignored the fae yelling to him as he picked up speed. It had been months since Griffin had his full strength, and now, nothing could stop him getting Tia to safety.

She bumped against his chest as he ran, and a million thoughts flooded his mind. He had to get her to Brea—or maybe to Brandon, her grandfather. He understood Fargelsian power more than anyone.

Dust kicked up underneath his feet as he clambered through the mountain pass, moss-covered boulders narrowing his escape route. The sounds of armored footsteps followed him through the pass, and he looked up to find three Slyph flying above his position.

He was out of time.

"I'm sorry, Tia." He wasn't her true father, the one who'd raised her. Griffin knew that. But he still felt the crushing knowledge that he couldn't keep her safe. Griff set her down, glancing over his shoulder to find two of the Light Fae criminals who led a contingent of Egan's army.

And they too had their magic back.

Blood red streams of power narrowly missed Griffin as he gathered his O'Shea magic in the tips of his fingers and drew a line in the air, a portal into the human realm.

Picking Tia up again, he prepared to step through the opening when an arrow flew past him, lodging in the throat of one of the Light Fae. The magic faded from his eyes as he crumpled to the ground.

Yellow ropes of magic shot up to the Slyph, narrowly missing one of them, but they weren't so lucky when a second arrow sliced through her shoulder, making her tumble from the sky and slam against a boulder.

Griffin looked from the portal to the path where his two allies must have been hiding. He'd recognize that yellow magic anywhere.

They'd come.

Brea and Lochlan barely knew him. They didn't remember their twins. And yet, they were here.

Another arrow hit the remaining Light Fae in the chest, while the Slyph above tried to avoid Brea's Eldurian magic, made powerful by the blinding sun overhead. Seeing his comrades fall, he took off back toward Myrkur.

The remaining Dark Fae lifted higher in the sky before following the other back toward Egan's camp.

Griffin's heart hammered in his chest as he tried to control his breathing.

"Wow." Lochlan stepped into view. "I guess that letter to myself was right. There was an O'Shea brother here that needed my help." He looked to the portal, one eyebrow raised. "You must be Griffin. You going to go through? I wouldn't recommend it. That kid in your arms can't be helped in the human realm."

Brea followed Lochlan onto the road. "I don't get to use my magic enough. That was fun." She looked to her husband. "And you wanted to wait to approach the barrier at night so you were the one with power. This man and his daughter would have died if you had your way."

Lochlan's armor had a crown etched on the helmet marking him as king. He creaked with each step. Brea, on the other hand, wore fighting leathers that suited her.

"We should get off the road." Lochlan looked back the way they'd come and turned to march down the road to the tree line.

Brea kept a sympathetic eye on Tia, but Lochlan didn't look at them again. "The barrier is down, isn't it?"

"It is." Griffin shifted Tia, looking down into her face. It had never struck him so hard before, the forgetting. That her parents could look into her face and show no recognition. No emotion. "The Light Fae inside the prison realm have had their magic returned."

"You mean the criminals?" Lochlan asked.

"Some. Not all." Griffin didn't have the energy to explain everything he'd already taught Lochlan, everything his brother forgot once Griffin returned to the prison realm. "I'd worry more about the Dark Fae army."

Brea looked back at him then down at Tia. "Those fae had wings."

Griffin nodded. "As do many others. Are you prepared for an onslaught of things you've never seen before?"

They stepped into a clearing, sloping down the side of the mountain, and Griffin stopped. Every inch of space was occupied by a tent or a soldier. They didn't wear Iskaltian blue, there were no Iskalt flags.

Instead ... "This is the Fargelsian army."

As if that called him forth, Myles sprinted through camp. "What happened?" He looked from Brea to Griffin. "Who is this guy?"

Before, having Myles remember him had been helpful. But now that Myles too was a part of the world that forgot Griffin, he had no time for get-to-know-yous. "Is there a healer here?"

Brea was the first to answer. "Myles, go find Neeve's personal healer."

Myles ran toward another part of camp. "Where are the Iskalt forces?" The Fargelsian army was impressive, but also the weakest of the three.

Lochlan looked sideways at him. "We have them meeting with the Eldurian army at the border in case this king of yours manages to get past us. They will be here soon."

"Uncle Griff?" Tia moaned as her eyes fluttered open.

"Hey, sweetheart." He smiled down at her. "You're going to be okay."

A tear trickled down her cheek. "I was strong."

"You were." He held her close. "You were so strong, Tia."

"I feel hot, Uncle Griff. There's magic inside me that isn't mine. I feel it moving under my skin. Get it out. Please, I don't want it anymore. I just want Toby."

"Riona went to get Toby. She'll bring him to us soon."

Neeve walked through the camp, looking every bit the warrior. There was once a time when kings and queens didn't stand with their soldiers.

That time was over.

Neeve reached them and looked down at the girl with a smile. "You brought down the magic. I can see the Fargelsian power lighting through you."

Tia hiccupped a sob. "I don't want this power."

"You're a hero." Neeve smiled down at her.

Tia shook her head. "I'm not. I want to go home. Mama." Her eyes found Brea's. "Take me back to Iskalt. I don't want to be here any longer."

Griffin could see the struggle in Brea's eyes as she tried to remember her daughter.

"Papa," Tia cried.

Tears shone in Lochlan's eyes. "I'm trying."

It was then Griffin finally realized the prison magic wasn't any easier for those who forgot. They had to live with that burden.

"Hey." Griffin hugged her closer as the heat from her skin permeated her clothes. "We're going to get Toby, and we will all find our way home. I've got you, Tia."

Griffin wasn't the true father of these kids. He didn't delude himself. But Lochlan currently looked at Tia like a puzzle piece he was trying to place, and Griffin didn't like it.

"Uncle Griff, can you put me down?" Tia asked, wiping away her tears.

Griffin set her on her feet, getting a good look at the pure white power thriving inside her.

Neeve looked to Tia. "Dear, I can try to draw the magic out if you'd like."

Tia nodded. "Just make it go away, Auntie Neeve, please."

Neeve looked startled at the endearment.

Brea walked off, yelling orders to her sister's army. They had to be ready to face creatures they'd never imagined.

And still, Griffin hated the sight of Brea leaving her daughter.

Neeve and Tia sat across from each other on the forest floor. "Repeat what I say."

Tia nodded and copied every odd word that fell from Neeve's lips. The power pulsed, a bright light shining out of Tia. She screamed as the light poured out of her, blinding those nearby.

Griffin covered his eyes until the light dimmed. As they continued the spell, tendrils of white magic floated from her, not altogether different from when Tia and Riona took down the wall.

Only this time, Tia didn't need help from a magical instrument.

Something tightened in Griffin's chest as a slithery bit of magic struck him, warming him from the inside out.

His heart pounded as beads of sweat dotted his brow. He searched frantically for the one fae who'd lessen the turmoil inside him.

Because it was back.

As magic wound through the camp, Griffin realized Tia returned to him the one bit of magic he did not want.

Marriage magic.

Broken by the prison realm barrier and healed by that same magic.

Brea stood across the clearing, but he could feel her eyes on him. He turned, meeting her gaze.

And he knew.

Tia had changed the course of their lives forever.

Tia slumped forward, her skin returning to its pallor, with nothing beneath the surface. She looked as if it took everything in her just to lift her head.

Griffin stepped toward her.

"Tia!" Brea shrieked, sprinting across the camp sobbing her daughter's name. Lochlan ran from another direction, scooping Tia into his strong arms.

"I'm sorry. I'm sorry. I'm sorry." He held her tight, repeating the words as if that could make them truer.

Brea reached them, wrapping her arms around both her daughter and her husband. Griffin watched their family, a pit opening in his stomach.

Neeve pushed herself off the ground with a weary sigh. "I didn't know." Something haunted her gaze. "When the wall came down, she internalized every forgotten memory."

"The outer wall was made of the memories it took from the world each time someone stepped through." Millions of memories spanning generations and they'd filled Tia, but they hadn't defeated her.

Myles walked toward them, rubbing his temples. "I'm guessing we don't need a healer anymore?"

Around them, Fargelsian soldiers prepared for war, but a different war raged inside Griffin.

Neeve slipped her arm through Myles'.

"I didn't remember you this last time." Myles gave him a curious look.

Griffin rubbed his eyes. "Because you were in the fae realm when I crossed the barrier."

Neeve couldn't take her eyes from Tia. "That girl ... I'm not sure there's another fae alive who could hold that much power and survive it."

Griffin nodded. It was on the tip of his tongue to call her his daughter, but as he watched Lochlan torment himself over not remembering her, he realized blood didn't make her his daughter. Lochlan raised her, he protected her, he loved her.

Tears stained Brea's cheeks. "Where's your brother? Where's my Toby?"

Griffin was the one who answered. "I sent someone to rescue him."

As if the words alerted them to Griffin's presence, all eyes turned to him.

Lochlan's jaw clenched.

"Hello, brother." Griffin didn't know what else to say. Ten years had passed, ten years of Lochlan and Brea not knowing Griffin existed, not remembering enough to even question the twins' births.

Brea looked to him with softer eyes. Even after everything he'd done, she was the one fae who'd always believed he could be better, do better. It was why he'd fallen in love with her in the first place.

Riona's words came back to him, questioning if his feelings for Brea were real. At the thought of Riona, the marriage magic wrapped around his heart, squeezing it painfully.

What he didn't know was whether they remembered his time in Iskalt recently, when he'd been a brother to Lochlan and a friend to Brea.

Myles stepped forward, despite Neeve trying to hold him back. "I feel like I need to step in here and remind everyone Griffin is not the same fae. Try to look for those recent memories, guys. He was kind of a mopey dude on our trip, definitely didn't get my jokes, but he still tried to save the world, and he risked his life to bring Tia home. So, you know, maybe we shouldn't kill him."

"Myles." Lochlan growled. "Shut up."

"Yes, douchey Loch, king sir." He gave an elaborate bow. "It's just..."

"Myles." Neeve yanked him back. "Maybe we should go prepare to meet the Myrkur army should they march."

"Prepare? Is this like that training you thought was so necessary? As if anyone in Fargelsi doesn't know how to march. One foot. Two feet. I mean ... it's not like anyone has three feet so they should know to go back to one."

"Myles." Lochlan sent him a dark look.

"Yeesh. Harsh crowd. Smile. It's not like we're about to march into a kingdom with no sun, an evil king, and an army of people who could just fly above us. Oh wait, this is totally like that. Come on, wifey. Let's go make sure our warriors know which end of their sword to use."

Silence descended as they walked away.

This was not how Griffin ever imagined a reconciliation. If it could be called that. "Look, Loch, I know you hate me, that you never expected to see me again. But I'm here now, courtesy of your daughter." He almost choked on the word *your*.

Brea reached up on her toes to whisper in Lochlan's ear.

"You saved my daughter." It looked like it pained Lochlan to say. "I won't kill you. Yet. But you, Griffin O'Shea, are not part of my family."

The words stung more than Griffin expected them to. He hadn't imagined any of this would be easy, but he'd hoped they'd give him a chance at least.

"Papa." Tia's eyes glassed over again. She pushed away from him, forcing him to set her down. "Uncle Griff isn't bad."

"You don't know what you're speaking of, Tia."

She shook her head and wrapped her arms around Griffin's waist, her face tilted up at him. "I love you, Uncle Griff. Even if my papa can't see it, you don't have to be bad anymore. You saved me just like the dream."

He crouched down in front of her. "You, Tia O'Shea, are the one who saved us all."

"And Toby."

He nodded, fear lancing through him at the idea of Toby still in Myrkur. "The path forward won't be easy, but I have faith in you." In his daughter who could do amazing things. "Never forget that, okay? Wherever I am, I will always believe in you."

She sucked her bottom lip into her mouth and nodded.

Griffin straightened and turned, preparing himself for the hike back to the boundary where Egan's forces were no doubt preparing for battle.

"Stay," a quiet voice said.

Griffin didn't realize how long he'd stood there looking into the mountains or that only one fae remained looking at him.

Turning to Brea opened a gulf between them. Pain flashed across her face, and she rushed forward at the same time he walked toward her.

They collided in a crushing hug, the marriage magic inside Griffin releasing, letting the pain ebb away.

"I've missed you, Griff." Her words were muffled by his shirt.

He rested his chin on top of her head. "You haven't remembered me, so I don't think that's true."

"There's been this hole in my memories, and I was never able to figure it out. For ten years, I lived my life knowing something was different. And whatever Lochlan admits, so has he. I remember everything now. All the bad you did, but also the good."

She looked up at him, tears glistening on her cheeks. "You belong with us, Griff."

He didn't know where he belonged, only that it was with his people. Brea and Lochlan were only part of what he needed. Gulliver ... Shauna ... Nessa. Riona. They were part of him now.

"It's back, isn't it?" Brea sighed against him, probably realizing what he already had. The only reason she didn't hate him as much as Lochlan was because of the magic tying them together.

"Yes."

"It hurts. The magic tying me to Lochlan is at war with the magic tying me to you. I don't think we're supposed to have both."

Griffin looked over her shoulder to watch Lochlan glare at them. He pulled away. "I love you Brea, I always have. But I'm not in love with you. Not anymore. Whatever the magic tries to tell me, I know the difference now."

She wiped her face and smiled. "Then maybe there's hope for all of us." She threaded her fingers through his. "Fight beside me. Beside your brother."

"He won't want me at his side." He slipped his hand from hers and crossed his arms, taking a step away from Brea.

"He's in shock, Griff. We all are. Just please ... don't give up on us."

He pulled her into another hug. "It's never been me giving up on you."

"We're here because of you. Our people have been called from their homes to protect the three kingdoms. Lochlan didn't remember you, but he trusted you in a way I've never seen him trust before. That couldn't have been fake. You're brothers."

That word ... brothers ... it stoked something deep inside Griffin. He wanted it. He wanted a chance to prove he deserved that trust.

Lochlan and Brea were family, and family never quit on each other.

He glanced toward the mountain path Egan and his army would traverse soon enough. "Okay, Brea. I'll stay. I'll fight at your side." For his people still stuck in Myrkur, for the twins he could never claim, and for the woman he needed to find.

If they all stood together, Egan didn't have a chance.

CHAPTER 29

RIONA

Riona had little experience carrying a fae as she flew. Her wings flapped harder, trying to get as much energy into each movement.

The kid—Toby—slipped in her arms, and she hiked him higher, needing a way to get him down the mountain to wherever Griffin went.

But Egan's soldiers were everywhere.

An arrow whizzed past her, and she veered to the left to avoid a contingent of ogres who were surprisingly good with the bow.

Egan's vast force spanned the length of the border, not letting a soul cross. She didn't know if Griffin was safe, but she had to believe he was to keep going.

If she couldn't get across the border, she had to find safety farther back in Myrkur.

The farther she flew, the heavier Toby became, until she had to find a place to rest.

Drifting toward the ground, she landed in a village that looked like it had been abandoned in a hurry. Smoke rose into the dark from nearby chimneys.

Choosing a small hut, she kicked the door open and set Toby on the simple bed. Stale air permeated the inside, and Riona stepped out, sucking in gulps of fresh air.

Toby had only woken once as she flew with him, but his skin was hot to the touch. She needed to find water.

Going from thatched-roof hut to hut, she kicked open doors, searching the belongings. Finally, she found two ceramic jugs. One was water, the other wine. She slipped two cups under her arm.

Hurrying back to where she'd left the kid, she poured him a cup of water and held it to his lips. "Toby, drink this."

The magic that had flowed through him wasn't his, so when it drained him, it found no magic to take, using his life force instead.

Sitting on the floor, she leaned back against the mud-brick wall with a sigh and uncorked the jug of wine, not bothering with a cup as she took a swig, letting it calm her.

"Tia." Toby groaned.

Riona scooted toward him. "We'll find her, kid."

She didn't know if the words were true or fantasy. A lantern sat near the bed, and she brought it to life, holding it up so the glow illuminated Toby's ashy skin. Sweat made his face shimmer.

She leaned her head back. "I tried, Griff. I promise I tried." Using the lantern, she pulled her wings around her so she could check the edges.

The black that had crept from the edges of her wings, now covered almost half of each wing. Was it the destiny? Did reading her tattoos change the color of her wings?

"I'm supposed to recognize the king when the time comes." She whispered to herself. What time? And how would she know?

And what happened if she died before fulfilling her destiny?

She closed her eyes and took another gulp of wine. As her eyes opened, she examined a tear in one of her wings. She reached for the wine again. "Griffin O'Shea, I hate you."

At least, she wanted to. Riona had never been the kind to risk her life for someone else. She didn't do favors or protect anyone other than herself.

And yet, she was here with blood sticking to her black leather shirt—it wasn't hers—and tears in her wings.

Toby said something in his sleep, and Riona froze. She'd thought the kid was dying, that she'd failed to save him in time. Exhausted, she crawled toward the bed and poured water onto a corner of the fur blanket before brushing it against Toby's heated face.

She leaned closer, her eyes widening as she saw tendrils of white magic swirl beneath his skin.

As she stared, it seemed to stop writhing. The first strands rose from his body, and she shrank back, watching the magic swim into the air, ignoring her altogether.

"She did it." Toby smiled. "Tia released the memories."

That was what the white ropes of magic were?

At this moment, people across the realms were remembering the ones they'd trapped here.

Commotion sounded outside, the sound of many footsteps and a rabble of fae.

Riona fortified herself with a long drink of wine. She struggled to her feet, keeping the jug in her grasp as she reached for her sword. Pain radiated down her wings and into her back as she tried to lift it.

It seemed she wouldn't go out with a show of skilled swordplay. Riona ripped a knife from its scabbard. Her other hand weakened, and she dropped the wine, watching as ceramic pieces shattered at her feet. Casting one more look at Toby, she ducked out of the hut.

She stumbled across the village, knife at the ready as her injured wings hugged her body.

A large group of fae—both dark and light—rested outside the village. Riona hid, watching them for a sign of Egan. But there was none.

"What are you doing?" Gulliver's whisper came from behind her, making her jump.

"Gullie." She panted.

He grinned, but his smile dropped quickly. "You're hurt."

She shrugged. "Nothing I can't handle. We need to be quiet. These warriors could belong to Egan." Though, she'd never seen his warriors with farm implements and rusted swords for their weapons.

A laugh burst out of Gulliver. "Riona, these are the people of Myrkur, the ones who didn't join Egan. Villagers, healers."

"What are you saying?"

"That we still have friends in the realm." He gestured toward the man she now recognized sitting in the center of their camp with a group of his soldiers. Hector. As soon as she talked to him, Toby would be safe, and she could return to his bedside.

Shauna smiled at her as she approached. "Hello, Riona." She got to her feet. "What's wrong?"

"I'm okay. But Toby ... Griffin's ... nephew. He needs help. Do you have any healers with you?"

"Show me where he is." Shauna slipped into a tent and returned with a sack of supplies. "Nessa and I went back for Toby, but he was already gone." There was hope in her voice.

Riona nodded. "He's asleep, but he'll be glad to be with you." She slid her gaze over the lines of men, women, and even some children stretching as far as she could see.

Magic wound through Riona, tugging at her the way she'd grown used to. Egan was looking for her.

"What's your plan with this army?" Riona matched Shauna's pace.

"There's no concrete plan." Her brow furrowed. "Griffin told us the other kingdoms were coming and that they would fight for us. Now, with the barrier down, we deserve the chance to fight for our kingdom rather than relying only on help from others."

Riona nodded because she understood. These people might not have much. They lived under constant threat from Egan. And this, here, was fighting back.

Riona tried to ignore the pain lancing through her from the damaged wing, but she couldn't hide her wince.

"I'll give you something for the pain once I see Toby." Shauna didn't look at her. "And you will take it. Because we need you at full strength, Riona."

Riona only nodded as she led Shauna into the room where Toby slept. She paced back and forth while Shauna checked the kid over before finally stepping back.

"I don't know what's wrong with him." Fear laced her voice. "I think all we can do is wait and see."

That wasn't good enough for Riona, but she didn't know what else to do.

Shauna fished something out of her bag and handed it to Riona. "Oiche bark. Chew on this for the pain. It'll help your wings heal. I'll assign a watch on you and Toby. I'm assuming you prefer to stay here with him."

"I'm not leaving him." Not an option.

Shauna nodded like she'd expected that. "Let me know when he wakes."

When she left, Riona let herself relax onto the floor as she chewed on the oiche bark. The effect was almost instant. Relief wound through her, pushing away the pain. Before long, she felt herself nodding off.

Movement made Riona jerk awake. She was on a horse.

How?

With a groan, she lifted her head to see a troop of soldiers wearing Egan's colors.

"She's awake," one of them yelled.

Another appeared in her vision, a young man with tiny horns. "Morning, my lady. It's good to see you awake."

"What's happening? Where are we?" None of this made sense.

"On the way to his Majesty's camp. We aren't moving out quite yet as he has another priority, so they'll still be there. The King will be right pleased with you, my lady. I always told people there was a reason you were his favorite. And look here! You found one of them kids he's looking for."

After that, it didn't take long for Riona to figure out what was going on. She looked to a horse-drawn cart beside her mount. Toby lay in the cart, his eyes wide. She wished she could reassure him, but that wouldn't save their lives.

"How did you get us out?"

The soldier who'd spoken before puffed out his chest. "We knew they were holding someone, so we slipped past their camp and killed their guards easily enough. The young one with the tail though ... he was a funny wee one."

Riona's chest squeezed. Not Gulliver.

"We only knocked that one out."

Relief flooded Riona.

Egan's magic looped around her again, pulling her toward him.

And this time, she had no choice but to obey.

Egan's lips curled up the moment he saw Riona stumble into his camp with a damaged wing. It would heal soon enough, but Riona hated anyone seeing her with a vulnerability. His smile fell, and she couldn't help but wonder if the concern on his face was genuine.

The army stood, ready to march from the only kingdom they'd ever known, something she was surprised hadn't happened yet. Dark Fae marched with their own kind. Riona averted her eyes as she walked through lines of ogres beating clubs on the ground in excitement.

Still, Egan hadn't given the order to march.

She walked past Slyph standing in narrow lines. Once the battle started, they would leap into the air, raining havoc from up above. Each had a bow in one hand and a quiver of arrows strapped to their backs.

What was Egan waiting for?

Next were the Asrai, in their land form. Their eyes held the power of the ocean as they wielded long, thin swords.

Riona couldn't keep track of the different species of Dark Fae who'd answered their king's call.

She stumbled, pain lacing through her. She kept moving. Egan didn't near her, instead standing perfectly still, watching her approach.

His power pulled at her, not letting her stop.

Riona could only watch as one of Egan's ogres stomped across the ground at the barrier, a boy dangling from his hands.

Toby's eyes widened as he yelled.

A strange fear awoke in Riona. She'd never counted on anyone, never had a fae she loved, one she wanted to make proud.

"Now," she whispered to herself. "I do."

It was those words that kept her going, those words that brought her to join this army of cruelty and despair. They didn't belong trapped in Myrkur, but they didn't belong outside it either, not in the rolling Fargelsian hills. Not in the beautiful danger of the Eldurian deserts.

And certainly not in the frozen tundra of Iskalt.

As she looked at the fae she passed, she wondered how many of them were here simply because they didn't know where else to be. They didn't have a side. No one fought for them. At least serving in Egan's army paid them a wage and provided their meals.

Riona lifted her chin as she reached Egan. "Are you going to let the boy live?" Her voice was cold, devoid of emotion.

Egan looked to the ogre who shrugged and tossed Toby's body onto the ground like a sack of grain. He groaned, and Riona released a breath, relieved he was still making any sound at all.

"May I?" Riona pointed to Toby.

Egan nodded.

Dropping to her knees, Riona pushed his hair out of his eyes. "We're going to be okay, Toby." She sat back on her heels. Looking up, she caught Egan's curious expression.

"Riona." He sighed. "My Riona. Have you chosen a side at last?"

She nodded, pushing to her feet as she said the words that betrayed every thought, every feeling she'd had over the last few months. "I have, sire. If it would please you, I would like to remain by your side."

He smiled. "Good answer." He pointed to her wing. "You are

injured."

Riona crossed her arms over her chest, knowing she had to do this. For Toby. For Griff. "My injury is nothing, Majesty."

"Good. Good. My army is prepared for battle, Riona."

"Prepared, sire?" She'd assumed the army would march as soon as the barrier came down, yet here it stood. And she wouldn't be asked to fight?

A smile slid across Egan's face. "There is a prize greater than the three fae realms, my dear. One that holds untold power. The lady Enis has told me of the magic we can possess. But there is an army on our border, and until young Toby here can learn his family's portal magic, our people must fight to give us time."

"Portal magic?" She took a step back from him, her eyes going wide.

He nodded. "I will find the ultimate power, the only thing greater than this book."

"And what is that, sire?"

"Its source."

Enis appeared at Toby's side, giving Riona no chance to ponder the king's true wishes. "The boy ... is he ready?"

Egan nodded. "Take him. We don't have much time. I'm counting on his power. It is the only use I have for him to remain alive."

Enis pulled Toby to his feet and wrapped an arm around him. "We won't fail you."

"See that you don't." Egan turned away from them. "Riona, you will join your Slyph brethren to attack from the skies, but your job is to report back to me. Do not let yourself perish. Retreat when you can and return here. Our army must battle this night, but you and I have until sun up before our battle truly begins."

Riona didn't trust Enis with Toby, but she didn't have much choice. Hardening her heart for the coming battle, she only nodded.

This time, she'd make sure no one questioned her loyalty. She'd stay just long enough to get Griffin's son to safety.

Stepping in line with the other Slyph had a surreal quality to it.

Yet, they'd never considered her one of them for the other half of her blood. Her heritage set her apart.

Riona had always been an "other" to each group of fae, even among the Tuatha Da Dannan, the land fae, she was *other*.

But not to Griffin.

Around her, fae jumped into the air, hovering above the army. Even if Egan was distracted for the moment, they had to be ready if the armies of the three kingdoms came for them.

Gritting her teeth against the pain, Riona leaped upward, letting the flap of her wings carry her higher still. Up here, the pain faded away, and everything became clear. She adjusted for the injured wing and spiraled up.

She would do whatever was necessary to save Toby and bring an end to this army.

"We will defeat our enemies!" Egan screamed. "Here and in the worlds beyond."

Slyph readied their bows, preparing for the deadly accuracy the Light Fae wouldn't be able to match.

Riona's thoughts turned to Griffin and Tia, hoping they were safe. Because this army ... it was a force of destruction.

And now, she must go to war against her allies, against the fae she'd fallen in love with.

Because, not all love is forever. Some faded away like the morning dew.

And others, the kind a father had for his children, was eternal. She spent most of the last year fighting with Griffin, and it seemed that would never change. But she refused to let this world break him, shattering his heart.

She refused to let him mourn his son, a son he couldn't claim.

As long as Toby remained with this army, so would she.

But she'd watch and listen and plan.

She'd find a way to break Egan's hold on her. And then, she'd fight harder than she ever had.

This time ... oh, this time ... Riona smiled. She had something worth fighting for.

Chapter 30

GRIFFIN

The ground trembled beneath Griffin's feet, and a cloud of dust rose into the sky, obscuring the rising moon.

"It sounds like a stampede." Brea stared down the mountain pathway into the Northern Vatlands. They waited for Egan's army along the open tundra of the Iskalt snow plains, hoping to trap the Dark Fae army against the vast mountain ridge.

"It *is* a stampede." Griffin didn't take his eyes off the narrow mountain pass where they would get their first glimpse of Egan's army any minute. Even now they could hear the grunts and snorts of Egan's foot soldiers and the grating sound of ogre's laughing. "I did tell you about the ogres, didn't I?"

"Ogres?" Myles took a step back behind the line of fae rulers. "For real?"

"For real." Griffin sighed. "But keep your eyes on the sky. The Slyph will arrive in the first wave along with the ogres."

"Myles, are you sure you won't go stay with Tia?" Neeve reached for her human husband's hand. "I know you're dying to see this, but I don't want you actually dying."

"Please, Myles," Brea pleaded with her best friend. Her fragile friend with no magic to speak of.

A rumbling filled the sky like rolling thunder.

"That'll be the Slyph." Griffin craned his neck to watch the sky.

"Okay, that's my cue to go babysit my niece who can protect me from whatever that is." Myles kissed his wife and squeezed Brea's shoulder. "Be safe, guys. I can't lose any of you. But I'm no help here."

"Go." Neeve gave him a shove, murmuring Gelsi protective spells under her breath.

"Get ready!" Lochlan shouted to the sea of Iskalt soldiers in formation behind them. His horse paced along their ranks. He would ride with his people against the ogres, while Brea commanded their magic wielders against the Slyph, and Neeve would lead the spell-casters of the Fargelsian army to help both.

Egan's brute strength was no match for their collective magic and their united front.

"Mother of God," Brea whispered as an army of Slyph shot across the sky, swooping low to rain down their arrows upon the Light Fae. Griffin's magic gathered in his palms and he threw a protective barrier into the sky. Most of their enemy's arrows bounced off magical shields like his.

"Magic, Brea!" Griffin shouted. "Use your magic, woman." Most of the Light Fae had reacted like Brea, too stunned to do anything more than shield themselves from the arrows.

"Right." Brea shook off her shock, shouting orders to the Iskalt magic wielders. She didn't have Iskaltian magic, but she knew enough about it to lead them. Her Eldurian magic was of no use at night, but her Gelsi magic was strong. "*Skjöldur*!" She called on her Gelsi shield magic to protect everyone around her.

"*Svero*." Her magic lashed out like a sword against the lunging Slyph coming at them from the sky.

Griffin's violet magic exploded from his hands, crashing into the chaos.

"What's happening?" Brea cried out, sending out spells to make the Slyph fall from the sky, but they didn't.

None of their magic was working against the Dark Fae. Only their shield magic protected them from their enemy's arrows.

"I thought you said they didn't have magic," Neeve shouted over the roar of wings beating against the sky.

Griffin frowned, searching for a target. Casting his night magic into the sky, he watched it burst against a Slyph with leathery wings like a bat. His magic engulfed the Dark Fae, but it didn't touch him. Instead the magic seemed to bounce off him and returned to Griffin. It would have killed him if not for the shields.

"Gullie's tail." Brea's voice rose above the din of war. "Gullie's tail!" She turned toward Griffin. "I've seen this before." She scrunched up her face as if trying to sift through memories that still didn't feel quite right.

"Get there faster, Brea!" Griffin reached for his bow and knocked an arrow, joining Neeve and her soldiers as they launched their arrows into the sky. Most of them found purchase where their magic hadn't.

"Toby came to get me that day Tia tried to fix Gulliver's tail. I saw it when I first walked into the room. Tia's magic seemed to bounce right off of Gullie at first, like she couldn't touch him with her magic. That's when he passed out. But they're still kids, so it ... got through somehow."

"They have defensive magic." Griffin launched another volley of arrows. It never made sense that Dark Fae had no magic at all. But, of course, they wouldn't have magic behind the barrier. But that didn't mean they never had it. "They have natural glamours that shield them from humans. It all makes sense. They can't wield magic, but they don't need it. Magic can't touch them."

"Griffin O'Shea! What is the meaning of this?" Lochlan charged right up to him, his horse nearly barreling over him.

"They have some kind of natural defense, Loch!" Brea called to her husband, putting herself between the brothers. Lochlan's scowl told them both what he thought about that. "Our magic can't wound them, Loch. We can only ... push back so they can't get through our protective wards."

"We've put up a wall to keep the ogres out, but they will barrel right through it, eventually." Lochlan glanced back at his soldiers. "I don't think our shields can outlast their brute strength much longer. Why didn't you tell us this?" Lochlan gripped his sword in his hand.

Griffin tried not to roll his eyes at his brother. "For the last three hundred years, they've been behind a wall that takes their magic along with the magic of every Light Fae who passes through the barrier. Just as our magic has been returned to us, so has theirs. We just never knew they had any to be returned."

"We need to retreat!" Neeve shouted.

"We cannot let these beasts into Iskalt." Lochlan's horse reared back.

"They are fae, Loch, not beasts," Griffin grabbed the horse's mane to still him. "Best you learn that lesson quickly, brother. We will leave up our protective magic long enough to retreat and regroup. Then we will come at them with weapons rather than magic. This is going to be a long and bloody war, brother, and I'm going to need you to fight with me, not against me."

Griffin looked to the Slyph raining arrows down from above, catching sight of a familiar set of wings as Riona turned, flying away from the battle as if called back to the master she'd always served.

The story continues in
Fae's Promise: Queens of the Fae Book Six.
Turn the page to dive in!

QUEENS OF THE FAE
BOOK SIX

FAE'S PROMISE

MELISSA A. CRAVEN
M. LYNN

PROLOGUE
TOBY

Fire ravaged the village, casting a wave of heat through the ranks of those begging for their lives.

Help us.

Please.

Stop!

Not my daughter!

Light Fae cowered as creatures they hadn't known existed tore through their homes. Homes that had once lain hidden safely behind the magic found in the book of power.

Tobias O'Shea skittered back, stumbling over something warm behind him. His eyes searched the square frantically until he saw what tripped him. A body. A young man lay at his feet, blood pooling in the grooves between cobblestones.

This was Aghadoon, the fae village his grandmother discovered in the human realm using the book's power.

The book.

Someone crashed into Tobias from behind, and he fell forward, diving to the left to avoid the dead man. His knees hit the stones, sending pain rocketing through his body. His hands slammed down next, the shock reverberating up his arms.

Blood seeped through the cracks in the stones, its warmth soaking into Tobias' scratched palms.

He scrambled back until he hit the side of a building that didn't burn. Fire from surrounding surfaces licked at the walls, yet it remained intact.

Tobias pressed his back against the cracked wood of a door and drew his knees in to his chest, hearing the words his grandmother, Enis uttered to him only hours before.

It'll be okay, Toby.

This book can give you magic, the kind of power you've never seen.

All he wanted was his sister, his twin.

But Enis was right. It hadn't been the first time he held magic in his fingertips, but it was the first time the power belonged to *him*. His sister wasn't channeling power through him, he wasn't strengthening her magic. This was his magic.

Enis taught him how to use the book to awaken the O'Shea magic in his blood, the portal magic. And it led him here.

Tobias closed his eyes, wanting to pretend the world wasn't coming down around him, that every time he heard a body thump to the stones it wasn't his fault. He'd brought them here, the Dark Fae king and his army.

The innocents of this village had only ever wanted to protect the magic of the book.

"Tobias!" Someone screamed his name, but he couldn't find them amidst the cacophony. A creature King Egan had called an ogre ran across the square, each stomp shaking the structures nearby.

A Light Fae, who'd been a prisoner until weeks before, used his magic, drawing power from the sun to keep the fires blazing. An Eldurian. He had to be.

Tobias knew the Eldurian queen. The future Eldurian rulers were his cousins since his mom and theirs called each other sister. It would hurt them to see their ancestral magic used for such evils.

There'd been a place for people who did evil things.

The prison realm.

But now...

"Tobias!"

He heard it louder that time, the voice. Uncurling himself, he searched for someone, anyone he knew.

A sword flashed, the sun glinting off its rusted blade, almost blinding Tobias as an unfamiliar fae ran for him.

He froze in the moment, wishing there was something else he could do. Tia would have had a plan. She'd have used her power to save the day.

But all he could do was open portals, though he'd only done it a total of once. He wasn't sure where to begin or if he could even manage it on his own a second time.

His eyelids slid shut. If he couldn't help Tia save the world from Egan Byrne, he'd rather not play a part in this war at all.

But the blow never came. Instead, warm droplets sprayed his face. He opened his eyes to find Riona kicking the slain fae off her sword. Her wings, a mixture of white and swirling black shadows, stretched out behind her, adding to the fear he already felt around her.

"Tobias." He recognized the voice. Had she been the one calling for him this entire time?

When Tobias didn't respond, Riona bent down to grab his arm and hauled him to his feet. She pushed him forward, kicking open a door as she did and shoving him inside before shutting out the battle ensuing outside. Her wings curled in, making her odd tattoos the only thing separating her from the Light Fae.

"Tobias." She shook him. "Toby, did you crack your skull?"

He shook his head.

"Then speak, child. Don't scare me like that again. I've been searching for you the entire fight. You ran from the king's side."

He had. When Egan killed the first fae, Tobias ran.

"You came for me?"

She nodded, the blood spattered on her dark skin giving her a harsh look. But if she wanted to protect him, did that mean she was still loyal to his Uncle Griff?

"The king would have my head if we let you get hurt. You're our way back to the fae realm, remember?"

His heart sank. Maybe she'd never been loyal to Griffin at all. Maybe it was all a plan to get here, where she could help the king find the power he sought.

Tobias couldn't look at her hard expression anymore. He breathed deeply, trying to get control of his heart the way Mom taught him. Mom. Tears welled in his eyes. What would she say when she found out what he helped the prison fae do?

He blinked away tears, hearing his sister's voice in his head. *Iskaltians don't cry, Toby. When we're hurt, we get back up again. We fight.*

She wouldn't have let anyone use her.

Wiping at his eyes, he scanned the room they'd entered. "Why isn't it on fire?" Everything else in this doomed village was.

Riona slid her sword into the sheath at her waist, her shoulders relaxing the tiniest bit as she glanced to the door. "Because it's been spelled."

Spelled? Tobias walked on shaky legs to one of the shelves where ancient looking leather-bound books and scrolls were stacked in tight rows.

The twin Prince and Princess of Iskalt were no strangers to tragedy or danger. They'd spent months in the human realm with their evil Uncle Callum and lived. But they'd been together. Now, Tobias couldn't even feel his sister anymore.

Riona sighed as she blocked the door with a heavy wooden chair she wedged under the doorknob. "The king has given strict orders that no one is to enter the library. We won't be found until the slaughter is finished."

Tobias flinched at the word slaughter. An entire village of fae who just wanted to live their lives while providing a sacred service. They were gone.

Grainne's lineage had protected the spell book for so many years, and now it was snuffed out in a single day.

A library that didn't burn and was obviously important to the king? Tobias reached for one of the scrolls, but Riona's voice stopped him.

"I wouldn't do that if I were you."

Tobias curled his fingers in, despite her protest, making him more curious than ever. He'd never been one to act on curiosities. That was Tia's way.

Riona slumped onto a wooden chair in front of a long, cherry wood desk. "I never thought this was possible." She rubbed a hand over her face.

Tobias inched closer to the fearsome warrior. "What are you talking about?"

"From what I've been told, kid, your O'Shea magic would have woken years ago if you had any potential for magic." O'Shea power was different from the Iskaltian magic he didn't have. It didn't wait to fully manifest until one came of age.

"I'm only ten." He crossed his arms, unable to look at her.

"Yes, which is my only hope."

When he didn't respond, she continued. "The book woke your portal magic, but it's different from the other O'Sheas. Your father, your uncle... they struggle to take more than a few people through with them at a time. Yet you brought part of an army into the human realm on your first go. There's also the time skew. If Griffin leaves the fae realm at night, it's daytime in the human realm, rendering him powerless until the moon rises again. But you... despite the darkness and the full moon, it was day in the prison realm when we left. And now..."

"It's still day."

She nodded, giving him a weary sigh. "Did Callum bring you to the village?"

Tobias nodded.

"So, you knew where to portal, but I wonder if the power that book gives you would let you portal to places you've never seen before." She rested her arms on the desk and shook her head. "That book breaks all the rules."

Tobias didn't get a chance to find out if the fear he heard in her voice were true because a flash of light blasted through the door. It didn't burst inward like Tobias expected, but the chair blocking it exploded into a thousand tiny shards of wood.

The door opened, revealing King Egan flanked by two Light Fae with wicked smiles.

Riona rose to greet her king. "Egan, you should know nothing can destroy this library." She dipped her head in respect.

A wide smile spread across his face. "Just a test, darling."

She lifted a brow. "And that." She pointed out to the square where Tobias caught a glimpse of the carnage and turned away. "Is that a test?"

Egan walked forward and put an arm around Riona. "No, dear. That was a victory."

Enis followed him into the room, her eyes searching the library before finally landing on Tobias. "Toby." For a moment, he wondered if the relief on her face was genuine, but as she wrapped him in a tight hug, he found he didn't care. His body shook in her arms, and he sent a silent apology to Tia, wherever she was.

It turned out, Iskaltians did cry.

At least this one did.

CHAPTER I

GRIFFIN

Retreat.

It was a strange thought. The army pulled back from the battle they'd been fully engaged in, but it didn't lessen what they'd already lost. It didn't clear the rocky valley of the bodies of their fallen friends.

It didn't wash the blood from a warrior's hands.

Griffin O'Shea wasn't a man to back away from a fight, but even he'd known they couldn't defeat Egan's Dark Fae army who had defensive powers he'd never imagined they possessed, powers that kept the Light Fae from decimating them with magic.

For a seventh straight day since the battle, he stood looking at the bloodied rocks spanning the distance from the trees at his back to the prison realm at his front. There was no longer a barrier separating the two, no magic keeping him on opposite sides from his family.

He'd fought for them, battled against an army of people who weren't altogether different from the ones he'd lived with for the last ten years, and yet suspicion followed him wherever he roamed among the Iskalt and Fargelsi camps.

The fae who remained, the ones who'd lived through the

onslaught until Egan's army pulled back for a reason they couldn't understand. Their eyes held a wariness.

Griffin walked past the pyres that had burned for an entire day after the battle. He didn't let himself avert his eyes from those who suffered, the ones who'd come because of him. If he hadn't set out on that fateful mission for Egan to find the book of power, maybe none of this would have happened.

But his people would have still been trapped.

"Why hasn't Egan returned?" Griffin kicked over an empty pot, letting his irritation get the best of him. "Nothing makes sense." They couldn't leave the Myrkur border, couldn't provide Egan with a clear path into the three kingdoms. But there'd been no sight of his people since they attacked from both sky and land.

He'd told Lochlan everything he knew about the Dark Fae king, every strength, every weakness. Griffin wanted to lead the advanced Iskaltian and Fargelsian forces into the dark realm to meet the enemy forces head on before they could recover, but Lochlan refused, saying he wouldn't lead his people into a realm they did not know to fight a king they'd never heard of before a week ago.

In this war, Egan would have to make the next move.

"And why the heck is my brother a self-righteous jerk who has to be right all the time?" He imagined if they'd grown up together, Lochlan would have been their father's favorite, mastering his books and his magic in ways Griffin never could.

But they didn't grow up together, a fact that had never been more clear when recognition finally lit in Lochlan's eyes only hours before the battle, when he knew Griffin for what he was—or, at least, what he used to be.

"You going to burn the camp down?" Myles looked up from the book he was reading. "Yesterday I sat by Lochlan when he ranted and raved about you, and I swear he almost set me on fire."

"Since when do you read?" Griffin plucked the book from Myles' hands and looked down at the cover. "The mythical fae?"

Myles took it back. "The grumpier O'Shea took me into the

human realm after you left for Myrkur—again—for a few of their books once he realized they knew more about our world than we did."

"It's just a book of myths."

Myles lifted a brow. "And you think their myths aren't rooted in fact? This book contains information about fae who live in the waters, in the skies." He shrugged. "Even ogres, though I'm still not sure I believe Shrek is out here running around."

Griffin sighed, lifting his eyes to the sea of tents winding through the thick forests in the mountains outside Myrkur. It was considerably less than it had been a week ago. He dropped to the ground next to Myles. "I don't know one named Shrek, but I've only met a few ogres."

Myles smiled in that human way he had whenever he thought fae were amusing for not understanding what he said. He closed his book. "Griff..."

"Spit it out, human." Griffin had never given Myles much thought after dragging him to the fae realm. He hadn't wondered where he was while Griffin spent ten years in the prison realm. Yet, he'd come to have a grudging fondness for the boy over the last few months.

"Are you okay? Like... really, really okay?"

"I don't look it?" He forced a smile, knowing how he must appear to those camped here, the ones who now remembered the stories of Griffin, the traitor, the Iskaltian prince who chose the wrong side.

"I mean... you always have that ugly mug... but lately it's been—"

"Uglier?"

Myles let out a humorless laugh. "I guess."

"I'm guessing the words are yours, but the question is not." He let his eyes follow the familiar trail to the tent belonging to the King and Queen of Iskalt. Queen Brea sat on a stump digging her hands into the bucket containing the day's washing. A servant stood by, horror plain on her face at the sight of the queen washing her own clothing.

Myles followed his gaze. "Is it wrong for her to be worried about you?"

"No. I feel it too." The worry, the remnants of a broken marriage bond that returned with the memories. It didn't return the love, exactly, but he was tied to her. A fact both she and her husband knew as well.

"I don't understand why you two can't just clear the air."

"Myles." Griffin shook his head as he pulled his knife free and reached for the stone he'd used to sharpen it. And sharpened it again. The steady sound of the blade kept him from focusing on the magic inside him.

"No." Myles rose up on his knees and inched closer. "Hear me out. Okay, so I know I'm like the only person in this entire camp who will talk to you."

"Not true."

"The only person who isn't a kid." He paused as if waiting for Griffin to contradict him.

But it was the truth. Griffin had been shut out of everything. Strategy sessions, war planning. Other than Myles, the only people in this camp who spent any time with him were Gulliver and Tia, the latter only because he didn't try to make her talk like Brea and Lochlan did.

"Go on." Griffin continued sharpening the already sharp blade.

"Like I said, I may be the only adult here who will talk to you, but I'm not the only one who cares about you. It's complicated, Griff. You have to understand that."

The truth was, he did.

"I need a walk." Or to hit something. Where was Egan and his army when he needed them?

After ten mostly peaceful years in Myrkur where they struggled to survive but didn't have to fight for their lives, he was back to his old self, yearning for a fight. Jumping to his feet, he ignored Myles' protests.

All Griffin had done for the last week was replay the events in his mind, talk to Myles, and sharpen his blade. He wasn't sure how much longer he could do it. He wound through rows of tents where Iskaltians and Fargelsians followed him with their eyes. He'd betrayed both peoples when sitting at Regan's side. Ten years didn't erase what he'd done.

Back then he'd longed to be known, to sit on a throne. And now... everyone knew him.

The smaller Fargelsian army and the advanced force Lochlan and Brea had led from Iskalt were bolstered just before the battle by the arrival of the rest of the Iskaltian army.

The remaining army of the three realms—the one loyal to Eldur, stayed back along the border of Iskalt and Eldur, a last defense if the Dark Fae broke through.

Griffin found Gulliver surrounded by a circle of soldiers who laughed and gaped at everything he could make his tail do. Seeing the soldiers laugh after the tough week they'd had was uplifting.

Tia leaned against a tree, keeping herself apart from the soldiers. She hugged her arms across her chest as if afraid someone would come along and rip her heart out. Maybe they already had. He knew the feeling.

"Hey, kiddo." She lifted dark eyes to his, and he wondered if he was mistaken at the relief on her face. Knowing she wouldn't respond, he didn't wait for an answer. He loved how much she liked human terms and belongings. She was as fascinated by the other world as Gulliver was. During the battle, Gulliver had named himself her protector—along with a guard her mother assigned—and he hadn't left her side.

Griffin tried not to think too much about the similarities he might share with Tia, not now that he knew a truth no one else did.

Other than Riona.

Pushing her betrayal from his mind, he wrapped an arm around Tia's shoulders. "How about you and I go find some quiet?"

She nodded, the brightness she once held in her eyes gone. He jerked his head toward the path they'd taken many times over the last few days. It twisted through the trees before bringing them to the edge of camp, where a small clearing let them escape without drifting too far from the safety of the army.

He saw Lochlan standing with two of his generals and pulled his arm back from Tia's shoulders. Still, she followed him.

He pushed through a curtain of branches and leaves, creating an opening for Tia.

They sat side by side on the bright green carpet of tall grasses. Above, the trees shielded them from the sun.

Tia lay back, her hands resting on her stomach.

Griffin watched her, not saying a word. It wasn't that he didn't know what to say, just that there was no reason to speak because he knew this girl had the same emotions rolling through her. It was like half of her was taken right along with Tobias.

Just like Riona.

And his mother.

The difference was Tobias never chose to leave her.

Griffin reached out, folding one of her tiny hands in his larger one. He didn't know if Tia would ever find out he was her father, but he wasn't sure he wanted that—to completely upend her world. To take that away from Lochlan—even if Lochlan was currently not on team Griffin.

Griffin didn't know how long they lay there before Gulliver's shouting broke their peace. He pushed through the opening to the clearing, his chest heaving.

Releasing Tia, Griffin jumped to his feet. "What's wrong?"

Gulliver's haunted eyes flicked from Tia to Griffin, and he swallowed. "I need to tell you something—"

Tia's scream cut him off as she pressed her hands to the side of her head and rocked from side to side. "Toby, no!"

Tears streamed down her face, and Gulliver dropped to his knees at her side, pulling her up to look at him. "Tia... what is it?"

More tears. Seeing Tia cry was such a rare sight, Griffin watched her carefully.

Gulliver dipped his head to meet her gaze. "Is it Toby?"

She nodded. "I see..." She couldn't finish.

Gulliver gripped her hands. "He's in the human realm, isn't he?"

How? Griffin watched them, not quite sure what was going on.

Egan didn't have an O'Shea with magic with him. They couldn't get to the human realm.

Gulliver looked to Griffin. "You can't ask me how I know, Griff. I won't tell you. But Enis used the book to awaken Toby's O'Shea magic. I think that's what she's seeing. Egan's army has destroyed Aghadoon, leaving only the library intact."

That wasn't possible.

But with the book of power in the mix, he still believed it. "I need to get to Lochlan. We have to march into Myrkur now." There were too many people he cared about still in there to forsake it. He had to make his brother see that. "Can you get Tia to her guard?"

Gulliver nodded. "Make him listen, Griff."

When Griffin pushed through the branches back into camp, he froze. Soldiers who'd been sitting idly by their tents on his way through now scrambled to don their armor and wield their weapons as brigadier generals shouted orders.

Griffin had to find Lochlan. He pushed through the hordes of men and women preparing for another battle, reaching the command tent as fast as he could. Shoving past the guard outside, he pushed his way in.

Lochlan stopped mid-sentence as his advisors turned to look at Griffin, not a single one hiding their disdain.

"Shouldn't you be preparing to run to the enemy, brother?" Lochlan didn't even bother looking up from his maps.

Griffin's jaw clenched. "I didn't deserve that after fighting Egan with you, but I don't care. Right now, you need to listen to me. Enis has used the book to awaken Toby's O'Shea magic."

"That is Prince Tobias to you," one of the advisors snarled.

"Enough. I *will* speak with my brother on this matter." Griffin wished he could call on his magic, but the sun prevented it from flooding into his arms. Still, he clenched his fists as if holding it back. "Egan has destroyed Aghadoon."

No one even blinked.

"Destroyed what?" one of the men near Lochlan asked.

Lochlan crossed his arms. "The village that once protected the book. Why is it of importance now?"

"You have no idea how this book works, do you?" Griffin would never forget what he'd read in it. He only understood pieces of the whole, but he couldn't ignore it for the tool it was. "The village… the book is the key to accessing every spell, every history, every piece of magic housed in the Aghadoon library, the most dangerous and powerful magic the realms have ever known."

"If Egan has the book, why does he need the library?" Lochlan asked.

There was no time for this. "Because a spell does not exist in the book if it is not in that library. When one has the book, they see what the book allows them to see. But in the library, there is no limitation."

No one spoke for a long moment as they stared at each other in confusion. A voice came from the doorway. "Is my son okay?"

Griffin closed his eyes at the sound of Brea's voice.

Lochlan cleared his throat. "The best way to save Toby is to meet this army head on."

"What army?" It made sense now why the soldiers were preparing to march.

"The one full of Dark Fae who just marched over the border where the barrier once stood. We fought them before, we've been preparing to do it again. This king has sent a much smaller force this time."

"No, that doesn't make sense. Egan's units retreated. If they come for another fight, they will lead with an air strike first."

Lochlan nodded to a guard. "Get my brother out of here and inform the rest of the generals we are prepared to march."

The guard grabbed Griffin's arm, but he jerked away and stormed from the tent to find Gulliver waiting. "Come on, Gullie. We need to find out what's happening before my brother leads us into ruin." Egan wouldn't risk one part of his army unless he needed to hide what the rest was doing—like Griffin suspected he'd done with the first battle, the one Egan didn't fight in, the one Riona retreated from in the midst of chaos. Was that when he'd left for the human world? He'd sent his army to fight as cover, hadn't he?

But now… why would he send a small force now?

"It can't be Egan, Griff." Gulliver's tail flicked in agitation. "They're still in Aghadoon. I'm sure of it."

At some point, Griffin would demand to know how he knew. But there was no time.

He didn't realize they'd been followed until he heard soft footsteps behind him. Turning on his heel, he prepared for a fight only to come face to face with Brea. The magic inside tugged at him, wanting him to move closer.

He refused to obey it. "Here to make sure I don't interfere with your husband's war?" The words came out harsher than he'd intended.

Brea didn't even flinch. Her eyes hardened. "Lochlan is a stubborn man. I know you, Griffin O'Shea. Something isn't right here."

He met her eyes for a brief moment. "You used to know me, Brea. But I'm not that man anymore. I have more people I'm fighting for than you and your husband."

"Your brother."

Griffin didn't give that a response. When Lochlan hadn't remembered him, he'd hoped they could be true brothers. But he realized now that was just a dream, a delusion. There were people trapped behind Egan's forces whose fates were unknown. They needed him, and he needed to remember who he was fighting for.

Hector… *he* was Griffin's brother. Shauna, his best friend. And Nessa. He worried for her like Brea worried for Toby, like a parent.

He stopped, facing Brea, as a horn sounded, calling all their forces to the front. "If you want to help, Brea, command one of your men to give me their horse."

Her eyes searched the camp full of soldiers leading their horses to the lines of cavalry. "Benjamin," she called.

The young soldier approached. "Yes, your Majesty?"

"Griffin needs your horse."

"My horse, Majesty?" The boy's ears turned pink with indecision.

"Yes. The king will not like it, but I trust Griffin. I will take any blame that comes your way."

The soldier bowed his head. "Of course, Majesty." He handed the reins to Griffin without hesitation. Griffin wondered if Brea was loved everywhere she went. First in Fargelsi, then Eldur, and finally she thawed the cold hearts of Iskalt.

Benjamin gave her one more long look before running to join the lines of foot soldiers.

"Thank you." Griffin took the reins.

"Don't let me down, Griff."

He wouldn't. Not this time. Pulling himself into the saddle, he looked down at Gulliver. "Stay with the queen. Keep her safe."

He didn't stick around to see the scowl he knew those words would bring to Brea's face. Digging his heels in, he snapped the reins and galloped through the crowded camp, forcing soldiers to jump out of the way as he approached the troops preparing to march out.

Breaking through the Iskalt line, he ignored the shouts from the generals as he raced through the trees and along the narrow mountain pass, determined to catch sight of this enemy army, to find out if it was a trap.

He rounded a bend and pulled up on the reins, a smile stretching across his face.

Griffin rode at the head of the army approaching the Iskalt forces. He waved a white flag high over his head. The sun sank on the horizon, meaning Iskalt would soon be at full power.

And Griffin had to make them see reason first. Lochlan sat atop his dark steed, ready to lead his army. "I'll go talk to him," Griffin shouted over his shoulder. "Stay here."

As he neared his brother, he wondered which family mattered more. The one at his front or the one at his back?

Lochlan tried to remain stone-faced, but Griffin caught the terrified glances toward the other fae. They'd seen what an army of Dark Fae could do.

"Joined the enemy again, brother?" Lochlan sneered.

Griffin sat ramrod straight atop his borrowed horse. "They are no more my enemy than you, Loch. These fae are from Myrkur, but they pledge no allegiance to Egan. In fact, they'd like to help us defeat him." Griffin glanced back over his shoulder, catching sight of a few Slyph flying above the army to intimidate the Light Fae.

He waved their leader forward.

"This is Hector." Hector stepped up to Griffin's side. "He's my brother." Griffin hadn't gotten the chance to tell Hector how much it meant to see him here.

Lochlan's stony expression cracked at that. "How did your force get past Egan, Hector?" Suspicion rang in his tone.

"Egan is gone." Hector's tone was flat.

Lochlan sat up straighter. "What?"

"Egan is no longer in Myrkur. A few of my people witnessed the army disappear, but I'm not quite sure how the magic works."

Griffin knew exactly where they'd gone.

Lochlan visibly paled. "Toby," he muttered, seeing the truth in Hector's words. He steeled himself and yelled to his people. "There will be no fight today. We are among friends."

As Hector's small army joined the ranks of the Light Fae, the two sides didn't mix, but there were furtive glances both ways. Lochlan's lines broke, allowing the new allies into camp.

Griffin barely noticed Brea ordering food to be made for Hector and his people as they tried to determine what was next. Instead, he jumped from his horse and ran through crowds looking for a few distinct faces.

Gulliver found them first, coming out of nowhere to cut in front of Griffin and barrel into Nessa, lifting her in a crushing hug. Griffin did the same to Shauna, pressing her so close their hearts beat in time with each other. A tear slipped down his cheek as he thought of the months since he'd seen them last, when he'd wondered if Egan had killed them.

But he hadn't, and they were right here.

Gulliver and Nessa joined their hug, and a hole in the center of his chest filled. His family was okay.

The four of them cried as they clung together, no shame too great to stop them.

They didn't break apart until a horse thundered into the camp, looking like it had been running for days. A haggard messenger stumbled from the horse, dropping to her knees, weary eyes lifting to the crowd of soldiers still recovering from the almost fight.

"She's wearing Eldur colors," someone murmured.

"Bailey!" Brea ran forward, Neeve at her side. They helped the young messenger to her feet and murmured in low tones.

Griffin inched closer, trying to figure out what was going on, why this girl would almost kill herself riding into their camp.

Her cracked lips parted. "Majesties. I have dire news," she said, her voice growing stronger with the message. "Eldur has fallen."

CHAPTER 2

RIONA

Riona followed the narrow stone path along the Dalur River through Raudur City. Even after weeks of occupying the city, she still couldn't get used to the exotic people of Eldur with their spicy food and robust personalities. Or the infernal blazing hot sun.

In Eldur, clear sunny skies were a daily occurrence—not even a cloud to offer a respite from the heat and endless bright light that still hurt her eyes.

Sliding her sunglasses back in place, she followed the directions Rowena had given her to the marketplace.

Rowena. Now there was a fae she wouldn't mind helping escape the Eldur Palace. Maybe then the woman would finally stop trying to be her *lady's maid.* In all her life, Riona had never known what it was like to be waited upon. Not until she arrived in Eldur with Egan's army and watched as he laid waste to the beautiful city, taking it for himself. He'd moved Riona into what Rowena said were Brea's old rooms and set the servant on her, saying the old woman was his gift to her for showing her loyalty by returning to his side.

At first, she thought she might like having a servant, but she found out rather quickly that lady's maids were an opinionated lot, and she avoided hers as much as possible.

Riona picked up her pace, feeling the fine hairs on the back of her neck and wings stand up straight, like she was being watched. The boarded-up windows and soot-covered mounds of rubble were a sorry sight to behold of the once beautiful city. Riona had never seen anything like it. Even in its current war-torn state, the city was incredible, carved right out of the canyon walls far above the Dalur River. She imagined crowds of Eldurians must have filled the narrow streets before the Dark Fae arrived. Now only the bravest of souls—or the most desperate—ventured out of their hiding places.

Taking a turn down a dark alley, Riona checked her directions again. She wasn't looking for just any marketplace. The mainstream market was all but closed these days, anyway. She was looking for someone with special skills. She just hoped they would be willing to help her.

She pushed through the screen door and stepped into the dark shop.

"Can I help you?" A kind voice met her in the cool darkness.

"Yes, please." She took her sunglasses off and approached the counter of the apothecary. It wasn't the usual shop. That was destroyed in the battle. This was the temporary shop the local apothecary set up to help the Eldurian people get through this difficult time with the essentials that could still be had. It was supposed to be a secret shop.

"You're one of them." The man's previous kind tone disappeared as soon as he caught sight of her wings. "We do not serve dark beasts in this establishment."

The cutting remark hurt, just as it was intended to, though the Dark Fae *had* destroyed their city. She'd heard all sorts of insults since her arrival in Eldur. She shrugged it off. If nothing else, Riona Nieland had a thick skin. "I have coin to spend. Coin I would rather see put to good use in this city than spend it in the human realm acquiring what I need."

"You have access to the human realm?" The tall, thin man stared down his crooked nose at her. "You're the one in charge here?"

"Yes. And as I said, I have coin to spend. I would see it used to help your people."

The man gave a doubtful snort before he approached her at the counter. "What do you need?"

Riona took her sunglasses out of her pocket. "I was told you might have the skills to create something like this."

The shopkeeper picked up the glasses, examining the dark lenses and their unusual construction.

"You want me to make dark glasses for your beast brethren? So they can see better to kill more fae?" He placed the glasses back in her hand. "Not interested."

"We are all fae," Riona said softly. "Light and Dark Fae."

"You are killers, Madame. All of you."

"By that logic, am I to believe all Light Fae are exactly the same? You are all good and kind creatures of magic who have never waged war against your brothers, usurped thrones from young princes, or imprisoned an entire nation of fae?"

The man met her gaze and shook his head. "You may have a point, my dear, but I cannot—will not help you."

"There is an entire army of Dark Fae fighting alongside the leaders of Fargelsi and Iskalt this very minute. They need the protection these glasses can give them. Not to fight against you, but to fight with you."

"I'd like to believe that, but it is difficult to trust such a thing."

"What if I hire you to make the glasses, but you can deliver them to one of your own kind? A friend of mine who works with this army will take delivery of the glasses, and he can vouch for their use." At least she hoped they were still friends.

"You will pay up front," the man relented. "I can make the dark lenses, but I will need a smithy to make the frames. How many do you need?"

"As many as you can make, sir. And the lenses as dark as you can make them."

"Evan." He held out his hand. "I hope I don't live to regret this."

"Thank you, Evan." Riona shook his hand. "You have my word, you will not regret this. Send word to Rowena at the palace when you have them ready."

Is operation 'make it stop' a go?

Riona rolled her eyes as she stared down at her journal. The boy had spent far too much time with Myles, and he had a fondness for talking like a human, but his idea for the sunglasses was a good one.

Yes, I found someone who has agreed to make them. You may tell Hector he can stop complaining about the blasted sunlight very soon.

You should also warn him, the light here in Eldur is more miserable than anything he's seen of this land so far.

I'll just let him find out that for himself. Gulliver's neat handwriting shot across the page. It was a lot more fun talking to him through the journals than it was when King Egan had the mate to hers.

How is your journey?

Awful. We've been riding forever, and we still haven't reached Eldur. We are out of the mountains now. Lochlan says we will reach the border soon, but then the journey across Eldur is a long one and very hot. He won't tell me what a desert is. Says I complain too much, and I should talk less.

Riona snorted a laugh at the thought of the icy King of Iskalt up against Gulliver's curious mind.

Give the poor man a break, he misses Toby.

How is Toby? I hope he isn't as bad as Tia. She won't talk much. She misses him something awful.

He is about the same. Riona cast a glance across the sitting room where Tobias sat looking out the window at the courtyard below. He sat there most days when the king didn't have need of him. Riona thought he intended to sit there and watch until his sister arrived.

"Toby?" Riona called. "Do you want to send Tia a message?"

"She knows I miss her." Toby didn't glance her way. He just kept staring at the palace gates across the courtyard as if he expected his sister to walk through them any moment.

"What about your parents? Do you want Gulliver to tell them anything?"

"No. I'll see them soon." His voice was so small and distant it broke her heart to hear the pain he fought to hide. He was a lot like Griffin in that way. A little softer and a great deal kinder, but that was likely Brea's influence. There was something about Toby that reminded her so much of Griffin it almost hurt to look at him sometimes.

She glanced back down at the book on the table in front of her. Gulliver's scrawl appearing on the page. *You know you can ask me about him, Riona.*

She knew she could. And she knew Gulliver would tell her. But she wasn't sure she wanted to know. Not yet.

I know. She wrote. *I'll ask you about Griffin soon. I promise.*

Where is Egan? Gulliver asked instead. The kid was good at not pushing her to talk about things she wasn't ready to talk about. He was wise beyond his years.

He is here in Eldur at the moment, gathering information from his generals. But he remains in the human realm with Enis at Aghadoon most of the time. I believe they are searching for ways to fight against the Light Fae, but Enis assures me, she will not show him anything of value. Riona wasn't sure how much she could trust that woman. She went wherever the book of power went. Right now, Egan had it and the library that contained knowledge of all magic.

And when he's gone, you're in charge of Eldur? Gulliver asked.

Yes. It wasn't something she was proud of.

Then why don't you just take control of his army and come join us when he's gone and can't do anything about it? His army will go where the money and the food is. And I'm guessing there's a lot of both of those in the palace.

Because when the king leaves Eldur for Aghadoon, he takes Tobias with him to open portals for him, and I will not leave without Toby.

That was why she was here. For Toby. For Griffin's son. As much as she might want to leave, she refused to turn against Egan when he had Toby O'Shea under his thumb.

Griff's yelling at me. Gotta run, TTYL.

Riona didn't know what that last part meant, but she wiped her hand across the page, letting the book's magic recognize her touch before their words faded away. She shut the book, hiding it in a secret compartment she'd discovered in the table beside the settee. Her journal could not fall into the wrong hands. It was her lifeline to Gulliver, and through him, Griffin too. It was the only thing keeping her sane.

"Tobias?" She crossed the room to sit on the empty chair beside him. The warm breeze blowing in through the open balcony doors was soothing. This oasis city was so beautiful, she could almost see herself living here if the world wasn't such a giant mess right now. War was coming for them all. She couldn't think beyond that. "Would you like some tea?" Rowena seemed to think tea was the answer to everything.

"No, thank you," Toby murmured.

"You want to go visit Logan and Darra? Your cousins might like to have someone to play with. Especially Logan, I hear he's pretty bored with just his baby sister keeping him company." Unfortunately, Riona could do nothing for the young Prince and Princess of Eldur, left behind with their grandmother, Faolan in the absence of their parents. Egan was all too eager to take the royal family as prisoners upon his victory over Raudur City.

"Maybe later." He turned toward her, his glassy eyes almost looking right through her. "I'm okay, Riona."

She sighed, sitting back in her chair. "I just can't believe that, Toby. Not when you look so sad."

"I'll be okay ... I think."

"Why don't you tell me what's on your mind? Maybe it will help."

Toby turned his sad eyes on her. "Do you think my papa will be mad?"

"Mad? At you?"

Toby nodded, his eyes misting over.

Riona leaned in closer. "Your papa could never be mad at you, Toby. Nothing that has happened is your fault."

"I led the king's army into that village through my portal. They killed all those people. It's all my fault." His lip trembled, and she was terrified he was going to cry. Riona never knew what to do with crying children. She found herself wishing for Rowena to return. The grandmotherly woman would know just what to say to make Toby feel better.

Riona took his hand in hers. She sympathized with the boy more than he would ever know. "That wasn't your fault, Toby. Sometimes when we're forced to do things we would never willingly do, it can feel like we've done a bad thing. But the responsibility for those things does not fall to us. You didn't kill all those people. Egan did. And he will pay dearly for all the wrong he has done. Trust me, your mother and father know exactly who is at fault for the destruction of Aghadoon and the sack of Eldur. They will never think badly of you for doing what you had to do to survive."

Toby leaned over and wrapped his gangly arms around her, nestling his face against her neck. "Thank you, Riona. I'm glad you're here with me."

CHAPTER 3

GRIFFIN

"My bum hurts."

Griffin ignored Gulliver's complaining as he focused on the feel of the horse beneath him. It was a stronger beast than any he'd seen in Myrkur, one that had done Griffin well in battle.

When he was fighting against the people he felt should be his.

"I'm tired."

Griffin glanced at Gulliver out of the corner of his eye but didn't respond. He had too much on his mind.

Like Riona who hadn't fired a single arrow in the battle weeks ago. He still couldn't get the image of her among the Slyph forces, turning to fly back into Myrkur for reasons he couldn't fathom.

"I'm hungry."

Griffin turned in his saddle to give Gulliver a scathing look. "Really? Is that all that's wrong with you? You're in pain, tired, and hungry? What about the heat? Would you like me to shield you from that too? Is the vast expanse of Eldurian desert not to your liking?"

"Griff." The disappointment in Brea's voice cut him, but he couldn't call the words back. He closed his eyes and released a breath.

"I'm sorry, Gullie." His eyes slid open to the stricken face of the boy.

Gulliver gripped the reins of his horse and pulled them back to slow. "I'm going to ride with Tia. She might not talk, but at least she won't yell at me."

Griffin sighed as he watched Gulliver ride toward Tia.

"We're all a little on edge." Brea sidled up next to him, her white mount keeping pace with his.

"So, we're talking now?" Over the weeks of their long ride through the Northern Vatlands and across Eldur, Griffin mostly avoided Lochlan and Brea. He'd fought Egan's army beside them, but none of them had known what to say next and the silence grew between them.

With Lochlan, it was deliberate. He hated Griffin. Griffin could see it in his eyes. But Brea... hers was born more out of mourning the loss of her son rather than regretting the return of her memories.

Griffin's hands clenched around the reins. "I'm sorry. I'm just..."

"Tired." She gave him a weak smile. "Griffin, you're preaching to the choir here. I'm riding alongside my ex-husband—something that doesn't exist among the fae—to the kingdom that became my first true home. Since the moment we learned of Egan's capture of the palace, I have spent every moment terrified for my people, but not only them. Egan now has more than my son."

Griffin hated himself for not considering how hard this was for her. Alona, the Queen of Eldur, was a sister to Brea. Finn, the king consort was Lochlan's best friend. Both were poised to fight Egan and terrified for their children's lives inside the palace.

Brea was quiet for a long moment. "I don't know this Dark Fae king or his people, but Griff, I need you to tell me... do you think my mother is alive?" Her steely eyes met his.

Griffin wanted to give her the hope she so desperately sought. He wanted to tell her Egan probably let Faolan dine on fine food and spend her time in the gardens. But he'd seen what the king did to amuse himself. His eyes caught on Shauna. Nessa rode in the saddle in front of her, not because she wasn't big enough to ride on her own, but because her sister wouldn't let her go far. Both of them sported lasting scars thanks to Egan.

Brea nodded as if his silence was the answer she needed. "Griff, you and I have never been exactly honest with each other. Our history is fraught with lies and deceptions, but also more. I remember every moment we spent together before you went to the prison realm, but I also have the more recent memories. You saved my daughter. Her dreams… they were about you, weren't they?"

He nodded. They had to be. Tia dreamed of the prison realm before she'd seen it, of a man saving her from it. Griffin.

Her father.

He shook his head to clear it of that thought. The long ride gave him a lot of time to think. Brea and Lochlan could never find out. They'd raised Tia, and she loved them. He wouldn't do anything to interfere. Instead, he'd be her uncle, her friend, and still get to love her.

Brea's lips pursed, and it was such a familiar look on her face a laugh rolled out of Griffin.

"What?" Her brow scrunched.

He fixed his eyes on anywhere but her, looking from the dusty desert road to the army surrounding them. "You just look like the girl I remember."

An errant strand of hair fell in her face, and she tucked it behind her ear. "I'm not that girl."

At the words, the magic that wanted him to love her sparked to life. "You'll always be the human farm girl I saved from Lochlan in the human realm."

One corner of her mouth quirked up. "You didn't save me from Lochlan. He broke me out of jail and wanted to take me to my real mother. You…" She shook her head. "You took me from him and brought me to Fargelsi where I was Regan's prisoner."

"You make me sound so evil."

She laughed, and the sound soothed something inside him. He'd longed to hear Brea's laughter since the moment he crossed into Myrkur.

"Well, you weren't exactly a good guy." Her laughter died. "But you are now, aren't you? We're finally on the same side."

"Your husband doesn't think so."

She glanced back over her shoulder to where Lochlan glared at them from atop his horse. "Well, you know Lochlan. He's kind of a grumpy gus."

Griffin couldn't help smiling at that. "I missed your odd human phrases."

Brea's smile dropped, and she looked toward the horizon where the sun had started to rise. Once they'd crossed into Eldur, they traveled at night to avoid moving their army in the heat of the desert sun. "I missed *you,* Griff. I didn't know that's what the feeling was, but for ten years it has felt like a part of our world was missing."

"I didn't deserve to be part of your world."

She shot him a scowl. "You're an idiot if you think that matters. You're family, Griff, whether my oaf of a husband will admit it or not. You and I weren't truly in love, but that doesn't mean I don't love you. I do. My daughter obviously does. For some reason, even Myles seems to think you've changed." She laughed. "That's probably one of the reasons Lochlan is so grumpy."

"Why?"

"Well, he and Myles have always had this bromance, but he wasn't able to go searching for our children with you, and now you return and Myles talks about the great Griffin O'Shea. Lochlan is probably jealous."

Griffin snorted. He doubted that had anything to do with Lochlan's anger. "Why now, Brea? Why have we waited two weeks for this conversation?"

She drew in a long breath. "My heart is broken, Griff. My son is a prisoner, and I just don't have the time to hold grudges anymore. I can barely think of anything else, but I'm not mad at you for what you did ten years ago. Our world has moved on. But... you didn't make me see. When you returned to Iskalt... we knew some of what you were to us, but you should have tried harder to make me see. There was a time you were all I had. You changed my life, and I *forgot* you. Why didn't you make me see?"

"I tried."

"I know." A tear rolled down her cheek. "But now I have two forms of marriage magic twisting inside me. I never wanted to star in my own reverse harem, Griffin!" Her voice grew so loud the fae surrounding them glanced their way.

"Um." Griffin lifted a brow. "A reverse what-now?"

"Nothing. Just another of my stupid human sayings. Ignore me."

He couldn't ignore her if he tried, but Queen Neeve's voice lifted through the riding party telling them it was time to set up camp, and Brea rode to join her sister. There was no tree cover nearby now that they were deep in the Eldurian desert so they'd have to rely on their tents to protect them.

There was a reason Griffin opted to brave Loch Villandi to get to Iskalt instead of going through Eldur.

The Iskalt and Fargelsian armies made camp together. Hector's Dark Fae separated themselves to set up their tents. They struggled during the day more than anyone.

Griffin remained atop his horse watching Lochlan lift Tia down and cradle her against his chest before Brea joined him. He watched Neeve help Myles down—being that she was stronger than him.

Around him, soldiers made camp, prepared to spend another day avoiding the sun before marching toward an inevitable battle in Eldur, ready to fight for a cause they believed in.

This truly was a new fae world, one in which the three kingdoms protected each other. Sliding down, he handed off his reins to Lochlan's groom who traveled with them and insisted on serving both O'Shea brothers.

Lochlan may hate him, but he'd still assigned a servant to help Griffin set up his own camp among the Iskaltians. Yet, Griffin couldn't fathom sitting in a sea of people he didn't know, people who didn't trust him.

He found Gulliver laying against his pack outside Tia's tent, a notebook in his lap. "What are you doing?"

Gulliver jumped at the sound of Griffin's voice and slammed the book shut. "Nothing. Just waiting on you." He leaped to his feet and tucked the book in his bag. "Is it finally time to eat?"

Griffin laughed. "They'll have the cook fires going soon. Look... I'm sorry I was—"

"A douche?"

"Myles," Griffin grumbled. "Stop listening to his human words."

Gulliver shrugged. "It's okay, Griff. It's not exactly the first time you've yelled at me, and it won't be the last. I figured you enjoy it, so I may as well let you."

Griffin stared at him for a moment before laughing and swinging an arm over the kid's shoulders, hugging him to his side. "I do love you, Gullie. No matter what I say."

Tia waved to them as she ducked into her tent.

Gulliver's cheeks heated. "Griff," he whined. "Let me go."

"Sure, sure." He ruffled his hair. "I think I'm going to find some friends to eat with if you want to join me."

He shook his head. "I have to stay near Tia, remember? You told me to protect her."

"In the battle, Gulliver."

"Well, the battles aren't over. Plus, I think she needs me more than you do right now. Is that okay?"

Griffin looked toward Tia's tent, knowing Gulliver was right. "Of course it is." He wanted to tell him how proud he was of him, but he thought that would embarrass Gulliver, so he stepped back.

"Tell everyone I said hi."

Griffin nodded. "I will. See you tonight when we leave? We should only have another day of hard riding."

"Sure, Griff. See you then." Gulliver ducked into the tent, and moments later Griffin heard Tia's soft voice. She wouldn't speak to anyone else, but Gulliver got her words. Griffin was glad she had him.

He started off through camp, planning to leave the Iskaltians and Fargelsians behind in favor of his family. The sound of two horses nearing camp had him walking in Lochlan and Neeve's direction instead. The two royals met the messengers at the edge of camp.

An older man slid down first. "I have an update from Iskalt."

"What's happening in Iskalt?" Griffin asked.

Neither royal questioned his presence, but only Neeve spoke. "Brea has messengers keeping her up to date on her children's safety as do I." She pointed to where Brea spoke with Myles, and the messenger headed that direction.

The second messenger jumped down, her sprightly move a surprise to Griffin. She pushed back her chain mail hood, and he realized she was even younger than he'd realized.

"I come from Queen Alona of Eldur."

"Go on." Lochlan urged her to speak.

"The Eldurian forces were camped on the border of Iskalt and Eldur when the palace and city were taken. The queen now has us north of the palace and patrolling the area. We've managed to get some news from inside. The old Queen Faolan is alive. We know that much. As are the Prince and Princess of Eldur."

Lochlan's shoulders dipped the slightest bit. He didn't show his relief most of the time, but Griffin could see it in him. He loved Faolan. She was more a mother to him than their own.

The messenger continued. "Both Queen Alona and King Finn are with the army, so they are safe. She will be relieved that I found Iskalt and Fargelsi so close."

"What of the city?" Lochlan asked.

The messenger's face fell. "It's been sacked."

That couldn't be true. Raudur City was the grandest city in the fae realm. Every kingdom aspired to create such a marvel.

It was no longer there...

"I'm sure you're tired." Lochlan rubbed the back of his neck. "And hungry. Eat and rest before returning to Queen Alona. I'm sure Queen Brea will want to speak with you."

Griffin drifted away from them, his steps dragging as he made his way through camp. This was real. Everything was real.

Egan truly held the crown jewel of Eldur.

By the time Griffin crossed the sandy clearing between the Iskalt camp and Hector's camp, he was ready to collapse. Until he caught sight of a number of fires the Dark Fae cooked over and Hector's people—Griffin's people—collected in one giant group, gathering their strength.

These fae were the reason he was here. They'd made the impossible decision to fight those like them, to do what was right after hard lives with bleak futures. Now, their future held too much bloodshed and uncertainty.

Yet, they were still here.

"Griff." Shauna's smile was exactly what he needed to soothe the turmoil inside.

"Hey, everyone."

Many of them shouted greetings to Griffin, welcoming him despite the fact he wasn't truly one of them. There was a royal meal waiting for him back with Brea and Myles, comfortable tents and servants.

But here there was family. No matter what Brea said, he'd never found this anywhere else. He lowered himself to Shauna's side and accepted a bowl of stew from Hector who was cooking it himself.

Nessa scooted toward him and curled up against his other side. Shauna looped her arm through his and leaned her head on his shoulder.

"Gulliver said to tell you all hi," Griffin started. "But he probably just meant it for Nessa."

They all laughed.

He closed his eyes, soaking in the sound, the feel of his people surrounding him. They didn't look like him with their horns, wings or their many other features. But they knew him, every part that mattered.

Every step that brought the two armies closer to Eldur was another move toward war. The battle of Myrkur was only the beginning, a distraction while Egan took a bigger prize. If he remained in control of the desert kingdom and the powerful book, the fae world would be divided like it was ten years ago by Regan and Callum.

This time, Griffin wouldn't let that happen.

He stood at the front of the armies with Hector to his right, watching smoke rise up from the city in the distance.

Two Slyph men glided through the morning haze, touching down in front of Griffin. They didn't have tattoos stretching across their skin like Riona, but there were other similarities to her. One of them had stark white wings while the other's were more of a dusty brown.

"Kristjan." Hector greeted the first before turning to the second. "Theo. What news have you brought to us?"

Kristjan stepped forward, his wings stretching wide as he pushed thick black curls out of his eyes. "We got past the guards into the city, but couldn't get far. Egan's soldiers patrol the streets. The Slyph were nowhere to be seen, but the ogres and Asrai were out in force."

"And the city?" Griffin asked.

Theo ducked his head, a sadness in his gaze. "It did not fare well. We only managed to get past some of the rubble before having to return, but the people who remain are shut inside their homes, not venturing into the city."

Hector put a hand on his shoulder. "You did well. Thank you. Go get your breakfast. We do not know what the next few days will bring and may have need of you yet."

Lochlan stormed toward them, ignoring the Slyph going the other way. "You sent spies into the city?"

Griffin sighed as he turned to face him. They'd sent Kristjan and Theo after the camp quieted for a reason.

Lochlan had barely spoken to Griffin in weeks, but now Griffin didn't have time to deal with an irate king. "How else did you expect to get information?"

"Egan could know we're here because of your stupidity."

Brea ran toward them, Queen Neeve at her heels. "Lochlan, stop."

Griffin crossed his arms. "We didn't send any of your people. Ours can blend in."

"Your people?" Lochlan scoffed.

Hector took a step toward Lochlan, ready to defend Griffin, but Griffin held him back.

Brea reached them and stepped in front of Lochlan. "Neeve approved it."

Some of the red receded from his face. The Fargelsian queen had just as much authority as he did.

Lochlan turned to Neeve. "Why wasn't this discussed with me?"

It was Brea who answered. "Because you're blind where Griffin is concerned. We knew you wouldn't like the idea since it came from him. Now, stop being a scorned brother. You are a king, Lochlan O'Shea. It's time to act like it. Our son's life may very well depend on us all working together."

That seemed to deflate Lochlan's anger.

Neeve, ever the calm ruler, turned to Griffin and Hector. "I take it the news isn't good from your expressions?"

Hector heaved a sigh. "I'm sorry, Majesty. Raudur City appears lost. Our men tell us some of what they saw is in ruin. The people are hiding from the Dark Fae patrolling their streets."

Her face remained an emotionless mask as she contemplated the words. "Thank you for asking your people to take the risk, Hector." She sent Lochlan a look. "We appreciate it and recognize the bravery your people exhibit by not joining Egan. It is always harder to do the right thing."

"Thank you," Lochlan grumbled, thoroughly shamed.

Neeve turned on her heel. "We must come up with a plan to meet Egan's forces, but also to make contact with Queen Alona again and maybe get someone inside the palace. Lochlan, you and I will confer with our advisors." Her next words appeared for Lochlan alone. "Hector and Griffin are welcome to join us, and their ideas will be considered." She marched away with a shake of her head.

Brea slipped her hand into Lochlan's and pulled him after her sister.

Hector let out a low whistle. "You said she was once a servant?"

Griffin nodded. He'd known Neeve most of his life. She had as much reason to hate him as anyone. While he'd lived in Regan's luxury, she'd been helping fae escape through the Vatlands to get away from Regan's influence.

Yet, she treated him as she would any new advisor, like someone who hadn't yet lost their last chance.

He looked to Hector. "She was never just a servant. Neeve has always fought for her people. But I think growing up in the lower class is what makes her such a good queen."

Patting Hector on the back, he realized it was the same thing that made Hector such a good resistance leader. He'd never given up on the good in his people despite living in Fela where every day was a struggle. It started with protecting his mother and sisters.

Now, he protected the idea that the Dark Fae could be good, that they too could live in peace.

"Come on." Griffin jerked his head toward where the others had gone. "When a queen invites you into the important discussions, you never say no."

Hector gave him a bewildered look like he wasn't sure he belonged among such royalty.

But when Griffin started toward Neeve's tent, Hector followed. It was the first step toward full cooperation between Light and Dark Fae. A peaceful future outside the prison realm had always been just a dream, but maybe one day it could truly join reality.

CHAPTER 4

RIONA

"The Eldurians certainly know how to build a palace." Egan gave a low whistle at the opulent gardens built at the apex of the palace grounds above the canyon city below. From here they could see for miles across the green oasis to the desert sands, illumined in the russet colors of the setting sun.

Where Egan's eyes fell to the beauty of the Eldur Palace, Riona's attention went to the endless sea of soldiers and tents reaching out to meet the horizon. The Iskalt and Fargelsi armies had the city surrounded to the south and east, but Egan didn't even flinch at the sight of their unified forces. As long as he had Tobias O'Shea in his grasp, he could evade his enemies with a simple portal.

But Riona was certain the Eldurian army, camped to the north of the city and isolated from the other armies would make a move to take back their city. And the Eldurian heirs Egan had taken prisoner.

"The flowers are beautiful here, are they not? Such rich colors."

"Yes, sire. They are lovely." Riona followed Egan around the winding paths of the exotic tiered garden.

"We shall hold a celebration here to reward our faithful soldiers for their hard work."

Riona nodded absently. No doubt the Dark Fae army would

destroy this lovely place in their enthusiasm for celebration and too much wine and ale.

"And what of our next steps, sire?" Riona paced beside him with her hands clasped behind her back, just under her wings.

"We have everything we could possibly need, Riona." Egan turned to face her in the fading light. Evening would be upon them soon. That always made her feel better, just knowing Griffin was out there with the full use of his magic.

"What will we do concerning the siege, my Lord?" She gestured at the surrounding armies.

"They can't touch us, dear girl. They will tire of this eventually and return to their kingdoms."

"And you will keep Eldur for yourself?"

"For now." She didn't miss his evasive tone. "With the discovery of the Dark Fae's defensive magic, the Light Fae have no way to resist us. Their magic can hurt us, but not without great physical cost to them."

It was true, their magic could breach the Dark Fae's natural defenses, but it took great effort on their part. "We should not forget their swords can still damage us, sire."

"I have the book, Tony, and the library. Even Enis remains at my side to study the secrets of magic only I control."

"Toby."

Egan frowned at her.

"The boy's name is Toby."

Egan shrugged. "This army is nothing but a show of force. These Light Fae may try to intimidate us, but they are weak, and they will grow weaker still as they lie in wait. They rely too much on their magic, and magic can't help them now. Once I have found the right war spells, we will deal with this nuisance, and then I will take Iskalt and Fargelsi too. It is time all fae were united under one king."

"And what of the Eldurian heirs, my lord?" Princess Darra was only four years old, and her brother, Prince Logan was eight.

"They're more of a nuisance than an asset," Egan muttered.

"Perhaps we could use them to negotiate the surrender of the

Eldurian monarchs?" Riona suggested. She hoped it wouldn't come to that, but for the time being, she wanted Egan to think of them as bargaining chips rather than something useless to cast aside.

"We don't need their surrender, and we don't need their children either." A vicious smile spread across Egan's face. "Perhaps what we need to lessen the boredom of a siege is a little demonstration? Have them bound and whipped at the city gates at sunrise. That should show them what we think of heirs around here. Throw the old queen in too."

Riona took a deep breath to steady her nerve. "Very well, my Lord." She nodded. In trying to make things better, she'd made them so much worse. "I shall see to it at once." Riona left him to marvel at the flowers.

Returning to her rooms in the palace, Riona groaned to find that woman rooting through her things again.

"What are you doing?" She snatched her undergarments from Rowena's aged hands.

"It's called laundry," Rowena snapped, jerking the dirty clothes from Riona's grasp.

"I can wash my own things."

Rowena turned to the washroom and scooped up the clothes Riona had discarded there. "A lady should never do her own washing."

"Good thing I'm not a lady," Riona called over her shoulder.

"I've heard that one before." Rowena shuffled around the bedroom and the sitting room, gathering items of clothing to be washed when they weren't even properly dirty yet. "I won't bother trying to get you into a dress for your king's grand dinner this evening. Even though you have a wardrobe full of beautiful dresses that dreadful king of yours ordered for you." She paused to dust a perfectly clean table. "They've even been altered to accommodate your lovely wings too. Pity they shall go to waste."

"I would gladly put on a dress if it would get you to leave."

"And then who would see to your ladyship?" Rowena moved back into the washroom.

"I've lived a very long time seeing to myself, Rowena," Riona called over her shoulder as she sat in the chair under the window, searching the side table for her journal. The nosey maid was into everything. She wouldn't be surprised if Rowena had found it in the false bottom of the drawer.

Breathing a sigh of relief at the sight of it still where she'd left it last, Riona sat back against the chair, kicking her boots off and taking up her journal and inkless quill.

The young prince and princess were being held in the palace nursery, and there was simply no way Riona could allow them to be punished as Egan had suggested. She needed to get them out of the palace.

How is the siege going from the other side? Riona scrawled the quick note to Gulliver. *I sure could use someone with your skills here on the inside.*

The rush of water brought her out of her thoughts. "What are you doing now, woman?" Riona rolled her eyes at the racket coming from the room with the enormous swimming pool that woman insisted was a bathtub. She stashed the journal into its hiding place just as Rowena marched back into the room.

"It's time you wash, my lady. I won't hear another word of protest. This has gone on long enough." Rowena tapped her foot against the brightly colored rug beneath her feet.

"I know you aren't suggesting I don't have enough sense to wash myself regularly." Riona scowled at the old fae woman.

"Bathing from a basin is not enough in this climate for a lady of your stature. You've been out in the hot sun, baking in those leathers you insist on wearing. You need a proper bath. Now march." Rowena pointed to the washroom. "I will get you in that bath one way or another."

"I'd like to see you try, old woman." Riona narrowed her eyes.

Rowena gave a knowing smile. "A servant to the queen's household is privy to many secrets." She placed her hands on her ample hips. "Secrets an enemy of that vile king would find useful. Especially an enemy he keeps right under his nose. One he doesn't yet realize is working against him."

"What do you think you know?" Riona's shoulders tensed. Had she been too careless and let something slip around this cursed woman?

"I am an old woman, child. I have served four queens, and I've learned much from observing among the shadows. You have no loyalty to the king you profess to serve. Your loyalty is to that boy you protect. The Iskalt prince is the only reason you are still here. Now, get in that bath."

"And you expect to trade this bath for what?" Riona stood, an amused smirk tugging at her mouth.

"Information, child." Rowena swatted her with a linen drying sheet.

"And what information do you believe you can share with me? Information important enough to warrant that bath?" She stepped into the washroom and folded her arms across her chest.

"A servant moves about the palace without notice, my lady." Rowena turned to toss a handful of dried flowers into the steaming bathtub built into the floor. She added several sprinkles of fragrant oil to the water too. "We have our own ways of coming and going so we never run into the royals or their court as we go about our work."

Riona shed her vest and belt. "Meaning the servants have their own hallways and stairways behind the scenes?"

"I am sure your king's palace is much the same." Rowena moved to help Riona out of her shirt, but Riona was quick to slap her hands away.

"Egan's castle is nothing like this. The servants frequently pass him in the halls." Riona chewed on her bottom lip. "He certainly wouldn't expect there to be passages and stairs meant for the servants alone." She slipped out of her leggings.

"To my knowledge, the Dark Fae king still loses his way around the palace, though he has yet to see much of it." Rowena placed a drying sheet along the edge of the bathtub as Riona took the first step down into the depths of the pool.

"Rowena, can you tell me how to get inside the royal nursery?" Riona sank down on her knees, letting the hot, sweet smelling water engulf her.

"I can, my lady." Rowena smiled. "I would be happy to show you where you might visit them this evening."

"Perhaps late this evening. After the king and his men are deep into their drink?"

"My thoughts exactly." Rowena moved faster than an old woman should and the next thing Riona knew, she was under water and the cursed woman was scrubbing her hair.

Riona moved slowly through the dark palace. It was late, but Egan and his court of favorites were still celebrating in the great dining hall. They'd gotten into the queen's special stash of sweet fae wine that was far more intoxicating than anything the Dark Fae had ever had the pleasure of drinking.

She was certain the king hadn't even missed her when she finally slipped away.

Smoothing her hand down over the rich fabric of the golden gown Rowena had chosen for her, Riona picked up her pace, her wings fluttering behind her like shadows. The few guards she'd passed in the courtyard were either snoring or carousing with their own small celebrations. No one noticed her. She was counting on that luck to stay with her throughout the night.

"Rowena, we must—" Riona nearly shrieked and reached for the dagger sheathed at her waist when she found someone waiting in her room. Someone who was not Rowena.

"The food here is way better than the crap we're eating at camp." Gulliver reached for a pastry stacked on a silver tray. With one hand he stuffed his face, and with the other, he drank down a mug of sweet cold cider, using the flat of his tail to dab at his mouth.

Riona let out a strangled sigh, resting her hands on her hips.

"What are you doing here, Gullie? And how have you gotten Rowena to feed you?"

"You said you needed me, so I came. And the lady maid is nice."

"Lady's maid." Riona pinched the bridge of her nose.

Gulliver snorted a laugh. "Are you a lady?"

"No. But you need to tell me how you got into the palace. Hopefully without being seen."

"Who do you think you're talking to, lady?" Gullie crossed his arms over his chest. "No one saw me, promise."

"Mr. Gulliver." Rowena swept into the sitting room with a tray full of meat pies.

"Don't wait on him, Rowena." Riona snatched up a pie for herself. She hadn't eaten a thing at dinner. "This one will have you running to the kitchens all night."

"The poor dear was so hungry. I don't think they were feeding him enough. Conditions with the siege must be dire."

"Probably not." Riona crossed the room to pull Gulliver into a hug. "This one is just a bottomless pit."

"You look beautiful, Riona." Gulliver chomped down on a pie. "I've never seen you in such a fine dress."

"You saw me in Fargelsi in that awful blue dress."

"That was not a pretty dress. The gold suites you."

"Well don't get used to it." Riona headed for the bedroom to change into her leathers.

"What do you need my help with?" Gulliver flopped onto the settee and put his feet up on the table beside his meat pies.

"Feet off the table, young sir." Rowena rapped his ankles with the end of her duster.

"Ow, that hurt." Gulliver rubbed his ankle.

"We have some children to rescue." Riona returned, munching on the last of her pie.

"Toby?" Gulliver turned to her with wide eyes.

"No, I'm afraid we can't reach Toby. Egan keeps him close and under guard. But there may be a few others we can help tonight. Rowena will show us the way."

"I have drawn you a map to the nursery." Rowena waved them over to the low table in front of the settee. "It will raise more suspicion if I escort you than if you go alone, presumably on the king's orders."

"Very well." Riona nodded and bent to look at the map.

"I'm afraid I won't be of much use in getting them out." Rowena twisted her hands nervously.

"That's what I'm here for." Gulliver popped half a meat pie into his mouth and dusted the crumbs off his tunic. "Let's do this." He reached out a fist for Riona to bump.

Riona tapped her fist against his. "You were in the human realm for such a short time, how did so much of it rub off on you?"

"What can I say? I really liked Television." Gulliver followed her to the door. "Thank you for the food, ma'am. It was the best I've eaten in weeks."

"Any time, dearie." Rowena's cheeks flushed pink. "Be very careful you two."

"We've totally got this."

"This boy sounds just like my Brea." Rowena chuckled as they stepped into the empty hall. Rowena rushed off back to the servant's quarters, and Riona and Gulliver made their way to the back halls the maid sketched for them.

It was a maze of dark narrow corridors, twisting and turning until they reached the first set of stairs that would take them closer to the queen's household.

Riona almost stopped breathing when they encountered a few servants running off to deliver late night snacks and drinks to whoever they were attending. But none of them paid her or Gulliver any mind.

The second set of stairs took them deep into the queen's quarters, ending with a short hallway with a single door at the end of it. Peeking out, Riona noted the rich plum colored carpet and the dim lighting of the royal residence where Egan himself was staying when he deigned to spend any time in Eldur away from his precious library.

Three guards stood outside the nursery doors as Riona and Gulliver approached. She could see it in their faces, her reputation preceded her. She was still known as the king's favorite and his most skilled warrior.

"Stand aside, the king has orders for the young prince and princess. They are to be whipped at dawn, and I must make them ready."

The guards shared a look and then stepped aside, not sparing a second glance for Gulliver who slipped into the room behind her.

The children slept soundly, and she wasn't sure how she was going to get them up and ready. Children were not her forte.

"Who are you?" A jeweled knife appeared at her throat.

Riona swallowed, uneasy with the knife pressing into her skin. "A friend, your Majesty." She took a hesitant breath. "I am here to take the children to Brea O'Shea." She knew it was a name that would get the knife removed from her throat.

"Brea is here?" The former Queen of Eldur stepped into the dim light of the moon sweeping into the room through the huge windows.

"There is a siege, my Lady."

"You are Egan's woman." She stared down her long nose at Riona's wings.

"I am loyal to Griffin O'Shea, not the king."

"Griffin? Lochlan's brother from the prison realm?" Faolan sat down on a stool beside her granddaughter's bed.

"Yes. I am only here to remain close to Prince Tobias. I cannot rescue him, but I may be able to help you and your other grandchildren."

"Why would you risk it?" Faolan swept a hand over Princess Darra's blond hair.

"Egan means to have you and the children flogged before the Fargelsi and Iskalt armies in just a few hours. I won't let that happen." She'd seen young children suffer at the end of Egan's whip many times, but she would tolerate it no more. Over the last weeks, Egan trusted Eldur to her while he was away in the human realm at Aghadoon. She'd regained his trust. He would never suspect her.

"Then we must get them ready to leave at once."

"You too, your Majesty," Gulliver said. "We cannot leave you here. Brea would have a fit if she knew we were here and didn't rescue you."

Faolan smiled at him. "It restores my soul to see Dark Fae working against this man who calls himself your king."

"He is not my king, your ladyship." Gulliver bowed at the waist.

"I must stay here with my people." Faolan moved to wake the prince. "I cannot leave them to the whims of Egan. I may not be able to do much for them, but I will stand with them." She lifted the sleepy princess from her bed and handed her to an equally sleepy prince.

"What's happening Grandmother?" Logan blinked his bleary eyes.

"You're going with Riona and her friend here." Faolan stooped to Logan's level. "She's going to take you to see Aunt Brea."

Logan's eyes widened in surprise. "Truly?"

"Truly." Faolan smoothed a weathered hand over the boy's brow. "I will see you again soon, but you must go now, darlings. Tell Aunt Brea and Uncle Lochlan I love them."

"Come with us, Grandmother? Please?" Logan shifted under the weight of his sister.

"We'll come back for your grandmother soon." Gulliver reached to take the princess from the small prince, settling her in his arms. She went right back to sleep, murmuring against his coat as his tail moved to stroke her hair. Gulliver took Logan's hand and had them moving toward the nursery door.

"Riona's a nice lady. And she has the prettiest wings," Gulliver said to the young prince. "But she's going to have to pretend to be mean until we can get you back with your aunt and uncle. And if you're scared, it's okay to cry."

Logan nodded, his eyes already bright with tears he was working very hard not to shed.

Riona stepped into the hall first. "Come, quickly, my patience is running thin." She let her voice take on an angry tone as she ushered the children down the hall. "And stop your sniveling." She yanked on the door to the stairway that would lead them back into the servant's halls.

Once away from the guards, they moved quickly down the stairs, retracing Rowena's directions until they were back on the main floor.

"This way." Gulliver crept down the corridor toward the kitchens.

"How did you make it all the way to my rooms without being caught?" Riona followed him, keeping the prince between them.

"Most people just don't see me. I'm nobody, so I can go anywhere and no one questions if I belong there are not. As long as I keep to the shadows."

"You clearly have a talent for it." She followed him past the kitchens to the rear of the palace to yet another set of winding stairs that seemed to go on forever. As Gulliver guided them through a heavy wooden door, they were suddenly outside, far above the canyon city.

"Where are we?" Riona glanced around at the empty yard. The sun would be up soon, and they needed to be far away from the palace by then.

"There's an orchard up this path. Just don't touch the trees, they're wicked hot."

"Fire nut trees," Logan murmured. "They get hot when the nuts are nearly ripe." Logan seemed to relax now that they were outside. He lifted his face to the sky, breathing in the fresh air. Taking his sister from Gulliver's arms, he nodded. "We should hurry."

Soon they were deep into the smoke-filled orchard, moving quickly toward the field lined with tents. Riona spotted Iskalt soldiers and slowed to a stop.

"This is where I leave you." She pulled Gulliver into a hug. "You're a good man, Gullie. Thank you for coming to help, but don't ever do that again. It's too dangerous. Let's keep our talks to the book."

"Well, I can't guarantee it. If I get hungry again, I might have to come pay you and Rowena a visit." Gulliver flashed her a smile and waved. "Love you, Riona. It'll be your turn next."

"Love you too, kid," she murmured with a wave as she watched them approach the soldiers who would take them back to their king and queen. The sky was just beginning to lighten, and she needed to get back to her rooms before the palace began to wake for the day. She would pay dearly for this if Egan ever found out, but it was worth it.

CHAPTER 5

GRIFFIN

"Where is that kid?" Griffin paced back and forth. He'd recieved a message from a Fargelsian soldier come to tell him Gulliver was seen sneaking out of camp in the middle of the night and still hadn't returned.

"He's probably fine." Shauna sounded like the words were for herself more than Griffin.

He turned to her. "Really? You remember what happened the last time he ran from us? He found his way into the stores of one of the most dangerous men in Myrkur who came back to capture him. I almost had to trade my life for his. If it wasn't for Ri..." He didn't want to say her name. It physically hurt.

And now Gulliver was gone.

Griffin started pacing again as Hector ducked out of a tent and joined them where Shauna had started a small fire—more to have something to do than of necessity.

Dark Fae roamed the camp, staying clear of the agitated Griffin. The night time hours made those of Myrkur more comfortable, allowing them to sleep in their tents during the day to avoid the Eldurian sun.

Across the sands, the Iskalt army remained in a similar state of unrest as they took power from the moon. The Fargelsian camp was far quieter, which was why Gulliver chose that route as his point of exit. He hadn't wanted to be stopped.

"Griffin?" Hector crossed his arms.

Griffin didn't respond as his mind ran through a thousand wild scenarios of what could have happened to Gulliver.

"Griff." Hector jerked his head to something behind them, and Griffin turned.

Tia stood at the edge of their camp, her eyes wide as she stared at the Dark Fae. Griffin didn't blame her hesitation after Egan held her captive. She'd met few Dark Fae who treated her well.

Griffin reached her in a few strides. "Tia, are you okay?" She was probably upset about Gulliver leaving her.

Her mouth opened like she wanted to say something, but the only person she'd spoken to since her brother was taken was Gulliver.

Griffin glanced at the fae behind him. Hector joined Shauna in front of the fire while Nessa dozed in Shauna's lap. They too were grieving. Everyone was. Shauna hadn't mention Sinead, but her loss was felt by them all. Yet none of them had been as profoundly impacted as the little girl in front of him.

A tear slipped down Tia's cheek as her mouth opened again.

A thought came to Griffin. Gulliver wasn't exactly secretive, and if he'd tell anyone, it would probably be Tia.

Griffin put a hand on each of her shoulders and dipped his head to meet her glassy eyes, so different from the confident, trouble-making girl he'd first met in Iskalt. "Tia, if you know where my son is, you need to figure out a way to tell me."

She hiccupped back a sob and nodded. "Uncle Griff." The words burst out of her as if forced, like a dam finally breaking free. "He went to the palace."

Fear ripped through Griffin. Lifting his eyes to the sandstone structure across the expansive canyon, he imagined Gulliver skulking about the halls avoiding Egan or Riona's detection.

Griffin had to believe Riona wouldn't hurt him.

He slid an arm around Tia's shoulders and looked back at his family. "We'll get him back." It was a promise to himself as much as them. He refused to lose that boy. "Tia, have you told your parents?"

She shook her head.

"Have you talked to them at all?"

One of her shoulders lifted in a shrug.

"Okay, come with me." He marched Tia toward the orderly rows of dusty gray Iskalt tents. Soldiers looked up as he passed, a weariness on their faces despite the newness of the war. The Light Fae had no taste for siege or battles after so many years of peace. Griffin could see it in their passionless expressions. In contrast, the force of Dark Fae Hector led had known nothing but struggle. This war was supposed to be the end of that.

Lochlan sat with Myles in front of his tent, a wry smile on his face—the kind of expression Griffin remembered from when Lochlan didn't know him, yet treated him as a brother, anyway. Just like Hector was Griffin's brother, Myles and Finn were Lochlan's. The three kings were family.

Myles saw Griffin and Tia approaching before Lochlan did, and his smile widened. "Yo, Griff! Here I thought you forgot we totally became friends before everyone else remembered you too. You here to wish me happy birthday?"

"It's your birthday?" He didn't claim they weren't friends because whether he wanted it or not, Myles was right. "That's human name days, right?"

"You're catching on, buddy." He gestured to the fire in front of them. "Take a load off." His eyes bounced from Griffin to Lochlan and back. "Unless you two would rather battle it out."

Lochlan, ignoring Griffin, reached a hand out to his daughter, a sight that made Griffin look away. "Hey, baby girl. Come here." Tia folded herself into her dad's lap. Lochlan and Myles were so different from the kings that came before them.

"I couldn't imagine Regan ever sitting on the ground."

Lochlan didn't look at him, instead resting his chin on Tia's head and staring into the flames.

Myles released a dramatic sigh. "You two make my head hurt.

Griffin, is there a reason you came to see this lump of a king beside me? Lochlan won't ever say it, but he's happy you're free of the prison realm and helping us set the world right. Oh, but he also wants you to know that no matter how close you guys get once he gets over himself you'll never replace me in his heart."

Griffin would have laughed if it wasn't for the scowl on his brother's face and the heaviness created by Gulliver's absence.

"Oh." Myles wasn't done. "Also, Lochlan is the one who sent the Fargelsian to alert you about Gulliver because he cares about you, and Gulliver is practically his nephew."

Lochlan shot Myles a scowl.

Myles lifted both hands. "Don't shoot the messenger, dude."

"While this is entertaining, Myles, my son is out trying to get into the heavily guarded Eldurian palace for reasons I doubt anyone knows." A thought occurred to him, and he looked to Tia. "Unless someone does know why he went."

Lochlan looked down at Tia. "She doesn't know anything, Griff. Don't even think about questioning her."

Griffin crossed his arms over his chest. "How do you think I know he went to the palace?"

"She..." Lochlan finally met his gaze. "*Spoke* to you? You?"

Griffin had never wanted to deflate Lochlan more than in that moment, but still, he couldn't reveal his true connection to the girl. "Does that matter right now? I want your permission to take a small force after Gulliver."

"Why mine? Hector could give you the soldiers."

Griffin shook his head. "Hector loves Gulliver, and he'd risk his own life for him, but he knows this siege is not his. He won't do this without your permission. I won't lie, we could all be captured. But I can't sit here and do nothing."

Lochlan started to say something but commotion at the edge of camp stole their attention.

"She's just a kid," someone said.

Lochlan pushed to his feet and set Tia down, taking her hand. "I'll be right back."

Griffin couldn't stay behind and wait, so he went after him with Myles behind him.

Before they reached the camp boundary where guards were spaced evenly apart, Brea ran past him.

"Darra?" she yelled, gaining speed.

Griffin didn't know who Darra was, but he kept going until he saw a little girl stumble and fall to her knees. Brea pushed past everyone and dropped at her side. "Darra? Can you speak? How did you get here?"

She coughed. "We... walked."

"From the palace? That's at least an hour." Under normal circumstances, an hour's walk wouldn't be a struggle. In Myrkur, that was an easy trek. But here in the deserts of Eldur, even without the blazing sun, the heat made any travel on foot difficult for fully grown fae, let alone a child.

"There's someone else coming!" a guard yelled.

The shout had Griffin peering into the dark to make out another figure making his way toward camp carrying a young boy in his arms.

"Logan." Lochlan ran forward to lift the boy into his arms, but Griffin couldn't take his eyes from the remaining figure, the one who left camp many hours ago and now returned breathing heavily, but alive.

Tia broke away from her dad and ran to Gulliver, wrapping her little arms around his middle.

"Gullie," Griffin whispered, watching the crowd engulf him.

Pushing his way through soldiers throwing questions at Gulliver, Griffin reached him. They stared at each other for a long moment before Griffin crushed him to his chest.

"Don't scare me like that again." Griffin couldn't let go.

"Let's be honest, I probably will."

A laugh wound through Griffin as he finally pulled away. "Make me understand this."

Gulliver shrugged. "A friend needed my help. That's what we do, isn't it?"

"You know these children?"

"They aren't the friend I meant, but they are important, Griff."

Brea backed away from the little girl to let one of the camp healers give her water and make sure she was okay. "He's right." She turned to Griffin. "This kid of yours just saved the Prince and Princess of Eldur."

Alona's kids. The number one reason the Light Fae armies hadn't been able to storm the palace. Griffin didn't know what to say, so he pulled Gulliver into another hug. "I'm so proud of you."

"A minute ago you were telling me not to do this again."

Griffin shook his head as he released him. "We will only beat Egan with bravery, and you, kid, are the bravest fae I know."

Red crept up Gulliver's neck. "I'm a thief. I just figured maybe it was time I stole something more important than hams."

Brea laughed as a tear tracked down her face. "In the human realm, stealing people is bad. But you did good, kid."

"Auntie Brea?" Logan wiped water from his lips and sat up.

"I'm here, honey." She shooed the healers away, reaching a hand to each of the kids.

Lochlan stepped up to Gulliver's side. "They look malnourished."

Gulliver issued a sad sigh. "They are. Egan kept them away from anyone else with their grandmother."

"Faolan?" Lochlan turned to him. "You saw her?"

Brea looked to them. "Where is my mother?"

"She wouldn't come." Gulliver's shoulders fell. "We tried to convince her, but she said her people needed her."

"That sounds like her." Lochlan took on a look of pride and love, the kind of look Griffin had never worn for Regan. He'd respected her, loved her even, but he'd never been proud of her.

The day Regan was chosen to raise Griffin and Faolan was chosen for Lochlan was the day their fates were sealed.

Darra crawled toward her brother, sobs racking her tiny body.

Brea gathered them both against her. "You're okay now." She tilted their chins to look at her. "Your parents are on the other side of the palace. They're so worried about you. Lochlan?"

"I know." He met her gaze, only hesitating a moment before turning to Griffin. "I need one of your winged fae again. It's the only way we'll get news of this rescue to the Eldurian army. Alona and Finn must know they're safe."

"Of course. I'll take care of it." He gripped Gulliver's elbow. "Come with me. I'm not letting you out of my sight."

Tia pushed her way forward, gesturing to Gulliver and then to herself. She turned hard eyes on her father and sucked in a breath. "I'm going with Gulliver."

He looked so stunned to hear her speak, he nodded.

As Griffin turned away, Lochlan called to him. "Take care of her."

Griffin met Lochlan's gaze over his shoulder, knowing it took everything Lochlan had to let his daughter go with him. "Always."

He didn't care if he embarrassed Gulliver when he took his hand. Gulliver in turn slid his free hand into Tia's and the three of them crossed from the Iskalt camp to return to their people.

Hector shot to his feet as soon as he saw them and yanked Gulliver forward, wrapping him in a strong hug. "You scared us, kid."

"That's what Griff said, but I saved a prince and princess. It was awesome. You have no idea how cool the Eldurian palace is. It has all these secret stairwells and hallways. It's like a thief's dream. But the only thing I stole was people, and Queen Brea told me that was okay. Well, I suppose I nicked a few pies while I was there."

Hector looked to Griffin for confirmation, and Griffin nodded. "It's true. The prince and princess of Eldur are now safe because of Gullie here. We need to get a message to the Eldurian queen. Can you send a Slyph with the news that we have her children, but the queen mother remained behind?"

"Sure, I'll assign someone the task myself." Hector looked to Gulliver once more. "Glad you're okay."

Gulliver grinned. "I'm always okay, Hector. Myles says surviving is like my superpower—whatever that means. But it sounds cool."

Shauna and Nessa approached next and Gulliver fell into their embrace.

When Gulliver pulled back, a grin stretched across his face. "You should have seen me." He tugged Tia forward to stand at his side as he regaled them with stories of his epic adventures right under Egan's nose.

But one thing was missing.

Gulliver said a friend needed him, but there were only a few people he could have known in that palace. Egan, Toby, Enis, and... Could that be it? Was Riona the part of the story Gulliver left out?

He didn't know how long they'd relaxed by the fire--Gulliver tired from his adventure and Griffin exhausted from the worry. The girls dozed off, leaving only Griffin and Gulliver. A comfortable silence stretched between them as they looked to the stars, the same ones shining over Myrkur.

"Griff, do you regret it? Helping to figure out how to take the magic down? We unleashed all of this on peaceful kingdoms."

Griffin had asked himself that question too many times. Did he regret his own actions that led to war? Again.

He leaned back on his elbows, his eyes falling on Tia and Nessa, one a princess of said peaceful realms and the other the product of a hard life in Myrkur. Yet, as they slept, they both looked like little girls, few differences between them. That was what they were fighting for.

For the Dark Fae of Myrkur to be able to live full, happy lives. For them to be seen as equals among the fae who didn't even know they existed. Yes, most of the Dark Fae fought with Egan, but at the root of it, they wanted the same thing.

To be seen.

To be known.

For the world to remember they were here.

"No, Gullie." The sun was just beginning to peek over the horizon, and Griffin's Iskalt magic faded away with the night, but the Dark Fae would still be who they were. Neither the sun nor the moon controlled them. They had no words of magic.

Their magic was inherent in who they were, integral to their very being. It wasn't meant to cause harm. That was the beauty of it.

Defensive magic kept them safe, a noble goal. They weren't weapons.

His eyes drifted from the stars to Gulliver. "I don't regret it." For once in his life, he knew what he did was right. "No matter what happens in these battles, the Dark Fae didn't deserve to be kept separate from the world. When something is wrong, Gullie, it is our duty to fight for change."

"I know." Gulliver failed to suppress a smile as the glow of the fire flickered across his face. "We have to do the right thing. I learned that from you."

Griffin never imagined in his life that he'd inspire someone to do good, that they'd look at him as the example for how to live their lives, how to fight. When he'd first entered the prison realm, he hadn't known who he was anymore. Redemption hadn't seemed possible, so he didn't try. That first year, he spent most of his time feeling sorry for himself.

Until Gulliver… until this kid made him want to be better, to be worthy of remembrance.

"Gullie…" Griffin rubbed a hand over his face, wishing whatever secret Gulliver held didn't have to be pried out of him. "This friend you have in the palace—"

"Riona." The name burst out of him. "It's Riona." Gulliver collapsed onto his back, staring into the dark sky. "I'm sorry, Griff. I should have told you, but she didn't want me to."

Griffin released a breath. He'd suspected, but the confirmation struck him like a bludgeon. "Why couldn't you tell me?"

He sat up. "I don't know. Honestly. Riona… she's not with Egan. She's still on our side, and she misses you so much she can't bring herself to ask about you. I know she does. But I think she's afraid she'll let you down, and it's easier if you don't know she's still doing what you asked."

Griffin rubbed the back of his neck. "What I asked?"

Gulliver met his gaze, lowering his voice to a whisper. "She's protecting your son."

At the words, Griffin's gaze darted to Tia, making sure she still slept. Her eyes remained closed, but Shauna's eyes slid open, locking onto him. Griffin would have some explaining to do, but now was not the time.

"How are you communicating with her?" He turned to Gulliver.

"The books she used with Egan. I managed to steal his. She has great ideas, Griff. She's having an Eldurian smith make some of those human sunglasses for the Dark Fae in our army."

"Did she ask you to come tonight?" He couldn't imagine Riona putting Gulliver in that much danger, but if she had...

"Not exactly. She just said she wished I was there to help her. Egan was going to have Darra and Logan whipped in front of all of us today. We had to get them out of there. Darra is only four, and Logan is Nessa's age. If I hadn't gone, they'd probably end up dead. You love Brea, right?"

"Well," Griffin sputtered, the marriage magic pulling tight. "In a healthy, non-romantic, she's-married-to-my-brother kind of way."

"Well, duh. How else would you love her?"

"Don't say duh."

"Why?" Gulliver's brow furrowed.

"It's too human." He put a hand on Gulliver's arm. "I understand. You were needed, and you went." He'd have done the same thing if Riona needed him, if he'd known she was still on their side.

That knowledge lifted a weight from his shoulders, and his heart came alive inside his chest once more. She hadn't betrayed him. She'd chosen differently than he had all those years ago when he went into the crumbling Fargelsi palace for Regan.

"Riona is stronger than me."

Gulliver pursed his lips as his tail curled around into his lap. "No, Griff. She just loves you. Yeah, I'm sure she also wants to do what's right, but she's in the enemy's camp because *you* asked something of her. She's staying for Toby, for you."

A choice he hadn't made for Brea even when the marriage magic tied them together. Sure, he'd gotten her to safety, to Lochlan, but he'd returned to the evil queen he called his mother.

Maybe Riona was right. Maybe he'd never truly loved Brea in

that way. He'd wanted her, sure. He'd liked her a heck of a lot, but love? That was staying with a dangerous man and working against him. Letting others think you betrayed them.

It was Riona.

"Gulliver, take me to your journal. Please."

Gulliver pushed himself to his feet. "Should we wake the girls?"

Shauna's voice joined in. "I'll put them to sleep in my tent. You two go."

"Thanks, Shauna." Griffin looked from Shauna to Nessa and Tia, knowing she'd keep his daughter safe.

Gulliver started walking toward the Iskalt camp. "So, I've been sleeping outside Tia's tent. She lets me keep my stuff with hers."

"Tia's tent? You mean—"

"The journal is in the mean Iskalt king's tent. That a problem?"

"No, Gulliver. Not a problem." He didn't care where he had to go to get the journal. He needed to speak with Riona.

Griffin leaned against a rock on the outskirts of the Iskalt camp with the journal in his lap. Gulliver left to seek a bed as the sun rose on the horizon.

The book sat in his lap open to the page Griffin had written a single word on. *Riona...* He hadn't known what else to say.

So, he waited. And no response came.

"Griff." Lochlan's grunt came as no surprise. Griffin had seen him approaching.

"Don't worry, I'm going back to my camp soon." He hadn't returned to Shauna, knowing he'd have a lot of explaining to do.

"You are of Iskalt. This is your camp too."

Griffin snorted, not taking his eyes from the page. "Sure, Lochlan." He expected his brother to walk away like he had so many times before, but instead, Lochlan lowered himself to the ground, kicking one leg out in front of him and bending the other.

Griffin tore his eyes from the book. "What do you want? I'm too tired to handle your scorn right now."

Lochlan gestured to the book. "Myles tells me that journal is supposed to contain messages from someone inside the palace."

Of course Myles had known about Gulliver and Riona before Griffin had. "It contains nothing except a lame attempt for me to contact Riona."

Understanding lit in Lochlan's eyes. "You know, I never really believed she'd changed sides."

"Lochlan, you hated her. Even when you didn't remember me, you didn't trust her."

"At first, I didn't. But neither did you. I saw it in your face when you looked at her. She was loyal to Egan. But she changed, didn't she? Just like you did."

"Is there a point to this conversation? You've refused to say more than a few words to me for weeks. And right now, I'm a little busy waiting for Riona to write back."

"You're in love with her."

Griffin pushed out a breath. "Of course I'm bloody in love with her, you oaf. She's tried to kill me... a few times... and she yells at me a lot. We don't really get along, actually. But I love her so much I hate myself for doubting her. And now... she's in that palace because of me."

"I'm sure it's not—"

"I asked her to protect Toby." Griffin pounded a fist into the book. "Before Tia destroyed the magic, they sent Toby to a different section of the barrier. I stayed to protect Tia, and Riona promised she'd protect Toby. I didn't expect that promise to take her onto the enemy's side."

Lochlan didn't respond for a long moment. "Brea thinks I've avoided you because of the partial marriage bond returning between you, but I can see you don't love her. Not now. But you and she were together, Griff. None of us remembered it, we didn't know she'd been married before when she announced she was pregnant."

He rested his arm on his knee and looked away. "We thought our kids were early. Twins often come a bit early. It was expected."

Griffin shook his head, wanting to deny it, to pretend Lochlan wasn't coming to the realization Griffin feared.

Lochlan sighed. "I don't know what the truth is, Griff. We will probably never know for certain, but even the possibility… I haven't been able to look at you."

Griffin could have told him what he knew, but the words clogged in his throat.

Lochlan went on. "Your Gulliver may have saved us tonight. We can now attack without worrying for the prince and princess. Alona may even forgive you for kidnapping her all those years ago."

"Yeah, I sort of did that a lot, didn't I?" Griffin looked down at his hands resting against the open journal in his lap. Words appeared on the page.

Lochlan stood. "I just… I don't know what I wanted. Maybe… Brea has been saying it's time I stop hating you. Maybe she's right." He looked like he had more to say, but he only nodded and walked away.

Griffin stared after him before looking back to the book.

This isn't Gullie, is it?

He smiled at the words. She could tell it was him based on one word. He dragged the inkless quill across the page. *It's me.*

Griffin.

He smiled, hearing her say his name in his mind. *Gulliver returned with the Eldurian prince and princess.*

That's good, Griff. Really good.

He released a sigh and closed his eyes, picturing her sitting next to him. *I doubted you.*

I figured you would.

She'd always been perceptive. *I'm sorry,* he wrote.

It took a moment for her response to appear. *I know. I'm keeping my promise to you, Griff. Toby is under guard when he's here, but I'm staying close.*

When he was there? Griffin knew exactly what she wasn't saying.

If Egan had taken Aghadoon, he and Toby spent time going back and forth. *Thank you for keeping him safe.* There was so much else he wanted to say to her. He missed her. He wished he could see her, feel her. But he couldn't find the words.

Instead, he did what he always did. He focused on the problem at hand. *Are you with him now?*

Her response was immediate. *I am. I have this servant who knows how to get to places unseen. I came to check on him and have been sitting by his bed for a while.*

Griffin released a breath. Talking to Riona made him feel closer to getting Toby home, back to his family. *Can you wake him? Someone here needs to know he's okay.*

Give me a moment.

Griffin pushed himself to his feet and trudged back to the Myrkur camp where he found Shauna watching over Nessa and Tia inside her tent.

"Hey." Griffin poked his head in the tent.

Shauna smiled. "I still have a hard time believing Nessa is safe. Makes it hard to sleep."

He understood exactly what she meant. He found himself watching Shauna and Nessa and Tia whenever they were near, unable to clear his mind of their imprisonment in the Myrkur palace.

"Wake Tia. There's someone she needs to talk to." He handed her the book. "Tell her to wait for her brother's words to appear and write back to him."

"Where are you going?"

His eyes found Tia once more, her angelic face relaxed in sleep. "They aren't mine, Shauna. And right now, my brother needs to know his son is okay."

By the time he reached Lochlan's tent once more, the sun already blazed hot against the dry cracked ground. His Iskalt magic no longer gave him strength, but he didn't need it.

Not this time.

Chapter 6

RIONA

Without the Eldurian kids to make an example of, Egan strapped Faolan Cahill to a post at the city's edge and gave her thirty lashes himself. By the final strike, blood poured from her wounds, and her head lolled forward.

Afterward, Riona sat by her bed. This woman was once the Queen of Eldur before abdicating for her adopted human daughter. She was the mother of two queens, a woman who hadn't ruled in ten years, yet there was a quiet strength within her.

A smile curved Faolan's cracked lips as her eyes slid open to find Riona.

"I'm sorry." Riona hadn't been able to stop it. She couldn't prevent Egan from hurting anyone. There was a profound powerlessness in her situation.

"My grandchildren?" Faolan wheezed.

"They're safe." Riona nodded as she tried to hold back her tears. "They made it to Brea and Lochlan." To Griffin.

Faolan's entire body relaxed at the news. "Thank you for saving them."

"I wish you'd have gone with them."

She gave a small shake of her head. "My job isn't finished here.

This palace is full of those who've served my family faithfully. They never abandoned us. I must not abandon them now."

"He's probably going to kill you. Egan... he's dangerous." A tear slid down her cheek.

"I have lived a beautiful life, my dear. Do not cry for me. I have raised two wonderful children in Alona and Lochlan. My daughter, Brea, came back to me many years ago, and I've had the joy of loving her. I am a grandmother many times over. And the love of my life, the woman I never wanted to live without, died fighting Queen Regan. So, my dear, save your tears for those who've never known my happiness. Whatever Egan does to me, it is okay because my family is safe."

Despite Faolan telling her not to cry, Riona couldn't help it. She'd never had anything close to a mother, but she could imagine what it was to be connected to someone so fully.

The door to the infirmary burst open, and Egan marched in, flanked by two Slyph. "Riona, you are spending too much time in this palace with these people." He stalked forward and reached out to clamp his fingers around her arm. The tattoos squirmed under the pressure, and she bit back a growl of pain. "I do not know how the children disappeared, but you do not want to see me question the old queen." He bared his teeth at Faolan. "It will not be pleasant. I'm sending you to Aghadoon. When we first attacked, we were able to use the book to allow us to see it temporarily, but we've been working on a permanent spell, and Enis has finally worked it out. So, you'll be able to see the village for good now. And I want you there permanently."

Riona tried to take a step back, but he didn't let her go. "Permanently, sire? You need me here." She needed to be here. With Toby and Faolan. There was so much to do to ensure Egan didn't win.

"I can spare you. The protection of that library is our top priority. The armies outside the city are merely a distraction. Pack your belongings. I'll retrieve the boy to open a portal."

Aghadoon looked different than Riona remembered. Egan didn't allow Toby to join her, forcing her to say goodbye to him in Eldur after he opened a portal, realizing she would never be able to keep her promise to Griffin.

Egan would always win.

The portal snapped shut behind her, and she stared at the village that looked like it hadn't faced a destructive battle. The destroyed homes and shops had been repaired, but that wasn't possible after so little time.

Dark Fae patrolled the streets, but they let her pass, her reputation preceding her.

She stopped outside the library, peering in but not crossing the threshold. Enis sat at a table in the center hunched over an ancient looking scroll.

Gone was the harsh sun of Eldur. Instead, rain drizzled from a gray sky. A chilled wind pushed the braids from her shoulders, sending a shiver down her spine.

Her pack hung heavy against her back, but there was one thing she needed to do before she could rest.

A grassy square stood in the center of the village. Black numbers were burned into the stone, changing each time the village moved.

Black numbers that could be the key to everything.

Pulling out her journal, Riona wrote the numbers across a worn yellow page. There was no other message, but Griffin would understand.

She thought her only purpose was to keep Toby safe.

But Egan had handed her another weapon.

Aghadoon.

They came two days later in the early morning. On this day, the rain didn't drizzle, it poured down as if the very skies wept at the battle of the fae world spilling into the human lands. Again.

Riona stood outside the village in a field awaiting the portal that would bring her closer to getting back to Griffin.

It opened in a flash of violet magic that was now so familiar to her. Dark Fae spilled through the portal with Hector at their lead. Griffin appeared last, shutting them away from the fae world.

"Are you ready for this, Riona?" Griffin stopped in front of her, his eyes skimming over her face like he wanted to see everything. But they had a mission. This wasn't a time for reunions.

She nodded. "Aghadoon is just now waking up. There will be guards patrolling the streets. The only fae remaining belong to Egan."

"Does everyone see it?" Griffin asked, looking to Hector.

"Of course we do." Hector lifted one brow. "It's a village. They don't just disappear. Fae! With me!" He took off running, his broad head bent to display his sharpened bull horns, and his thick legs thundered toward the village. Slyph jumped into the air, zooming ahead, their bowstrings drawn. Others with tails and horns and a myriad of other features joined in a battle cry, their voices rising together as one. It wasn't the full army Toby had managed to bring through before, but maybe it would be enough.

These people of Myrkur were united—not like Egan's army where each race kept to their own lines and units.

Riona didn't fly, choosing instead to keep pace at Griffin's side. Drawing her sword, she crashed into the village, slamming into the first guard she saw. Her sword sliced through him, and she moved on to the next.

Blood sprayed her face, feeling like warm tears on her cheeks before the rain washed it away. Griffin shot her a grin, his hair dripping, as he dove into the fight, and it gave her the strength to keep going, to fight fae she'd claimed to be allied with, the ones she was supposed to lead in Aghadoon.

Some stared at her in shock as she cut them down, others ran for their lives in the face of the onslaught.

The battle wouldn't last long as Egan's soldiers rose from their beds to fight for their lives. All Riona could focus on was her next move and the man at her side.

Griffin didn't leave her, and she stayed with him as they worked together to clear a path toward the library. Unlike when Egan took the village, Hector ordered his fae not to burn the village or destroy what they'd come to take.

Riona's chest heaved as she dodged an arrow from an airborne Slyph. The flying fae drew another, and Riona watched as the arrow sailed through space, aiming for Griffin's back.

Running toward him, Riona slammed into Griffin, shoving him as hard as she could into the open doorway of the empty library. They both lost their balance and fell to the ground.

Riona recovered first, jumping to her feet to close the door. It brought back the memory of hiding in the library with Toby as Egan took the village. Only this time, the right side would come out victorious.

Griffin rose to his knees, clutching his side.

"Are you okay?" Riona stepped toward him.

He nodded. "I took the hilt of a sword to my ribs, but I've felt worse." Pain flashed across his face as he got to his feet. The sounds of battle drifted into their sanctuary, swords clanging, soldiers yelling.

It had to be almost over by now.

Riona and Griffin stared at each other for a long moment, both sucking wind. She didn't know who moved first or which one of them was faster as they collided in a searing kiss that sent warmth racing through her limbs, despite the rain-soaked clothing clinging to her skin and water dripping from her wings.

Griffin's kiss was as good as she remembered, as she'd dreamed about. For this small moment in time, he filled her mind, chasing away thoughts of a queen who might not be alive any longer, a king trying to destroy the fae kingdoms, and the battle they'd achieved a momentary escape from.

But one never forgot the impact reverberating in their bones of their sword making the killing blow.

"Griffin," she whispered against his lips.

His hands wiped the rain from her cheeks, and she met his dark gaze. "I missed you. The magic inside me is saying this is wrong, that

I need to obey the shreds of the marriage bond that returned with the memories, but still, Riona, I missed you. No magic could make me stop."

Her brow furrowed. Those words weren't the ones she wanted when she knew this moment of theirs couldn't last. "Kiss me again."

He didn't hesitate, but this time he went slow, as if savoring every second of their connection. His touch burned into her, reminding her this time didn't belong to them, that their mission was bigger than anything they felt for each other.

Griffin pressed his forehead against hers. "I know we have to get back out there. But first, where is Toby?"

"Egan kept him in Eldur. He's supposed to return here when Egan wants me to come back."

His eyes searched hers. "What you did here, Riona... we'll control this library now. The magic in the book is all from here. With this power, we can win."

A smile tilted her lips as her wings wrapped around them, enclosing them in a cocoon. "You will. I believe that. Egan must be stopped."

He sighed. "You're returning to him, aren't you?"

"I have to. He still has Toby. I have to find a way to contact Toby for a portal. As soon as I do, you need to move the location of the village. There's a spell kept under the stones in the square where the coordinates appear."

He smoothed a hand over her hair and pulled her into a hug. "Riona, I l—" The door flew open, and Riona pushed away from Griffin, cutting off whatever he wanted to say.

"You can't keep me here," she yelled, reaching for the sword that had fallen when she'd tumbled to the ground.

Enis stood in the doorway, the book clutched to her chest. "Riona, leave him. We have to go."

Riona wished she didn't see the hurt in Griffin's eyes at his mother's callousness. For Toby, she told herself. And Faolan and every other Eldurian in the palace. She had to go back.

Giving Griffin one final look, she followed Enis out into the rain.

"I contacted Egan." She started running, using the buildings to hide from Hector and his soldiers who dragged corpses from the village, the battle over.

"How?" Riona chased after her. She didn't know they'd been in contact.

"I copied the spell that created your journals. It's a rudimentary version, but it works for emergencies. We need to get to the edge of the village before they change the location."

The ground rumbled beneath their feet, and an unnatural fog rolled across the village. Griffin had found the spell, and he didn't require the Iskalt magic he didn't currently have, not with the Fargelsian words. Magic zipped through the air, tingling along her skin and forcing her defensive magic to the surface.

"Come on," Enis yelled.

The cobblestone streets heaved under foot, rattling against each other. Riona turned the corner, running for the road out of the village.

"Jump." Enis hurled her body through the ancient pillars that served as the village boundary.

Riona lunged after her, her shoulder slamming into the stone as the village shook and disappeared behind them.

A laugh escaped Enis. "We made it."

Riona watched the empty field where the village was only a moment before, unable to help feeling like everything she truly wanted just vanished.

Before she could think much about it, a violet portal, looking very similar to the ones Griffin created, opened, and Toby stepped through followed by Egan.

Egan stared at the empty field, his face red as a scream escaped his throat.

Someone would pay dearly for losing Aghadoon.

And Riona suspected that someone would be her.

CHAPTER 7

GRIFFIN

Griffin stumbled from his tent after a few hours of much needed sleep, but he still felt like something was off.

In some ways he was almost happy, knowing Alona's children were safe, his brother might not hate him after all, his Dark Fae family was back together, Aghadoon was safely moved to a location at the center of the army encampment, well beyond Egan's reach, Riona hadn't betrayed him, and he was pretty sure she was in love with him. Despite the imminent war, things were going great for Griffin O'Shea.

But something kept him on edge all morning as he joined his family for breakfast over the remnants of last night's fire. He wasn't sure if he was waiting for the inevitable bad news to tear his world apart again, or if he simply wasn't used to having good things happen.

"What is with you today?" Shauna nudged him to still his fidgeting.

"I don't know. Something's ... not right, but I can't put my finger on it."

"Griffin!" Lochlan's gruff voice was laced with panic. "What magic is this?"

"What's wrong?" Griffin stood to greet his brother as he rushed across the clearing between their camps. "Is it Tia? News of Toby?"

Lochlan's face grew hard as stone as he stared at his brother in surprise. "Tell me, Brother, did you not notice the sun failed to rise this morning?" He cast a glance around the Dark Fae camp. "Did none of you notice? Sunrise should have occurred more than an hour ago, and still the moon sits high in the sky as if it were midnight."

That was it. The thing that felt off. Griffin stared up at the unnaturally dark sky hanging over the palace and the army camped outside it. "I spent ten years under such darkness, Loch. It feels more natural to me than the sun."

"You really didn't notice?" Lochlan shook his head, running his hand through his hair. "This is magic like none we've ever seen before. Everything is twisted. My magic hasn't faded, and we received a frantic message from the Eldurians. They are beside themselves because they are powerless under this veil of darkness."

"It's Egan's doing." Griffin frowned. There was something too familiar about this particular darkness. Too convenient. "With the knowledge contained in the book of power, it's like he has gained a kind of power we don't understand, but a bit of darkness won't hurt us, Loch. It's just an adjustment we will have to make."

"It's not just darkness, Griff." Lochlan turned, pacing back toward him. "This magic, whatever it is, we cannot break through it. It is like a ... shield keeping us out of Raudur City. We can't attack."

"Then we will have to break through the magic keeping us out. We need to find the spell he's using. The one Enis is performing for him. Then maybe we can reverse it."

"I don't have the patience or the desire to figure out what Mother is up to in all of this nonsense." Lochlan tried to hide the pain it caused him, knowing his own mother was working against them, but Griffin felt the same pain. There was no hiding it for either of them.

"She goes wherever that book goes, and as long as Egan has it, she will be his puppet." Griffin shook his head. "We need to find the spell in the library."

"Neeve and Myles are already there with Brea, trying to learn what they can, but Myles is asking for you. He says you have more experience with the village and the book."

"They are almost the same thing." Griffin turned to wave to Shauna and Nessa before he followed his brother back to the center of the huge camp. Aghadoon stood in the middle of the sprawling army camp, but Brea managed to find the spell that would conceal it from their enemies. Neeve performed the spell the moment they moved the village from the human realm to Eldur. Even if Egan managed to defeat them, he would never find the library perched right at his doorstep.

"How?" Lochlan scratched his head.

"The book contains everything the library contains. It is a key with severe limitations. It will only show the reader what pertains to them. Or what it thinks they need to know. I believe the book shows the reader certain magic that is needed for current events. In the future when this war is won and a new conflict arises, the book of power will show its reader contents we've yet to see from it. But the library holds the secrets of all magic, we just have to look for it."

"I don't like it. A book should not have the power to make decisions." Lochlan charged through the crowds of Iskalt soldiers brimming with magic that should have faded hours ago. Griffin wondered how they would fare throughout the day. Would they grow weary, or would it become too much for them to bear, holding on to more magic than they could reasonably contain? He remembered well what it felt like to have his magic in a kingdom that saw no light, but before getting his power back, his body had been used to the constant darkness. Did that mean he could handle it more?

"I agree. The book cannot be trusted when its source is unknown. We don't know who created it or why." Griffin and Lochlan stepped through the crumbling pillars that had become familiar to Griffin during his visits to Aghadoon. The streets and homes were filled with women and children from all the kingdoms who had accompanied the armies. Brea and Lochlan had decided the invisible village that could be moved at a moment's notice was the safest place for them.

Tia made her way through a group of young girls, her eyes round and bloodshot from lack of sleep.

"She's having nightmares," Lochlan explained, scooping her up into his arms when she came to greet them. She still wasn't talking much, but as she laid her head on her father's shoulder, she reached a hand out for Griffin.

"Thank you for letting me talk to Toby in the magic book again, Uncle Griff."

"You're welcome, sweetheart." Griffin smoothed a hand over her strawberry blond hair that was a perfect blend of his auburn hair and Lochlan's blond hair. "Riona is taking good care of him."

Lochlan grunted as they approached the library, setting Tia back down. "Why don't you go find Gulliver, and try to get some rest, baby girl? I know you must be tired."

"I'll try, Papa." Tia left them to find her way back to the cabin where some of the other children were playing.

"Loch, get in here!" Brea called from inside the library.

"I take it you found something?" Lochlan raised his brow at her tone.

"Oh good, you brought Griff." She waved them over to the long table where she and Myles had a sea of books opened and scattered across the surface.

"Have you found anything useful yet?"

"Useful" Three pairs of eyes turned toward the King of Iskalt. Neeve stood on a ladder between two bookshelves that reached the ceiling.

"Lochlan O'Shea, this library is nothing short of enlightening," Neeve said, her tone one of reverence.

"For a Gelsi magic wielder, I suppose it is." Lochlan moved to sit at the table.

"No, Loch, that's not it at all," Brea said. "This place holds more than just Fargelsian spells. There are references and lesson books for Iskaltian magic I've never seen before, Eldurian too. And it's not just a catalogue of magic. The history of our world is right here. Histories we've lost. It's incredible."

"This library is priceless, Loch," Myles said, pulling his nose out of a book reluctantly. "We could study these books for the rest of our lives and never learn everything Aghadoon has to teach us. It's like ... finding the complete contents of the library at Alexandria."

"While that is exciting," Griffin interjected before someone else could sing the praises of the Aghadoon library. "Have you found anything that will help us defeat Egan?"

"We have discovered something." Brea picked up a book of Iskaltian magic for beginners. "See this instruction on how to use night magic to create a small cyclone of wind?"

"Most kids learn how to do that sort of thing when they first come into their power." Lochlan pulled the book closer to him. "And this method is convoluted."

"Do it." Brea said. "Just like the book says."

Lochlan read over the instructions with a scowl. "There's a much easier way to do this, Brea."

"Not the point, Loch." She sighed with impatience. Griffin knew that sigh well. And apparently, so did Lochlan.

The blue light of his magic flickered across his palms as Lochlan formed the small, slow moving cyclone, setting it free to circle about the room.

"Now watch this." Brea ripped the page from the book. "*Dóiteán,*" she whispered the Gelsi word for fire and the page went up in flames.

"Nothing happened." Griffin watched the lazy cyclone circle around them.

"It means there is another record of this magic here." Brea reached for a heavy volume on Iskalt wind magic and flipped to the page she'd marked with a piece of paper. Tracing a finger over the lines of the spell, she spoke the word for heat, letting the lines of the page smolder and darken under the heat of her finger. When the last of the instructions were destroyed, the cyclone stumbled and collapsed.

"You destroyed the records of the magic." Griffin's voice rose in excitement as he realized what this meant.

"What am I missing?" Lochlan frowned.

"Try to do it again from memory," Brea said.

Lochlan's magic sparked to his fingertips, but the cyclone didn't form.

"Destroy the record, and you destroy the magic." Lochlan stood, staring around the large room with shelf after shelf of books and scrolls covering every available surface. "This is a record of all magic."

"It's the source of everything we can do," Brea said in a breathless voice.

"But the book is a duplicate, isn't it?" Myles asked, sitting back in his chair, running a weary hand over his eyes.

"Think of it like an iPad." Brea turned toward her human friend. "It can access anything on the internet, but it doesn't contain all the knowledge found on the internet."

"The library is the internet, and the book is just a window that shows you what's here." Myles shot up from his seat. "So, if it's destroyed here, then the book can't access it."

"Exactly."

"Care to dumb that down for us non-humans over here?" Lochlan asked.

"We destroy the records of the bad magic Egan is doing to make it dark and keep us out of the city, then that magic will fail just like that little cyclone failed."

"Wait." Griffin dropped into a chair next to his brother. "Are you saying all we had to do to destroy the prison barrier was burn a page in a book here?"

"Yes." Brea's shoulders stiffened. "If we'd known that, we'd have saved my children a lot of heartache they're far too young to have endured. But I can't think about that, or I'll go crazy. Right now, we need to find the records of this awful magic and destroy it. That's something tangible we can actually do to help bring Toby home. So, that's what we're going to do."

Brea sat down and pulled a stack of books toward her. She would exhaust herself sorting through all these books, looking for any reference to a spell that would cause permanent night.

"I'll help." Griffin picked up a large volume on Iskalt air magic. "Wait." He put the book down. "The only person Egan trusts who can perform this complex level of magic is Enis." He refused to call her mother. "The Light Fae under his control are much too new at magic to possibly execute such difficult spell work."

"Yes, she would be the one responsible for this current mess." Lochlan scowled at the mention of their mother's name.

"She can no longer wield Iskalt magic. She was never very good at it because her family ties to Iskalt weren't strong. She only has Gelsi magic."

"Which means we need to be looking for a Fargelsian spell book." Brea sorted through her stack of books, handing more than half of them off to Neeve to return to the shelves. "That just narrowed it down by a lot."

"We've got this, Brea." Myles and Neeve set off to the back of the library to search for more advanced books containing Gelsi magic.

"You need to rest, Brea." Lochlan leaned over her shoulder. She moved to place her book on top of another open book in front of her.

"I will, I promise. I just want to finish searching this book, and I'll go take a break to check on Tia. I promise I'll take a nap."

"Griff, make sure she actually does that," Lochlan said, turning toward him. "I need to make my rounds at the front and see to our soldiers, but I'll be back soon to help with the search, though my knowledge of the language of power is minimal at best."

"We can handle this part, Loch." Brea assured him. "Go do your kingy things." She leaned up to kiss his cheek.

"We've been over this, Brea. *Kingy* is not a word I'm willing to recognize."

"Love you," she called over her shoulder as she scanned the page in front of her.

Griffin smiled at their easy banter even in the midst of so much heartache. They were good together. The remnants of the marriage bond didn't like that thought, but he couldn't deny that things had worked out for the best for the two of them.

"This book isn't nearly advanced enough." She slammed the

leather volume shut. "It will be an excellent tool for Tia, though. She's far beyond the spell work of a typical student her age. This is more intermediate magic that actually might interest her. She likes nothing more than a challenge, but I'd prefer she tackle some of the fun stuff in this book than take on destroying a three-hundred-year-old barrier spell all by herself."

"You'd have been so proud of her, Brea." Griffin said. "She was so strong and brave. It scared me to death to see her do it, but I don't think anyone else could have. She's special. She and Toby both."

Brea forced a smile as she stood. "All my babies are special," she managed to say over the tears that threatened to spill. "I'm just going to go find another book." She darted down an aisle, and Griffin could hear her sobs as she tried to stifle them. Marriage magic or not, it killed him to see her so distraught over her children.

Griffin sifted through the books still left on the table, sorting them by their root magic, Iskalt, Eldur and Fargelsi magic. He pulled the last book closer to him. The one Brea had shielded from Lochlan when he leaned over her. And Griffin could see why she had.

He studied the chart that traced the lineage of the O'Rourke Queens, ending with Brea O'Rourke-O'Shea and her four children. Just as in the book of power, Kayleigh and Ciara's names connected with Brea and Lochlan's names. But Tierney and Toby O'Shea were connected with their father's name, Griffin O'Shea.

He wasn't sure how he felt about Brea knowing the truth. He would have spared her that heartache if he could have. The fact that some fragment of their marriage bond had survived was more than enough for her to be dealing with. As Griffin looked around the library, he wondered if there might be a way to permanently break their bond. If it was possible, the way to do it could be found somewhere within these walls. He could do that much for her at the very least.

"Griffin!" Brea raced back to the table with a scroll clutched in her hands. "O'Shea magic." Her hands trembled as she set the scroll down.

"What about it?" Griffin moved to her side to help her spread the ancient-looking scroll across the table.

"This is it. The record of your family's signature magic. It was granted to your ancestors eons ago. It's rooted in Fargelsian magic." She traced the fine print with her fingertips. "This is how Enis was able to awaken Toby's portal magic when it never showed in him."

"He should have inherited the O'Shea magic when his sister did. I can't imagine how he's creating such powerful portals at his age."

"This is how." Brea's eyes flew across the parchment. "She's enhanced his natural ability using the source magic to ... essentially redesign it to be stronger."

"That sounds dangerous." Griffin would gladly throttle his own mother the next time he saw her for daring to tamper with his son's magic.

"From what I can tell, it's not exactly dangerous, but there are consequences for abusing the power. He shouldn't be traveling as often as Egan is forcing him. Especially, because he is so young. Too young to be wielding such magic when he's never shown any signs of having magic at all." Brea's tone grew angrier as she read the complicated spell work that went into enhancing her son's dormant magic.

"We have to rescue him, Griff." She reached out and gripped his hand. "If he keeps this up, his magic is going to fall out of balance. He will fall ill with a fever that can't be controlled. He could have hallucinations and struggle to get the rest he needs to recover. Griff." Brea looked up at him with terror in her eyes. "This could kill him. Toby needs to find a balance with his portal magic. He can't keep creating these massive portals to move Egan's army between the worlds."

"We're running out of time." Griffin pulled her into his arms as she sobbed. "We have to find that record and burn it. We have to get into Raudur City and bring Toby home to his parents and his sisters. He needs you both, Brea." It was as much as he could bring himself to say, but he saw the recognition in her eyes. She knew he was trying to tell her. Lochlan was Toby and Tia's father in all the ways that mattered.

CHAPTER 8

RIONA

Riona's eyes snapped open. It was the middle of the night, but shouting from the halls outside her door had her leaping out of bed and reaching for her sword before she was fully awake.

"Riona!" The pitiful wail shot right through her.

"Toby." She rushed from her bedroom and across the sitting room, not bothering to grab a robe to cover the ridiculous sleeping gown Rowena made her wear.

Riona darted into the hall, fully expecting to see another battle between Dark and Light Fae. For the last few weeks, Egan sent portions of his army to attack the Light Fae camps surrounding the palace. It was only a matter of time before Griffin and his brother found a way through the magic protecting Raudur City from the invasion they were all waiting for.

"The snakes! They're coming!" Toby screamed, writhing in the Asrai soldier's arms.

"For the last time, there aren't any snakes in the palace."

"Unhand him." Riona drew her blade along the Dark Fae's throat. He was Egan's man, but if he harmed a hair on Toby's head, she would kill him without blinking.

"He escaped his rooms again," the soldier hissed in the creepy way of the Asrai who normally resided at the bottom of the Black Sea of Myrkur.

"Can't you see he isn't well?" Riona reached for Toby as the soldier released him.

"The snakes, Riona, they're everywhere." Toby turned his bloodshot eyes on her, his face flushed with fever.

She wrapped her arm around his shoulders and steered him toward her room. "He will stay with me for the rest of the night. His hallucinations are getting worse."

"Very well." The soldier relented and skulked away with two of his brethren. Asrai were the last creatures that should be guarding the boy. Some were acclimated to the land and its customs, but others were the stuff of nightmares. Egan must be desperate to keep his hold on Tobias.

"The snakes." Toby's bottom lip trembled.

"It's okay, Toby. There aren't any snakes in my room. We'll stay here for the rest of the night." She guided him into her rooms and closed the door behind them. Toby turned and threw his arms around her waist and burst into tears.

"I want to go home, Riona." He shook in her arms.

"I promise, I will get you home to your parents, Toby." She smoothed her hand over his dark curls, so like his mother's. He couldn't last much longer. Egan was abusing Toby's magic, and it was taking a toll on him.

"I heard the commotion." Rowena let herself into the room without knocking, balancing a tea tray with two steaming mugs. "Eldur Blossom tea. It will help you both sleep a nice dreamless rest." She pressed a mug into Toby's hands.

Riona helped herself to the other mug of sweet smelling tea. She could do with a nice dreamless rest herself.

Rowena soon had them both tucked into bed, and Toby was finally calm, curled up beside Riona.

"We have to get him out soon," Riona whispered. "It will throw us all into the war we'd all like to avoid, but it's time."

"We've fought wars before, and we likely will again." Rowena sighed. "I can't think of a better reason to fight a war than for the safety of an innocent child."

"Especially this child." Riona's eyes drooped from the effects of Rowena's tea. "He reminds me of his father."

"Where is that worthless brat?" Egan kicked in the door of Riona's bedroom. "I will not lose this war because of a stupid useless child." He dragged Toby from Riona's bed.

"Your Majesty." Riona scrambled to her feet. "He was ill. Out of his head with fever. I thought it best to keep him here where I could see to his care."

"He looks fine to me."

"He is feverish."

"All children are feverish."

"I'm afraid his magic is too erratic. It's making him sick, my Lord. We must be careful—"

Egan's fist shot out, striking her with a bruising blow to her jaw.

Riona stumbled but managed to keep her balance, dropping her head with a show of remorse. "I am sorry, your Majesty. I overstepped."

"It is not for you to tell me what must be done."

"Of course, your Majesty." She made a show of groveling—the one thing that was sure to please him the most.

"Come, boy. You will open a portal for my troops."

"My Lord, if I may?" Riona put herself between Egan and Toby. "I agree, the boy's portals are vital to your strategy, but I fear it is too much for him, portaling to the human realm so often, and with such large numbers, and immediately portaling back to Eldur."

"How else are we to lead an attack on the Light Fae?" Egan rounded on her, and she feared he might strike her again.

"You remember what Griffin said about Tia's magic? She and her brother are very young. They are powerful, each in their own ways, but they haven't come of age yet. Think of how useful Toby will be to you when he's older and more capable of welding his portal magic? I fear—if he uses his O'Shea magic too often, it could kill him, sire. And I would hate to see you lose such an important tool."

"Perhaps." Egan shrugged. "But perhaps his death will buy me a victory. Come boy. We have a battle to wage." Egan shoved Toby from the room, sending him with his soldiers to the courtyard where he frequently made his portals.

For nearly two weeks, Egan launched surprise attacks on the Eldurian camp closest to the palace grounds where those of Iskalt and Fargelsi couldn't help them. The Dark Fae's defensive magic put them on an even playing field, and the Eldurians couldn't use their magic in the perpetual night. The two sides clashed in bloody battles almost daily now. The Eldurians were skilled with their weapons and their battle tactics. But the Dark Fae were fast and their brute strength made them formidable foes. Riona shuddered to think of what this war could turn into if it went on much longer.

Making her way along the servant's halls to the dowager queen's rooms, Riona was determined to get them all out of the palace as soon as possible. It was time. She'd done what she'd set out to do. Protect Toby and keep Egan from destroying this world. But he wasn't listening to her anymore, and if she wasn't careful, she'd be the one under guard before much longer.

"Any progress?" Riona asked as she closed the queen's door behind her. It was getting harder to talk her way past the guards.

"Nothing." Enis paced the length of the queen's sitting room, wringing her hands together. "Egan won't let me take the book to study on my own anymore, so I have to be careful when I'm searching the book for answers. He's losing faith in me."

They all were. Riona was never sure where Enis' loyalties lay. She was faithful to Egan, for now, but she worried for her grandson. "Have you considered that maybe magic isn't the answer to everything?" Riona asked. "Maybe what Toby needs is an absence of magic. He is the boy who was born without it, after all."

Enis stared at her like she'd suggested the boy should visit a human doctor to treat his symptoms.

"It is time to make our move, ladies," Faolan said, wincing in pain. "Toby's health isn't improving. His mental state is getting worse with every portal the king forces him to open. The poor child blames himself for all the Fae who have died or been injured in battle. A thing like that weighs heavily on a grown man, but he's just a little boy."

"Will you go with us, your Majesty?" Riona asked, but she knew the answer already. Faolan would never leave her people.

"I must stay."

"I don't understand what you can do for your people cooped up in this room." Riona shook her head.

"It's the simple fact that they know she is here," Enis said. "They are trapped within the city, and the one thing that gives them hope is knowing their queen's mother is right there with them. If she abandoned them, it would kill their spirit."

"So I must stay." Faolan nodded. "But you three must go."

"I will help Riona get our grandson to safety," Enis said. "But I must return—"

"For the book." Riona finished for her. "The book Egan wouldn't know what to do with if you weren't here to interpret it for him."

"I fear he would destroy it if I left. The book of power must be preserved." Enis continued her nervous pacing. "But not at the cost of my grandson's life."

"Perhaps you should have thought about that before you awakened O'Shea magic that he'd shown no ability to wield." Faolan glared daggers at the woman who gave birth to the son she raised in her stead.

"I had little choice."

"Maybe you shouldn't tell Egan everything you discover in that book," Faolan shot back.

"Enough." Riona moved between the two former queens. "We will get him out tonight."

"Get him out of here." Egan kicked Toby's chair away from the high table in what Egan was referring to as the King's Hall.

The chair tipped over, and Toby went sprawling to the ground, shrieking about snakes and writhing on the floor like a madman with tears running down his gaunt cheeks.

"My patience grows thin with his childish lunacy." Egan tipped his wine glass and drained its contents. "I've a mind to toss him into the canyon and be done with him."

"I will escort him away from your presence, your Majesty." Riona jumped at the opening Egan gave her. It was just what she was waiting for. With the king sufficiently drunk, there was a chance she could get Toby to safety before Egan suspected anything.

"Thank you, my dear." Egan reached for her hand. "You are the only one I can count on not to disappoint me."

"It is my honor to serve you, my Lord." Riona dipped her head toward the man who had raised her to be his greatest weapon. She longed for the day when she would never have to lay eyes on him again.

"The snakes!" Toby screamed, his eyes wild with fright. "Riona, they're everywhere. They want to destroy the king." He scrambled to her side, kneeling before her, he wrapped his bony arms around her knees. "Can you hear them whispering?"

"Get up." She jerked him to his feet, hating herself for treating him so roughly. "The king has no need of your antics tonight, boy." She marched him from the great hall toward the inner sanctum of the palace and the rooms where Egan kept the boy imprisoned.

Once in the shadows of the dimly lit corridors, Riona crouched in front of Toby, running her hand over his forehead. He was blazing hot with fever. "It will be okay, Toby. The snakes won't bother you anymore."

"Did it work?" He quirked a mischievous smile at her. One she'd seen often from Griffin.

Riona stared at him in awe. "You were faking it?"

"Grandmother Enis said I should be extra irritating tonight."

"You did good, kid. Now let's get you out of here." Riona took his hand, clammy with sweat, and steered him toward her rooms. She wasn't sure she could risk escaping with Toby the same way Gulliver had with Logan and Darra. She had half a mind to walk through the front door and dare anyone to stop her. But she couldn't take such a big risk with Griffin's son.

In the quiet corridor outside her rooms, the outrageous fountains trickled and gurgled. The whole palace was ostentatious, but those fountains were ... extra, as Gulliver would say. She wished he were here. That kid knew how to sneak around better than anyone, and she caught herself asking, *what would Gullie do*?

She glanced at the winding stairs that led up, all the way to the highest points in the palace. Gulliver might not walk out the front door, but he would use the quickest means of getting where he needed to go and then take that route like he owned it.

"This way." Riona led Toby toward the stairs. "And if we run into anyone along the way, do exactly what you did for the king just now."

"Yes, ma'am." Toby gripped her hand as they climbed the steep stone steps. There were hundreds of them, winding in an endless loop, all the way to the top of the tiered gardens that sat above the canyon.

Toby grew weary quickly, sweat trickling down his face. Riona had to carry him the last several flights, and even she was panting by the time they stepped into the cool night air. Toby groaned as she set him back on his feet.

"Quiet, Toby," Riona hushed him as she took his hand in hers. "Can you walk?"

He nodded, his eyes bright with fever in the moonlight.

"Wait here one second while I check for guards." Riona left him in the shadows, searching the garden pathway for sentries. They were posted at the base of the pyramid-like structure at the main entrance, but no one guarded the path that led to the stables and the myriad of pathways that wound back to the city streets. That was their way out. They just had to avoid the soldiers near the stables and make their way to the canyon road that led to the Eldurian army camp.

"Who's there?" a slurred voice called in the darkness that was like home to Riona and her kind. The soldier peered at her through a haze of drink.

"I am on the king's business." She lifted her head at the Light Fae sizing her up.

"Yeah? And what business is that?"

"Nothing that concerns you." Riona grabbed her knife from the sheath at her waist and hit him over the head with the hilt before he could gather his wits about him.

He sank like a stone to the ground in a puddle of wine.

Riona took up his cloak, wrapping it around her shoulders to conceal her wings. Pulling the hood down low, she returned to Toby.

"Riona?" His voice quavered. "Is he ... dead?"

"No, but he'll probably wish he were come morning. Let's go." She reached for his hand, and they set off through the shadows to the lowest tier of the garden. Once through the rear gate, they crouched in the tall grass where Egan's soldiers not welcome in the palace made their camp nearest the stables. The hour grew late, and the men were deep in their cups beside the warmth of their fires by now. But they weren't safe yet. And they wouldn't be until they found the Eldur camp.

With the solid stone of the city streets beneath them, Riona moved more confidently, one hand on her sword, and the other gripping Toby's hand.

Few roamed the streets at night, but with a soldier's cloak on her back, no one questioned her presence. Riona didn't know Raudur City well enough to navigate it in the dark, but she was determined to leave it behind, once and for all. Once Toby was safe, she had no need to return to Egan's side.

They walked quickly along a winding pathway at the cliff's edge. Much of the city lay sprawled out beneath them, but she was searching for a route that would lead them up and away from the canyon roads. The longer they walked, the fewer soldiers they saw, but destruction blocked their path.

"I'm tired, Riona." Toby's voice was soft, and his breath was shallow. This kid needed a healer. And soon.

"We're nearly there." She bent to pull him into her arms, wrapping his gangly legs around her waist. He was too old to carry, but he'd lost weight in his time with Egan, and Riona was determined to get him out of this city one way or another, even if she had to carry him the rest of the way.

Her legs shook with the effort, but she kept walking for miles over mounds of rubble and around deep holes in the ground. Magic and weeks of battle had destroyed this end of the city.

Crouching low, Riona studied the lines of tents and smoldering fires that belonged to Egan's front-line soldiers. The ones keeping the Eldurians out of their city. But Riona knew a thing or two about these soldiers. They were nothing more than mercenaries. Soldiers here for a full belly and their fair share of wine and ale, and the spoils of war. They had no real loyalty to Egan or any king. That kind of army wasn't exactly diligent in their watch, and she was counting on their preference for a warm fire and a cup of ale to get her through the lines.

Toby's hot breath against her neck alarmed her. She wasn't entirely sure if he was sleeping, or if he'd passed out from the illness that plagued him.

Riona made a wide berth of the camp as it gave way to the lush forest of the oasis surrounding Raudur City. Under the cover of trees, she moved faster, her chest burning with the effort of carrying Toby. Part of her wanted to take to the skies and stretch her wings, but that was a good way to get shot. Her defensive magic would shield her from magical attack, but that would leave Toby vulnerable.

She walked all night along the aimless paths through the forest and grassy meadows until she reached the desert sands. Tattered tents stretched out before her as the moon settled along the horizon. It was morning.

Riona felt them before she saw them as they moved on silent feet.

Eldurian soldiers swarmed the area, their weapons at the ready.

"Who is the child?" a gruff voice asked.

"I am a friend," she gasped as she fell to her knees, dropping Toby onto the sandy ground.

"Dark Fae are no friends of ours." A soldier flicked his sword at her wings fanned out behind her under the cloak she wore.

"I am not your enemy." Her voice was like sandpaper in her throat. She was so tired and so thirsty. "I've brought—"

"Stand aside." A woman's weary voice joined those of her soldiers. "Tobias?" The Eldurian queen fell to her knees in front of her nephew.

"He is ill." Riona tried to swallow.

"Who are you?" Alona demanded as she reached for the boy. "Toby." She patted his flushed face. "Finn!"

"Your Majesty, we should send this woman and her child back where she came from."

Alona stood to her full height, which was somehow still intimidating, though she wasn't very tall—and she was human. "Soldier, that child is my nephew and the Prince of Iskalt."

"Alona, what's going on? Is that..." Her husband and King Consort of Eldur came to her side and quickly bent to lift Toby into his arms. "He's burning up."

"He needs a healer." Riona tried to stand, but with a dozen swords pointed at her, she decided to stay where she was.

"What's wrong with him?" Alona looked from Toby to Riona.

"His magic, it's making him sick." The look in the human queen's eyes sent a shiver of fear through her. She was as fierce as any fae.

"Take this woman to the queen's tent and give her whatever she needs," Queen Alona ordered. "She's just saved my nephew's life."

CHAPTER 9

GRIFFIN

Aghadoon sat in the middle of the army camp, yet walking from the village into the sea of tents felt like taking a long journey, leaving Griffin tired and wanting to seek his bed.

They'd seen no sun for a week now as reports came to them of attacks on the Eldurians to the north. Without their day magic, the army couldn't use magic to defend themselves.

And his Iskalt magic... During his time in Myrkur, he'd longed to feel it buzzing underneath his skin, the warmth when it pooled in his fingertips. But his body wasn't meant to hold magic for such a continuous period.

Griffin stumbled toward the Dark Fae camp, wanting nothing more than to collapse where he stood. His fellow Iskalt soldiers lazed around their tents, unable to rise while their Fargelsian counterparts cooked the day's first meal. There was a reason their magic was so much weaker than any other type of fae's. Because it was always there, always ready to funnel into their spells. If it wasn't weak, their bodies would break down.

Before he could escape the depressing Iskalt camp, he noticed a crowd of people near Brea and Lochlan's tent. With a sigh, he changed direction, trying to remain upright for just a little longer.

He'd left Brea, Neeve, and Myles in the library, searching for the spell creating the endless night. They said he was needed in camp, but he wasn't sure about that. As his legs weakened beneath him, he wondered if he was really worth anything at all at the moment.

Lochlan stood in front of his tent, his face an ashy gray. His body swayed like he too struggled to remain standing. Beside him, Hector looked like the symbol of health, and Griffin almost hated him for it. A few other Iskaltians stood nearby, also looking close to death.

Lochlan saw Griffin first, his expression not changing as he moved aside to reveal the fae he'd been speaking to.

Steps faltering, Griffin thought he imagined her at first. Riona.

A smile curved her lips when she saw him, but Griffin didn't understand. She wasn't supposed to be here. Fear wound through him. Had something happen to Toby?

He forced his legs forward, pushing the questions to the back of his mind because she was here. Riona stood in front of him, weary with dark circles under her eyes, but otherwise seemingly okay. And with Lochlan, of all people. Griffin swayed on his feet, unsure if he was dreaming.

"Riona?" Griffin only had to say her name once for her to rush toward him, concern in her eyes.

"You shouldn't be standing." She reached him, neither of them touching the other as their gazes connected.

"You shouldn't be here."

Her lips curved up again. "I am done fighting for Egan, Griff. I need to be on the right side in this, your side."

He reached a tentative hand out, letting the tips of his fingers trail over her dark skin. "Toby?"

Lochlan was the one who answered, pushing back the flap of his tent to reveal two sleeping children curled around each other. Tia and Toby should never be pried apart again.

"He was able to muster enough strength to portal us to the human realm and then to here," Riona whispered. "You should be proud of him."

He was. Griffin couldn't have been more proud of the boy sitting on the ground in front of him if he tried.

This was the missing piece, the last thing they needed before attacking Egan. He couldn't take his eyes from Toby as the remaining energy drained from his body. He didn't feel himself falling before his knees hit the ground. And when he crumpled forward, the only thought on his mind was that at least all of his kids were safe.

A damp cloth wiped sweat from Griffin's face as his eyes slid open to find the most beautiful face he'd ever seen hovering over him.

"Hi." Riona smiled in the way he'd so rarely seen. "You slept longer than I did." It hadn't been a dream. She was safe and here, just like Toby.

"You saved him." It was all he could think to say.

"I promised you I'd protect him." She pulled the cloth away and sat back on her heels. "I've broken a lot of promises in my life, done a lot of bad, but that was good. I like this feeling."

"What feeling is that?"

"Like we have something to fight for, something good to protect."

"Me too." He sat up with no difficulty and looked around the tent he recognized as his own. "Why don't I feel sick?" Had they found the magic that created the perpetual night? Did Brea burn the spell and bring back the sun?

Crawling to the doorway, he pushed aside the hanging canvas and peered out, surprised to see darkness still covering the land.

"Brea is kind of amazing, isn't she?" Riona crawled to his side.

"What?" He lifted a brow as he looked to her.

"They found a spell in the library, one that Lochlan tried to keep her from performing. It's pretty dark stuff and not altogether different from the prison magic."

Griffin sat back, finding her face in the dark. "What do you mean?" He didn't like the sound of this.

"They're still searching for the magic to destroy the darkness, but once they do, we can't attack Egan with a half-dead army."

"Riona, what did Brea do?" He got the feeling she didn't want to tell him.

"She found a spell similar to the one that infused the prison barrier with the magic of those who crossed." Griffin didn't need her to explain any longer. He pushed to his feet and darted out into the dark camp, winding through rows of tents to reach the Iskalt camp where soldiers looked to be regaining their strength. He sprinted for the village, not noticing when the sand turned to stone underneath his feet.

He burst into the library to find the table pushed against the shelves in the back and two fae laying in the center of the library.

"What did you do?" he murmured.

Brea and Tia clasped hands, holding tightly to each other as something lit their skin from beneath.

"I tried to stop her."

Griffin turned at the sound of Myles' voice. He sat in the dark corner of the room, a sword across his lap as if he, a human, was their protection.

Myles rubbed his eyes, not looking up when Riona entered behind Griffin. "She waited until Neeve left, knowing her sister wouldn't approve. But me… I'm just Brea's goofy best friend. The human. She didn't listen to me. And then Tia found her trying to perform the spell." He lifted bloodshot eyes to Griffin. "Brea was the most powerful magic wielder this world knew… until her daughter. She couldn't do this on her own, and Tia was so adamant about lending her strength." He shook his head.

Griffin took a tentative step toward the girls to stare down into their open eyes. "They took all the Iskalt magic into them, didn't they? What were they thinking?"

An irrational anger rose within him. Brea wasn't only risking herself, but his daughter's life was on the line too. No one knew the risks of such magic.

Riona crossed her arms over her chest. "They did it for all of *you*, for Lochlan. The two of you should be ashamed for doubting them after everything that has happened. Griff, you collapsed in front of me almost two *days* ago. Iskaltians were all on the brink of death. You think we could have fought Egan with a large part of the army dead from exhaustion before the battle even started?"

"It's only temporary." Myles pushed to his feet and set the sword on the table. "That's what Brea said. She needed to let the Iskaltians recover just until the spell to end the darkness was found. Then, when their magic returned, they could fight."

Griffin couldn't deny how horrible he'd felt and the strength that now coursed through him. He lifted a hand, testing his magic. The Iskaltian power didn't come, but he felt his O'Shea portal magic within his reach. Brea was right. The Iskaltian army would have been destroyed.

And if she could risk everything for this—even her own daughter —he could fight for it too.

The door burst open once more, and Lochlan ran in, his chest heaving. He took one look at his wife and daughter and advanced on Myles. "You let her do this?"

"You think I could stop her?"

"Lochlan." Neeve walked in behind him and froze, her gaze going to Brea. She didn't voice her thoughts on the matter as she turned to Myles. "I promised I'd bring help, and I have." Her eyes flicked to Brea once more. "We will find the spell we need so we can bring Brea and Tia back to us."

Griffin looked to his brother. "They can find the spell. You and I must prepare for the battle that will come when they do." He stepped forward and put a hand on Lochlan's shoulder. "Do you have your portal magic?"

Lochlan nodded.

"Then it is time we bring the three kingdoms together."

Griffin and Lochlan chose not to use the magic they'd found that enhanced one's ability to travel through portals. Instead, they worked together as neither of them had ever dreamed they would, to bring the bedraggled Eldurian army into the Iskaltian camp, using Toby to direct their portals to the Eldurian camp. They might not have had their Iskaltian magic, but the O'Shea power still bent to their will.

The usual time skew between the fae world and the human world didn't occur because of the endless night, allowing the O'Shea brothers—and son—to make their jumps quickly.

For weeks, the Eldurians had fought small skirmishes with parts of Egan's army as he tested their magic and attacked during the night when they had none. He probably assumed they were the weaker force being led by a human queen, but he didn't know Alona.

She'd stayed behind, letting each of her people go through the portals before her. Griffin and Lochlan couldn't take entire armies like Toby had been able to, so it was slow going. They refused to let Toby open his super portals—for lack of a better word—he could only help direct theirs.

As the brothers had prepared for their first portals, Toby came to them, steel in his gaze.

"I want to help."

Less than two days ago, he'd been at Egan's side. There was no way Griffin wanted him to become involved in the very thing that was draining his own energy.

"Okay." Lochlan had walked toward his son.

Griffin shook his head. "Lochlan, no."

They both knew at this point Griffin was Toby's biological father, but this wasn't his choice. Lochlan's hard gaze told him that.

"Brea and Tia are laying at the center of that library holding the magic of an entire army. You and I are shuttling the Eldurians here while Neeve and her people search for a way to end this night. And *my* son has more reason to fight than any single fae. He deserves to be in this just as much as his sister."

Toby's eyes had glassed over as he stared at his dad. Growing up without magic, Griffin could only imagine how useless he'd felt in the fae realm. But now they could give him the chance to do something good.

"We are O'Sheas." Griffin had stepped toward them, completing their triangle. "We do this together."

Toby's magic appeared first, a violet rift in the fabric of the world. Griffin's matching power opened a portal. Before he stepped through, he caught sight of the icy blue O'Shea magic escaping Lochlan. The whole of Iskalt magic might be inside Brea and Tia right now, but their family power, their heritage, had bonded the three of them together, giving Griffin the strength he needed for a few final portals.

Now, here they were six portals deep and exhausted.

They only stayed in the field outside Brea's family home in the human realm long enough to catch their breath before portaling into the center of what Toby said was the Eldurian camp.

At the edges of camp, ditches had been dug as a defensive measure that wouldn't have been effective against sylph.

A breath rushed out of Alona the moment she saw the three of them. The remaining force protecting her and her husband rose to their feet.

Lochlan stepped forward and folded the Eldurian queen into his arms. "Now, we fight together."

When Griffin used to think of Lochlan with Alona and Finn, jealousy overcame him. He'd been raised alone while Lochlan grew up with the eventual Eldurian royals. They were more siblings than Griffin had ever been.

Yet now, he saw what he had with Shauna and Hector, a bond that didn't exist purely because of the blood in his veins, a family that chose each other.

Finn lifted Toby in a hug before patting Griffin on the shoulder in an awkward "I remember you now" meeting.

"We should go." Griffin looked toward the smoke rising from Raudur City.

Alona ran a hand through her tangled blond hair and offered him a nod. "You're right." She turned to her remaining people. "Be prepared to enter the human realm before we make it to the Iskalt camp."

The moment they stepped through the final portal into their camp, Griffin's shoulders sagged, his magic retreating into him. Commotion sounded around them as Alona asked someone to take her to her children and walked off.

Lochlan kept a hand firmly on Toby's shoulder as Neeve rushed across the camp to him and murmured in a low voice. "That's good, Neeve. Are they... okay?"

She nodded. "I believe so. Brea took certain precautions according to Myles. She did not let Tia take the Iskalt magic into herself. That could have caused permanent damage before she is of age for her body to handle it. From what I can tell, Brea is simply drawing on Tia's strength. Tia was the only magic wielder strong enough to make sure we didn't lose Brea."

He rubbed a weary hand across his face. "When can we bring them out of the spell?"

"As soon as we find what we're looking for. We're close. You should prepare your soldiers to attack within the next six hours. I am going to do the same."

Finn sighed. "We'd hoped to rest our warriors, but Eldur will be ready as well. Though, we won't be much good without our magic."

"You will have it." With that, Neeve walked toward the Fargelsian camp.

Lochlan looked to Griffin and for once, there wasn't a hint of scorn or distrust in his gaze. "Will you help me, brother? We must convince our Iskalt brothers and sisters their magic will return before the fight."

Griffin wanted to say yes, to tell Lochlan he'd waited his entire life for someone to tell him the Iskalt people were truly his.

But what if they weren't?

Not anymore.

"I have to find my family." The words were only meant for himself and not to hurt Lochlan, but he saw his brother's face fall. Was it possible that Lochlan spent his life wanting to be a true brother to Griffin as well? "Loch, I will fight beside you. You are my brother, and that will never change, but I need to find my son." His eyes fell on Toby and Lochlan's hand on his shoulder. It confirmed what he knew.

If a battle was coming for them, Griffin wanted to spend the last hours with the Dark Fae, with Gulliver and their family.

Lochlan gave him a nod before steering Toby to follow Finn. They too had to be with their family.

He found Gulliver sitting at the edge of Aghadoon, his shoulders slumped. He straightened when he saw Griffin. "You're back!"

"Stand up, Gulliver." Griffin stopped in front of him.

Gulliver jumped to his feet, his cat-eyes narrowing. "What's wrong? Are you mad I helped Tia get into the library to help her mom? I didn't mean to do anything wrong, I promise. Are you disappointed in me, Griff? Oh wow, you are, aren't you?" His eyes glassed over. "Please don't be. She asked me, and... then I couldn't leave the village, but Myles kicked me out of the library, waving a sword at me. So I've been sitting here. I don't want you to be mad at me."

Taking mercy on him, Griffin reached out and pulled him into a hug. "I'm not mad, Gullie. Not disappointed. You're everything I could ever want in a son."

"Whoa, I don't know what made you all sentimental, but this hug is kinda nice." Gulliver wrapped his arms around Griffin's waist.

Griffin laughed and pulled back. "I just wanted to see you. We're going into battle soon. When we do, I'm going to ask you to stay in Aghadoon."

Gulliver opened his mouth to protest but Griffin cut him off. "Tia and Brea won't be in any shape to fight. You'll need to stay with them, to protect them."

That was the one thing that could keep Gulliver away from the fight. Protecting Tia.

"I won't let you down, Griff."

"I know you won't." Griffin slid an arm over his shoulders and steered him toward the Myrkur camp. "Until then, we should be with our family."

They found Hector speaking to some of his soldiers, having already been informed of the impending battle by an Iskalt general. Griffin smiled at the thought Lochlan considered this force a part of the true army.

There'd be no sleep tonight. Fires dotted the landscape, as soldiers waited for the sun to come—a sun they'd never imagined in all their years in Myrkur.

Griffin lowered himself between Shauna and Riona as they sat with a group of fae around a small cookfire that thankfully gave off light but little warmth. Hector's mom, Kiaran, smiled at him across the fire where she sat with her younger children.

Pressing a kiss to the side of Riona's head, he pulled her closer. A smile played on her lips as she relaxed against him.

Shauna knocked her shoulder into his. "We didn't know if you'd be with us tonight."

Hector joined them. "Of course he's here. Griffin is one of us." He winked at Gulliver. "We don't know what tomorrow will bring, but tonight we can give each other strength."

Griffin replayed Hector's words in his mind. *Griffin is one of us. One of us. One of us.* He wasn't Dark Fae. He'd been broken for so long. Yet these people had never once questioned his place among them since the moment Shauna found him. He never had to earn their affection.

And they'd taken Riona in as one of them despite her history. He'd always be grateful to them for that.

Wrapping one arm around Shauna and extending a hand to grip both Riona's and Gulliver's hands on his other side, he prepared himself mentally for the battle to come. His eyes fell to Nessa, curled up in Shauna's lap, the girl who'd started his adversarial relationship with Egan when he'd tried to save her.

And he was still trying to save them all.

Now, it was possible in a way it never had been before.

They spent most of the night talking in low tones, their laughter punctuating the darkness.

He didn't know how long he'd been there when a familiar buzz raced along his skin, his Iskalt and O'Shea powers curling together.

Lifting a hand, he watched the violet power spark in his fingertips.

"It's almost time, isn't it?" Riona asked.

Griffin nodded. "We must prepare."

Darkness still coated the sky, but if the magic had been returned, it could only mean they'd found a way to bring the sun back. For now, they had to take it on faith.

Hector rose and started issuing orders to his soldiers. Any who weren't going to fight made their way to the village. Gulliver pulled a crying Nessa away from Shauna and held her hand as he led her away.

"He'll take care of her." Griffin slipped a chain mail shirt over his head.

"I know." Shauna sighed as she strapped on her sword belt.

Grooms brought the few horses the Dark Fae had, and Griffin pulled himself into his saddle. Riona jumped into the air with a flap of her wings, now nearly half black against the darkened sky.

"Riona." He looked up at her hovering beside him.

"I know, Griff. Be careful."

He nodded. "That... and I love you."

Her mouth opened, but no words came out. He didn't need a response from her, not now. He'd just needed her to know.

The Dark Fae joined the lines of Iskaltians, Fargelsians, and Eldurians preparing to march. It was a united fae realm like Griffin had never thought possible.

At the front of the combined force, Lochlan rode with Finn and Myles. Alona led the archers, their fingers curled around bows as they sat atop their horses.

Brea should be there, but she'd done her part. She'd made this all possible. And Queen Neeve had one more task to perform. She had to bring back the sun.

Operating on faith, knowing Neeve would come through for

them, the army marched across the sands separating them from the city.

And still, the sky remained dark.

Egan's forces scrambled to form lines at the edge of the western canyon, Dark Fae running and flying from the streets behind them.

And still, the sky remained dark.

Griffin drew his sword, the metal scraping against its sheathe. He was ready to fight.

And still... A cry wound through the Iskaltian, ranks and Griffin looked back over his shoulder to see a fire raging through the tents they'd left behind.

But the sky... Light appeared on the horizon, a dim ray of hope for an otherwise hopeless battle.

Looking toward the moon, Griffin caught sight of the blazing ring of light growing larger as the sun appeared from behind the moon until it was halfway visible.

"A partial eclipse," a soldier nearby cried out.

An event where both night and day existed together at the same time. Something the humans experienced, but no fae alive had ever seen. He looked to the Eldurian lines where they tested the magic returning to them after too long away.

The Iskaltian magic didn't fade from Griffin. Instead, it pulsed inside him, eager for an escape.

His eyes hardened as he readied to ride into battle.

Iskaltians. Eldurians. Fargelsians. Dark Fae.

Only when good bonded together could they wipe evil from their kingdoms.

Chapter 10

GRIFFIN

The noise of battle filled Griffin's mind and stirred his blood. Swords clanged, and warm blood spurted from fresh wounds. Iskaltian fought beside Eldurians, their magic working together against their enemy. It defied nature, and should never be, yet it was a thing of beauty to see them united together under the partial eclipse.

Gathering his magic close to his core, Griffin fought alongside Riona with Hector and Shauna, Dark Fae and Light Fae fighting for the good of them all. Casting his magic toward the desert sands beneath their enemy's feet, an explosion of ice and sand sent them scattering, blinded by the sand in their eyes.

They'd learned quickly that the Dark Fae's defensive magic could be penetrated with much effort. But the Light Fae could expend too much energy trying to get through their defenses. It was a far better use of their magic to use it on their surroundings, creating explosions and obstacles to block their enemy's path and cause confusion. After that, it came down to which side was better with a sword.

Beside him, Hector snorted like a bull, sinking into a crouch. As the dust cleared, he charged ahead, locking horns with a fae twice his size.

Riona and Griffin moved to flank him with Shauna at their backs, their swords making quick work of those moving in to surround Hector and his opponent.

"Griffin! Above you!" Riona called as she leapt into the air and sank her dagger into the thick neck of an enormous ogre. She held on as the ogre fell to his knees.

Griffin whirled around just in time to block a volley of arrows with his magic. The roughly hewn arrows fell to the ground, and Griffin sent out a blast of icy wind to blow the angry Slyph off course.

"What you said back there." Riona hacked away at the ogre's back to ensure he was dead. It was hard work, killing an ogre. Gore smeared her face and wings.

"I've said a lot of things, Riona." Griffin moved to block an Asrai from barreling over her. "Can you be more specific?" His sword glanced off the Asrai's scales. They were even harder to kill than ogres.

"You know I feel the same way, right?" She called as she climbed down off the ogre, just in time to help him take on the Asrai. She blocked the creature's massive sword, shoving her back.

"I know." Griffin shot her a grin as he threw a punch, sending the Asrai woman to the ground. Her scales were like stone against his fist.

"Well that was stupid." Riona moved in, hip checking him out of the way. Tossing her dagger from one hand to the other, she moved like quicksilver until her blade found purchase, and the Asrai went down like a dead fish on dry land. "Aim for the gills." She panted, wiping the gore from her dagger against her boots. "If you hit them like that, you'll be the one coming away with broken bones."

"I'm going to need to hear you say it." Griffin jumped in front of Riona, throwing up a shield to block a Light Fae's killing curse—a Fargelsian criminal from the prison realm. They would have to do something about all of them when this war was over. They couldn't leave the worst criminals of their world roaming free.

"Say what?" Riona leapt over him to clash with a Slyph with massive black wings. A ripping sound followed by screams and a shower of blood had Griffin looking up to the sky to make sure she was okay. The huge Slyph came crashing to the ground, his wings a bloody mess.

"I said the words, Riona, now it's your turn," Griffin shouted over the din of battle.

"Fine!" She turned toward him, her sword dripping blood. "I love you, Griffin O'Shea!"

"I love you too." Griffin grinned, making his way toward her. "Now was that so hard?" He threw a knife at an oncoming fae with tusks, the blade sinking into his forehead.

"Is this really the time for your nonsense?" Hector raged at them both. "We have a battle to win here, and we need you to focus."

"We're focused," Riona shot back.

"It's Griff." Shauna rolled her eyes. "He's never had the best timing."

"Quit your antics and come help me take this side of the canyon so we can get into the palace." Hector waved to his troops, and together they charged toward the western side of Raudur City. The palace sat perched among the city streets carved right into the sides of the eastern canyon below. Egan would be manning his forces from the safety of the palace.

"This isn't over until Egan is dead!" Griffin cried as they surged toward a line of Dark Fae protecting the Western road into the city.

Swords clashed, and Griffin's magic sent the Dark Fae scrambling for cover. They were almost through the ranks when a contingent of Slyph came surging up from the canyon, and Griffin barely managed to get his shields up in time to block the arrows raining down on them.

"Griffin!" Riona shrieked from the sky. Her brethren had swooped in to grab her, pulling her high above the battle.

"Riona!" Griffin called for her as he sent shards of magic toward the Slyph carrying her toward the palace, not stopping until the sharp bite of a blade tore into his leather armor, getting to the flesh beneath. Riona's panicked eyes met his once more before he stumbled back, losing sight of her.

Pain lanced through him, quickly chased away by the adrenaline surging in his veins. Hector's heavy axe ripped into the Asrai who'd wounded Griffin, dropping him to the ground.

Having no time to think of his injury or the warm blood seeping through the tear in his armor, Griffin charged toward the palace, Hector right behind him. His steps only faltered slightly before he regained his pace.

"Griffin, focus on what's in front of you," Hector reminded him. "You're no good to her if you get killed because your mind is elsewhere."

Griffin let out a scream of frustration as he hacked his way through the Dark Fae standing between him and Riona. His wound stretched and widened with each movement, but he did not stop. They would not take Riona away from him now that they'd found each other. Not now when they were finally on the same side. She'd risked her life to keep his son safe and again when she brought him home to his parents. He was not about to let her die for it, no matter how many times their swords struck him. He knew as sure as if they'd told him where they were going, the Slyph were taking her to Egan, and he would make her pay for her betrayal.

"She can take care of herself, brother," Hector called to him.

"I'm going to her. I have to find her."

Shauna's hand slipped into his. "We will help you." She turned her back to him as a swarm of horned fae came at them. Together they fought back to back, making their way closer to the canyon road that would lead them into the city.

Griffin's body ached with the effort of swinging his sword and wielding his magic, but the adrenaline of battle kept him focused on the fight ahead instead of his wound. The eclipse kept his night magic alive, but like everything, it came at a cost, sapping his energy faster than it should, faster than even his wound did. He absently wondered if the Eldurians were experiencing the same. They needed to win this battle quickly.

The last of Egan's defenses gave way, and Griffin ran with Shauna into Raudur City. The streets were empty, Eldurians hiding in their homes with windows and doors boarded up.

They met a troop of Egan's soldiers along the road up to the tiered gardens that overlooked the canyon from the eastern side. Griffin caught a glimpse of Egan pacing along the top tier of the garden. Beyond him, Enis—Griffin's traitor mother—worked to perform spells from that cursed book.

The only good thing was they didn't have Tia this time. Enis might know a lot about magic, but she wasn't as strong as Tia.

Griffin and Shauna darted up the road to the gardens. When Griffin's feet stumbled, Shauna shot him a worried look, her eyes flicking to where he hadn't realized his hand pressed to his side. She knew him better than anyone, so she let him keep going. Griffin had to dig deep, but he kept a shield over them, letting the arrows from Egan's crossbows bounce right off them.

Egan had strategically placed ogres and vicious Asrai at intervals along the pathway up through the gardens to the top where he directed his side of the battle. Griffin could make out Egan's angry shouts and the crack of a whip.

A woman's screams filtered down through the din of battle.

"Riona!" He cried, rushing in to help Hector and Shauna take down an enormous ogre. The ground shook beneath them as the Eldurians charged down into the canyon to take back their city.

With the Iskaltians coming in from the south, they would take this battle as a win. But they had to get to Egan now. Even with their numbers, they weren't able to fully surround Raudur City because the canyon and the Dalur river cut them off, leaving an escape route wide open for Egan.

"To the top!" Hector roared. He understood as well as Griffin that they couldn't let Egan escape down the back side of the pyramid-like structure of the gardens. They fought their way up each level, tearing through Dark Fae Egan had left to slow them down.

"Egan!" Griffin roared just below the top tier. He couldn't get through the swarm of bodies.

"This is not the end, young Griffin." Egan leaned over the side of the garden wall, his beard and arms covered in blood and gore as if he'd been fighting among his men this whole time. But men like Egan didn't fight their own battles. They hid behind others, forcing them to do the fighting for him. "Well, it may be for you." The Dark Fae king flashed an evil smile before he disappeared behind the wall.

"Egan." Griffin shoved his way through the swarm of battle, Shauna hot on his heels. When they reached the top, Egan was gone, Enis and his last remaining loyal soldiers with him. Griffin stumbled to the other side of the garden only to see Egan fleeing on horseback through the fire orchard and to the road that would lead him into the unforgiving deserts of Eldur.

"We need to go after him!" Griffin shouted, knowing he'd be no good in any chase.

"We will." Hector panted beside him. "I'll go myself once we know this battle is done. He won't get away, Griffin. We will see him pay for his crimes. But that day is not today." Hector waved overhead to call down his Slyph from the skies. "I'll send a few sylph to track him and then follow once I can leave here." He turned to Griffin. "But you... Shauna needs to tend your wound." He walked away to talk to his fae.

"Who is she?" Shauna reached for Griffin's shoulder, having not heard Hector. She pulled him back to the aftermath of a battle just winding down and the force almost sent him falling to the stones.

"Who?" Griffin let his gaze wander across the gardens. And then he saw her. Strapped to a whipping post, the former Queen of Eldur lay slumped against it. "Faolan?" His voice shook as he ran to her side. He didn't want to have to tell his brother that the woman who raised him as her own might be dead.

Her back was a mass of shredded skin and welts. Some half healed and scabbed over as if she'd succumbed to this treatment on multiple occasions.

Shauna reached to check her for signs of life.

"She's Brea and Alona's mother." Griffin moved to cut her down from the post, using his last bits of strength as pain replaced the adrenaline inside him.

"She lives," Shauna whispered, making the swift adjustment

from soldier to healer in an instant. "Bring her into the shade." She guided him toward a corner of the garden shaded under a canopy of trees with enormous waxy leaves. "Lay her on her stomach. I will tend her wounds." Shauna reached for the herb kit hanging over her shoulder. "You, Griff, stay. Don't think I forgot your wound. It needs tended to. Remove your armor while I help Faolan." She turned her attention from Griffin.

Faolan was in good hands, and Griffin needed to find Riona more than he needed Shauna to bandage his wound. He feared Egan might have taken her with him.

"We need to address the Dark Fae," Hector said, returning to Griffin's side. "Now that Egan is gone, most of them are laying their weapons down. You need to tell them it's time to choose which side they're on. The side of a king who has treated them like slaves all their lives or the side that will give them something they've never known. Free will."

"They need to hear that from one of their own, brother." Griffin clapped him on the back and winced. "And you are far more eloquent than I am."

"Me?" Hector stared blankly at him.

"Yes, you. Like it or not, you are a leader, and your soldiers respect you. The other Dark Fae will too if you give them a chance to come to your side."

"Mine?" Hector shook his head, his great bull horns nearly gored Griffin.

"It's time, Hector." Griffin led him to the garden wall overlooking the carnage below. Most of the fighting had stopped as news of Egan's escape spread like wildfire through the armies. "Stand still." Griffin placed his hands along Hector's throat, his magic pooling in his hands to enhance Hector's voice. "They will all hear you now." Griffin stepped back from the wall, each movement harder than the one before.

The Griffin of old would have jumped at a chance to take the reins after an epic battle, wound or no. The old Griffin would have seen it as an opportunity to seize power now that Egan was on the run and no longer in a position to rule over the Dark Fae.

But Griffin learned the hard way that power corrupts, and he wasn't that man any more. The thirst for power had long since died out of him. All he wanted now was to make sure his family was safe.

"Dark Fae." Hector's voice boomed across the city. "What are you fighting for?" His steady gaze swept the crowds below. "Why do you fight for a king who does nothing for you? It is time to make a choice, my brothers and sisters. Myrkur is our home. It will always be our home, but we are no longer enslaved to a king who demands loyalty, but gives none. We are no longer held in bondage by a magical boundary erected hundreds of years ago to keep us contained. The people who did that to us are long dead and long forgotten.

"This is a new day." Hector gripped the edge of the wall, looking down over the people of all the realms. "We stand on the precipice of a new future. But we must decide what kind of future we want. I for one, stand for peace. Peace among the Dark Fae who wish to live openly in whatever land they choose to call home. I stand for peace between those of Myr and those of the three kingdoms. We are all fae. I ask my Dark Fae brethren to lay down their weapons in the name of peace."

A great roar of approval swept through the city, surprising Hector with its vehemence.

"Wrap it up, big guy, you've won them over." Griffin was eager to search for Riona and check on Gulliver. He needed to know all of his family had survived the battle before he could tend to himself.

"But to those who insist on resisting peace," Hector's voice grew harsh. "Light or Dark Fae, know this. We are coming for you. We stand united as the four kingdoms never have before. Fargelsi, Iskalt, Eldur, *and* Myrkur are united as one, and we *will* have peace."

Just as Hector stepped back from the wall, the magic that created the partial eclipse subsided. The sun burst free from its place behind the moon, and light swept across the land, chasing the darkness away.

Griffin watched as those of the four kingdoms rejoiced. Dark Fae moved in droves to lay their weapons down, but he saw those who would resist as they crept away in small groups here and there. They were the ones who would find their way back to Egan.

The kingdoms won a huge battle today, but the war was not over. Not by a long shot.

CHAPTER II

RIONA

Riona slumped against the wall as the Eldurian troops surged into the palace. Blood trickled from a cut near her hairline, but other than that, she was unharmed—unlike the Slyph who'd carried her into the palace. Unlike Griffin who'd taken a sword to the side as her captors carried her away. She'd never forget the cold dread of that moment, the calm efficiency she'd used to dispatch the fae keeping her from protecting Griffin.

Loosening her fingers, Riona let her sword fall to the ground, its blade coated in the blood of her own kind. She leaned her head back, breathing heavily.

They did it.

She hadn't seen Hector give his speech, but his voice had carried throughout the halls as she dispatched the remaining attackers with a quiet efficiency. During the battle, she'd enjoyed fighting the army she'd pretended loyalty to, resisting a king who abandoned his troops while their enemy cut them down.

He lost. Egan had one chance to take control in the fae realm. Now, he had his life and the book but no army.

Her wings pushed against the wall, and she stumbled forward, needing to get outside, to escape the halls that were now stained with blood as well as the filth from Egan and his soldiers.

The grand palace of Eldur had been reduced to a hovel for Dark Fae who didn't know any different. It wasn't hard to see why the palace of Myrkur had been in such disrepair.

Riona crept up the winding stairs, finally bursting through the doors that let out into the gardens. A woman lay on her stomach on a stone bench with Shauna applying a paste to her back. As she neared, Riona recognized the Dowager Queen of Eldur, Faolan. A groan escaped her lips, and Riona released a breath. Leaving Faolan in the palace had been on Riona's mind, but she'd had no choice.

Across the garden, Hector also tended to his people with a surprising softness as he bandaged wounds. She turned as someone ran into the garden, expecting to see Griffin.

But it wasn't him.

Alona dropped her bow and sprinted down the path toward her mother, dropping to her knees at her side. Blood streaked through her blond hair, giving her more of a warrior queen look than the human she was. It suited her.

Everywhere Riona turned, injured fae tried to pick up the pieces of the battle. Walking to the wall looking down into the streets, she watched fae mourn over the dead as their blood still warmed the streets. In the distance, Eldurians tentatively came out of their homes.

Riona jumped into the air and flew the short distance into the city, landing among the people. They gave her a wide berth, and she looked down to find blood gleaming on her leather armor.

Above, the sun beat down on them, bringing with it the harsh Eldurian heat they'd avoided during Egan's endless night spell.

A fae she recognized ran toward her, a canvas sack over his shoulder. "My Lady!" He waved a hand over his head.

Riona paused, waiting for him to reach her. "I'm not a lady, sir." That title implied a status she didn't pretend to have, especially not after a battle where the enemy looked like her. She'd noticed the only

Slyph who'd stayed were the ones already a part of Hector's army. The others were either dead or scattered.

The fae shoved his bag at her. "I tried to reach your army before the battle, but my wife forced me back into my home."

"Your wife is smart." She looked into the bag, finding the sunglasses not unlike what Gulliver wore in the human realm.

But the Dark Fae no longer cringed at the light during the day. She shook her head. If they were going to have peace, they had to adapt to this world. These glasses wouldn't help. "I'm sorry, sir. You can keep the payment, but we have no more need of a device to protect us from the sun. It is our sun too." She handed the bag back. There was no time for this when Griffin was out here somewhere injured.

He gave her a confused look but didn't try to follow her as she stepped onto the road heading outside Raudur.

The battle hadn't lasted long, but it drained every bit of energy she had. As she walked, she pulled on her wings, checking them for tears. The darkness that had crept into them since she first left Myrkur now covered more than half of the delicate surface. She didn't know what that meant. Nihal's wings were dark, but she'd questioned everything about him since Enis revealed herself to be in league with Egan.

Even now, she escaped with him.

She reached the edge of the city and kicked her toe against the ground, letting her wings stretch to their full span. Before her, Iskalt, Fargelsi, and Dark Fae soldiers trudged across the hot sands to return to their camps. Riona lifted into the air, hovering for a moment before letting her wings carry her to the camps.

As she neared, she caught sight of burned out tents and black marks scorching the sand. Soldier's belongings lay in charred messes. Spotting Lochlan directing the healers, she touched down. They'd done what they could to set up an area for the wounded, but it seemed they lacked supplies.

Lochlan didn't scowl as she approached—a welcome change in their relationship.

"You're hurt." He crossed his arms. "Take a seat, and I can have one of my healers help."

She shook her head. "I just need to find Griffin."

"Another who refused my help." Lochlan released a tired sigh.

"So, he's alive?"

He nodded. "He's a fool, but alive."

Riona's gaze searched the destroyed camp. "What happened here?"

"From what Myles says, the spell bringing about the eclipse went awry the first time they tried it. It sent streams of fire through the camps, lighting up the dark with flames instead of the sun."

Riona didn't know how magic worked, but she nodded, knowing the explanation was as good as she'd get. A familiar face looked up from a spot laying on the ground.

"Your Majesty?" Riona moved closer. "Do you need help?"

The King of Eldur stared at her like he was trying to figure her out. "You're the one who saved my children."

She wasn't sure how he knew that, but she opened her mouth to refute it. It had really been Gulliver who saved the Eldurian kids. Lochlan jumped in, cutting her off. "Finn, this is Riona. I don't know her last name, but I'm sure I'll learn it. And yes, she saved Darra and Logan." His eyes met hers. "And our Toby too."

Finn offered a weak smile. "Then never again call me Majesty. I'm Finn... just Finn."

She wouldn't remind him they'd met before in the human realm, not now when his brow scrunched in confusion, and his eyes slid shut.

"No, Finn." Lochlan kneeled at his side. "Come on, brother, keep your eyes open."

"Alona," Finn whispered. "Where's my Alona?"

Lochlan cursed as his hand came away covered in blood seeping from the back of Finn's head.

Riona dropped to his other side, her wings helping her keep her balance. Lochlan called for one of the healers as Riona gripped his hand. "Alona is alive, Finn. She's well. I saw her at the palace with her mother."

Lochlan's eyes snapped to hers. "Faolan... she's..."

"In rough shape, but alive and being tended to."

He nodded, releasing a breath. "Good, that's good."

An Iskaltian healer ran toward them, and Riona got to her feet, backing away.

"Riona?" Lochlan turned from the healer to her, a worried frown on his lips as his eyes flicked to Finn.

"Yes?"

"I can't leave him." He gestured to the hordes of injured. "Any of them. We're going to prepare to move the badly injured to the village while tending to minor injuries here. More will pour in, and I'm determined to help all we can. But I don't know where my brother is. Will you find him and make sure he's not bleeding out in an Aghadoon alleyway?"

He didn't have to ask. She wanted nothing more than to search for Griffin. But she sensed Lochlan needed to say the words, to know he'd tried to do something to help his brother.

Lifting into the sky, she flew over the destroyed camps to reach Aghadoon, dropping to the stones outside the library. The door stood partially open, and she pushed it wider, finding Brea collapsed in a chair next to her equally exhausted looking sister. Neeve leaned forward with her head on the table.

Myles bustled in behind Riona, a silver tray balancing on one hand. Blood caked under his fingernails, providing a contrast to the small moment of having tea sitting in a library that didn't belong near a battlefield.

The human looked unharmed, which surprised Riona. She'd struggled in the battle even with her fae advantages.

But there was someone missing.

Tia.

The young girl had been a part of their magic too.

Brea lifted her pale face, fixing her eyes on Riona. "I heard Griff was seen back in Aghadoon. You can find him if you go look." Riona hadn't needed to ask any questions.

Riona paused at the door. "Lochlan is with the healers tending the wounded."

Brea released an audible breath. "I've been so scared since he didn't come find me right away."

"Finn has been hurt."

Brea closed her eyes for a brief moment and nodded. "Only his family could keep him from me. Will Finn live?"

"I don't know." It was honest, at least.

A tear slipped down Brea's cheek. "Go find Griff. He's hurt too and wouldn't let me help him until he found that boy of his."

Just like Lochlan, family was the most important thing to Griffin. Riona rushed from the library. She stopped when she noticed drips of blood on the stone, all leading the same way.

A soldier bumped into her as he led a large group through the streets, cheering in celebration. A huge battle had been won this day, but Riona didn't feel like there was anything to celebrate.

Egan and Enis got away. They still had the book. This wasn't over. Not yet.

But no one knew what they'd do next.

Riona couldn't help feeling like this battle was only the beginning. This wouldn't end until Egan was dead.

The trail of blood led her to the door of a shop with an image of a loaf of bread hanging crooked over the door. A bakery.

She braced herself for what she'd find inside. It was only when a scream pierced the air she forced her way in.

CHAPTER 12

GRIFFIN

Griffin managed to get back to Aghadoon atop his horse after giving Hector instructions to go after Egan with the journal that would let him report back. As soon as he's reached the village, he slid from the saddle and crashed into the stones below. He watched his blood fill the cracks between stones, remembering Shauna stitching up a similar wound from another lifetime.

But Shauna wasn't there this time. He'd managed to crawl toward the library, but his blasted horse left him. The door had been so close, but he hadn't made it before two sets of arms dragged him across the road into a nearby shop that smelled of yeast.

He hadn't had the energy to fight them, but he forced himself to look up at them as they leaned him against the counter.

Two familiar faces frowned down at him.

"Griff." Gulliver slapped his cheek. "Don't you dare pass out on us."

A crease formed between Tia's brows. "I can fix you."

He wanted to tell her no, that they'd seen what happened when she tried to fix Gulliver's tail with a spell she'd forged together herself. Fargelsians weren't supposed to be able to craft their own words of power, but Tia seemed to defy every rule.

Gulliver turned his cat eyes on her. "Are you sure?"

"Gullie, there is no one else here to help us. If we don't fix Griffin, he could die. It's up to you and me." Griffin tried to focus on the ten-year-old manipulating the older boy, but he couldn't get his mind off the pain throbbing through his side.

Gulliver studied Griffin for a long moment.

Tia bent to look into Griffin's eyes and took his hand. "I don't want you to die."

She knew. Griffin could see the truth of it in her eyes. "How long?" How long had she known Lochlan wasn't her biological father?

"Since I first saw you in my dream."

The dream. Tia had seen the prison realm and Griffin in her mind before ever seeing either in person. She'd known Griffin would save her before they'd ever met. And with that knowledge, knowledge she'd kept to herself for so long, there was a bit of trust.

Seeing no other option, Griffin nodded, preparing himself for whatever consequences of her uncontrollable magic he had to face.

"What do you need?" Gulliver asked her.

"Focus. To craft spells, I need to draw on Toby's strength."

Gulliver slid onto his butt at Griffin's side. His tail curled into his lap as he reached forward to wiggle the leather armor over Griffin's head. It took some doing, but Griffin breathed more easily without the weight on his shoulders.

"Take his shirt off," Tia said. "I want to see the wound."

Opting to tear it instead, Gulliver ripped the already fraying and faded shirt so nothing stood between Tia's magic and Griffin's bare chest. He breathed heavily, wondering how these two kids would ever look at him the same after seeing him coated in blood.

This wasn't his first battle, but it was the first where he wondered if it would be his last. The moment the Asrai sword bit into his flesh, he saw the last few months flash before his eyes.

Had he brought this upon the realms? If he'd never gone in search of the book for Egan, if he'd never left Myrkur in the first place, maybe none of this had to happen.

But then his eyes met Gulliver's, knowing the kid would get to live in the sun. He'd see himself as an equal to Tia and other Light Fae. And there was power in that. Some things were worth fighting for, worth giving up peace.

Because peace could not truly exist if it wasn't peace for all fae.

Tia closed her eyes, trying to call on Toby's strength.

Gulliver leaned down. "Where's Riona?"

A tear slipped from Griffin's eye. Riona. He'd tried not to think of her being carried away by her own kind. Did she now lay among the bodies in the palace? Or had Egan taken her with him? This time as a prisoner rather than a loyal subject.

Either fate was almost too much for him to bear.

"She loved me." She'd admitted as much. There was a time Griffin didn't think he'd ever have what Lochlan and Brea found in each other. Something to overcome even the sharpest pains of the marriage magic.

And he never once imagined Riona would say the words.

Gulliver's eyes glassed over. "Is she..."

Griffin nodded. "But she didn't die before making a difference, before doing something good. I think that's all she wanted." He knew because he'd wanted the same thing. After Regan, he'd arrived in Myrkur thinking there was no good in him.

He'd been wrong.

And Riona had been wrong about herself too.

Tears flowed down Gulliver's cheeks, and his eyes flashed in anger. "He took her from us."

"What?"

"Egan. He took Riona, and for that we'll make him pay." Seeing his own anger reflected in the kind-hearted Gulliver scared him.

Tia's eyes snapped open, breaking their moment. "Something is wrong."

"What do you mean?" Gulliver wiped his cheeks.

"Toby..."

"Is your magic broken?" Gulliver would probably never truly understand how magic worked.

She shook her head. "My brother isn't in the village."

Alarm shot through Griffin, and he tried to push himself up but Gulliver had a surprisingly strong grip and held him down.

Tia tried to hide the fear on her face, something Griffin had learned she did often. Toby was more open with his emotions like his mom, but Tia was more like him. She got to her feet. "I… I can feel him but not close. Where is he?"

Gulliver looked up to her, his voice pleading. "We can find Toby, but we still have to close Griffin's wound."

Griffin shook his head. "I changed my mind. Don't fix me with your magic. You need to find Toby."

Tia pursed her lips. "I'll be back." She disappeared, leaving Griffin alone with Gulliver.

Gulliver pressed the ripped shirt to the wound. "You're going to be okay. I won't lose you like we lost Riona. I refuse."

We.

Griffin tried to muster up some encouragement, to tell Gulliver it would be okay.

But he didn't want to lie to the kid.

"Everyone else?" Gulliver met his eyes, looking scared of whatever answer was coming.

Griffin forced out the words Gulliver needed. "Hector and Shauna are uninjured. Lochlan is fine as well."

He bit his lip. "But someone else isn't?"

"The King of Eldur—Finn—he's badly injured." Gulliver barely knew Finn, and Griffin had never been friends with the guy, but still, he couldn't help the ache at the thought of what his loss would do to Lochlan. "A lot of fae are dead, Gullie."

"But we won? Soldiers came through here celebrating and saying we won."

Griffin nodded, his breathing growing labored. "But Egan got away." It was Griffin's biggest regret, not capturing the Dark Fae king and his mother. They wouldn't know what to do next until Hector made contact.

But Griffin had never been good at waiting.

Tia burst through the door with Nessa on her heels. A steely look replaced the youth in Nessa's eyes. She was an eight-year-old on a mission.

Nessa clutched a bag in one hand.

"The village healers have left to go transport the injured. This girl says she's going to fix you, Griff, but she's just a kid!" Tia paced in agitation. "I can still do it with Toby far away, I can still draw strength from him over the distance like I've done before, but I'll have less control, and I could hurt you, and..."

On a normal day, Griffin would have laughed at the thought of Tia saying someone was "just a kid." He'd seen enough things now to realize youth did not mean a lack of necessary skills.

And Nessa...

"Go, Tia. You need to find Toby." If he was near the battle... "Please, go."

Nessa lowered herself next to Gulliver. "I can help you, Griff. I swear I can."

Nessa had spent her entire life helping her sister tend to the villagers, learning everything she possibly could about healing. He looked from Gulliver—the child thief who'd saved the Eldurian prince and princess—to Tia, the child who'd brought down the prison magic.

And finally Nessa. "Do it."

"I'm going to find my papa." Tia turned on her heel and ran from the room, her words trailing behind her. She might know who Griffin was to her, but Lochlan was Papa, the man she wanted when every fear came to the front of her mind.

Gulliver watched after her, torn. "Lochlan can protect her."

Pain seared through Griffin as Nessa probed his wound. "I don't have any of that gross brown liquid my sister gives patients or even the numbing herbs. This is going to hurt, Griff."

"Just do it."

Nessa looked so much like Shauna as she bent forward, a crease between her brows. This was better than using Tia's magic, more controllable, the outcome sure.

The moment she pierced his skin with the needle, he bit back a cry. Not everyone was as strong. Gulliver screamed as if it had been his skin Nessa stitched.

Griffin was so focused on Gulliver and on not passing out, he didn't notice the door opening or the woman rushing in. Not until her gasp drew all his available energy.

Riona stood in bloody leathers, half dark wings curling into her back and light pouring in behind her.

Griffin grit his teeth as Nessa continued to stitch his wound, but he couldn't take his eyes from the woman he'd seen carried away. The one he thought dead or a prisoner.

But she was here.

"Riona?" Gulliver choked back a sob. "You're dead."

Riona rushed forward as she took in the scene before her. "What are you doing? Nessa, stop right now, and I'll find a healer."

"I am a healer," she squeaked in her little voice. Her tongue poked out between her lips as she concentrated.

"Let her finish, Riona." Griffin's voice was weak.

She lowered herself to the ground on the opposite side of Gulliver and Nessa, taking Griffin's limp hand in hers. "You're okay." It was like the whispered words were only for herself.

He looked up at her. "You're okay."

"I'm okay," Gulliver piped in.

Riona reached across and gripped Griffin and Gulliver's clasped hands. There'd be time for explanations and worrying about Egan later when Griffin didn't have to worry about losing too much blood if he stood.

"Shauna is going to be so mad." Gulliver shared a smile with Nessa as if this here was their contribution to the fight. They too got to be a part of it despite their ages.

Worry for Toby mixed with relief at being with these three warred within Griffin. Squeezing Gulliver's hand tighter, he bit back another scream.

Riona's brow furrowed. "That's got to be painful, Griff. You don't have to be silent just because I'm here. I heard you scream."

Red crept up Gulliver's cheeks. "That was me."

"I'm done." Nessa sat back on her heels and wiped her brow. "It's not perfect, Griff, maybe not even good. I had nothing to clean it with and don't have any salve now. But your guts won't fall out, and the bleeding will stop."

Griffin nodded, staring down at the jagged stitching holding his skin together. "Ness, thank you."

She shrugged. "You and I save each other. It's what we do."

She spoke with the words of a much older fae, but Myrkur stole any hope of a childhood from her. Nessa didn't grow up playing with toys. From the time she could walk, she accompanied Shauna to treat patients. The children of the village worked from a young age. They too had to fight to survive.

Gathering his remaining strength, Griffin pushed himself up, so he was sitting. "We need to find Toby."

"Griff." Riona sat back to stare at him. "Nessa just stitched you back together. You aren't going anywhere."

"No choice."

"His father is out there looking for him." She said the words pointedly, telling him Toby wasn't his responsibility. Not anymore. Both Griffin and Riona had done their job protecting the kids. Now it was up to their parents.

"I love them, Riona." Whether he was their father or just the uncle he was supposed to be, that wasn't something he could forget. He loved Toby and Tia from the moment he'd met them.

And he'd do anything to keep Brea's children safe.

"Let me bandage you." Nessa dug through her bag for a roll of bandages.

"There's no time."

"Griff." The kid gave him a stubborn look. "You love Toby. Well, we love you."

"Yeah, we sort of don't want you to die." Gulliver matched Nessa's stance.

Griffin sighed, inching forward so Riona and Nessa could wrap the bandage around him.

The door opened, and Myles peered in, his floppy hair soaked with sweat and who knew what else. Curses flew from his lips. "I wondered where the blood was leading. Yikes, Griff, you don't look so good. Was it an ogre?" He said it as if an ogre was the only creature who could defeat Griffin.

"Asrai." Griffin winced as Nessa tied the bandage. "Myles, can you get me a horse?"

His words faltered. "Uh, Griff, you really don't look like you should be riding a horse."

Griffin leaned forward, trying to push himself to his feet. "I'm guessing Brea hasn't recovered from the magic. If you don't help me, I'll have to tell her we don't know where her son is, and then you'll have a weak Brea demanding to join the search. So, that horse?"

Myles stared at Griffin in stunned fascination. "Who knew Griff could be such a manipulator? Oh wait, everyone." He laughed. "If you want to kill yourself for Toby, who am I to stop you?" He turned on his heel and marched back out of the bakery.

"Help me up." Griffin reached a hand out to Riona. When she didn't move, he looked to Gulliver. "I am going to find the boy."

Reluctantly, Riona and Gulliver helped him to his feet. He tried to step away from them, but his body tilted forward, and Riona slid one of his arms over her shoulders and gripped his waist before he could fall. Pain shot through side. Yet, he couldn't sit here and recover while Toby could be out somewhere on that battlefield injured.

Riona helped Griffin outside to where Myles lead a horse toward them. It was already saddled, and Griffin knew all he had to do was get to the city. He had to find Lochlan and Tia and make sure they didn't lose one of the people they loved most.

Injured soldiers streamed into the village, directed to one of the many homes and businesses that had been set up for them, filling the village streets with hobbling fae. The people would recover, but Griffin was more worried about his family.

Before they reached the horse, Riona pulled Griffin to a stop and turned to face him. Some emotion he didn't recognize sparked in her eyes. She reached up, trailing her fingertips over his cheek. "You'll find him, Griffin."

"No one has ever had such faith in me before." He didn't understand how she could stand with him, holding him up because his strength had failed him, and still look at him like he was a battle-ready warrior.

Rising up on her toes, Riona pressed her mouth to his. He wished their moment didn't have to end, that it wasn't just another in a steady stream of dangers.

"I meant what I said before the battle." He ran a finger over the cut on her head, making sure she was okay.

"Well, I thought the ogre was going to kill me. And in that moment, all I could think, all I wanted, was for you to know this isn't like your battles ten years ago. Now, you're fighting for people who love you, people who will fight for you too."

"Come on, lovebirds." Myles waved to them, lifting the reins in the air. When a curse slipped past his lips, Griffin turned his head to see Brea stumbling from the library, her face pale.

"What's going on?" She looked from Myles standing next to the horse to Griffin leaning on Riona just to stand at all. "You're injured. We should get you to a bed."

He shook his head, not wanting to utter the words he had to say. "It's Toby. We don't know where he is."

Only hours ago, Griffin ran through the streets of Raudur City fighting the fae who now stood on their side. Dark Fae and Light Fae together cleared the dead from the streets. Eldurian families watched in horror. The stain of battle would never be scrubbed free.

And now, Griffin held on to a saddle, doing everything he could not to fall off. It was a slow ride from the village to the city, especially because he was not the only person on this horse who could hardly sit up on their own.

Brea clung to him, refusing to be left behind as they went in search of her son. They left without Myles, but he caught up with them after going in search of a second horse. Riona had flown ahead to lend her assistance to Lochlan.

Now, as Griffin surveyed the carnage, he wondered if they would ever find Toby alive. There were too many dead in a war that hadn't had to happen. The Dark Fae that had turned to their side once Egan fled, outnumbered the Light Fae.

They could've prevented this by realizing sooner the way to gain freedom from the prison realm was not by controlling the other kingdoms, but by seeking peace with them.

This battle would fade to the back of their minds, but there were many Dark Fae out there who ran rather than surrender, and they would have to be dealt with. As would Egan and Enis. It wasn't even close to being finished.

But this wasn't about that. They had to deal with the consequences of this battle before moving onto the next. And one such consequence was a missing prince.

Griffin found Lochlan in front of the wall where Hector had given his speech. Lochlan and Tia called for Toby, using Tia's magic to make their voices carry through the streets.

Sliding down from the horse, Griffin stumbled when his feet touched down. Brea managed to be slightly more graceful than him.

When Tia caught sight of Griffin, she hiccupped back a sob. Running toward him, she jumped over the body of a hooved fae. Riona caught up to her before she could reach Griffin. "Careful."

She skidded to a halt in front of him, careful not to touch him for fear of his injury.

"Hello to you too, daughter." Brea held out her arms.

Tia fell into them. "I'm sorry, I've just been so worried Griffin died because I left."

"Still here, kid." He gave Lochlan a nod. To his brother's credit, he made no comment about his wife being here when she hadn't regained her strength. "Now, let's find your brother."

Riona helped Griffin walk through the streets calling for Toby. He could hear Lochlan, Brea, and Tia ahead of them.

"Do you feel him?" Griffin yelled up to Tia.

She looked back over her shoulder. "Sort of. He's struggling."

"So, that means he's alive?" Griffin's heart ached at the hope in Brea's voice. He hoped she didn't have to lose it.

Tia nodded. "I think so. But it doesn't mean he'll stay that way. We have to hurry, Mama."

"What was he doing joining the battle?" Brea's shoulders dropped. "And how could I not have kept him safe?"

It was Tia who answered. "Because he wanted to do something. Toby's life has always been about me. But he was held hostage for much longer than me, he has more reason to fight. Just because we're kids, doesn't mean this isn't our war too."

Griffin wanted to say that he was just ten years old, but that didn't matter anymore. He continued to call the boy's name. He didn't know how long they'd been searching or how he remained upright when his side radiated pain, but when he heard a faint reply, it was worth it.

Lochlan took off running with Tia at his side. Brea tried to keep up, but she wasn't in much better shape than Griffin. By the time they reached the others, they found the body of an ogre and something moving underneath.

"I'm here." The cry that reached them was weak.

"Under the ogre?" Brea's eyes widened. Only months ago, she hadn't known such creatures existed.

"Help," Toby cried. "Please. I can't breathe."

Lochlan clenched his fists, probably realizing what Griffin already had. Griffin and Brea would be no help, and Lochlan and Riona couldn't lift it alone.

But it seemed they didn't have to. Tia crouched down next to the ogre, not showing an ounce of intimidation as she pried the giant green arm away to peer down into the small space created underneath its twisted body. "Toby, are you hurt?"

"Tia," he cried. "You're here."

"Of course I am."

"It's on my legs. I can't move them."

"Tia." Lochlan put a hand on his daughter's shoulder. "Back away. We're going to try to move the ogre."

She didn't move except to look up at him. "No."

"What?" Lochlan crossed his arms. "This is no time to—"

"Save the day? Again? Yeah, I think it kind of is. Please stand back, Papa. I don't want to have to make you."

Riona snorted and shared a smile with Brea.

Lochlan, obeying his daughter with amusement in his eyes, joined them in backing up. Griffin shook his head, pride blossoming inside him. "She's her mother. Every bit of her."

"I know." Lochlan groaned. "It's going to be the death of me."

And yet, he remained back, trusting his young daughter. Griffin was proud of him too. The Lochlan he'd known was prideful, arrogant. He'd had trouble trusting anyone.

"Okay, Toby," Tia started. "I don't want to move the ogre off you in case it hurts you further. You're going to have to do it."

"I can't."

"Yes, you can. You survived a battle all by yourself." She patted the slimy shoulder of the ogre. "I'm guessing you killed this ogre here. My brother, the ogre killer. You didn't need magic to be great, Tobes, because great is who you are."

Griffin sent himself a mental reminder to go to Tia when he needed a pep talk. Every moment with the twins amazed him just like the time he spent with Gulliver and Nessa. When he was their age, he played with other kids at the Fargelsi palace and spent time at his studies. He didn't go to war, stitch wounds, or travel across four kingdoms and the human realm.

Tia kept going. "It's just like taking down the prison magic. I couldn't have done that without you, and I can't do this alone either. I'm going to funnel magic into you, Toby, and this time, you're going to save yourself. Are you ready?"

A moment passed before he said, "I'm ready." Griffin couldn't help noting the added strength in his voice.

Tia concentrated on the ogre as she muttered Fargelsian words under her breath. The ogre shifted, its other arm dropping to the ground, cracking the stones underneath.

It shifted again, its giant body rolling to reveal the boy they'd all been searching for.

Lochlan, Brea, and Tia rushed forward as Toby scrambled out, covered in the ogre's blood. Together, they collapsed into a family hug.

Griffin watched their reunion, reaching a hand out for Riona, this time for a different kind of strength, the kind that let him turn away. He stumbled over his own feet.

"That's it." Riona kept him steady. "We're going to the palace."

"What's at the palace?"

"Not what, who. Shauna is there caring for Faolan and other wounded. Come on."

By the time they reached the palace gates that stood open, Griffin wasn't sure how much longer he could keep going. Servants bustled by, returning the palace to its pre-Egan grandness.

Soon, there'd be no sign of the battle. But they'd always remember.

Dark Fae wandered listlessly, no one giving them orders.

Griffin's shoulder slammed into the corridor wall, and pain lanced through him. He started sliding down the wall, but Riona wouldn't let him.

"You," she called to someone Griffin didn't see. "I need help."

Strong arms scooped him up, and he looked into the hairy face of a horned fae with a giant red beard.

Riona directed them through the palace to the infirmary where not a single bed was open. "Set him near the wall."

The fae put him down and walked off.

Riona crouched next to him. "We'll get you some help, Griff. You should have stayed in Aghadoon to rest."

Even if Tia hadn't needed him, he'd needed to be there. "I-I... know." It was all he'd had the energy to say.

"Griffin?" Shauna rushed toward them, wiping a bloody hand on her apron. "What are you doing here? And where's your shirt?"

He looked down at his chest and the bandage where dots of red soaked through. Shauna followed his gaze. "I told you to stay and let me treat this, you big oaf."

"Had to get to Gulliver." He couldn't admit he'd thought had Riona died and needed to be with the one person who'd feel that as deeply as him.

Shauna lowered herself to her knees, ignoring the bustling infirmary around her. "All right, let me see the wound." Riona helped her remove the bandage, and Shauna pursed her lips as she began muttering. "You idiot man. This wasn't cleaned before it was stitched, was it? Whoever did it has some skill, I'll admit, but it should have been me."

She reached into the bag slung over her shoulder, producing a tiny ceramic pot he recognized as the salve she put on to help wounds heal. "I'm going to have to open it up again to clean it out and make sure it's just a flesh wound." She shook her head. "You need to start caring what happens to you."

"It was Nessa." He leaned his head back.

Shauna froze for a moment before slapping him upside the head. "She's better than most of Egan's healers, but Griffin! My sister is eight. Eight!"

"It was either that or die, Shauna. What would you have me do?"

"And how many healers did you pass on your way to almost dying, you idiot man?" He couldn't tell what else she muttered as she searched the room. "I need a bed for you."

Riona shrugged. "This palace is full of beds."

Shauna's eyes lit up. "Riona you're a genius. Will you return to Aghadoon and let Gulliver and Nessa know what's happened?"

Riona stood, and Griffin appreciated that she trusted Shauna to take care of him. She met his gaze. "Do *not* die." With that, she hurried away.

Shauna rubbed a hand over her face. "This is going to hurt, Griffin. A lot." She stood. "And it's all your fault, so I don't want to hear any complaining."

He closed his eyes. "I can handle it, Shauna."

He could. The battle was over, and the people he loved lived through it. It was a miracle, one he hadn't expected but had been afraid to hope for.

Now, they had to survive what came next.

Chapter 13

GRIFFIN

Griffin's hand drifted down his side. The bandages wrapped tightly around his torso made it difficult to get a deep breath.

But he was healing. They all were.

"We're going to be late." Riona tugged his hand as they made their way through the battle-torn streets just days after Egan fled Raudur City with his few remaining loyal followers.

"Hurry, Griff." Gulliver ran ahead of them. "I'm starving."

The Eldurians had spent the last two days cleaning their city. They still had a long way to go, but they were in high spirits. Now that their king—though he wasn't conscious—and queen had returned with the young prince and princess, they could see the light at the end of the tunnel. For them it was a matter of celebrating their victory and picking up the pieces to continue on, hoping King Finn would wake to join them soon. And celebrate they did. Even now, Eldurians danced in the streets, singing ballads of the epic battle for Raudur City.

But for Griffin and his family, there was no light at the end of the tunnel. At least not yet. Egan would be back. He was not the type to disappear after failing to get what he wanted. He would rise again.

This would never be over until he was dead and the book of power was somewhere safe.

Griffin leaned on Riona for support as they made their way up the winding path to the tiered gardens that sat above the canyon city.

Egan and his brutish followers had destroyed the once beautiful garden—mostly through neglect—but Alona would have it put to rights again soon. For now, the pathway danced with light from the torches perched at intervals to light their way.

Though none of them felt like celebrating, the banquet was just that. A celebration for their victory over the Dark Fae king.

Griffin was sweating by the time they reached the top. Alona's court was in full attendance. Tables lined the open terrace, and Eldurians mingled with Iskaltians and Fargelsians as well as Dark Fae. Griffin even spotted a few ogres among them.

"Over here, Griff!" Gulliver called them over to his table. For a moment, he was torn between the two sides of his family. Part of him wanted to seek out Tia and Toby and their parents, and another part of him was desperate to hear how things were going for Shauna and the others.

"Look, Griffin." Riona nodded across the room, giving his hand a gentle squeeze.

Gulliver sat between Tia and Nessa. Hector's mother and Lochlan were in deep discussion over something serious. And Brea and Shauna were discussing Faolan's condition. For once, all his family were together, except for Hector who'd gone to track Egan, and for a moment, he couldn't catch his breath.

Griffin O'Shea didn't get this. He didn't get to keep both his old and new families.

"Let's find a seat. You're dead on your feet." Riona guided him toward the long table.

"There he is." Lochlan's smile caught him off guard. "It's about time you showed up."

"Griffin." Brea beamed a smile at him. "We saved you two seats."

"Right here between Toby the Ogre Killer and Shauna the Mighty Healer of Myrkur." Lochlan clapped a hand on his son's shoulder, and Toby's ears turned red just like Griff's did when he was that age.

"I have yet to hear the full tale." Griffin groaned like an old man as he took his seat.

"There's not much to tell." Toby shrugged. "I wanted to fight. I've trained with Papa for years, and I thought I was ready." Toby cast his eyes down at his lap. "I'm thinking there's not much that can prepare you for what battle is truly like."

"Wise words, young prince." Riona raised her glass, and the others followed suit.

"I was mostly staying out of the way, looking for ways to help our soldiers who might need an extra hand. I helped a few fight off their opponents, and then the ogre caught me. He picked me up by my collar and waved me around like a feather. I thought he would kill me."

"Ogre's like to play with their enemies first."

"That they do." Toby nodded. "And that's what got this one killed. He dropped me to the ground and was going to kick me, but I rolled out of the way and tried to gut him with my sword. Their skin is awfully thick."

"You have to get them from the back," Griffin said. "Right at the waist where their skin is fleshier."

"That's where I stuck him. Several times." Toby's eyes glassed over at the memory. "He started to fall back. I knew I wouldn't get out of the way fast enough so I lunged for a gouge in the ground, left over from some explosion, but I couldn't get my legs out of the way. The great stinking ogre landed right on top of me, but the hole in the ground kept me from getting smothered. Did you know ogre blood is black like sludge? And it stinks. Like, really stinks."

"He was covered in it when we pulled him out of that hole," Lochlan said proudly. Griffin was certain the Iskalt king had partaken of copious amounts of wine.

"How are your legs?" Griffin leaned in to ask his son. When they pulled the ogre off him, the boy's legs were badly bruised and swollen. Brea feared there might be permanent damage.

"All healed," Toby said, rubbing his leg under the table. "Shauna took care of me."

"It still twinges a bit, doesn't it?" Griffin nudged him.

Toby nodded. "That numbing salve she uses makes me feel funny."

"It'll feel that way for a while, but you'll be good as new soon enough." Judging by the somber look in his eyes, Griffin was certain the battle with the ogre would haunt Toby for years to come.

"Have some wine, brother." Lochlan filled a glass for Griffin. "It will help with the pain of Shauna's stitches."

"My stitches are what's keeping his guts inside him." Shauna shoved him playfully.

"How is Queen Faolan?" Riona asked.

Shauna's smile wavered. "She is going to pull through. I've never seen anyone take such a beating and still hold on. That woman is a force of nature."

"It would take more than a whip to break Mother's will," Brea said softly. "But if you hadn't been there to care for her when you did, I shudder to think what would have happened to her." Brea reached for Shauna's hand. "I can never repay you."

"I'm just glad we were able to keep her pain under control with the Eldurian medicines. I've learned much from your healers."

"And I've heard they've learned much from you too." Brea squeezed her hand.

"How is Finn?" Griffin asked, not sure he wanted to know.

"He still isn't awake." Shauna sighed. "The healers from all the kingdoms have been working together to treat him. We believe he will wake soon as the swelling from his injuries continues to improve."

The crowd murmured behind them as Alona entered the gardens with Prince Logan and Princess Darra holding her hands. Of all the things Griffin might have expected to see tonight, he never would have imagined Alona, the human Queen of Eldur to be accompanied by Egan's highest ranking general, Padraig—an ogre.

Alona looked weary but every inch the queen she was. With both her mother and her husband gravely injured and a hurting kingdom to run, she hadn't slept in days.

Alona stood at the front of the gardens with all of Eldur spreading out behind her to the east. "My friends." Her voice rose above the silence that had fallen at her arrival. "Eldur thanks you for everything you've done to aid us in this terrible war." Her fierce gaze fell across the terrace. "Tonight we celebrate our victory and our unity, but we are not done. We have a common enemy."

Cries of agreement rang out across the crowd.

"Egan must be defeated, and the book of power must be contained," Alona continued.

"Burn it!" several shouts rang out.

"Burn the library!" others agreed.

"I invite the leaders of Eldur, Iskalt, Fargelsi and Myrkur to join me this evening for a council meeting in the throne room where we will discuss what must be done in that regard." She turned toward the tables where the nobles sat. "General Padraig and I will meet you there in an hour."

With that, she took her children and made her way back to the palace.

"I am looking fer one called Tobias the Ogre Killer." The gravelly voice made Griffin flinch. Both Lochlan and Griffin reached a protective arm over Toby at the sight of the massive General Padraig towering over the little boy.

Griffin and Lochlan stood together, but Lochlan spoke for his son. "You seek my son, Prince Tobias of Iskalt." Lochlan's voice grew icy.

Padraig cleared his throat, a sound like an avalanche of boulders crashing down a mountainside. "I wish ter shake yer son's hand, Majesty. It's na small feat ta kill an ogre in the heat o' battle. Tobias is already a great warrior. You should be proud."

Lochlan looked stunned.

"The ogres have great respect for those who manage to best them in battle." Gulliver leaned forward to explain. "It happens so rarely, they recognize the great skill of their enemies."

"Tobias the Ogre Killer isna our enemy, nor tis his father, the mighty King o' Iskalt." Padraig gave a courtly bow.

"Go on, son. Shake the general's hand." Lochlan stepped aside.

Toby stood on shaky legs and approached the ogre with more confidence than Griffin would have in his shoes.

"I am sorry I had to kill one of your soldiers, sir." Toby stuck out his hand.

His little hand disappeared in the ogre's massive gray hand. Padraig leaned down to Toby's level and winked. "Now tha' we're on the same side, see that it doesna happen again." He chuckled, patting Toby's shoulder as he turned to shake Lochlan's hand. "I ha' never agreed with Egan's way o' ruling, and I'm grateful for a chance fer my people ta do better."

"Well, that is something I've never seen before in all my life." Riona shook her head. "An ogre playing at diplomacy."

"We should head to the throne room, Loch." Brea took her husband's hand. "I've asked Rowena to take Tia and Toby to spend the night with Logan and Darra. Gulliver too." She turned to Griffin.

"We'll take Gullie back to the village with us." Griffin draped an arm around Riona's waist.

"If you think you two are getting out of this council meeting, you'd better guess again," Lochlan said.

"We aren't leaders." Griffin looked to Riona in confusion.

"You forget you're a Prince of Iskalt, and though Riona might not have a title, you've each played integral roles in this war. You're coming with us." Brea tilted her chin in the stubborn way Griffin remembered.

"I wish Hector was here to represent the Dark Fae," Lochlan said.

"He has a more important mission." Griffin stood. "We can't lose Egan. Shauna and I can represent the people of Myrkur. Nessa can go with the other kids."

"What? How did I get dragged into this?" Shauna frowned.

"You're going to give us a report on the injured." Brea linked her arm through Shauna's, and they all made their way down the winding path to the palace.

Griffin and Riona walked with Lochlan down to the throne room. It was going to be a very long night.

"Thank you all for coming." Alona sat at the head of the long table in the throne room.

Myles and Neeve were already there, pouring over maps of the three kingdoms. Finn was still under the care of the palace healers, but it seemed that General Padraig and Alona had become fast friends.

Lochlan and Brea sat to Alona's right, and that left Griffin, Riona, and Shauna feeling uncertain about where they fit into this war room.

"My brother is here as a Prince of Iskalt and a representative of the Light Fae who have lived in Myrkur all these years."

"And we've asked Shauna to stand as a representative of the Dark Fae of Myrkur," Brea added. "She's also our resident Dark Fae healer." Alona gave her a grateful nod.

"And why am I here?" Riona cast an uncertain glance at Griffin.

Brea patted the seat beside her. "You, my friend, are here because of all the fae in all the lands, you know Egan's mind. You have insight we desperately need."

"We have much to discuss." Alona sat forward. "And everyone in this room is vital to the future of all the kingdoms."

"The people cry out for us to burn the library," Brea said. "We do not have the book, but burning the library would destroy the book and the source of vital magic. My sisters and I do not believe this is a solution."

Neeve nodded in agreement. "We believe to destroy the library or the book would destroy far too much magic. The Fargelsian's in particular would suffer greatly for the loss of the ancient language of power contained in the library."

"Forgive me, your Majesties," Shauna interjected. "We do not know the ways of magic. Could you explain how burning a building would affect your knowledge of magic?"

"Of course," Brea continued. "We discovered a way to destroy any bit of magic so long as we can find the corresponding spell in the library. Destroy the record, and the magic will never work again. It will fade from the minds of those who once knew it. We believe the library contains the origin records of all magic. It cannot be destroyed, at least not all of it."

"We must study everything within the library and destroy the records of the most dangerous magic there." Brea turned toward Alona. "We would like to leave the rest as a public record for everyone to study and benefit from."

"Do we all agree this is the best measure to take?" Alona asked the room.

"Perhaps a committee should be selected to study the contents of the library," Shauna said uncertainly. "With representatives from each kingdom?"

"That's an excellent idea," Lochlan said. "And a task to tackle after we win this war."

"Of course," Alona said. "We're in agreement not to burn the library."

"We should move it," Griffin spoke up for the first time. "It's not safe here. Most still can't see it, but they know where it is and they see it as the source of all our problems."

"I have a suggestion." Brea stood up to address the room. "I want my kids with me. All of them. And I know Neeve and Myles want their kids with them too. The village could be the safest place for the realm's princes and princesses. We must protect them."

"We could portal to the three kingdoms," Griffin suggested. "Get the kids and bring them to the village and then move the village somewhere safe."

"We can't let Toby use his portal magic any time soon." Brea shook her head. "He's able to do more with his portals than you two can, but I can't risk his health. He needs time to recover from his ordeal."

"I can do it," Griffin offered. "At least, I think I can."

"I'm lost again," Shauna whispered to Riona. "What's a portal?"

"The O'Shea's have portal magic that allows us to travel from the fae realm to the human realm," Griffin explained. "But we can only travel to a place in the human realm where we've visited before, and once there, we can only return to the place where we portaled from here."

"You think you can portal from here to the human world and then to Iskalt and back to bring our children here?" Brea asked.

"I did it once before. I portaled from Myrkur to the human realm and then from the human realm to Gelsi."

"Wasn't that because the prison magic wouldn't let you return to Myrkur?" Riona asked.

"Yes, but since then, we also managed to get to the Eldur forces. Toby was with us and directing the magic then, but I can do it without him. I can at least try."

Lochlan nodded. "So maybe it's possible. But you need to rest, brother. I should travel to get the children."

"I'll go with you through your portal to the farm. Once we're there, I'll open the portal to Iskalt for you. So, even if we must return to the place we've left, your portals have only been opened between Aghadoon and the human realm. Mine will have been opened between the human realm and Iskalt."

"I think I followed that... it might work," Lochlan said. "We will try it after you've rested tonight."

"Who is watching over your throne, brother?" Griffin asked. It hadn't occurred to him how long Lochlan and Brea had been away from Iskalt.

"My advisor, Lord Brennan Cormac of Isvasi serves as my regent when I am not there."

"I know that name." Griffin frowned.

"He served as father's general. We used to call him Uncle Bren when we were children."

"Very well, once we have the children here, we will move with Aghadoon to somewhere safe in Fargelsi, then our children can join us there." Neeve scribbled notes in a journal. "Aghadoon should rest somewhere remote in the country where Egan won't find it."

"Brandon should be an invaluable help with researching the contents of the library," Lochlan said.

"I believe we might be able to study the darkest magic in the library and discover what Egan might do next." Neeve lifted her nose from the book in front of her where she made notes. "If we can find and destroy the magic he seeks before he can have Enis perform it, then we might be able to cut him off at the knees."

"Brandon has been busy since we left," Myles said. "Droves of confused Dark and Light Fae who did not join Egan's army have been making their way across into Fargelsi, refugees fleeing the harsh conditions of Myr with nowhere else to go. We will have to move them from the current camp Brandon has set up to more permanent lodgings."

"You can count on Iskalt's help to create a place for our Dark Fae friends who do not want to return to Myrkur," Lochlan offered.

"Eldur as well," Alona added.

"They will need a province, perhaps in northern Fargelsi near the shores of Loch Villandi," Neeve offered. "The country is wild, and few villages call that part of the kingdom home. Perhaps we can appoint a Dark Fae governor of the region, though they would need to abide by Gelsi law."

"It is decided." Alona leaned back against her chair. "We will gather our children and send them to Aghadoon, which we will then move to Gelsi. The library and our children will be safe there. I must remain here in Eldur to see to my people while Mother and Finn are recovering. I would ask that General Padraig go with you in my stead until I can join you."

"I would be honored ter serve ye, my Queen." Padraig gave a bow as if he'd spent his life in the court of the highest queen in the lands.

"Then the only thing that remains is Egan. What will he do now that he has lost Toby, Riona, Aghadoon, and Eldur?"

All eyes turned to Riona, and Griffin could sense her distress. She didn't like to be in a position of leadership. He reached for her hand under the table, giving her as much reassurance as he could in that gesture. Her fingers wrapped around his, and she held on tight.

"He will seek power wherever he can find it." Riona spoke softly. "If that is no longer possible here in the three kingdoms, he will probably return to Myrkur and those who have remained. He will gather his followers, creating an army once again. If given the time to gain his footing ..." Riona paused, casting a look at Lochlan. "I believe he will set his sights on Iskalt, and if he cannot reach for your throne in your absence, he will grasp power by any means necessary. Whenever he makes his next move—whatever that might be—we will know immediately."

CHAPTER 14

RIONA

Making changes to the way the O'Shea magic worked wasn't as hard as they'd imagined it would be.

Making changes to the way the O'Shea brothers *viewed* their portal magic was a different matter entirely.

They couldn't break the rules that had existed for hundreds of years, not like Toby could. Instead, they had to learn to work together.

And they figured it out.

Three weeks ago, Griffin and Lochlan left Aghadoon together through Lochlan's portal. It took many attempts, but they soon learned if they then used Griffin's magic to come back to the fae realm, they didn't have to return to the exact spot Lochlan had left.

Riona expected the brothers to celebrate when they managed it the first time, but they'd come back arguing instead, and they hadn't stopped since.

"I found another one." Lochlan dropped a heavy book onto the table, and a cloud of dust erupted from the pages. He opened it to the page he'd marked, and Griffin sidled up next to him, his eyes scanning the words.

"Absolutely not." Griffin scowled down at the book. "Loch, you can't be serious. That spell isn't even dangerous. Veto."

Lochlan sighed. "You can't veto everything." They'd been having the same argument for weeks. Lochlan wanted to destroy Fargelsian spells Griffin thought needed to be preserved. "It lets the spell weaver create a barrier. Haven't we all had enough of those?"

Now, he'd done it. Riona hid a smile as she stared into the book in her lap. They searched the library in shifts to avoid getting in each other's way, shifts Brea scheduled. Riona got the feeling the Iskalt queen had some ulterior motives throwing the brothers together so often.

Griffin grit his teeth and ran a hand through his already messy auburn hair. He'd made Riona chop the length off last week as the Fargelsian humidity made anything touching his neck unbearable—his words.

"Loch." Griffin dropped into a chair beside his brother. "I feel like I've said the same thing over and over. Not all spells are the same even when they appear to be. I know because I—"

"Grew up in Fargelsi." Lochlan rolled his eyes toward the ceiling. "Yes, Griffin, I remember."

"Plus he's said it a million times," Riona muttered.

Both brothers looked to her as if they'd forgotten they weren't alone. They looked as exhausted as she felt with dark circles under their eyes and rumpled clothing.

No one had gotten much sleep over the last few weeks. The royal children were now in Aghadoon, even Darra and Logan whose parents weren't here, and it gave the village some much needed life after all the death Riona had seen here. But it had become the unofficial center of the fae realm, with four of the six rulers spending the majority of their time here.

And that meant no one had a moment to breathe.

They'd destroyed hundreds of dark spells. Even if they didn't find Egan, they were making this world a safer place. Yet, they hadn't found anything that looked like something he'd attempt.

He'd been quiet since the battle, returning to the palace of Myrkur according to the messages in the journal they'd started receiving from Hector. It wouldn't last long. Riona knew he was up to something.

The majority of the army stayed in Eldur to bolster their own decimated forces and help Alona rebuild. They'd come if needed.

And Riona knew eventually they would have to fight again.

Lochlan and Griffin continued to argue, their voices filtering through her mind.

"Loch," Griffin groaned. "Do you see these words here?" He pointed to a Fargelsian phrase. "Those are safeties, preventing the spell from growing in power over time. This is the kind of boundary spell Fargelsians use to keep their chickens from escaping, to keep intruders from entering their homes uninvited. It is impossible for it to grow large enough to cause the kind of problems you're suggesting."

Lochlan's shoulders dropped, and he slumped into a chair. "I feel like we're still in the dark here." He rubbed his eyes and pushed the book away. "You're right."

"I'm what?"

"Don't make me say it again, Griff. These aren't the type of spells we're searching for. But my Fargelsian is rusty at best and staring at these words is making my head hurt."

"Then take a break." Brandon entered the library, looking way too wide awake. Brea and Neeve's father knew more about this place and the book than any of them because he was part of the Fargelsian royal line. But it didn't mean he knew a lot.

Brandon stopped behind Lochlan's chair and put a hand on his shoulder. "I passed Brea on my way here. She's feeding the children, and then she'll come. You all should go get some rest and come back with fresh eyes."

Neither Lochlan nor Griffin argued with that as they pushed to their feet. It was only when they stood side by side one could see the similarity between them. It wasn't in their looks, but their mannerisms, the way they held themselves.

Riona couldn't look away.

Griffin paused at the door and met her gaze. "Are you coming?"

She shook her head, not wanting to stop when she'd just found what she was looking for. "Not yet."

"Don't stay too long."

"I won't."

He attempted a tired smile, but it fell quickly and he ducked out, leaving Riona alone with the intimidating Fargelsian. She'd heard the stories about Brandon O'Rourke. Kept in the dungeons for eighteen years by his own sister, Regan, he hadn't known Faolan gave birth to a baby girl—Brea—or that she'd exchanged her with the human Alona as an infant for her own safety.

"Which book are you reading?" He had a kind voice, one that held none of the pain she imagined he hid.

Lifting the book from her lap, she showed it to him. "I don't know Fargelsian, so I'm not much help with finding the spells. But there's a section of books on the histories of the fae realm, and these, I can read."

"Ah." He smiled. "Yes. After my sister studied in this library when she was young, she told me about such books. The books themselves are spelled to appear in whatever language the reader wishes to see. It was once a way to make sure no one was able to forget. If everyone could read our earliest beginnings, they could not be denied. And then the books were hidden in Aghadoon, and much of the histories were forgotten behind the prison magic."

He walked to the back of the room and retrieved a black leather-bound book. "I found this yesterday. It may be of more interest to you than—" he looked over her shoulder at the book in front of her. "—Iskaltian histories."

Taking the book from him, she set it on top of the other. It had no title, but the moment she opened it, she knew what it was.

This was an accounting of Myrkur.

A kingdom only those in this village in the human realm knew existed, and they'd kept it secret for generations.

It was a handwritten book, the calligraphy hard to read. But something kept her eyes pinned to the words, straining to know their meaning.

Brandon gave her a knowing smile and went to another shelf to dive back into searching the spells.

Others came and went while Riona read. Brea and Neeve both had children on their laps as they focused on their research. Myles came, leaving when Neeve kicked him out for being annoying.

Riona read first of the depiction of Dark Fae, creatures with horns and tails and wings. She flipped through hand drawn images showing them as vicious animals with sharp teeth. "This book was obviously written by a Light Fae." She shook her head and kept going, ignoring the rumbling of her stomach, her dry mouth.

A heading started a section on origins of the Dark Fae, and the image drawn made her breath stutter. It was a Slyph with the gills and scales of an Asrai. Rubbing a hand up her arm, Riona needed to feel her scale-less skin. There was no denying what the drawing was supposed to be. Someone like her, like Nihal.

Half Slyph.

Half Asrai.

The story of Riona had always been that she was the product of a Slyph and an Asrai coupling, that her village had been full of such fae until it was destroyed. That was what Egan told her.

But this book said something different. "They come from us."

"What?" Brea lifted her eyes.

Brandon and Neeve stopped reading to focus on Riona.

"This book... is it possible it can be wrong?"

Brandon studied her for a long moment. "There's always that possibility, but I wouldn't think so. Not here. You found something, didn't you?"

She held out the book to him, needing him to confirm what she was really seeing.

"The Slyph and the Asrai come from the same ancestors," he read. "Creatures of both the sea and the sky, they are the earliest known Dark Fae. Their fates intertwine with that of Myrkur."

Fates. She'd tried not to think of what the book said about the tattoos on her skin, but there was no hiding from it. Her fate was to find the rightful ruler of Myrkur.

Shoving that from her mind, she shook her head. "I... I've always been treated with such scorn as if my very existence was wrong. An abomination." A tear slipped down her cheek as she remembered how those in Myrkur looked at her.

Brea handed her daughter to her grandfather and stood, crossing the room to Riona. "Riona...," she paused as if trying to figure out the rest of Riona's name.

"Nieland." Riona wiped her cheek.

"Well, Riona Nieland, no matter your birth, whether your people were the first Dark Fae or a mix of others, it doesn't matter. Not here. We accept everything you are."

Embarrassment flooded Riona when she couldn't hold back the tears. She'd never had a friend, not until Griffin. And now, this perfect queen didn't look at her as something different from her.

"Warning." Brea smiled. "I'm going to hug you now. I know we aren't the hugging type of friends yet, Riona, but I think that's friend goals for us." She wrapped strong arms around Riona. "I mean, a part of me wants to squeeze the life right out of you for being in love with my first husband, but lucky for you, I won't let the marriage magic win. And oh, holy cow, your wings are so soft. Neeve, get over here and hug Riona."

Neeve crossed her arms. "No. Can we go back to saving our kingdoms now?"

Myles walked in, one hand held up in surrender. "Don't make me leave again, wifey. I know I can't read the spells, but we have a problem." He dropped the journal they used to communicate with Hector. They'd tasked Myles with handling these communications.

Riona reached for it, flipping through the pages that had told them Egan was back in Myrkur struggling to gain many new followers. They hadn't erased any of the intel in case they needed it. She reached the last page with writing and stopped, reading the words. "We've been found."

No one spoke for a long moment until Brea stood. "Gather everyone in the center of the village. Lochlan won't like this, but I'm going to have Toby take him to Eldur." She walked from the room with the air of a queen. For someone who claimed she didn't want to rule, she was good at it, going from sentimental human to fae queen in minutes.

A million scenarios filtered through Riona's mind as she thought of Egan and what he'd do next. Would he return to Eldur now that they'd left? Try to make a move on the weaker Fargelsi, not knowing Aghadoon was within its boundaries?

There had to be something more, something none of them had thought of.

Night had fallen on Fargelsi by the time Riona reached the crowded square. Once, this village was home to many families who'd lived here for generations.

Until the slaughter.

Riona still saw their faces in her mind, and she wondered if Toby did as well. She met the watchful black gaze of Padraig, a general she'd worked with many times before when they both served Egan. The Light Fae had been so desperate to trust those who'd put aside their weapons in the battle she worried they didn't really know who they were dealing with.

She'd never met an ogre she could trust, one with the intelligence for true leadership—until Padraig.

The other fae in the village gave him a wide berth, and she didn't blame them.

Tearing her eyes away, she searched for Griffin. Only he'd understand this foreboding feeling inside her. He too would have guessed Egan wouldn't be content just sitting in an empty palace with Enis and the book.

Not when there was still so much dark magic left in it.

It would take years to finish combing the Aghadoon library for dangerous spells to destroy. They didn't have years.

Brea clapped her hands together, and the sound reverberated against the stone, amplified by her magic. All chatter died down.

Neeve and Myles joined her, the only other royals currently in the village. "A moment ago, King Lochlan and Prince Tobias left for the human realm. They will portal from there into Eldur to make sure our brothers and sisters in the desert kingdom are secure." She kept emotion out of her voice, and Riona didn't know how she did it. Brea O'Shea was the most emotional fae she'd ever met—other than Gulliver, of course.

"What's going on?" Gulliver hissed, joining her.

Riona slipped her arm around his shoulders but didn't answer him as Brea continued. She couldn't voice the words she knew would hurt him. Hector, he...

"When Egan Byrne fled the battle like the coward he is, a group of the noble Slyph went to follow his movements led by the Dark Fae leader, Hector. I'm sad to say we no longer believe them to be alive." She lifted her chin. "But their deaths will not be in vain. We know where our enemy is, and we will prepare to meet him once more. Our troops who have been resting and recovering in Eldur while helping to protect Raudur City will be recalled to join the fight. This time, we take the fight to—"

Her words cut off as icy blue magic ripped through the air, a portal opening right in the middle of the crowd. Fae scattered out of the way as Lochlan and Toby practically fell through. Lochlan snapped the portal shut and turned to the expectant faces. "It's dark."

Riona never would have imagined seeing fear on the face of the seemingly fearless king. But it was there, and she wasn't the only one who noticed.

Griffin appeared at his side, his face stony with a lack of emotion over Hector's fate. She knew it was a lie. "What's dark?"

Lochlan shook his head, unable to get the words out.

Toby's next words carried over the crowd, settling an ominous weight around them. "The human realm. It's daytime there, but their light... it's gone."

Riona wouldn't believe the blinding sun of the human realm was gone until she saw it for herself. She shook off any lingering sadness and weariness from the last few weeks as she clothed herself in the least fae looking thing she could find. Brown trousers that gave her ample room to move, a white linen shirt, and black boots she'd scrubbed the blood off only days before.

She left her sword behind to join the traveling party.

This was it, she could feel it. The darkness in the human realm had something to do with Egan's next step. It had to.

Which was the worst thing of all. The fae realm wasn't supposed to have an impact on the humans—unless an O'Shea was involved of course.

In this moment, nothing else mattered. Not the histories she'd uncovered or even the spells Neeve and Brandon would continue searching with their team. Even Hector's unknown fate, his possible death after being found and the journal destroyed, had to fade into the background.

Lochlan and Toby had only spent a few minutes in the human realm before portaling back, so no one knew what they'd find at the familiar farmhouse in Grafton.

Which was why their party wasn't small.

Brea insisted on leading them herself, and no one argued. It was her home, after all. She and Myles had more stake in this than anyone.

"Are we ready?" Lochlan asked, his power winding through the air.

Griffin nodded. "Let's do this." His violet portal opened, and he held out a hand for Riona. There'd been so little time to spend together over the weeks that just a simple touch had her heart speeding up.

She'd been prepared for the darkness after suffering through so much of it, but there was something wrong about it in the human realm. A familiar feel of magic buzzed through the air. Did the humans feel it too?

It took her a moment to get her bearings as she stood in the field across from Brea's house. The last time they were here, Aghadoon stood where she now did. Well, according to Griffin. Riona hadn't been able to see it then.

Memories of that time came at full force. Nihal sitting under the drooping tree by the front porch playing his music.

The sun blazing down on them.

"This isn't right," Brea whispered. "Do you feel it?"

Griffin tugged Riona close to his side, whether for his comfort or hers, she didn't know. Her wings stretched out behind her, ready for a fight should that become necessary.

"Myles." Brea gripped his hand, and Riona wondered how much worse this was for them.

Riona was used to her home being shrouded in darkness, and that's when it hit her. The thickness in the air, the way something felt so off. It wasn't a feeling she'd have noticed if she'd never left Myrkur, but then she'd experienced the fresher air of the other kingdoms.

This felt exactly as Myrkur had.

The hairs on her arms stood on end.

None of them spoke as they walked toward the house. It was as if they were afraid of voicing what they were all thinking.

Egan was coming after the human realm, and the humans would stand no chance.

But how? How did he get here to use the book? That was the question no one could answer.

"I thought we destroyed the darkness spell when we created the eclipse." Myles' voice was low.

It was Griffin who answered. "We did."

That was the problem. They'd destroyed it, and still, the human realm was dark.

Brea pulled a key from her pocket and ran up the steps to unlock the house. "Okay, first thing's first. Myles, you know the box in my room under my bed?"

"The one you used to hide things from your parents in when we were kids?"

She nodded. "I'm still paying for internet here, so it should be up and running. I want the laptop and the phone from that box."

He ran off to retrieve the items, though Riona wasn't sure what a laptop or internet was.

Brea turned to Lochlan and Griffin. "Don't just stand there. Be useful. We don't have to stay the night here since we don't want your magic lingering too long like last time, but I don't want to sit in the dark. Turn on lights, open up the house."

"What can I do?" Riona rubbed her suddenly cold arms.

Brea ticked her head toward the sitting room. "You and I are going to do some searches."

Riona nodded. "Tell me where to look and what I'm looking for. I can fly further into town if you'd like."

"Any other time you'd be cute, Riona, but right now I really just wish you spoke human. Okay, short lesson." Myles returned and handed her a slim silver metal thing. "This is a computer. It will tell us any information we need to know." She sat on the couch and opened the computer to reveal a bright light and rows of letters.

Riona perched on the arm of the couch.

"We don't have time for your stand-offishness." Brea patted the seat next to her.

Riona reluctantly joined her.

Myles threw himself into a chair and started hitting letters on the phone.

Lochlan and Griffin watched from the doorway.

Brea's fingers flew over the letters, and before long, a list appeared. She used her finger to choose an item.

Riona read over her shoulder. "A week?" She sat back. "The human world has been dark for a week."

Brea nodded. "It looks like it's only Grafton right now, but it's spread from where it began. The reporters are calling it a weather phenomenon and linking it to global warming."

"Global what now?" Lochlan asked.

"Warming. The humans are killing the planet, but that's not our issue right now. This isn't a global warming issue. How could they even consider that? It's not weather! The sun is just gone." She huffed out an angry breath.

Griffin pushed away from the doorframe. "When something unexplainable happens, humans will find logical explanations—they just won't be right. Humans do not know magic exists, so what else can help them understand an entire town going dark?"

Lochlan nodded. "The bigger issue is you said it's spreading. The computer told you that?"

Myles held up his phone. "Look, there's a map showing how it's grown. These articles... the humans are freaking out. I mean, I would have too before I knew another world existed."

Riona met Griffin's gaze, wondering if he felt the same similarities to the prison realm. "This... thickness, that lack of fresh air... it feels very much like the prison realm, like whatever magic caused the endless night in Myrkur."

But that wasn't supposed to be possible. The humans would be helpless against magic.

Leaning forward, she rested her elbows on her knees, not looking away from Griffin. "Is it time to consider if there's a breach between the fae and human realms?"

Everyone spoke at once, denying that could happen.

Except Griffin.

Because, like Riona, he knew Egan. He'd seen the book. Anything was possible.

Myles stood. "I need to call my folks."

Brea nodded. "Then we must get back to Aghadoon." She rubbed a hand across her face. "If we're to entertain the notion that Egan has caused some kind of rift between the worlds—since he has no O'Shea to bring him here—we at least know what to look for in the library."

The moment they returned, those who'd stayed behind had a million questions. Riona wanted to seek her bed, to curl up and forget this day for a few hours. But she didn't get that luxury.

Not now that she knew Egan's next steps.

The others might be skeptical, but she'd never been more certain of anything.

Brea led them to the library for a meeting before they decided what to do next.

She spoke much more calmly than any of them felt. Griffin sat next to Riona and reached for her hand.

Her entire body relaxed at his strong grip as she listened to Brea tell the others what they'd discovered.

Neeve had many questions, but Riona watched Brandon, noting how quiet he'd become.

She cut off whatever Neeve had been saying. "What is it, Brandon?"

The man who knew more about this world than any of them sighed. "I never wanted to speak Regan's final truths. I figured she's dead so her true mission didn't matter."

"She wanted to control the fae," Griffin said. "What does that have to do with this?"

He shook his head. "No, son. She wanted to control all life. My sister... she was much darker than even you realize. I may know how Egan managed this. But... we're going to need Regan's grimoire."

Griffin's breath quickened as they spoke of Regan, and Riona leaned closer to him, letting him know she was there. "That book was destroyed when she died."

Brandon shook his head. "I saved it."

CHAPTER 15

GRIFFIN

"It's happening." Brandon's hands shook as he paced the span of the library. He'd left to retrieve Regan's Grimoire. A book Griffin had grown up seeing. It was never far from Regan's reach, but she never let him touch it.

It was spelled so that no one could open it without her permission. It seemed her death was her final permission because Brandon O'Rourke set the book on the table, letting it fall open.

Griffin gasped at the sight of Regan's handwriting. It shouldn't hurt to see it after all this time, but it did. Like a knife right through his heart.

"I am so sorry, Griffin." Brandon turned his sad gaze on him. "I hoped the truth of her darkness had died with her." He thumbed through the grimoire, searching for whatever he believed was relevant now. "She was your mother." He slid the book toward Griffin.

"The legacy of her darkness is my burden to bear." Griffin's voice came out strangled, and he couldn't seem to meet his brother's gaze.

"It is not, brother." Lochlan placed his hand across the book, forcing Griffin to meet his eyes. "She was your mother, and you loved her. You remained loyal to the woman who raised you. We ... I should never have blamed you for that."

Griffin nodded, not trusting his voice as he pulled the book toward him and began to read. It took his breath, reading his mother's words. He could hear her voice as clearly as if she stood behind him reading over his shoulder.

Shock and revulsion rolled through him as he realized how truly unhinged Regan was. He'd always known she craved power. Absolute power.

Griffin stood to pace as he read through pages and pages of research and dark spells. Dangerous spells. Some she'd constructed herself—a perilous pursuit that rarely ended well for the fae involved in such things.

"Well?" Lochlan finally spoke as Griffin flipped through the pages.

"Give him a moment, Lochlan," Brandon said. "It's likely a shock."

Griffin sat back in his chair, dropping the book on the table in front of him as if it burned him.

"She was ... insane." Griffin reached for Riona's hand, needing her strength. "We all know she craved power. She wanted to unite the three kingdoms as one under her rule. In her twisted mind, she found her pursuit to be a noble one.

"She used to tell me about a world where there was no more war or conflict. She painted a picture of a beautiful life for all fae, one I wanted to help her create. But I was wrong. So very wrong." Griffin leaned forward, pressing his forehead against the table.

"She writes of her time studying here in the Aghadoon library. She was an O'Rourke descendant, so they could not deny her access, but they wouldn't let her copy the spells she studied. She writes of one spell in particular." Griffin pulled the book closer. "A complex weave of magic she describes as wickedly beautiful in its construction. It came from an ancient scroll filled with dark magic. She tried to tear the spell from the scroll, but the paper wouldn't rip. The main subject of this scroll was on the fragile veil that exists between our world and the human world. She wished to destroy it. To bring magic to the human world where she would rule as mistress over all." Tears welled in his eyes and splashed on the page in front of him.

"How did I let her become this? This monster? How did I not see that she wasn't in her right mind?"

"That fault lies with me, son. Not you." Brandon laid a weary hand on his shoulder. "You were just a boy who loved his mother. You believed her to be right and true. Whereas I was her elder brother. I knew what she was when we were young, and because I loved her, I looked the other way when I should have done something about it. I should have gotten her the help she needed."

"The fault is Regan's." Brea stood up, coming to Griffin's side. She leaned down until he couldn't help but meet her gaze. "She went down a dark path that lead to her end. This is not your fault, Griffin O'Shea. It was never your fault, and I can't believe we let you enter the prison realm to pay for the crime of believing in the wrong person."

"I did terrible things, Brea. Don't kid yourself. I deserved what I got. But right now we need to find this scroll."

"Griffin is right." Neeve placed a careful hand on Regan's grimoire, as if asking his permission to see it. He nodded, letting her take it from him. He never wanted to see it again. "There are thousands of scrolls here. But knowing we are looking for a scroll and not a book narrows our search considerably. We will find this bit of magic, and we will destroy it."

"If Enis has somehow found this magic within the book," Lochlan began. "And created a tear in the veil between our worlds, allowing the darkness of Myrkur to ... leak into the human realm, will destroying the magic repair the tear?"

"It should." Brea came back from a far corner of the library with a stack of dusty scrolls. "At the very least it's the first step to making sure that fool who calls himself a king doesn't destroy the veil completely."

"Enis is likely not powerful enough to do that," Neeve said, helping Brea shift through the scrolls. "It will only be a matter of time before Egan realizes he needs a stronger spell caster. And comes for one."

"Griffin!" Brea stormed into the room he shared with Riona and Gulliver. Aghadoon was bursting at the seams with people, and the royals were sharing one small house.

"Oh, I'm so sorry." Brea's face flushed at the sight of Griffin and Riona in the same bed together. Not that there was anything remotely interesting happening between them with no privacy to be had these days.

"Whas happening?" Gulliver sat up from his pallet at the foot of the bed. His tail flicked nervously over his head. "We being invaded?" His tail knocked over a stack of scrolls Griffin and Riona had spent most of the evening poring over.

"Go back to sleep, Gullie." Griffin slipped out of bed, feeling nervous and ashamed to have Brea find him here in a completely innocent embrace with the woman he happened to be head over heels in love with. They had to do something about this marriage bond holding them together. He'd always seen the marriage bond as a romantic thing one shared with the love of their life. But what happened to free will? He didn't want to be connected with Brea like this. Not anymore.

"What have you found, Brea?" Riona asked, rising from the bed in the clothes she'd slept in. They'd fallen asleep reading late into the night.

"We found it. Early this morning, Lochlan found the spell we've been looking for. We need to destroy it, but we want everyone in agreement before we destroy the whole scroll."

Griffin and Riona gathered the scrolls they borrowed the night before and followed Brea across the narrow cobblestone road to the library.

"It's truly awful magic," Brea called over her shoulder as they rushed through the library doors. "Neeve has read each spell carefully to make sure we don't destroy anything important."

"Whoever created this magic hated humans." Neeve set the scroll down when they all gathered around the table. "I mean, really despised humans. This is written on some kind of leather I'm truly afraid might be human skin."

"It's just like I've always said." Myles sat back in his chair looking like he hadn't slept in days. None of them really had. "Human legends are always rooted in truth somewhere. Listen to this." He gestured to Neeve, and she began to read.

"This is a spell designed to fool humans into believing the fae are beautiful souls who only want the best for them. And this one creates spelled music that will force a human to dance for the fae's entertainment. It says here they will dance until their feet are bloodied and they finally die from exhaustion."

"That's horrifying," Riona said.

"It's also the kind of magic that shows up in every human fantasy book with fae characters." Myles looked ill at the thought that such magic existed. He held the evidence of it in his hands.

"This magic cannot be allowed to exist." Neeve sat back with a sigh. "It's always bothered me that we are sitting here destroying magic. No one should get to decide what magic should exist and what shouldn't. It's a dangerous precedence that cannot be helped. We are dealing with such an extreme situation. It calls for extreme measures."

"Are you saying we should preserve these spells? And others like it?" Brea asked.

"No, but I worry what the future kings and queens of the realms will have to say about us. What happens generations from now when we are all long dead and others look back at what we've done here and either judge us for it, or use it as a precedence to ... censor all magic, or worse, destroy it completely. Who are we to decide these things?"

"We do what we must," Lochlan said. "We cannot look back, and we cannot look forward. We must do whatever we can to ensure our survival and that of the human world. Let history mark us as traitors or heroes. None of it will matter if Egan wins."

"You are right." Neeve nodded.

Griffin cleared his throat, wondering if what he was about to suggest would force them all to remember he was the criminal in the room. "No one needs to know what happens here. Neeve is right to worry about how history will judge us for how we deal with this threat. But who says history needs to know any of this? If we all take this to our graves, we aren't setting a precedence at all."

Silence fell across the table, and Griffin immediately regretted the suggestion.

"I'm good with that," Lochlan said as he stood, taking the scroll from Neeve.

"Yeah, I can live with it," Neeve agreed as her husband nodded his consent.

Lochlan dropped the scroll into a charred bucket at the center of the room. They had burned dozens of spells they deemed dangerous, but none so complex as this. Unlike the books, most of the scrolls they destroyed refused to burn by magical means. Lochlan struck a match —a human match—and dropped it on top of the aged leather.

Fire blazed as the scroll burned followed by an unnatural green flame that destroyed the words of magic written with such hate and vengeance it couldn't be allowed to exist.

They stood around in silence, watching the scroll burn to ash.

"By destroying such a dark part of our history, may we not be doomed to repeat it," Neeve whispered.

"This history will die right here, sister." Brea took her hand. "Because we will teach our children not to harbor such hate in their hearts."

It didn't work.

After burning the scroll, Lochlan and Griffin traveled to the farmhouse to find the darkness still spreading from the breach in the veil. A breach they could not find because it was invisible. But with the destruction of the dark magic that created the breach, they had ensured that Egan would not be able to destroy the veil or create a larger tear.

"This is the sort of darkness you lived in for ten years?" Brea asked as they stood in the field near her childhood home the following morning. The sun was still absent from the skies over this part of Ohio. But they were here to rectify that situation.

"It is." Griffin nodded. "But you get used to it. Myrkur has its own beauty if you know where to look. The darkness wasn't so bad. I still enjoyed this time of day."

"How do you know what time it is when it's always the same?" Brea asked.

"It's in the subtleties. The early mornings are quiet. Fresh and cool with the morning dew. The darkness is still there, but it's not as heavy when the day is young."

"You always could find the beauty in everything." Brea smiled as she moved into the clearing with her daughter and her sister. The three women held hands. As they performed the magic that would chase the darkness back into Myrkur, they leaned on each other so the strength the spell demanded of them would not drain them.

Griffin only had eyes for Tia as she spoke the words of power with confidence. She was incredible, his daughter. He would never cease to be proud of her. Together with her mother and her aunt for support, Tia guided the darkness back through the invisible veil, sealing the rift behind it.

Sunlight burst through the clouds, and they all cheered in triumph. They thwarted Egan again. And this time, they wouldn't let him recover. This time, they were going to bring him to justice.

CHAPTER 16

RIONA

Riona sat on the edge of her bed as her thick black hair hung in wet braids around her face. She tried to dry her hair with a bath sheet, relishing the feeling of being clean. Time away from the library was hard to come by, and she closed her eyes, letting the rare quiet wrap around her.

Reaching behind her, she pulled the tips of her wings to the front to study the inky darkness that seemed to expand almost daily now. Would she end up with entirely dark wings like Nihal had?

Thoughts of Nihal always left her confused and a little angry. He'd pretended to be on their side, to give them answers, but it was Enis who held his loyalty in the end.

And none of them quite knew what that woman's goal was yet.

Nihal died for his trouble, to save Enis, taking the rest of the answers Riona needed with him.

"You took a bath?" Gulliver walked into the room and stripped off his shirt. "Griffin told me I couldn't bathe for another few days."

She hid a smile. He'd surprised her this morning with the bath, lugging the water himself. "Carry the water yourself, and you don't have to listen to him."

He shrugged. Riona had never spent much time around kids, but now she was surrounded by them. She'd learned quickly that they didn't prioritize privacy, nor cleanliness, especially if it meant extra work. "No time today. I have a game to play." He flashed her a smile and slipped a new shirt on before running out the door.

From what she'd learned of Fela, the village in Myrkur where he grew up, there'd been so little time for playing. But now, with all of the royal children in the village, they spent hours playing a game Myles called soccer, running through the town square without the heavy burdens on their parents' shoulders.

That was one thing the adults had all agreed on. Other than occasionally using Tia's magic or Toby's portals, they wouldn't put this weight on their children. Not after all they'd been through.

After all everyone had been through.

Had they done it? Had they thwarted Egan's grand plan? Kept him from the human realm?

It felt like a win.

But she had no delusions about it. This wouldn't be over until he was dead.

Standing from the bed, Riona twisted her braids to wring out the water. She laid the bath sheet over the back of a chair and walked from the house into the sun she'd come to appreciate. The brightness still bothered her at times, but its warmth on an otherwise chilly Fargelsian morning was welcome.

Signs of life entered the village with shops opening to keep the royals and soldiers supplied. They'd managed to change the village magic once again, allowing all those with honest intentions to see it, which meant trading with the Fargelsians was possible.

Yet, the people who'd lived here before were never far from her mind. They too had lived lives with purpose.

She crossed her arms as she reached the square near the library at the center of the village. Gulliver kicked a ball in front of him with Tia and Logan chasing. Little Darra trailed along after them. It was good the Eldurian prince and princess were occupied. It kept them from asking too many questions about their father who still had yet to wake.

Riona barely knew Finn, but she could see the worry in Lochlan's eyes.

As if the thought of him called him forth, cold blue light flashed in front of her moments before Lochlan stepped through a portal with a familiar little girl at his side.

"Nessa?" Riona walked toward them.

Lochlan met her gaze, and it still surprised her whenever he did so without scorn. The battle changed him, learning the truth about his world changed him. "Where are the others?"

"In the library, I'm guessing. I was just headed there."

He nodded and took off toward the most important building in the entire realm.

Inside, the realms' rulers looked fresher than they had in a long time. They were still searching for dangerous spells, but there was a sense of hope that what they were doing had worked.

Griffin stood from his seat at the table and walked toward them, bypassing Lochlan and Riona to get to Nessa. "Hey, Ness. I thought you were staying in Eldur with Shauna."

"Eldur." Lochlan sighed. "Just one of our problems. I spent the last few days with Alona and Faolan—who is mostly recovered thanks to Shauna's attentive care. Bands of fae who'd chosen to leave rather than join us after the fight have been attacking the city, forcing Eldur and Iskalt soldiers to work day and night to keep them out. We need to call our men back, but I won't leave Eldur unprotected. For now, they will have to stay."

He looked down at Nessa. "Shauna thought the village would be safer for her."

Nessa crossed her arms. "I was helping. That's more important than safety."

Griffin smiled and put a hand on her shoulder. "Shauna just worries, but you can still help here."

"Help you figure out why the human realm is dark again?"

Riona sucked in a breath as every eye in the room focused on Nessa.

Lochlan rubbed a hand across his face. "I was getting to that. We just portaled through Grafton on our way back. Our bigger problem right now... whatever we did to save the human realm... it didn't work."

Weeks of darkness did something to a fae... or a person. Riona and Griffin were well versed in living without light in the sky, but most were not.

Which was why it didn't surprise her when the news out of the human realm was of societal breakdowns. Their governments had no answers, nor any solutions to the increasing crime and dissolution of order.

This time, the darkness didn't linger over Grafton. It spread rapidly and without slowing to the neighboring towns and beyond. Nearly all of Ohio was dark now.

Weeks had gone by, and they still hadn't found the tear or how Myrkur's darkness leeched through it.

Griffin, Riona, Brea, and Lochlan had started a rotation at the farmhouse. There was never a time when two of them weren't in the human realm searching for answers while the other two searched in the library.

Riona flopped onto the bed, too exhausted to keep her eyes open. They'd spent the entire day scouring Grafton for any sign of the breach. Just like they'd done every other day. At least they could return to the village soon for a break.

Griffin crawled into bed beside her and released a long sigh as he rested his face on one of her soft wings. The hope that bolstered them after they thought they'd sealed the breach and chased the darkness away had long since evaporated, leaving them drained.

"Riona," Griffin whispered.

She didn't open her eyes. "Hmm?"

"Do you think we'll be able to stop this?"

Turning onto her side, she slid her eyes open to study him, this beautiful fae she'd once tried to kill. "Do you remember what you said to me in the arena?"

He hummed in the back of his throat. "Not really. What I remember was how fierce you looked as you tried to gut me. I like to picture warrior Riona."

She pinched him. "I was being serious."

"So was I."

"Griff, I will never forget your words that day. I think they were the start of everything changing for me. You told me you weren't scared of me. When I asked why, you said it was because you had something to fight for." She put a finger under his chin and turned his face up. "I didn't understand it then, but I do now. I don't fear Egan or the book of power, because we will never stop fighting until he's gone. Do you know why?"

"We have something to fight for."

She nodded. "We do. That day in Myrkur, you did not let fear control you, and you bested me because of it. The only way we will beat Egan is if we do not fear him."

Griffin wrapped an arm around her waist and pulled her closer. Riona had never before considered love as something she sought. But this fae... he changed that too.

Riona wrapped a blanket around her shoulders as she stared out on the back deck where Griffin watched the moon overhead, his shoulders hunched forward. Beside him lay a book he'd taken from Aghadoon to study while they were here. He'd been using his magic to light the pages, but now he looked deep in thought.

Tomorrow they'd return to Aghadoon for another never-ending round of reading in the library until no one could make out another word and waiting to come back to the human realm.

It was all they had.

And it wasn't enough.

Riona walked into the bedroom and lifted Griffin's bag onto the bed. She knew he still held out a small hope that Hector was alive somewhere and would contact them. He blamed himself for his death, claiming he should have been the one to go after Egan. It was his mother helping him after all.

That had led to one of the more epic arguments between Griffin and Lochlan—who held more blame for their mother's actions, a mother neither of them knew. Both of them were way too self-sacrificing for their own good.

She dug through Griffin's bag until she found the book only he cared about now, needing to see what it was he wrote in it every day.

Flipping the cover open, she thumbed through the pages, watching his desperation play out. He wrote to Hector, begging him to answer, to let him know if any were alive. There was no information regarding troop movements or plans, nothing about burning spells in the library.

Griffin was too smart for that. An idea struck her, one that probably wouldn't matter. If Egan found the Slyph, he probably had the book now. Was he too smart for them to deceive him? Wanting to test her theory, Riona reached into the bag for the quill.

Her hand bumped against a worn leather scroll, tied with a fraying silk cord. Glancing toward the door to make sure Griffin wasn't there, she untied it and rolled it flat. It looked old, older than anything they'd seen thus far. Instead of parchment, leather held the words she realized belonged to a spell. A complicated one. She couldn't read much Fargelsian, but she recognized the language. Why did Griffin have an ancient spell from the library hidden away with him in the human realm?

So many questions rolled through her mind, questions she wasn't sure she wanted answers to. If he'd kept it with him, it had to be important, something he wanted to protect.

The back door slammed, and Riona jumped, shoving the journal back into the bag and putting it on the floor. The scroll, however... if it was something that could help them, she had to know.

Gathering her strength, she sucked in a breath and marched from the room, ready to confront whatever this was.

"Hey." Griffin had his head in the strange ice box when she approached. "So, there are what Brea calls frozen burritos. They're not awful if we want them for dinner. I can heat them again with my magic." Brea refused to let him touch the new microwave after the old one blew up when he'd tried to reheat leftovers in a metal pan two weeks ago and almost set the house on fire.

When Riona didn't respond, he shut the ice box and turned to her, his eyes going to the scroll in her hand. His mouth opened, but he didn't say anything.

Riona stepped forward, letting only the kitchen island separate them. "Why do you have a scroll from the library with you here? The books, I can understand for studying purposes, but a single spell? Why this one?"

It seemed like such a simple question.

He placed a hand on the countertop, his fingers curling in. "That's none—"

"If you finish with 'of my business,' I know what that human phrase means. It means you're hiding something. Griffin, we are in the human realm that has been dark for weeks, and it's still spreading. We can't find the breach or why it didn't close when we tried. Nothing we do works. This is not the time to keep spells hidden. What could possibly be so personal from that library that the rest of us don't need to see it?"

Griffin leaned against the counter. "I don't owe you an explanation."

"You know what? You're a coward. The only reason you'd keep that spell from us is if it scared you."

"It's the marriage magic," he burst out, stealing the breath from Riona's lungs. "The scroll... it's the origin magic that every marriage bond in the three kingdoms stems from."

Riona stepped back, taking a moment to let this information filter through her mind. The marriage magic... if it really came from a Fargelsian scroll, it could be destroyed just like all the others. "And you couldn't let her go?" It was the only explanation.

For months, Riona told herself Griffin didn't love Brea, but they were connected, and that meant something.

Something more than she'd ever mean to him.

Neither of them spoke for a long moment. "Have you told her what you found?"

He shook his head. It was the answer she'd expected.

"You don't understand, Riona," he pleaded. "The bond... do you think I like being connected to my brother's wife? That I like flashes of long past memories invading every thought when she's near? And yet, most of the time it's awful, but it's also a connection like something you could never imagine. The minute it returned to me, I knew I wasn't alone in this world. There's power in that. As long as I have the marriage bond, I'll never again have nothing."

"Have nothing?" Her voice was low. "Nothing? Gulliver isn't anything? Shauna, Nessa, Hector? Griffin, you were never alone in Myrkur. Their love for you wasn't tied to some piece of magic. That isn't how love should work. It shouldn't be a compulsion. There has to be choice, it has to be allowed to grow out of nothing instead of just appearing. Or else, what value does it have?"

Griffin stared at her with glassy eyes. "How would you know? You and I both grew up with false love, false belonging. Neither of us knows how to love, let alone be in love."

"That's what you think? Griffin, I hated you. But even when I hated you, there was something more. I saw the way you protected Gullie, the way you risk everything time and again for kids who will never call you father. And your brother... even Brea. I don't think all your affection for her is the magic. I envied them all, because even when I hated you, Griff, I still fell in love with you."

She stepped around the corner, wanting him to see what she'd learned in her time around him and his two families. "You don't have to learn to love, just like you don't need magic tying you to someone to keep you from being lonely. Regan and Egan never loved us like parents should." Her steps stopped in front of him. "But we are different than them. Because we choose to be. You taught me that."

"I... Riona." There was so much desperation in his voice.

Riona set the scroll on the counter because it didn't matter anymore. There would be more discussions to come once they showed it to Brea. But right now, Riona just wanted to prove to Griffin, to herself, that they could have this. Despite all their trials, everything they'd done and said to each other, they could hold on to some kind of hope in the darkness. Hold on to each other.

The thought was so unlike her, but she was tired of never taking what she truly wanted.

"I love you." They seemed such simple words, and it wasn't the first time she'd told him. But there was a difference between declarations in a battle and standing in front of each other laying themselves bare.

Reaching up, Riona trailed a hand over the curve of his neck and repeated herself. "I love you. I'm not saying it because we might die, not this time." She pulled him down, and when their lips met, his sigh gave her life.

"I love you," she whispered against his lips.

There was a time he was the wise one, giving pep talks and making her question her loyalties. Now, she had to be the strong one for him. Give and take, that was what love meant.

Griffin's kiss turned more forceful, and he picked her up, setting her on the counter. Her wings stretched out behind her, the pleasure tingling all the way to the tips as Griffin's lips trailed to her ear. "You're right." His breath warmed her skin. "I don't need the magic."

His hands dipped under the loose t-shirt she'd borrowed from Brea's room, his fingers sliding along her rib cage. It had been so long since they had any privacy, and Riona needed more. She needed Griffin to prove to her his hesitation about destroying the marriage magic had nothing to do with her.

She slipped her shirt over her head as he pulled his off, revealing strong muscles shining in the moonlight. Only a tiny bulb illuminated the kitchen, casting them mostly in the darkness they knew so well.

Needing to touch him, she leaned forward, kissing a line across his shoulders, wishing they could stay this way forever.

Griffin lifted her up to slide her pants down her legs, and it was just the two of them with nothing separating their bodies, their souls.

Riona's wings splayed out, the white and black plumes stretching as far as the tendons could go as she cried out.

"I love you too," Griffin whispered as they collapsed against each other.

Riona trailed a finger down Griffin's chest. The air felt like early morning, meaning they'd slept through the night after eating dinner sans clothes in the kitchen. He was beautiful when he slept, when the lines of worry eased from his face.

One day, she hoped their days could be filled with as much peace as their nights.

But today would be another day of fruitless searching before returning to Aghadoon.

"Mmm." Griffin's lips curved into a smile. "I like waking up to you."

Riona couldn't believe moments like these existed in either world right now. Moments of being content, despite everything happening around them.

"I had an idea yesterday before you distracted me." She didn't want to think of the marriage magic that had been the cause of her distraction.

Griffin's eyes slid open. "It involves getting out of this bed, doesn't it?" He sighed as his hand gripped the curve of her waist, the other massaging the joint where her wings met her back.

Riona tried not to give into the pleasure, but she couldn't help moaning.

"So, this idea?" Griffin smirked.

"Right." She pushed his hand away. "I noticed you still have the journal that can communicate with the other."

He nodded. "But it's useless. I've tried. Our spies are truly dead."

"Which means Egan probably has the book."

Griffin sat up, the sheet pooling at his waist. "He wouldn't get rid of something like that."

Riona pushed herself up and rested her chin on his shoulder. "Maybe we can use that to our advantage."

"I'm such an idiot."

"Well, I won't argue with that."

"I've been trying to communicate with Hector as if it's truly him. But if Egan has the journal—"

"—we can feed him information," she finished for him.

He turned to her, taking her face in his hands and planted a kiss on her lips. "Riona, you're a genius. We need to get back to the village." He jumped from the bed in all his naked glory and marched from the room.

"Might want to put on clothes, first," Riona yelled after him. "Don't want to scare the children!"

CHAPTER 17

GRIFFIN

Griffin's bloodshot eyes ran across the page in front of him, the ancient Fargelsian words and letters a jumble of nonsense.

"Drink this, it'll help." Brea poured him a steaming cup of Eldur brew. The stuff she claimed was the fae equivalent of human coffee. It was the one human vice she refused to give up. "This is the good stuff too. Straight from the human realm."

"Not Eldur brew?" He peered into the mug with slightly less contempt.

"Of course not, I wouldn't dare serve a royal fae such a common drink." Her sarcasm dripped like venom from her smart mouth.

"And here I thought you liked me better than you did when we were married." His tone was teasing, but his words reminded them of the bond they still shared. The bond that made everything awkward between them. He glanced at his bag where the scroll sat hidden from her. It was time they had that discussion. "Brea, I—"

"You drink it with cream and sugar, and it'll perk you right up." Brea mixed the dark brew until it was the color of sweet toffee. He had to admit it smelled much more appealing this way. Taking a tentative sip, he refused to admit how it warmed him from the inside out and revitalized him with its potent jolt of caffeine. Not that he knew what that was, only that Brea had constantly whined about needing caffeine in the mornings.

With a sigh, Griffin kicked his bag under the table, vowing to find the right moment later. And soon.

The words on the page began to make more sense as he read through the complex spells for growing buildings and structures from the ground using nature as the source for the power to fuel the spell. It was really fascinating to learn just how complex Fargelsi magic was. His Iskalt magic came to him intuitively. He'd had to study growing up, and practiced for years and years before he mastered his natural abilities, but he'd never had to work as hard as those with Gelsi magic did.

He mustered up his courage again. "I need to tell you—"

"We have a problem." Neeve came to sit with them. Blowing her dark hair from her face, she gave a big sigh. Griffin hated how relieved he felt at the interruption. "At least I think it's a problem. That or I truly need to rest and possibly see a healer."

"Care to tell us what you're rambling about, sister?" Brea sipped her coffee looking more refreshed than either Griffin or Neeve.

"Come with me." Neeve stood, guiding them through the stacks to the desk she and Myles were using toward the back of the library.

"What's going on?" Griffin asked, watching the way Myles stared at a stack of books like he thought they might disappear.

"We cleared out a whole shelf of books on primary Eldurian magic this morning. We were going to ask Brea to give it a quick look before we moved on. Myles has been shifting the books and scrolls around, creating a system to set aside those books we've reviewed and deemed safe."

Brea nodded. "So, what's the problem?"

"This." Myles stood and turned her around to face a bookshelf bursting with leather-bound tomes.

"Use more words, Myles. I'm too tired to guess what you're trying to tell me." Brea frowned.

"That's the shelf we cleaned off this morning," Neeve said.

"The one with all the kid's books on Eldur magic," Myles added. "It's full again."

"So just move these books back to wherever you found them."

"We didn't move them here." Neeve sighed. "The library did."

"What now?" Griffin turned to her, confused.

"Come again?" Brea echoed his confusion.

"I think our little pea brains have made some rather dumb assumptions." Myles scratched his head.

"Like?"

"Like this rather smallish library houses everything in a pretty substantial collection of knowledge... at first glance. But I think what we've got here is your basic Room of Requirement situation."

"Oh." Brea's eyes widened. "Oh my." She looked around the room, seeing more than Griffin saw.

"Explain using more fae words." Griffin rolled his eyes.

"If we took all the books off the shelves and moved them outside, the shelves would just fill up again. Not everything housed here is altogether ... visible."

Neeve sank back down to her chair. "Which means we've barely put a dent in this search for dark magic."

"So you're saying this is going to take longer to accomplish."

Neeve nodded. "Once we figure out how to get the library to show us everything on record here."

"Guys, we can't keep this up." Brea rubbed a tired hand over her eyes. "What we are doing here is important work, but we have to move on. We're in the middle of a war, and Egan is getting stronger every day we let him live."

"I think you're right. Father can spearhead this project," Neeve said. "He's the most knowledgeable fae we could ask for in terms of researching what magic is catalogued here."

"It's time we make a big move." Griffin set down the book he'd spent the morning reviewing. "Let's get everyone here."

"It's clear we need to move against Egan." Lochlan stood at the head of the rough plank table in the library. "But we need our army to do that, and most of them are still in Eldur helping Alona deal with the remaining Dark Fae roaming around Raudur City."

"We can't wait the weeks it will take for them to arrive." Brea twisted her hands in her lap. "By then it could be too late."

"We will have to ask Toby to create a portal large enough to bring at least a small force of soldiers ready for battle."

"I don't like it, Loch. He's just a baby, and he's just getting back to his normal self after being sick for so long from the way Egan abused his portal magic. We're his parents, we should do better by him."

"He is not a baby, Brea. No matter how much you might like him to stay one, our boy is growing up. He killed an ogre all by himself. I don't like it either, but what choice do we have?"

"Um, we could use this rather fancy party bus we're sitting in and go pick up an army and bring them back." Myles looked at them both like they were rather dim.

"You mean the village?" Brea smiled.

"That's a rather smart idea." Griffin shot Myles a patronizing smile.

"I've been known to have them from time to time," Myles muttered.

"But the village is so full," Neeve said. "We'll have to move the children into the Gelsi palace as well as the injured and anyone not needed for battle. Myles and I could watch over them with Father's help. We'll keep the young royals safe. That is, if you can do without me in the coming battles with Egan? We aren't the most useful leaders in a fight, and my soldiers will follow Lochlan."

"You have done enough, sister." Brea reached for her hand. "We all need to face the fact that Eldur and Fargelsi need to stay strong while the rest of us deal with this threat. Lochlan's regent is strong enough to hold Iskalt should we fail. Should that happen, it's more important than ever for the realms to stay united."

"You will not fail," Myles said. "You two don't have it in you."

"Then it's decided," Lochlan said. "We will empty out the village and then move Aghadoon to Raudur City. It will be a good time for us to check on Alona and Faolan. And Finn," he added uncertainly. His best friend still had not recovered from his battle wounds. Griffin feared he might never recover and wondered what that would do to Lochlan. Finn was the brother Griffin never had a chance to be. Like Hector was to Griffin. The pang of loss struck him, but there'd be time to mourn fallen friends. Right now, he had to focus on the task ahead.

"From there we will fill Aghadoon to bursting with strong soldiers ready for battle and we'll move to Myrkur near Egan's palace. None who are our enemies will be able to see the village."

"And once we are there, we will seek out Egan and make our move against him," Griffin said. "His days are numbered." He'd pay for Hector's death and every other dark deed.

"Don't argue with me, Gullie. You're not going. Not this time." Griffin crossed his arms over his chest and stood his ground against the persuasive Gulliver.

"But Griff, you know I can be useful." Gulliver's tail thumped irritably against the wooden floorboards of their room. Getting Gulliver packed and to the palace had proven to be an undertaking. The kid did not want to go, and Griffin couldn't blame him.

"Know and should are two different things. I know you're more than capable of helping us fight this war, but you are only twelve years old—"

"Thirteen." Gulliver's tail wilted to a lifeless coil behind him. "My name day was weeks ago."

Griffin felt like the worst father in the world. He'd forgotten his name day. He'd given Gulliver his gift months ago, right before their world turned upside down. He'd seen Gulliver using the carving kit whenever he had free time. But he should have recognized his name day.

"I should have remembered." His shoulders drooped as lifeless as Gulliver's tail.

"We were kind of busy, Griff. Truth be told, I forgot it too until it was over."

"We were kind of busy." Griffin smiled, draping his arm over his son's shoulders. He would be a man before Griffin could blink. "You've been right by my side through all of this Gulliver." He leaned down to look him in the eye. "But I need to know you and the others are safe. Go with Tia and Toby to the palace and help Myles and Neeve."

"I'm a lot more useful in battle, and you know it."

"You're not going anywhere near Egan and his men." Riona marched into the room, giving them both a glare. "And that is final."

Gulliver opened his mouth like he was about to argue.

"Final." Riona glowered. "Egan is a desperate man, and desperate men do desperate things. He's used you against Griffin in the past, and I will not let that happen again. Do you hear me?"

Gulliver's tail coiled around his leg, and he dropped his head. "Yes ma'am." Grabbing his bag, he tossed it over his shoulder and shuffled toward the door.

"Hey, where's my goodbye?" Griffin pulled him back by the scruff of his shirt.

Gulliver grinned and threw his arms around Griffin's waist. The kid couldn't stay mad at him for long.

"Do try to behave yourself while we're gone."

"Don't I always?" Gulliver blinked up at him.

"You do not want me to answer that. Just don't steal the crown jewels while you're a guest in Neeve's palace."

"I swear, I will only steal food."

"You know." Griffin pulled Gulliver against his side. "They'd probably just give you whatever you want if you'd go to the kitchens and ask for food."

"It's more fun to steal it. It tastes better."

"Take care of yourself." Riona pulled him into a hug.

"Love you guys." Gulliver squirmed out of her arms. He leaned back in to whisper in Riona's ear. "Take care of Griff for me."

"You got it." Riona winked.

"I heard that." Griffin scowled at them both.

"Later gaters." Gulliver tipped his hat onto his head and made his way to the center of the village to meet the other kids traveling to the palace this afternoon.

"You're the mean one, you know." Griffin moved to put his arm around Riona. "I'm the nice one."

"That's why the kid never listens to you."

"We have a system."

"Whatever, he likes me better." Riona elbowed him playfully.

"Does not. I'm his favorite. He just thinks you're pretty."

Riona smiled and took his hand, leading him to the small table in the corner of their room. "I have an idea."

Griffin pulled up a chair to sit beside her as she shuffled through her bag for the spelled journal. "We talked about using the journal to manipulate Egan. Feed him some false information. Now that we have a plan in place, I think we should test it."

"What did you have in mind?" Griffin folded his arms against the table and leaned closer.

"The message needs to be subtle at first. Similar to the messages you've written to Hector previously. But we make it look like a careless slip of too much information. A tip we didn't realize we'd given."

"Enough to get Egan to respond, hoping for more." Griffin nodded.

"Exactly." Riona handed him the quill.

Griffin stared at the blank page, letting his eyes drift over his previous messages before he began to write.

Hector,

It has been some time since we've received word from you and your team. Should you be in need of assistance, please respond. We are nearly in position to aid you if you can let us know where in Myrkur you're being held.

Griff.

Griffin leaned back, hoping the hint that they would soon be within striking distance of Myrkur would spurn Egan to respond. They waited not so patiently until it was clear he would not be responding so soon.

"It's nearly time." Griffin sighed.

"I think I prefer portaling." Riona winced. She didn't like the disturbing sensation of an entire village moving of its own accord.

"It's definitely not my favorite way to travel." Griffin took her hand and left for the town center. After weeks of living on top of each other in the confines of Aghadoon, the village was eerily quiet without the children and their families.

"Feels huge now with just the four of us here, doesn't it?" Brea asked as they joined her and Lochlan on the green lawn surrounded by the ancient numbered stones.

Brea spoke the words of power that set the stones in motion. The village turned in a slow circle, gaining speed as Brea finished the traveling spell that would transport Aghadoon to Eldur. A thick fog crept across the village as they disappeared from the rolling green hills of Fargelsi.

"Yeah, I'd definitely rather portal." Riona clenched Griffin's hand, her wings spreading to wind around them. As the spinning village came to an abrupt stop, Griffin smiled down at her from the cocoon of her silken wings.

"You freaked out," he teased.

"That was a freaky thing we just did." She let her wings slip from his shoulders with a shrug.

"We are so not in Kansas anymore," Brea said.

As long as he lived, he would never understand that woman.

As the fog cleared from Aghadoon, the vast night sky stretched across the Eldur deserts. They would leave for the palace in the morning to meet with Alona and catch her up to speed with their plans. But for the evening, they would do what they had done every night since leaving Eldur. Study.

"If I never see another book on Fargelsi magic, it will be too soon." Lochlan slammed his book closed and leaned back in his chair. "The spells are a nightmare, I don't know how any of you actually learn to perform your magic."

"It's tedious work." Brea nodded. "But it's fascinating." She hummed as she kept her nose stuck in a book on the complexities of spell work involving herbology. "I never knew there were so many poisonous plants in Fargelsi. Everything there really is trying to kill you." She turned the page.

Lochlan shared a bored look with Griffin. If he knew his brother at all—and he was getting to know him quite well—Lochlan was ready for a chance to fight. Anything to bring them out of the mind numbing task they'd been at for months now. Griffin was of the same mind.

"This is interesting." Riona paced back to the table with a weathered scroll trailing behind her. "It's about the book of power."

"So you're saying you've found a book about a book?" Lochlan leaned his head against the table.

"It seems to explain the nature of the book and how it works as a key to the library. Neeve was right, the contents of the library are vast." Her eyes scanned the faded script, and her breath hitched.

"What is it?" Griffin pressed a hand against her back as she sank into the seat beside him.

"For the book to function properly, it must have a keeper. A fae tasked with tracking the movement of the book. This keeper is responsible for what the book chooses to show those who come in contact with it." Riona lowered the scroll to the table looking to Brea for confirmation. "Like some sort of ... filter."

"Grainne must have been the last keeper," Brea mused. "I wonder ... do you think she and her descendants created this village to ... take over the role of keeper? So a single fae keeper couldn't become corrupted by the power of the book?"

"If she was the last, then Mother has surely taken on that role now." Griffin ran his thumb across the spine of the book he'd been studying.

"Which would make her responsible for the tear in the veil." Lochlan's jaw grew rigid with tension. "She's responsible for Tia and Toby's suffering. All of it." He pushed back from the table. "I need some air." He stormed out of the room, his footsteps thudded across the cobblestones leading away from the library.

"I'll go check on him." Brea rose from her seat.

"Let me." Griffin moved to follow his brother.

Griffin found Lochlan sitting on one of the ancient stones in the town center, his elbows resting on his knees as the moonlight illuminated his blond hair that was so like their mother's. In many ways his older brother was a lot like their mother. Stoic and firm. But he had a nobility that came from their father. A strength of character Griffin completely lacked.

Griffin sat on the ground beside the stone.

"Do you remember her?" Lochlan asked.

"Not really." Griffin pulled his knees up toward his chest. "I have vague ... feelings of her. But no clear memories."

"I don't have a single memory of her." Lochlan's gaze drifted toward his. "Not one."

"We were both terribly young when they died."

"I remember Father." Lochlan shook his head. "I remember so much of him. Yet, I can't recall anything about the woman who gave us life." He leaned back, lifting his face to the moon. "This whole time I've been trying so hard to see the good in her. Father was a great man. A respected king. He would not marry a woman without honor. At least that's what I told myself."

"I have struggled with similar thoughts. Unable to decide which side she's on or if she can be trusted at all." Griffin turned toward his brother, hoping to find the right words to comfort him.

"I am afraid Enis is on Enis' side," Lochlan scoffed.

"The book has been her life for so long—"

"Don't make excuses for her, brother. She could have come home when we were young. She and Father took Brea to the human world when she was a baby. After Father died, she was trapped in the human realm. But Enis knew where Brea lived. She knew one of us would be watching over her. She knew one or both of us would come for her when the time was right. She could have found us."

"She didn't want to, Loch. It's as simple as that. She gave us up for the power of the book. I know that hurts. It cuts deep. But the fact is, we were both raised by loving mothers that were nothing like Enis. As unhinged as Regan proved to be, she was still there when Enis was not. She loved me as much as if she'd given birth to me. As much as Faolan and Tierney loved you and Alona."

"Aye, they loved me well." Lochlan looked down at his hands.

"Perhaps the O'Shea brothers are destined to choose their own family?" Griffin said softly. "Blood has never mattered to us."

Lochlan nodded, laying a hand on Griffin's shoulder. "Maybe it's never mattered before, but you and I are brothers through blood and by choice."

"It took us long enough to get here." Griffin snorted a laugh.

"Thirty years too late is better than never, I suppose." Lochlan grinned.

"It's getting late, maybe we should call it a night. I do have a rather pretty Dark Fae waiting for me. And I'm sure Brea is twisting herself up into knots wondering if you're okay."

"Riona is good for you, brother."

"I don't think you approved of her much in the beginning." Griffin and Lochlan trudged through the dark streets back to the temporary home they shared with Riona and Brea.

"I did not trust her."

"What changed your mind?"

"She took care of my son when I could not. For that, she will always have my loyalty and respect. And she has very good taste in fae. She had the good sense to choose my slightly less handsome brother." Lochlan clapped him on the back.

"You underestimate the red hair. The ladies—and the males—quite like it."

"I said slightly less." Lochlan shrugged. "That's the most you'll get out of me."

Griffin let them into the dark house with a laugh. "You are every inch the ice king they call you."

"Who calls me that?" Lochlan blanched.

"Everyone. Night, Loch." Griffin chuckled at the blank look on his brother's face.

Without the kids running amok, the house was quiet.

"Riona?" Griffin stepped into the room they normally shared with Gulliver.

"Everything okay?" She turned to him from her seat at the table.

"We're good." Griffin nodded, not wanting to let himself think overmuch about what just passed between him and his brother, not when he was keeping the key to breaking the marriage magic a secret.

"Good, because we got a response." The spelled journal sat on the table in front of her. "But it's not who we thought it would be."

"Who's the response from?"

"Your mother."

CHAPTER 18

GRIFFIN

Raudur city looked as if a battle had never taken place among the streets. The windows that were boarded up after Egan's arrival now stood open, letting the Eldurian people resume their lives once more. Shopkeepers sold their wares in the marketplaces across the city where the people congregated.

As Griffin followed Lochlan and Brea through the busy streets, he took everything in. It all seemed so... normal. Even the Dark Fae mingling with the Eldurians didn't look out of place.

It was mid-morning when they rode past an ogre standing guard at the palace gates. He stared down at them, his dark eyes finding Riona, recognition lighting in their depths. With a simple nod, he let them pass.

Eldurian, Iskaltian, and Dark Fae soldiers stood at intervals, guarding the royal family and all others inside the palace from dangers Griffin hated that they faced. The human queen had been left to fend off waves of stragglers from Myrkur, Light Fae prisoners—now released—and Dark Fae who didn't know how to live in peace.

And yet, the city thrived. Griffin didn't know what he'd expected. Egan had all but destroyed parts of the palace, but now it looked as it always had.

They reached the inner courtyard doors, and a familiar figure sprinted out, her pale pink dress bunched up in her hand to keep her from tripping. Griffin jumped from his horse to wrap his best friend in a hug. "Shauna." He squeezed her tighter. "You have no idea how good it is to see you."

Lochlan slid down and handed his reins to a groom who'd come running when they entered the courtyard. "I'm going to find Finn." He marched inside without another word.

Shauna slid her arm through Griffin's. "He's friendly, that one, isn't he?"

"Takes some warming up to." He laughed.

Brea joined them, turning a hopeful smile on Shauna. "My mother... is she—"

"She's well, Majesty." Shauna grinned. "And she awaits your arrival with your sister in the gardens."

Brea gripped her arm. "Shauna, thank you. For taking care of them." Griffin knew who she meant. It was the reason Shauna stayed in Eldur. To care for Faolan and Finn.

"Oh, it was a simple thing, your Majesty."

"Stop calling her that," Griffin hissed, jabbing her with his elbow playfully.

"Don't embarrass me in front of the queen," she hissed back before turning her attention back to Brea and dipping into a curtsy. "Your mother has been telling me stories about you, your Majesty."

Brea laughed at that. "You mean she's been filling your head about the great Brea Robinson." She held out a hand, urging Shauna to take it. "Come. We aren't strangers just because you now know my story, Shauna. On the way to the gardens you can tell me what lies my mother has filled your head with. And my name is Brea. I'm not really a queen, you know. I just married a king."

Shauna's eyes widened as she stepped away from Griffin and took Brea's hand before walking into the palace.

Griffin shook his head, wondering if it was wrong to smile when everything else was so dour. Maybe it was the only thing that was right. "And Brea steals another heart." She and Shauna had met briefly a few times, but Griffin hadn't seen them speak to each other directly before. Brea was a warm figure, one who was easy to love. And Shauna took to people easily, wanting, needing to trust them.

Riona lifted one brow and followed the other women. Griffin brought up the rear. He'd never spent much time in Eldur, always begging Regan to send others on missions to the kingdom his brother had grown up in.

Now, he saw it with new eyes. It was beautiful in its own way. Too hot and too crowded. But there was a kindness in the way servants met their eyes as they passed, offering smiles and nods, a warmth in the way the palace was designed to feel like one was almost outdoors. Archways lined the halls leading into various courtyards where fountains sat to be admired and gardens to be enjoyed.

But there was no time to enjoy Eldur. They had to be gone by nightfall. There was a purpose in their arrival here, a dark purpose.

Shauna led them to the tiered gardens where hanging vines wound up the archways leading to beauty that could only be found among the oasis cities of Eldur.

Alona saw them first, jumping from her seat. "Brea." She rushed forward to give her sister a hug. "We didn't know you were coming until we saw the village arrive last night. I will never get used to that." She pulled back.

Brea gave her a sad smile. "I'm afraid we can't stay long." She crossed the garden to hug her mother.

Griffin watched as Shauna took a seat next to Faolan and the two shared a smile. No. That couldn't be right. He hid his gasp behind a cough and thumped his chest. Ten years ago, he'd seen Faolan's wife die in the battle against Regan. Since then, she'd lived in the palace she once ruled, though she abdicated the throne for Alona.

"Ignore Griffin." Brea shot him a look. "He seems to have forgotten how to breathe."

"Would you like tea?" Alona waved to a tea cart at the edge of the garden with a queenly flick of her hand. Of all the fae queens, the human was the only one who'd been bred as royalty, and it showed. There was a stiffness to her the others didn't possess.

Only her husband softened that in her.

"Brea." Faolan smiled. "There's also Eldur brew."

Brea pumped her fist and ran toward the cart while Riona stepped to the edge of the gardens, peering out over the city.

Griffin sat on a stone bench across from the two Eldurian queens. "We have a lot to tell you. And none of it is good."

It took longer than Griffin wished to explain everything that had happened with Alona's frequent questions interrupting him, and even longer to tell of their plan.

She leaned forward. "So, your plan is really that you have no plan?"

He bristled at that. "That is not a fair assessment. We are going to Myrkur."

"With soldiers. And once you get there, you will find this rift... somehow. Then you will seek out King Egan by doing... something."

"My mother." Lochlan's voice shocked them all as he stepped out into the gardens. "Enis will tell us what to do."

"And you trust her?" Alona gave him a skeptical look.

"We have no other choice." His face softened. "Finn is asking for you."

Alona shot to her feet. "He's awake?"

Griffin leaned against the door to Finn's room, wondering if he should be here. They'd moved Finn from the healer's ward so he could rest in his own bed. Alona and Lochlan wouldn't leave his side. His father, a member of Alona's guard, came by, speaking in low tones with Faolan.

As Lochlan sat on the edge of the bed laughing with his friend, Griffin waited for the jealousy to come. He'd spent his life watching them at dual state functions act as brothers in a way Griffin never got to. Envy was a normal feeling for him.

But now, it didn't come. Instead, he only felt an immense relief his brother didn't lose someone who meant so much to him.

Riona and Brea had left to gather a unit of soldiers to bring them into the village. Griffin tried to go with them, but Alona had more to speak with him about.

She crossed the room to stand at his side and folded her arms across her chest. "You told me my children are in Fargelsi with Neeve, and I trust her with their lives, but I need you to tell me they're okay. That I will get them back when Eldur is safe."

Despite her skepticism of him, Alona was not only a queen, but a worried mother, and he had to remember that. "They're smart kids. It's hard on all of us, you know. I left my son in Fargelsi. Brea's four children are there as well. It is the safest place for them with Neeve and all of Fargelsi protecting them. I know you think we are trusting the wrong person in Enis, and I'm as skeptical of her as anyone, but we can no longer just sort through a library we'll never get through to prevent Egan from doing evil. We have to stop him."

"I know. We will not be safe until he is gone."

"I don't make promises about children anymore." He pushed away from the doorframe. "But I can say we won't stop fighting Egan until every last one of us is dead. Because we are fighting for your children, and for mine and Lochlan's, and every other fae child."

A small smile curved her lips. "You're not such a bad fae, Griffin."

"We are who we choose to be." It was a lesson he'd had to learn the hard way—by making the wrong choices.

Alona returned to Finn as Lochlan walked toward the door. Faolan stepped in front of him, and Griffin couldn't help watching them, imagining if things had been different, if a better version of Regan could stand in front of him now.

Faolan reached down to take both his hands. "I just need to say this, Loch. Enis O'Shea was once my best friend. She gave birth to you and saved Brea. I never imagined she was still alive or that she'd get mixed up in such a mess. But Lochlan, whatever that woman does to you, she is not your mother. She cannot break your heart because she does not belong in there. Do you hear me? *I* am your mother."

Griffin didn't like to see his brother so vulnerable. As Lochlan let

Faolan wrap him in a hug, he turned away, needing to escape the palace before everything became too much. There was too much emotion that sounded like goodbye.

And he refused to say any goodbyes.

Marching through the halls, he burst out into the courtyard, not bothering to call for a groom as he started up the road to the stables. It was time for him to be a soldier, to prepare for the next step in this war.

He led his horse from one of the stalls and saddled him quickly before pulling himself up and thundering down the road and across the bridge into the desert sands and the village that would take them to the final battle.

Faolan's words to Lochlan ran through Griffin's mind. *I am your mother.*

She was right. Enis didn't deserve to be trusted just because she gave birth to two Iskalt princes.

Griffin held the quill hovering over the journal. It was strange knowing his mother was on the other side of these messages now, talking to him more than she ever had.

But he needed to know he could believe her when she said it was time to get the book away from Egan. If she truly was this keeper of the book, she only wanted it safe.

And she'd have to prove it.

Enis, I need to know everything you tell me is the truth. How will I know you won't betray us to Egan again?

He waited a long moment, staring at his own words before closing the book and setting it aside. She'd respond when she saw the message.

A crash sounded from the room next to his, but he was supposed to be the only one in the house. Taking silent steps, he retrieved a knife from the table near the door and walked from his room. Rounding the corner, he prepared to fight an intruder. It was probably a Dark Fae who'd found their way into the village by tricking it with their intentions. When they'd altered that magic, they all knew it was a risk.

The door stood ajar, and Griffin pushed it open slowly before bursting into the room, his knife raised. He froze when three familiar and terrified faces looked back at him.

"Oh, it's just Griff." Gulliver relaxed and flashed his ornery smile at Tia and Toby. "It's okay."

Griffin lowered the knife slowly, anger burning in him at his son. "What are you doing here?" he grit out.

Gulliver backed up. "Okay, I know you're mad, but Griff, there's a good reason. I promise."

Setting the knife down, Griffin crossed his arms. "Speak, boy."

"Well." Griffin shot Tia a helpless look. "We... uh... we wanted to stay."

That was his good reason?

Tia jumped in. "He means you need us."

"Oh, we do, do we?"

She nodded, her hair bouncing around her shoulders. "You're going into Myrkur, and after everything, you can't tell us we're too young for this."

"Don't tell me Nessa is hiding somewhere here too." He searched the room.

"Oh, no." Gulliver rolled his eyes. "She's *such* a rule follower."

"Well, at least one of you has sense." He rubbed a hand over his face. "Brea and Lochlan are going to—"

"Freak?" Gulliver smiled proudly at his human phrase. "We know. Sooo..."

"You could just not tell them," Toby finished.

"You too?" Griffin sent him a look of betrayal. "I figured these two dragged you into this."

"No way." Gulliver gave Griffin a stern look. "I'm a good boy. This was all Toby's idea."

Toby snorted-laughed, but Tia ignored them both, stepping in front of Griffin.

"What if we're right?" She looked up at him with pleading eyes. "Hasn't everyone kept saying we'll do what it takes? What if it takes me and Toby?"

"And me," Gulliver piped in.

Tia continued. "We brought the prison magic down. Please, Uncle Griff, let us finish the job. This is our world too, and we don't want to keep having to fight. Maybe if we're there, it can be the last time. For all of us."

Griffin sighed, unable to tell Tia she was wrong. When Lochlan told him he was making the twins stay in Fargelsi, something hadn't felt right about that. Maybe their magic would be needed, and he didn't want to fight anymore—just like her. "I have to tell your parents."

She shook her head, her eyes glassing over. "They'll take us to Fargelsi. Please, just keep this a secret a little while longer."

Brea would hate him for this. He thought about the marriage magic sitting in his room. She'd hate him for keeping a lot of things from her. But if it meant defeating Egan... he'd do whatever it took.

Gulliver gave him a triumphant smile the moment he recognized they'd won.

A knock at the door had the kids scrambling for cover. Except it wasn't their parents. Shauna pushed open the door, her brow arching as she caught sight of Gulliver's tail poking out from under the blanket he'd covered himself in.

Griffin joined her in the hall. "Shh, we aren't supposed to tell anyone they're there."

Shauna shrugged. "You'll have to give the kid a hug for me then. I just wanted to see you before you left."

His shoulders dropped as they stepped from the house to survey the activity of soldiers entering the village. "I was hoping you'd come with us." He eyed her, wondering if she'd admit what he suspected.

Her lips curved down. "I want to. For Hector. But I can't leave this place, Griff. I'm needed here. They lost a lot of their healers in the battle, and..." She pushed out a breath. "I can't leave her."

He wrapped an arm around her. "I know." His eyes found Riona directing a handful of soldiers. They planned to leave most of the Iskaltians who hadn't already returned to Iskalt in Eldur to continue keeping the roving bands of fae at bay and take most of the Dark Fae with them to Myrkur. "I would go where she is too."

Shauna leaned into him. "Be safe, yeah?"

"Always."

"This isn't goodbye."

"Definitely not." He kissed the side of her head, wondering how long it would be before he saw her again.

As Shauna turned to leave, Gulliver burst from the house. "Shauna!"

She turned to catch him in a hug. "Take care of our guy, Gullie."

"I will. I won't let anything happen to him in Myr."

She smiled and pressed her lips to the top of his head. "I know you won't."

They hugged for a moment longer before Shauna walked from the village. Griffin turned to Gulliver and swatted him toward the house. "Get inside before Brea sees you." He couldn't believe the words leaving his mouth, but he'd made his choice to keep their secret.

Gulliver skipped back to the room where the twins hid, and Griffin returned to his own, flipping open the journal to find his mother's message.

You want good faith information?

Your fae inside Myrkur are alive. They gave this journal to me freely.

Hector. Could it be true? Griffin always figured Hector would have destroyed the journal before letting Egan get it again. But now... he was alive?

Griffin had to believe her. He scrawled his response across the page.

Okay, I'm listening.

She took little time to respond.

You cannot wait any longer if we are to save the human realm.

It is time.

CHAPTER 19

GRIFFIN

Rain soaked the village, welcoming the Dark Fae home to Myrkur. Griffin stood on the edge of the village, staring out at the sparse forest where trees struggled to keep their leaves. They weren't far from the rocky mountain passes leading to Kvek's stronghold he'd once broken into when he was injured.

When he'd thought he was going to die.

There were very few memories he had of Myrkur that were good, but a few hours ride from here was Fela where he'd become the person he was.

Somewhere in this harsh terrain was Hector, once again trying to survive under Egan's rule.

"This darkness feels familiar." Brea stepped up beside him. "There's a coldness to it, isn't there?" She had a hood pulled up over her dark hair, shielding her face from the drizzling rain.

"For a long time, it was all I knew." Brea and Lochlan experienced the darkness twice before, but they never had to live with it for a prolonged period. "But we cannot stay here long. A few days at most."

She nodded. They'd had this discussion many times. With Griffin and Lochlan having night magic, being in a fae realm where darkness was all they saw would exhaust them, maybe even kill them if they stayed too long. They'd seen it before.

"Is it day or night?" she asked, looking to the sky.

"It's early morning." Even with the rain, the air held a freshness in the mornings.

She nodded. "I've pictured the kind of place you lived, Griff, but I don't think I even imagined this." She gestured to the dark, barren land.

He had no energy for explaining the harshness of a life in Myrkur, so he turned away, eyeing the soldiers who went about their morning routines preparing for whatever was to come. The Dark Fae were used to the inky mornings.

"Have we heard from Enis today?" Brea asked.

Griffin sighed. His mother was supposed to send them the location of the rift. It seemed so simple, but she'd been silent for days. "No. But I'll keep checking."

She nodded. "So, there's a reason I came to find you before Lochlan woke."

He didn't like the sound of that. "And?"

She sucked in a breath. "So, this marriage bond. I've been thinking about it. It's something we haven't completely discussed between the three of us, well four with Riona. But I think we can live with it. I think we both know how much it'll hurt after this battle is over and we go our separate ways, so I have a proposal."

"Brea—"

"No, listen to me. The worst part last time was when we were too far apart. But we don't have to be. You and Riona can come to live in Iskalt. She can help any Dark Fae settle there who so choose, and you can join Lochlan's counsel where you belong."

"Brea—"

"Think about it, Griff. Both Iskalt royals back in the palace? The people would rejoice."

"I know how to break the magic."

Brea froze, her lips no longer moving.

A sigh rattled through Griffin. This was the moment she lost faith in him. Again. "Come with me."

Brea silently followed him back to the house. Lochlan slept still, and the kids didn't make any sounds. Riona had left in the middle of the night, telling Griffin she wanted to explore the village being rebuilt near the palace. She'd covered her tattoos, and her head, making her look like any other Slyph.

She knew what she was doing.

Unlike Griffin.

He led Brea into his room and retrieved the leather scroll from its hiding place. Handing it to Brea, he waited as she unrolled it, her eyes scanning the words. "Griff." She sounded more surprised than angry. "When did you find this?"

"A few weeks ago. I know I should have told you, but this magic... if we burned it and saved ourselves this pain, it doesn't only affect us. Every married couple in the kingdoms would lose their marriage bonds."

Tears gathered in the corners of her eyes. "We shouldn't have to make that choice."

He sat on the corner of the bed. "I've studied the scroll. Marriage magic once had a great purpose. It says it was created hundreds of years ago when fae couldn't perform magic on their own. They borrowed strength from others, and the bond made that easier. But the world has changed, fae and magic have evolved. Our powers have grown to immense levels, and we no longer need one another to use it."

Brea slumped onto the bed next to him. "It's like O'Rourke twin magic. Tia borrows power from Toby. Every fae used to do that?"

He nodded. "Twins were once the only fae who didn't need the marriage magic to... boost their natural abilities. Now, only O'Rourke royal twins do, and marriage magic has become an obsolete power, meant to hold people together for long fae lives. In the end... it strips us of our free will." He took her shaking hand in his. "You and I weren't meant to be together, yet the magic forced it on us. Loving someone should be a choice. Not once, but every single day. Magic can't take its place."

He knew that now, the difference between love and magic, his feelings for Brea and what he felt for Riona.

Brea swallowed a sob and leaned her head on his shoulder. "Every single day."

"Are you mad at me?"

She shook her head. "I can't say I know what I'd have done if I found it either. We all do the best we can, Griff. But I don't think it is only for us to decide what to do with it."

She was right. Of course she was. He looked down at her. "When this is over, once Egan can't torment us anymore, then we will make a decision."

"Griffin O'Shea!" Lochlan's voice echoed through the house.

Brea bolted up, and Griffin walked out into the hall to find Lochlan staring into the spare room where the three kids gave him sheepish smiles.

Now, this... this angered Brea. She rounded on him. "Why is Lochlan yelling at you?" There was an accusation in her voice. "Toby, did Uncle Griff know you were here?"

Gulliver groaned. "He already told Lochlan he had." He shot Toby a betrayed look.

Griffin wished he could disappear right then.

Lochlan and Brea both advanced on Griffin, their eyes holding a kind of anger he hadn't seen in them. He backed up until he hit the wall.

"Hey," Gulliver yelled. "It wasn't his fault."

"It's okay, Gullie." Griffin met his brother's eyes. "I made my choice."

"You let them come." Lochlan's eyes narrowed. "To Myrkur!"

"Actually, he didn't know we were here."

"Quiet, Tia," both her parents yelled.

"No." She stepped between them and Lochlan. "It's our fault. You leave Uncle Griff alone. We just want to help."

"You don't know what you're getting in to." Lochlan looked over her, not taking his eyes from his brother.

"I do. We all do. I've done more in this fight than you, Papa!" Her words echoed down the hall.

Some of Brea's anger dropped as she looked to her daughter and sighed. She wrapped an arm around Tia. "Let's let them talk."

"Mama, I deserve to be here."

"I know, honey." Brea sounded more tired than anything as she led the kids back into the room. "Now, tell me how you managed to keep yourselves hidden? That's impressive." She closed the door, leaving Lochlan and Griffin staring at each other.

Lochlan's jaw clenched. "You are not their father, Griffin."

"I know. Loch—"

"No, I need you to hear this. I don't care whose biological children they are. I have raised them since birth. I named them and held them when they hurt. I have feared for them every day of their lives because I love them so much it physically hurts. If anything happens to them—"

"I know. Loch, I know." He always had. It didn't matter who'd fathered them over ten years ago, only who'd been a father to them for ten years. "You have to believe me. I would *never* take that away from you. You, Brea, and the kids... that's *your* family. I'm their uncle and will never be anything more. But you also have to see how amazing they are. Tia and Toby could be the difference in this fight. They have been before. I've seen it."

"I don't want them to be the difference, I just want them to be my kids." He hung his head and moved to lean against the wall next to Griffin. "This wasn't your decision to make."

"I know."

"Then why did you make it?"

Griffin was quiet for a long moment. "Because I want them to grow up in the kind of world we never had."

"And what world is that?"

"One at peace. If they stay here, Loch, maybe they can get to be kids when this is over."

Lochlan leaned his head back. "Why do I always love the special ones?"

A laugh burst out of Griffin. Lochlan had fallen in love with Brea when she was destined to defeat Regan. "I am sorry, Loch. I should have told you they were here."

"I understand why you did it. I don't agree, but I understand." He pushed away from the wall. "I'm going to go be with my family." He gave Griffin one final look, nodded, and entered the room.

Griffin left the house behind, stepping out into the rain that had grown steadier as the day wore on. He walked toward the center of the village where their coordinates were burned into the stones. The human numbers transformed to ancient runes in the fae realm, but it still led them to their specific location.

Shaking wet hair out of his face, Griffin looked to the sky, ready for whatever came. He found a stone bench and sat down.

Movement caught his eye moments before someone sat beside him.

"You sure like to create trouble, Griffin." Gulliver nudged him. "You should try not to do that."

Griffin laughed. "Says the thief." He bumped Gulliver's shoulder.

"I'm sorry you can't be their father."

"You heard all that, did you?"

Gulliver nodded.

Griffin wiped rain out of his face. "Well, I'm not sorry. I still get to be your father."

He bit back a smile, water dripping from his lips. "True. Just stop fighting with Lochlan, please. It's kind of embarrassing for all of us."

Griffin wrapped an arm around Gulliver and pulled him close. "I'm embarrassing, huh?"

"Very much."

"Good." He smiled.

"You're very strange."

He only shook his head with a laugh. Through the rain, he caught sight of mostly dark wings and the fae they belonged to.

Riona had returned, and it warmed him despite the rain to have her near.

She approached the bench and both of them stood to greet her. Griffin pulled her into a hug with him and Gulliver.

"What has gotten into you?" Riona groaned. "And how is Gullie here?"

"Old news, Riona. You know what's also old news? Griffin is acting odd." Gulliver agreed. "If you two are going to kiss now, I'm definitely leaving." He practically ran from them.

Griffin laughed, knowing this feeling of contentment should wait until after they defeated Egan. But maybe it didn't have to. "I'm definitely going to kiss you."

The rain dampened the kiss, sliding his lips against hers. He'd wanted to prepare for whatever came here in Myrkur, and this was the best preparation there was.

CHAPTER 20

RIONA

Riona and Griffin led the way along the rocky trail through the mountains far above Chieftain Kvek's fortress. Part of her worried they were walking into a trap. The other part of her genuinely hoped Enis would come through for her sons. They needed to know there was some spark of goodness within her.

She'd cared enough to help the children escape Eldur, perhaps she cared enough for her sons to help them defeat Egan.

"It's just up ahead." Griffin studied the map Enis had sketched in the journal for them.

The Iskaltians and other Light Fae trailing along behind them complained about the darkness, but to Riona, this was her natural habitat. She could make her way through these mountains in her sleep. As they crept along the narrow trail, they came to a ridge. A barren valley stretched out below them. Wide and grassy, it would have seemed beautiful to her had she never witnessed the rolling green hills of Fargelsi.

"The rift lies at the north side of the valley." Griffin moved to pick their pathway down the steep ridge into the valley. Riona followed, moving between boulders and dry patches of dirt where nothing grew. Their friends trailed them, with the small force of soldiers they brought with them from Aghadoon.

"I think I can see it," Riona said, peering ahead of Griffin.

"Can you?" He gave her a skeptical look.

"No she's right. I can see it too." Gulliver squinted in the moonlight.

"I don't see anything."

"Well, we are Dark Fae, we can see better than you." She could just make out the faint edges of the tear. She couldn't see into the human world beyond, but she could almost feel the darkness seeping out of Myrkur through the narrow gap. "It's just there." She pointed with a shaky hand. "Can't you feel it? Evil magic has happened here." Riona and Gulliver grasped hands as if they could feel the taint of it. Riona had the sudden urge to leave the valley at once. "Do not leave my side." She pulled Gulliver closer.

"I don't feel or see anything." Lochlan pushed past her. "But if you do, that's good enough for us."

"I wonder if it's their defensive magic at work?" Brea moved forward, clutching Toby and Tia's hands. Riona knew their parents didn't want them here any more than she and Griffin wanted Gulliver here, but they had each played important roles in this war. It was fitting they get to witness the end of it.

"Let's get this done." Lochlan turned to direct the small army to surround them for protection should Enis betray them and show up with Egan and his dwindling forces.

"Can you handle this alone?" Griffin looked to Brea as she approached the rift clutching a book from the library. It contained the spells she and Neeve had used in the human realm to try to seal the rift once before. They were hoping it would be more successful from this side of the rift, and now they were staring right at it.

"I can handle it." Brea nodded. "It was easier with Neeve's help, but I can manage it alone just as well."

"And I'll be here if you need me, Mama," Tia called from the sidelines where Lochlan stood guard over her and her brother.

"Good luck." Riona patted Brea on the shoulder and went with Gulliver to stand with the others.

Riona watched as Brea opened the book of spells and began muttering the ancient words that meant little to Riona. Griffin came to stand beside her, clutching Gulliver between them.

"I should fly up to the ridge and circle overhead to make sure we aren't taken by surprise."

Griffin grabbed her hand tight in his. "Please stay. We have sentries posted all across the valley."

Riona nodded, comforted by the thought he wanted her near.

Brea's Gelsi magic was different from her Eldur magic that glowed yellow whenever she embraced her power. When she used her Gelsi magic, it wasn't as flashy, but the massive effort and focus it took was so much more impressive.

"That's not gonna work, Mama," Tia yelled, causing Lochlan to shush her. "Well, it's not going to fix it," she muttered to herself. Having witnessed what Tia and Toby could do with their magic, Riona was inclined to agree with the kid.

"The darkness is shifting," Griffin said. "She's pulling it back through the rift." They watched in silence as Brea moved through page after page of complicated spell work. She reminded Riona of an adult version of Tia when she'd brought down the barrier surrounding Myrkur. If Brea was any indication of what her daughter would be like when she was grown, Tia would be a force of nature when she came into her full magic.

"It is done." Brea stumbled forward as she closed the book.

"It's gone." Gulliver looked up at Griffin. "I can't see it anymore, can you?" He turned to Riona.

"I don't see the tear either. It's sealed."

A cheer went up behind them as the news spread through the ranks of soldiers surrounding them.

"Lochlan, can you go check it?" Brea scowled up at the place where the rift was only a few moments ago. "Something doesn't feel right."

"Should we give it some time first?" Lochlan turned to his brother.

"We can portal to the farm once we get back to Aghadoon. I don't like being out in the open here."

"Agreed. Especially with the children and the eventuality of me and Griff growing weak without the sun to relieve us of magic for a time." Lochlan took Tia and Toby's hands, and they returned to the path they took to get here.

Riona looked over her shoulder, but she wasn't sure if what she saw was part of the rift or an afterimage of it. She agreed with Brea, something didn't feel right.

"The darkness is returning. Again." Griffin emerged from Lochlan's portal and dropped down beside Riona on the grassy lawn of the village center where she and Brea waited.

"So, it didn't work?" Brea's shoulders fell.

"No." Lochlan said as he followed his brother back from the human realm just moments after they'd left. "We will have to find another solution." He joined his family on the blanket Brea had set out for their evening picnic.

Griffin and Lochlan should have been gone for hours, waiting in the daylight of the human realm to return to the darkness of Myrkur once the moon rose. They arrived to discover it was already night in the middle of the afternoon, meaning the rift was still open.

"You didn't fix it right, Mama." Tia sat in the middle of the grassy lawn, making flowers grow up around her for the daisy chains she was making. She braided the long-stemmed flowers into crowns for Gulliver and Toby.

"I know, baby," Brea muttered absently. "Loch, I just don't think I can take another minute of searching in that library for a spell that might or might not work. It's exhausting."

"I second that." Griffin lay back in the cool grass, tugging at Tia's flower chains, trying not to laugh when she shot him a death glare just like her mother's.

"So where does that leave us?" Riona asked. She would be all too happy to never set foot in that library again, but they had to find a solution. Who knew what atrocities might happen to the humans if the rift was left open much longer.

"Why can't we just make a new one?" Tia said with a shrug.

"A new what?" Brea turned toward her daughter with a frown.

"A new spell. If the old one didn't work to close the tear in the veil, I should just make a new one instead of wasting so much time looking for some old spell that might not even work." Tia tied her chain of violets in a loop and placed it on Griffin's head. Then she went to work growing blue flowers for a new chain.

"No." Lochlan and Brea said in unison. "Absolutely not."

"Crafting new spells is dangerous, honey," Brea said. "Even the simplest spell can go wrong if you don't construct the words of power just so. For something as complex as this situation, it's impossible."

"No it's not, Mama." Tia glanced at Toby, sporting a crown of red poppies on his brow. "I know I could make a spell that would work."

"I don't know, maybe we should move the village back to Gelsi and brainstorm with Neeve and Dad. Between all of us, we have to find a solution that will work." Brea ignored her daughter, but Riona was beginning to think the girl might have the fresh perspective they needed. She was a child, but she was an inherently gifted one.

"We do need to move on soon. We can't take too much more of this endless night before it starts to affect our Iskalt magic." Lochlan scowled at his daughter when she stood to place a crown of blue irises on his head.

"That seems like an awful lot of moving around just to come right back here, Papa," Tia said, patting her father's long blond hair.

"Griff." Gulliver rolled his cat eyes at him. The orange marigolds on his head bobbed in the breeze.

"What?" Griffin stared blankly at him. But Gulliver just glared at him.

Finally Griffin sighed. "I think Gullie might have a point. We should listen to Tia's ideas."

"Griff, I don't want my daughter involved in this kind of dangerous magic. She's just a child." Brea was quick to put an end to such a discussion.

"And that decision falls to you and Lochlan." Griffin cast a worried look at Riona. She knew he was afraid of overstepping.

Well, Riona had no such hesitations. She'd never worried about overstepping in her life, and she wasn't about to start now. "If I may, neither of you were there when Tia and Toby worked together to dismantle the prison magic keeping thousands in bondage."

"How dare you." Brea bristled like an angry cat. "Our children were taken from us."

Griffin sat up to move beside Riona. "I think Riona just means that we actually got to witness your children performing complex magic better than most adults could on their best day. Tia was in control the whole time. It was astounding."

"I meant no disrespect," Riona rushed to say. "Your children were nothing short of incredible. If I hadn't seen it with my own eyes, I wouldn't have thought it possible of any child. They are young and innocent, but they are gifted with strong intuition. Tia's knowledge of Fargelsian magic seems unparalleled. I just wonder if we should hear her out."

"Thank you, Auntie Riona." Tia placed a chain of silver rosebuds around her neck.

Riona looked down at the flowers Tia had grown for her and something swelled inside her. It was an unfamiliar feeling, this ... emotion for a child that wasn't hers to love.

"You don't like it? I didn't want to give you dark flowers, so I thought silver would match your pretty wings." Tia stroked the silvery gray part of Riona's wings where the black and white met.

"They're beautiful." Riona smiled, patting the blanket beside her. "Why don't you sit and tell me why you think you can just make a new spell."

"I make new spells all the time." Tia shrugged and sat down on

Riona's lap, still braiding a chain of yellow daisies. "It's easy for me. Even the hard stuff. Mama and Papa think I'm being reckless, but I know what I'm doing. The language of power comes to me easily."

"Sweetheart, I know you are talented," Brea said. "I don't want you to ever think I don't believe in you. I do. I just don't want you to *have* to do this kind of magic before you're ready."

"But I am ready, Mama."

"Before we go so far as to make an entirely new spell, let's think about other options," Lochlan interjected. "What can we do that isn't so drastic, but also doesn't send us back into that library to chase phantom spells from now to the end of time?"

They all fell silent trying to think of a solution. Riona didn't have a clue when it came to all things magic, but she watched Tia's hands move through the motions of braiding. The little girl's mind was clearly somewhere else.

"What if we reversed it?" Tia finally said, picking up her chain of daisies.

"Reversed what?" Brea moved to sit in front of her daughter.

"The spell you did, Mama. The one that didn't work the other two times."

"Reverse it how?" Brea frowned.

"If you won't let me make a new spell, we could reconstruct that one. Reverse the magic so it doesn't pull the darkness from the human realm back into Myrkur, but instead pushes the daylight from the human world back here."

"This land has always been dark," Riona said. She couldn't imagine a version of Myrkur that existed in daylight.

Tia leaned her head back against Riona's shoulder and looked up at her. "Yeah, but what if it wasn't?"

"Can you do that?" Riona asked Brea, though she had no doubt in her mind the child sitting in her lap playing with flower chains could do it with one little hand tied behind her back.

"That is ..." Brea trailed off, staring at her daughter in awe.

"Brilliant," Lochlan finished for her. "Our daughter is a magical genius."

"I told you, Papa." Tia rolled her eyes, draping the chain of yellow daisies around her mother's neck.

Riona stared at the colorful flowers Tia had used for each of them. In her own way, she'd given them each a flower that represented the color of their magic.

CHAPTER 21

GRIFFIN

It turned out that Lochlan made Tia nervous with his loud pacing and grumbling, so Brea threw him out of the library. But then Tia asked if Uncle Griff could stay since he knew more of the ancient Fargelsian language.

That did not go over well with Lochlan.

"Loch." Griffin stood on the front porch of the building. "She's just afraid of disappointing you. It's messing with her work."

Lochlan gave a curt nod before he left them to their work.

Brea had turned the reconstructive magic project into an art project. The library table was covered in brown paper and an assortment of crayons and markers.

"Darling, is this part right?" Brea pointed to the childish blue scribble Tia had just handed her.

Tia rolled her eyes and read the phrase.

"Snúou töfrunum við til ao koma ljósi til lands þar sem aeins er nótt."

"That's right, Mama. It basically means, 'turn the magic around to bring light to a land where there is only night.'"

"Are you sure? Do you think the intent should reverse with the subject?"

"No," Toby said from his end of the table where he and Gulliver were drawing crayon doodles. "Tia said it right. The subject of the spell *always* comes first, even in a reversal. Intent comes last because it's the most important part of each phrase that makes up a complex spell. Unless it's just one word. Then the intent is in the body movement and state of mind."

Brea and Griffin exchanged looks of confusion.

"I knew that." Brea erased what she'd just written on the brown paper.

"Toby can't perform the spells himself, Mama, but he knows the language and construction as well as I do. This is right." Tia slid the scrap of scribble back to her mother. "Can you trust us?"

"You know what, kiddo? This is your rodeo." Brea copied the partial spell into the notebook so they had a clear record of their work that wasn't in crayon. "I came into my magic when I was a lot older than you, but my magic was unique, like yours and Toby's. I need to remember how irritating it was when people used to tell me what I could and couldn't do with it."

"It is irritating." Tia's eyes scanned the spell they were trying to reverse engineer. She started to scribble more words and phrases, the tip of her pink tongue poking out between her lips. Some words she copied straight from the book—just in a different order that made little sense to Griffin—and some words he was almost certain she'd made up on the spot.

"What does this mean, honey?" Brea pointed to a word Tia had written in black marker surrounded by other phrases in pink crayon.

"*Sköpurn.*" Tia wrinkled her nose. "That's a bad word, Mama. But it's necessary for the intent."

"I have a whole new appreciation for what my mothers went through when I was learning my magic." Brea bent to copy the new phrases into the book.

Pretty soon, Brea stopped asking questions and let Tia work her translations. Occasionally, Tia would call Toby over and the two would have what amounted to a philosophical discussion on the construction of sentences.

Brea looked up at Griffin as the two kids worked together on a particularly difficult part of the spell. "Am I a bad mother because my kids' power scares me?" she whispered, leaning in close to Griffin. "They're freaking me out."

"No, you're the best mother in the whole world, Brea. But I'm glad it's not just me." Griffin ran a hand through his hair. "How did they get to be so much smarter than us?"

"And they're only ten." Brea shook her head, stifling a laugh. "What happens when they're twenty?"

"They'll have solved all the world's problems by then." Griffin shared a look of pride with Brea and for the first time, he didn't feel uncomfortable about their unique family situation.

This time when they traveled to the valley where the rift in the veil was, they took as many soldiers with them as they could. They were lucky the first time, and neither Griffin nor Lochlan felt like their luck would hold out much longer. Egan was bound to make his next move soon.

"According to Enis' communications, Egan has been busy trying to browbeat her into widening the tear between the worlds, but she has told him that's beyond her abilities. It probably is." Griffin and Lochlan made their way into the valley with the others following close behind. The rear guard would protect them until they were in position.

Lochlan nodded. "He will figure out soon enough that Brea and Tia are more powerful than Enis, and he'll come for them."

"I have every confidence in our daughter's spell work." Brea and Riona came to stand with them. "We will fix this matter today, and then you two can go kill that awful man who calls himself a king." Brea patted Lochlan's arm and took Tia by the hand to approach the rift with Riona and her sharp eyes guiding them.

"You do realize we're just the brute force here?" Griffin stood watching with his arms folded across his chest.

"They don't even need us," Lochlan agreed with a grin.

"Speak for yourselves." Gulliver cupped his hands around his mouth. "A little to the left, Riona."

Riona guided Tia and Brea where Gulliver directed until they were right in front of the tear in the veil.

"I still don't see anything," Lochlan muttered.

"It's okay, your Majesty. I've got this." Gulliver patted the king's arm, and Griffin coughed to cover his laughter.

"It's cold in front of the tear." Riona rubbed her arms as she came to watch with them, their soldiers fanning out around them for protection.

Tia's clear voice joined Brea's as they worked together to perform the complex magic.

"This makes me insane." Lochlan paced. "I want to run up there and take my baby girl home to play in her nursery until she's forty. She shouldn't have to do this."

"No, but I'm grateful she *can* do this." Griffin clapped a hand on his brother's back. "She's so much like you, Loch."

Lochlan snorted irritably.

"I'm not just saying that. That kid adores you, and she's as stubborn and loyal and smart as her papa."

Lochlan shook his head. "She's smart like her mama. But I did always wonder where she got that red-blond hair from."

"Majesty!" A Slyph swooped down from the sky, her eyes wide with fright. "King Egan's guard is marching this way."

Lochlan immediately started issuing orders. "What are his numbers? Captain Macleod?"

"Slightly more than ours, your Majesty."

"Take your Slyph and prepare your archers."

"Yes, sire."

"And Macleod, please be careful. There are precious few of you, and we don't want to lose any of you."

Captain Macleod looked startled at Lochlan's kind words. "Thank you, your Majesty. We will be careful."

Lochlan shouted orders to his guard, sending them marching

around the valley to protect Tia and Brea.

"I'll take the east side, you take the west?" Griffin gripped his sword.

Lochlan pointed to the line of soldiers across the grassy glade in front of them. "Nothing that passes through our soldiers goes anywhere near Brea and our kids."

"Nothing." Griffin grasped his brother's hand.

"*We'll* take the east side." Riona came up beside him with Gulliver gripping a pair of daggers Riona must have given him.

"And I'll go with you, Papa." Toby stepped beside his father, lifting his chin in defiance. "I killed an ogre all by myself. I can handle this."

Lochlan nodded, handing his son a bow and quiver of arrows from his shoulder. "You're as good a shot as me. But stay behind me, son. Be prepared to help your sister if she calls for you."

"Yes, Papa." Toby gripped the bow, reaching for an arrow as the first rumble of Egan's guard rushed down from the ridge to the south of the valley. A swarm of Slyph beat their wings as they soared above them.

Griffin and Lochlan threw up shields just in time to keep the archer's arrows away from Brea and Tia.

"Back up." Lochlan called pointing to the sky and the line of Slyph coming in to land behind their guard. Even with Gulliver and Toby, they were outnumbered by half.

"Gulliver, stay behind us," Griffin called as he and Riona moved to block the approaching Slyph.

Toby fired off shots as fast as a grown fae, hitting his target every time.

Griffin's sword clashed with the Slyph in front of him, and he cut through wings and flesh without hesitation.

Riona and Gulliver fought together. Gulliver moving so quickly, their opponents didn't even see him until it was too late.

Lochlan and Griffin crashed through the Slyph, armed with bows and little more than their incredible strength. The brothers hacked through them, but Egan's guard pushed their forces farther and farther back. Soon, Lochlan and Griffin fought back-to-back, protecting Brea as she worked through the magic with Tia.

The ground trembled beneath their feet, and Griffin looked to the mountain paths behind them. "Ogres." More than a dozen of them ran down into the valley to clash with Egan's army.

A contingent of Slyph flew in from the mountains behind the rift. Six of them circled above Brea, flying low to protect them from the enemy's archers.

"It's Hector!" Gulliver shouted, pointing to the foot soldiers flooding the valley.

At their helm was Hector, his bull horns catching in the light.

Light? Griffin looked over his shoulder to see faint daylight streaming in through the rift. "She's doing it, Loch! The reversal is working."

"Griffin!" Hector shouted over the din of battle. "Enis said you would be here soon. We've been waiting up in the mountains for days."

"I am glad to see you, Brother." Griffin gripped his arm.

"My soldiers will take care of Egan. You take care of your spell casters and then get them out of here." Hector charged into the fray. Little by little, the battle moved to the north end of the valley, leaving Griffin, Riona, Lochlan, and the boys to stand guard over Brea and Tia.

"I need you, Toby!" Tia cried out, sounding weary from the stress of the last hour.

"I'm here, Tia." Toby ran to his twin's side, taking her hand, even though she didn't need to touch him to draw from his strength. His touch and his calming presence were what she needed now. "I'll always be here when you need me."

Griffin listened to the spell, trying to determine how far into it they were. By the time Tia had finished deconstructing and reversing the spell, nearly half of Brea's notebook was full of neatly penned phrases that made up the complex magic.

He watched as Brea turned the page, her voice rising in sync with her daughter's. They were nearing the end of the spell. Daylight flooded the valley, causing confusion and pain among the Dark Fae on Egan's side.

Tia's voice rose like a clear bell drowning out the chaos of battle.

"Risastór ljúka er lokio og allt er rétt mei heimana!" Tia and Brea's voices filled with the power they wielded together.

"Hafou pao opi en láttu engan fara í gegnum pessa opnun!" Tia said these final words alone.

Griffin held his breath. The last time his daughter finished performing such a spell, she passed out from the demand of more magic than she could handle.

This time, she stepped back, looking weary but elated as she high fived her mom.

"Toby, portal." Lochlan shouted as he charged toward Brea, grabbing Riona and Gulliver as he went.

Toby's O'Shea magic gathered in a crimson swirl in his palm, and as he spread his hands wide, a huge portal opened, and all seven of them charged through it. Toby leaped through his portal, letting it close behind him. Unlike his father and uncle's magic, Toby's allowed him to take them straight to the stone pillars marking the entrance into Aghadoon instead of going through the human realm.

"Did it work?" Lochlan panted, picking Tia up to keep her from falling over. She was dead on her feet but in high spirits.

"Did you see all the light, Papa?" Tia smiled through a yawn.

"I did, baby girl. I'm proud of you and Toby."

"What am I, chopped liver?" Brea stood with her hands on her hips.

"You know I don't know what that means." Lochlan carried Tia into Aghadoon, holding Toby's hand.

"Of course it worked." Brea scrambled along behind them. "My daughter is a genius."

"Oh, so she's *your* daughter when she's smart, but *mine* when she's done something horrid?"

"I don't do horrid things, Papa." Tia's head drooped to his shoulder, and she gave Griffin a wink before she fell asleep in her father's arms.

CHAPTER 22

RIONA

Hector walked into Aghadoon like a hero returned from battle. Blood streaked his hair, and he could barely hold his sword up, but a smile curved his normally stoic face.

Riona caught sight of him from the doorway of the library and walked out to meet him.

Gulliver raced past her. "Hector," he cheered. "You were amazing."

Hector dropped his sword to the stones and wrapped an arm around Gulliver's shoulders. "That battle was a long time in coming."

Riona crossed her arms. "And we're not done yet."

His smile fell. "No. We're not."

Riona had wanted to head to the palace as soon as they finished with the rift. Sunlight from the human realm streamed in through the rift and spread slowly across the surrounding areas. It would take some time, but Brea believed the daylight would reach across the land, eventually fading in the distance to leave parts of Myr in its natural darkness.

What they didn't have time for… sitting around.

But Griffin insisted they needed to recover, that going to the palace could wait a couple of days.

"Where are the others?" Hector searched the streams of soldiers who'd taken up residence in Aghadoon.

"The library. Doing more talking. Now isn't the time for talking. We need to act."

His shoulders fell, and he leaned on Gulliver support. "Can you take me there?"

She turned on her heel and marched back to the library.

"I've got you," Gulliver told Hector. "You're barely standing upright."

Riona led them into the library where all talk ceased until Griffin shot from his chair. "Hector." He grabbed his arm and led him to a seat. "You have no idea how good it is to see you."

Hector slumped into a chair. "Egan's force is destroyed."

"I brought all those who wanted to come marching through the night to get here. They're setting up camp outside the village. We're maybe two hundred strong. Many chose to return to their families and prepare for whatever comes after Egan."

"After Egan?" Griffin leaned against a set of shelves.

Hector nodded. "You plan to kill him, right? I have fae blocking all exits from the palace so he cannot leave."

That was good to know.

Lochlan rubbed the back of his neck. "We're trying to come up with a plan to enter the palace."

That was the problem. Riona sighed. "And I keep saying that you Light Fae and your need to plan everything is going to allow him time to get away. Is that what you want?"

"Yes," Griffin said to Hector. "Egan must die."

It was as if Riona hadn't said anything.

Hector nodded at that. "Well, I have been living among the remaining Dark Fae in Myrkur since I followed Egan from Eldur. Most of them expect Griffin to assume the throne once the king is gone, and they will support that."

Griffin pushed away from the shelf. "Me?"

He said it like it was an incredulous notion, but Riona would be lying if she said she hadn't had the thought as well. He made sense. This war wouldn't be won without him. Despite his lack of Dark Fae heritage, the fae loved him, and he had experience leading. After the very first time she'd faced him in the arena, his name was all she heard in the villages.

It was one of the reason's she'd spared his life in Kvek's stronghold. Who wanted to kill the hero? It would have made him a martyr. Now, he was perfect for the job. Even his magic could keep them safe. But the dark expression on his face told her a storm brewed inside him.

Hector went on telling Lochlan and Brea of how Enis found him and how they'd started working together, but Riona's only focus was on Griffin.

Without a word to anyone, he walked from the library into the dim light. This far from the breach, the daylight was a subtle glow on the horizon throughout the afternoon. Riona followed him without a word.

"Go back to the library, Riona," Griffin said.

"Not a chance." She caught up with him in the middle of the street and grabbed his arm, forcing him to turn.

Pain swirled in the depth of his gaze. This was not a man who had just been told the crown could be his if he chose. "None of what Hector said matters, Riona. You will recognize the rightful ruler when the time is right. That is your destiny."

"Forget about destiny, Griffin. This isn't about that. You and I understand each other. I know you." She stepped closer, her voice dropping. "You're scared."

"Scared?" he scoffed.

"Yes." She advanced on him, her wings reaching out behind her in dark intimidation. "You, Griffin O'Shea, are afraid to want power."

She could see the truth flash across his face as the stubbornness faded away. "I spent so many years being told I was going to be king of Fargelsi, and I did horrible things to make that come about. I can't be trusted, Riona. What if that yearning for power is what separates who I was from who I am?"

It was a similar question Riona had once. What if her yearning to be loved—once by her father figure in Egan—was what made her who she was? But she knew now it wasn't. "Griffin, your choices are what separates your past from your present. I don't think you could go back if you tried. I don't know if you have any right to be king of Myrkur, but even without the crown, you have power. Look at what you've done, what you've set in motion? It's because of you this war has happened, because of you we will finally be free."

He didn't speak for a long moment before reaching for her, folding her in a strong embrace. "Thank you."

"For what?" she murmured against his neck.

"Believing in me."

He kept an arm around her as they walked to the center of the village, neither ready to return to the library where those who didn't know Egan talked of what needed to be done.

"I get to kill him." She didn't need to explain her words.

A sigh rattled from Griffin. "Yes, you do."

"Come on." Riona tugged Griffin away, leading him to the edge of the village where they could see Hector's Dark Fae setting up camp.

Riona leaned her head on Griffin's shoulder. "This is why we need to leave as soon as we can. These fae... they deserve to be free. So do we."

She knew what Griffin would say.

"We have to get back to the library." He turned and hurried away. Griffin's movement was so sudden, she turned to stare after him, but he was already heading back the way they'd come.

Riona ran after him, following him in.

"Brea... Lochlan... Hector," he started. "We've been trying to find a way to repair the breach now that the magic has been reversed. But what if we don't?"

They stared at him, not saying a word.

"Think about it. The humans know something isn't right after weeks of darkness. If there was ever a time to leave the worlds open to each other, it's now. We could spend our entire lives trying to find whatever spell in this endless library would close it. I don't want to do that."

It wasn't a horrible idea. Riona couldn't stand the thought of more time within these walls with books she couldn't understand.

Lochlan stood. "Absolutely not." He walked from the library, unwilling to even discuss the possibility.

Brea rubbed her eyes. "It's... Give me tonight to talk to him. I lived in the human realm for the first eighteen years of my life. Humans are stronger, more resilient, and more open-minded than most fae think they are. But, Griff, this is a big thing. It is not a decision for only the four of us." She stood and put a hand on Hector's shoulder. "Most of us have been up all night. Let's discuss this more tomorrow with fresh minds. If we do this, the decision won't be made until after we face Egan."

Brea followed her husband's path, leaving only Hector at the table. "We have to worry about the Light Fae accepting us, and you'd like us to appeal to the humans as well?" Hector shook his head.

Riona thought of Nihal and how he'd lived his life in the human realm. "Hector, I think you'd be surprised how many Dark Fae live as humans." It made so much sense. To the human eye, they appeared no different. How many lived among the unsuspecting humans?

"Get some rest, Hector," Griffin said. "You've earned it."

Now, there were no more questions in Riona's mind, no more battles to fight save one.

And she had to do it alone.

Slipping out from under the mound of furs Griffin slept with, she rummaged in his bag for the book that would let her talk to Enis O'Shea. They'd conspired once before, but this time was different.

This time, they were on the same side.

Finding the quill, she wasted no time writing to her, her Dark Fae eyes seeing the words even in the dark.

I am coming to the palace. She didn't mention it was her and not Griffin. *Can I expect your aid to get in unseen?*

Enis didn't respond at first, but then her words appeared.

I will meet you at the fighting pits.

The fighting pits. It was perfect. The tunnels would take her straight into the dungeons.

Closing the book, she set it on the table next to the bed, placing the quill on top of it. Griffin would see the messages she hadn't erased and know where she'd gone, but by then it would be too late.

Pulling on leather armor, she prepared herself for the battle she knew was waiting for her. She tied her black braids back away from her face and slipped into her boots.

With one final glance at Griffin, she picked up her sword and left the room behind.

Once outside, she walked toward the edge of the village, flexing her wings as she looked up into the clear night sky. A sliver of a moon provided little light, and not a single star hung overhead.

Kicking off the ground, she leaped into the air and circled the village, looking down on it once more.

Violet eyes stared up at her from a doorway, his magic sparking along his skin.

"I'm sorry," she whispered, knowing he wouldn't be able to hear her.

Turning away from Griffin, she headed toward the palace where the fight she'd dreamed of awaited her arrival.

CHAPTER 23

GRIFFIN

Griffin couldn't seem to shift his eyes away from the starless night sky, hoping for a glimpse of Riona's wings. There was still enough of their original white, he should be able to spot her.

"She's long gone, Griff." Lochlan urged his mount to keep up with Griffin's.

"That blasted woman is going to get herself killed." Griffin drove their horses to a breakneck pace over the barren plains. "Her and her blasted wings," he muttered, wishing he could travel by horse as quickly as she could fly.

"She's a capable warrior," Brea reminded him as she and Gulliver struggled to keep up with Griffin, Hector, and Lochlan. "But are you certain she's gone after Egan?"

"Positive." Griffin gripped the reins, urging his horse to go faster. "I know she can take care of herself, but this is not a fight she should face on her own. She shouldn't have to."

"Maybe she needs to face her demons, Griff." Brea reached out to ease his grip on the reins. "A chance to slay them once and for all."

"I would slay them all for her if I could." Griffin reluctantly slowed their pace to give the horses a break.

"You know, that's where you and I went wrong," Brea said, and Lochlan gave a derisive snort.

Brea returned in kind. "Long before Loch was in the picture, when we first arrived in Fargelsi, I was just a scared kid, and I needed time to get my feet under me. You were there to take care of me when I really needed you, but then once I had my head wrapped around the fae world, you still wanted to take care of me. Sometimes, Griff, you have to let the people you love deal with their demons on their own."

"Easier said than done." Griffin slowed his horse to a walk as they approached the edges of the King's Forest along the road to the Castle of Myrkur.

"We should go in through the front and then sneak around back through the fighting pits." Gulliver steered his mount between Griffin and Hector.

"Surely you don't mean to let Gullie go into Egan's palace with you?" Brea sounded just like the concerned mother she was.

"Yes, but only because he's the best man for the job," Griffin replied.

"Gulliver has a way of sneaking into places he's not supposed to be." Hector clapped the boy on the back as if to congratulate him on his skill.

"People don't notice me till it's too late." Gulliver took a bite of an ochie fruit he'd pilfered from somewhere, wrinkling his nose when the bitter fruit no longer appealed to his more experienced pallet. "We'll ditch the horses in the forest and then head toward the castle gates." Gulliver tossed the fruit over his shoulder—something no inhabitant of Myrkur would ever do no matter how odious the fruit could be.

They found a spot for the horses to graze among the underbrush near a ridge overlooking the crumbling castle below.

"That's it?" Lochlan looked confused. "That... ruin is Egan's pride and joy?"

"It used to look a lot nicer." Gulliver slipped from his horse, seemingly oblivious that the castle hadn't changed since the last time he'd seen it. Gulliver was the one who had changed.

"Wait. This isn't going to work." Gulliver frowned at the adults, giving Hector an eye roll.

"What's wrong?" Brea looked around in confusion.

"It's you three, your clothes are too nice." Gulliver looked down at his own clothes. "Even mine are too new. The guards at the gates will never let us pass if they think you have coin to spare."

"He's right," Hector turned to examine them. "You need to rough up your clothes and get your hands dirty.

Griffin ran a weary hand through his hair. "We have to hurry, she's had too much of a head start."

"I'll be right back." Gulliver mounted his horse and took off down the road toward the nearest village. The one where most of the king's favorites lived with their servants.

Gulliver returned quickly, carrying a pile of garments he'd no doubt stolen right off some old village woman's clothesline. "Put these on over your clothes." Gulliver passed the heavily mended cloaks and robes to the others, stepping back to inspect them.

"Brea, drop your shoulders some," he instructed. "And maybe rub some dirt on your face. And Loch ... try not to look so much like a king."

"He can't." Brea fidgeted with her robes. "It's physically impossible."

"I *am* a king." Lochlan stood ramrod straight in his peasant garb, looking exactly like a king who wanted to blend into the crowd.

"Put your hood up and stay in the back," Gulliver ordered the King of Iskalt. "And don't speak. You sound too proper-like." Gulliver rubbed dirt on his face and ripped the neck of his tunic.

"You heard the man." Griffin smeared some dirt on his clothes and slumped his shoulders.

"All right. You'll do." Gulliver nodded, leading them down the ridge to the castle gates. Dark Fae streamed in and out of the gates, though their numbers were drastically diminished from what Griffin remembered of his last visits to Egan's fortress.

"Wait for my signal," Gulliver whispered as they approached the entrance. The adults followed Gulliver's lead, shifting through the crowd queuing up at the castle entrance. Some were there for work, others trying to get work and others were looking for a handout to keep their families from starving. Gulliver jerked his head toward the entrance. The guards didn't give them a second glance.

Once inside, Gulliver led them through the tents of the castle slums. Hector had worked hard to move the poorest souls to the nearby villages, but in his absence, the slums were once again bursting with the king's castoffs. Their numbers far outweighed what was left of the king's guard.

"It's like we did nothing," Hector muttered. Following Gulliver to the other side of the slums where they took the path around the back of the palace toward the kitchens and the fighting pits.

"This way." Gulliver waved them toward a smelly drain ditch that ran the length of the outer castle wall.

"This is just awful." Brea shook her head. "These poor people. Have they come to the castle from the villages?"

"No, Majesty." Gulliver shook his head. "The slums are always here. It's where Griff found me when I was three."

"Right near here, actually." Griffin winced as he remembered that day. "He was looking for water." He gestured at the stagnant drain water.

"We have to help these fae." Brea took Lochlan's hand.

"We have to find Riona first." Gulliver glanced over his shoulder and urged them all down into the steep ditch. "Keep your heads down."

"Gullie, how did you know this was here?" Griffin stooped down to help him move the grate from an opening in the ground.

Gulliver shrugged. "I pay attention." He bent to crawl inside. "It's not gross or anything, Brea. Just a little smelly till we get to the tunnels under the fighting pit." He disappeared into the drain, and they followed.

Griffin bent nearly in half as he shuffled down the tunnel a short distance where Gulliver moved another drainage grate aside. From there, they entered the wide tunnels where they could stand up straight and catch a whiff of fresher air now and then. But the tunnels spread out in every direction.

Griffin's heart nearly seized in his chest when he heard the sound of swords clashing, unaccompanied by the cheers of a crowd.

"You've done enough damage, Egan. You've lost." Riona's ghostly voice bounced off the stone walls, sounding as if it could have come from any direction.

"Where is she, Gullie?" Griffin reached for his son's hand.

Gulliver took a few steps in every direction before leading them to another tunnel, racing along in the darkness until they could hear Riona's struggle growing louder.

"You forget, my dear." Egan's laughter reached them. "I taught you to fight. You cannot hope to win against me, child. You don't have the experience. But if you surrender now, I can be convinced of your remorse ... in time."

"You will have to kill me first." Riona's weakening voice sent chills down Griffin's spine.

CHAPTER 24

RIONA

"Griffin O'Shea, if you think for one moment you came here to stop me, you can think again." Riona darted toward Egan across the sandy fighting arena she'd fought in countless times. Her sword arced wildly, crashing against his again.

Her arms felt like lead weights, but she would finish this. It was time, and Egan was hers to kill. He'd done her more harm than anyone else.

The sight of Griffin and Gulliver gave her strength. They were her family now. Even Hector, Brea and Lochlan were part of that family.

"You slaughtered my people." Riona charged Egan, barely registering the sensation of his knife slicing through the delicate flesh of her wings. She would feel it later, but right now the bright red blood splattering across the sand might as well have been his. It would be before she was finished toying with him.

"Riona!" Gulliver started toward her, but thankfully Griffin stopped him.

"Stay with Griff," Riona called over her shoulder. The kid had seen enough bloodshed to last him a lifetime, he would not see her death here today.

"I am your people, Riona." Egan's voice took on a kinder tone. The one he'd used with her to get his way. "Haven't I always been a father to you, my darling? And this is how you repay my kindness? I saved you from the extinction you would have succumbed to like the others of your village."

"Kindness?" Riona slashed with her dagger and grazed Egan's side, drawing blood. "You don't know the meaning of the word. Your fatherly affection always came with a price. You've manipulated and bribed me since the day you brought me to this crumbling ruin you call a castle. You handed out scraps and called them riches."

Egan's form faltered, and he showed the first signs of tiring. "How dare you scorn me now when I've given you everything!" Spittle flew from his mouth, and she took the opportunity to strike another blow, scraping her sword across his cheek. "I should have let you burn with your father."

"My father?" Riona stumbled back. "You told me my father was never around. He was of the sea. An Asrai. I was raised by my mother."

"Your father was Chieftain of your people, and he thought to rise above me." Egan parried her attack, but she drove him back across the cold dark arena. "He spoke of the prophesies your people carried in the form of their tattoos. That one of his people would rise up to name a new king of Myrkur. One who would be just and fair. I could not let others learn such magic existed within Myrkur. I had to kill them all."

"Except me." Riona parried his next blow, but gave him no ground, she had him nearly backed up against the high wall below his dais. "Why did you let me live?"

"The fighting was brutal and bloody. Your village burned, and my soldiers found you hiding in a barn. They dragged you out. You were just a child. Hardly more than a babe, but you lashed out at my men, screaming and biting at them. I saw something in you that day. I knew you would be my greatest warrior and champion. So I let you live. And for a time, you were everything I could have wanted in a daughter of my own. Until you betrayed me." Egan pushed back in a sudden surge of energy and emotion. He was truly saddened by her betrayal. Hacking with his sword, he drove her back.

"You don't know what family is, Egan. You called me your favorite and treated me like a beloved daughter when it pleased you and ignored me when you had no use of me. That is not was love is!" Riona screamed, emotions dangerously close to the surface.

"You are not my blood, Riona. What would you have of me?" Egan shouted back. "I did right by you. You never needed anything."

"You made a mistake, Egan. A fatal error." Riona drew back, circling him. "When you sent me out into the world to be your eyes and ears, you allowed me to see everything I've missed. I've seen the love of a father for a boy who was not born of his blood. I've seen families who choose each other, not based on their blood ties, but through their bonds. You owned me once, Egan Bryne, but not anymore."

She charged him, swinging her sword with ruthless strength, driving him back against the wall. Caging him in, she leaned forward. "You failed the moment you let me live, my king. You saw me as a child, too worthless to be a threat." She drove her dagger into his gut and gave it a twist. Egan's eyes widened with shock.

"I have learned my true destiny while I've been away." She gave him a maniacal grin. "You see, I am that fae you feared the day you slaughtered my people. The one you so desperately needed to kill has been under your protection all this time. I will name a new ruler of Murkur, and she will be everything you are not." Riona stepped back, letting Egan slump forward as his blood stained the sandy ground beneath his feet.

"You lie," he spat.

"I already know who the rightful ruler of Myrkur is. An heir to the original kings your family murdered. I will raise her up and name her queen, and the people of Myr will know I speak the truth when they witness my destiny fulfilled. It is why my wings grow dark. My destiny is upon me." After reading the histories of her people in the library, Riona began to suspect that was what her darkening wings meant.

"She is right." Enis called from the dais far above the arena floor. "The book has told me as much." She held the book of power to her chest. "She was always meant to name a new ruler of the Dark Fae."

Egan clutched his wound as if to keep his guts from spilling on the ground.

"Then let us get on with it." Riona raised her sword and ran it through Egan's heart, letting him slide to the ground with his lifeless eyes staring at her.

"Riona?" Griffin ran to her side, taking the bloodied sword and dagger from her clutches. "It's over."

She nodded, too numb to speak.

Gulliver approached her, a wary look on his face. She draped her arm across his shoulders, leaning on him for strength. "I am all right." She squeezed his arm in reassurance.

"Riona, you were so brave." Brea gave her a regal nod.

Griffin still hadn't said anything, and when Riona lifted her eyes to him, she caught him staring at Egan's lifeless form. "He's dead."

A sob rose in her throat, but she held the emotion back. Whatever Egan had been to her, in the end, he was just an enemy. Crossing to Griffin, she slid her hand into his.

He turned glassy eyes to her. "You did it. You ended this."

"It's not over yet." Gulliver gripped her other hand. The three of them had faced Egan's torment for so many years, it was hard to believe he was really gone, that all their suffering had meant something in the end.

It was a feeling Brea and Lochlan would never understand.

Hector cleared his throat, the sound echoing through the hollow arena. "What now?"

"Burn it." Riona's voice was a rasp in her throat.

"Burn it?" Lochlan frowned. "The arena?"

"All of it. The castle, the slums, the arena, everything. Get the fae out to the villages and then raze this awful place to the ground."

"I've had some experience with destroying palaces that hold bad memories." Brea nodded again. "It's therapeutic. We'll get right on it." She turned to Hector. "Can you issue the orders for everyone to evacuate the ... er ... castle?"

He looked from Griffin who hadn't moved away from Egan to Brea. "Yes, your Majesty." Hector left with Brea.

"My boys." Enis nearly skipped down the steps to the arena floor. "I am so pleased to see you." She came to stand before them, her arms wrapped around the book.

"Mother." Lochlan gave her a cold stare.

"Enis." Griffin's voice grew colder.

The Iskalt king and his brother had nothing but ice in their veins for their mother.

Riona pulled Gulliver aside, letting the O'Sheas have their privacy.

"I trust you have won your war with the Dark Fae?" Enis pasted on a smile that seemed fake even to Riona, a smile that didn't belong on such a dour day.

"No thanks to you," Lochlan said.

"My boys." She frowned. "The book—"

"The book is all you're here for, so why don't you just take it and go?" Griffin folded his arms across his chest, his voice resonating with a hard edge. "You are the keeper. It's your duty, is it not?"

"Yes. I—"

"You've made it clear, Mother." Lochlan towered over her. "Time after time, you've chosen the book and its power over us."

"Let's give her a final choice, brother." Griffin took a step toward their mother. "Give up the book. Let us place it somewhere safe where it can never be used again. Then you may rejoin your family. Get to know your sons and your grandchildren. Be there for us."

"Or," Lochlan interjected. "We will send you back to the human world with your book of power, and you can continue protecting it."

Enis lifted her chin. "You boys do not understand. As keeper of the book, it is my duty and my privilege to decide how the book is used and how it is protected. Grainee's descendants protected the book to the detriment of all magic. The book should be studied. Revered. It is the key to our future. You have access to the library.

Surely by now you understand the wealth of knowledge stored there? The book is the key to the library. It can show the keeper things you will never find in a lifetime of research."

"Shall we create a portal for you?" Lochlan raised a brow.

Enis nodded. "You are grown men. You do not need your mother."

"That's not entirely true." Lochlan's icy blue magic swirled in his palm. "I am not ashamed to say I still need my mother. I value her counsel. My mother is Faolan, and Griffin's mother was Regan. You have never been a mother to either of us."

"Go." Griffin nodded toward the portal Lochlan created. "It is fine, Enis. I hope the book will love you and comfort you throughout what remains of your life."

Tears pooled in Enis' eyes as she took a step toward the portal. "One day I hope you will understand my choices. I always loved you both, and I always will." As she moved into the portal, she sang the song Griffin only vaguely remembered from his childhood before his family was ripped from him. It was a fitting farewell from the woman he would never truly understand.

She would keep the book, but the magic inside it could be controlled from the library. It wouldn't be able to hurt their world again.

And neither would she.

CHAPTER 25

GRIFFIN

Fire.

It shouldn't have soothed Griffin's nerves, but it did. He continued to stare at the place where Lochlan's portal took his mother and the book to the human realm before closing her off from them forever.

A sob echoed behind him, and he turned to find Riona staring up at the flames bursting from the palace windows. Brea's magic kept the flames from reaching the slums until Hector evacuated every last fae, but it seemed she hadn't wanted to wait to begin.

Another sob escaped the always strong Riona, the woman who never shed a tear, who fought her sort-of father with a coldness that left them all chilled.

"I'm going to help Brea." Lochlan walked away, leaving Griffin to stare at Riona and Gulliver.

It was over.

Egan was dead.

He pulled Riona against him as he cleared her tears with a scorching kiss. He put everything they'd been through, every bit of pain and heartache, fear and doubt into that moment, letting it wash away.

Leaning his forehead against hers, he sucked in a breath. "You really did it," he whispered. "You killed him." And the people Griffin loved were still alive. It was an outcome he hadn't allowed himself to imagine, but now it was here.

"You came." Her eyes found his. "I left you—again—and you still came."

"Always." He wiped her tears away with his thumbs.

"I killed my father today."

Griffin pulled her into a hug, letting her bury her face in his shoulder. He knew what it meant to lose the one fae who'd always been there, but even he hadn't had to kill Regan. Brea took care of that. "Everything is going to be better now, Riona." He didn't know where they'd live or how they'd live. Lochlan and Brea both wanted them to move to Iskalt, but something about that didn't feel right. It wasn't home.

But wherever they went, they'd be together.

"Gullie," he called. "Stop staring at Egan like he's going to come back to life and get over here."

Gulliver stood from where he'd crouched next to the dead king and jumped over him.

Griffin pulled him into their hug.

"Griff," he complained. "Let me go."

"Never."

Something crashed nearby, a tower succumbing to the magical fire, stones and wood raining down. "We should probably go." Griffin urged Riona and Gulliver into a run.

They passed familiar crumbling structures, and Griffin wondered how they'd ever thought of it as more than it was—a symbol of oppression that no longer belonged in this world.

They found Brea and Lochlan, both using their power to control the flames, weakening the castle walls and freeing Myrkur of its dark past.

"Go help Hector," Brea grit out before mumbling a few Fargelsian words. Flames exploded from an untouched tower.

Griffin tore his eyes away and found the stream of fae carrying their few belongings through the gates, emptying the slums of the remaining indentured servants and soldiers of Egan's, the ones who hadn't joined his march into Eldur.

"Gullie." Griffin pushed him toward the gate. "Go get the horses."

"Griff—"

"No arguing. I have taken you into more danger than you should see in a lifetime, and you have proven yourself more capable than I could have imagined. Which is why I'm trusting you to bring our horses to the gate." If he knew Brea, there'd be a big finish once the slums were empty and a quick getaway was always a good idea.

Gulliver straightened his shoulders. "You trust me." He said it almost like an accusation, poking Griffin in the chest. "As much as Lochlan or Myles or anyone else."

"I wouldn't say I trust Myles," he grumbled, though he did. "Don't make a big deal about it, Gullie. Just go. Take Riona with you, she's barely able to stand."

Riona opened her mouth to protest, but closed it with a sigh as she turned to him. "Promise me you won't be long."

He pressed a kiss to her cheek. "I promise I'll come to you once this place has burned to the ground."

She wanted that more than anyone, but he knew the toll the fight with Egan took on her, and she seemed to realize her own weakness. With a nod, she followed Gulliver into the crowd fleeing the castle grounds.

Wasting no time, Griffin ran back to where Brea and Lochlan stood facing the flames.

"I told you to help Hector." Lochlan didn't look at him.

"I need to be the one to do this." He hadn't destroyed Regan's palace, and in the end, he'd tried to save her. Unlike Riona who'd had the courage to kill Egan. He hadn't gotten that moment.

But now... this place... he could make sure no fae ever again set foot inside.

Lochlan turned to him, pulling in his magic. He studied him for a long moment, and Griffin didn't know what he saw before nodding and running toward Hector.

"Come on then." Brea shot him a smile. "Let's destroy a castle."

It felt right, standing there with her. Everything that had happened began many years ago when he made the fateful decision to follow Regan's orders to abduct a girl from the human realm.

Now, they finished it together.

Flames ripped through the halls he'd walked as a prisoner, through the rooms his kids had been held against their will, the fighting pits where he'd first fought for his family and made the decision not to kill Riona.

Every part of this place held a memory, a hint of pain washed clean in the scorching heat of the fire.

The flow of fae from the slums slowed to a trickle until only four remained. Brea stepped back when Lochlan and Hector joined them, letting Griffin continue. He pulled on the flames, yanking stones from the walls as he did. When he turned, the fire spread along the high walls, speeding through the tents and hovels of the slums until they encircled the group.

Redemption was an odd thing. Griffin hadn't wanted it. He never searched for it or believe he deserved it. But as the flames erased this evil from Myrkur, they wiped it clean from his soul.

Maybe that wasn't redemption. He'd done so much bad, and nothing could make up for that. Forgiveness was a better term.

As Griffin let the heat of the flames wash over him, he forgave himself.

Forgetting wasn't the answer—Myrkur proved that. It only led to more pain, and Griffin didn't want to forget the things he'd done. The evil, though... it didn't define him, not anymore.

He hadn't realized Brea, Lochlan, and Hector all screamed his name as the flames closed in until their collective voices struck him.

"Griff!" Brea cried. "We need to get out of here."

"Time to go, brother." Lochlan tried to pull him back.

"You've done enough." Those were Hector's words, and they swirled through him. He'd done enough. Myrkur was free.

There was more work ahead, but with freedom, none of it seemed so daunting.

Turning, he realized Brea had to use her magic to keep the flames from overwhelming them. His eyes lifted to the burning castle, knowing it would be nothing but ash and soot stained ruins soon.

"Yes." He nodded. "We've done enough." Turning his back on it, he parted the flames even as his magic weakened. "Well, what are you waiting for?"

The four of them sprinted through the raging fires, nearing the crumbling gate. They burst through a wall of fire, all rolling to the ground on the other side.

Griffin's chest heaved as he looked up at the horses waiting for them, a smile curving his lips. He closed his eyes for a brief moment and opened them when a cheer wound through the darkness.

The fae who'd escaped the slums crowded together, lifting their voices in the kind of joyous sound that was foreign to Myrkur.

Pushing himself off the ground, Griffin watched as the fae who'd just lost the only home they had cheer for its destruction.

Riona rounded one of the horses and slid her arm through his, wiping black soot off his face. "I never knew it before, Griff, but this is Myrkur." She gestured to the fae who'd been little more than slaves and the villagers who'd come to help them. "Egan wasn't Myrkur. He was the one holding us back."

The inexhaustible Hector walked out among the people, a smile stretching his lips.

"Look!" Gulliver shouted, pointing into the distance.

Griffin strained his eyes to see to tiny bit of light streaking across the horizon, so different from the bright glow of the fire behind them. That was about desperation.

This... the dawn coming to Myrkur for the first time was hope.

"It worked." Gulliver bounced on his toes. "It's the light from the human realm."

The crowd of fae watched the brilliant pinks and oranges light up their dark world.

Gulliver turned to Griffin with a wry smile twisting his lips. "They're so going to need sunglasses."

"Aghadoon feels empty." Griffin lowered himself to the blanket Gulliver had spread in the village square.

Gulliver insisted they do this post-victory—his word—meeting outside instead of in the stuffy old library (also his word).

No one protested.

Throughout the morning, Hector worked to dispatch the Dark Fae soldiers who'd been staying in the village to aid those who'd escaped the slums, setting up temporary camps until some of the nearby villages could be improved to accommodate them.

Griffin had known Myrkur was a harsh place, but the sunlight streaked across the sky, illuminating the barren landscape in a way they'd never seen before. Yet, among the dying forests and shriveled crops, there was a beauty. In the distance, snowcapped mountains towered over the land with a majestic strength.

Lochlan lay sprawled on the blanket, soaking up the warmth. Both O'Shea brothers were happy to let their magic rest as it was meant to.

Tia and Toby had a thumb war. Griffin smiled at the memory of Brea teaching him the human game.

Brea joined them, kissing her husband before sitting with her kids.

They were only missing Riona. She walked toward them in her traditional dark clothing, but that wasn't what caught Griffin's eye. Her wings... the white was gone, leaving a thick inky blackness covering the surface.

She stopped before sitting down. "I know about the wings, okay? I don't need your comments. I'm choosing to believe not all darkness is bad. Maybe this is a good thing. Nihal had dark wings."

"He was also a liar who gave his life for a bad fae who might also be not bad? I don't really understand," Gulliver muttered.

Griffin pulled his tail. "Stop. Enis had a mission she wanted to devote her life to. End of story." Lifting his eyes to Riona, he arched one brow. "Finished? We have things to discuss."

Riona shut her mouth, crossed her arms, and took a spot next to Griffin.

Lochlan rubbed a hand over his face. "We had no choice but to let Enis leave with the book. She's the keeper. But, how do we control her now?"

Griffin met Tia's gaze. "This isn't about the book. Maybe it never has been."

Brea's brow furrowed. "What do you mean? My kids were taken. We fought a war over that thing."

"The book is dangerous because it has no conscience, nothing to decide whether showing someone a spell is right or wrong. If it thinks a fae needs a spell, it gives it—assuming that spell exists in the library. There is nothing good or evil about the book."

"Griff—"

"We already know how to control Enis and the magic. We've been doing it for months now. The book doesn't recognize evil, but we do. It doesn't control the library, the library controls the book."

"The fae can be its conscience," Riona said, her eyes widening.

Griffin nodded. "And now we have two realms to protect. The breach into the human realm can't be closed, so we must do what we can to control that as well. All of us."

"No." Toby's single word surprised them into silence. He shared a look with his sister. "Not all of us. You, Griff. You can protect it."

Tia unfolded her legs and stood, reaching a small hand down to Griffin. "We need to show you something."

"Now?" He looked to the others. "Tia... is it in the village? Because, honestly I'm exhausted and there's still so much to do to help the Dark Fae."

"This will help, Uncle Griff." Toby pushed to his feet. "We promise."

"Come on, Griff." Gulliver jumped up. "Don't be an old fae. It's not like you destroyed an entire palace last night or anything."

A tired laugh wound through Griffin, and he sighed. These kids were going to be the death of him. "Fine."

Tia smiled in triumph. "Good, because Papa definitely won't let us take the horses on our own."

Lochlan groaned, but the rest of them made no move to come. Traitors. Lazy, rotten traitors who'd rather sleep after everything they'd gone through than ride off with kids who had too much energy.

And yet, as the three kids surrounded him, they gave him life.

Wrapping an arm around Gulliver, he pulled him close. "Do you know what we're doing?"

Gulliver shrugged. "I trust Tia."

Griffin did too. Despite how young the twins were, they'd done well. They possessed more Fargelsian power than he thought possible.

The four of them rode the short distance to the ruins of Fela. As Griffin slid down, he realized it looked no different than it had before.

Walking through the rubble, he kicked over a pot, finding a tiny doll beneath it. With a sad shake of his head, he turned back to the kids. "Why are we here?"

Tia skipped forward, her hands clasped behind her back. "Do you know how Fargelsi was built?"

"Of course. I grew up there. The Fargelsian's grow their villages from the ground, calling forth treehouses and houses made of stone and sod. I've even heard about old villages grown right into the hills."

Toby kicked at a rock across the ground.

"We read all about it in the library." Tia nodded, the corners of her mouth twitching. "Lots of Gelsi villages sprout right from the forests, but we don't think that's necessary."

"I don't understand what any of this has to do with Fela." Or why it was so important it couldn't wait.

Tia and Toby shared a grin. Tia held out her palm, and Toby

slapped his into it. They both closed their eyes, old Fargelsian words even he didn't understand falling from their lips.

"What are they doing?" Gulliver whispered.

Griffin was about to say he didn't know when the ground beneath his feet shook, the vibration traveling up his legs. Vines shot from the earth, twisting in the air, and Griffin yanked Gulliver out of their path, his eyes widening. He'd seen such magic in his youth, but seeing his own children wield it was startling.

All around them, a wind whipped through the destroyed village, clearing the debris as the ground shifted.

Griffin watched as several small buildings took shape from the stones beneath them, magic etched into their very core. Moss and vines grew up the walls just like in Fargelsi. Silvery black flowers sprouted from the vines, and their sweet fragrance chased away the pungent odors left from the fires that destroyed Fela.

Small cottages dotted the narrow roads, now paved with moss-covered stones still shifting into place. Rock fences closed in yards covered with fresh green grass and wildflowers in the darkest shades of red and purple bobbed in the breeze.

The village square shifted, and the ground churned as the twins called up more grass and sweet smelling clover to carpet the square. A thick, gnarled tree rose from the cracked, dry soil at the center of the village. Griffin watched in awe as it morphed into a gazebo with smooth bark covering every surface. Vines twisted around the gazebo, hanging heavy with purple fruit he didn't recognize.

Communal buildings took shape from new trees the twins called forth. And at the end of the cobble stone street, a large two-story house emerged from the cliff-side with shale shingles along the roof and big open windows. Ivy vines crept up the sides of the house and shrubs of night berries rose in the beds along the foundation.

With the village still morphing around them, Tia fell silent and released her brother's hand. Their chests heaved with a matching rhythm, but Griffin couldn't take his eyes from what they'd done.

Fela, looking like a quaint Fargelsian village, stood tall and proud. Cobblestone roads and paths wound between the structures. Griffin made note of everything there was to do to show his people the modern fae world. Crops to plant that would thrive in the sun, roads to pave, trade routes to create.

And it was all possible.

They could return.

Griffin was from Iskalt. He grew up in Fargelsi.

But Myrkur was home. These people were home.

"I know Papa wanted you to come home with us." Tia met his gaze. "But you don't belong there." She took his hand and led him down the street to the biggest house.

She was so young and yet saw so much.

No, he didn't belong in Lochlan's court. He never had.

"Plus." Toby took up Griffin's free hand "We're right by the tear into the human realm, and someone has to watch it."

He was right.

"Can I go inside?" Gulliver asked.

Griffin nodded, a tear sliding down his cheek.

Gulliver's shouts reached them from the second story. "It's huge!" He stuck his head out of the window over the front door. Windows that would need glass in the coming months. "It's not a palace, it's way better." Gulliver's head disappeared from one window to appear in another. "Griff, I have my own room! And there are extras too."

Toby coughed. "That's... uh... for us when we come visit."

Tia smiled. "Do you like it, Uncle Griff?"

Wrapping one arm around each kid, his rested his chin on her head. "It's perfect. Absolutely perfect."

"We love you, Griff." She dropped the word uncle as she looked up at him, the truth in her gaze. Even if Lochlan would always be their father, it was okay for him to love them too.

"I love you too, kiddos. Now, what were you thinking putting a window in Gulliver's room? He's just going to sneak out all the time."

"Hey!" Gulliver appeared in the doorway. "Okay, that's probably true. But does it matter? Myrkur is safe now."

Griffin stepped past him into his forever home—the first he'd ever had—and shook his head. "Someday, Gullie, we'll discuss the difference between not under the control of an evil king, and safe to resume a life of thievery."

Griffin continued to argue with his son as he walked through the empty home. He couldn't wait to bring Riona here. And the others. He couldn't wait to fill the village with his family.

CHAPTER 26

RIONA

One Month Later

Riona stood beside Shauna, shielding her eyes from the sunlight shining across Fela, a sight she'd never expected to see in the land of perpetual darkness.

"I never get tired of looking at it." Shauna sighed, a blissful smile on her face. She'd arrived more than a week ago with the former Queen of Eldur. When Riona had first met Faolan, she'd seemed old and feeble, like she'd given up on life. But after Shauna's careful nursing, Faolan was a new woman.

It was amazing what love could do to a person.

"The sunlight or your beautiful queen?" Riona nudged her playfully.

"Can I say both?" Shauna laughed. "She's not a queen, though. Not anymore."

"I don't think you can ever take the queen out of a lady like Faolan."

Faolan walked with her grandchildren and their friends through the newly established berry patches, watching for signs of new growth.

New growth was everywhere in this part of Myr. Green grass and trees were just beginning to flourish under the sun. This close to the rift between worlds, the sunlight was at its brightest—though still not as bright as it was in the human realm or even Fargelsi. Riona's eyes were grateful for that.

Farther away, the light was dim, like a lingering sunset all day. And at the far reaches of Myrkur, it was still dark. The night realm had never known light, and for those Dark Fae who preferred it that way, they would always have a home that felt natural to them. But for those who relished the sun's rays, Fela and the villages growing up around it, had become a beacon of hope for a new life without the tyranny of a king who did not care for them.

That was why Shauna and Faolan had come to visit. Why Riona waited anxiously for the others to arrive. Nerves churned in her belly. It was time to choose a new ruler. Time to fulfill her destiny and name the true heir of Myrkur—should she choose to accept the role.

"I'll never get used to that." Shauna winced at the surge of magic sweeping through the center of town.

"Neither will I," Riona agreed. "Let's go greet our guests." Riona and Shauna set off across the grassy slopes leading down to the orchards. Griffin and Gulliver were already there with Hector.

The stone pillars appeared first—the markers of Aghadoon. The rest of the village emerged from an unnatural fog. Brea and Lochlan stood at the center of the magical village with their four children, and Alona and Finn walked up next to them with Logan and Darra.

Griffin waved frantically at the twins who were already running toward him and Gulliver.

Brandon emerged from the library with Myles and Neeve and their brood of little ones in tow.

"Riona!" Myles called as they all made their way down to the pillars. "We carpooled." He flashed the goofy grin Riona had come to expect from the lovable human.

"I am more than a little disturbed that I know what that means." Riona leaned in to give him a hug. "I've spent way too much time with this one." She smiled at Brea.

"He has a way of rubbing off on you, doesn't he?" Brea linked her arms through Shauna's and Riona's. "Now show us what you've been up to for the last month—besides mooning over your new loves."

"No one has been mooning over anything." Shauna frowned at the odd expression. "We have sunlight now."

Brea threw her head back and laughed. "You Myrkurians are a hoot, you know that."

Riona shrugged at that. There was no way she'd ever really understand this queen and her human ways.

"Brea!" Griffin called as he ran up the slope with Tia and Toby, wrapping her in his arms for a brief moment. "Lochlan, it's good to see you brother." He gripped his brother's hand.

"Daylight agrees with you and your new homeland." Lochlan slapped him on the back.

"It does." Griffin flashed a wink at Riona.

"Are you ready for this?" Brea asked as they made their way toward the center of Fela.

"As ready as I will ever be, I think." Riona sighed. It was a heavy burden, her destiny. "I would like to speak with you all privately first, if I may. Before we make anything official."

"We have a town hall now," Griffin said eagerly. "It's nothing fancy, but we love it." He guided their party of visiting royals to their modest building, looking as proud of it as he would if it were the finest castle anyone had ever seen. He and Hector had worked hard with some of the villagers to build it themselves.

The wooden structure opened to a great hall, a single room with high ceilings and exposed beams. One wall of windows faced the east, to catch the early morning light. Everyone filed into the hall, taking up their seats in a circle around the center fire pit. Griffin and Riona had laid the bricks themselves. It was a unique experience for Riona. Creating something meant to last. It was a simple building, but it had character. She imagined generations of villagers meeting here to discuss the town's communal system, and it made her feel like she was truly part of something greater than herself.

With an encouraging nod from Griffin, Riona stood to greet their guests. All the royals from the three Light Fae kingdoms, along with their children and the current leaders of Fela were here today to discuss the making of a queen. They just didn't know it yet.

"Thank you all for making the journey to Fela. We are so happy to have you here as our guests." Riona's voice shook for a moment. It wasn't like her to be so nervous. "Some of you know why we are here. I am the last of my kind. After much research, we've come to learn I am the last of the original Tuatha De Dannan. From us, all Dark Fae came. The Asrai, the Slyph, the land fae, even the Ogres owe their origins to those like me. Egan massacred the last of my people, a small village near the Black Sea. I was the only survivor."

Riona lifted her chin. "He killed my people because of a prophecy that said one of my village would rise up as a kingmaker to name the rightful ruler of Myrkur. Our tattoos hold the keys to our purposes in life. Egan knew one such as I could destroy his reign, and he sought to prevent that from coming to pass. He didn't know it, but when he chose to let me live, that prophecy survived the bloodshed of that day. He killed my mother and father, who was the village chieftain. But I have come today to fulfill my destiny. This heir to the last true royal family of Myrkur sits in this room today." Riona cast a glance around the Light and Dark Fae faces staring eagerly back at her.

"I think it is fitting that this heir is the child of both Light and Dark Fae." Murmuring spread across the room. "Shauna and Nessa could you please join me for a moment?" Riona reached her hand out to Nessa. She'd discussed this with the sisters the previous morning. She wanted to be certain they understood what she was asking of them.

Nessa smiled shyly and came to stand in front of Riona. Shauna stood uncertainly beside them.

"Shauna and Nessa's mother was Light Fae. The daughter of a convicted felon from Fargelsi. Shauna's father was also Light Fae, but he died when she was very young. Nessa's father was Dark Fae. A beloved man of Fela, but he also died when his daughter was just a baby. For most of their lives, Shauna and Nessa have only had each other. But Nessa's father was the great-great-great-grandson of the last king of Myrkur. A fact he likely didn't even realize. Nessa is the true heir to the throne."

Nessa beamed a beautiful smile at the room as everyone present fell into astonished whispers.

"I thought for sure it would be Riona," Brea said.

"You thought I would name myself queen?" Riona shook her head with a laugh.

"We'll you deserve it. If it wasn't you, I thought it would be Griffin."

"No way." Griffin shook his head. "Our queen should represent the Dark Fae. Nessa hasn't come into her Dark Fae features yet, but she will. Our people need to see someone just like them on the throne."

"May I speak?" Nessa turned to Riona.

"Of course." Riona lifted her onto the edge of the cold fire pit so she could see everyone.

"I am young," Nessa said in her clear voice. "But what Riona says feels right inside here." She held a hand over her heart. "Maybe my ancestors were kings once upon a time. But that shouldn't make me a queen by default. I understand it is my right if I want to be queen. But ... this is a new world." Nessa's smile lit the room. "We should not look back to what was, but look to the future. To what Myrkur will be some day."

"Are you saying you don't want to be our queen, Ness?" Shauna asked carefully. "You may feel differently when you are older."

"I was never able to just be a child. Egan's Myrkur didn't allow for such lives. I have that chance now, and I want to take it. Before it is too late. Besides, I am a healer, like my mother and my sister, or at least, I wish to be. There are others here who would do a much better job at governing us." Nessa waved Riona over to her side and stood up on tip toes to whisper in Riona's ear.

Riona looked back, surprised. "You think so?"

Nessa nodded.

"You know, that's exactly what I was thinking too." Riona winked and took the young could-be queen by the hand as she jumped down from the fire pit and returned to her sister.

"I can choose another," Riona announced. "This magic that manifests as prophecy among my tattoos can guide me to whoever would fall next in line for the throne. But I'm not sure I believe that is the right course either." Riona looked to the circle around the fire pit, meeting each eye. "I believe Nessa has shown great wisdom today. We should look to the future. But we can't ignore the past. Specifically the recent past. One among you has risen to the challenges of recent months. One of you has acted like a king." Riona stopped pacing and turned to the man standing beside Griffin.

"Hector. You have proven your worth. Since the moment this all began, you've worked tirelessly to help those in need. You've headed armies, bested Egan's finest soldiers, and fought for your freedom."

"I can't think of a better man for the job," Griffin said softly.

"Me?" Hector looked at them like they'd lost their minds. "I'm just a farmer."

"You're a leader, Hector." Griffin clapped him on the back.

"When Nessa declined, my purpose shifted." Riona glanced down at her swirling tattoos. They moved faster, the colors whirling together like paint in a bowl. "I believe you are the leader we need, Hector. And Nessa herself suggested it."

"It takes more than the right lineage to make a king." Lochlan moved to stand behind Hector. "You have what it takes to rule. I would be honored to call you my ally and fellow king."

"I—I can't be a king." Hector shook his head.

"That is precisely why you will make a good one, my friend." Griffin took a knee before him. "I have thirsted for power before, and I have seen others who have coveted crowns that did not belong to them. True kings and queens are humble. Like you, your Majesty."

"Get up, Griff," Hector pleaded.

"King Hector, ruler of Myrkur." Riona placed her hands on his trembling shoulders. "You will serve your people well." Riona's voice came out formal and tinged with a hint of ancient magic. Her tattoos stilled, growing dark as the color drained from them, like magic washed away once its purpose had been served.

Sadness echoed through her to see her markings go still and dark.

"Riona, your wings," Gulliver gasped. "They're beautiful."

As she'd fulfilled her purpose, the color from her tattoos faded away, switching places with the darkness of her wings that were once white—like a blank page—and had recently turned black. Now her tattoos were black and her wings swirled with the vibrant colors of her markings. She wrapped her wings around herself, overcome with the sheer beauty of such color.

It seemed over the last months as she moved closer and closer to fulfilling her destiny, her wings had grown dark in preparation for this moment.

"She's breathtaking," Griffin whispered in awe. For a moment, she stood before him, and all the others faded away. They had nothing but good things coming for them in the near future. A future of their own making.

EPILOGUE
GRIFFIN

"I believe we have some unfinished business." Brea lowered herself to the ground beside Griffin.

Myrkur celebrated their new king with a bonfire in Fela's town square. Hector was a reluctant king, but he took to the role like a natural. He was a good man who would never let the power of ruling over others go to his head. He would be a benevolent and kind ruler.

"What business is that?" Griffin watched the young people of Myrkur dance and sing in the growing darkness.

Brea pulled something from her bag.

"Ahh, the marriage magic. I'd wondered when that would come back to haunt us again."

"I've studied this scroll with my sisters and Lochlan. We're all in agreement that this kind of magical bond is no longer necessary." Brea glanced down at the scroll in her lap. "More than ever, freewill is vital to our people and the future we are trying to build for our children. But still, a part of me—"

"Hates the idea of letting it go?" Griffin finished her sentence.

"Isn't that crazy?" Brea scoffed. "I shouldn't want or need magic to keep me in love with my husband. To keep me feeling close to you. I fear what will happen when it is gone. I know Lochlan and I will be fine. Most married couples will be just as strong without it. But I don't want to lose you, Griffin. You're not my husband, but you are family. You know that, right?"

Griffin reached out to take her hand. "I do, Brea. And part of me will always love you, but I need ... we both need to let our relationship evolve naturally. The fragments of magic holding us together will only hinder us. I think it's time we trust in ourselves and our relationships to keep us strong." Griffin's eyes searched through the crowd of revelers to find Riona. She was easy to spot with her brightly colored wings that seemed to suit her better than her white wings ever did. "Someone once said magic isn't the answer to everything. I feel those are wise words we should heed."

"She is a smart lady." Brea watched Riona dancing with Gulliver and Toby. She lifted the leather scroll holding one of the oldest bits of magic either of them had ever seen. "Would you do me the honor of finally divorcing me?"

Griffin stood and offered her his hand. "No human custom would please me more."

Together they walked through the crowd to the bonfire.

Griffin hesitated a moment. "Are we doing the right thing, Brea? This will affect everyone."

"It should be a choice, Griffin. Loving someone, creating a family with them. We owe it to our people to give them the freedom to choose."

"She's right, you know." Lochlan came up behind them. "It's not about us anymore. We get to choose our family." He turned to watch the twins playing with the other royal children. "It's not about blood or magic. It's about love."

"Are we doing this?" Alona and Finn approached the fire with Neeve and Myles.

"This is going to change everything," Brea said, holding the scroll toward the flames.

"Do it." Myles took his wife's hand. "We'll find a new way forward."

"We always do," Alona agreed.

With a smile for her family, Brea dropped the scroll into the flames, and they all took a step back.

Griffin felt it the moment the last fragments of his bond with Brea shattered. It was like losing a thousand pound weight from his shoulders. It felt like freedom. For a man who'd spent so much of his life beholden to others, it was everything.

Thank you for reading Queens of the Fae. We hope you enjoy the next book, **Fae's Rebellion, book 7!**

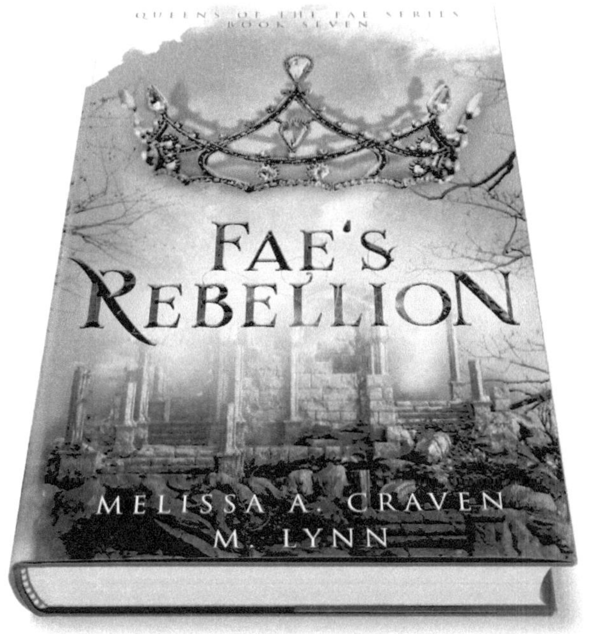

FAE'S REBELLION
QUEENS OF THE FAE BOOK 7

A powerful fae princess
desperate to escape her future.
A broody prince holding her captive.

Tia O'Shea just wants to go home, back to the palace among snowy fields where her twin brother amplifies the power inside her, and her father tries to secure the future of the throne through her marriage.

A marriage she doesn't want and refuses to consider. As a future queen, Tia only wants a choice in this one part of her life.

On the night of the ball to introduce all possible suitors for her hand, she escapes to the human realm, planning to return after everyone has come to their senses. She never expected anyone to follow her, let alone her best friend and two of her suitors.

When the portal home goes awry, she finds herself separated from the others, without her magic, and stranded in a kingdom she knows nothing of, a kingdom torn apart by generations of war.

Tia has been through her fair share of war, she knows what happens to those caught in the middle, but avoiding it might not be possible if she wants to find her friends.

To recover her missing magic and find a way back home across the treacherous fire plains, she might have to wade right into the fight.

But first...
She has to escape the prince claiming her as prisoner.

ABOUT MELISSA A. CRAVEN

Melissa A. Craven is an Amazon bestselling author of Young Adult Fantasy. Her books focus on strong female protagonists who aren't always perfect, but they find their inner strength along the way. Melissa's novels appeal to audiences of all ages and fans of almost any genre. She believes in stories that make you think and she loves playing with foreshadowing, leaving clues and hints for the careful reader.

Melissa draws inspiration from her background in architecture and interior design to help her with the small details in world building and scene settings. (Her degree in fine art also comes in handy.) She is a diehard introvert with a wicked sense of humor, and an addiction to iced coffee.

Melissa enjoys sitting on her porch when the weather is nice with her two dogs, Fynlee and Nahla, reading from her massive TBR pile and dreaming up new stories.

Visit Melissa at Melissaacraven.com for more information about her newest series.

Want to see more books by Melissa A. Craven?
You can view them at
https://books2read.com/ap/ng5y22/Melissa-A-Craven
Join Melissa and Michelle's Facebook Group:
Fantasy Book Warriors
Follow Michelle and Melissa on TikTok
@ATaleOfTwoAuthors

ABOUT M. LYNN

Michelle MacQueen is a USA Today bestselling author of love. Yes, love. Whether it be YA romance, NA romance, or fantasy romance (Under M. Lynn), she loves to make readers swoon.

The great loves of her life to this point are two tiny blond creatures who call her "aunt" and proclaim her books to be "boring books" for their lack of pictures. Yet, somehow, she still manages to love them more than chocolate.

When she's not sharing her inexhaustible wisdom with her niece and nephew, Michelle is usually lounging in her ridiculously large bean bag chair creating worlds and characters that remind her to smile every day - even when a feisty five-year-old is telling her just how much she doesn't know.

See more from M. Lynn and sign up to receive updates and deals!
michellelynnauthor.com

Join Melissa and Michelle's Facebook Group: Fantasy Book Warriors

Follow Michelle and Melissa on TikTok
@ATaleOfTwoAuthors

Want to see more books by Michelle?
You can view them at
https://books2read.com/ap/R5my46/M-Lynn

Want More From Brea's World?

Don't miss the FREE prequel,
Fae's Dilemma
Grab your copy at https://BookHip.com/VJMXVGD

Don't forget your bonus chapters.
right, there's more! Get your bonus chapters here:
https://michellelynnauthor.com/fpbonus

www.ingramcontent.com/pod-product-compliance
Lightning Source LLC
Chambersburg PA
CBHW020347310726
48979CB00015B/2537/J
9781970052183